The
MX Book
of
New
Sherlock
Holmes
Stories

Part XLV
2024 Annual
(1898-1917)

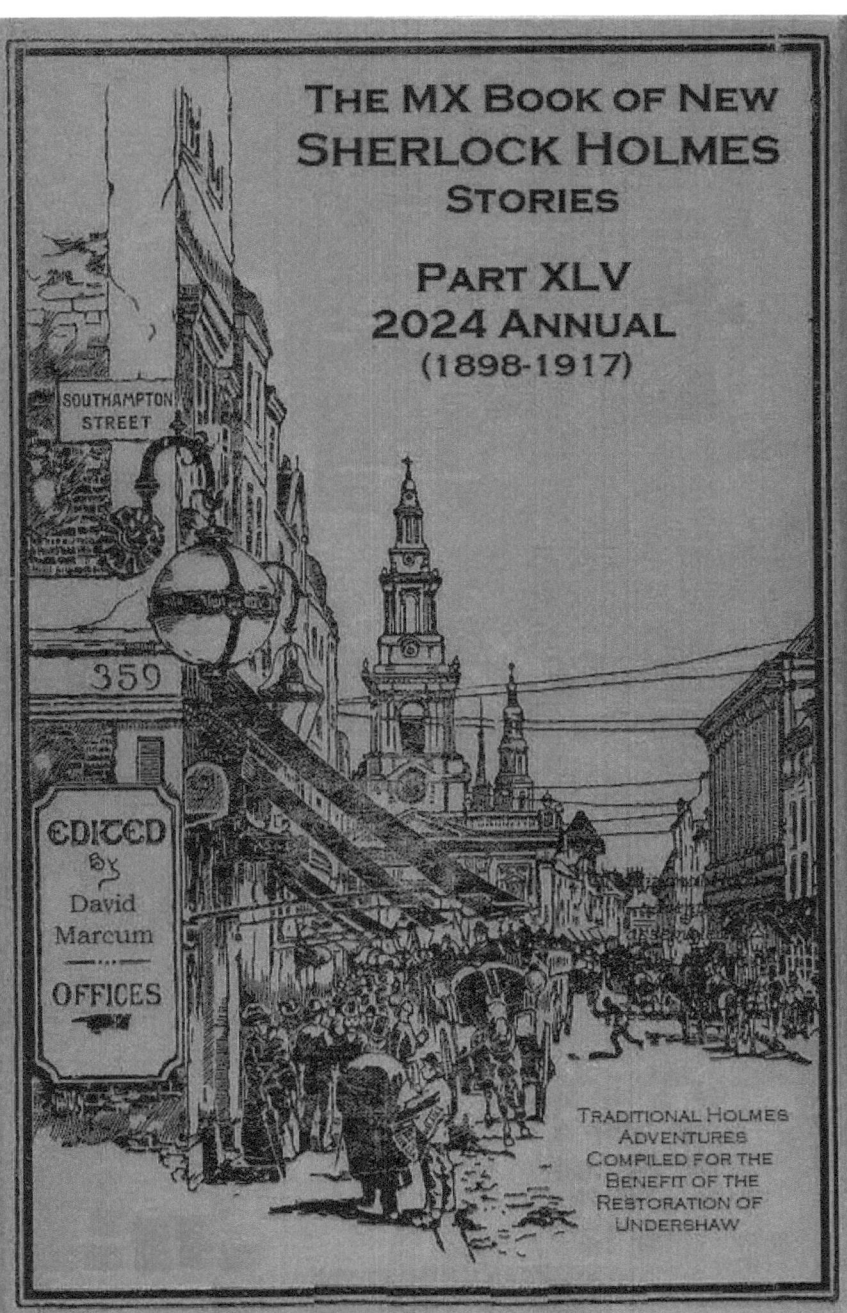

The MX Book of New Sherlock Holmes Stories

Stories

Part XLV
2024 Annual
(1898-1917)

SOUTHAMPTON STREET

359

EDITED By David Marcum

OFFICES

TRADITIONAL HOLMES
ADVENTURES
COMPILED FOR THE
BENEFIT OF THE
RESTORATION OF
UNDERSHAW

ISBN Hardback 978-1-80424-486-9
ISBN Paperback 978-1-80424-487-6
AUK ePub ISBN 978-1-80424-488-3
AUK PDF ISBN 978-1-80424-489-0

Published in the UK by
MX Publishing
335 Princess Park Manor, Royal Drive,
London, N11 3GX
www.mxpublishing.co.uk

David Marcum can be reached at:
thepapersofsherlockholmes@gmail.com

Cover design by Brian Belanger
www.belangerbooks.com and *www.redbubble.com/people/zhahadun*

Internal Illustrations by Sidney Paget

CONTENTS

Forewords

Adventures

(Continued on the next page . . .)

(Continued on the next page . . .)

(Continued on the next page . . . .)

These additional Sherlock Holmes adventures
can be found in the previous volumes of
The MX Book of New Sherlock Holmes Stories

(Continued on the next page . . . .)

(Continued on the next page . . . .)

PART V – Christmas Adventures

(Continued on the next page . . . .)

PART VI – 2017 Annual

(Continued on the next page . . . .)

PART VII – Eliminate the Impossible: 1880-1891

PART VIII – Eliminate the Impossible: 1892-1905

(Continued on the next page . . . .)

Part IX – 2018 Annual (1879-1895)

(Continued on the next page . . . .)

The Lambeth Poisoner Case – Stephen Gaspar
The Confession of Anna Jarrow – S. F. Bennett
The Adventure of the Disappearing Dictionary – Sonia Fetherston
The Fairy Hills Horror – Geri Schear
A Loathsome and Remarkable Adventure – Marcia Wilson
The Adventure of the Multiple Moriartys – David Friend
The Influence Machine – Mark Mower

Part X – 2018 Annual (1896-1916)

Foreword – Nicholas Meyer
Foreword – Roger Johnson
Foreword – Melissa Farnham
Foreword – Steve Emecz
Foreword – David Marcum
A Man of Twice Exceptions (A Poem) – Derrick Belanger
The Horned God – Kelvin Jones
The Coughing Man – Jim French
The Adventure of Canal Reach – Arthur Hall
A Simple Case of Abduction – Mike Hogan
A Case of Embezzlement – Steven Ehrman
The Adventure of the Vanishing Diplomat – Greg Hatcher
The Adventure of the Perfidious Partner – Jayantika Ganguly
A Brush With Death – Dick Gillman
A Revenge Served Cold – Maurice Barkley
The Case of the Anonymous Client – Paul A. Freeman
Capitol Murder – Daniel D. Victor
The Case of the Dead Detective – Martin Rosenstock
The Musician Who Spoke From the Grave – Peter Coe Verbica
The Adventure of the Future Funeral – Hugh Ashton
The Problem of the Bruised Tongues – Will Murray
The Mystery of the Change of Art – Robert Perret
The Parsimonious Peacekeeper – Thaddeus Tuffentsamer
The Case of the Dirty Hand – G.L. Schulze
The Mystery of the Missing Artefacts – Tim Symonds

Part XI: Some Untold Cases (1880-1891)

Foreword – Lyndsay Faye
Foreword – Roger Johnson
Foreword – Melissa Grigsby
Foreword – Steve Emecz
Foreword – David Marcum
Unrecorded Holmes Cases (A Sonnet) – Arlene Mantin Levy and Mark Levy
The Most Repellant Man – Jayantika Ganguly
The Singular Adventure of the Extinguished Wicks – Will Murray
Mrs. Forrester's Complication – Roger Riccard
The Adventure of Vittoria, the Circus Belle – Tracy Revels

(Continued on the next page . . . .)

Part XII: Some Untold Cases (1894-1902)

PART XIII: 2019 Annual (1881-1890)

(Continued on the next page . . . .)

PART XIV: 2019 Annual (1891 -1897)

(Continued on the next page . . . .)

(Continued on the next page . . . .)

Part XVII – Whatever Remains . . . Must Be the Truth (1891-1898)

Part XVIII – Whatever Remains . . . Must Be the Truth (1899-1925)

(Continued on the next page . . . .)

Part XIX: 2020 Annual (1882-1890)

(Continued on the next page . . . .)

(Continued on the next page . . . .)

Part XXII: Some More Untold Cases (1877-1887)

(Continued on the next page . . . .)

The Dundas Separation Case – Kevin P. Thornton
The Broken Glass – Denis O. Smith

Part XXIII: Some More Untold Cases (1888-1894)

Foreword – Otto Penzler
Foreword – Roger Johnson
Foreword – Steve Emecz
Foreword – Jacqueline Silver
Foreword – David Marcum
The Housekeeper (*A Poem*) – John Linwood Grant
The Uncanny Adventure of the Hammersmith Wonder – Will Murray
Mrs. Forrester's Domestic Complication– Tim Gambrell
The Adventure of the Abducted Bard – I.A. Watson
The Adventure of the Loring Riddle – Craig Janacek
To the Manor Bound – Jane Rubino
The Crimes of John Clay – Paul Hiscock
The Adventure of the Nonpareil Club – Hugh Ashton
The Adventure of the Singular Worm – Mike Chinn
The Adventure of the Forgotten Brolly – Shane Simmons
The Adventure of the Tired Captain – Dacre Stoker and Leverett Butts
The Rhayader Legacy – David Marcum
The Adventure of the Tired Captain – Matthew J. Elliott
The Secret of Colonel Warburton's Insanity – Paul D. Gilbert
The Adventure of Merridew of Abominable Memory – Tracy J. Revels
The Affair of the Hellingstone Rubies – Margaret Walsh
The Adventure of the Drewhampton Poisoner – Arthur Hall
The Incident of the Dual Intrusions – Barry Clay
The Case of the Un-Paralleled Adventures – Steven Philip Jones
The Affair of the Friesland – Jan van Koningsveld
The Forgetful Detective – Marcia Wilson
The Smith-Mortimer Succession – Tim Gambrell
The Repulsive Matter of the Bloodless Banker – Will Murray

Part XXIV: Some More Untold Cases (1895-1903)

Foreword – Otto Penzler
Foreword – Roger Johnson
Foreword – Steve Emecz
Foreword – Jacqueline Silver
Foreword – David Marcum
Sherlock Holmes and the Return of the Missing Rhyme (*A Poem*) – Joseph W. Svec III
The Comet Wine's Funeral – Marcia Wilson
The Case of the Accused Cook – Brenda Seabrooke
The Case of Vanderbilt and the Yeggman – Stephen Herczeg

(Continued on the next page . . . .)

Part XXV: 2021 Annual (1881-1888)

(Continued on the next page . . . .)

(Continued on the next page . . . .)

Part XXVIII: More Christmas Adventures (1869-1888)

(Continued on the next page . . . .)

(Continued on the next page . . . .)

The Adventure of the Chained Phantom – J.S. Rowlinson
Santa's Little Elves – Kevin Thornton
The Case of the Holly-Sprig Pudding – Naching T. Kassa
The Canterbury Manifesto – David Marcum
The Case of the Disappearing Beaune – J. Lawrence Matthews
A Price Above Rubies – Jane Rubino
The Intrigue of the Red Christmas – Shane Simmons
The Bitter Gravestones – Chris Chan
The Midnight Mass Murder – Paul Hiscock

Part XXXI: 2022 Annual (1875-1887)
Foreword – Jeffrey Hatcher
Foreword – Roger Johnson
Foreword – Steve Emecz
Foreword – Emma West
Foreword – David Marcum
The Nemesis of Sherlock Holmes (A Poem) – Kelvin I. Jones
The Unsettling Incident of the History Professor's Wife – Sean M. Wright
The Princess Alice Tragedy – John Lawrence
The Adventure of the Amorous Balloonist – I.A. Watson
The Pilkington Case – Kevin Patrick McCann
The Adventure of the Disappointed Lover – Arthur Hall
The Case of the Impressionist Painting – Tim Symonds
The Adventure of the Old Explorer – Tracy J. Revels
Dr. Watson's Dilemma – Susan Knight
The Colonial Exhibition – Hal Glatzer
The Adventure of the Drunken Teetotaler – Thomas A. Burns, Jr.
The Curse of Hollyhock House – Geri Schear
The Sethian Messiah – David Marcum
Dead Man's Hand – Robert Stapleton
The Case of the Wary Maid – Gordon Linzner
The Adventure of the Alexandrian Scroll – David MacGregor
The Case of the Woman at Margate – Terry Golledge
A Question of Innocence – DJ Tyrer
The Grosvenor Square Furniture Van – Terry Golledge
The Adventure of the Veiled Man – Tracy J. Revels
The Disappearance of Dr. Markey – Stephen Herczeg
The Case of the Irish Demonstration – Dan Rowley

Part XXXII: 2022 Annual (1888-1895)
Foreword – Jeffrey Hatcher
Foreword – Roger Johnson
Foreword – Steve Emecz

(Continued on the next page . . . .)

Part XXXIII: 2022 Annual (1896-1919)

(Continued on the next page . . . .)

(Continued on the next page . . . .)

Part XXXVI: "However Improbable . . . ." (1897-1919)

(Continued on the next page . . . .)

(Continued on the next page . . . .)

(Continued on the next page . . . .)

Part XLI: Further Untold Cases (1877-1892)

Part XLII: Further Untold Cases (1894-1922)

(Continued on the next page . . . .)

The following contributors appear in this volume:
The MX Book of New Sherlock Holmes Stories
Part XLV – 2024 Annual (1898-1917)

The following contributors appear in these companion volumes:
Part XLIII – 2024 Annual (1874-1888)
Part XLIV – 2024 Annual (1889-1897)

Editor's Foreword:
"A fake, is it? Well, strike me!"
by David Marcum

Once upon a time, in long-ago days that are receding inexorably away from us into the misty past, the opportunities for admirers of Mr. Sherlock Holmes to enjoy his adventures were quite thin on the ground. For the first six years between late 1887 and late 1893, there were only twenty-six published Holmes narratives – *Twenty-six!* – with the last of those telling of Holmes's supposed death at the Reichenbach Falls. Then there was nothing – officially and Canonically, that is – until *The Hound of the Baskervilles* was serially released in 1901-1902. The next thirty-three Canonical tales appeared over the following twenty-five years, with more than one-third of those appearing as *The Return of Sherlock Holmes* (1903-1904), while publication of the others were sometimes separated from one another by years.

And then, the well might have dried up. At the end of the 1920's, both Watson and then the First Literary Agent had died, and Holmes was long removed to Sussex. He wasn't exactly retired from detection, but the majority of his time was then more involved in his apiaristic studies, and also working on his *magnum opus*, *The Whole Art of Detection*. For the admirers of Mr. Sherlock Holmes, there was a vast Holmesian vacuum.

Of course, there were other detectives who had filled the void when Holmes left Baker Street, although their arrivals didn't occur overnight. Dr. John Thorndyke was accepting clients at 5A King's Bench Walk in the late 1890's, so he overlapped Holmes's London practice by a few years. Solar Pons went into private practice in 1907 – possibly at 7B Praed Street, or perhaps somewhere else in those early days before moving so close to Paddington Station. Sometime after arriving in England as a war refugee in 1916, Hercule Poirot made his way to London and set up a consulting practice at No. 14 Farraway Street. The 1920's welcomed Lord Peter Wimsey to 110A Piccadilly Street and Albert Campion at 17A Bottle Street, with plenty of work for both. Their various biographers and literary agents provided information when news of Holmes was lacking, but what was needed – then and now and always – were more of Holmes's cases. *Lots more.*

In the early days, there were many Holmes parodies, but they're bogus and forgettable wastes of time. Seeing the supposedly "clever" and "humorous" ways that Holmes and Watson's names were misspelled and

1

distorted is now quite painful. Why go down those dead-end rabbit holes if stories about the True Holmes can be obtained?

The earliest extra-Canonical adventure was William Gillette's 1899 play (and later film and radio show) *Sherlock Holmes*. It had some painful inaccuracies – that bizarre romance that Gillette awkwardly jammed onto the conclusion, and ignorantly naming Professor Moriarty *Robert* instead of *James* – but it helped to fill the chasm. Then, decades later, Edith Meiser brilliantly realized that Holmes's adventures would be perfect when dramatized for the young radio medium. After multiple broadcasts of many of the pitifully few sixty Canonical stories, she brought forth additional previously unrevealed adventures – "The Hindoo in the Wicker Basket", "The Haunted Clock", and possibly the first explanation behind the events of "The Giant Rat of Sumatra". After Meiser's association with the radio show ended, other chroniclers – like Denis Green, Leslie Charteris, and Anthony Boucher – carried on her important work.

Although many details of these early extra-Canonical adventures ended up being incorrect, courtesy of script writers adding their own poorly informed touches to Watson's notes, it was still good news when a number of new stories also appeared in the 1930's and 1940's by way of films starring Clive Brook, Arthur Wontner, and Basil Rathbone. In the 1950's, Adrian Conan Doyle, son of the First Literary Agent, and John Dickson Carr revealed *The Exploits of Sherlock Holmes*. While Adrian, along with his brother Denis, had made many enemies within the Sherlockian community that resulted in attacks on this particular Holmesian volume, it's actually an excellent collection of stories about the *True Holmes* – set in the correct period, and with no non-Sherlockian aspects and agendas awkwardly grafted on.

1959's Hammer version of *The Hound* was notable for several reasons: The first time Holmes was excellently acted by Peter Cushing. The first Holmes film in color. But also because it had a vastly altered and fictional ending. (This wasn't the first time that *The Hound* had been violated. Several German versions leapt in entirely absurd directions, and even Rathbone's version added a séance and left out Lestrade.)

The 1960's gave us, in addition to the Canonical offerings of Peter Cushing and Douglas Wilmer, the first film encounter between Holmes and Jack the Ripper, *A Study in Terror* (1965 – although the first print encounter was *Wie Jack, der Aufschlitzer Gefast Wurde* [How Jack the Ripper Was Caught] in 1907). The book version of *A Study in Terror* contains extended alternating chapters of both Holmes's investigation and Ellery Queen's contemporary follow-up as he's reading Watson's account – and along the way, it happily provides another book in the Queen Canon.

The parodies had continued all along, of course. All sorts of films over the years indirectly referenced Holmes when they placed characters in deerstalkers – Laurel and Hardy, The Three Stooges, The Marx Brothers, Abbott and Costello, and even The Little Rascals (a.k.a. Our Gang, depending on your generation). 1956 brought the brilliant *Deduce, You Say,* starring Daffy Duck and Porky Pig as Dorlock Homes and Dr. Watkins. Throughout, no one ever said that Daffy Duck or Harpo Marx or Lou Costello had actually *played* Sherlock Holmes. People had enough sense to realize that Holmes was *Holmes* – separate from these completely different characters displaying Sherlockian aspects. But in 1971, the shift between harmless Holmesian parody and more detrimental Holmesian replacement began to occur with *They Might Be Giants* starring George C. Scott. He portrayed a modern-day judge, Justin Playfair, who slides into mental illness after the death of his wife. He believes he's Holmes, and those around him seem to believe it, but there is never any question – Scott is playing *Justin Playfair*, a man with a debilitating delusion, and he is *not* ever actually *Sherlock Holmes*.

And yet . . . when people now make lists of Holmes on screen, they list George C. Scott as Holmes – *although he never actually played Sherlock Holmes!*

This terrible trend of slapping Holmes's name on any character and then asserting that this *was* Holmes, as if Holmes was some body-and-time hopping Time Lord, began to gain traction. In *The Return of the World's Greatest Detective*, Larry Hagman plays *Sherman* Holmes, a modern-day policeman whose motorcycle falls on him – and he wakes up believing that's he's *Sherlock* Holmes – and now some people think that Larry Hagman played Holmes. 1984's *The Return of Sherlock Holmes* was a new twist – Sherlock Holmes had been frozen in the 1890's and was thawed out in the 1980's. The same sad gimmick was repeated in *1994: Baker Street*. In neither case did the actors actually play Holmes, as Holmes was *not* frozen and thawed out in the latter Twentieth Century – but people still credit these as actual Holmes films, and indicate that these actors played Holmes – which they did not. These films eroded the actual facts about Holmes in people's minds, wherein they forget or willfully ignore that Holmes was a man born in 1854, and not a thawed-out Holmesicle in modern times. Nor was he a mentally ill judge or brain-damaged motorcycle cop.

In between these two frozen films, Michael Caine played Reginald Kincaid – and not Sherlock Holmes – in *Without a Clue* (1988). This is another parody Holmes film, and not a legitimate post-Canonical work – and yet, lists and artwork regularly include Caine as "Sherlock Holmes", despite the fact that he never played him.

3

Meanwhile, the idea of using Holmes in non-Holmes ways continued to grow as well. There have been more versions of Sherlock Holmes-versus-Dracula than I care to list here, and sadly, in almost every case the authors forget Holmes's dictum of "No ghosts [*or vampires*] need apply,", and they essentially and simply re-tell Bram Stoker's *Dracula* with Holmes replacing Van Helsing. This opened the door to all kinds of other Holmes-as-Van Helsing encounters with Frankenstein, the Wolfman, demons and devils (including Satan himself), mummies, Lovecraftian Gods, steam-punk monstrosities, dinosaurs, sea monsters, space aliens, brain-eating spoors, brain-eating space-alien spoors, and just about any other supernatural critter imaginable. *No ghosts need apply? Pfui!* In these cases, no normal client need apply, because Holmes is too busy looking for his cross and his garlic and his holy water and his silver bullets for the next monster encounter.

And as *Fake Holmes* became even more un-moored from *True Holmes*, it was easier to graft on various other aspects – taking him from the person described in the Canon to a various levels of dysfunctional brokenness, to the point that certain television shows presented him as a full-on sociopathic murderer or a tattooed New York drug addict paying off a prostitute at the exact moment he meets his new Watson (and that we, the viewer, first meet him too).

But thankfully, the *True Holmes* has *not* been lost in this red tide of Holmes-in-name-only.

In 1974, Nicholas Meyer inaugurated the new (and still ongoing) Sherlockian Golden Age with his discovery of *The Seven-Per-Cent Solution*. The story is flawed, of course – the parts about Moriarty being a victim, for instance, and that the Great Hiatus never occurred, were apparently grafted onto the manuscript by Moriarty's heirs in an effort to rehabilitate his reputation. Still, the world was electrified when this book was released, for it became apparent that there were unknown Watsonian manuscripts out there in the world, waiting to be discovered – in scattered Tin Dispatch Boxes (for there were apparently more than one of those,) and hidden in people's attics and buried in their grandparent's papers. In 1975, *The Seven-Per-Cent Solution* became a major film, further pouring gas on the previously smoldering *True Holmes* fire. Stories began to trickle forth from authors like Sean Wright and Nick Utechin and Daniel Stashower – slowly at first, and then more and more and more. That particular genie, thank God, was out of the bottle for good.

But imagine a world where Nicholas Meyer and the rest *didn't* discover Watson's manuscripts – first *The Seven-Per-Cent Solution*, and then others. Would the misdirection taken by George C. Scott's *They Might Be Giants* have become more influential? Would the parodies and subversive versions of *Fake Holmes* have become even more established with no Sherlockian Golden Age to hold them in check? Would Holmes as Van Helsing become the new norm, replacing in people's mind the Canonical Holmes, and making the latter original adventures no more than footnotes or a jumping-off place? Or would Holmes have irrevocably become the poster child for murderous sociopaths, as almost became the case in the early 2000's after the frantic and urgent efforts of that television show's producers to permanently hijack him that way?

In 2015, *The MX Book of New Sherlock Holmes Stories* was specifically created to remind people of the *True Holmes* – a hero and not a villain. A consulting detective, and not a monster hunter. Someone to be admired and taken seriously, and not a subject of comedy and ridicule. A champion born in 1854 and set in a specific era, and not a Doctor Who wanna-be who can be dropped into any timeline.

Now, nearly ten years later, with 45 volumes (and more in preparation) and over 920 stories, more weight has been added to the scales on the side of the *True Holmes*. But *Fake Holmes* is still sitting over there, grinning and gibbering on the other side of the see-saw, and the work isn't done.

We can but try.

* * * * *

"Of course, I could only stammer out my thanks."
– *The unhappy John Hector McFarlane,* "The Norwood Builder"

As always when one of these collections is finished, I want to thank with all my heart my incredible, patient, brilliant, kind, and beautiful wife of nearly thirty-six years, Rebecca – Every day I count my blessings and realize how lucky I am, for she is the finest and fairest of them all!!! – and our amazing, funny, creative, talented, and wonderful son, and my friend, Dan. I love you both, and you are everything to me!

With each new set of the MX anthologies, some things get easier, and there are also new challenges. For several years, the stresses of real life have been much greater than when this series started. Through all of this, the amazing contributors have once again pulled some amazing works from The Tin Dispatch Box. I'm more grateful than I can express to every contributor who has donated both time and royalties to this ongoing project – both for the current set, and also the 200+ contributors from around the world since the beginning. It's amazing what we've accomplished – as just mentioned, over 920 new Holmes adventures in 45 volumes (so far), and over $120,000 raised for the Undershaw school for special needs children!

I also want to give special recognition to the multiple contributors of this set: Arthur Hall, Tracy Revels, Marcia Wilson, Daniel D. Victor, Susan Knight, Alan Dimes, Paula Hammond, Mike Adamson, Jonathan Schneer, and Daniel Lenois.

Additionally, I cannot express how thankful I am to all of those who keep buying these books and making them the largest and most popular Sherlockian anthology ever.

I'm so glad to have gotten to know so many of you through this process – both contributors and readers. It's an undeniable fact that Sherlock Holmes people are the *best* people!

I wish especially thank the following:

- *Daniel Stashower* – I first became aware of Mr. Stashower in 1985, when his Holmes adventure *The Adventure of the Ectoplasmic Man* was first published. That was during those dark days when only one or two good traditional Canonical Holmes pastiches were published per year – and that's if it was a good year! I was halfway through college, and bought it and devoured it, impressed at the meeting between Holmes and Watson and Houdini, and also learning a lot more about Houdini than I'd previously known.

  From there, Mr. Stashower went on to write and edit a number of other works, including several volumes about the First Literary Agent (*Teller of Tales: The Life of Arthur Conan Doyle* and *Arthur Conan Doyle: A Life in Letters*, both multiple winners of the Agatha, the Edgar, and the Anthony awards, and *Dangerous Work: Diary of an Arctic Adventure*) and co-editing four Holmes anthologies (with Martin H. Greenberg): *Murder in Baker Street*, *Murder, My Dear Watson*, *Ghosts in Baker Street*, and *Sherlock Holmes in America*.

  I was thrilled to finally meet him in 2020 when I attended the Sherlock Holmes Birthday Weekend in New York, when he signed for me another volume he'd co-edited, *The Worst Man in London* (containing the facsimile manuscript of "Charles Augustus Milverton", along with a number of related essays). His work has been important and impressive, but personally I'm most grateful for what he's done to bring more Holmes adventures to light. Having admired his Sherlockian work for nearly forty years, I'm thrilled that he's a part of these books.

6

- *Steve Emecz* – From my first association with MX in 2013, I observed that MX (under Steve Emecz's leadership) was *the* fast-rising superstar of the Sherlockian publishing world – and more than ten years later, that has not changed. Connecting with MX and Steve Emecz was personally an amazing life-changing event for me, as it has been for countless other Sherlockian authors. It has led me to write many more stories, and then to edit books, along with unexpected additional Holmes Pilgrimages to England – none of which might have happened otherwise. By way of my first email with Steve, I've had the chance to make some incredible Sherlockian friends and play in the Holmesian Sandbox in ways that I would have never dreamed possible.

  MX has become *the* powerhouse premiere Sherlockian Publisher, providing new stories for those (like me) who need them, and writing and editing opportunities for those (like me) who might not otherwise have had the chance.

  Through it all, Steve has been one of the most positive and supportive people that I've ever known.

  From the beginning, Steve has let me explore various Sherlockian projects and open up my own personal possibilities in ways that otherwise would have never happened. Thank you, Steve, for every opportunity!

- *Roger Johnson* – From his immediate support at the time of the first volumes in this series to the present, I can't imagine Roger not being part of these books, and once again he has heeded the call. His Sherlockian knowledge is exceptional, as is the work that he does to further the cause of The Master. But even more than that, both Roger and his wife, Jean Upton, are simply the finest and best of people, and I'm very lucky to know both of them. Many many thanks for being part of this.

- *Brian Belanger* – I initially became acquainted with Brian when he took over the duties of creating the covers for MX Books, and I found him to be a great collaborator, and wonderfully creative too. I've worked with him on many projects with MX and Belanger Books, which he co-founded with his brother Derrick Belanger, also a good friend. Along with MX Publishing, Derrick and Brian have absolutely locked up the Sherlockian publishing field with a vast amount of amazing material. It's very gratifying to see the old

7

dinosaurs trembling with every new and worthy Sherlockian project, one after another after another, that these two companies create. Luckily MX and Belanger Books work closely with one another, and I'm thrilled to be associated with both of them. Many thanks to Brian for all he does for both publishers, and for all he's done for me personally.

And finally, last but certainly *not* least, thanks to **Sir Arthur Conan Doyle**: Author, doctor, adventurer, and the Founder of the Sherlockian Feast. Honored, and present in spirit.

As I always note when putting together an anthology of Holmes stories, the effort has been a labor of love. These adventures are just more tiny threads woven into the ongoing Great Holmes Tapestry, continuing to grow and grow, for there can *never* be enough stories about the man whom Watson described as *"the best and wisest . . . whom I have ever known."*

David Marcum
April 6ᵗʰ, 2024
The 141ˢᵗ Anniversary of
the first day of
"The Speckled Band"

8

Foreword
by Daniel Stashower

"*This I am sure of,*" Arthur Conan Doyle once declared, "*that there are far fewer supremely good short stories than there are supremely good long books. It takes more exquisite skill to carve the cameo than the statue.*"

The comment reflected hard-won experience. Early in his career, while practicing medicine in Southsea, Conan Doyle seemed on occasion to begrudge the time he spent pursuing the short story form. "*I realized that I could go on doing short stories forever and never make headway,*" he would recall. "*What is necessary is that your name should be on the back of a volume. Only so do you assert your individuality, and get the full credit or discredit of your achievement.*"

He soon reversed course. In April of 1891, even as his novel *The White Company* was enjoying notable success, Conan Doyle's career as a medical practitioner reached a turning point. Having recently abandoned his practice in Southsea to study diseases of the eye, the thirty-one-year-old physician moved his family to London and declared himself ready to "*put up my plate as an oculist*", setting up a consulting room at 2 Upper Wimpole Street. His lease entitled him to a consulting room and a share of a waiting room, but, as Conan Doyle ruefully admitted, "*I was soon to find that they were both waiting rooms.*"

His thoughts naturally turned to literature, and he now approached the subject of short stories in a more congenial spirit. It struck him that there might be some benefit in writing a series of stories featuring a single, continuing character. This offered an advantage over the more conventional serialized novel, because the reader would not lose interest if one installment or another was missed. "*Looking round for my central character,*" he wrote, "*I felt that Sherlock Holmes, whom I had already handled in two little books, would easily lend himself to a succession of short stories.*"

This proved to be a life-changing decision. Not only had Conan Doyle made a canny marketing decision, but he had also found the natural showcase for the talents of Sherlock Holmes. In the two previously published Holmes novellas – *A Study in Scarlet* and *The Sign of the Four* – the detective had been obliged to trundle offstage for long patches of exposition. The short story format offered a compact execution and brisk pace, and highlighted Conan Doyle's singular talent for puzzle plots.

Within weeks, Conan Doyle began sending the first of his Sherlock Holmes short stories to a new magazine called *The Strand*, and the rest – in a cliché he would have abhorred – is history.

"I've written a good deal more about him than I ever intended to do," Conan Doyle would observe in 1927, forty years after Holmes first saw print, *"but my hand has been rather forced by kind friends who continually wanted to know more. And so it is that this monstrous growth has come out, out of what was really a comparatively small seed."*

The phrase *"monstrous growth"* admits a number of interpretations, with a heavy suggestion of Conan Doyle's ambivalence towards his famous creation. One naturally wonders what he would have made of the present volumes, the latest in a series of forty-five – *Forty-five!* – collections of short stories, all contributed by kind friends continually wanting to know more. Even so, I feel confident that Conan Doyle would look upon the MX book series with a kindly eye. *"If every man who receives a cheque for a story which owes its springs to Poe were to pay a tithe to a monument for the master,"* he once declared, *"he would have a pyramid as big as that of Cheops."* Each of the stories in this series owes its springs to Conan Doyle – unabashedly so. As yet there is no Egyptian pyramid dedicated in Conan Doyle's name, but at last count these books had raised some $120,000 for the Undershaw school, which provides a specialist setting for children with learning difficulties and additional needs, under the banner of *"eliminating the impossible"*. It is difficult to imagine a more fitting monument to the master; one that preserves the legacy of his Hindhead home even as it helps to insure – as someone once remarked – that education never ends.

Daniel Stashower, BSI
January 2024

A Letter From Scotland Yard
Discovered by Roger Johnson

My dear Dr. Watson,

Further to our correspondence of the 15th *ult* . . . .

No, scrub that. This is strictly unofficial and off the record, and if you so much as think of publishing any part of it, *I will have you, sunshine,* good and proper.

Right. Where was I? Oh, yes . . . .

I see that Mr. Sherlock Holmes has decided to pack in the detective business and retire to the south coast. Very nice, too! I also am about to become a gentleman of leisure, having been detecting, I may say, for quite a few years more than Mr. H, but I don't expect to be moving from my little house in Camberwell – not till they carry me out feet first, anyway.

Well, well! I can't say I begrudge Mr. Holmes his retirement. Goodness knows he's earned it, and I'm not too proud to admit that he was a great help to me on many occasions, and to some of my colleagues as well. Toby Gregson – He hates being called that! – *Tobias* Gregson is probably indebted to Mr. H. for his promotion. Did you know that? At all events, he became an Inspector shortly after the successful conclusion of the Arnsworth Castle affair.

Come to think of it, I may even owe *my* rise in the force to Mr. Holmes, though I like to think that my own good qualities had something to do with it. If I remember correctly, Mr. H. once said I was the best of the professionals, and I've always taken that as a high compliment, even if he did also call me "that imbecile Lestrade"!

Dear me, but we've seen some times, haven't we, Doctor – You, me and Mr. Sherlock Holmes! "We have heard the chimes at midnight, Master Shallow."

Hah! That surprised you, I'll bet: *Me* quoting the Bard! The fact is that I once saw Beerbohm Tree play Falstaff, and I've never forgotten his performance. I couldn't tell you which play it was – "The Merry Wives of Whatsit" or "Henry Ivy" – but it was the best evening I ever had in the theatre, outside of the Drury Lane pantomimes, of course. (I say, can you imagine Herbert Campbell as the fat knight and Dan Leno as Justice Shallow? That *would* be something, now, wouldn't it?)

We have seen some times, though, haven't we? That Norwood affair, the business out in Herefordshire, the Black Pearl of the Borgias . . . Great days, Doctor, great days! And, you know, I was right about that last case: The Mafia *was* involved, after all, even if its involvement did turn out to be a bit of a red herring.

Do you recall our first proper meeting? Well, of course you do. It was at an empty house in Lauriston Gardens, Brixton – empty, that is, apart from Toby Gregson and a *very* ugly corpse. Gregson was at his most pompous, I remember, and Mr. Holmes was at his most superior. I don't need to tell you that he was always keen to prove himself a better detective than any of us, and in those early days, I sometimes suspected that that outweighed his wish to see justice done. Later, of course, I discovered that I was mistaken, but it was a close-run thing on occasion.

That, as I say, was our first *proper* meeting, though we had seen each other a few times before then, without either of us knowing just who the other one was. I quickly realised that you were sharing digs with Mr. H., and in time he told you that I was – Let me see – "*a well-known detective, who got himself into a fog recently over a forgery case*". Yes, well . . . it's true enough, as far as it goes, though the case was a good deal more complicated than Mr. H. would admit.

You weren't exactly complimentary about me yourself, were you? A "*little sallow, rat-faced, dark-eyed fellow*" you called me then, and not so long after, you said I was "*lean and ferret-like*". Well, I suppose a ferret is a more useful creature than a rat! I rather like ferrets, as it happens. My old dad used to breed them – lithe, handsome things they were, very cat-like in their ways, wonderful for getting in and out of tight corners, absolutely fearless, and unbeatable for rabbiting. You know, I really don't mind being called ferret-like! A ferret's as good a model for a detective as any sort of *dog*.

Come to think of it, you've compared me to a dog on occasion as well. Not a hound – I think you kept that particular simile for Mr. Sherlock Holmes – but a "*small wiry bulldog*". That made my wife sit up, I can tell you! She's always the first to admit that yours truly is no oil painting, but even she couldn't work out how the same person can resemble both a *ferret* and a *bulldog*!

Let's see. That was the Dartmoor business, wasn't it? Why I ever let Mr. Holmes talk me into these things I shall never know. You wouldn't *believe* the trouble I had with my own Superintendent and the Deputy C. C. of the Devonshire Constabulary! I'm sure it put my career back two years. Ah, well, it's all water under the bridge, and I wouldn't have missed it for the world, though I don't know whether Sir Henry would agree. Still, he seems to be getting on all right these days, thank goodness.

12

What was that stuff about an *unsigned warrant*, though? "*Coming down with* unsigned warrant." I can only imagine that you had lost the telegram I sent and wrote the first thing that came into your head. After all this time I can't remember just what I did say, but I'm certain I never mentioned an *unsigned warrant*! What's the use of a warrant if it isn't *signed*?

And while I think of it, I've often wondered why you described me as *little* and *small*. I'm *thin* – always have been, eat like a horse and never put a pound on – and I'll grant you that I'm shorter than Mr. H. Well, most people are, aren't they? He's a fraction over six foot, I think, and, as you said yourself, he's so *very* lean that he seems to be considerably taller. (It's odd, but *my* leanness seems to have the opposite effect!) I'm shorter than *you*, if it comes to that, but only by half-an-inch. In fact I stand – or did, in my prime – exactly five-foot-ten, the absolute minimum height for an officer in the good old Metropolitan Police.

I hope you don't mind me letting off a bit of steam. It's not really anything personal, you know. Only things are rather slow here at the moment. If I weren't writing to you, I'd just be tidying up my desk and clearing out my cupboard, getting ready to leave the Yard.

I'll miss the old place, of course I will. Old, did I say? This is *New* Scotland Yard, mate, and they don't let you forget it, especially if you've been around as long as I have, and remember working at *Great* Scotland Yard, the other end of Whitehall! Well, you'll remember what that was like. We occupied half-a-dozen buildings around Whitehall Place and Great Scotland Yard. It was dark, poky, and uncomfortable. This place is like the Langham Hotel by comparison, but that's not why I'll miss it.

It's the *people*, the fact that every day is different, the knowledge that you're helping to keep London safe . . . but there's more to it than that. We work hard here, you know (and it is mostly brainwork, whatever Mr. Holmes may say to the contrary). Sometimes it can be dull, but *most* of the time – Well, you've written about the "Adventures" of Sherlock Holmes. I can assure you that the adventures of G. Lestrade have been no less exciting!

Still, I can't deny that the best of them have been the ones I shared with you and Mr. Holmes. The Baskerville case really was a corker, and it would have been hard to top that business of the stolen submarine plans. Police work isn't always appreciated, despite what you may read in the papers, so it's nice to get a bit of public recognition – Ah! I know what you're thinking, but you're wrong. True, there was no public recognition in *that* case: You said yourself that it was part of "*that secret history of a nation which is often so much more intimate and interesting than its public chronicles*". But we all knew, didn't we, that we'd done the country good service, and that we had the approval of the people who matter.

If anyone should ask me, though, what was the most memorable adventure in my forty years with the force, I'd have to say the arrest of Sebastian Moran. Not just because it cleared up a particularly baffling murder case. Not even because it put an end to the Moriarty gang at last, but because it rather gloriously confirmed my suspicions that Mr. Sherlock Holmes *was* still alive and that he would eventually come back to London. You know, Doctor, I was never so glad in my life as when I got his message asking me to be in Baker Street that night!

And now, even though only one of us has reached what I'd call retirement age, we're both packing it in. Goodness knows what Mr. Holmes will find to do down there in Sussex, but I intend to spend my time in the garden. Mrs. L has made it very clear that she doesn't want me in the house all day, getting under her feet!

You've got yourself a good practice now, haven't you, just off Harley Street, and I can't somehow see you retiring for a good many years. Well, if anyone deserves success, Doctor, I reckon it's you. You've said a lot in your memoirs about the remarkable qualities of Mr. Sherlock Holmes, and you've even come to appreciate that we in the C.I.D. aren't lacking in skill and intelligence! But you've rather tended to hide your own light under a bushel. On occasion, you've made yourself out to be a bit of a booby, which is something you're definitely *not*!

Your military service may have been fairly short, but it was by no means ignominious. You're intelligent, skilful and courageous. Unlike Mr. H, you have a gift for making friends – and you're a better shot than he is, for all his fancy pistol-work indoors. (My word, wasn't Mrs. Hudson's face a picture when she saw what he'd done to the wall of your sitting-room!)

Above all, Doctor, you're honest and straightforward. It's been a pleasure and a privilege to know you. If I may adopt the language of the streets for a moment, and use a phrase that I'm sure Mr. Holmes would recognise, you, Dr. John H. Watson, are a *Diamond Geezer*!

Please give my best regards to Mrs. Watson, and believe me to be,

Yours very sincerely,
G. Lestrade . . .

. . . by way of Roger Johnson, BSI, ASH
Editor: *The Sherlock Holmes Journal*
February 2024

An Ongoing Legacy
for Sherlock Holmes
by Steve Emecz

Undershaw
Circa 1900

With over six-hundred Sherlock Holmes books in print, we continue to have lots of fun publishing Holmes stories. *The MX Book of New Sherlock Holmes Stories* is by some way our largest and most successful project.

Since 2023, every book bought on our website means we donate a meal to a family in need through ShareTheMeal from The World Food Programme (WFP). I am proud to have been a member of the external advisory council and a mentor with the WFP for several years, and part of the team in 2020 that was awarded the Nobel Peace Prize. You can find links to all our projects on our website:

https://mxpublishing.com/pages/about-us

Coming into 2024, it is audio that has been the fastest growing segment – though we do see some fans still wanting print, so we will continue to produce paperback and hardcover versions – especially of this series.

Steve Emecz
March 2024

The Doyle Room at Undershaw
Partially funded through royalties from
The MX Book of New Sherlock Holmes Stories

A Word from Undershaw
by Emma West

Undershaw
September 9, 2016
Grand Opening of the Stepping Stones School
(Now *Undershaw*)
(Photograph courtesy of Roger Johnson)

"Until you spread your wings, you'll have no idea how far you can fly."
– Napoleon Bonaparte

There are so many attributes to an Undershaw education, both within the classroom and in the world beyond. Who we are and the strong Undershaw character we show to the world are as real on the outside as they are on the inside. We are who we say we are. Our sense of community, our strong culture, and the values which shape our behaviour all become the very tangible qualities of an Undershaw student.

We have had such a wonderful start to 2024, and at this juncture of being halfway through our school year, it's such a pleasure to recount some of our achievements that go so far in illustrating the cultural fabric of our school.

Under the leadership of Will Milner-Smith, Undershaw's Physical Education Lead, we have seen an exponential increase in participation in sports, particularly football. We have four teams across the school, all of which compete across the county in accessible leagues. Our girls' team has just returned from a tournament hosted by Fulham FC (London's oldest professional football club, established in 1879) where they were not only triumphant, but congratulated for their 'tournament values' by the staff and students from the opposing teams. Illustrating their football skills alongside their inter-personal skills has been the focus of our physical education curriculum, and it was wonderful to see these skills shining through.

To continue the theme of resilience, a group of students have just completed their Duke of Edinburgh Award Bronze Expedition, which involved two days of walking and an overnight camp. The technical skills on show (map reading, setting up camp, fire lighting, and campfire cooking) were balanced beautifully by their life skills and school values of respect, kindness, and resilience – and obviously a huge dose of teamwork.

We are also excited to bring you news of our first collaboration with an international school: Kampinda School in Zambia. PEAS (Promoting Equality in African Schools) is one of our partner charities supported by the Leo Lion Foundation. This is the first of many opportunities of this type for Undershaw, and we're excited for the future of this partnership where we can share best practice and get to know more about the world, our friends in other geographies and cultures, and shape a new way of working.

Undershaw continues to recruit and retain the very best talent, and to that end, all our Teaching Assistants have just been awarded the Open University qualification in 'Understanding Autism'. Not only does this illustrate their significant passion and commitment to our students at Undershaw, but also Undershaw's belief and investment in our staff. Careers at Undershaw are sought after, and working at a Centre of Excellence for SEND education is an enviable role.

We are so proud of our school, and of the staff and students who showcase our vision every day. I continue to be proud of our relationships outside the gates too, some with people who have never set foot in the school but know from our reputation of the abundance of good that we do here. I thank you for sharing your talent with us and for your keen commitment to us and to our remarkable students. Thank you for being by our side as we look forward to end of the academic year, awash with all its celebrations, fun to be had, and the promise of the new beginnings in the year beyond. I look forward to writing again in the Autumn with more news from Undershaw.

Emma West
Headteacher, Undershaw
March 2024

"Undershaw," Hindhead Conan Doyle's House.

Editor's *Caveats*

When these anthologies first began back in 2015, I noted that the authors were from all over the world – and thus, there would be British spelling and American spelling. As I explained then, I didn't want to take the responsibility of changing American spelling to British and vice-versa. I would undoubtedly miss something, leading to inconsistencies, or I'd change something incorrectly.

Some readers are bothered by this, made nervous and irate when encountering American spelling as written by Watson, and in stories set in England. However, here in America, the versions of The Canon that we read have long-ago has their spelling Americanized, so it isn't quite as shocking for us.

Additionally, I offer my apologies up front for any typographical errors that have slipped through. As a print-on-demand publisher, MX does not have squadrons of editors as some readers believe. The business consists of three part-time people who also have busy lives elsewhere – Steve Emecz, Sharon Emecz, and Timi Emecz – so the editing effort largely falls on the contributors. Some readers and consumers out there in the world are unhappy with this – apparently forgetting about all of those self-produced Holmes stories and volumes from decades ago (typed and Xeroxed) with awkward self-published formatting and loads of errors that are now prized as very expensive collector's items.

I'm personally mortified when errors slip through – ironically, there will probably be errors in these *caveats* – and I apologize now, but without a regiment of professional full-time editors looking over my shoulder, this is as good as it gets. Real life is more important than writing and editing – even in such a good cause as promoting the True and Traditional Canonical Holmes – and only so much time can be spent preparing these books before they're released into the wild. I hope that you can look past any errors, small or huge, and simply enjoy these stories, and appreciate the efforts of everyone involved, and the sincere desire to add to The Great Holmes Tapestry.

And in spite of any errors here, there are more Sherlock Holmes stories in the world than there were before, and that's a good thing.

David Marcum
Editor

Sherlock Holmes (1854-1957) was born in Yorkshire, England, on 6 January, 1854. In the mid-1870's, he moved to 24 Montague Street, London, where he established himself as the world's first Consulting Detective. After meeting Dr. John H. Watson in early 1881, he and Watson moved to rooms at 221b Baker Street, where his reputation as the world's greatest detective grew for several decades. He was presumed to have died battling noted criminal Professor James Moriarty on 4 May, 1891, but he returned to London on 5 April, 1894, resuming his consulting practice in Baker Street. Retiring to the Sussex coast near Beachy Head in October 1903, he continued to be associated in various private and government investigations while giving the impression of being a reclusive apiarist. He was very involved in the events encompassing World War I, and to a lesser degree those of World War II. He passed away peacefully upon the cliffs above his Sussex home on his 103rd birthday, 6 January, 1957.

Dr. John Hamish Watson (1852-1929) was born in Stranraer, Scotland on 7 August, 1852. In 1878, he took his Doctor of Medicine Degree from the University of London, and later joined the army as a surgeon. Wounded at the Battle of Maiwand in Afghanistan (27 July, 1880), he returned to London late that same year. On New Year's Day, 1881, he was introduced to Sherlock Holmes in the chemical laboratory at Barts. Agreeing to share rooms with Holmes in Baker Street, Watson became invaluable to Holmes's consulting detective practice. Watson was married and widowed three times, and from the late 1880's onward, in addition to his participation in Holmes's investigations and his medical practice, he chronicled Holmes's adventures, with the assistance of his literary agent, Sir Arthur Conan Doyle, in a series of popular narratives, most of which were first published in *The Strand* magazine. Watson's later years were spent preparing a vast number of his notes of Holmes's cases for future publication. Following a final important investigation with Holmes, Watson contracted pneumonia and passed away on 24 July, 1929.

Photos of Sherlock Holmes and Dr. John H. Watson courtesy of Roger Johnson

The
MX Book
of
New

Sherlock Holmes Stories

Part XLV
2024 Annual
(1898-1917)

Heaven's Guise
by Alisha Shea

Hours crawl and minutes pass
And here I sit upon my arse.

A silly rhyme, I softly giggle
Perhaps I *should* cut back a little.

But life is tedious, dreary and dull
And thoughts run rampant though my skull

Formulae and ancient texts,
Symphonies and pirate wrecks,
Poisons, pashas and Poseidon,
Falcons and the drafts they glide on,
Architecture, gleaming steel,
A sawmill with its turning wheel,
Serpents scales, ouroborous,
Stolen jewels, treasures lost,
Pleading faces of clients I have met,
Memories of losses I'd prefer to forget . . . .

I puff my pipe until my clenched jaw aches.
And ashes fill a nearby plate.

I fiddle for hours. My fingers grow numb,
Horsehair worn; a string has sprung.

I survey my books on shelves and on floor,
But they contain nothing I've not read before.

I start an experiment, but quit halfway through.
I find I care not if it turns red or blue.

I stalk empty streets from dusk until dawn.
Though my muscles may tire, my mind rushes on.

I finally arrive at the end of my wits

And wish for a friend to distract me a bit.

But I've been abandoned for love of a wife.
Thus only one recourse remains in my life.

The needle, the vial, one tiny injection
Will preserve me from ceaseless introspection.

My thoughts slowly drift. Focus is lost.
Relief found at last, but at terrible cost.
I do understand this course is unwise.
That the devil will tempt us in Heaven's guise.

But I succumb to temptation anyway.
After all – It is just for today.

The Adventure of the Awakened Mummy
by Tracy J. Revels

My friend Mr. Sherlock Holmes was often a very difficult man. For example, it was almost an impossible feat to convince him to take a holiday, to commit to a brief respite from the noise, crowds, and crime of London. He believed the evil elements within the city would run amuck if he was absent from Baker Street for more than a fortnight. However, I once persuaded him that a brief retreat to a pleasant country house in Hampshire would be good for avoiding the nervous collapse which, as both his friend and physician, I judged to be imminent. By good fortune, an old army comrade of mine, Mr. Charles Lane, a former artillery sergeant in the Berkshires, had recently inherited a small country residence, and was gracious enough to invite us both for seven days of shooting, fishing, or simply lounging about, as it struck our fancy. Once assured that it was a bachelor household, and there would be no expectations of sociability with the neighbors, my friend acquiesced.

Trouble, however, followed us to the country.

We had been in residence less than twenty-four hours. Holmes, who favored the ever-changing metropolis to pleasant scenes of nature, demurred from accompanying Lane and myself on a morning constitutional, preferring instead to lounge about my friend's library. Meanwhile, I was delighted to set out with Lane, accompanied by his faithful dog Vino, an odd-looking canine whose heritage baffled even Holmes.

"Beagle and foxhound, but with some terrier, bulldog, and perhaps schnauzer as well on his family tree," Lane said, as we slowly made our way down the road. "Ugly creature, but always on the prowl, never losing a scent. Rather like your companion, I suppose."

I gave a hearty laugh. We were just cresting a hill, and in the distance, across the fields, I could see a gray, gothic building surrounded by an imposing wall. I pointed to it, inquiring as to what it might be.

"Ah, that is the Manor School for the Reform of Wayward Youth," Lane said. "Lads who have run afoul of the law, but aren't judged to be incorrigible, are sentenced there. A few even emerge truly reborn to good morals, or so I am told by several local notables who happen to be donors." He lit a pipe, musing for a moment upon his neighbors and his good fortune to reside among them. "Lord Hewell and his Lady live just east of the institution, and Baroness Nettle is to its west. Who would have thought an old sergeant like me would have settled in such distinguished company, heh? And there's also Mr. Topher Reilly, who lives at Ra House."

"The Egyptologist?"

"You've heard of him."

I nodded. "I attended one of his lectures when I was at the university. He presented on Egyptian tomb art." I shook my head. "I'm ashamed to admit it, but I dozed off and when I woke up, the room was empty!"

"That doesn't surprise me in the least," Lane chortled. "Reilly is a pompous old windbag. But he possesses a fine home, a fat checkbook, and a lovely unmarried daughter."

I was about to make a jest about Lane's sudden interest in all things Egyptian when Vino, who had darted away from us, came running across the field with something in his jaws. Lane shook his head.

"Ah, you scoundrel, what do you have now? It had better not be one of Lady Hewell's riding gloves. I'll end up in Broadmoor if those go missing again and . . . ."

The words died on his lips. I leaned forward, my jaw dropping in astonishment. The dog looked back and forth between us, as if awaiting praise for his discovery.

Clenched in his jaw was a withered human hand.

"How good of you to return so quickly," Holmes said, as we came bounding into the foyer of the house, sweating profusely from our gallop. "I feared I would have to order the serving lad out to find you, Lane, as you have a visitor. You also have – Good Lord!"

I thrust the grisly object into his grasp. Holmes carried it to the closest window, while Lane quickly combed down his hair.

"Who is here?"

"A young lady, fair-skinned and plump, in a great state of excitement."

"Constance!" my army companion gasped. "Did she say what she wanted?"

Holmes was lost in thought, turning the relic over and over. Lane shook his head and ran for the parlor.

"Holmes," I said. "Is it murder?"

"Perhaps. This flesh is dry and desiccated, but hardly ancient enough to have come from the Nile Valley, or the tomb of a king. Where did you find it?"

I related the story of the dog. Holmes immediately asked where Vino had come from, and I could do no better than to say from the general

36

direction of the school, as we hadn't noticed the hound until moments before he delivered his treasure to us.

"Intriguing. But let us hear what the lady has come to consult your friend about. When young girls come driving hell-for-leather in dogcarts, something is clearly amiss."

Together, we made our way to the parlor. A striking young woman of some twenty years was sitting on the sofa, with Lane beside her. She was clearly in a state of agitation, her brown hair hanging loosely from her hat, her soft face flushed, and her eyes red and swollen. She gave a gasp as we walked inside and might have bolted had Lane not quickly caught a fluttering hand.

"No, Constance, wait – This is my friend the doctor, and his friend, the detective. Do you remember me telling you that I should be hosting these gentlemen for the week? You must share with them the story you have told me. Mr. Holmes is famous for setting things right and getting to the bottom of all kinds of mischief."

I doubted Holmes appreciated his gifts described in such a delusionary fashion, but he bowed to the lady and offered his services.

"Oh, sir – Are you a priest as well as a detective? I'm not certain which I require, for a dead man is walking and has driven my father's wits from him."

I was grateful Holmes had placed the corpse's hand on a table outside the parlor. He settled in a chair across from the nervous young woman. His slow movements seemed to calm her.

"I will not claim to be a clergyman, but if your trouble has a human source – as virtually all troubles do – then I am certain I can assist. Tell us what brings you here, in such a panicked state that a lady of fashion dons mismatched boots."

She looked down at her toes. Indeed, one boot was black, the other almost red. A pretty blush stained her cheeks.

"You are correct, sir. Let me put my problem to you quickly, for the medicine the doctor gave Papa will soon wear off, and I wouldn't wish him to awaken and find me gone. I only came here because . . . I didn't know where else to turn."

She glanced to Lane, who gave her an encouraging nod.

"My father is Mr. Topher Reilly, a member of the Royal Society and a noted Egyptologist and antiquarian. For years he lectured in London, and briefly held the Pendleton Chair at Oxford. My mother died five years ago, and after she passed away, Papa felt there was little left for him in the world. We therefore came to Ra House, so he might rusticate. However, Papa is a restless man, and retirement doesn't suit him. It seems that every other week he is travelling about the country with Sabatok-Nafi, to give another speech and demonstration."

Holmes raised a hand. "And who is this gentleman? A student or a servant?"

"Neither sir. He is a dead man."

I confess this answer startled both Lane and me. Holmes merely nodded for the girl to continue.

"You see, my father is an expert on ancient Egyptian mortuary practices. He has a collection of mummies, but they are fragile items. There was once a craze for acquiring mummies and hosting parties where they would be unwrapped – As you might imagine, the damage was irreparable, once the process was complete. Therefore, Papa wanted some way to demonstrate to students how the mummies were prepared, but without ruining his own legion of the dead. He made a special application to the Royal Society and received permission to take the body of a man who had died, friendless and nameless, in a London almshouse, and prepare it in the way of the pharaohs. Father did so, two years ago. He rewraps the body before every exhibition."

I hold myself to be a man of science, but this bordered on the macabre. "Why did he not use a statue or some kind of wax figure?" I asked, and perhaps my indignation was sharper than I intended. The lady sniffled.

"I know it sounds wicked – but Papa used the process to test his theories about the nature of Egyptian embalming, and subtle differences between the Middle and New Kingdom techniques. No disrespect has ever been intended, and no morbid gawking is allowed. Papa will not allow me to assist him, even though I could. And last evening – Oh, how I wish I had been with him!"

The girl seemed about to weep, but a glance at the clock upon the mantel abruptly restrained her tears.

"Yesterday, he had an appointment at the Manor School. The warden, Mr. Maxwell – They call him the headmaster, but in truth he is the boys' jailor – had asked Papa to give a talk for the boys who had been good for a month. Baroness Nettles and Lord Hewell attended as well, as they are great patrons of the institution and always interested in the boys' instruction. There is an old surgery in the building, for it was once an insane asylum, and Papa brought Sabatok-Nafi – as he has named his otherwise anonymous gentleman – in his casket. It is a wooden sarcophagus from the time of Cleopatra, brightly painted with images of gods and monsters and the portrait of the man who had hoped to spend eternity inside, but whose mummy was lost long ago.

"Papa said that he lectured for two hours, and that while many of the lads were very interested as he removed and then rewrapped the linen bandages, others were bored, and some, very rudely, went to sleep. Afterward, the boys were dismissed to their room, and Papa, along with the noble patrons, were invited back to Mr. Maxwell's office for a libation. They talked longer than they had intended, for Mr. Maxwell was hopeful Papa would agree to become a patron of the institution. My father said that he would consider it, but only after I married, and my inheritance was settled. Papa arrived home at almost midnight. I had already sent the servants to bed, and so it was I who helped him shift the mummy's casket from the wagon to his study."

"How could you do that?" Lane asked. "You are just a girl, and the coffin must be heavy."

Miss Reilly shook her head and managed a somewhat exasperated look at her admirer. "It isn't heavy at all, and our mummy is almost as light as a feather, because he is nothing but a dry husk of a human. However . . . the box did feel heavier last night, but I assumed it was only because I was tired. Papa was, I confess, a bit worse for having indulged in spirits, and he wobbled so badly that I insisted he put the casket down in the hall. Fortunately, Ross, our butler, is a bit accustomed to our strange ways. I cannot imagine most butlers walking down to find coffins blocking the staircases! I tried to get Papa to go to bed, but he insisted he wished to work some more on his book, and so I left him in his study. I barely remember blowing out my candle after reaching my bedroom, I was so exhausted.

"I awoke once during the night. I could have sworn I heard footsteps, and an odd, swishing sound, like someone dragging a cloth about the floor. My chamber door creaked open. I lifted on my elbows, calling to Papa. The door closed immediately, and I suspected that Papa was lost in his own house, due to his excessive intoxication. It wouldn't be the first time such a thing occurred. I shook my head, laughed, and immediately returned to sleep.

"I awoke at six, pulled on my dressing gown, and started down the stairs. I was midway down when I halted in alarm. The mummy's case was open, the lid shoved off to the side. I couldn't imagine what had possessed my father to open it, or to leave it in such a strange fashion. I descended, looked inside, and gasped. The linen bandages, which Papa so carefully rebinds with each session, were piled in a great heap inside the sarcophagus. And Sabatok-Nafi had vanished!

"'Papa!' I called. 'Papa, what has happened?'

I heard a moan coming from the study. I ran inside and found my father crumpled upon the floor, shaking like a leaf. His eyes were wide, his face was deathly white. I screamed for Ross to run for the doctor. Meanwhile, our housekeeper came to my aid. We made Papa as comfortable as we could upon a divan, and I begged him to speak to me. All he could mutter, between chattering teeth, was '*He walks! The mummy walks!*'"

At this point the girl broke down, leaning upon Lane's shoulder. He assured her that Holmes had the situation well in hand.

"What is the physician's diagnosis?" I asked.

"He says that Papa has experienced a terrible shock and must be watched carefully. Papa's many years in Egypt, doing fieldwork, exposed him to fevers and left him with a weak heart. The doctor gave him a sedative, but . . . Oh, I must return. Please, Mr. Holmes, come to Ra House and help us make sense of what has happened!"

The lady darted from the room, with Lane in pursuit. I went to the door, watching as she whipped her pony into a brisk trot. Holmes returned from retrieving his coat, looking highly amused. He quickly buried any hint of humor when Lane rejoined us after seeing the lady on her way.

"I have called for my carriage," Lane said. "We shall be at Ra house less than ten minutes behind Constance."

Holmes smiled. "Ah – I felt you had an understanding with the lady."

"Oh. Oh, no, I merely . . . I have hoped Constance will favor me. But at my age – "

"She fled to you in her time of need. That, I think, bodes well for your wooing. But we shall not be going to Ra House immediately. We are needed at the school."

"Why?" I asked.

"That shall be obvious as soon as we ride through the gates. Ah, what a handsome bay mare you have."

Lane drove for us, dismissing the stable lad. My army friend swallowed further questions, and I knew better than to ask any. Holmes made random comments about the fine weather and the lovely countryside. We reached the gloomy, imposing structure in less than half-an-hour.

Holmes's prediction was astute – the institution was clearly in a state of turmoil. Shouts rose from open windows, and a small cadre of lads in stripped denim pants and loose tunics milled about the yard, looking confused and angry. A guard with a club stood just a few paces away, snarling and snapping at the boys to get in line. The gate was closed, and it took several minutes before Lane was able to convince another guard – an older man who Holmes quickly placed as a former naval officer – to admit us. Lane, who had visited more than once, quickly led us to the office of Maxwell, the warden.

"My God, what a disaster!" the man, a heavy-set fellow with a dark shadow of a narrow beard across his face, swore as we entered. He was clad in an ill-fitted, greasy coat, and still reeked of the previous evening's drinking party. "We are searching in every nook and cranny of this school. How in Heaven's name could he have disappeared?"

Lane introduced us. The man scowled at Holmes.

"The private detective?"

"Consulting detective," my friend answered smoothly. "Forgive me for saying so, Mr. Maxwell, but I believe you could use my assistance."

"If you can tell me where that rapscallion has gone, I shall be very grateful indeed for your assistance. I am sure that our patrons will reimburse you. But as for now . . . What shall I do?"

"You can begin," Holmes said tartly, as he took a seat before Maxwell's desk, "by supplying me with the name of the inmate who has escaped. Who is he and how did he elude your authority?"

"His name is Howard Williams," Maxwell sighed. "He is called 'Seashore' by the boys, because he was arrested at Brighton, taken in for stealing wallets and watches from the towels of the bathers. The first night he was in residence, he tried to escape and was sent to the hole for it. I thought that had cured him of disobedience."

"The hole?" I asked. Maxwell raised his head.

"A special cell. No light is permitted, except while eating. A naughty boy may be sent there for five days, or longer if he doesn't repent sufficiently."

I saw Holmes's eyes narrow, his lips compress. I knew instantly he was thinking of his Irregulars, the little street Arabs who served him so well. His tasks kept them occupied and he paid them regularly, so they didn't need to beg or steal. But there were other lads who he couldn't help, bright children who might fall afoul of constables and become jailbirds for life. I felt Holmes was imagining Wiggins caught in such a horrible place, where the punishment would far outweigh the crime.

"Describe Seashore to me," Holmes said.

"He is small, and underweight for his age, which is almost thirteen. He has dark hair, a sharp nose, and barely speaks at all."

"How did you misplace him?" Lane inquired. Maxwell glared, clearly not appreciating the tone of the question.

"There was a lecture last night, by Mr. Reilly. Seashore – I mean, Howard – was among the twenty or so boys permitted to attend in the old surgical theatre. Afterward, the boys were told to go to the dormitory room they share in the eastern tower. We don't like to keep them in cells, though when they disobey, we do not hesitate to lock them up. Last night, we dismissed them, and then my men came to my office for a moment before returning to check on the lads and lock their door."

"Is this customary after a special lesson?" Holmes asked.

"No. Usually, the two guards would follow the boys directly. But Baroness Nettles insisted the guards have a toast with us, and they were glad to oblige. They were only here for a few minutes, certainly not long enough for any of the boys to break out of the institution. They returned to the tower and looked the dormitory chamber over. All the boys were in bed."

"And nothing memorable occurred during the night?"

"No."

A burly guard, who had been standing silent in the corner, abruptly coughed. Maxwell twisted in his chair.

"You have something to add, Byron?"

"I was walking along the wall at about two in the morning, sir, and I heard a splash outside the tower. But of course, it couldn't have been the lad."

Maxwell waved a hand. "Did you not investigate?"

The guard shrugged and looked to us for understanding. "There is a stream that runs on the eastern side of the tower. Sometimes the lads throw things from the windows into it – shoes, books, plates. They are always punished severely when they do. But the windows of their chamber are all old arrow slits. Even the skinniest of the young fellows couldn't slide through. I thought the matter could wait until the morning."

Maxwell glared at the guard. "You should have told me this earlier. You are dismissed!"

The man shrugged and walked away. The warden pulled out a handkerchief and mopped his face.

"I still cannot understand how Seashore got out," Maxwell muttered. "The boys claim they know nothing, but of course they are lying. Maybe a few days on bread and water, down in the hole, will loosen their tongues."

Holmes rose. "That will not be necessary. Mr. Maxwell, I assure you that the lad shall be dealt with, but not by you. Might you have a photograph of the young offender? Ah, thank you, this will do nicely." Holmes slipped the small image into the pocket of his coat. "I suggest that you gently chastise his associates, but don't inflict any bodily harm upon them. It would hardly be the thing to have special visitors from Her Majesty's Government witness."

The man's face turned ashen. "Special visitors?" he stammered.

"Good day to you, sir."

Holmes spun and marched out with military precision. Lane and I trotted behind.

"I say, aren't you going to visit the dormitory?" Lane asked. "I've read Watson's stories. Don't you need to walk around the premises, to make deductions?"

"That would be a waste of time," Holmes said. "I already know how young Howard Williams, fondly known as 'Seashore', made his daring escape. I know who on the outside aided him, and where he most likely is hiding. The only aspect I am ignorant of is why this individual is taking such a risk, though at least three theories have suggested themselves to me."

Lane stopped in the hallway, his jaw hanging open. I had to grab his sleeve to pull him along.

"Is he always like this?" Lane asked.

"One becomes accustomed to it," I assured him.

We returned to the carriage and Lane asked whether we would now hurry to Ra House. Again, Holmes shook his head.

"Circle the wall, so I may judge the strength of the stream."

Lane nodded and cracked his whip. The school was situated amid plowed fields, but at one corner, just below the high tower, a brook made a sharp curve before shooting out across the farming country. It was wide enough that a plank bridge was necessary to cross it. Rain had fallen the two days previous, and the waters were higher and more turbulent than was normal, for the bridge was almost flooded. Holmes didn't get out of the open carriage, instead signaling that he had seen enough.

"Thank you, Lane. Now – which road will take us to Baroness Nettles's establishment?"

"Why – we must turn around. She lives almost two miles west of the school, not far from Ra House."

"Ah, a pleasant drive then. Carry on."

I shook my head at Lane, preventing more useless questions. Holmes sank down in his seat, folded his arms, and gave the impression of a man who was thoroughly enjoying himself. I looked up to the tower where the boys were nightly locked into their "dormitory". It was a high drop, perhaps as much as seventy feet, straight down into the stream and its scattered rocks.

"I doubt anyone could have survived a fall from that window, if he did squeeze through it."

"I assure you, Watson, that wasn't how it was done."

"Then why did you wish to see the water?"

"Only to ascertain the directional flow and ponder who we might hear from next."

43

"I don't understand."

"The village of Thornston lies downstream. By this evening, the constables of that charming little town will have a murder on their hands. If the news travels that Sherlock Holmes is in residence nearby, they will ask me to solve their grisly case."

"Really! Holmes, this is too much, even for you. Are you now claiming to possess the second sight?"

"Watson, you and I have seen and heard exactly the same things. Nothing has been withheld. At this moment, you should be able to tell me exactly what I am thinking."

I folded my arms and gave a loud snort. "Yes, I could . . . but I refuse to do so."

My friend laughed so loudly he almost spooked the horse.

I held my peace until we approached the home of Baroness Nettles. At Holmes's request, Lane offered a bit of local gossip about the lady. She had wed Baron Nettles some five years earlier, but was now a widow. The couple had no children, and the lady divided her time between London and her country estates.

"She's an attractive person," Lane informed us, as the red roof of her house came into view. "Perhaps thirty-five years of age, with a splendid figure. Her hair is as black as ink, and she is always very well dressed. Our paths haven't crossed much, but I have seen her in church, and Constance says she is generous and kind. She is also a patron of the Manor School."

"How long ago did the baron die?" I asked. Holmes smiled at me.

"The first anniversary of his passing was last month," Holmes said. "Really, Watson, I thought you followed the society news." Holmes turned back to Lane. "But how long has the lady been in residence at this property?"

"I believe she arrived here about two months ago, but you really should ask Constance these questions." He twisted in the seat, peering over his shoulder in exasperation. "Mr. Holmes, don't you think we should be going to Ra House instead of paying a social call on the baroness? What if Reilly is dead?"

"Then the best thing for us to do would be to capture his murderer. Please exercise patience, Lane. Let us hope the noble lady is willing to receive us. I wouldn't wish for this encounter to become unpleasant."

A smart young butler took our cards and, after ten minutes of cooling our heels in the foyer, we were admitted to a room that had clearly been a gentleman's study. Baron Nettles had built his career in the colonies, and maps of various Oriental regions were hung on the walls, along with taxidermized trophies and strange weapons. His lady rose from behind a massive mahogany desk to receive us.

She was indeed a spectacular woman, fair of face with luxurious black hair set in surprisingly girlish curls about her head. Her dark-gray dress was elegantly trimmed, and a delicate gold watch hung from a chain that encircled her tiny waist. She radiated both poise and kindness, and spoke in a low, soft voice.

"It is good to see you, Mr. Lane. We missed you at church last Sunday, and the vicar's message was very interesting." She turned to shake hands with my friend. "And I have heard of you, sir. In fact, you solved a problem for a friend of mine, Lady Lyle."

"A matter of an emerald bracelet," Holmes said. "A simple case, easily resolved."

"I am glad to hear it was so elementary, as you are fond of saying. Had that bracelet disappeared forever, I doubt my friend would still be married, as her husband was so furious with her for misplacing it he threatened to divorce her! But pray, sir, what can I do for you?"

Holmes had dropped into the chair that sat in front of the desk. He had, as the lady was speaking, removed the photograph of the boy and was glancing back and forth between it and his hostess.

"Madam, you can answer one question for me: *Where is your son?*"

Lane made a sound as if he'd been shot. The lady gasped, her hands flying to her mouth. Even I, who trusted Holmes's instincts and abilities beyond all others, feared for an instant that he had made a horrible and humiliating mistake.

The baroness tumbled into her chair, gripping its arms like a swimmer seizing upon a life preserver. She swayed but didn't faint. At last, just as Lane had begun to sputter out oaths and demand apologies on her behalf, she raised a hand.

"Howard is upstairs, asleep. He ate up half the kitchen before he nodded off. I thought it best to allow him to rest."

I heard a thud. It was Lane, dropping down onto a divan at the back to the room. I stepped beside Holmes's chair, watching the lady as she slowly gathered her courage and resolve.

"Are you here to take him from me?"

Much to my surprise, Holmes shook his head.

"No, Madam. Whatever offense your child committed, he has paid for it a hundred times over. My only concern is for the old gentleman at Ra House, whose fate we have yet to learn."

Baroness Nettles put a trembling hand to her forehead. "Howard told me Mr. Reilly fainted. I imagine anyone would do the same, upon viewing a mummy that had awakened and risen from its casket."

"We shall do all we can," Holmes assured her. "Clearly, it wasn't your son's intention to harm the gentleman. But to protect your child, we must know your story."

The lady sighed. "Not even my own husband knew of him, and yet here you are, a complete stranger, asking for his history. Very well, Mr. Holmes, I shall throw myself upon your mercy.

"I was a bold and foolish girl in my youth, and I made my living with my face as a model, a beauty whose image appeared on soaps and medicine bottles. It was only a matter of time before I gave myself heart and soul to a worthless cad who promised me marriage but cast me aside when I told him I was carrying his child. I knew that if the public learned of the infant, I would be an outcast, unable to make my living. Heaven, however, had sent me an answer in the form of Lizzie Williams.

"She was my dearest friend, and she longed for children but had been unable to bear them, and her husband had just died. Together, we devised a plan. We would go on a long Italian holiday. I would give birth in Rome, and she would adopt my child as her own. For eight years all was well. Howard couldn't have had a better mother. I was introduced as a favored 'Auntie' so that I could watch him grow up. I never stopped loving him – I hope you believe this, sir! – but I knew Lizzie's home was better than any I could provide.

"When Howard was six, Lizzie married a man called Tucker. Her second husband was disliked Howard, because he was a stepchild, but was never openly cruel, and I know Lizzie wouldn't have tolerated her husband hurting him. But then Lizzie died – she was run down by a cab in London – and as he settled Lizzie's affairs, Tucker somehow learned the truth about Howard." The lady paused. A single tear slipped down her cheek. "Just weeks before her death, Lizzie had been my bridesmaid when I married Baron Nettles. Our honeymoon was a protracted one, and when I returned home, I found an abusive letter from Tucker informing me that if I didn't retrieve Howard within a week, he would be cast into the streets. My poor son had been ejected from his home with nothing more than the clothes on his back, while I was on safari with my new husband.

"Mr. Holmes, I dared not tell my spouse the real reason for my distress, because he had no inkling of the past affair which had produced my child. I loved the baron, but he had a sanctimonious streak and might well have thrown me over for my 'sin'. Any chance I had of saving my son required me keeping my husband in the dark. I claimed Howard was my late friend's child, and that I wished to find him and see to his upbringing. The lie satisfied the baron, who never objected to my efforts. I spent money like water, paying dozens of detectives, but no one could find him. I see now that I was a fool not to come to you instead, to lay my entire sad history at your feet.

"My husband passed away, and four months after his funeral my son was found – Howard had been arrested in Brighton for stealing from the tourists. My late husband's title bore influence, and I was finally able to have Howard transferred to the school here, close to my estate. When he arrived, I learned that he had been sentenced to serve five years! I visited in the guise of a generous patron, hoping to arrange some type of parole for Howard, but the warden bragged to me that he didn't care if even a royal prince was incarcerated at the Manor School – no prisoner would be released before his time.

"Howard recognized me at once. His horrid stepfather had revealed his origins, but had also lied, telling Howard that I had abandoned him. It took several visits, and many tears, before my son learned to trust me again. Howard was clever enough to keep our relationship a secret, and I feared that if I told the truth, the warden might abuse my child even further, to make an example of him to the other boys. Yet Howard's health grew more fragile every day. Therefore, I began to plan how he might escape."

The lady gestured to the walls, with their maps of the East.

"My husband told me many strange tales of his time in India and of holy men who could lapse into such a deep trance that their followers might bury them for days, and then dig them up, to great acclaim. Perhaps that is what inspired me."

Holmes leaned forward. "Please, allow me to state my perception of what happened, and you may correct me if I err."

Baroness Nettles looked relieved and gave a quick nod.

"You arranged for the lecture and by some subterfuge told your son what to do on that evening. Following the lecture, you entertained Maxwell, his guards, Reilly, and your neighbor Lord Hewell with strong spirits and a discussion of Reilly's potential status as a patron. It was essential that you keep the men occupied, for your son was busy taking the mummy's place inside the casket. Of course, he had co-conspirators, for he could hardly have removed the current occupant, wrapped himself up completely in the bandages, or lowered the lid by himself. The actual mummy was stripped and transported to the dormitory, where he took his place in Howard's bed, thereby fooling the guards when they came for a final check. The lads knew they needed to dispose of the desiccated corpse afterward, so they broke him apart and slipped him through the arrow slot, dropping him into the stream below the tower. One hand was later discovered by Lane's dog, thus beginning our involvement in the affair."

Holmes looked back to Lane, who could only nod dumbly.

47

"While I cannot imagine that impersonating a mummy was a pleasant task, the wooden sarcophagus wasn't airtight, so there was no risk of him being smothered. Miss Reilly noticed their burden was heavier than normal but put it off to her own exhaustion. You had already made sure that her father was too intoxicated to notice the difference.

"The pair left the coffin on the floor by the stairs. Your son waited until the household was asleep, then he freed himself. He feared that his 'uniform' from the school would give him away as an escapee, should he meet anyone along the road, and so he went upstairs in search of fresh clothing. He hadn't completely unwound the bandages, for Miss Constance heard a swishing sound, like cloth being dragged on the floor. She awakened and called out to her father just as Howard – unfamiliar with the house – opened her door. The lad very sensibly backed away and travelled down the stairs, abandoning his quest for new attire. But just as he reached the threshold, the door of Reilly's study opened and the old man, still somewhat in his cups, beheld him. Reilly collapsed and your son fled. Where is he now, Baroness?"

"I am here, sir," a small voice said. From the hallway, an emaciated child entered the room, came forward, and threw his arms around the lady. They had the same hair, skin, and striking profile. "I am so sorry for scaring Mr. Reilly. I didn't mean to do it. He gave us a very interesting talk last night, all about how mummies are made. I promise, I listened closely and didn't go to sleep, like Jacky did."

Holmes rose from his chair with an indulgent smile. "Let us see if we can make everything right. Baroness, I would suggest you that you take your son to a trusted friend in London and reclaim him when the furor of this escapade has somewhat calmed."

The lady gasped. "You will not turn him in to the authorities?"

"I think it is safe to say that Howard has learned his lesson about stealing from tourists," Holmes answered, with a wink to the lad. "He will be an upright and law-abiding citizen for the remainder of his days. I have friends in Her Majesty's government. A strongly worded letter and a visit from certain officials will prevent any repercussions upon the lads who assisted him. In fact, I predict the school will soon be under different management. Perhaps as a patron, you may even be asked to be involved in the selection of a new headmaster or mistress. As for Mr. Reilly, we should visit him now and see how he is faring."

We left the lady with her son, hurriedly preparing for a trip to London. When we arrived at Ra House, Miss Reilly raced down the steps and carelessly threw her arms around Lane.

"Papa is saved! He woke an hour ago, with a terrible headache, but able to speak. He said he understands now that it was all a dreadful nightmare and has promised to take the pledge and never touch spirits again."

"A happy ending all around," Holmes said, preventing me from descending the carriage. "Lane, it would be better to leave Mr. Reilly to his recovery," he warned, clearly not wishing us to become caught up in the household drama. "And besides, we seem to have forgotten our luncheon. You promised your cook is exceptionally talented."

Lane gave Holmes a look that indicated my friend clearly didn't understand how he was interrupting a splendid opportunity for courtship. Still, Lane bid his lady to send a note if he was needed, then climbed back into the driver's seat. The girl rushed forward before Lane could take up the reins.

"But what of our mummy? Even if Papa only had a bad dream, what happened to Sabatok-Nafi?"

Holmes leaned forward and patted her hand. "The mummy was the victim of prank committed by naughty boys at the Manor School. You wouldn't wish them to be in further difficulties, would you?"

"Oh, no! The poor little lads . . . I feel so sorry for them."

"I sensed you have a kind heart,' Holmes said. "Therefore, allow the esteemed late gentleman named Sabatok-Nafi pass from your memory into eternal rest and encourage your father to acquire a wax figure to replace him."

Miss Riley nodded and waved farewell. Lane looked back over his shoulder, once we were away from the house.

"I say, Watson, following this nosey chap around, getting into all manner of trouble, and never being allowed a moment alone with a pretty lady . . . How did you ever manage to acquire a wife?"

"Such selfish behavior is best avoided," Holmes quipped, before I could speak. We all enjoyed a laugh, and Lane whipped up the horse so that we were soon approaching his home. Just as we made the turn into his drive, Holmes commanded him to halt.

"What is it?" Lane asked.

"That is an official looking vehicle," Holmes noted, motioning toward a conveyance parked at Lane's door. "It smacks of the police."

"I've seen it in Thornston village," Lane noted. "And I recognize the man on the box. He drives for the local inspector and the constables."

"They have found the other pieces of the mummy," I said. "And now they think there has been a murder. Holmes, it seems your prophecy has come true."

"If so, they are persons best avoided," Holmes said, opening our door and leaping out, then tipping his cloth cap to my army friend. "Mr. Lane, it has been a pleasure, and I thank you for a most entertaining diversion.

The train station is just a mile in the southern direction, is it not? Watson and I shall take a brisk stroll through the woods and arrive in time to catch the five-fifteen to London. Will you be so kind as to forward our luggage? The address is 221b Baker Street!"

The Adventure of the
Unknown Traitor
by Arthur Hall

Of all the eccentricities of my friend Mr. Sherlock Holmes that I became accustomed to during our long association, I always considered his aversion to exercise for its own sake the least understandable. It was with some surprise, therefore, that I accepted his invitation to accompany him on a stroll in Regents Park immediately after breakfast one frosty March morning.

Clad in our heavy coats and wearing scarves and gloves, we walked along glistening paths still strewn with the leaves of the previous autumn, beneath skeletal trees that waited to again burst into life. The freezing air stung our faces. We spoke little, not unusually for him, but something of a rarity for myself. I knew of course that Holmes would quickly notice my reticence, for his powers hadn't noticeably declined over the years, and so his enquiry as we regained the streets of the capital wasn't unexpected.

"What's troubling you, Watson?" he asked as we waited for a landau to pass before crossing the road. "You have spoken hardly a word since we left Baker Street."

"I am caught on the horns of a dilemma."

He laughed shortly. "I deduced as much. After reading the fourth letter in your post after breakfast, your mood changed instantly. It goes without saying that I'm at your disposal to assist if you find yourself in difficulty."

"I'm exceedingly glad to hear that, for no one else could aid my decision."

"Then pray enlighten me. Beginning with the letter, tell me all."

The morning crowds grew thicker, and young men in particular strode purposefully past us after dismissing their transportation, presumably late in attending their employment. Holmes nimbly avoided a young and, I thought, probably inexperienced nanny pushing a perambulator at a fast rate. He apologised with his usual good manners before I answered.

"It was a communication that I didn't expect. The sender was an old army comrade, Carlton Ferrers."

He nodded. "But why has it caused you such apparent anxiety?"

"For the first time since my army days, I'm invited to a meeting with him and three other survivors."

51

"I would have thought the renewal of old friendships a pleasant experience. Where is the dilemma?"

I half-turned to see his expression and gauge his response. "My dilemma was whether or not to put this to you. Ferrers specifies that you should accompany me, if that is possible."

"Could that be because he anticipates a need for my services?"

"That is what I surmise." I shrugged. "But I haven't seen these men for some years, and know nothing of their lives since Maiwand."

A beggar, wrapped in an old blanket and visibly shivering, staggered across our path and hesitated as he decided whether to accost us. Before he could speak, Holmes dropped some coins into his tin cup and he mumbled his thanks.

"Poor fellow," I said.

"Indeed. Tell me, were these men particular friends of yours?"

"Not at all. They were unknown to me, apart from our service. You could say that the war threw us together."

"When is this gathering to be?"

"Tomorrow evening at eight o'clock. A room has been reserved at the Langham Hotel."

I saw his expression lighten. "Very well. I confess to having become curious about this. I will accompany you, as you have me on so many occasions. How are you to notify Mr. Ferrers, as he now is, of your acceptance?"

"He requested that I do so by telegraph, at his address in Kent."

"I see that we are almost in Baker Street, and just ahead is a hansom that has just delivered its fare. I suggest that you procure it to get to the nearest Post Office from where you can send your message. On your return to our rooms, I think a brandy is in order, to dispel this infernal chill that seems to be worsening by the minute."

Less than half-an-hour later, we sat in our usual armchairs on either side of our sitting room fireplace. As he had promised, Holmes had already poured the brandy, and it was only after the restorative effect of the fiery spirit that he referred to the matter again.

"Tell me." he said as we replaced our empty glasses, "all that you know of these men. It may give us some notion of what to expect tomorrow night."

I leaned back in my chair and searched my memory. "To the best of my recollection, they were part of a larger group. Our detachment sent out an expeditionary force when we were camped three days out of Kandahar. We were to meet some of our spies from Ayub Khan's forces, who were to tell us of his intended movements, but something went horribly wrong.

In the darkness there was chaos, with gunfire all around and men dropping like flies. The remnants of our party arrived back at camp eventually and we made our reports, after I had done what I could for the wounded survivors. The following day, we arrived at the Maiwand Pass where, as you know, we were defeated and I received my wounds."

"Quite so." Holmes spent a few minutes in quiet thought, before adding, "Well, I expect we will discover your former comrades' intentions tomorrow night. For now, I see that you have yet to complete your notes on the cases you mentioned yesterday, while I have a chemical experiment in progress that could save Jason Morrell from the gallows. We have two hours before luncheon, and after that I have a promise to keep. One of my informants is appearing in an appalling drama at the Lyceum, and I'm quite certain that she would be doubly gratified if you were to attend also."

I spent most of the following day with a dying patient who, in late afternoon, took an unexpected turn for the better. On returning to our lodgings, I found Holmes seated on our sitting room floor, surrounded by several open volumes of his index.

"Ah, Watson," he said, looking up. "Allow me a moment or two to replace all this and we can indulge ourselves in an early dinner. I have informed Mrs. Hudson of our plans for tonight."

For once, Holmes did justice to Mrs. Hudson's steak-and-kidney pie. For my part, I enjoyed it as ever. No sooner was our meal concluded than he selected a book from the shelf. I saw that he was consulting *Who's Who*, and surmised that he searched for information about my former comrades. At length he replaced the volume and handed me my hat and coat. Minutes later, both wrapped up against the cold, we left our lodgings.

The pavement twinkled as the evening grew colder and the frost returned. Thankfully a hansom appeared quickly, and the short distance to the Langham Hotel was traversed without incident. We passed from Regent Street into Portland Place and left our conveyance near the entrance of our destination. The fellow at the reception desk, on learning of our purpose there, called a uniformed boy to show us to a small conference room. He accepted Holmes's tip and opened the heavy door for us to enter.

The room, panelled in dark wood, was lit by a candelabra at each end of a long table. Four men sat around it, each looking in our direction. I noticed that there were two empty chairs, and that a carafe of water and a glass stood untouched by each place. Like ourselves, each man wore evening attire, and in a moment, I recognised my old comrades, despite the changes that the years had wreaked upon them.

No one spoke until the door closed. Then a man carrying rather more weight than I remembered got to his feet.

"Doctor Watson, Mr. Holmes: Welcome, and thank you for attending. It was I whose letter you received at Baker Street. I am Carlton Ferrers."

We both gave a small bow in acknowledgement.

"Thank you for the invitation, Mr. Ferrers," Holmes answered. "Whatever your difficulty, I am at your disposal."

Ferrers at once became embarrassed. "My thanks, sir. I have asked my former three comrades here under a deception. This isn't to be simply a reunion, but hopefully the occasion when a mystery that has lain heavily on my mind since our days in Afghanistan is finally made clear."

I saw that the other three at the table had begun looking at each other in surprise.

"Be seated and hear me out," Ferrars invited us. "I beg of you."

There was a moment of complete silence, and Holmes's expression gave no indication of his thoughts. I confess to my curiosity as to Ferrer's purpose.

"Very well," my friend remarked, "although I fail to understand how anything arising from that war can be my concern."

"After my explanation, you will realise that the presence of a man of undisputed integrity is necessary to conclude the matter. Watson was an obvious choice, the more so because of his association with yourself."

Another short silence passed, before Holmes nodded. "Very well."

Ferrers looked relieved as we took our seats. I introduced my friend to the remaining three men.

"Mr. Godfrey Stone, Mr. Henry Gillespie, Mr. Harcourt Vernon – my former comrades in the Second Anglo-Afghan War – Mr. Sherlock Holmes."

Holmes acknowledged them, and they responded with nods and mumbled greetings. I studied each man briefly. Ferrers appeared heavier, as did they all, and age had turned his hair and beard white. Stone had lost much of the shock of red hair of his youth, while Gillespie had added a magnificent handlebar moustache to his gaunt features. Vernon alone seemed closest to my recollection of him, except that his face was now excessively flushed. At first, I wondered if his heart was ailing, and then I noticed that his eyes repeatedly wandered to the water carafe. He wished it, willed it, to be magically transformed to a flask of whisky or brandy. I had seen that look many times before, in patients long addicted to strong drink.

"I believe our group was more numerous," I remarked.

"Indeed it was," Gillespie remembered. "I have kept track of the others since the battle. Mullins, Inman, and Updike fell in engagements subsequent to Maiwand, and McBride, Quirner, and O'Fallon died since from various natural causes."

A momentary wave of regret swept over me, as I recalled these men as they had once been.

"I assume then that this mystery, as you have called it," Holmes ventured, "originates either before, during, or immediately after you gentlemen served in Afghanistan. If I am to assist in any way, I must have the facts. Reasoning is impossible without them."

"I cannot imagine how there can be any question attached to the affair," Vernon retorted. "I have no recollection of anything except gunfire and death."

"Nor I," Stone agreed.

"To refresh your memories if need be, and for Mr. Holmes's information, I will relate what occurred on the day before the Battle of Maiwand," Ferrers began. "Should my own recollection be less than accurate, I'm sure that Doctor Watson will correct me – assuming, that is, that his memory retains the accuracy of his youth." He smiled faintly and paused to glance at the others, who remained silent.

"Pray continue," Holmes urged with a trace of impatience.

Ferrers shifted in his chair. "You will recall, at the very least, that three days after leaving Kandahar, we were to join the main forces of Brigadier-General George Burrows to engage those of Ayub Khan. Our group, comprising twenty-five men, were sent out from the camp at night to meet and obtain information from paid spies from within his ranks."

"An appalling mess," Stone said quietly.

"Quite," Ferrers allowed, "for we met a detachment of Khan's forces and were taken by surprise. In the slaughter that followed, fifteen of our men lost their lives. We always believed the incident to have been a chance encounter, but I now have reason to suspect otherwise."

He broke off to pour himself water, and then drained his glass. I saw that a curious expression had crept onto the faces of the others.

"I should explain," Ferrers resumed, "that I decided some time ago to write a memoir of my military experiences. I journeyed back to Kandahar, and to some of the nearby villages from where some of our guides and assistants were drawn. After considerable effort I found some of them, now much older of course, who were willing to talk at length to me of the events that transpired on the eve of the battle and the days after. It was during this research that I realised the truth of that fateful night."

"What can you mean, Ferrers?" Gillespie asked.

"My meaning, and the true purpose of this gathering, will become abundantly clear, when I tell you that I discovered and proved beyond doubt that we were betrayed. Khan's soldiers were waiting, ready to destroy us – not by chance or circumstance, but because one of our own had informed them of our intended liaison with the spies who, incidentally, were executed after torture."

Now the other three became visibly uncomfortable. Each looked at the others suspiciously, and shock was written on all their faces. The atmosphere in the room seemed to cool.

"Your purpose tonight then," Holmes said, breaking the silence that had fallen on the room by addressing Ferrers, "is to presumably unmask the traitor?"

"Indeed. This has occupied my every waking moment since I saw the truth of the situation."

"It will have occurred to you that the traitor could have been one of those comrades who later died in other battles, or even those who survived to meet a natural end?"

Ferrers nodded. "My first task was to ascertain the innocence of the dead by further research. I succeeded eventually. I confess to being appalled and saddened to conclude that the man who betrayed the company can only be one of the remaining comrades. One of the three with me at this table, now."

The effect on the others ranged from dismay to anger. Stone, white-faced, said nothing.

"This is preposterous!" Vernon exclaimed. "How can you tell? It was all so long ago."

Gillespie shook his head slowly. "I wouldn't trust those natives for your information. They'd sell their souls for a few coins."

"They weren't my only source," Ferrers replied.

Vernon and Gillespie got to their feet.

"I will not sit here and listen to this piffle!" Vernon said loudly.

"Nor I!" added Gillespie. "The past is dead. That war is part of the history of each of us and cannot be changed. I say leave it, and let us all depart from this place."

Both men made to move from their positions at the table, but Ferrers would have none of it.

"Resume your seats at once!" he ordered in the sharp voice that I remembered from his service as a colonel at Maiwand. Then, more calmly, "In any case, Gentlemen, I have requested that the door be kept locked for the duration of our occupancy. Kindly be seated again."

They obeyed reluctantly. Holmes, I saw, had remained impassive.

"I see now why they need someone neutral but known to them," I said to him in a low voice. "In this situation, not one can trust the others. How do you think we should proceed, or should we leave?"

My friend adopted a thoughtful expression, but decided in a moment.

"Gentlemen," he began, glancing at each in turn, "I cannot doubt that you are men of honour."

There was a unanimous murmur of assent.

"Excellent. I have a suggestion which is extreme, but will permanently remedy the mistrust and shame that one of you has brought upon your group and your regiment." He took a revolver from his pocket, emptied the chambers and put away the bullets. From a waistcoat pocket he produced a single bullet which he loaded into the weapon. "If guilty, an honourable man will recognise that there is but one way out – that of atonement. Then all will be clear, and the doubt in the minds of his comrades will be erased. I propose that I leave my revolver here," he slid it to the centre of the table, "so that the guilty man can make use of it. Watson will extinguish the candles at the far end of the table and I the other, at precisely the same instant. When the report is heard, the light will be immediately restored. Otherwise, the candles will be re-lit when, by my calculation, three minutes have passed." He again glanced at each face. "Are we all agreed?"

A babble of outrage commenced immediately, but was short-lived. The others, appearing confused and, I thought, a little afraid, stared at Ferrers as if for guidance. The silence that fell upon the room then didn't last.

"I think Mister Holmes's suggestion most appropriate," the former colonel judged, "and compassionate, inasmuch as it allows for the traitor to retain a semblance of honour by adopting a manly course. That should spare the shame of his relatives and dependents somewhat."

They responded with reluctant sounds, like tortured breaths, which were taken as the agreement of each man. This plan seemed far from secure, and I glanced at my friend doubtfully, but his answering look told me that, as always, he had already considered every likely outcome.

All eyes were fixed on Holmes's weapon, as if it were a venomous serpent, as he rose and moved to the end of the table. I left my seat, and from the opposite end looked past them all while awaiting Holmes's signal.

Silence descended again, and it came to me that the guilty man must be suffering agonies of fear and indecision at this moment. Then my friend extinguished every candle near to him, some with a large snuffer and the remainder with a mighty exhalation. I tried twice, before achieving the same effect.

Because the windows were heavily curtained, the darkness was complete. Faint movements, I couldn't tell from exactly where, disturbed the silence. A coldness, like that within a tomb, seemed to envelop me, and I told myself that the time limit must surely expire in an instant. Then a cry of fearful surprise was immediately followed by the flare of a vesta as Holmes re-lit the candles, after which I did likewise to those in the candelabra before me.

Everyone blinked and looked around cautiously as the scene was again illuminated. From Holmes's expression, I knew that he had learned from the situation.

The revolver was now in Ferrers' hand, but he appeared confused rather than guilty.

"I didn't pick it up," he stammered. "My word on it. Someone forced the weapon into my hand and tried to press it to my head!"

"And in another moment," Holmes concluded, "you would have appeared to have taken your own life, and it would be forever thought that you yourself were the traitor." His glance took in the table. "His task would have been easier had the traitor shot you before throwing the weapon down, but would have been easier also for me to deduce his identity. Evidently, he realised this."

"Yes," said Ferrers, still somewhat dazed by this unexpected event. "I suppose that must have been the intention." He gave the others a curious look. "Thank you, Mr. Holmes."

"Well, whatever that little demonstration was intended to prove, it failed miserably," Stone commented.

Holmes shook his head. "Much to the contrary, it proved exactly the one point about which I was uncertain."

"And what might that have been?" asked Vernon.

"That Mr. Ferrers was correct when he stated that the traitor wasn't among the dead of your group. Had that been so, none of you here would have found it necessary to make it appear that he himself is the guilty man."

"Whose true identity we have failed to establish," observed Gillespie.

"Only as yet," I corrected. "Holmes rarely fails to expose the truth, in the end."

"Do you realise the needless danger you placed us in with this?" Vernon asked Holmes. "Any one of us could have accidentally handled that revolver, and it could have fired unintentionally in the darkness causing injury or death."

"Not so, I assure you. It may have occurred to you to wonder why I emptied the weapon and then produced another bullet for the experiment, if we may call it that, when I could simply have left one of the original bullets in the chamber and proceeded from there. The bullet I used had remained in my waistcoat pocket, forgotten from a previous affair, and it was on discovering it that the idea came to me. There was no possibility of injury because, for another purpose entirely, I had previously removed the gunpowder."

"You are telling us that, if the guilty man had attempted to kill himself, he couldn't have done so?" Stone enquired with some surprise.

"It would have been impossible, but he would have identified himself, and all that remained would have been to notify Scotland Yard."

"Would his actions in Afghanistan still be considered a crime?" Gillespie asked.

"That would be for the courts to decide, of course. At the very least, he would be considered a pariah by all who know him."

Ferrers seemed to have recovered himself by now.

"But unfortunately, we have failed to establish his identity after all," he said. "Mr. Holmes, I must apologise once more, this time for arranging for you to attend an occasion that has been fraught with failure. Please feel free to send me your account, for your attempt was indeed ingenious."

Holmes rose, and I followed.

"That will not be necessary, Mr. Ferrers," my friend responded. "Nor is this incident concluded. If you will make the arrangements with the hotel, and you gentlemen are free, I propose that we meet here again at the same time on the evening after tomorrow. I have every reason to expect that I will be able to throw light upon the situation by then."

Ferrers, appearing eager to comply with Holmes's suggestion, turned to the others. Stone nodded his agreement at once, but Gillespie merely shrugged. Vernon smiled faintly for the first time and raised a hand to concur.

"Very well," Ferrers said a little wearily.

"Then if you will summon someone to open the door, Doctor Watson and I will be on our way."

The next morning, I breakfasted alone. Holmes, I knew because the teapot was cold, had eaten some time previously. Mrs. Hudson informed me that he had said it was unlikely that he would return until dinner-time.

I was unusually busy that day, but most of my patients suffered from minor ailments only. I arrived back at Baker Street in the late afternoon and drank a welcome glass of port while attending to my neglected notes.

Dinner-time came and went. I enjoyed our landlady's excellent game pie, while expecting the arrival of my friend at any moment. To my disappointment he failed to appear, and I had been settled in my armchair reading for several hours before I heard his tread upon the stair. He burst into the room with blood on his face, and suffering obvious pain.

"Holmes!" I cried. "Good Heavens! What has happened to you?"

He sat down awkwardly. "I was attacked. I believe that one of your former comrades intended that I shouldn't complete my investigation."

"Are you certain that they were connected with this incident?" I enquired as I helped him remove his coat. "I'll call Mrs. Hudson to bring hot water."

"So much ado isn't necessary, Watson. My body is bruised from receiving several blows from a stout stick, but the cut on my face is slight. There were two of them, but I'll wager they came off worst."

Our landlady responded to my request nevertheless, and I tended to Holmes's wounds with him complaining throughout.

"Why are you so certain that your attackers were sent by one of my old comrades?" I asked again when my examination was over and we each held a glass of brandy.

"I can think of no one else likely to be responsible. The Marrason brothers are behind bars awaiting trial, Miss Shirley Christopher has begun a long sentence in Holloway and, according to today's *Standard,* Morton Chiles has committed suicide. As you will recall, I have had no more recent cases."

"You weren't able to learn anything from either of your assailants?"

"I was not, regrettably. They came at me out of the shadows near Tottenham Court Road, where I had led them after discovering that I was being followed. Both were men of considerable size, but neither too skilful nor intelligent. I left one of them bleeding from a stomach punctured by my sword-stick and the other, I suspect, with a broken arm."

"Will you tell Lestrade?"

"Possibly, but I think that will have little effect. I am aware of their usual haunts, should their arrest prove necessary."

"Have you made any progress towards learning the identity of the traitor in Afghanistan?"

"I have identified him as the only one of your former comrades that could have betrayed your regiment."

"So quickly?" I retorted in surprise. "How did you accomplish that?"

He took a final sip of his brandy and replaced his glass on a side-table. "Let me tell you how my day was spent." He smiled faintly. "You may someday be able to include the incidents in one of your over-dramatised accounts of my little enquiries."

I had long since become accustomed to his remarks concerning my work, so I made no reply.

"Kindly proceed," I said encouragingly. Fortunately, my notebook was close at hand, and I retrieved it as he leaned back in his chair and began his reminiscences with closed eyes.

"As you will be aware, I left Baker Street after an early breakfast. My intention was to arrive at Whitehall before Mycroft began his daily routine, in the hope that he would spare me sufficient time to arrange access to the National Archives. He wasn't pleased to see me, but I was able to persuade him of the importance of the matter and he eventually complied. Once installed in that labyrinth, I was able to search at my leisure, sometimes with the assistance of the resident curator, and the records of your comrades' actions, as far as they are known, were discovered. When all was known, I left the establishment, suddenly aware that it was now late in the day. As I neared our lodgings, I came to realise that another hansom had followed my conveyence for the last half-mile, so I directed my driver to Tottenham Court Road, where I took to walking and led my persuers a merry dance until they attacked me. When that unpleasant incident had passed, I engaged another hansom to bring me back here."

"I wish I had been with you," I said sincerely. "Those roughs might have inflicted less damage against two of us."

"Good old Watson. I confess to believing that I had eluded them, but at least one must know the streets there as well as I. It was a surprise attack but, as I have explained, I was able to prevail."

The question on my lips was of course the identity of my traitorous former comrade, but I knew that Holmes would reveal nothing until the second meeting of the following night. I was about to suggest that he retire early because of his exertions when he stood up to stretch and announce that this was his intention. Left alone, I read one of my accumulated medical journals before taking to my bed.

Holmes hadn't risen by breakfast-time, so once more I ate alone. My day was spent treating several seriously ill patients and also some little time at Barts before I was able to return to Baker Street. As I approached our lodgings, I saw a tall, serious-faced elderly man emerge, and wondered what new problem my friend had been confronted with during my absence.

"Nothing to occupy me for long," he informed me when we were seated and awaiting Mrs. Hudson's entrance with our dinner. "I had the unenviable task of revealing to Mr. Oliver Fortesque-Jones that the much younger woman he was about to marry is actually his estranged daughter of many years. The poor fellow was so shocked that I found it necessary to refill his brandy glass several times. He had apparently almost forgotten the original marriage of his youth."

"That is an incredible situation!" I exclaimed.

"Indeed, but it is not unique. Remind me to tell you of Miss Isabelle Coultier and the circus clown, a small matter that I was presented with while living in Montague Street, when we have a moment to ourselves. It was a farce that might prove amusing. Today's enquiry, however, was conducted entirely within this room." He inclined his head towards the door. "Ah, but I hear our good landlady on the stairs. The accompanying aroma tells me that we are about to partake of some excellent fish, and after that we must discuss briefly what is to take place at the Langham Hotel."

To a man, we all arrived early for the second meeting. When we were seated as before, I scrutinized the faces of each of my former comrades, but learned nothing. Every countenance showed strain and anticipation. I wondered how many memories of that bloody war of yesteryear would be shattered by the exposure of unexpected truths.

"This will not take up much of our time," Holmes began when he was certain that he had their attention, "and then, in the light of the truth, the blameless ones among you will be exonerated."

I saw that Ferrers' gaze remained on him, while the remaining three regarded each other nervously. The candles flickered, projecting a shadow on each man's expression that lent a sinister air. Vernon, I thought, looked paler than before.

"The guilty man stands accused of conveying vital information – in this case of the movements of your expeditionary force – to the enemy," my friend continued. "To do this, he had to have been absent from your camp for some little time immediately before the mission began, and after the orders were issued. My method of procedure, therefore, was to consult the official records of the actions of each of you at the time and the journal of your immediate commanding officer."

"You were able to gain access to such information so quickly?" Ferrers asked incredulously.

"Indeed. The results of my research were surprising."

Concern was etched into the faces of Stone, Gillespie and Vernon. Each radiated guilt, and I wondered if Holmes had uncovered a conspiracy. Ferrers, I saw, was aware of their uneasiness.

"I will begin with Mr. Gillespie," Holmes paused as the man fiddled nervously with his moustache, "who is exonerated from this charge since he had been confined to his quarters for several days." Gillespie stared at the table-top, unable to meet our eyes. "The records are rather vague concerning the reason, but it is clear that it involved his actions towards a local girl and the resulting dispute with her family."

All eyes were now on Gillespie, who shook his head slowly but made no comment.

"With Mr. Stone it was different," Holmes revealed then. "According to the daily journal, he was at that time secretly involved with the exposure of those among the native bearers who sold opium to the servicemen. Unfortunately, he was found to have accepted payment from the offenders rather than to be instrumental in their arrest. Hardly commendable, but once again it does exclude him from the charge of betrayal."

"It was never proven," Stone protested. "Sergeant Brooker wrote down his opinion, that was all. The man disliked me from the beginning."

Ferrers fixed both Gillespie and Stone with a frosty glance, and said simply, "You disappoint me," but the effect on their expressions was as if they had received a whipping.

"And so," Holmes concluded, "we are left with you, Mr. Vernon. At first I could see no opportunity when you could have conversed with the enemy, but then I discovered that you volunteered to ride out to search for and bring back to camp a certain Private McLellan. Apparently the poor fellow had previously suffered some sort of mental blackout and wandered off unobserved. The sergeant's journal mentions surprise that you were away for so long, and regret that McLellan was dead when you caught up with him."

Vernon was now visibly agitated. He turned his head this way and that, but there was no avoiding the contemptuous glares of every man in the room.

"I didn't want to do it," he said in a voice that shook with fear, "but I was desperate. My run of bad luck at the tables before we left England had put me in deep debt. I knew what I would have to face when the war was over and we returned home, and I could see no way out until one of the bearers offered me a solution. He arranged for me to meet Ayub Khan's man with the information." He paused, his tone heavy with shame. "When I had disclosed it, the money was thrown at my feet and the man turned and rode off abruptly."

"No one has respect for a traitor," Ferrers said in a voice that surprised me with its deadly calmness. "You do realise how many of your comrades died because of you?"

"There is one thing more," Holmes added before Vernon could reply. "The journal recounts that McLellan was dead when you returned to the camp. Since there was no obvious cause," he held Vernon's eyes and spoke in a harsh but level voice, "the eventual verdict was that he died of exposure, but is the truth that you killed him because he witnessed the meeting?"

Vernon appeared shocked, and I wondered if this was because he considered Holmes's supposition to be outrageous, or because the final discovery of his act was unexpected. His pallor was now darker than before, and a violent trembling had come upon him.

"Also," my friend continued, "I should mention that the two blackguards who you sent to silence me last night were totally incompetent. It is to be hoped that they put you to no great expense."

Receiving no answer, Holmes turned to make a remark to Ferrers as Vernon made a frenzied dash for the door at the instant his glance was averted. On reaching it and discovering that it held fast against his attempts to wrench it open, he beat upon it while beginning to stagger and cry out hysterically.

Holmes, Ferrers, and myself were across the room quickly, and my friend caught Vernon before his body hit the ground. I saw at once that the immense strain and the years of strong drink that he had used to numb the pain of his guilt had taken the ultimate toll.

"The end of an evening that has been far from the finest in the regiment's history," Ferrers said somewhat sadly. "Was it his heart, Doctor?"

"I am sure that an examination will prove so," I agreed. "He could bear his burden no longer."

"He is beyond the vengeance that I see written on your faces," Holmes told the others. "While this is understandable, I couldn't allow it. As I had no way of predicting Vernon's death, I took the precaution of arranging for Inspector Lestrade of Scotland Yard to attend for the arrest. Possibly his journey hasn't been entirely wasted, since he may require a few words with Mr. Stone. If you would signal for the door to be opened, Mr. Ferrers, I believe you will find that he is waiting."

My recollection is that our conversation with the inspector was over quite quickly, and of Ferrers voicing his appreciation of Holmes's efforts once more before we left.

"I'm sorry, Holmes," I said to break the silence shortly after, as our cab neared Baker Street.

"Whatever for?"

"I meant for involving you in that sorry affair."

"Its conclusion brought no satisfaction, it is true, but the truth needed to be exposed. You must have wondered how it was that your group's foray was expected, that night all those years ago."

"It isn't a recollection that I dwell upon often."

"Nor would I. However, it's getting late, and I'm expecting a client to be at our door in the morning with a most intriguing tale to tell. I therefore suggest that, after a restorative beverage in our sitting room, we retire a little earlier than usual."

The Yorkshire Chieftain
by Robert Stapleton

For once in his life, my friend Mr. Sherlock Holmes had acceded to my professional advice to relax and, together with myself, had left Baker Street for more healthy climes. Namely, the northern edge of the Yorkshire Wolds. An area of rolling chalk downland, to the east of the city of York, south of Scarborough, and bordering on the German Ocean or, for those with an aversion to our Teutonic cousins, the North Sea.

One of my friend's family members had arranged for a cottage to be placed at our disposal there for a couple of weeks during the month of June, and we were at this moment enjoying a restful morning with no distractions. I was reading through a few old editions of *The Strand Magazine*, while Holmes was staring with great intensity at a leaf he was holding in his right hand.

It was Holmes who broke the easy silence that had developed between us.

"You know, Watson," he began. "During my travels through the lands of the East, I came across a great many strange and wonderful things. People, places, and animals, but also singular varieties of plants, such as would have amazed even that most famous of all explorers: Marco Polo. I have to tell you, my good fellow, that however impressive those plants might have been, there is nothing among them that compares to the humble plant life to be found in our own homeland."

"What on earth has brought this on?" I inquired, as I lifted my attention away from my magazine.

"You see this leaf?"

"Hmm. It looks like a clover leaf from here."

"That is indeed what it is. But do you not see something unusual about it?"

I put down my journal and looked more intently at the article in his hand. "Now, on closer observation, I see that it has *four* leaflets rather than the usual three – not that such a thing is entirely unknown."

"Precisely. However ordinary things might appear to us on first encounter, further and deeper investigation can reveal the most unusual details."

"Is that a fact?"

"Noticing *minutiae* like that, Watson, is the basis of all investigative detection. The recognition of details."

"And what use to you is a four-leaf clover?" I asked. "Apart from the popular superstition that it is considered lucky to possess one."

"The beauty of a flower, or indeed a leaf such as this one, has nothing whatsoever to do with the power of mindless Fortune to supply our daily necessities. These flowers are extras. They are gifts to us from a higher Providence. If there is another purpose to them, then we aren't made aware of it at this precise moment. Perhaps such a significance will emerge for us in due time. I collected this particular specimen from a patch of clover while out on the moors. You might remember that we passed it on our walk yesterday. In that same small patch of land, insignificant as it was, many of the clover plants bore four-leaflets."

"It sounds to me like a simple mutation – a single metamorphosis which has then spread throughout the local population," I replied.

"That is indeed the logical reply I would expect from a man of science," said Holmes, with a chuckle. "But life also possesses other richer aspects, which we need to keep in mind."

Still puzzled by his comments, I watched as my companion opened his pocketbook, slid the clover leaf between two of its pages, and carefully closed it shut once more.

For a few minutes, we sat together in agreed renewed peaceful contemplation of life in general and of our current agreeable sunlit surroundings in particular.

"We have a visitor," declared Holmes, emerging from his reverie.

"Visitor? But nobody knows we are here."

"However that may be, it seems that at least one person knows of our presence at this cottage."

"Now who is being logical?"

I opened the front door and watched as a horse and trap pulled up on the turning circle some twenty yards from our cottage. A man stepped down. I have spent sufficient time watching policemen in action to recognize an upholder of the law when I see one – even from that distance.

His well-built appearance belied his agility, which became evident as he hurried toward me.

"I'm looking for a Mr. Sherlock Holmes," said the policeman. "Someone at Scotland Yard told me I might be able to find him at this address."

"I'm Dr. John Watson," I informed him, "and I can confirm that you have indeed reached the place where Mr. Holmes is staying. But I'm not sure he is seeing visitors today."

Fortunately, Holmes proved to be in a good-enough mood to be willing to welcome the policeman.

"*Come in!*" he shouted from the main room. "I'm Sherlock Holmes. From time to time, I assist Scotland Yard with some of their problems, so they like at least to know where I'm going to be when I'm away from London."

"And I'm Inspector James Newlyn," said the policeman as he stepped across our threshold. "From the North Yorkshire Constabulary, currently assisting with the Scarborough Borough Police. And I'm immensely glad that I've found you, Mr. Holmes."

"Take a chair, Inspector," said Holmes, still seated but now with an affable smile. "Now, kindly tell us how I might be of service to you."

"A break-in has been reported to us," replied the Nelwyn, sitting down. "At the Rotunda Museum in the town of Scarborough. Not far from here."

"Oh, indeed?" I responded. "We're hoping to pay a visit to that particular museum at some point during our stay."

Newlyn nodded and then continued. "It's a somewhat-unusual building, as you shall see for yourselves. Although a couple of wings have been added onto the place in recent years, it's essentially circular in structure, its design having been based on that of the Pantheon in Rome. The place was constructed to house and display the geological collection assembled by William Smith in 1829."

"Ah, yes, William Smith," said Holmes, as though a light of recognition had been turned on in his mind by the very mention of that name. "He was the genius who produced that famous map of the geological strata of Great Britain."

Newlyn nodded. "I'm glad you're aware of the place and of its famous founder."

"Aware, though not yet familiar with the place," added Holmes. "But perhaps we might remedy that before long."

"I hope so."

"And what appears to have been taken during this break-in?"

"A body. At least, it's a skeleton that has been taken from among the exhibits."

"If such an exhibit has been on show, then logically it cannot be somebody recently deceased."

"Not at all. It is quite ancient, in fact. The skeleton is that of a Bronze Age warrior chieftain, discovered in 1834 at a place not far from here: The village of Gristhorpe. The skeleton was cleaned and then displayed in the Museum, together with the hollowed-out tree trunk which had functioned as the coffin. Though almost black with age, the bones have remained there for most of the last sixty years or so. Until today."

"Or," Holmes added with a knowing smile, "sometime during the night, presumably."

"That is correct," replied Newlyn. "The man in charge of the Rotunda Museum arrived there as usual first thing this morning, only to find that the lock to the front door had been forced."

"Did it rain during the night?" Holmes inquired.

"Rain? What does that have to do with the matter?"

"Maybe nothing – though perhaps a great deal."

"Well, yes, I think there might have been a light shower late in the evening."

Holmes nodded. "I seem to remember, from my reading about the exhibits at the Rotunda Museum, that there were some significant grave-goods uncovered along with the skeleton," mused Holmes. "A knife, for example."

"Indeed, there were some grave-goods."

"Were any of those taken by the thief?"

"Not as far as I'm aware," said the inspector.

"Just the skeleton?"

"So it seems."

"But why would you call upon me to help you? It sounds to me like a routine police matter."

"I know something of your methods, Mr. Holmes," said the policeman, "and, with you being so close to hand just at the moment, I thought you might be willing to give us the benefit of your professional opinion."

Holmes drew in a deep breath. "It also seems to me that the problem you face will shortly remedy itself. Though not entirely to the advantage of the Museum."

"How do you mean?"

"Inevitably, the thief will shortly send the Museum a ransom note. If they pay the ransom, the museum will have their exhibit returned to them, but at a cost."

"If we can trust the thief to keep his word."

"Quite right," I muttered.

"As things stand at the moment," said Holmes, "I can see no alternative course of action."

"Will you not at least yourself come and examine the scene? I have left explicit instructions that the place should remain closed and untouched until you have visited the Museum."

Holmes stood up. "Very well, Inspector. Since you have gone to such lengths to prepare the place for our investigation, we are at your service. Come along, Watson. We are to pay a visit to Scarborough this morning."

We found that the town of Scarborough was gathered around two bays, north and south, separated by a promontory, on which stood the impressive remains of an ancient castle.

The inspector's carriage took us close to the bottom of the Vernon Road, not far from the Cliff Bridge, with the sea beyond. The salt smell of the sea was blowing in toward us on the light breeze.

"Here we are, Mr. Holmes, Dr. Watson," said Newlyn. "This is the building we call the Rotunda. As I said before, it is essentially circular, along with the couple of recently added wings."

"As you also told us before, Inspector," said Holmes, "the place does resemble the Pantheon in Rome. The designer clearly had classical tastes."

We were all glad to be at the end of our ten-mile drive as our carriage turned off the road and took us up a slight incline to where the building stood on a rise above the main road.

After climbing out of the carriage, we found ourselves standing beside the front door of the somewhat odd-looking building we had come to visit.

Holmes examined the door and the forced lock. "The culprit was certainly not trying to be subtle in his methods or conceal his intrusion," observed Holmes. "He had no intention of hiding the fact that he had broken into the place."

"So it seems," Nelwyn commented.

In his habitual manner, Holmes examined the thoroughfare immediately outside the Rotunda Museum building. Occasionally he nodded to himself, storing away some obscure information he had gleaned from these observations. Then he stood up again, appearing satisfied, and turned towards the front entrance.

Once we had entered the building, we were introduced to the Honorary Curator of the museum, a man in his mid-seventies by the name of John Phillips.

"Mr. Holmes," said Phillips, "it is indeed an honour to meet you, sir. I've heard a great deal about you and your exploits."

Holmes returned an indulgent smile. "In his publications, my colleague, Dr. Watson, does have a way of elaborating and even exaggerating some of the exploits we share together."

"But people love to read of your triumphs all the same," I countered.

Holmes nodded. "Now to business. Is everything here still exactly as it was when you discovered it this morning?"

The man looked gloomy and nodded. "As near as we could keep it, although a couple of us had to ascend the stairs in order to ascertain what had been taken during the break-in."

"Namely, the Gristhorpe skeleton."

"Indeed."

Holmes again nodded, took out his magnifying glass, knelt down on the floor, and began to examine the entire area, emitting the occasional non-committal grunt.

Eventually he stood up again. "I think I've learned sufficient down here," he declared. "Now, kindly take me up to the place where the exhibit was being displayed."

A short flight of steps led us all up to the floor above.

Holmes told us to stand back while he once more examined the floor space.

"And, finally," said he, "the place where the exhibit was on display."

"The skeleton had enjoyed its own place, elevated on a plinth," said the Honorary Curator. "It was therefore visible to viewers without them having to bend down to any extent."

After removing one or two almost-invisible items from around the hollowed-out tree trunk which had served as a coffin, Holmes stood back to pronounce his verdict.

"Gentlemen," he began, "it seems to me that there is evidence of two people having entered the museum during the night. Possibly three, since they would have needed someone to hold the lantern."

Newlyn nodded, as though Holmes were stating the conclusion he had already reached.

"Traces of mud brought in from outside reveal that one of the intruders wore boots with cleated soles," continued Holmes, "while the other wore hob-nail boots. One distinguishing feature of those hob-nails is that one of the nails is missing from the heel of the right boot."

Newlyn chuckled. "So, we are supposed to look for a man with a nail missing – is that it?"

"Not as bluntly as that," returned Holmes, with a scowl, "but it will be a feature contributing to the identifying of the thief when you find him. Sufficient grounds, I suspect, on which to retain him on suspicion. But, as I've already told you, there is insufficient evidence to take the inquiry any further, until such time as the ransom note has been delivered."

"In that case, I hope we will indeed receive such a note. And very soon."

"And what about the third man?" I inquired.

"Ah, yes, the third man," replied Holmes. "So far, we have little more than supposition to go on, supported by a dirty thumb mark on the handrail beside the museum staircase."

"But that could have been left there by any number of people," objected Newlyn. "After all, the museum was open to the public all day yesterday."

"But the thumb mark is made with lamp-oil – not something people would be likely to leave during the daytime. Particularly during the summer."

"That is true," admitted Mr. Phillips

"The bucket and mop standing near the entrance shows that you have a lady who comes in each morning to clean the place. I assume you have asked her not to come in here this morning, at least until I've concluded my visit to the place."

"As is the case with the rest of the staff," said the septuagenarian with a nod.

"Is this cleaning lady available?"

"I imagine so. At present, she'll be enjoying a cup of tea at the café down the street."

"In that case, I should like to have a word with her."

The cleaning lady, a stout middle-aged woman by the name of Mrs. Cragson, confirmed that she hadn't touched the stairs or the floor area of the Rotunda that morning.

"The regular staff are well aware that I shall be coming in to clean the place, but they are always most careful not to leave the place unusually dirty, with footprints all around the place," she told us. "Or even thumb prints on the banisters."

"I'm indeed glad to hear that," said Holmes.

"Otherwise," she continued, "I would give them a piece of my mind."

"Quite right," answered Holmes.

"Mind you," she added, "I have to confess, I really am glad that the skeleton has been removed. At least for the moment. It always gave me the creeps."

"But it's three-thousand years old," I pointed out to her.

"That is just what old Mr. Williamson's son decided. Not that he had much experience of life. He was only seventeen years old when he wrote his book about it and determined how old the thing was – in his not-so-humble opinion. But I have my own views. I don't think the skeleton is anywhere near as old as what he makes out."

Holmes nodded. "You may well be right about that, Mrs. Cragson. However, I'm not here to decide upon the age of the bones, but only to retrieve them for the museum."

"Well, good luck with that, Mr. Holmes."

"I hope I don't have to rely too much upon luck," he replied with a chuckle. "But we shall see."

When we returned to the Rotunda Museum a few minutes later and reported back to Inspector Newlyn, he was dismissive of what we had achieved so far.

"And where does all this take us now?" he demanded.

Holmes stood to his full height and looked around at the rest of us. "We are now, gentlemen, in a position to sketch out, with reasonable accuracy, the sequence of events surrounding the theft of the skeleton."

"In that case," said Newlyn, "please continue, Mr. Holmes."

"Very well. It's plain to see that at some point during the night, after a rain shower had softened the ground outside, a horse and cart drew up directly outside the front door of this museum. Three men climbed out, leaving the horse to enjoy a nose-bag of oats. Traces of this are still visible on the ground outside. One of the men, the one who was wearing a pair of boots with hob-nails in the soles and heels, carried a crowbar, or some such length of iron. With this, he forced open the front door and led the way inside. The second man was wearing boots with distinctive cleats. He was also carrying a woollen blanket. The third man had footwear that way somewhat less distinctive, but the job of this man would have been to hold the lantern and illuminate the interior of the museum so that the others could see to carry out their work of removing the exhibit. He might even have been directing the operation."

"This is all very speculative," complained Newlyn.

"Speculative, no," said Holmes, with an acerbic note to his voice. "Deductive, certainly. The first man led the way up the stairs, to where the skeleton was on display. The second man followed him and spread out the woollen blanket beside the exhibit. Then, together, they removed the skeleton and wrapped it up in the woollen blanket. This is obvious from the fact that traces of wool from the blanket are evident to anyone who cares to look for them. The three men then made their way back outside to where the horse and cart were waiting for them. The thieves then went to some specially prepared destination."

"Which is where?"

"I have an idea, but I don't yet possess sufficient information with which to arrive at a definitive conclusion. However, as the horse showed signs of having a slight limp in its right foreleg, it cannot have been particularly far away from here."

"Then," concluded Inspector Newlyn, "we must wait for events to develop."

For the rest of the afternoon, Holmes and I were free to wander the streets of that seaside town. With the weather being dry, holiday makers crowded the thoroughfares. Many of them wandered along the seafront, visiting shops and amusements. Some explored the quayside and waterfront, ambling along the jetties. Others sat in deckchairs on the sands, or wandered along the water's edge with a mindless nonchalance. A few people had hired small boats in which to venture out into the south bay and engage in a couple of hours of fishing.

As was his habit, Sherlock Holmes spent time watching the people. Occasionally, he would chuckle and suggest that Scotland Yard might spend a fruitful day investigating many of the suspicious characters, either inhabitants or visitors.

We watched an ice-cream vendor selling his wares. The penny-lick, a serving of ice-cream on the top of a small egg-cup shaped glass goblet, was particularly popular.

Farther along the foreshore road we noticed a man taking photographs, using a large plate camera. To be more precise, he was offering to take photographs of passing holiday makers, in order to sell to them at the end of the day.

"This fellow looks a likely lad," said Holmes.

"Likely for what?"

"We shall see. Perhaps we should avail ourselves of this facility and have him take our photographs."

I was surprised at this suggestion. It wasn't the sort of thing that Holmes might usually consider. But I'm often surprised at the suggestions he comes up with.

We each in turn sat against a decorated cotton backcloth while the young man with the tripod camera fitted his dry photographic plate and uncovered the lens cap for the required five seconds, before covering it again and removing the exposed plate to the box at his side.

He handed us his card, which stated that he was *Luke Barrowbridge, First-class Photographer*, and promised to have the photographs developed and ready for us to collect by the end of that afternoon.

Our resumed promenade was soon interrupted by a young police constable, breathless after having run like a greyhound among the crowds in search of us. The young officer told us that the ransom note that Holmes had predicted had now been delivered, and asked if we would please return to the Rotunda.

Holmes led the way back to the museum where we were greeted by Newlyn, whose face showed a mixture of embarrassment and evident relief.

"I understand you have now received the anticipated ransom," said Holmes as he stood in the entrance hallway.

"Indeed we have," replied the policeman. "You were quite right to anticipate it, Mr. Holmes. However, it was delivered in a slightly unusual manner."

"Please elaborate."

"A young boy arrived here a few minutes ago, carrying a canvas bag."

Newlyn turned to the reception desk and lifted up a canvas bag that had been hiding on the floor behind it. "This bag."

"What did it contain?"

"On investigation, the receptionist found that it held a skull. *This* skull, gentlemen."

Newlyn reached into the bag and retrieved a human skull, black with age.

"And it's from that skeleton that was stolen last night?"

"It is indeed," said Mr. Phillips, who now joined us from a nearby office. "This is without doubt the skull of our Bronze Age warrior chieftain."

Holmes took the skull and examined it with great respect and care.

"What became of the small boy?" continued Holmes.

"It seems that he vanished as quickly as he had arrived," said Newlyn.

"Can anybody give a clear description of the child?"

"Nobody took much notice of him at the time."

"And what does the ransom note say?"

"Ah, now this is where we reach the interesting part," said the policeman, as he handed a single sheet of crumpled paper to the detective.

Holmes began by examining the paper itself. "Common letter-writing paper," he announced. "The sort that might be purchased at any normal stationery store."

"We have plenty of those in this town," said Newlyn.

"The style of writing suggests a man with an advanced level of education. Perhaps more than an ordinary shopkeeper or artisan might be able to achieve."

"But the contents of the note, Mr. Holmes?" the inspector prompted him. "What do you make of that?"

Holmes read it.

"It merely demands the payment of twenty-thousand pounds sterling for the return of the remainder of the skeleton. Hmm. I presume the museum can afford such an amount – otherwise the whole enterprise would have been pointless."

"I suppose that sum could be accumulated from the town finances. So, yes. Just about."

"The note clearly requires you to place the money into a leather bag and leave it outside the front door of the museum after closing time this evening. That seems straightforward enough."

"So, said Newlyn, "all we have to do is follow whoever collects the bag."

"Apprehending the culprit is a police matter," concluded Holmes in a dismissive tone. "As is the apprehension of the other two men involved. But first I suggest that you make arrangements to do as the thief demands."

"He also requires that we put a notice in the Personal Column of this evening's edition of the local newspaper, confirming our intention to pay the ransom."

Holmes nodded. "Then I suggest you hurry up and do just that. You might just catch the '*Stop Press*' of the early evening edition."

Holmes took the canvas bag that had held the skull and began to search through it. "I see that the skull was carefully cushioned in a protective layer of heather. Now, let us make a closer examination of this heather. It isn't in full bloom just yet because of the early season."

"That's right, Mr. Holmes, said the inspector. "The moors burst out into purple blossom later in the summer."

"Ah, now that is interesting," continued Holmes.

We watched as he reached into the mass of heather and drew out one small flower.

"A flower?" scoffed Nelwyn.

"Indeed," replied Holmes. "A simple flower. Perhaps not quite as simple as one might at first imagine."

"It is quite attractive," I opined. "An evergreen flower with four large white petals."

"And yet I suspect that they aren't petals," said Holmes.

"But whatever is it," I asked him, "is it of any significance?"

"That, Watson, is what I intend to discover," said Holmes as he took out his pocket book, opened it, and placed the flower between pages not far from where he had pressed the clover leaf earlier that day.

"What now?" Newlyn asked.

"I think that concludes our business for this afternoon," announced Holmes. "But I would be obliged, Inspector, if you would kindly directly me towards the nearest telegraph office."

"In the meantime," said Newlyn, "we shall have to arrange to fill the leather bag with the money they're demanding in return for the skeleton."

As the evening began to draw on and the museum prepared to close its doors for the day, one of the members of staff placed a leather

Gladstone bag immediately outside the Rotunda Museum, beside the door which had now been fitted and fastened with its new lock.

In the shade of the adjacent wall sat an old tramp, with his hat pulled well down over his face. He wasn't the sort of person that any passer-by would take much notice of, except to stay as far away as he or she could manage.

Almost at once, from out of one of the side streets, a small boy emerged, looked around, ignored the old man, grasped hold of the leather bag and began to hurry away.

With the speed of lightning, a hand stretched out from the old tramp and fastened around the small boy's wrist. He cried out with alarm and pain.

"Now, boy," snapped the old tramp, "where are you taking that bag?"

"This man told me to collect it," said the boy as he struggled to free his arm from the grip of the vagrant.

"What man? What's his name?"

The boy shrugged. "I don't know."

"How much did he promise to pay you to pick up this bag?"

The boy continued to wriggle, but the grip on his hand remained firm. "A shilling."

"Very well, then. You take that bag and allow me to follow on behind you. Do that, and I shall give you half-a-crown. Do you understand? You can then go home with three-shillings-and-sixpence in your pockets, and you will be as rich as Croesus."

"Who?"

"Just do it."

"All right. Follow – if you can keep up with me."

Carrying the bag, the boy hurried off, with Sherlock Holmes, casting off his disguise, in hot pursuit. Inspector Newlyn and I followed apace.

We watched as the boy approached a man sitting in an open cart, stationed at the side of the main road.

We caught up with Holmes just in time to see him hand the boy his promised reward.

I failed to recognize the man in the cart, but before any of us could take hold of the driver, the man whipped up the horse and drove away at a trot. The cart turned a corner, and it seemed to vanish into the backstreets.

As Holmes hung back, Newlyn and I ran after the man in the cart. We felt sure he had something to do with this business, as he had at least paid the boy for the leather Gladstone bag.

Turning the corner, we saw that the cart had already stopped. Newlyn was quick to notice the driver step down, hugging the leather bag to himself and scurrying down the lane which would take him back the way we had already come, although on the far side of the shops and establishments which line the waterfront.

I did my best to keep up with both the driver and the policeman.

Newlyn pursued the man down another turning and in through a side entrance to one of the buildings.

I followed and found myself in a photographer's shop.

As we approached from the rear entrance, Sherlock Holmes joined us through the front doorway.

"There was no need to hurry," he told us. "It was quite clear where he was going to end up."

I took in our new surroundings. A man was sitting on a chair beside a shop counter. I recognized him at once. It was the fellow called Barrowbridge, the photographer. Beside him was another less-reputable citizen.

"Ah, good evening, Mr. Holmes and Dr. Watson," he said. "I have a couple of photographs waiting for you to collect."

He handed me the two-tone photographs he'd taken of us earlier in the afternoon. Grudgingly, I handed over the money due to him on that account."

"Although," Barrowbridge continued, "under the circumstances, I'm inclined to be less cordial to your companion there: Inspector Newlyn."

"I see you now have the bag containing the ransom money," said the Nelwyn.

Barrowbridge opened the leather bag, searched through it, and gave a sick smile as he considered what had occurred. "Presumably you are going to arrest me for receiving a dozen copies of *The Evening Post*." He laughed as he pulled out the folded copies of the newspaper and dropped them onto the floor.

"We knew you were responsible for the theft of the skeleton. We weren't going to risk losing all that money as well."

"But what evidence do you have against me?"

"Plenty," replied Holmes. "Firstly, your boots left clear muddy impressions in the Museum. I'm confident that the right boot heel has a hob-nail missing."

The photographer raised his foot and examined the heel.

"How clever of you, Mr. Holmes."

"Then there was the smell of silver bromide, the chemical used by you in preparing the glass for your dry plate photography. The smell is distinctive – even after you tried to cover it with the smoke from your Turkish cigarette. You have become used to the chemical smell of it, but to someone not so accustomed to your work, it was still evident in the still air of the museum."

"All this is hardly overwhelming evidence," replied Barrowbridge. "You will have to do better than that."

"And, what about your companion here?" asked Holmes.

"His name is Sewersby," explained Newlyn. "He is a well-known local character."

"I'm a rag-and-bone man," said Sewersby with pride. "A scrounger. Some would say a freeloader. But every man has to make his living some way or other. And that is nothing to be ashamed of. Neither is it unreasonable for a man such as myself to seek additional money when it's offered to him."

"Offered?" Holmes now took a new interest in the second man. "Who offered you money to steal the skeleton? Who was it who hired you?"

Barrowbridge snarled at his friend. "Don't dare say another word! You know what the Gaffer will do to us if he finds out we've betrayed him."

Sewersby swallowed hard and lapsed into silence.

"The more you can help us discover what happened last night," said the inspector, "the more it will help you when you come to stand trial."

"Trial?" demanded Barrowbridge. "What trial? You can't even find the skeleton you claim that we have stolen."

"True," replied Newlyn, "but it must have been one of you two who sent the boy along to the Museum with the skull."

Barrowbridge shrugged. "You have no proof. Even if the child could identify one of us, it would never stand up as evidence in a court of law. And you know that, Inspector."

"Will you at least tell us where we can find the rest of the skeleton?"

"Certainly not," replied the photographer. "Unless you can make that payment."

"The twenty thousand?"

"Together with a guarantee of immunity from prosecution. Only then might I tell you where you can find the bones. But not until then. Find the rest of the bones if you can, but I refuse to help you any further."

"You admit to taking the skeleton."

"I admit to nothing," said the photographer.

Sewersby remained silent and looked down at his hands, with which he continued to fidget. However much his companion was playing his part, he at least looked to me like a guilty man.

"Is that so?" replied Newlyn. "Well, just for the moment, Barrowbridge, you are going to have to come with me, along with your friend here. We have a cosy little cell waiting for each of you."

The photographer scowled and, with the utmost reluctance, allowed himself to be escorted from his own premises.

Sewersby followed, attached by handcuffs to another police officer.

I stood with Holmes, looking around the newly vacated the office of the photographer.

Newlyn looked back at us as he prepared to leave. "Please make sure you close the door after you, Mr. Holmes. There are thieves about tonight."

"Though not as many as last night, perhaps," replied Holmes.

"True."

"Have no fear, Inspector," I said. "We'll make sure the place is secure when we leave."

When the policeman had left, Holmes and I began to search through the contents of the premises. Piles of photographs covered most of the surfaces, while prints and negatives hung from a washing line, drying.

"Now, this is interesting," said I after a few minutes."

"What have you found there, Watson?"

"Photographs of churchyards. A dozen or more of them. I wonder where these places are."

"Not far from here, I would wager," said Holmes as he took them from my hands.

"What would somebody like Barrowbridge want with all of these photographs?" I wondered. "Not one of them has a person in the picture."

"He was certainly intense in carrying out his research," mused Holmes.

"Research?"

Holmes looked up at me. "Where would you hide a stolen skeleton?"

"Hide it? Well, along with a whole collection of other bodies, I suppose."

"Which you would be likely to find where?"

"A churchyard or cemetery would be ideal. Perhaps. But there are so many of them around here, as witnessed by these photographs. Which one?"

Holmes slipped the bundle of photographs into his pocket and turned toward the door. "I need to check with the telegraph office," he told me. "I expect to have received a reply to my wire by now."

"From whom?"

"Ah, now that is tomorrow's business. Tonight, we must take a cab out to our cottage and have a good night's sleep. I think we're going to need it for our escapade in the morning."

The following morning, we were awakened with the dawn by a hammering at the front door of our cottage.

I opened the door and found Inspector Newlyn on the doorstep. He appeared greatly distressed.

"Come in, Inspector," I told him.

"I'm here to see Mr. Holmes," he explained.

"Of course."

At that moment, Sherlock Holmes himself entered the lounge from the kitchen.

"Now, Inspector: How may we help you this bright and sunny morning?"

"There is precious little to be bright about, Mr. Holmes," Nelwyn replied, "but I wish to bring you up to date on the developments in our case."

"The case of the stolen skeleton."

"Indeed."

"Then proceed, my dear fellow."

"Late last night we had a surprise visit at the police station. A man arrived claiming to be an Inspector Graham from Scotland Yard."

"I cannot recall that name," said Holmes.

"He had a warrant card, which seemed to authenticate his claim."

"Hmm. Can you describe the man?"

"Not at all well. It was dark at the time – the middle of the night – and he was wearing dark clothing. I'm quite certain he was wearing make-up to hide his identity."

"So you doubted his identity as well."

"Only upon later reflection."

"And what did this imposter want?"

"He demanded that we release our two prisoners into his custody, ready for him to take with him down to London."

"That sounds odd," said Holmes. "But you did allow him to take your two prisoners."

"Indeed. Although we remained dubious about him during the night, our doubts were confirmed this morning, when the body of that fellow Barrowbridge, the photographer, was found floating in the south bay. His throat has been cut."

"And the other man? Sewersby?"

"There is no sign of either of the other two men – Sewersby or Inspector Graham."

"This is all very odd," said Holmes. "The death of Barrowbridge sounds like an execution, revenge being meted out on someone for failing in his job of securing the ransom money for the skeleton."

"But who is behind it?"

"The third man," said Holmes.

"And who is he?"

80

"That is the big question," replied Holmes. "But this all sounds very much like the work of a man who is dead and gone: A villain by the name of Professor Moriarty."

All eyes were fixed upon Holmes as we thought through the implications of what he had just said.

Eventually, Inspector Newlyn stood up and headed for the door. "I have to get on with clearing up as much of the mess as I can."

"While Watson and I are planning to visit the city of York this morning," Holmes added. "I hope you will not consider it an unwarranted impertinence if we asked you for a lift to the railway station at Malton."

Whatever Newlyn genuinely thought, he kept to himself, but he did indeed permit us to journey with him

The weather that day was dry, the sun shone down from a clear sky, and the smell of spring growth filled the air. There were certainly worse parts of the world to be out and about on a day like that, in spite of the dark nature of our quest.

The train took us west to the ancient city of York. The structure of the mediaeval cathedral stood high above the surrounding buildings and crowded streets. From the railway station, we made our way to the Museum Gardens, not far away.

A man was standing waiting for us there. He was perhaps slightly older than Holmes, but with an upright posture and a bright face.

"Mr. Holmes," said the man, approaching us with an outstretched hand, "welcome back to York. It is good to see you once again."

"It is good to see you in the flesh once more, Dr. Storn," said Holmes. "We usually communicate with each other by written correspondence."

"And this must be your colleague, Dr. Watson," said Storn. "I've heard a great deal about you."

"Of course," said Holmes. "You two will never have met before. Watson, this is Dr. Andrew Storn, a well-known authority on botany. He has written a number of books on plants, and his specialist subject is flowers of the moorlands of North Yorkshire."

"I'm pleased to meet you," I replied.

"Now," said Dr. Storn. "I understand that your visit here is as much about business as pleasure. Come, let me take you into the Yorkshire Museum and we can find a room where we can talk the matter over in private."

We soon found ourselves in a side-room of the museum, with the morning sunshine lighting up the dust motes hanging in the air.

Holmes took out his pocket notebook and opened it up to reveal the mysterious flower he had placed there on the previous day.

Dr. Storn's eyes lit up in recognition. "A dwarf cornel – *cornus suecica*, without a doubt."

"What can you tell us about this flower, Dr. Storn?" Holmes asked him.

"The dwarf cornel is one of the species of plant left over from the Ice Age," he began. "The plant itself is small, rising to no more than six inches in height. The flowers are also small, purple structures gathered together in the centre to form an *umbel*. You see, the bloom itself is deceptive. The four structures that might be taken for petals are in fact white *bracts*."

"Would we be able to find these flowers locally?" Holmes asked him.

"Possibly. These flowers are common in the lands of the north. North America, Scandinavia, even Greenland. They also occur in Scotland. But in England they can be found nowhere south of the upland moors of North Yorkshire. Unlike the chalk landscape of the Wolds, this moorland is a mixture of limestone and sandstone. This area is bounded by Cleveland to the north, the Vale of Pickering to the south, the Vale of Mowbray to the west, and the ocean to the east. The moorland supports grouse and sheep, and in the summer it is covered with a carpet of purple heather."

"That is most interesting," commented Holmes.

"But where exactly did this specimen come from?" asked Dr. Storn.

"That is what we'd like to know," said Holmes. "You may have read in the local newspaper that the famous Gristhorpe skeleton has recently been stolen from the Rotunda Museum in Scarborough."

"Indeed. I was sorry to hear about that."

"The skull was returned to the museum a few hours later, together with a ransom demand for the rest of the skeleton. The skull was wrapped in heather, but amongst the heather I found this one small flower. I believe that it is the key to finding the rest of the skeleton."

"Do you have anything in particular to help find it?" asked Dr. Storn.

From his pocket, Holmes pulled out the pile of photographs he had taken from Luke Barrowbridge's photographic studio of and laid them out on the table. "The man who was arrested in connection with the crime was a prolific photographer, and a careful planner. One of these places, churchyards perhaps, might be the site of the missing bones. Fortunately, he has inscribed each of them with pencil notes on the reverse."

Storn rubbed his chin in thought. Then he pulled from another drawer a large-scale map of the moors. This he laid out upon the table and began to lay the photographs out on the map, each according to its location.

"I know these places reasonably well," said Dr. Storn. "They are all close beside stretches of heather moorland. And, as far as I know, they're all sites where the dwarf cornel grows. But."

"Yes? Is there a problem?"

"Perhaps. One of the sites I might have expected to find here among these photographs is missing."

"Interesting. Then perhaps that is the site we need to investigate. Do you know where that might be?"

"I do. And, better than that, I can take you to see it this afternoon, if you gentlemen and willing to accompany me onto the wilds of the Yorkshire moors."

"If you can help us find this missing relic, then we would be very pleased to have you guide us."

After a brief repast, we made our way back to the railway station and caught a train which would eventually take us to the moor-side town of Pickering.

"This line might have taken us across the moors to Whitby," said Dr. Storn, "but the place I have in mind lies out of range of the railway. From here, we need to take a carriage and head up onto the high ground."

That is indeed what we did. Although the trackway across the moorland was rough, we were urged on by our hunt for the missing churchyard.

The June sun was still high in the sky when the coach driver drew up outside the dilapidated walls of a country churchyard. A small church building, much battered by the winds which habitually swept across the unprotected moorland, stood in the middle of a walled cemetery. The three of us climbed out of the carriage and began to examine the place we had now reached.

"This one is certainly not among the photographs," said Holmes.

"We have no idea how long the church building has been standing here," said Dr. Storn. "Some people think it was a church from many hundreds of years ago, but that it was taken into use as a sheep barn. Only later, when the antiquarians began to take an interest in place, was its previous use restored, and it once more became a place of worship. Dedicated to 'All Saints' because nobody knew what the original dedication might have been."

"But the graves appear to be ancient," noted Holmes, examining some of the headstones. "Some date from a hundred years ago, and much more. This place is so isolated from any human occupation that there is little wonder it remained unused for so many years. Centuries indeed."

"True. But you must admit that its setting is spectacular. Heather moorland stretching to the horizon. The building is mainly used as a cemetery chapel nowadays, although there are services here several times each year."

"Just the sort of place to hide a body," I said.

"Quite," replied Holmes. "Now, Dr. Storn, where are these flowers to be found? There must be some close by."

"Indeed there are, Mr. Holmes," replied the naturalist. "Come. I shall show you."

Together, we ventured out onto the nearby moorland and stopped almost at once beside a patch of white flowers just about visible amongst the heather.

"Well," said Holmes as he stood to his full height, "this certainly could be the place we are looking for. But where might they place the skeleton for safe-keeping?"

We all looked around the burial area, until Holmes spotted a likely site.

"There is the sort of place I would choose," he informed us. "Standing proud of the surrounding area is a stone box tomb with a removable lid. The grass around it has been disturbed very recently. The impression of carriage wheels is evident, as indeed are some footprints. And look – there are the imprints of our two suspects. The hobnail boots of Barrowbridge and the cleated boots of our second intruder. Sewersby, no doubt. But who do these other imprints belong to?"

"The mysterious third man," I concluded.

"Quite right, Watson," said Holmes. "And they look to be much fresher than the others. Come, let us see if we can open the lid on top of the grave. It looks to be slightly ajar, so it may be easier to lift than otherwise."

The three of us gathered around the monument and together heaved on the stone lid.

The cover slid aside, to reveal the dark depths of the tomb.

"Can you see anything?" I asked Holmes.

"Yes, but this isn't what I imagined."

I joined him and looked inside. A dead man was lying there: The scrounger, Sewersby, his contorted gaze looking up at us. I felt his skin. It was still warm.

"He cannot have been dead for very long," I concluded.

"Look at his feet," Holmes suggested. "This is the man with the cleated boots. The second of the three man who entered the Rotunda Museum during the night. And it is obvious how the man died: A knife is still protruding from the man's belly. It was pushed in at an angle and thrust up into his heart. Instant death."

"I wonder where the Gristhorpe skeleton is," I dared to say.

"Immediately beneath and to one side of the fresh corpse," said Holmes. "Wrapped up in its protective white woollen blanket. The outline of the bones are just visible in the darkness of the tomb."

At that moment, we heard a voice from behind us.

"Hello, there," it said. "Can I help you?"

We looked round and found that we had been joined by a gray haired man wearing a tweed suit. He was walking towards us from the direction of the church building.

"I don't remember seeing a carriage or horse," I said in a low tone.

"Nor do I," returned Holmes.

"Look out, Holmes!" whispered Dr. Storn. "He's carrying a gun."

"We are looking for a body," said Holmes in reply to the inquiry.

"There are plenty here," replied the man in the suit. "But it seems to me that you have found the one you were looking for."

Holmes stared at the newcomer, until a light of recognition lit up his face.

"I'm Sherlock Holmes," said my companion. "And these gentlemen with me are my companion and friend, Dr. John Watson, and a botanical expert from York, Dr. Storn. But you and I are already acquainted."

After an embarrassing pause, the man replied.

"I think you're mistaken, Mr. Holmes, or whatever your name is. I'm the churchwarden of this place, and I'm here to prepare for a service in the church tomorrow."

"Carrying a rifle?"

"Personal protection."

"You're good at putting on a disguise," said Holmes. "Indeed, almost as good as I am. But I still recognize you."

"Who is he?" I demanded. "Ought I to know him?"

"Possibly," replied Holmes. "He is a fellow who goes by the name of Harry Dunsdale. One of the last members of Moriarty's gang who is still alive and at liberty."

"I have no idea what you're talking about," replied the man.

"Oh, do drop your futile pretence, Dunsdale," said Holmes.

Dunsdale smiled and shook his head. "I must learn never to underestimate you, Mr. Holmes."

"That is a wise policy," replied Holmes. "So please tell us what you are doing here."

"Me? Have you not realized yet that this whole affair has been organised by myself?"

"This fiasco of a theft, you mean?" said Holmes. "Your boss would have been bitterly ashamed of you."

"Be careful what you say, Holmes, or you might end up in the same state as my two former colleagues – dead as a doornail."

"Like Barrowbridge? You seem to prefer the knife to the gun."

"I'm still a crack shot with my rifle," replied Dunsdale. "The fact that you aren't dead at this moment is merely down to the fact that I wanted to talk with you."

"Talk? About what?"

"About getting us both out of this current situation."

"How do you imagine I can help you out of this mess?"

"A mess not of my own making, I can assure you. That's where my colleagues, Barrowbridge and Sewersby, slipped up. They had to be dealt with."

"You used your skills at disguise to persuade the police to release those two men to you."

"I had it all prepared in advance," said Dunsdale. "But it turned out to be easier than I had imagined."

"So you killed Barrowbridge but you kept the other man alive, because you wanted to know find out much he had revealed to the police in Scarborough."

"That's right."

"And?"

"He'd already told them everything. Names and places."

"And do they know about you being up here this afternoon?"

"Inevitably. After they have searched the town, they'll head in this direction. I expect them to turn up here any minute now."

"Your theft of the skeleton has turned out to be a disaster," said Holmes.

"Oh, the Yorkshire Chieftain. You can have him back if you like. That theft was merely a smoke-screen. A deception."

"For what?" I demanded.

"I knew that one or two precious stones had been included in the special displays at the museum," said Dunsdale. "I helped myself to a small but perfectly formed emerald. I have it with me now. So, you can see that my time here hasn't been entirely wasted."

"You have my admiration," said Holmes. "Moriarty's evil genius certainly seems to live on in you."

Dunsdale nodded graciously, then looked around. "But it's time for me to leave. I trust you won't try to stop me."

"Trust all you like, Dunsdale," Holmes replied. "I'm not going to let you break free again, if I can help it."

Dunsdale lifted the rifle he had been carrying. "I shall once more spare your life," he said as he took to his heels and fled.

"Come along, Watson," said Holmes. "There may yet be something we can do to bring this present business to a satisfactory conclusion."

"I don't see how."

"We shall see."

Leaving our learned friend in the churchyard, Holmes and I set off in hot pursuit of the man with the gun.

He ran like a gazelle, jumping over tufts of grass and leaping over streams, until he reached a line of trees, where he came to an immediate halt. And stood listening.

As we joined him, Holmes and I could hear the sound of shouted voices and the baying of hounds. The police had arrived in the vicinity, no doubt armed to the teeth, in pursuit of Dunsdale.

"Where are we now?" I asked Holmes, as we drew almost level with Dunsdale.

"On the brink of some yawning ravine. Possibly the Forge Valley. Steep. Tree lined. Deep."

Dunsdale turned to face us.

"Now we have come to a pretty pass," he said. "If I stay here, I shall have to face the police and die either in a shooting match or at the end of a rope, convicted of murder. If I jump, I shall inevitably break my neck."

"I leave the choice to you," said Holmes. "But I agree that a jump from this height would appear be fatal."

"I ought to have been halfway to London by now," said Dunsdale. "But I decided to stay. I wanted to find out which of us was the cleverer, you for finding the whereabouts of the Gristhorpe skeleton, or me for committing the perfect crime. You see, I replaced that stolen gem with a glass replica, and then I killed the only two witnesses. What a shame! And now I've outwitted the famous Sherlock Holmes. The perfect crime, you see. And, of course, I win. So, farewell, Mr. Holmes."

At the sound of voices coming to us from the policemen gathering behind us, Dunsdale turned his back on us, threw the rifle aside, and leapt into the void.

With no sign of Dunsdale, we tried to explain the situation to the newly arrived Inspector Newlyn.

One of the younger policemen climbed down carefully into the ravine.

"Excuse me, sir," the policeman shouted up to us. "I think our man is gone. If you look down into the gorge, you'll see a rope, knotted and extending down to the bottom. The fugitive must have used it to climb down and effect his escape. There's ample evidence here of a horse having been tethered recently."

"That must be how Dunsdale and Sewersby arrived," said Holmes.

"I'm sure you are right, Mr. Holmes," said Nelwyn.

Holmes examined the rope.

"The cunning devil," he said. "I suggest, Inspector, that you conduct a detailed search of the valley, just to make sure he really has gone."

"This explains why we saw no other means of transport up by the churchyard," I agreed.

"The appearance of this fellow, Dunsdale, shows that we haven't yet seen the end of Moriarty's gang," said Holmes. "I wonder how many more of those devils are hiding among the criminal underworld of our country."

I was able to certify the deaths of the men who had been killed that day – the one on the moors, and the other in the fishing harbor.

The Rotunda Museum gladly received back the Gristhorpe bones, and once more put them on display to the public.

A few days later, Sherlock Holmes and I returned to London, to our Baker Street rooms and our normal lives. Whatever that meant.

Holmes appeared somewhat more refreshed than he had been. Possibly the change had done him some good, in spite of the gruesome interlude. Perhaps the stimulation of a case had also helped him.

"Do you think," I put to him through a haze of tobacco smoke, "that the Gristhorpe bones really are those of a Bronze Age warrior Chieftain?"

Holmes thought about it for a moment, puffing even more tobacco smoke into the atmosphere, before giving his considered response. "People are free to believe whatever myth, true or contrived, they choose to accept," he told me. "Just so long as it does no harm to others and enhances the reputation and income of such a place as the Rotunda Museum. I consider that we are in no position to give a definitive response. Perhaps we should merely leave the question to lie unasked and unanswered in the imagination of the public."

"And the stolen emerald?"

"Ah, now that is interesting, Watson," he replied. "I've received a message that yesterday the men from Scotland Yard descended upon a certain jeweler's establishment in the East End. There they were able to retrieve the stolen jewel. But they were just too late, by a matter of a few seconds, to apprehend Dunsdale."

"Did you have anything to do with the retrieval of this jewel?"

Holmes smiled. "Perhaps I did suggest the name of a certain jeweler's shop. The emerald has now been found, even though the villain is still at large."

"Perhaps to continue his crimes another day."

"I'm sure we shall meet him again before too long."

With that, the case of the Yorkshire Chieftain was laid to rest, so that Holmes and I were free to turn our attention to other matters.

As I was busy clearing out my traveling bag, I discovered the pictures taken by the photographer on the seafront at Scarborough. So much had taken place since that day that I might have thrown them away or burned them. Instead, I decided to give them to Mr. Hudson who, for some strange reason, seemed oddly delighted to receive them.

Why she felt this way, I have no idea.

But when Holmes opened up his pocketbook and presented Mrs. Hudson with the pressed four-leaf clover he had hidden away in there, she became so delighted that she gave us a most delicious supper.

It is a well-known fact that, in spite of my experience of marriage, I still find it difficult to understand women and, I have to admit the truth of it, I sometimes comprehend Mrs. Hudson least of all.

The Little White Lie
by Jeffrey A. Lockwood

My constitution had been hardened by the searing heat of Afghanistan during service as an Assistant Surgeon with the 66th Foot. But looking at Holmes draped across our paper-strewn settee, one would think we were in the midst of a triple-digit summer day in Candahar, rather than a muggy but altogether tolerable August afternoon in our Baker Street lodgings. For my part, I was uninspired by the recent issue of *The British Medical Journal* on my lap which offered few articles of keen interest.

So, between my companion's suffering and my own lassitude, the sound of footsteps on the stairs up to our sitting room promised a welcome break from our languor. Holmes sat up eagerly and noted, "A youngish woman of modest means, I would say, given her well-worn soles and rather sprightly pace." Thence came a soft knock at our door, and he called out for our visitor to enter.

She was a simply attired, handsome woman who I judged to be not yet in her thirtieth year. Her cheeks were flushed, and she dabbed at her forehead with an unadorned handkerchief. I might say that her most attractive features were thick, raven locks and a confident, womanly presence which she struggled to sustain. I rose to pour a glass of water from the pitcher on the sideboard for our visitor.

"Mr. Holmes," she began tremulously with a slight bow, "I am Miss Caroline Jennings. I understand that you are a discreet investigator, and I am in desperate need of someone who has the skills to navigate a most urgent situation."

"Please sit down and tell us how I might be of assistance, along with my friend and colleague, Dr. Watson," replied Holmes, courteously gesturing her toward the basket chair.

"Oh, it is a terrible mess that my brother and sister have gotten themselves into," she began upon taking a sip of the tepid water to steady herself.

"Now then, my dear, rarely are problems as intractable as people imagine," Holmes said, leaning forward paternalistically. "My years of experience with those who face the seemingly insurmountable vexations of personal, financial, and even legal conundrums have provided me with unusual insights into the human condition."

Holmes had a peculiarly ingratiating way with women which allowed him readily to establish their trust. Having put our humble visitor at ease, he settled back into the cushions, closed his eyes, and placed his fingertips together, thereby conveying to our uninitiated visitor either disinterest in her plight or his deepest attention. She looked toward me quizzically, and I nodded for her to continue.

"My younger brother, Charles, has fallen deeply into debt," she began, having recovered her nerve. "This, despite our parents having been killed in a fire a year ago and providing a goodly inheritance to the three of us."

"Three?" I interjected, inducing a subtly arched eyebrow from Holmes who silently scolded my interruption.

"There is also my younger sister, Eleanor, whose life is in danger from Charles's recklessness. You see, my brother became possessed by the demon of gaming, frequenting a notorious gambling house where he lost all of his money. There is a good reason these darkened places are called 'Hells', Mr. Holmes." Her voice now elevated from assuredness to the edge of anger, and Holmes gave a slight, knowing nod.

The young lady continued. "In a foolish effort to recover his losses, Charles claimed to have the assets necessary to secure a loan that would allow him to make further wagers. You see, Eleanor often accompanied Charles to dinner before he spent the night throwing dice, and she flaunted the diamond necklace that had been my mother's prized possession and her sole inheritance. The gambling den's proprietor became a moneylender, and his underlings evidently affirmed that Charles had the jeweled security to pay back a loan. Of course, he managed to squander the money and told his creditors that Eleanor would turn over the necklace to save him from a terrible fate.

"When he took the despicable leeches to her apartment, Eleanor disclosed that she had recently sold the necklace to place a very large bet of her own at the Ascot races earlier this summer, as she had been corrupted by Charles and received inside information that the heavily favoured horse had been injured in training. Her source was mistaken, and the favourite easily won the race, which meant she just as readily lost her entire inheritance."

Bringing himself out of his focused reverie, Holmes directed a sympathetic gaze at our visitor. "And might I presume that your brother's creditors were unmoved by Eleanor's dire situation?"

"Oh, Mr. Holmes, they've kidnapped Eleanor and said that she will be killed – or worse – if Charles fails to pay his debt by Friday at sunset! That is just three days from now, and I do not know where he could possibly acquire the nearly two-hundred pounds that he owes."

Holmes pricked up his ears at this formidable sum. "I might further surmise that you aren't in a position to rescue your imprudent sibling," said he.

"I have very little of my inheritance left. I used most of my funds to pay the doctor's bill for my closest childhood friend. She developed cancer of the – " Miss Jennings paused uncomfortably.

"I am a physician," I reassured her. "There is no cause for embarrassment about the human body."

"Well then," she said quietly, looking down at her feet, "it was a tumor in her breast."

"As such, I would suppose that the surgeon performed a Halsted mastectomy," I said, "which is a most traumatic procedure. However, it provides nearly fifty-percent survival from the cancer."

"She was horribly disfigured and in pain afterwards," said Miss Jennings. "Her husband left her, and I stepped in to buy her a crumbling cottage in the country, which was all I could afford. At least it gave her a place to garden and make a few shillings by mending."

"And that is why you are unable to cover your miscreant brother's debts," said Holmes, slowly shaking his head in dismay. My companion doesn't often express such solicitude, but sometimes his cold, calculating mind sympathizes with the plight of common folk.

"I would fain take your case," he said and gestured dismissively when Miss Jennings asked about his fee. "Your commitment to family and friends is laudable, if perhaps overly benevolent. However, I shall need a bit more detail to begin an investigation. Time is short, and it would appear that options are limited, but there is no reason to abandon hope of a suitable resolution until doing so becomes absolutely necessary. As a starting point, tell me what you can about the blackguard who is holding your sister as ransom."

"I don't know much," Miss Jennings said, although I could see a sense of fierce determination in her countenance. "As I understand the situation, Charles is indebted to a very shady and private man known as Mr. White. He is the reclusive Hell-keeper of The Alabaster Club, where my brother accrued his losses."

"Indeed," said Holmes, "it isn't unusual for those who extract money from gamblers to turn around and lend them money so as to dig the hole deeper. Now then, I would advise you to do two things: First, tell your brother to be absolutely quiet about this matter. He can only further aggravate the situation at this point. And second, take some rest for yourself, as you are most surely exhausted with anxiety. I shall call you when I have a firmer grip on the case and a plan for how to proceed."

Our client took her leave, and Holmes turned to me. I knew that he didn't think well of my gambling proclivity which sometimes amounted to half of my wound pension, but I also anticipated that he would want to tap into that unsavory side of my life to pursue the case.

"Watson, we shall set aside my judgments regarding your penchant for wagering on cards and horses so we might help this poor lamb with her predicament. Such vices have surely provided you with social connections that you can exploit to gain knowledge of this Mr. White. For my part, I shall head to The Alabaster Club and see what might be gleaned from those who frequent this contemptible establishment." With that, he rose energetically, having been rejuvenated by the promise of a challenging case.

Holmes and I spent that evening and much of the next day separately delving into the nature of Mr. White and The Alabaster Club – both of which turned out to be rather repugnant. We decided to exchange our findings over an early dinner at Simpson's, as my companion suggested that there was no reason to deprive ourselves of culinary pleasures, however distasteful our respective discoveries had been. I began with a smoked haddock omelet, while Holmes chose the fishcake with a poached egg and chive butter sauce. While we enjoyed these starters along with our pre-prandial whiskies, I shared what I had learned.

Having connected with my most-reliable gaming associate and parted with half-a-sovereign for his time, insights, and beer, I discovered that Mr. White was either fortuitously born into an *apropos* surname, or he had taken this appellation to reflect his most striking feature. The man was an albino. And he was as wealthy as he was pallid.

To gain further insight as to this queer fellow, I risked an interview with Langdale Pike, one of Holmes's most reliable sources of scandal, rumour, and impropriety. I knew well that my companion would be perturbed by my doing so without first consulting him, but I explained that time was precious, and Holmes acceded to my reasoning. Having located the disreputable gossip monger at his usual post in the bow window of a St. James's Street club, I was provided with the background of our Mr. White. Although shunned by the public, many albino men and women do well by displaying themselves in the ever-popular circuses. As a medical man, I am appalled by the exploitation and exhibition of Siamese twins, bearded ladies, dwarves, and giants who are deemed monstrosities or marvels of nature. But at least sideshows provide these pitiable people with a means of supporting themselves.

I had heard of Tom Jack, a Bohemian albino who was known as The Ice King and performed with Tom Thumb across the Continent. Pike knew of several others, including the American, Nellie Walker, who was known as the "White Negro Girl". He seemed disappointed that one of his degenerate associates had repeatedly failed to draw her to London. However, Pike was evidently pleased that London's own "Alabaster Boy" was a regular at The Egyptian Hall in Piccadilly, where the fellow earned twenty pounds-per-week. This young fellow would eventually accrue such wealth that he was able to buy a gambling den, name it The Alabaster Club – and name himself Mr. White – the man we were seeking.

Given Mr. White's substantial fortune, I inferred that he was likely a patient of Dr. Archibald Garrod, London's leading expert on skin disorders. I knew of his work, as he had given lectures at St. Bartholomew's Hospital when I was a student, and through this professional connection I was able to gain entry to his principal consulting room in Harley Street. He had a phlegmatic bearing with sympathetic eyes and a thick, greying moustache that provided the sort of countenance that would give a patient confidence. Dr. Garrod explained that he had been attending to Mr. White for several years, and his furtive patient suffered from a range of symptoms including severe vision problems, extreme light sensitivity, and an exceptional propensity for sunburn, even on cloudy days. He never ventured out before sunset. As much a scientist as a physician, Dr. Archibald was anxious to explain his researches on the inheritance patterns of *alkaptonuria*, based on Mendelian principles and how he was extending his early findings to understand the appearance of albinism in family lineages.

Being an ordinary practitioner, I was soon lost in the technical jargon which I was trying to share with Holmes when I was rescued by a portly carver, dressed in white, and pushing a trolley featuring an array of meats. I chose the rib of Scottish beef with horseradish, along with roast potatoes and Savoy cabbage, while Holmes opted for the saddle of lamb with buttered carrots and Yorkshire pudding. My companion poured us each a generous glass of claret as he began to recount his own findings.

"I managed to make my way into The Alabaster Club last night, although it was something of an affair to gain entrance." My mouth was full of beef, so I gestured for Holmes to continue while already being familiar with what he'd encountered at the doorway. "I had first to pull a bright-knobbed bell, after which the door was opened silently by a most severe man who closed it quickly behind me. Then I confronted another door, sheeted with iron. A small, glazed opening allowed a second person to scrutinize me, and I was evidently deemed trustworthy, as I was then allowed to pass up richly carpeted stairs into the first floor where roulette, French hazard, and other games were being played with stakes ranging from a few shillings to five-pound notes. Substantial sums were being won and lost without any display of excitement."

"That all sounds rather typical," I offered to Holmes's disapproving gaze, "but pray continue, as I expect that there were some unusual features."

"Indeed," said Holmes. "The curtains, carpet, and furniture were all pure white, as if putting lace over a feather. However, what is more important is that I was able to befriend the head croupier during his break, while I had supper from the buffet in the back room. I was able to secure an appointment with him for the next day to ask about his employer. Since he was clearly anxious about such a meeting, I paid him five guineas on the spot and promised the same amount on the morrow."

"We shan't be coming out ahead on this case," I murmured, but quickly followed this with, "but the real payoff comes with knowing the game is afoot," to which Holmes nodded approvingly with a steely glint in his eyes.

"My generosity made it worth his while to report to his superior that he had fallen ill. Indeed, so worried was he that Mr. White would somehow discover his perfidy and wreak revenge that he felt it necessary to leave London for the interview with me. It required most of today for me to travel to and from Alfriston, where my informant had a relative to provide him with lodging. We met in the back room of his favored pub along the River Cuckmere."

By this time, a dessert of treacle sponge and jam roly-poly had arrived, along with our glasses of port. Holmes leaned forward, as if remembering bodily the secrecy with which his source shared intimate knowledge of Mr. White.

"My stool pigeon had no love for Mr. White, which surely made it easier to 'deliver the goods', as the Americans say. In short, Mr. White is cruel, violent, and disturbed. My informant personally knew of Mr. White's having torn out the tongue a man who double-crossed him, and he had heard that his employer isn't averse to meting out equally cruel punishment to women who betray him. Most notably, he wears only white clothes and eats only white foods."

"How is that possible?"

"It is evidently not as difficult as we might imagine. My source has been told that Mr. White breakfasts exclusively on oatmeal and egg whites with white bread and milk. His dinner table on the top floor of the club is typically filled with cod and haddock filets, chicken breasts with mayonnaise, along with a selection of potatoes, cauliflower, turnips, onions, leeks, and parsnips. His standard dessert is rice pudding with white sugar and blanched almonds, although sometimes he eats poached apples and pears that have been peeled so they are without color."

"That is utterly remarkable," said I. "He is surely in greater need of an alienist than a dermatologist. I gather that he has the funds to secure any sort of medical assistance."

"Perhaps so, given his reported wealth. However," continued Holmes, holding up a cautionary finger, "it is also the case according to my source that Mr. White has paid enormous sums for rare, white objects. There are rumors of his having acquired the skin of an albino tiger from Bengal at a price of a thousand pounds, and an absolutely colorless water opal from Australia for a similar sum."

We finished our meal in contemplative silence, as Holmes labored with knitted brows to assemble the puzzle pieces that we had acquired into a picture of dangerous madness. After paying our bill, we walked back to Baker Street to settle our stomachs. Having also cleared our heads from our oenological indulgences by the time we reached 221b, we agreed that after a light breakfast in the morning, we would pay a visit to Mr. White.

I was up betimes in the morning and went down to our sitting room to find almost every surface covered with Holmes's scrapbooks and references. He had evidently been pursuing some arcane subject, perhaps all night as was often his wont. In any case, Holmes was so insistent to get the day underway that I forwent my toilet to devote myself to drinking two cups of strong coffee and then grabbed a slice of toast and hard-boiled egg on our way out. We took a hansom to St. John's Wood, with the morning breeze providing a bit of cool refreshment before the heat of the day was sure to arrive. We stopped at one of the poshest corner-houses of the West End. Holmes wanted to reconnoiter Mr. White's setting to get a better sense of this strange man, and my companion suggested that given the peak working hours of the gambling establishments and our subject's aversion to sunlight, arriving rather early in morning would provide our best chance of finding our quarry in his natural environment. Moreover, on our expeditious cab ride, Holmes had shared his ingenious plan to lure the object of our hunt into the open.

We rapped at the gleaming door using its brass knocker inlaid with ivory. A butler in an unconventional attire of a stark white, rather than black, coat, albeit with the typical pepper-and-salt trousers, looked disapprovingly at his household's unscheduled visitors. Holmes gave the dour servant a card on which he had written: "*I have the Gogibus Pearl.*" The slightest cock of his head betrayed the butler's recognition of the potential value of a pearl so extraordinary as to be given a name. Holmes had hoped such a tempting bait would draw out his master.

As Holmes had explained on our way over, his late-night research had revealed that this mysterious gem had been discovered in 1620 by a Spanish merchant named Gogibus, who sold it to King Philip IV of Spain. The pearl subsequently passed through various hands and essentially disappeared while being rumored to have been seen in private collections around the world. The incredible fact was that this long-lost gem weighed at least one-hundred-twenty-six carats, making it the largest pearl in all of Europe. The most important feature for our purposes was that it was said to be exquisitely lustrous. Surely anyone claiming to possess such a treasure would capture the attention of our quarry, obsessed as he was with whiteness, and likely to be aware of such a famed and mysterious object.

The butler directed us down an opalescent hallway to a door leading out to the garden, where we were commanded to wait. We found ourselves amidst a bizarre botanical and zoological collection. In the reflecting pool, a swan was gliding past a school of snowy white carp. Hanging from the tree branches were cages filled with white canaries, cockatoos, and lovebirds. The most spellbinding denizens were a pure white peacock which looked warily at an albino wallaby that seemed to want avian companionship in a strange scene that seemed to belong in Alice in Wonderland. As I marveled at the creatures, a stooped gardener appeared with his pruning tools and shuffled toward beds of snowy roses. He paused to deadhead the white carnations which were, like him, past their prime. Then he noticed us sitting quietly on a marble bench.

"Great Heaven!" he said, standing upright and reaching for his lower back to assuage the pain of assuming an erect posture. "You nearly frightened me to death, sitting there so quietly at this early morning hour. What brings you to Master White's estate?"

"We have business with Mr. White and were directed to wait in the garden," replied Holmes. "We are quite taken with the menagerie, as well as your beautifully cultivated flowers. Mr. White is indeed fortunate to have a man of such evident horticultural expertise."

The grizzled old fellow smiled his appreciation as Holmes swiftly endeared himself. "I also look after the animals, which I rather enjoy, although there is a white mole that I would just as soon be done with. If you look under the shrubbery, you might find the albino toad and hedgehog."

"Indeed," said Holmes. "I gather that your master is quite fixated on all things white."

"You don't know the half of it," said the fellow, putting aside his shears and sidling over while glancing around to make sure that he wasn't being overheard. "Mr. White is so obsessed that the servants call him 'Captain Ahab' when he's out of earshot, after the madman who devoted his life to chasing the white whale, you know." With this, the gardener gave a slight wink, clearly pleased with the literary cleverness of the household staff regarding a rather obscure work of fiction. "Mr. White has a madness that is surpassed only by his money," he continued. "His greatest passion is for any creature that shares his condition. I was told to plant cabbage for the sole purpose of attracting white butterflies that infest the plant. He imported live, pearly-white beetles from Siam, but they needed sugarcane for their food, and I couldn't get the plant to grow well enough, even in the conservatory. He is positively crazed to have white insects kept in captivity or, failing that, to add to his collection of pinned specimens. That seems to be his newest mania."

By this time, the gardener's voice had dropped to a whisper, which was probably for the best as a tall, lean-jawed man had quietly come into the garden and announced himself as Mr. White's secretary. The gardener tottered away to tend to the plants, evidently hoping that he hadn't been speaking to us. The prim-faced man scowled in the gardener's direction and announced, "My employer wishes me to convey his deepest doubts that you bear the treasure you claim to possess. But if you do, then I am empowered to examine the gem and report back to Mr. White as to its apparent authenticity so that a further inspection by a qualified expert can be arranged toward the eventuality of determining a purchase price." He extended his hand, as if to receive our supposed treasure.

At this, Holmes rose haughtily and expressed our profound offense at Mr. White's insinuation that we were less-than-honest. I played along, doing my best to appear aggrieved and echoing my friend's assertion that only a fool would carry an object of such value on his person. I followed Holmes out of the garden as he declared that he would offer the pearl to a less-libelous and obstreperous buyer. By good fortune, there was a cab passing as we came out of the house, and Holmes hailed it.

Once comfortably seated, I turned to Holmes and said, "Well, I suppose there was nothing lost in that encounter other than a bit of our dignity. But alas, nothing was gained."

"My dear Watson, your lack of insight never fails to amaze me. We gained enormously valuable knowledge. Indeed, this data evidence provides the foundation for our next move."

"I do hope such a move happens quickly, as we must act decisively by tomorrow if we are to save Miss Jennings' sister."

"I am well aware of the situation," said Holmes with uncharacteristic testiness. The strain of having to develop and implement a plan in such short order was weighing on my companion. He lapsed into a focused silence with abstracted eyes that indicated the depth of his thought as the heat and hubbub of the city conspired to discomfort me no less than did my friend's intense consternation.

By the time of our arrival at Baker Street, Holmes's countenance had changed from disquiet to energetic resolve. I knew better than to inquire as to the strategy he had formulated, given his usual reluctance to share his full plan out of professional caution and a desire to maintain control and preserve the element of surprise. Having engaged an urchin in muted conversation, he remained on the street while I went up to our rooms to attend to my neglected toilet. When he arrived a few minutes later, his first move was to send a message for Miss Caroline Jennings to return to our humble quarters. We then took our lunch of cold beef sandwiches while Holmes explained the initial stage of his plan.

"Do you recall an incident last month in which Mrs. Hudson intercepted us on the way up to our rooms and insisted that we come into the kitchen to see what she called a 'ghost cockroach' that she had trapped beneath a teacup?"

"Indeed, I do." Our usually calm and eminently practical landlady reported that she had issued a bloodcurdling scream upon seeing the spectral creature. "Having captured the bizarre beast, she managed to calm herself and wanted us to witness the remarkable insect."

"And what did we find upon lifting the cup?"

"Nothing but a typical cockroach – perhaps a bit lighter brown than usual, but hardly what one would describe as ghostly."

"Yet the poor woman was distrait, insisting that somehow another creature had displaced her captive. I assured her that I would investigate the phenomenon. So it was that I spent the better part of two days researching the nature of insect color, this being a topic that had never drawn my attention beyond some chemical features associated with the use of these creatures for the extraction of dyes. Of course, you well remember some time ago that I had reason to consult with a first-rate lepidopterist at the British Museum, who revealed that that a collector named Vandeleur was associated with a particular moth. And this queer connection provided a vital clue to solving the murder of Sir Charles Baskerville.

"When I returned to this entomologist's laboratory after Mrs. Hudson's ghostly encounter, he loaned me a copy of Kirby and Spence's acclaimed four-volume *Introduction to Entomology*. In particular, he directed my attention to the section on the metamorphosis of insects. The authors wrote incisively about the stages of growth in cockroaches, crickets, and grasshoppers, wherein the larval form doesn't differ markedly from the adult. However, with each shedding of its cuticle, the insect emerges as a soft, white creature with a body that subsequently expands, then soon hardens and darkens its covering to take on the familiar color of its kind."

"So what Mrs. Hudson found and trapped beneath the teacup was a recently molted cockroach."

"Precisely. And in the intervening hours between its capture and release, the cockroach turned from a pallid form into the familiar brown insect. She was rather relieved, but less fascinated than you and I as to the normality of this developmental process."

Having now gleaned a clue as to Holmes's plan for recovering Mr. White's hostage, our conversation was interrupted by the arrival of our client. Holmes issued his orders in very precise terms. Miss Jennings was to inform Mr. White that she had acquired something that might well be of far greater value to him than mere money. She would trade her sister for an exquisitely rare, albino specimen of a cockroach, the likes of which are virtually unknown in all of Europe. The exchange was to take place in The Alabaster Club precisely at precisely six o'clock the following evening.

Next, Holmes commanded that she pack for herself and her sister whatever would be needed for a prolonged journey, and tell her brother to do the same without question. They were to secure a carriage large enough for them and their younger sister, when rescued, along with all their luggage and meet us across the street from The Alabaster Club at the scheduled time. The poor girl was perplexed, but savvy enough to ask for no further details, trusting that Holmes would procure such a precious specimen and had reasons for their abrupt travel. She headed off with the final order for her to call Holmes as soon as Mr. White agreed to the terms.

Once she had departed, I asked my companion, "What if Mr. White already knows of insect molting or, barring that, doesn't find the terms of the exchange to his liking?"

"Fine questions, and it is for such inquiries that I find you to be a valued colleague. As for Mr. White's knowledge of entomology, I strongly suspect that his interests are focused on the physical specimens rather than a scientific understanding of insects. And regarding the viability of the transaction, it is reasonable to infer that his mania for whiteness will trump his lust for money."

"Indeed, although it would be desirable to have had more time better to grasp the nature of his greed."

"I concur. However, time isn't our ally. And mine is as promising a plan as can be contrived, given our constraints. Remember Voltaire's admonition that one ought not allow the perfect to be the enemy of the good."

100

"But how good are the chances of finding another recently molted cockroach?"

"That is a calculation for which I lack the essential data. For your card and dice games, probabilities can be determined, but for biologic phenomena such exactitude is impossible. However, I have contemplated various assumptions about the frequency which with cockroaches might shed their outer covering, how much time is required for them to darken their bodies, and how long these creatures live."

"And?"

"And I would estimate that perhaps one in a thousand is in the stage we are seeking at any given time. But the odds might well be far less."

"Great Heaven! Where shall we find such a number of cockroaches by tomorrow afternoon?"

"Not 'we' my friend, but 'they'."

Just as I was to inquire as to the identity of "they", there came a barefooted stampede upon the stairs, along with a cacophony of high-pitched voices. Into our sitting room rushed a dozen dirty and ragged little street-Arabs. Stepping to the front was the tallest and oldest of the disreputable mob.

"I go' your message, Guv'nor," said he.

"Very well, Wiggins. I have an assignment of the utmost importance for you and the others, who will report you and not again invade our quiet home." The boys looked almost apologetic, although any sense of decorum was surely beyond their ken.

"Yes, I'll make 'hem behave like civilised lads," said Wiggins, casting a censorious glance over his shoulder at the others who had retreated to the landing outside our door.

"Now then," continued Holmes, "let me explain the assignment. You and your able but motley gang are to seek out the refuges of cockroaches wherever they may be found – whether sewers, basements, alleyways, or dust yards. And in your searching for these insects, you are to locate and collect any specimens that are white in coloration."

His instructions were cut short by a telegram from Miss Jennings, reporting that Mr. White had agreed to the deal, but had indicated that Eleanor would suffer a terrible fate if there was any chicanery. He wanted the specimen to be alive so that there was no possibility of bleaching, dying, or other alteration. Holmes took this news in stride and continued his orders.

"Be careful in handling the insects, as they might be rather softer than normal. They are to be taken alive, and I will provide each of you with a stoppered glass phial for holding your quarry. The white cockroaches must

101

be delivered to me by tomorrow afternoon at four o'clock. Not one minute later. Do you understand?"

Wiggins nodded and the boys who were now gathered behind him murmured their assent as Holmes distributed the phials and concluded his contract by specifying, "I shall provide the usual scale of pay, but allow for extra time in the expectation that you might well work through the night." As he then went to his desk and returned with two shillings for each filthy lad, Holmes smiled and sweetened the deal. "For each white cockroach that is returned to me by the deadline, the captor will receive a guinea."

The next morning, Wiggins was at our door after we had breakfasted and were smoking our morning pipes. He was disappointed that his Baker Street Irregulars had worked long into the night and hadn't captured a single white cockroach. Their grimy leader explained that his boys had found the insects to be reticent to expose themselves, although they had found some impressive masses of the vermin. It suddenly occurred to me that a method to flush the insects into the open was at my disposal. I told Holmes and the urchin that I would dash out on an errand and return within the hour, at which time I should have in my possession just what was needed. I admit to taking some satisfaction in being evasive as to my plan, given how often I had been left in the dark by my companion.

I took a hansom out to Penhaligons's, which I knew from my courtships was the city's center of perfumery and, in particular, lavender oil production. I also knew well that ladies used dried lavender to repel clothes moths from wardrobes and bedbugs from mattresses. I returned to Baker Street with an ounce of pure lavender oil and handed the phial over to Wiggins who had returned to our quarters.

"Pray tell, Watson," asked Holmes, "what are you proposing?"

"I have applied the deductive skills you have so ably taught me. By my reasoning, if dried lavender effectively protects garments and mattresses from insects, then the concentrated oil might well have a repellent effect on cockroaches."

"A most intriguing prospect," Holmes averred with an approving nod.

"You should distribute a small amount of this material to each of your chums," I said to young Wiggins, "and dilute it with the strongest gin you can obtain, as I have no doubt that you have your sources. Sprinkle the concoction into cracks and crevices that you have reason to believe harbor masses of cockroaches to flush them into the open."

As the chief urchin dashed off to his compatriots, Holmes lit a cigarette and turned to me with his grey eyes as bright and keen as rapiers. "Really, Watson, you excel yourself." He need not have said more, as

102

these few words filled me with pride to think that I had so far mastered his system as to apply it in a way which earned his approval. "Now then," he continued, "I have one other task that requires your attention."

"But of course," I replied.

"At half-past three, find Mrs. Hudson and secure a quarter-pound of ice from the ice box. Crush it finely and keep it cool in a canvas bag."

Feeling emboldened by Holmes's approval of my contribution to his plan, I asked, "Might I inquire as to the purpose of the ice?"

Holmes was a bit taken aback, given his usual reticence about revealing details in the midst of a case. However, after a moment of silence, he offered his thoughts. "It is my understanding from Kirby and Spence's scientific disquisition that the rate at which insects age is a matter of the ambient temperature. As such, if the Baker Street Irregulars are successful, I think it advisable to keep their ghostly captives cool to prevent their darkening before they can be exchanged for Mr. White's human captive."

"A most ingenious tactic," I said and began pacing to relieve my mounting anxiety of whether the whole plan would come together. For his part, Holmes settled into his chair and smoked like a chimney.

At precisely four o'clock, Wiggins arrived breathlessly at our door, holding not one but three glass phials containing pearly white cockroaches. He energetically noted that, "The smaller one is missing i's 'ind leg. Bu' the othuh two are in fin' shap', Guv'nor. Tha' flowery oil did the 'rick an' made the li'l b------s come swarmin ou' like tenants in a boardin 'ouse fire!"

Holmes nodded approvingly and took the phials. He went to his desk and paid the lad – who had never smelled better in my experience with him or his grubby associates – three guineas to distribute. Having packed our barter on ice, Holmes provided us both with rather simple disguises of wigs and whiskers. These were intended to change our appearances sufficiently so that should Mr. White or his minions wish to find us among London's teeming masses after he discovered the true nature of the white cockroaches, we would be unrecognizable.

We hailed a cab and in short order, thanks to Holmes's promise of an extra two guineas to the driver for exercising breakneck speed, pulled up across from The Alabaster Club where Miss Jennings and her brother, Charles, were waiting in a carriage. Holmes ordered Charles to stay put, as he had already done enough harm and could only make matters worse by his presence when we met Mr. White. The young man looked chagrined and slumped into his seat.

We readily passed through the doors of the gambling hall as the men guarding the entrance had been apprised of our arrival by their leader.

Climbing up two flights of stairs, we arrived in Mr. White's luxurious sitting room. Unsurprising, but nevertheless remarkable, everything in the room was stark white, including a piano without black keys and a massive oil painting of a landscape using only variations of white and cream with touches of pale grey, surrounded by a polished silver frame. As for our host, I hadn't been so close to an albino before. I must admit that even as a medical man, I was taken aback by the extreme pallor of his skin, the startling whiteness of his hair, and the icy blueness of his eyes. He was gaunt beneath a white linen suit and appeared sickly in every sense of the word.

Rising slowly from his satin upholstered settee, he took the phial in which Holmes had placed the two undamaged cockroaches, brought out a lens, and studied the insects for a full minute. Mr. White gave an approving grin to Holmes which transformed into a chilling leer as he stared at Miss Jennings. He then nodded toward the doorway through which we had entered. The door had a minute aperture through which Mr. White's sentry monitored the situation, ready to inflict grievous harm should we fail to uphold our end of the deal. Instead, the enormous brute brought Eleanor Jennings into the room, and she fell sobbing into her sister's arms. Mr. White dismissed the lackey with a flick of his thin, effeminate hand and spoke his first and only words.

"You are indeed fortunate, young lady, to have such protectors who are able to provide me with not just one but a pair of six-legged gems for my collection. Perhaps I can induce them to mate, which might have been your fate had I been dissatisfied with these creatures. I assure you that your sister and her companions would have suffered a far more terrible punishment for disappointing me. However, I do hope that your imprudent brother has learned a lesson. Speaking of lessons, I wish to learn just one thing before releasing all of you to pursue your pathetic lives: Where did you acquire these remarkable specimens in such a timely fashion?"

Holmes smiled and replied, "London is a remarkable city, Mr. White. A man can acquire most anything if he has the right connections and sufficient funds. Why, it's even possible for a circus owner to acquire almost any freak of nature that he can imagine, including individuals who are devoid of both pigment and morals."

Mr. White sneered and dismissed us with a foppish flutter of his fingers. We came out into the final rays of the setting sun and crossed the road to the awaiting carriage occupied by Charles, who could only manage to mumble his remorse over and over again. Holmes reached into his coat pocket and brought forth an envelope and handed it to Miss Jennings.

"Here are three train tickets to Manchester, and ten pounds to get settled."

"But Mr. Holmes," exclaimed Miss Jennings, "we cannot take your money after all you've already done for us!"

"It isn't my money, but Mr. White's."

"His? Then how did you come by such a sum?

"One could say that I earned the money during my visit to The Alabaster Club two days ago. If one employs a bit of distraction and swift sleight of hand in the presence of an inattentive Faro dealer, it doesn't take long to come out ahead of the game. But you need not concern yourself with such matters. Rather, it's vital that you take the next train and don't return to this city for a very long time."

"Why must we be exiled from our homes?" asked Charles woefully.

"Because, young man, I secured your sister in exchange for two supposedly albino cockroaches which will, within the next hour or so, gradually transform into unremarkable, brown insects. At that time, your creditor will be livid at having been fooled, and he will spare no expense in tracking down and brutalizing those who swindled him. That is why we shall shed our disguises and you must abandon London."

With that, Holmes signaled the carriage driver to make haste to Victoria Station.

The Riddle of
Parsons Lodge
by Mark Mower

"Perhaps it was a political gesture," said Sherlock Holmes unexpectedly, "or an attack reflecting some deep personal loss."

I moved my copy of *The Times* to one side and looked up to see that he was leaning on a corner of the mantelpiece, briar pipe in hand, staring at me with some intensity.

"How did you know what I was reading?" I said incredulously. "There must be two-dozen or more articles and news items on these pages, and from where you're standing, you couldn't have seen my face. Have you developed some new talent for seeing through paper?"

He chuckled at the thought. "There's no great mystery. For the past five minutes, you've been fidgeting in that chair and have twice rubbed your leg. On no less than five occasions, you snorted with derision at the piece you were reading. Having digested the contents of the paper a little earlier, I can recall all the items of a criminal nature. One of which concerned the defacing of a military memorial in the early hours of Sunday morning. My supposition is that you read the piece and were at a loss to understand why anyone would wish to despoil such a magnificent monument to those brave men. Your bewilderment and anger then triggered some sub-conscious recollections of being injured at the Battle of Maiwand, which in turn gave rise to both the fidgeting and the leg rubbing."

I was a touch annoyed to admit that he was right, and then made a deduction of my own. "You clearly have nothing to occupy your mind. I take it that you have no cases at present?"

He smirked. "Correct on the first, incorrect on the latter. I have agreed to assist a man called Lawrence Munsey in his search for a missing document. A telegram received earlier has confirmed that he is due to brief me on the particulars today. I stand here idly, pondering your reading habits, merely because I'm awaiting his arrival, which should have occurred some ten minutes ago."

I had no time to respond, for at that very moment there was a loud knock downstairs. I hastily folded the newspaper and placed it down. Holmes moved towards the sitting room door, and in no time at all our guest was ushered into the room by Mrs. Hudson, whose expression suggested that she hadn't welcomed the interruption to her planned morning of baking.

"Ah, Mr. Munsey! A pleasure to meet you. This is my colleague, Dr. John Watson. He'll be sitting in on our consultation. Now, could we offer you any refreshments?"

The young gentleman looked most anxious and didn't seem to know what to say first. In the event, he offered up an apology: "I'm so sorry to be late, Mr. Holmes, but my cab was being followed. Three or four streets away, I asked the driver to stop and, having paid him, I then followed a circuitous route here to lose my pursuer. As for refreshments, a small brandy would suffice, for my nerves are quite on edge. And the pleasure is all mine, for I have long awaited the opportunity to meet both you and the esteemed Doctor."

He shook our hands eagerly, apologising once again and explaining that he'd read with much satisfaction all the published narratives I had thus far penned on my friend's career. When we had managed to coax him into a seat and supplied him with the beverage, he seemed to calm down a little and finally stopped talking. Holmes immediately interjected.

"I was intrigued by the letter you sent a few days back and your quest to find the missing document. But to assist you, I must first have all the pertinent facts. I would be grateful if you could start at the very beginning, even if that means repeating some of the information you've already shared with me. Dr. Watson hasn't had an opportunity to read your original correspondence."

Our client raised no objection and, having drained the glass, began his narrative. He was in his mid-thirties, flaxen-haired, and extremely thin. In height, I took him to be a little under six foot. His long, gaunt face was accentuated by a pair of thin-framed spectacles with round lenses, which testified to his myopia. He spoke with a slight West Country burr. "I grew up in Exeter, the son of a vicar. My father paid for me to have a good education and, when I was sixteen, I left home and took a job with a small legal firm on the outskirts of Hitchin, in Hertfordshire. In the ten years that followed, I was able to qualify as a solicitor, taking on conveyancing work on commercial and industrial buildings. It has been a steady profession, and the salary I received enabled me to live a comfortable life. And in that time, I also married my wife, Dorothea, and was blessed with two sons, Henry and Charles.

"I have always been something of a shrewd investor and set aside a proportion of my earnings each month to buy stocks, bonds, and shares in companies and commodities that looked to be attractive. My speculative investments paid off, so much so that by the time of my twenty-sixth birthday, I was able to leave the firm and set up my own legal practice a couple of miles away in the village of Ickleford. Since then, my business has flourished, and I have continued to make a healthy return on my investments.

"Earlier this year, in mid-March to be exact, Dorothea and I purchased a property on the outskirts of Ickleford known as *Parsons Lodge*. The house has a long history, and had been occupied since the reign of Henry the Eighth by successive generations of the Parsons family. The last occupant of that name was Denby Parsons. I had acted for him on several occasions, as he frequently bought properties across Hertfordshire which he rented out to tenants. He always conducted his business from home, so I came to know Parsons Lodge very well.

"It would not be unfair of me to say that, as well as being a very demanding and brusque man, Denby Parsons was something of a reckless businessman. Many of the properties he insisted on purchasing were agricultural cottages requiring significant repairs and costly ongoing maintenance. In total, he had a portfolio of around fifty properties, but the rental income from these was never quite sufficient to offset the investment he made in bringing the buildings up to scratch. Over the years – often against my professional advice – he funded this shortfall by taking out more loans and mortgages, many being secured on the value of his ancestral home.

"Two years ago, Denby was struck down with a debilitating bout of enteric fever. In preparing for the worst, he was keen to draw up a will to ensure that Parsons Lodge would pass to his younger brother, Eldred, in the event of his death. He explained that while he and his only sibling had never been close, Eldred was the last in line, so he should inherit what was left of the estate. Being a conveyancer, it had been some time since I had done any work of that nature, so I thought to pass the job to a legal friend, Howard Ogilvie, who specialises in wills and inheritance matters. However, our efforts were in vain, for events then overtook us. When news of the man's rapid deterioration reached the banks, all of his loans were called in. And in seeking to pay off the amassed debts, he was forced to sell all his properties. In his already weakened state, the news was too much for him, for he died within days, leaving instructions for me to complete the work required."

I listened to this grim narrative with some uneasiness, remembering just how ill I had been with typhoid. And it struck me, as it had many times over the previous few years, just how fragile the human condition can be – how one event can alter the whole course a man's destiny.

"In winding up the estate and paying off the creditors," continued Munsey, "Ogilvie and I did our best to secure the best sale prices we could on all the cottages. However, as most were being sold with sitting tenants, the value of the portfolio was severely reduced. Eventually, it became clear that Parsons Lodge would also have to be put up for sale to ensure that Eldred Parsons received something by way of an inheritance."

Holmes interjected. "How did Eldred Parsons receive this news?"

Munsey looked bashful. "None too well. He was livid that his brother had given me power of attorney, rather than appointing him as executor of the estate. And he badgered me for days, saying that there had to be other options to prevent the property falling out of his hands. I made it clear that unless he could raise a mortgage himself to buy the property, I had no option but to sell it to the highest bidder. Eldred indicated that this was out of the question, as his meagre salary as a schoolteacher would barely cover the interest payments on such a mortgage.

"Howard Ogilvie suggested that we should invite sealed bids for the estate when it was advertised. I reflected on this, for I was keen to put in an offer myself, having a great affection for the property. Yet I was conscious of the ethical position I was in and how this might be perceived by others – particularly Eldred Parsons. With Ogilvie's support, I agreed to let my old firm manage the sale, so there could be no suggestion of impropriety on my part. My former colleagues agreed that this would be legitimate. I duly submitted my tender and was delighted to learn later that I had secured the property, having outbid more than a dozen other offers. Meanwhile, with all the debts cleared, Eldred Parsons received what was left to him from the estate, a not-insubstantial sum of money, which enabled him to retire from teaching."

I was not sure that his purchase of the property sounded very ethical, but said nothing. As it transpired, this convoluted introduction had little to do with the man's reason for engaging Sherlock Holmes. That was an entirely different matter. Just before he moved on to expound on this, the detective fired another question at him.

"If I may just backtrack somewhat – would I be right in assuming that the person who was following your cab today was Eldred Parsons?"

"Yes, Mr. Holmes, I am certain of it. Since March, he has taken every opportunity to discredit my name and disrupt my business and personal affairs, telling everyone that Parsons Lodge is rightfully his and how I acted to steal it from him. I have seen him hiding in the garden and sneaking up to the windows on occasion. My wife is quite terrified by the man. Most recently, he has taken to following me. And it seems clear that he pursued me to London this morning, for I saw him on the platform at Hitchin Station, trying to look inconspicuous."

Holmes now looked to direct our guest towards the specific reason for his visit. "Mr. Munsey, thank you for this background information, but perhaps you could now move on to tell us what it is you're seeking."

"Certainly. I require your assistance on another matter, albeit one which relates to the property. Despite Eldred's protestations and public outbursts, Dorothea and I have been readily accepted in the village. The Parsons family were universally despised by the locals, as they set themselves apart and were the most unscrupulous of landlords. Two evenings a week, I take a stroll down to a tavern in the village called The Plume of Feathers. Over a glass of fine stout and a friendly game of cribbage, I have come to learn a great deal about the history of the family and their ancestral seat, the most significant revelation being the so-called 'Riddle of Parsons Lodge'.

"It is said that when the Catholic aristocrat, Sir Edward Leeming Parsons, first built the property in 1536, he created a secret chamber somewhere within the grounds of the lodge in which he concealed a treasure of great value and significance. Fearful that supporters of the Protestant Tudor King might seize this, he was desperate to ensure that the treasure remained hidden until such a time as it was safe to reveal it. Fearful about whom he could trust with the information – even within his own family – he decided to tell no one about the location. His only concession was to inform his three sons that he had also hidden, within the house itself, information which, when deciphered, could be used to find the chamber.

"As a prominent and influential Catholic, Sir Edward was eventually arrested on a bogus charge of treason and imprisoned within The Tower of London. As a result of the torture he endured, he never made it to his trial and died a day before his fortieth birthday. Most significantly, he went to his grave without revealing the location of the hidden treasure.

"Subsequent generations of the Parsons family have searched long and hard to find the document which purports to be the map or directions to the treasure chamber. Some have taken to digging up random sections of the ten-acre estate, hoping to strike gold. Others have doubted the authenticity of the story entirely. Denby Parsons had been one of those."

While a fascinating tale, I was already beginning to wonder how Holmes might view this, given that Munsey seemed set to ask him to assist in what was essentially a treasure hunt to add further wealth to the man's already-bulging coffers. And a glance across at my colleague showed that he was indeed beginning to show some signs of agitation at the direction of travel. He began to pick at some lint on the arm of his chair and was drawing more rapidly on the briar pipe. And yet, with what followed, both Holmes and I had underestimated the solicitor.

"Gentlemen, it must be clear to you now that I intend to pursue this matter to its logical conclusion. If the chamber does exist, I wish to find it. And if the whole matter is nothing more than a hoax, it would do no harm to expose it as such. Now, having told you that I am a shrewd investor, I would like to offer you a proposition. I have no greater insight into the location of this document and its associated treasure chamber than any of the people who previously resided at the lodge. But I have every faith that the two of you can lay this matter to rest. I am prepared to pay whatever fees you deem appropriate to do so. If we do uncover some treasure and it has a monetary value, I would like you to assist me in ensuring that the return on our investment is well spent. I therefore propose to set up a research fund with seventy-five percent of the proceeds, which could be used to further what Dr. Watson has affectionately referred to as your 'Science of Deduction and Analysis' – a pot of money which could help to promote advances in the numerous sciences which support criminal investigation and detection."

There followed a period of some silence. Munsey waited for a reply, while I felt it only proper to allow Holmes the first opportunity to respond. When he did, it was with a curiously practical query. "That is a very interesting and generous proposal, Mr. Munsey, but who would oversee the distribution of these funds?"

Our guest seemed reassured that the detective had focused on a legalistic matter which he clearly felt comfortable to answer. "The fund would be established formally as a charity, and the distribution of its research grants would be overseen by a board of trustees. And, if you are willing, I would advocate that you should be the chairman of that board, with Dr. Watson, myself, and a few other chosen individuals, assisting you as the other appointed trustees."

Holmes looked towards me and smiled as he digested this. "I would be content to go along with the proposal, on one condition: That Dr. Watson be appointed as chairman. I believe his skills in handling people and managing debate would be far superior to mine."

I was flattered at the praise and quick to confirm that the proposition sat well with me. Munsey was delighted and rose from his seat to shake us both by the hand. He left a short while later, saying that he planned to spend some time in town before returning to Hertfordshire.

It was only after the fellow had left 221b that Holmes voiced an immediate and obvious concern: "After all of that, let's hope this treasure does exist and we can find it. It wouldn't be the first time we've been led on a wild goose chase!"

We had arranged with Munsey to travel up to Hertfordshire two days after his visit to Baker Street. It was a dry but cold October morning as we boarded the train at King's Cross for the hour-long journey to Hitchin. Holmes was content to sit in silence for most of the time, smoking and reading a scientific treatise on gunshot residues. I was absorbed in the details of the Football World Championship match which had taken place in Glasgow the day before between Third Lanark and Preston North End – a thrilling encounter which had ended in a 3-3 draw.

The train pulled into the long station platform at Hitchin and we stepped down from the carriage to find Lawrence Munsey waiting for us – the diligent solicitor having already organised a vehicle for the short journey to Ickleford. A while later, we were being transported along a gravel track flanked on each side by three tall oaks in the approach to Parsons Lodge.

The house itself was a sizeable timber-framed building laid out in an *L*-shape, with an impressive front gable of traceried bargeboard. Set within this, below a diamond-paned window, was a large wooden corbel carved with the heraldry of the Parsons family. As we alighted from the carriage, we were greeted by a friendly, red-faced housekeeper who introduced herself as Mrs. Parkin. She insisted on taking our bags, explaining that rooms had already been prepared for our arrival. Munsey allowed the middle-aged woman to take charge, and the three of us followed her in to the house where we were greeted by Dorothea Munsey, an elegant young woman with a charming countenance and striking blue eyes. She explained that a cold buffet awaited us in the dining room.

The hospitality of the Munsey family was second to none. Our rooms were spacious and well appointed, and we each had access to a private bathroom. Dorothea could not have been more welcoming. Seated for the luncheon, she spoke freely on a range of topics, and seemed to enjoy entertaining us. Their two boys, Henry and Charles, sixteen and fourteen years respectively, were well-turned out and exceedingly polite. Young Charles took great delight in explaining how he too aspired to be a published author and quizzed me for some time about my own literary efforts. Henry was a little more reserved and, in looks at least, appeared to be more like his father. For the most part, Lawrence Munsey sat quietly, eating his food, and listening attentively to the conversations which unfolded.

Shortly after two-thirty, we began our quest to find the fabled treasure.

Munsey had given us free reign to explore all areas of the house and estate. We began by scouting out the grounds. The approach to the house we had already seen, a flat expanse of grass populated only by the tall oaks which flanked the long drive to the property. Holmes focused first on the areas around the house and the land beyond.

To the right of the main building was an ornate rose garden hedged with box. The neat rectangular plot covered an area of some five-hundred square feet. The pathways running through the rose beds were comprised of thick flagstones which ran away from, or were parallel to, the lodge. Beyond this, and around the other areas of the garden, the careful planting of trees and shrubs gave way to more open ground, which rose up beyond the back of the property in a noticeable gradient. Having ascended this, heading to the left, we were surprised to find a sizeable lake set within the estate, one which had not been visible from the house.

"Curious!" said Holmes, first scanning the landscape around the lake, before turning his gaze back down the slope towards the lodge. "This is clearly man-made. I suspect that the normal lie of the land would prevent water pooling here without draining down towards the property. Looking at the age of the trees here, it does suggest that the water feature was created in the sixteenth century, by Sir Edward Leeming Parsons."

I concurred, but as we began to walk around the front of the lake to the right, I spotted another unexpected anomaly: Beyond the main body of water sat another, intrinsically smaller pool, this one no bigger than a modest garden pond.

We lingered directly in front of this second feature and looked back towards the house. It was aligned with the rose garden we had seen earlier.

"Something to ask Munsey about later," uttered my colleague, pressing on around the pool towards the back of the estate, which we found to be populated with dense woodland. Beyond this, we came upon a long flint wall which, it transpired, ran around the whole of the property, broken only by the front gates of the drive.

As we stood looking at the wall, Holmes lowered his voice. "We are being watched by someone in the woods to our right. He has field glasses, and seems to have been observing our every move since we left the house. I anticipated as much – it was only a matter of time before Eldred Parsons appeared."

Ignoring the presence of our stalker, we continued the reconnaissance for the better part of an hour before heading back to the house. Approaching a rear door which provided access to the large kitchen of the lodge, Holmes confessed that he had not observed any features of interest beyond those we had already noted. "I could be wrong, Watson, for I am speculating on extremely limited data, but I think that any treasure which does exist is most likely to be found in or close to the building. Sir Edward Parsons was clearly an extremely cautious man. Fearing his enemies, I don't believe he would have risked undertaking any visible earthworks away from the lodge. Any such activity would be bound to attract attention and leave immediate tell-tale clues to the whereabouts of whatever he was trying to hide. No, I think our investigations must continue indoors."

Back in the house, Holmes began to explore each room of the property. After an hour or so, I left him to it, as he was clearly in a reflective mood and given to prolonged periods of silence. Some thirty minutes later, he reappeared in what Munsey had referred to as the "family room", a long rectangular library which ran to the right of the house. At the end of the this, overlooking the rose garden, was a large, stained-glass window, made up of three distinct sections and decorated with various motifs. Holmes spent some time scrutinising every aspect of its construction and depictions.

In a similar fashion, he seemed drawn to the largest of the bookcases running along the left wall leading to the window. Opening its various glass doors and removing from its central shelves several of the leather-bound volumes contained within it, he overlooked no detail. At one point, he even dropped to the floor, examining the floorboards beneath the solidly built cabinet with his magnifying glass.

By this stage, the family had rejoined us, no doubt eager to hear whether we had made any progress. I feared that we would have little to tell them, yet Holmes was surprisingly ebullient when he addressed the four. "I am pleased to say that Watson and I have made a particularly good start in our quest, and I already have some telltale clues as to our next steps. But before we continue, I should mention that we've already encountered the enigmatic Eldred Parsons. He was watching us from the woods at the back of the estate."

Dorothea Munsey let out a sigh. "That man is a constant irritation. I am fearful of letting the boys out of the house for fear of what he might do. I have instructed the grounds staff to watch out for him, but he finds ways of moving around the estate without being challenged."

Her husband concurred. "Yes, I may need to take more direct action to stop these encroachments. I'm considering what legal recourse I might have, beyond the usual laws of trespass."

"What more do you know of the man?" I asked, without much thought. "Is he known to be a violent or aggressive character?"

"Those I have spoken to at the tavern say he is extremely intelligent. And while seen as generally quiet and insular, he can be extremely tenacious. Before his retirement, he was a history teacher at the local Catholic school, and was known to be a staunch defender of his faith and a strict disciplinarian. The boys at the school were terrified of him."

"Interesting," ventured Holmes obliquely, before asking Munsey a different question. "What can you tell us about the rose garden beyond this impressive glass window?"

Munsey seemed a little thrown by the question. "Eh . . . Well, I understand it was first added to the grounds when the lake was put in at the back of the estate. Sir Edward Parsons created it for his wife, to ensure that her roses were never short of water, and he installed some pipework running from the lake area. The tiny pond to the right of the lake provides a supply of water to this day, although the tap is a recent addition."

Holmes seemed fascinated by this revelation. "Most instructive. And do you know whether any parts of the rose garden have ever been dug up in the quest to find the hidden treasure?"

Munsey smiled. "Yes, indeed, Mr. Holmes. I understand that Denby Parsons's grandfather had all the flagstones removed at one point, and he had his groundsmen dig six exploratory holes. Reaching a certain depth in the soil, two of these filled with water, preventing further excavation. It was believed that the diggers had ruptured the water supply to the rose garden. The other four holes revealed nothing. The family concluded that the chamber was unlikely to be in the area as a result."

"I see," said Holmes. His gaze turned to the stained-glass window at the far end of the room. "This window is very impressive. I have rarely seen better craftsmanship outside of a cathedral. Sir Edward Parsons must have spent a tidy sum on this."

"Yes," replied Mrs. Munsey. "We still have the account books from the time. The window cost more to make and install than the whole of this library building."

My colleague continued. "It suggests that the aristocrat wanted to make something of a statement with this . . . ."

We all looked towards the window. At the centre of the lavish design was the Coat of Arms of the Parsons family: A shield of white, with three black horizontal bands, supported on one side by three lions, and a depiction of three stags on the other. Beneath the escutcheon was the family motto, the familiar maxim: *Honi soit qui mal y pense.* In the section of window to the left of the crest was a depiction of Parsons Lodge, while on the right was the large figure of a Catholic priest in robes, holding a golden key and a Bible.

"What do you make of it, Mr. Munsey?"

Our host recounted what he knew of the design. "Well, the family motto is quite common on heraldic arms. In the Anglo-Norman language, which was spoken in England by the old Norman French, it translates as *Shamed be whoever thinks ill of it*, which I understand was the motto of the chivalric Order of the Garter. In modern parlance, we might say *Shame on anyone who thinks evil of it*.

"Indeed," replied Holmes. "But I would also add that in French usage, the phrase can be used ironically to insinuate the presence of a hidden agenda or a conflict of interest. In relation to our quest, that may be significant. And what of the priest?"

"Again, a common feature in Catholic iconography. Sir Edward Parsons was clearly demonstrating his faith, with the priest holding a copy of the Bible and a key to The Gates of Heaven."

"True enough, but I suspect that this once again hints at more." There was a degree of theatricality in the way that Holmes said this. He moved over to the large bookcase that I had seen him examine a little earlier. "Would I be right in concluding that Parsons Lodge has its very own *priest hole*?"

Munsey beamed. "You don't miss much, do you Mr. Holmes? Yes, beneath that very bookcase is a concealed entrance to the priest hole which Sir Edward had constructed when the house was built. It was designed to hide up to three people, should the need arise. I suspect that it was never put to use. I was first shown how to access the chamber by Denby Parsons when he still lived here and I was acting for him. I went down there when we first moved into the house in the search for the treasure, but discovered nothing. How did you know it was there?"

"It wasn't difficult to surmise that a prominent Catholic family would build such a security feature into a new home at that time. If you look again at the priest in the stained glass, you will see that there are two telling words beneath his right hand, *Clavis aurea*."

"*Golden key*," I added, "as we see in the picture."

"Yes, but the Latin phrase is often used to indicate the means of discovering hidden meaning in texts."

I was as intrigued, as was the family, when Holmes said this. "Then you believe the window is indicating that we should find a genuine golden key?"

"That is precisely what it is saying."

Mrs. Munsey spoke up. "I'm familiar with all the nooks and crannies of this house, Mr. Holmes. If there was a golden key to hand, I am sure that I would have found it."

Holmes continued with his performance. "There is no need to fret, my dear lady, for I have already located the key."

The faces of the two boys reflected the astonishment and delight that we all felt.

Holmes continued. "The key is in the middle drawer alongside the family Bible which it unlocks."

Lawrence Munsey looked confused. "But that is an old iron key, surely. I have used it to unlock the small padlock on the Bible several times. It is almost black in colour."

"Exactly as it was intended to be viewed." The detective stepped over to the middle drawer, opened it, and removed the said key, holding it up for us all to see. "What looks to be an ordinary, if dull, key, to open a quite unremarkable family Bible. But if you were to examine the key closely, you would recognise that it is too heavy to be made of cast iron. The outer case of this key is certainly made of a base metal, but it has been moulded around a genuine key of precious metal."

"How can you be sure?" asked Mrs. Munsey.

"Because the key tells us so. You would need a magnifying glass like my own to read the inscription, but carefully etched along the underneath of the key's barrel are the same two words we see in the window, *Clavis aurea.*"

"Splendid!" cried Mr. Munsey.

I remained confused. "Why did Sir Edward go to so much trouble to conceal the true nature of the key?"

"To disguise the importance of the locked family Bible. I believe it holds another important clue in our treasure quest. The 'golden key' unlocks the padlock on the front." Holmes removed the sizeable book from the middle drawer, placed it on a table in the centre of the family room, and invited us all to gather around as he demonstrated. "The key opens the lock, enabling us to remove the leather strap around the edge of the Bible. We can now open the pages at our leisure. And we can see here, on opening the cover, that it is inscribed with the names of all the descendants of Sir Edward Parsons. This has been passed down through the generations, while still retaining its hidden message."

It was Mrs. Munsey's turn to voice some concern. "I have spent many happy hours leafing through that Bible. I have never seen any message or wording that should not have been there."

Holmes smiled, before responding. "That is because the message has been cleverly disguised!" He turned the edge of the Bible towards us and lifted the top cover, before gently fanning the pages up at an angle. What had previously been a book edge decorated with gold leaf had now become an exquisite painting, recreating the crucifixion of Jesus Christ. Below the painting were the words *Familia supra omna – Family over everything.*

"Remarkable!" I exclaimed.

"Straightforward enough," countered Holmes. "The art of fore-edge painting can be traced back to the Tenth Century. Water colours are used to create an image when the pages are presented at a particular angle. When the leaves of the book are resting in their normal position, the painting remains hidden. The technique has been used for centuries to hide messages."

"But how did you discover all of this, Mr. Holmes?" asked Henry Munsey, with evident enthusiasm.

"By simple observation – one of the tools of my trade. But now we come to the significant part of the discovery. It's no coincidence that you have continued to refer to this library as the 'family room'. I imagine that it was called that originally by Sir Edward Parsons. Suspecting that the family room was indeed *over everything*, I began to speculate on what might lie beneath the bookcase. The obvious wear to the floorboards nearby indicated that the bookcase could be moved. In other older Catholic properties where I've seen this, it usually signifies the existence of a hideaway or priest hole. The Bible is clearly directing us towards that."

Mrs. Munsey could barely contain her excitement. "Then you believe the priest hole might be where the treasure is located?"

"I wouldn't go that far, but I would like to undertake a thorough examination of the hideaway."

Mr. Munsey was happy to oblige. The mechanism for moving the bookcase was surprisingly sophisticated. Our host opened the right drawer of the piece some three of four inches. This had the effect of releasing a small metal lever on the inside of the left-hand drawer – an action which would have been unseen by anyone unaware of its operation. Reaching to the back of this second drawer, Munsey pulled the lever to its full extent. There was a distinct click at the back of the bookcase to the right and some small movement of the cabinet away from the wall. With some effort, Munsey was able to swing the bookcase to the left, further away from the wall, assisted by a small set of wheels hidden beneath the piece. Over time, it had been the action of these wheels which had left the telltale signs of movement that Holmes had observed earlier with his magnifying glass.

An opening some three feet wide had been created with the movement of the bookcase. The wall behind was lined with the same oak panels which ran either side of the furniture. Inset to the right of one of these panels, I could see a small catch protruding from the wall by two or three inches. This was clearly part of the mechanism which had earlier secured the bookcase to the wall. I looked down at the floorboards which had now been revealed, expecting to see some sort of hole or hatch, but was disappointed. There appeared to be no obvious hideaway.

Munsey turned and smiled. "Here comes the clever part!" He grasped the small catch and twisted it to the left. It had the effect of releasing a small square door just above the wooden skirting board. This was comprised of four oak panels, hinged to the left. "The opening is a bit tight, I'm afraid, and we will need some form of illumination when we get into the tunnel. Once inside, we can stand, but will have to move single file for about ten feet. There will only be enough space for the three of us, so Dorothea and the boys will have to remain in the library."

Mrs. Munsey looked a little dejected on hearing this and the boys groaned. Holmes placed his hand on the shoulder of young Chàrles and addressed the pair. "As soon as we've scouted out what lies ahead, I promise I will give you a guided tour of the hideaway." This placated the youngsters, who beamed excitedly.

Five minutes later, with a hurricane lamp and two heavy candle holders to hand, we crawled in through the small entrance which extended to a depth of about ten feet. Beyond this, the space opened into a full-height stone corridor, sufficient for us all to stand upright. We edged forward, following Munsey's lead towards what looked like a dead end. Having reached this, the solicitor stooped and placed the hurricane lamp down upon one of the flagstones beneath his feet. He concentrated his attention on the stonework to his right, and in one smooth movement pushed on one particular stone. To my amazement, a section of the seemingly solid stone wall pivoted to reveal a small stone chamber. Munsey invited the two of us to enter, saying that he would remain outside so that we could move a little more freely.

The space was no wider than five feet, and extended for a length of around eight. We had to crouch to enter the chamber, and when inside could only sit on a solid wooden bench positioned to the right. It wasn't possible to stand up fully, as the ceiling was too low. The air was cold and musty, and I shuddered at the thought of being trapped in the space for any length of time.

Holmes began a thorough and silent examination of the interior. Sensing my discomfort, he suggested that I leave him to it – an action with which I was only too pleased to comply. Having rejoined Munsey in the tunnel, we made our way back out into the family room. Mrs. Munsey and the boys were nowhere to be seen. We learned shortly afterwards that the lady of the house had gone off to arrange for dinner to be served within the hour.

While waiting for Holmes, Munsey and I played some billiards with Henry and Charles at the far end of the room. It struck me again that the two boys were exceedingly good company and very well mannered.

Holmes reappeared after half-an-hour. He had a wry smile on his face and set about pacing the length of the wall from the entrance of the tunnel to the stained-glass window at the far end of the room. Having done this, he then asked Munsey for a jug of water. Our host didn't seem in any way put out by this, and complied with the request within minutes. With the jug in hand, Holmes said that he would take Henry and Charles in to view the priest hole. Their father raised no objection, so Holmes disappeared for a second time. The three re-emerged from the entrance to the tunnel just as the dinner gong sounded in the hallway. The boys continued to look excited, and Holmes promised to tell us all over dinner what they had discovered.

With the help of a young kitchen maid, Mrs. Parkin served us a most delicious meal of braised pheasant, roast potatoes, red cabbage, peas, and carrots, all topped with a thick onion gravy. For the adults, there was also a glass of Burgundian Pinot Noir.

As we ate, Holmes explained all. "Initially left alone in the priest hole, I examined every part of the chamber in minute detail. Underneath the wooden bench was an inscription, reading *Salus in arduis* – *A stronghold,* or *refuge, in difficulties*. Perfectly apt for the hideaway. I then examined and tapped each of the flagstones with the base of my candleholder. All but one appeared to have been laid on a solid base, for there was little sound beyond a dull thud. But the flagstone on the right, at the far end of the chamber – hidden beneath the wooden bench – gave a distinctly different sound, hinting at some sort of hollow or void beneath. Using my penknife, I was able to scrape away at some of the lime mortar around the stone until I had opened a small hole some four inches in length. With this section of the mortar removed, I was even more convinced that there was a void beneath. When Henry and Charles joined me on the second visit, we tested my theory. Sure enough, the whole jug of water drained through the hole without pooling and could be heard trickling away."

Holmes looked directly at Mr. and Mrs. Munsey. "With your permission, I would like to remove the flagstone tomorrow morning and explore the void below. At present, I believe it to be our best lead in this search."

The couple gave their wholehearted agreement to the plan, and Mr. Munsey said he would ask one of the groundsmen to assist. At this, Holmes frowned and shock his head. "I would prefer to conduct the work myself, assisted by Watson. At this stage, I don't want it to become common knowledge that we're trying to locate the treasure. It could bring all sorts of unwanted attention."

Munsey responded unequivocally. "Of course, I'll be discreet in arranging for all of the necessary tools you require to be taken to the family room tonight."

The remainder of the evening passed by very pleasantly, with Holmes and me joining the family in the parlour for a game of charades and a few hands of whist with Henry and Charles. I retired to my bed a little after ten o'clock, excited about the prospect of what we might find the following day.

With our breakfast complete by nine-thirty the next morning, we set about our task. The Munseys agreed to let the two of us work without interference and had planned a carriage ride into Ickleford with the boys, who were to spend some hours with their tutor who resided in the village.

With bolsters and mallets, we chipped away at the thick lime mortar around the flagstone. Then, with the help of a crowbar, I gently lifted one corner sufficient to enable Holmes to grasp an edge. The two of us then manhandled the heavy stone out from its position. My colleague's supposition had proved to be accurate, for we were now staring down into a brick shaft which appeared to drop down to a depth of about twelve feet.

Running down one wall of the shaft were positioned some iron handrails, much corroded since their installation, but still perfectly serviceable. We were also able to see that the flagstone had been positioned on the top layer of bricks forming the shaft. A damp, musty, aroma rose up to greet us.

Holmes said he would lead the way and began to descend using the handrails, while I held a lamp above to illuminate his passage. When he was wholly in the shaft, he paused and looked up at me enthusiastically. "We may indeed be on the right track, Watson! Look here – there is another inscription, reading '*Sic infit*' – *So it begins!*

Using a piece of rope, I lowered a kit bag of tools and our two lamps into the void, before climbing down myself. At the bottom of the shaft, the space opened into a tunnel running in an easterly direction. It looked like a mine, lined with beams, planks, and prop shafts, the height being just sufficient for us to move slowly by crawling on our hands and knees. When we had travelled some twenty-five feet, the tunnel opened into a taller and wider space, eight feet square, which enabled us to stand to our full height. Ahead of us, it was clear that there had been some sort of tunnel collapse, for there was a significant quantity of rocks and timbers strewn about, and it was clear that we would have to move the debris before being able to continue our passage.

"What do you make of it?" asked Holmes, holding his lamp out ahead of him. "We're about ten feet clear of the house and below the rose garden."

"It could be one of the collapsed test pits that Denby Parsons's grandfather commissioned."

"Precisely, and one of the two that filled with water. You can see the staining on the timbers. They clearly sat in water for a while before the liquid drained away. I think the best thing we can do is to move as much of this as we can to the sides of the tunnel to clear the space ahead. But be careful – we don't want to risk any further collapses."

It took us over two hours of back-breaking lifting and shovelling to move the soil, timbers, and rocks we uncovered. Heaviest of all was what looked to be a long stone lintel lying at the bottom of the pile. Holmes spent some time examining this and the space around what remained of the ceiling above the tunnel. When we had moved the lintel out of the way to the right-hand side of the tunnel, my friend let out a sudden exclamation. "A-ha! A detail I very nearly overlooked!" He knelt beside the lintel and pointed to an inscription which ran in large letters along one face of the stone. It read: '*Abundans cautela non nocet*'.

"'*Abundant caution does no harm*'", I said in response.

"Indeed. In other words: *One can never be too careful*. This final clue tells me all I need to know about the construction of this tunnel. It has been careful designed to protect whatever lies ahead of us. Sir Edward Parsons went to extraordinary lengths to prevent intruders from stumbling across his treasure. The inscription was to give genuine family members a clue as to the trap he had set."

"Then you believe this collapse to be no accident?"

"No, it's clear from what remains that this section of the tunnel originally contained a barrier of timbers supporting this stone lintel. Furthermore, the left-hand side of the stone held in place several rocks which covered the outlet of a stone culvert filled with water – water which was engineered to run down from the lake area. Anyone knocking through the barrier of timbers would dislodge the lintel and rocks, effectively flooding the tunnel – "

" – And drowning them in the process," I added, suddenly aware of my own vulnerability. "There is no way that anyone could crawl back through that tunnel if it was full of water."

"Yes. The design must have allowed for just a single release of flood water, for there is no longer any evidence of water draining down through the soil. And the water that did pass through has drained away over time. Of course, the trap didn't work quite as it was expected to, for the collapse was triggered by the test pit being sunk into the earth above, not from someone knocking through the timbers here in the tunnel. It's quite clear that we're the first people to venture into this space since the tunnel was first created."

I sounded a note of caution. "Yes, and I suspect we need to be vigilant about what lies ahead."

"Absolutely. It's likely that the other test pit which filled with water had exposed a second culvert containing flood water. Who knows what else might lie ahead."

Beyond the taller section of the tunnel, the space was once again at a height which required us to move slowly by crawling. We had covered about twelve feet, carrying the heavy tool bag between us, when Holmes turned and announced, "There is a second, more open, section coming up. Let me go in first to ensure that it's safe."

122

I stopped where I was, glancing back momentarily with the lamp to determine how far back I would have to travel should the tunnel flood with water. After only a few seconds Holmes called for me to join him. This new space had similar dimensions to the first, but the floor area was covered with flagstones rather than compacted soil. And while I could see a second stone lintel above the exit, there appeared to be no timbers barring our way.

"We're dealing with something different here," said Holmes, raising his lamp up to reveal yet another inscription on the lintel: "'*Obtineo et teneo*' *—To obtain and to keep*. It suggests something hidden."

"The treasure perhaps?"

"I think not, for the tunnel seems to continue beyond this point." He began to look all around the space, first examining the flagstones and then stooping to tap each with a bolster. He then looked around at the walls, left and right, before declaring that he had found something. I edged closer, raising my own lamp to the area he had focused on. At his own head height, he was scrutinising a patch of wall about six inches in width which sat between two wooden props. I could see why it had drawn his attention, for it was a distinctly different colour to the rest of the wall. "That looks to be clay, rather than compacted soil," I suggested.

"You aren't wrong. And it has been placed here deliberately. There are no other clay deposits in this section of the tunnel. This small telltale cross, etched into the clay, suggests it is covering something." He reached down into the tool bag and retrieved a hammer and chisel. With two or three smart taps, the dried clay cracked in half and fell from the wall. We could now see a small niche into which had been inserted an open metal box. With Holmes's lamp repositioned, we looked in to see that it contained a small metal key. "*To obtain and to keep*, indeed!" he said retrieving it. "I'm glad I took the time to look around. Otherwise, we may have exhausted ourselves lifting all those flagstones!"

We continued our onward journey through another smaller section of tunnel before reaching a third more expansive space. This time, Holmes looked to be exercising considerable caution. "Step carefully, Watson. You will see that our exit is barred by those heavy upright timbers. I have no doubt that this has been constructed in the same way as the earlier section which collapsed because of the test pit. The inscription on this lintel provides some confirmation, for it reads, '*Festina lente*' – *Hurry slowly*, or *More haste, less speed*, if you like. If we knock through these timbers, I have no doubt that our progress will be halted or slowed considerably because of a cave-in or a flood. We cannot afford to take such a risk."

I could only concur and, following a brief discussion about our best course of action, we agreed to leave the tools where they were and head back along the tunnel with our lamps. Given the time and energy we had already expended, our plan was to return the following day refreshed, and with some heavy-duty building props, to shore up the stone lintel. With that task completed we would be able to carefully remove the timbers. Before leaving, Holmes took a precise measurement of the height of the uprights to facilitate this.

It was close to one o'clock when we emerged from the darkness into the light of the family room. We found Mrs. Parkin in the kitchen baking some fresh bread and scones. She guffawed loudly when she saw the state of us, covered as we were in mud and dust from head to toe. Rather than risk dirtying up the dining room, we agreed to have a light luncheon at the kitchen table and spent a good hour being entertained by the housekeeper, whose anecdotes about some of the characters in the village had Holmes and me in stitches.

After lunch, we left the house to locate some suitable building props. In the sizeable barn and stable block which housed the Munsey's horse and carriage, we found just what we needed: Two oak beams, which we later learned had once formed part of the timber frame of a now derelict potting shed. While each took some time to cut to length, we had, by the late afternoon, assembled four suitable props. And to assist us in manhandling the timbers into the tunnel, we had also managed to locate a hoist, lift, and winch, which we carried across to the family room. By the time the Munseys returned home in the early evening, we felt as if we had done a solid day's work, and took some time to wash, dress, and relax before being called down for dinner.

Our evening meal was once again a splendid affair, with a main dish of Beef Wellington, mashed potatoes, and greens. The family were enthralled by Holmes's account of what we had discovered, and the boys hung on his every word. Mr. Munsey expressed his amazement at the engineering required to create the tunnel and install the traps. Holmes agreed, and pointed out that the design was particularly sophisticated, as it would have required calculations of the amount of water needed to fill the tunnel, without rising up into the priest hole and flooding the house. Some sort of valve or shut off facility must have been created to prevent any excess water draining into the space.

It was at this point that Holmes entertained us further with an account of a similarly impressive "treasure" tunnel which had been discovered in Nova Scotia, Canada, in 1795. On a tree-covered island in the Mahone Bay area, a young man had noticed a sizeable indentation in the ground and, with the help of a group of his friends, began to dig down. What they discovered was a man-made shaft, in which were set, at ten-foot intervals, some solid wooden platforms. As they began to remove some of these barriers, water flooded into the shaft from an unknown source, slowing their progress. It was discovered that the shaft had been sunk to a depth of over one hundred feet. And yet, despite their efforts, the group found nothing.

Other excavations were to follow, and various theories as to contents of the fabled "Money Pit" began to be published from 1856. Holmes ended by saying that no one had yet discovered the buried loot or historical artifacts that the treasure hunters hoped to find.

Mrs. Munsey asked us what we planned to do the following morning, having made such good progress. I explained that we were going to try and shore up the newly found lintel to prevent the tunnel flooding, and then remove the timber barrier. The family were once again excited at the prospect of us getting closer to finding whatever had been hidden all those years ago.

We retired to bed not long after this, exhausted but elated.

Having enjoyed another fine breakfast the following morning, we made our way to the family room in the same mud-stained clothes we had worn the previous day. We had little choice, for neither of us had packed an extensive wardrobe.

Entering the priest hole ahead of me, with a candle in his hand, I saw Holmes stiffen immediately as he looked towards the corner of the chamber.

"Someone has gone down into the tunnel!" he exclaimed in a hushed tone. "One of the lamps is missing!"

"Eldred Parsons, no doubt," I replied quietly.

He nodded in agreement. "He's been watching our comings and goings. If he saw us carrying the props and hoist into the house yesterday, he would have guessed what we were up to. No doubt, he then secreted himself in here after we had stopped work for the day."

"Why do you say that?"

"If he had forcibly entered the property last night, the servants would have reported the signs of a break-in. During the afternoon, the house was unlocked and the Munseys were away. He had only to wait until we left the family room to sneak in unseen." He stepped forward to look down into the shaft with the light of the candle.

I was suddenly aware of the atmosphere in the chamber. The distinct mustiness, which had characterised the smell of the place the previous day, had been replaced by a fresher aroma, like sea spray. Holmes's next announcement clarified all.

"The tunnel has been flooded! Parsons must have tried to break through the timbers and succeeded in bringing the lintel down, releasing the water. The fool! I would have thought that a former history teacher might well have heeded the warning on the lintel. Still, I suppose he would have had no knowledge of the lengths to which his forbear went in protecting the tunnel."

He quickly lit the remaining oil lamp to afford him a better view of the shaft. "It looks as if the bulk of the water has already drained away. From what I can see, there is about two-and-a-half-feet left. I'll climb down and search the tunnel. There's a slim chance that he may have survived. You must go and raise the alarm. If he has drowned, we'll need to inform the local constabulary."

I was reluctant to leave, but realised I had to comply with his instructions. I urged him to take care and found my way out of the chamber and along the short corridor to the family room. Heading to the kitchen, I found Mrs. Parkin mopping the floor. She looked up with some surprise as I raced into the room and very nearly slipped over on the wet floor.

"There's been an accident," I spluttered. "We believe that Eldred Parsons has gone down into the tunnel we discovered yesterday and may well have drowned. I need to alert the police."

It was a credit to the very able housekeeper that she took charge immediately. Quickly placing the mop and bucket to the side of the sink, she wiped her hands on the front of her apron, and headed for the door. Before departing, she announced, "I'll send Mr. Barton, our senior groundsman, into the village to rouse Constable Dunwoody. He can take the pony and trap."

Mercifully, Mr. and Mrs. Munsey had taken the boys off for the day, so they were spared the spectacle of seeing the drowned body of Eldred Parsons being pulled from the shaft in the priest hole. Holmes had reached the second section of tunnel, beyond the first collapsed lintel, to find the retired history teacher. The man had clearly tried in vain to crawl back through the passageway before the flood water overcame him. By the time that Dunwoody arrived at the house, Holmes had managed to move the body to the foot of the shaft. With the aid of the hoist, rope, and winch, the three of us were able to retrieve the corpse.

The doughty constable insisted that we remove the body from the house. With some effort, we lifted the drowned man outside and into the stable block, covering the cadaver with some tarpaulin. And while I had already pronounced Parsons to be dead, Dunwoody sent dear old Mr. Barton into the village for a second time to collect Dr. Gessner, the local surgeon.

126

In the time that it took for the elderly doctor to arrive, Holmes and I gave Dunwoody a short statement of the events leading to the death. I noticed that Holmes made no mention of the alleged "treasure" we had been pursuing and the carefully engineered culverts we had found, saying only that Lawrence Munsey had commissioned us to survey an unstable tunnel which ran under the house and grounds of Parsons Lodge. He explained how Eldred Parsons had been disinherited and had felt aggrieved at the loss of his family home. We were careful to tell the officer that Parsons had been seen loitering around the house on many occasions and had been watching us since our arrival at the property.

"But why would he want to sneak into the house and go down into the tunnel?" asked Dunwoody at one point.

"Perhaps he believed that the tunnel concealed a family heirloom," replied Holmes, mischievously.

The burly Scot snorted at the suggestion. "From what you've told me, it doesn't sound like a particularly good place to hide anything. And you say that the water which flooded the tunnel drained down from the lake area at the back of the house?"

We both nodded. In response, the constable asked us to show him where the lake was. We obliged and led him towards the back of the house and up the gradient leading to the lake. When we reached the large expanse of water, it was clear what had occurred in the tunnel when Parsons knocked out the lintel, for the pond to the right of the main lake had been pretty much drained, with just a small trickle of water flowing in from the direction of the lake.

Constable Dunwoody looked a little bewildered. "Why would the water drain down from here?"

Holmes was quick to respond. "As I understand it, the original owner of Parsons Lodge installed a water supply for the rose garden which sits above the tunnel. Perhaps there was some damage to that."

Dunwoody regarded him keenly, before replying. "Aye. That sounds plausible enough." He turned and looked down towards the house and garden. "Well, I think I've seen enough. I will await the arrival of Dr. Gessner. He will want to have the body removed to his surgery to conduct the *post mortem*. I will, of course, inform the local Coroner about the death, given the circumstances. You will need to come down to the station this afternoon to provide me with a full statement. And I have no doubt that you will be called to attend the Coroner's Inquest into the accident."

Holmes nodded and said that we would both be pleased to assist. I fancy that I saw him smirk a little at the mention of the word "accident".

When Dunwoody had left us, we walked down into the rose garden. "The engineering of this tunnel is every bit as sophisticated as I suspected

127

it to be. The pond was constructed to hold just the right amount of water to fill the space, without flooding the rest of the house. Once drained, the pond is slowly refilled from the lake, in readiness for any further breaches of the tunnel. Very clever indeed. And there must be some mechanism for shutting off each culvert after it has served its purpose."

I nodded in agreement but voiced a practical concern. "How are we going to continue? Surely it will be too dangerous to go back down into the tunnel while the water remains?"

In his familiar unflappable manner, Holmes patted me on the back and laughed. "Of course. We will have to arrange for a water pump to be installed, and it may take a while for the residual water to be drained. In the meantime, we'll comply with Constable Dunwoody's request and, in due course, attend the Coroner's Inquest. Given the attention the story is likely to receive from the press and public, it may be as well to cease operations for a couple of weeks. First off, we must inform the Munsey family about this unexpected turn of events."

It was to be a full four weeks before we were able to return to Parsons Lodge and resume our mission. In that time, the local constabulary had conducted a perfunctory investigation into the death, and we were also called to attend the inquest. Despite some of the questions posed by the jury of locals – no doubt inspired by the wild stories circulating about the legendary "treasure" of the Parsons family – the coroner directed them to focus on the events which had led to the death. At the end of the proceedings, the verdict reached was one of *Death by Misadventure*.

Lawrence Munsey had been proactive during the hiatus. With the help of his groundsmen, he had hired and installed a small, steam-powered water pump to drain the flood water from the tunnel. Over a period of three days, they had managed to complete the task. It remained to be seen whether the tunnel was still secure enough to facilitate our onward passage.

On our first day back, we managed to reach the space where Eldred Parsons had triggered the flood. The collapse was more severe than the first one we had encountered a month earlier. In the event, it took us the best part of two days to clear the debris and shore up the entrance to the next section of tunnel. Having done so, we were disappointed to discover a third collapsed area further along the passage. This took a further day to clear, at the end of which we decided to return to the family room rather than push on.

Each evening the Munsey family entertained us. Their excitement had continued to grow, despite the setbacks. On the fourth day, we encountered a challenge of a slightly different kind. Holmes calculated that the tunnel now extended some ten feet beyond the area of the rose garden above. He postulated that we were unlikely to face any more flood risks as we climbed down into the shaft. I was intrigued.

"Sir Edward Parsons was a devout Catholic. He seems to have been fixated with the number *three*, possibly referencing the *Holy Trinity* – three oaks on each side of the gravel driveway, three sections of the stained-glass window, and depictions of three lions and three stags on the family crest. I could be wrong, but I would be surprised if we encounter a fourth timber barrier."

We navigated our way through the new section of tunnel, only to find another more open space, once again around eight-feet square. This time, however, there was no timber barrier blocking our way. Instead, there looked to be a further section of tunnel set at a height of roughly five feet. A stone lintel framed the entrance, on which were inscribed the words *Ceteris parabus – All things being equal.*

"This is curious," I said, looking to the floor of the entrance. "There are two flagstones here running across the width of the space. Each one is three feet square. Yet only the one on the left leads into the tunnel. It's as if the tunnel was originally going to be twice the width we see."

"True enough," replied Holmes, holding his lamp ahead of him to provide more illumination. "And that's not the only feature which is unusual. While the tunnel starts off at a height of some five feet, you can see that after six feet or so, it opens into a taller space."

"Well, it looks safe enough. Let's crouch until we get through this first section." I picked up the heavy kit bag and slung it over my shoulder while stepping towards the tunnel entrance. In a sudden and violent move, Holmes slammed into my side throwing me off balance and sending me to the floor. Angry and bewildered, I looked up at him, seeking an explanation.

"I'm sorry, Watson! I couldn't let you go any further, for you may well have plummeted to your death." He held out his arm to help me back to my feet. "Let me explain. If you look carefully at the space between the flagstones, you'll see that some of the soil has been washed away. I believe that to be the result of the flooding initiated four weeks ago. These flagstones are not set into solid ground, but are, instead, on a pivot, which runs down the middle between them. That is what the Latin phrase is hinting at. *All things being equal*. The stones must be kept in balance."

While holding on to me for support, he tentatively placed the toe of his boot on the left flagstone and pushed down. It tilted, sufficient for me to realise that there was an empty void beneath. If I had crouched and stepped onto it moments before, I would have disappeared into a hole.

"That is why the passage for the first six feet is set lower. It is to prevent people jumping across the space. To successfully stand on the flagstone to the left, you must have something of equal weight on the right. That said, now that we know what we are dealing with, we will circumvent the need for weights."

So saying, he disappeared back down the tunnel, only to reappear some minutes later, dragging two timbers with him that he had retrieved from one of the earlier tunnel collapses. "If we strap these together," he said, with evident glee, "we can fashion a makeshift ligger and avoid the trap altogether!"

His plan worked perfectly, and with the timbers in place we were able to crouch and walk across the flagstone and into the new stretch of tunnel. With the space then opening to a height of over six feet, we were hopeful that our quest had finally come to a point of some conclusion. And after walking for another fifteen to twenty feet, the sight which greeted us seemed to confirm this. We were now faced with a solid oak door on which was carved in large letters, *'Finis coronat opus'* – *The end crowns the work.*

"Time to use the key we found earlier," said Holmes, relishing the moment. He retrieved the small key from his pocket and turned it in the lock. It was some credit to the original locksmith that the movement met with no resistance. With the door unlocked, it was a simple task to turn the handle and pull the door open. What greeted us was a sight I will never forget. The short space beyond contained wooden shelves running from floor to ceiling. On each was laid out a wealth of religious artifacts, from golden crucifixes encrusted with precious stones, to silver chalices and scent burners. On a middle shelf lay a large, encased book, which we were later to learn was a rare, illuminated Bible of Italian origin. There were also several cloth bags containing gold and silver coins. The display was dazzling.

Even Holmes seemed genuinely stunned by the discovery as he scrutinised all that lay before us. "It appears that there was a treasure after all . . . ."

Alongside my friend, I had already enjoyed countless thrills, adventures, trials, and tribulations, but the discovery of the Parsons treasure had to rate as one of the finest achievements of our time together. We removed one or two of the smaller items from the display to take back to the Munseys before re-locking the door and retracing our steps back along the tunnel.

It need hardly be said that the family were overjoyed at what we had to tell them. The two boys asked if they could descend into the tunnel to see the treasure for themselves, but Mrs. Munsey voiced her disapproval.

In the end, it was left to Holmes and Lawrence Munsey to return to the secret chamber to remove the valuable items we had discovered in solving "The Riddle of Parsons Lodge".

The financial value of the Parsons treasure could only be guessed at. So rare were some of the pieces in the collection that one or two of the experts called in to assess their worth and saleability refused to commit to an auction estimate – all of which helped Lawrence Munsey to reach the decision to which he eventually came. With the exception of the gold and silver coins, which were indeed auctioned at Sotheby's some months later – achieving auction prices way beyond those anticipated – the whole collection was gifted to the British Museum.

The decision was one that Holmes and I applauded. On display at the museum, the religious relics could be enjoyed by all and cherished in perpetuity. In any case, the sale of the rare coins had still given Lawrence Munsey a return which he could hardly have imagined, enabling him to retire from his work a very wealthy man.

True to his word, the former solicitor did donate seventy-five percent of the auction proceeds to the charity which Holmes and I went on to establish later that year. The Baker Street Foundation was created *to further the science of deduction and analysis*. Meeting four times a year, the Board of Trustees considered grant applications from individuals and organisations looking to contribute to the burgeoning number of sciences supporting criminal investigation and detection. It also set up an endowment fund for the specific purpose of supporting initiatives aimed at crime prevention. One of its primary areas of focus was the publication of academic papers supporting all of the new science. And it was through this channel that Sherlock Holmes was able to publish a multitude of monographs on topics related to his own methods of deduction and analysis.

In the years that followed, beyond my own brief tenure as the charity's chair, the organisation was to be led by several distinguished figures approved by both Holmes and Lawrence Munsey. One of these was the retired Scotland Yarder, Inspector MacDonald. Another was the one-time Baker Street Irregular, Charlie Wiggins, who had followed in Holmes's footsteps by creating his own successful detective agency. The charity served as another fitting legacy of that great man – and very cherished best friend – who once occupied that setting we have all come to know and love as 221b Baker Street.

The Arthritic Beneficiary
by Dan Rowley and Don Baxter

"Doctor, there is someone here to see you."

"Please ask them to depart," I informed the officer. "I have no desire to have anyone see me in this wretched place. I've suffered humiliation enough for a lifetime."

"Well, Watson, might you not make an exception for me?"

I lifted my gaze in sudden surprise at the sound of the voice I know best. "Holmes! How did you come to be here in Kent? I thought you were on the Continent dealing with the Russian Grand Duchess' missing necklace. And is that Gregson behind you?"

"Indeed, old friend, we're both here. The local constables informed the Yard of your arrest, as required in cases of suspected murder. Gregson saw the report, contacted Mrs. Hudson as to my whereabouts, and telegraphed me. Luckily I was in Amsterdam with the Grand Duke, who – by the way – I suspect is the culprit. In any event, I made my apologies to him, promising to return soon, and hastened here. I must say, Watson, I've seen you in many unpleasant situations, but a prison cell does not at all suit you. Come, Gregson, bring those stools over here, and we shall listen to Watson's story. As you know, Watson, leave nothing out."

Once they had settled themselves, I commenced. "As I believe you know, I was here in Bexley visiting the family of my friend, Sir Edward Doyle, at Tenderden Place."

"For Gregson's benefit, please elaborate on your relationship with Sir Edward."

"Yes, of course. Inspector, I was in school at the same time as Sir Edward. He was a bit older than me, but we belonged to some of the same societies and shared some common interests, such as military history. He was a striking man, tall, broad shouldered, quite imposing. He inherited a sizable fortune from his father and, after school, took over the family businesses, which centered on shipping, factoring, warehouses, and numerous investments in the Americas.

"Unfortunately, Sir Edward was killed several years ago when he was visiting a factory in Liverpool to view the test of a new boiler for one of his ships. The boiler exploded during the test, killing several men, including him.

"I had stayed in contact with Sir Edward and his family over the years, coming here periodically to visit. In fact, his only son, Jonathan, is my god-son. Since Sir Edward's death, I've felt it my duty to mentor Jonathan more intensively, especially given that he's working on becoming a physician. We anticipate the planned formation of the Royal Army Medical Corps later this year may provide an opportunity for him."

"Very, good, Watson. Let us move on to this particular visit."

"Well, I knew Jonathan would be here, and his older sister, Liza, had recently become engaged, so I could see him and offer my congratulations to her in person. I came two days ago at about five p.m. Upon my arrival, Martha, Sir Edward's widow, informed me that Liza was suffering horribly from arthritis. After dropping off my things, I proceeded to Liza's room, which is on the first floor at the back of the house, a combined sitting room and bedroom. She and a gentleman were seated at a table to the right of the doorway. After we greeted one another, Liza introduced me to William Reed, the family solicitor. She explained that they were going over some papers in light of her recent engagement. Upon my stating the purpose of my visit, Reed politely withdrew into the hallway, indicating he would return when I had finished.

"I had Liza sit on the edge of her bed and examined and questioned her. She was clearly in agony from the pain of her arthritis. I advised I would order some Fowler's Solution to alleviate the pain."

I saw Holmes give me a skeptical look, and I nodded.

"Fowler's is a quack nostrum, I know, but I have prescribed it on rare occasions in the past – typically as a placebo, and always in a low dose. Liza told me that it helped her before, and since she believed so strongly in it, I reluctantly decided to use it."

"She had used it before," clarified Gregson.

"She had, but nevertheless I proceeded to write out instructions for its use, which I placed on the nightstand next to her bed."

"And where was the nightstand?"

"On the right side of the bed as you face it."

"Continue, please"

"I went to the door to call Reed back into the room. I explained what treatment I was recommending and said that he should leave so that Liza could lie down to rest. He graciously agreed and began to gather up his papers. Liza and I walked to the door and conversed a few minutes as acquaintances will do, while Reed bustled around behind us. He bade us *adieu* and left the house.

"I went downstairs and located the butler, asking him to send up a maid to prepare Liza for bed. I also wrote out a prescription for the medicine, and he dispatched a footman to town to obtain it."

"What time did you leave Miss Doyle's room?"

"I would say approximately six o'clock."

"Recount for us the rest of the evening."

"I went up to my room to dress for dinner. We had sherry in the drawing room at seven, and dinner immediately after. We ended at about nine."

"Who all was at dinner in addition to yourself?"

"Lady Martha and Jonathan, of course. The younger daughter, Rosalyn. And a chap by the name of Arthur Thorpe. I would say he is in his mid-twenties. He had been a clerk for Sir Edward, and apparently stayed on after his death to assist with managing the various family enterprises. I must say that he seemed quite attentive to Rosalyn, and may have intentions toward her.

"After dinner, Lady Martha, Jonathan, Rosalyn, and Arthur retired to the game room at the back of the house. I believe they mentioned something about playing some variation of backgammon. I went over to the library in search of reading material, and sat by the fire with a copy of the latest *Strand*."

"Did anyone come into the library while you were there?"

"*Ahem* – I *may* have fallen asleep for a bit."

"I'm familiar with your penchant in that regard. What happened next?"

"There was a great commotion at about midnight, up on the first floor. I heard Lady Martha calling out for help. I ran to the back of the house and rushed up the stairs. Lady Martha was in the doorway sobbing, and Jonathan and Rosalyn had come out of their rooms. Arthur Thorpe was coming down the stairway from the second floor, which is where his and my rooms are located.

"Not being able to ascertain the reason for Lady Martha's distress, I went into the room. Going over to the bed, I quickly ascertained Liza was dead. Soon everyone was crowded in the room, and there was some confusion."

"What was the nature of the confusion?"

"Everyone was crowded by the bedside, all talking at once. I believe some items on the bedstand may have fallen to the floor when someone jostled it.

"Jonathan and I went downstairs. I told him that I had noticed Liza appeared somewhat yellow rather than pale – which, as you know, wouldn't normally be the case with a death by natural causes. I also knew that, other than the arthritis, Liza was quite healthy. Typically arsenic poisoning can take a while, and if discovered, the patient can be treated. But in Liza's weakened condition, she was likely too weak to call for help, and she died alone in the hours before she was discovered."

"So you suspected foul play?" summarized Gregson.

"Or that it was an accident of some sort. To be on the safe side, I thought it better for everyone to call in the authorities immediately."

Gregson smiled and nodded. "Quite right, Doctor. It is always best if we're called in as soon as possible, even if Mr. Holmes feels at time we're a heard of trampling beasts."

"But not you, Gregson. Watson, proceed. I assume the police questioned everyone that night."

"Yes, they talked to everyone, including the servants. When they had finished, we all went to bed.

"I slept late that morning, and we were having a late breakfast when the Chief Constable placed me under arrest. I've been in this miserable dungeon since then."

"Did he provide any explanation as to the reason for your incarceration?"

"No. And I have absolutely no idea as to why he has done this. I wouldn't harm Liza, or any other woman for that matter."

"Quite. Gregson, would you kindly ask the Chief Constable to join us."

While we waited for Gregson to return, I must have looked miserable, as my friend attempted to cheer me up by telling me that the situation with the Grand Duke would provide excellent "fodder for one of your romances". Before I could reply, Gregson returned with Francis Austen, the Chief Constable, a short, plump, red-faced man in his fifties – very self-important but (if I may be allowed the observation despite my circumstances) entirely out of his depth.

Gregson performed the introductions. "Chief Constable Austen, this is Sherlock Holmes, of whom I'm sure you have heard. He consults with Scotland Yard, with a remarkable degree of success. Given his relationship with the Good Doctor, who also has been a help to us, I thought it useful to bring him along so that he could assist me."

"*Hurrumph*. Highly irregular. We have no need of 'consultants' here. Solve things ourselves with good old fashioned methods."

Seeing Gregson bristle, Holmes smoothly intervened. "I'm confident that is the case, Chief Constable. If you would perhaps explain to us your reasoning, the Inspector and I can be on our way."

"What? In front of the prisoner!"

"Surely no harm can come of that. I assume there will be a Coroner's Inquest in the next day or so, at which time the three of us will hear it all. We can expedite this and save time by doing it now. I, for one, would be honored to hear your thoughts, as I'm a keen student of crime, as I'm sure you are as well."

Seeing an opportunity to impress the Yard and the renowned Sherlock Holmes, Austen's vanity overcame his reluctance. "Well, as you put it that way, I suppose it would do no harm to share my thoughts."

"Capital. Please proceed."

"*Hurrumph.* Following standard procedure, my constable and I interviewed the inhabitants of the household. We learned that the Doctor ordered Fowler's Solution for Miss Liza to ease her arthritic pain. I had my constable check with the local pharmacy, which confirmed there were no dosage instructions printed on the bottle's label. They also explained the composition of the medicine, which contains a solution of one-percent arsenic. A dram contains less than one-half of a lethal dose for a person Liza's size and weight. But the Doctor's written instructions call for *four* drams – well above a lethal dose."

I started to protest, but Holmes motioned me to remain silent. "Proceed, sir."

"We ascertained that one of the maids read the Doctor's instructions and poured out four drams in a measured glass next to the bed. That was approximately at eleven. Liza was awake and conversed briefly with the maid. She then drank the medicine and the maid left. Given the size of the dose, Liza likely died in less than five minutes. That also accounts for the yellow cast of the corpse.

"During our search of the room, we discovered that the Doctor's instructions were under the bed. My assumption is that, during the confusion, the Doctor pushed the instructions under there, planning on retrieving them later."

"And what would be the Doctor's motive?"

"According to some members of the household, he's quite the ladies' man and was fond of Miss Liza. I assume he made advances, which she rejected, enraging him enough to perpetrate this cowardly deed."

"This is preposterous!" I interrupted. "I did no such thing. I made no advances to Liza. And my instructions were for *one* dram of the Fowler's Solution, not *four*!"

"Yes, Watson, we'll get to that. Chief Constable, why would Watson call in the police if he is the culprit?"

"Well, as a medical man, it might look suspicious if he ignored the yellow cast to Liza's skin. If he retrieved the instructions and destroyed them, it might have appeared to be an accident. And he couldn't know that a maid, rather than Liza, poured out the dose, and so he assumed no one would know the dosage he'd prescribed. In my experience, criminals commonly make simple mistakes like this."

"I'm sure that is the case. May the Inspector and I examine the instructions?"

Austen left and returned with a piece of paper, which he handed to my friend. Holmes studied it intently for several minutes. Probably no one but me noticed the glint in his eyes, which always indicated that his mighty brain had reached a conclusion.

"Well, Chief Constable, allow me to explain why the Good Doctor didn't murder Miss Doyle. No, no, please be patient. I have several reasons for my conclusion, some based on my long study of human nature, and others on irrefutable facts.

"Let's commence with the Doctor's character. I've known him for nearly eighteen years. He is a man who has dedicated his life to saving lives, and assisting me in uncovering those who wish to end them. Committing a murder of the type and in the manner you suggest is utterly inconsistent with that character, while calling in the authorities when he suspected foul play is entirely consonant with it.

"As to the motive you suggest, it is true that the Doctor enjoys the company of women. But he does so in an entirely honorable fashion. He doesn't make an overture until he's satisfied it will be welcome. I've observed him numerous times admire a woman, but seldom does he act on it. And, even assuming he was rejected, he would apologize and withdraw – not murder the object of his admiration." I must admit that, at this point, I was never so willing to have Holmes expiate on my attitude toward the fairer sex. Normally he does it to tease me, but here he turned it to noble use.

"And, if those animadversions on the Doctor's character and nature don't convince you, there is the matter of the instructions. They indeed are in Watson's handwriting for the most part. But there is one exception. Note how the numeral *four* is written. There is a main upright, a cross-bar perpendicular to it, then, to the left another short upright parallel to the main one. In other words, the top of the four is open. But the Doctor inevitably draws the short upright at an angle so that it joins the tops of the main upright. It is always closed, unlike this open four. To prove this: Watson, I know you always carry your notebook on your person. Please hand it to the Chief Constable so that he can confirm that, in every case, your fours are closed."

Austen studied my notebook with growing consternation. Holmes added, "So you see, Chief Constable, someone altered Watson's original *one* into a *four* by adding the two strokes, making the mistake of leaving the altered number open at the top. And I believe the ink used to make the one into a four is slightly different from that used to make the one. Examination under a microscope will confirm this, but I've made an extensive study of various inks, and I'm confident I'm correct.

"And, before you raise the objection that the person who altered the instructions might worry I would come and exonerate my friend: Watson, did you tell anyone about my whereabouts?"

"Yes, everyone. Even Liza, in her pain, asked after you. They were all anxious to meet you. I explained you were on the Continent and that I had no idea when you would return."

"I'm sure that gave the culprit more courage to make the alteration."

Gregson spoke up. "Chief Constable, I've come to learn that Mr. Holmes is invariably right in matters such as this. And I agree with his assessment of the Doctor's character. I would prefer not to have Mr. Holmes testify at the Coroner's Inquest and embarrass a fellow guardian of public law and order. May I make a suggestion?"

Austen sat for a moment, then looked at each of us in turn. His face was contorted by indecision, but he finally said, in a muted voice, "What do you suggest, Inspector?"

"I vouch for Mr. Holmes and Doctor Watson. Allow Mr. Holmes, accompanied by me and the Doctor, to go to Tenderden Place to re-interview the inhabitants. Given the new light Mr. Holmes has shed on this, perhaps he can discover who altered the Doctor's instructions."

"Hmm. This is highly irregular, but if the Yard will assume responsibility, you may proceed. Is there anything else you need?"

"Thank you, but no." Holmes graciously replied. "And I assure you that, as Gregson can tell you, I want no credit, public or otherwise, for my efforts. One more thing would be helpful: Could you please arrange for the solicitor to come to Tenderden Place so that I can ask him about the papers he was reviewing with Miss Doyle?"

Austen gave his assent, unlocked my cell, and ushered the three of us out of the station. I began to offer thanks to Holmes, but he waved that aside. We procured a cab and made our way to the Doyle residence. As we went, it was manifest that Holmes was deep in thought, so Gregson and I remained silent, knowing nothing could penetrate his keen concentration.

Shortly we arrived at Tenderden Place, a stately structure with beautiful gardens. The original building had been constructed by an Elizabethan merchant and consisted of two spacious stories, with dormers on the second floor. It was of red brick with white touches, large windows, and several chimneys. The left side of the house was of different architecture and coloring, with a fanciful turret, bay windows, no dormers, and alternating red-and-white stones. Sir Edward had told me the portion to the left was a seventeenth-century addition by another merchant. He'd stated that his father had purchased it in part so that he could jokingly tell visitors it was made for a merchant, so he wanted to maintain that tradition.

It might assist the narrative to offer a brief description of the relevant layout of the main, older part of the building, which is where the sad events had occurred. On the ground floor, a long hallway bisected the house. Standing at the entrance and facing the back, on the right side, in order were a study, library, and game room. On the left were the drawing room, dining room, and a breakfast room. At the back of the hallway were stairs leading to the first floor and dormer rooms. Liza's bedroom was on the right at the back of the house, directly above the game room. Lady Martha, Jonathan, and Rosalyn also had bedrooms on that floor. Thorpe and I had dormer rooms on the second floor.

We alighted from the cab, knocked on the massive oaken door, and were admitted by the butler. I explained the reason for our visit and asked to see Lady Martha. He left us for a minute and, upon return, indicated we should follow him to the drawing room. As we entered, she was sitting by the fire, with an absent look in her eyes. Lady Martha was about forty-five, of medium height with auburn hair, a full figure, and glittering green eyes. The room was comfortably appointed with stuffed chairs, Davenport, end tables, and a sideboard.

Seeing me, she quickly arose and rushed to me, giving me a vigorous embrace. "Oh, John, I hope this means the police have abandoned the absurd notion that you murdered Liza."

"Yes, it appears so. Allow me to introduce my friend Sherlock Holmes, about whom I've spoken on numerous occasions, and Inspector Gregson of Scotland Yard."

Holmes gave a slight bow. "Madam, we're here to determine who or what caused your daughter's untimely demise."

"Oh, my! So you believe someone did murder her."

Sensing she was about to begin weeping, Holmes kindly smiled. "May I presume to ask you a few questions?"

"Of course. Anything that will help."

"Did you see your daughter after Watson left her, which was approximately at six o'clock?"

"No, I was in my room dressing. My regular maid is taken ill, so I was doing it myself."

"And then you came straight down to dinner?"

"Yes. We gathered here in the drawing room for sherry, then went to the dining room. Everyone but Liza was there until we finished at about nine."

"I understand that you then went to the game room to play a version of backgammon."

"John said he was tired and going to the library to read a bit before bed. Rosalyn, my other daughter, suggested we have a backgammon tournament. So she, Jonathan, Arthur, and I played that for several hours."

"Could you explain for us what you mean by a '*tournament*'?"

She smiled. "It is something the children and I came up with when they were younger. The four of us would start in teams of two each, and each team would play a game of regular backgammon. The two winners of the first game would then play each other, as would the two losers. Each winner received one point. We would continue with several rounds like that, winners and losers playing each other in each following round. At the end of our 'tournament', the person with the most points would receive a prize, something like an extra dessert at dinner, some candy, or a similar treat. Edward would often sit in a chair while we played, often making comments on individual moves. It was great fun."

"Do you recall how many rounds of play there were that evening?"

"I do not, but I believe there should be the sheet I used to keep a tally in the game room. John, would you be a dear and fetch it? The sheet should be on one of the tables."

I left and returned with a sheet of paper that had a number of letters and arranged on it. I handed it to Holmes, who scrutinized it carefully.

"I believe I comprehend the notation system, but allow me to flesh it out to ensure I'm reading it correctly. For example, the first entry is: '*Round 1. M(w) J. R(w) A*'. I take it that means you played against your son and you won the round, and your daughter played Arthur Thorpe, and she won."

"You would be excellent at games Mr. Holmes. That is exactly correct."

"I assume that, in each round, one team normally would finish before the other. What would the two players who had finished do while the other team continued?"

"Well, sometimes they would watch the game still in progress, or perhaps chat with one another, or leave the room for some reason."

"Can you recall which team finished first in the initial round."

"Jonathan and I are fairly evenly matched, so Rosalyn and Arthur were done before us."

"And what did they do while waiting?"

"I think Arthur sat by the fire reading a newspaper. Rosalyn may have left. She was rather discreet about it, so I assumed she needed to freshen up a bit."

"Did you ever leave the room? Please use the sheet to refresh your recollection."

"Let me see. Yes, I remember now. In the second round, Rosalyn and I finished before Jonathan and Arthur. I slipped out to talk to the cook about some preparations for the next evening's dinner."

"Very well. It appears that you played nine rounds."

"Yes, we ended a bit before midnight and chatted for a while. Jonathan and Rosalyn had some amusement pretending to argue about the prize."

"I wish I didn't have to bring this up, but could you describe how you discovered Liza. Please take your time."

She looked on the verge of tears again. I rose and went over to hold her hand for a few moments. Finally, she sighed and composed herself. "On my way to my room, which is across the hall from Liza's, I decided to look in on her. She was so still. I went over to the bed, and believed she wasn't breathing. I reached out to touch her, and her skin was cold. I probably screamed, but don't recall much after that. Very quickly everyone else was in the room, crowded by the bedside. John made his way through us and gently placed his hand on Liza's wrist and then her neck. I do recall how soft his voice was when he informed us she had passed away. He motioned for Jonathan to follow him, and they left the room. Rosalyn, Arthur, and I stayed there until Jonathan returned to say the police were on the way. I was confused, until he explained that John said this was standard procedure in cases of sudden death such as this."

"Thank you, Lady Martha. I have a fairly good idea of what happened from then until Watson's arrest. Now, I beg your pardon, but I must ask some questions that, while painful, are a necessary part of routine in a matter such as this. Would any of your servants have any reason to harm your daughter – especially the maid who poured out the medicine?"

"What a horrible thought! Absolutely not. Eunice, the maid, is extremely distraught. We have assured her this isn't her fault, but she is so upset I had her sent off to her family near Dover. And the others have been with us for years. They are all devoted to us, as Edward was kind and generous to them, a practice I have continued."

"What about the other members of the household who were present that night."

"Jonathan and Rosalyn loved Liza. They have always been close. I cannot imagine either of them wanting to harm her, let alone cause her death."

"And Mr. Thorpe? Anything about him – whatever the nature."

She hesitated, and I urged her to continue. "Well, it has nothing to do with Liza, but I'm a little concerned he pays too much attention to Rosalyn. That was never the case when Edward was alive, but started soon after he passed away. Rosalyn takes more after Edward than me, and men have never been that interested in her."

"Given the financial situation of your family, what mother wouldn't have such concerns. I comprehend perfectly, and you need say no more."

"Thank you, Mr. Holmes. John has always sung your praises, and I can now see why."

Holmes nodded. "Now, may we impose on you further. I would propose to inspect Miss Doyle's room. Then, if it meets with your approval, I would like to talk to your children and Thorpe individually. And, oh yes, your solicitor should be stopping by."

"Certainly. I believe the study, which is across the hall, would suit you. John knows his way around and can take you upstairs."

"Thank you again, Madam. I hope we won't need to disturb you further in your period of mourning."

The three of us left and went into the hallway. Holmes indicated he wanted a word in private with Gregson. I pointed out the door to the study, which they entered. About five minutes later, they emerged, Gregson retrieved his hat and overcoat and left, promising to be back whenever he had accomplished whatever tasks Holmes had set for him. I was accustomed to Holmes's behavior of this nature, so I didn't bother to question him.

I led to the back of the hallway and up the stairs to Liza's room, which overlooked the gardens. The room was much as when I had left it, except the bed was made and everything was back in place on the nightstand to the right of the bed. The room was decorated with rose-coloured flocked paper, with matching duvet. All the furniture, including the table and chairs, bed, armoire, dresser, wardrobe, and dressing table were of solid mahogany. Some paintings adorned the walls, mostly of flowers and pastoral scenes.

Holmes stood for several minutes, surveying the room. He then proceeded to give it his usual minute scrutiny. He first paced back and forth from all conceivable angles, eventually covering what seemed every square inch. He then got on his hands and knees by the nightstand, crawling around on all fours and peering under the bed and stand. He opened all the drawers and windows, for what reason I couldn't fathom. Finally, he again stood at the doorway, first facing into the room then out into the hallway.

At last he looked at me and indicated we should go down to the study. It was also furnished in mahogany, with a desk in one corner, a large fireplace across from the door, ceiling-to-floor bookcases, and large windows at the front of the house. There was a working table by the windows, and Holmes arranged two chairs on one side and another facing

142

them. He asked me to have the butler find Jonathan, and to tell him that we would see Rosalyn and Thorpe separately after that.

When I returned, Holmes was inspecting the various books with quiet intentness. As he turned to me, I asked, "Are you also going to speak to the servants?"

"At the moment, I think not. While the Chief Constable may have his faults, lack of attention to routine isn't one of them. The only one I might have wanted to speak to is the maid who poured out the four drams, but given that she was sent away, that obviously cannot happen. In any event, we know your note must have been altered by eleven, so the poor girl likely didn't realize the implications of the dosage. She probably didn't even know that the Fowler's Solution contained arsenic. Also, I asked Gregson to stop by the police station to look over the notes from Austen's constable. As you know, he, along with Lestrade, is the pick of a bad lot. He will notice anything of importance, if there is something."

At that moment, Jonathan Doyle entered the room. Like Liza, he took after his mother, with the same coloring and eyes. Unlike Liza, he was tall and built like his father. I was quite fond of this twenty-four-year-old, not least because I believed my example had prompted him to a career in medicine. I greeted him and introduced Holmes. We took our seats at the table, and Jonathan looked inquiringly at me.

"Uncle John, I'm so glad you're free, but Mother tells me there is still some question as to whether Liza's death was an accident. What in Heaven's name is going on?."

"Jonathan, my advice is to allow Mr. Holmes to ask some questions. As I've told you, he is without parallel in matters of this kind."

"Very well. Fire away, Mr. Holmes, although I don't know if I have anything to add to what Mother already has told you and what I told the police."

Sherlock Holmes smiled. "This won't take long. I just like to have in my mind everyone's perspectives on the evening in question. Let's start with what you were doing between approximately six, and when you came down for sherry before dinner."

"Well, let me see. Thorpe and I were playing billiards in the game room, I believe until a bit after six. Then I went to my room to prepare for dinner. I came down a little after seven. Arthur was there already, and everyone else came in shortly, but I cannot recall the order."

"After dinner, you played backgammon with your mother and sister and Thorpe. Your mother explained this tournament variant of the game. She said some people left the room if their team finished first. We were wondering if you did. Here's the tally sheet, if that helps."

"Oh, yes. In round three, I was playing Rosalyn, and we finished first. I went out for a cigarette because Mother doesn't like smoking while she's playing a game. I'm fairly sure Mother left at one point, but I'm not positive about Rosalyn or Thorpe."

"I realize this is a delicate question, but in situations of this nature, it's often necessary to delve into certain matters. Was there any tension or unpleasantness within your family?"

Jonathan looked at me, and I nodded. "Mother could be extravagant at times," he answered. "She often complained to me about the insufficiency of the portion of Father's estate that had been left to her in trust. She never asked me for money, but I overheard her and Rosalyn once arguing over a loan. I know no more than that."

"Very well. That's all for now. Could you please ask your sister to join us?"

Jonathan gave me a forlorn smile and left the room. Rosalyn must have been in the drawing room, because she came in quickly. I had always felt a bit sorry for her, as she took after her father, and consequently was tall with a rather squarish build. I could understand why her mother might be cautious about any potential suitor of this ungainly twenty-year-old. She smiled at me, darted a glance at Holmes, then took the seat across from us.

"Hello, Rosalyn. Mr. Holmes has a few questions for you. It will only take a few moments."

She nodded and again glanced at Holmes. "I'm not sure what I can tell that might help, but of course I'll answer anything, Uncle John."

"Thank you, Miss Doyle. To start, where were you about an hour or so before coming down to dinner?"

"I was in my room writing some letters, and then dressing."

"Fine. And after dinner, you participated in the backgammon tournament. I understand you left once when your team finished, but you need not tell us where you went." I appreciated Holmes's delicacy, given what her mother had said – always the consummate gentleman.

"Yes, that is correct. I returned before the next round commenced."

"I apologize for asking, but I've heard that you and your mother once had an argument about a loan. Could you elaborate for us."

"Oh, Uncle John, must I?"

"Yes, child. I know it's painful, but Mr. Holmes wouldn't bring it up unless we needed to know all the pertinent dynamics of the family, given the terrible tragedy that has befallen Liza."

"Very well. About a month ago, Mother asked me to advance her some money from my inheritance. When I inquired what it was for, she said she wanted to re-cover the chairs in the dining room and purchase matching curtains. I told her I thought the current fabric was just fine and declined to give her any money. I didn't receive that much from Father's estate, and I'm saving it for a trousseau. Besides, I know that, when Father was alive, he told Mr. Reed to be generous with us. He did that in front of the three of us. You can ask Mr. Reed about it. He has a rather odd verbal tic of repeating things, but he knows what he's about."

"Perfectly understandable, and we'll talk to Mr. Reed later. Again, I apologize, but I'm sure you want us to get to the bottom of your sister's unfortunate demise. That's all for now. I assume Thorpe was with you right before this, so could you please ask him to come in?"

She nodded, left us, and Thorpe entered. I wondered whether he'd been trying to listen at the door, given how quickly he came in. He was about twenty-three, of medium height with black hair and a sharp face. I always had the feeling he was looking at people and objects as if evaluating their possible worth or usefulness to him. I introduced Holmes and we all took our seats.

"Master Jonathan has already informed us you and he were playing billiards until a little after six. I assume that you, like the others, went up to your room to prepare for dinner."

"That's correct. I had gotten into the habit when Sir Edward was alive of being downstairs first, just in case he had any instructions for me or needed something taken care of in the evening. I've maintained the habit."

"I see. I've discussed the backgammon games with the other participants. Did you leave the room during the games?"

"Hmm. Yes, I believe in the fourth or fifth round, when we finished first. I wanted a different drink than what was available in the game room, so I went to the sideboard in the drawing room to get some brandy."

"You've been with the family some time now?"

"Yes, approximately four years."

"Persons in your position often observe things about a family of which they themselves are unaware. Do you have any such observations."

"Well, I would rather not say. "

"Come, come, man. A woman is dead. Now is not the time for delicacy."

"Very well. I know that Sir Edward and Master Jonathan had arguments about the son's gambling habit that he had picked up in London. And about a week ago, I came upon Jonathan in the study looking over his bank statements. He looked quite distraught, but when I asked if I could be of assistance, he hurried to cover the papers and asked me to leave."

"Thank you, Thorpe. That is all for now."

After he left, I started to protest that I'd never known anything about gambling on Jonathan's part, but the butler came in to inform us that Reed, the solicitor, had just come to the house. Holmes asked that he be ushered in.

William Reed was in his sixties, but I couldn't venture to say at which end of that decade. He was tall, stately with white hair, and very deferential. He gently sat in the chair and looked at Holmes with interest.

"Thank you for coming, Mr. Reed. We have just a few questions."

"Of course, of course. What a terrible thing about Liza. Terrible thing."

"Yes, it was. I believe that, on the evening of her death, you were with her, reviewing some papers, when Doctor Watson arrived at her room."

"Yes. Reviewing papers. Doctor, I must apologize if I seemed a bit hurried. You see, my partner, Millard Phillipson, has been the Justice of Peace here for some time. Justice of the Peace, you see. Poor Millard is a bit older than me, and has become a bit hard of hearing. There was a meeting that evening of local dignitaries to discuss arrangements for the Fall Festival. Poor Millard doesn't want people to know about his hearing issue, so I often accompany him to ensure nothing is overlooked. Overlooked, you know. The meeting was to commence at half-past-six, and I feared I would be late. Cannot abide being late, you know."

Holmes politely listened to this rambling narrative and its odd repetitious quirks with polite interest, which I assumed was feigned. "I see. And did you arrive on time?"

"On the dot, sir, the dot. These meetings can be tedious, especially when, like this one, food and drink was included. We didn't finish until close to midnight."

"I'm positive the Doctor wasn't put out by your need to leave. Could you tell us what was the nature of the papers you were reviewing with Miss Doyle?"

"Well, I'm not sure it would be proper for me to do so."

Holmes took a leaf from Gregson. "It likely will come out at the inquest, and will be public soon."

"I suppose you are correct. Yes, correct. The papers related to the content of Sir Edward's will and Liza's upcoming nuptials. Wedding and will related, as it were."

"How so?"

"Sir Edward left a sizable bequest to each of his three children, all three, and to Lady Martha. The assets are held in trust, and I have the honour of acting as trustee for each of them. An honour indeed. Prior to the marriage of each child, only the interest, but not the principal, may be distributed. But once they marry, the trust in question dissolves and the principal is distributed free and clear to the child. Free and clear. I was explaining all this again to Liza and showing her the paperwork she would need to sign once married to Worthington, her fiancée. Given that he is a stockbroker, I also wanted to explore whether she wanted him to invest it, but didn't get that far due to Doctor Watson's arrival. And my upcoming meeting."

"You said you explained 'again'. What did you mean by that?"

"Well, Sir Edward was quite insistent that the entire family understand the terms of his will. If I may be permitted a bit of professional pride, I had my own small part to play in that. Small part. It is my experience that many disagreements over an estate can be avoided if the testator explains his wishes forcefully and clearly to the beneficiaries while still in good health. Avoids many disagreements. So when Sir Edward made a new will a few years ago, he gathered his wife and children together and had me review the relevant provisions. In this very room, if you please. This room."

"What about Lady Martha?"

"There is a similar interest – only it's set up as a trust for her, and the principal distributed to the surviving children upon her death. Distributed into their trust, or directly if they are married. "

"And what happens under the will if a beneficiary dies before marriage?"

"Well, that was a bit peculiar. Sir Edward felt he had made adequate provision for everyone. So instead of distributing the money in the trust where the beneficiary is deceased directly or into the trusts, he provided that the trust for the deceased would remain in place, and the survivors would become the beneficiaries. The only difference would be that I could, in my discretion, distribute principal in addition to interest to the new beneficiaries. When I objected to this structure as being a bit unusual, he told me he trusted me to be generous as they were my own family. He repeated that when we went over the will with the family. And I would have been generous. Would have indeed."

"This has been very helpful. If we need anything further, we shall contact you."

Reed bowed deeply and left us alone. Holmes turned to me and asked if I could procure some coffee. When I returned to the study, followed by the butler with coffee and serving implements, I discovered that Gregson had returned. He and Holmes were deep in conversation, so I busied myself with supervising the layout of the coffee service, after the butler had retrieved another cup and saucer.

Once the three of us were settled by the fire, Holmes reviewed for Gregson what we'd learned from our interviews. He then smiled at both of us. "So, what do you both think of all this?"

I indicated Gregson should begin. "I reviewed the constable's notes of the interviews with the servants, and I could see nothing that suggests any of them has the slightest motive. And, as I mentioned a moment ago, they were all together after dinner until the maid went up to Miss Doyle's room."

"Yes, Gregson. Let's rule them out for now. And, of course, we know Watson didn't commit the crime." Holmes lit a cigar, leaned back, and closed his eyes. But I knew he was listening to every word.

Gregson glanced at his notes. "That leaves Lady Martha, her son and daughter, and Thorpe. Someone altered the Doctor's instructions, changing the *one* to a *four*, between six when he left Miss Doyle and eleven, when the maid, Eunice, poured out the four drams. Everyone was together for sherry, and dinner from about seven to nine. The change must have been made between six and seven, or nine and eleven.

"But no one has an alibi. All four were preparing for dinner until seven. During the backgammon tournament, each of the four left the game room at least once – Lady Martha to talk to the cook, Rosalyn to freshen up, Jonathan to smoke, and Thorpe to get a fresh drink. It would have been an easy matter for someone to slip up those stairs at the back of the hall, which lead right to Miss Doyle's room. Presumably she was sleeping, but if not, the murderer could have pretending to be checking up on her and straightened up items on the dressing table with his or her back to Miss Doyle. In either case, it would have been a simple matter to quietly enter the room, swiftly make two short strokes of a pen, and be back downstairs before anyone noticed. I admit it would take some daring, but murderers often take risks like that.

"Doctor, what about motive? You were here and heard everyone."

I shifted in my chair, groping for words. "Despite my fondness for the family, I'll do my best to follow Holmes's methods and simply state the facts. I had no idea Edward had established a will such as Reed described. With Liza expiring before her marriage, the others could expect to benefit financially because they could have access to the principal in Liza's trust, not just the interest. Reed said Edward told him, in front of the family, to be generous with the principle in such a case, so Martha, Jonathan, and Rosalyn could all expect to receive potentially large sums if they could convince Reed to distribute them,, which seems likely. And, if Martha is right to be wary of Thorpe, he too could expect to be able to persuade Rosalyn to obtain money from Liza's trust. Although I'm reluctant to admit it, Martha can be rather expensive in her tastes. I would want more confirmation about these gambling debts that Thorpe alleges for Jonathan. But, if true, that also provides a motive."

"And as to means, Doctor, young Jonathan was studying to be a doctor and would understand the dosage situation."

"Yes, but there are medical books in this study that Thorpe could have used to learn that information."

Holmes stirred himself. "You two are assuming that the murderer knew about the instruction note. Watson, did anyone know?"

I hesitated. "While we were having sherry, Martha asked me how Liza was doing. I did mention that I had given instructions for application of Fowler's Solution later in the evening. I didn't mention the dosage, but everyone was there."

Gregson smiled grimly. "So either the murderer knew about the solution, or came in here during the backgammon games to look it up. Perhaps he or she planned on substituting a different instruction note, and then switching the original back during the confusion when the death was discovered. But on entering the room, a different opportunity to change the *one* to a *four* and cast suspicion on you."

"That is even riskier than your earlier theory."

"True. But criminals usually are caught because they have an innate belief in their superior intelligence."

Holmes stirred himself. "True enough, Gregson. I believe it's time for a visit to the Chief Constable. Watson, could you arrange for Lady Martha to see us so that we can take our leave?"

As we were donning our overcoats, Martha came out. Despite her entreaties, Holmes politely declined to give any indication regarding his thought process and thanked her for her gracious hospitality under such trying circumstances. The butler had kindly arranged for the Doyle's driver to take us to town, so we were soon at Police Headquarters. We were ushered into Austen's office, where he had clearly been waiting for us."

"*Hurrumph.* So did your 'consultation' uncover anything new, Mr. Holmes?"

"If you will allow me, I would be pleased to go over all the facts." Another grunt, which Holmes took as assent.

"The inspector has reviewed your constable's notes, and it would appear you correctly concluded none of the servants has any reason to harm Miss Doyle, In fact, they seem to have been devoted to her. Also, those notes suggest it was the custom of the servants to dine together in the kitchen after the main dinner was concluded and then socialize together. It seems they did so that evening. Between six, when Watson left Miss Doyle, until dinner was concluded, there was too much movement in the halls for someone to slip into her room to alter the medication instructions, as the servants were preparing the beds, laying out toiletries and linens, and so forth for someone to go into her room unnoticed."

"So you are still holding your theory that the murderer altered the number 'one' on the instructions?"

"As I demonstrated earlier, it is a fact, not a theory."

"Good gracious, man! That means either Lady Martha, one of her children, or that clerk – What is his name? Thorpe? – is the murderer."

"Turning to those four," continued Holmes, "we now come to some new conclusions. All four had opportunity. Shortly before dinner, they heard Watson tell Lady Martha he had prescribed Fowler's Solution. Young Jonathan may have understood the composition from his medical studies, but in any event, there are reference materials in the study containing the requisite information. And after dinner, although the four of them played backgammon together, at one time or another each of them left the game room. I can give you the exact details later if you wish, but suffice it to say such an absence would have allowed a murderer to go up the back stairway, alter the number, and return to the game room. Inspector Gregson has speculated that the murderer may have carried a draft containing false instructions, but realized the one could be altered on Watson's document, even if Miss Doyle was awake."

"But why on Earth would any of them do it?"

"Our discussion with Reed, who I believe your constable did not interview, revealed that all of them could have benefitted financially from Miss Doyle's demise. Given the delicacy of these family matters, I trust you will allow me to defer disclosing the exact details for the time being."

"Blast it, man, who do you think did it?"

"I don't think, I *know*. One thing that was puzzling from the beginning was why the murderer left the altered instructions in the room to be found. In the confusion, the murderer could have removed the instructions, assuming the police would either not notice, or would assume that the servants had disposed of them inadvertently when cleaning up, which might lead to the conclusion that it was an accident.

"That didn't seem correct, because the instructions *were* left in the room, which left too much to chance. No, it seemed more logical that the murderer *wanted* the instructions to be found. Presumably, the instructions were knocked to the floor along with other items on the nightstand during the confusion when the body was found.

"But the murderer, not shocked by the discovery of Miss Doyle's death, would have been watching the nightstand carefully. Wanting the instructions to be found, the murderer could have unobtrusively placed them back on the nightstand. That didn't happen. Why?

"One other fact points to the murderer wanting the instructions to be found. The culprit couldn't be sure if Miss Doyle or a servant would pour out the four drams. If a servant poured out the medication, and which would have been the more likely assumption, and if the note was gone, the servant, who had no earthly reason to lie or to kill her, would swear that the instructions called for four drams. If Miss Doyle poured out the medication, if there were no instructions in the room, it would be unclear what happened. In either case, if there were no instructions in the room, one might assume either the servant or Miss Doyle made a mistake. That seems to have been contrary to the *murderer's* intent, and again suggests the murderer wanted the instructions to be found and would have placed them back on the nightstand so they couldn't be missed.

"This leads me to the conclusion that the murderer wasn't in the room at the time of the discovery of the body."

"You're talking in circles. Are we talking spirits or ghosts?"

"No. As I always say, when you rule out absurd possibilities, you are left with the truth.

"I asked Gregson to make certain inquiries in town and to send a telegram to a broker in London for whom I performed some services regarding curious ink spots on his trading records. He confirmed there is a person here in town who has had large losses on the exchange recently. Gregson visited the local public house, always an excellent source of information, and learned that person has recently married a much younger woman. I'm sure your knowledge of human nature includes the notion that an older man may feel a bit insecure in such a situation, and feel the necessity of spending lavishly on his new bride."

I still wasn't sure who Holmes meant, but I could see the dawning realization on Austen's countenance. He stuttered, "Do you mean to say – But that still doesn't explain why Liza . . . ."

"Yes, I mean Solicitor Reed is the murderer. He is the only person who had an opportunity and also wasn't present when the body was discovered. When Watson was finished with Miss Doyle, Reed came back into her room to gather his papers. Watson and Miss Doyle stood at the doorway with their backs to the room talking for some moments. I paced the room several times and determined it would be a matter of seconds for Reed to quietly go over to the nightstand, read the instructions, and recognize his opportunity. He quickly changed the one to a four. When you search his offices, I suspect you will find some medical reference books, a common possession of solicitors – especially for one who is a Justice of the Peace, as is Reed's partner. He also would have heard Watson tell Miss Doyle about my unavailability while standing in the hallway."

"I still don't understand how Liza's death benefits Reed."

"Ah, that is rather simple. Reed was likely embezzling money from the trust funds in his care as trustee. The size of his stock speculations in London suggests he was using someone else's money. If Miss Doyle married and her trust was distributed, the discrepancies would be discovered, especially as the family knew the details of the trusts, and her fiancée, as a broker, would be financially astute.

"That also explains why Reed wanted the instructions to be found. As I pointed out, the murderer didn't want any confusion about who was to blame for the amount of medicine administered. He didn't want suspicion to fall on any regular member of the household. Reed believed the police would conclude that Watson had made a mistake, or wished to murder Miss Doyle. He especially wanted suspicion thrown away from the family, because such suspicion could also lead to the discovery of his defalcations."

We all sat in stunned silence. Finally, Gregson spoke up. "Chief Constable, I suggest you and I adjourn to another room to plan our next steps and their sequence. We'll need to question Reed and search his offices, but we need to discuss obtaining a warrant for the search from someone other than his partner, the order of questions, how to examine the trust accounts, and so forth." Austen mutely nodded, and the two left us alone.

"Holmes," I said, "I don't know how I can ever thank you for exonerating me."

"Nonsense, my friend. That was the easiest part of the case."

NOTE

About the dosage of Fowler's Solution – Don Baxter and I calculated it this way: There are 3.6 milliliters in a dram. With a 1% solution, one dram would have 21 mg of arsenic. The references checked stated that 50 to 150 mg is fatal, depending in the person's weight, etc., which is why Liza was described as so slight. So 1 dram, with 21 mg, was less than the lethal dose for a slight person. 4 drams would have 84 mg, more than enough to kill a small person.

– D.R.

The Bell-Ringer's Requiem
by Daniel Lenois

Throughout the years that I've spent faithfully transcribing, to the best of my ability and memory, those select cases of peculiar curiosity of my friend, Mr. Sherlock Holmes, accounts of which I believe will prove of the greatest interest to the general public, several obstacles have remained in the path of widespread publication. It is in the interest of preserving the identities of those involved that I have chosen here to omit or revise certain names, locations, and details – none of which, of their own merits, have any particularly pressing bearing on the account at hand.

The winter of late 1898 had initially proved a mild-enough affair. However, it soon-enough bore down its unrelenting maw upon the streets, rooftops, and alleyways which so comprised the heart of London as the year gradually approached its inevitable conclusion. Between my languorous disposition and aged shoulder wound, the latter being a parting souvenir from my experiences in Maiwand, and which throbbed most acutely in such weather, there had been little indeed to draw me away from the comfortable amenities afforded in our rooms at 221b Baker Street.

With no particularly stimulating cases to further sharpen his already well-honed mind, Holmes passed the time engaged in a variety of theoretical and practical experiments, best understood by himself alone. However, it soon became evident to those that knew him that, like a hound held back too long on a leash, Holmes was all but frothing to resume his ceaseless pursuit of criminality in all its duplicitous forms.

Having always been an admittedly light sleeper, a mere touch to the shoulder brought me to my senses in the pitch-black predawn hours. "I am terribly sorry to rouse you from your deserved and well-earned rest, Watson – " Holmes's voice sounded in my ear, his lean frame outlined, a darker shadow than all else in the room. " – but there is a certain matter I believe warrants our attention. What say you? Care for a small expedition this particular morning to Norwich?"

While I couldn't make out his face, the unspoken gleam of newfound intrigue lingered in his tone. Eagerly, I sat up. "I shall pack at once," I replied.

It was but a few minutes before we were off, clattering away in a jostling carriage toward the station. Holmes's face was introspective as he stared absentmindedly out the side window. Having long accustomed myself to my companion's periodic bouts of taciturn silence, I remained unbothered. It wasn't until we had made our way inside, bought our tickets, and stepped into the newly arrived train that he next deigned to speak.

Holmes fished around in his breast pocket, eventually withdrawing a folded cream-coloured envelope. "I received this letter from one Inspector Martin, who you might recall from our last, most tragic, endeavour in Norfolk not six months past."

He handed the letter to me. "What do you make of it?" I took it and closely examined the envelope, feeling the indents of the letters and numerals upon its surface, and taking note of where the ebony colouring ran darker in certain places than others.

"It seems to me," said I, "the inspector was in some great hurry. See here, where the ink is discoloured upon key letters compared to its compatriots. I can only assume he wrote hastily, and then once finished, smoothed over his blunders. The surface he wrote on must not have been particularly thick or steady, as I can feel their weight readily when I run a finger over them. Other than that . . . I confess I perceive little else."

Holmes smiled. "Often have I said it, Watson, but perhaps not often enough: You do yourself an injustice in your own admittedly fanciful depictions of our past cases. All too often, you take gratuitously liberal excesses in depicting my own deductions, while at the same time, understating or omitting your own."

My pleasure at his compliment was tempered by a momentary flair of irritation at his literary remonstrances. Holmes's inclinations toward conceit, and even arrogance, rose prominent among his few truly profound flaws.

He went on. "Your assessment of the principal facts is adequate. However, where you err, at least in part, is in the inferences of those observations. The letter was written in a hurry. However, the haste, and the seeming carelessness it produced, was not due to an absence of solid surface. You will see that each line begins evenly and without any strong quiver. However, within seconds, it inevitably devolves into something almost bordering on illegibility. No, reason suggests the root cause here is fear, or at least, some great excitement which so unnerved the author, despite a conscious attempt to master it. A mere glance at the letter within confirms this as a working hypothesis."

I pulled the letter loose. It read as follows.

Dear Mr. Holmes,

A most dire situation of a curious nature has arisen just north of the city of Norwich, of which I should be glad of your

154

opinion. I have attached some record of the events, courtesy of a local newspaper, whose editor, most unfortunately, happened to be present at the time. If you would be so good as to come, I feel confident that we shall have the matter soon in hand.

Warmest regards,
Inspector Martin

I reached within the envelope again and withdrew an enfolded newspaper cutting from a local paper, dating back from the previous evening. I read it aloud:

Macabre Display at St. Adelaide's Church

At approximately half-past eight this morning, in the midst of an ongoing service delivered by one Reverend Oliver Walker, proceedings were suddenly halted by a single resonate note, followed by a pronounced steady sounding, emitting from the priory bell. As attendees and clergy alike hurriedly made their way outside and cast their eyes upward, however, a more grisly spectacle met their eyes: The form of a man, hanging from the bell rope below. The identity of the individual is, as of yet, unknown. The identity of the deceased is, as of yet, unknown.

Immediately following this discovery, all those in attendance were advised to return home, and the matter has been taken up for further investigation by the appropriate authorities at Scotland Yard.

I looked up.

"A distinctly theatrical affair, is it not?" Holmes observed sardonically.

"I should think so," I responded. "Were one to consider suicide, why a church, and why at a time when all would surely be in attendance? Is this merely some obscene expression of the ego?"

Holmes shook his head. "Hardly, Watson, hardly. While I have no doubt that yours is a sentiment we shall see readily mirrored by the good officers of Scotland Yard, I myself am more inclined toward a sinister cause and effect. What we have before us is murder – one as cold-blooded as it is in the nature of man to undertake."

"On what evidence?" I asked, taken somewhat aback.

155

"The single ring, Watson. The single ring."

His eyes locked on some distant point, and he would say nothing more.

I turned my attention to the rolling countryside visible through the window as the miles passed by.

We arrived in the coastal city of Norwich only a few hours later. Following a brief consultation with a local constable upon the platform, Holmes and I set off. The cold drifts of snow present throughout London here turned to sheets of rain lashing the ground, melting away what snow remained into a distinctly undesirable slush, and likewise transforming the dirt pathways into mud. The foul weather showed little inclination toward relenting as we made our way eastward toward the coast.

St. Adelaide's Church stood atop an inclining hill, its far end only a slight distance from a jagged coastal cliff. The building itself was of a modest, utilitarian design. Consisting of an approximately rectangular frame, its sole ingratiating nods toward beautification consisted of several decorative arches, and one prominent bell tower near its front. From where we stood, emerging from the carriage which brought us from the station, we paused for a moment to take in our surroundings.

I pointed to the bell tower, whose centrepiece rested, immobile and implacable, in plain view to all below. It was clear that the police had, at some point prior, cut loose the body, for nothing out of the ordinary could be seen from our positioning.

The constable who guarded the front door, witnessing our approach, raised one hand as if to turn us away, but, upon identifying my companion, lowered it at once and saluted promptly. The name and visage of Sherlock Holmes alone was enough to part the ranks of Scotland Yard.

Inspector Martin was standing directly below the altar, jotting down notes in shorthand as he spoke with a younger, auburn-haired man, the latter clearly no older than thirty. Martin spun around smartly and inclined his head toward Holmes.

"Ah, Mr. Holmes, Dr. Watson! So good of you to have come. I know how busy you keep." Martin gestured toward the man beside him. "This is Redmond Byrne. He's the deacon hereabouts."

Byrne smiled ingratiatingly, although his face was drawn and haggard.

"It's our honour to have such an illustrious man as yourself cross our threshold, Mr. Holmes," he remarked, shaking Holmes's hand. "Your involvement in the Cubitt case particularly hasn't gone unappreciated."

Holmes inclined his head, and it was clear the compliment pleased him. Then he looked past the deacon and instead surveyed the scene with that keen dispassionate focus that bespoke louder than words that his interest had been aroused.

"Have there been any new developments?" I inquired, breaking the silence.

"Not as far as I can tell," the inspector shrugged. "I've been interviewing witnesses all morning, from clergy to ordinary folk alike, and yet, I'm no closer than when I started." He shivered, although there was little chill in the air. "It's an eerie business, to be sure, and I should be right glad to wash my hands of it." He waved his pocket notebook in hand. "Everyone's accounts appear to corroborate the central facts. Their alibis are nigh on bulletproof, and no potential external agent or force has been identified as the cause."

Holmes turned back to the deacon. "Mr. Byrne. I take it you were present at the time?"

Byrne nodded solemnly. "As was Father Lewis, the Reverend here." His face tightened for a moment. "I trust I can depend on your discretion, gentlemen?"

We nodded.

Some of the tension left Byrne's face. "Thank you. To speak plainly, Father Lewis' health has been in some decline these past few years. His heart – Well, it is not what it used to be. The shock of it all came upon him rather hard. Following upon the heels of the crowd already forming outside our doors, he took one long look up to where every finger was pointing and collapsed there on the spot. Of course, I went to his aid but, finding him unconscious, I took hold of him and carried him back to his bed. His niece, Elsie, who likewise suffered a swoon from nerves, cares for him now. She herself is still quite shaken, but has recovered quickly enough, all things considered." He shrugged. "Since then, I've done what I can in the interim."

"It would probably be best to speak with the young lady at some future point," remarked Holmes, "but first, I should very much like to examine the place where the body was found." The slightest trace of impatience now coloured his tone. "Would you be so kind as to show us the way?"

"Certainly," responded the deacon, inclining his head.

The three of us, Holmes, Martin, and myself, were escorted up a series of winding unstained wooden stairs, until we finally alighted within the belfry.

The floor was sturdy enough, although I confess a certain private uneasiness at the continual creak of my weight upon the floorboards. It hardly indicated this elevated point as an ideal location for a prolonged struggle. I surveyed the layout around me. The space was not particularly large, such that only two men of the leanest disposition might walk abreast. The dimensions were square in design. The open design of the walls, which admittedly afforded a magnificent view of the surrounding lands, did little to inhibit the potentially rapid descent of an unwary victim.

"Indeed, Watson. It begs the question as to why the same thought did not occur to the perpetrator. Or if it did, why he disregarded it in favour of this as the alternative."

I nodded my agreement, then caught myself.

"Really, Holmes," I exclaimed.

Holmes smiled faintly.

"Surely," he commented, with the patient air of a professor initiating an instructive lecture, "it is a small enough thing to observe your astute study of the floor, followed by a momentary flash of introspection as you glanced, perhaps unconsciously, at the bell here." He gestured beside him, where the bell hung overhead. "You then considered the walls, focusing your eye not necessarily upon the construction, but the view outward, particularly downward. The likeliest explanation was that you noted that such a fall could easily lead to one's death, and thus made the connection to the case at hand, wondering why the killer did not choose this less exotic methodology. I then agreed with your conclusion."

Holmes turned to Byrne. "When was the body moved?"

"Some minutes after it was discovered. It seemed best to relocate it to a more appropriate resting place until it could be properly examined."

"Who was responsible for moving it?" Holmes inquired.

"Myself, along with Mr. Williams, the groundskeeper." Pain crossed his face. "Were it but anyone else at my side!" he proclaimed. "No father should come to a sight such as this."

I waved a hand to the bell. "You mean to say it was his son?" I was aghast.

Byrne nodded. "It was ever the two of them. Mother dead of the pox, or so I'd heard. They live apart now, but it's a small town, and the two were still on good terms, as far as I was aware."

"Very good," said Holmes. "Now, who else readily knew the way to the top of these stairs?"

Byrne shrugged. "Most every one of us, not to mention the attending members. The bell is a monument of local history, and it isn't uncommon for us to show it off to new members or visiting family of our longstanding members."

A trace of sadness crossed Byrne's face.

"If you'll excuse me, Mr. Holmes, I really should return to my duties. Don't hesitate to send for me if I can be of any further service."

Byrne excused himself. We heard his footsteps descending the stairs.

"A pleasant enough chap," I remarked. "A tad reserved, perhaps, but more than understandable, given the present circumstances."

"I believe there might be more than humble reservation lingering under the surface there," Holmes intoned.

"Why, whatever do you mean?" I asked, surprised.

"I'm not entirely sure yet," said he. "However, it's quite clear that he knows more about this business than he lets on, and just as equally, is very much keen to leave us in the dark. Observe the evasions in his answer, pivoting from fact in favour of a more emotionally charged response."

"Perhaps it might be the shock," I suggested. "It isn't unheard of for men to deal with grief in their own due time."

"It is certainly possible," Holmes admitted. "However, he didn't show any immediate symptoms of shock. His breathing was steady. There was no evidence of chills, sweating, or other irregular palpitations, nor did he have any difficulty reliving what he witnessed in the aftermath. In any case, I chose not to press him at present. Our priorities are in ascertaining the facts. Only then can we begin, with any certainty, to dispel the heavy fog of uncertainty and deception that so obscures our perception."

Holmes examined the hangman's rope.

"Whatever else he may or may not have disclosed, Byrne has at least done us one invaluable favour." Holmes was leaning over the narrow railing in the centre of the room directly below the bell, staring up into the bell's underside. He pulled loose a knife from one pocket and stood on his toes, cutting loose the hanging rope from its highest point. I put a hand out to steady him. A few seconds later, with a triumphant cry, he stepped back down, holding a crudely tied noose. "Recognize this, Watson?" He asked.

I examined it. "I've seen its like before," I remarked. "However, the name escapes me."

"It's a bowline knot," Holmes identified clinically. "It's popular among sailors and others familiar with the sea." He grimaced. "Given our current proximity to said waters, I can't say that alone significantly narrows the list of credible suspects." Some time elapsed as Holmes pulled out his magnifying glass and minutely examined the noose and the length of rope below.

"As a medical man," Holmes expounded, "I trust you recall the specific causes and basic symptoms of strangulation in instances of hanging?"

"Asphyxia by the sudden closure of the blood vessels and air passageways, leading to cerebral hypoxia, and ultimately death," I recalled by heart. "In his final moments, the victim would experience coughing, discoloration caused by the subconjunctival petechiae, and involuntary bodily spasms."

"Just so," Holmes approved. "It would be reasonable then, to assume there to be some indication of fraying or other violent movement along the inside of the noose – flakes of skin, or something to support the notion that our victim, consciously or otherwise, did not meekly go into the abyss."

"I would think so, yes."

Holmes extended both the noose and his magnifying glass to me. "Then how is it that no such sign is in evidence?"

"What?" I started violently. "There would have to be."

"And yet, there is not."

I took both of the proffered objects and studied the rope closely. It was just as Holmes had described.

"What does this mean?" I spluttered.

"The most suggestive inference one could reasonably identify is that clearly the victim here did not die of asphyxiation, but rather, was conveyed here posthumously."

"Whatever for? And if that is true, what then killed him?"

"I have a theory. It might very well be simple conjecture, but there's only one way to find out." He made his way back toward the stairs. "I think it's time we introduce ourselves to the man at the heart of this mystery."

Martin conveyed us at once to a small antechamber where the body rested on a table. The man was powerfully built and profoundly tall. A carelessly trimmed mane of coarse black hair and beard seemed to almost obscure his other features. "A Mr. Clarence Williams," Martin declared, reading from his notes. "Age twenty-seven or so. A bachelor." As he spoke, Martin gestured to Williams' neck. "Neck broken cleanly from the fall," he observed. "Died right there on the spot. No sign of foul play, save for this." He turned the victim's head upward and pointed to the nostrils. Holmes and I leaned in closer.

From within those two singular crevasses, we could clearly see marks of dried blood. "I've attended the occasional hanging in my day, sirs," Martin stated confidentially, with the air of a ringmaster revealing his star act, "and not once can I recall witnessing a man develop a nosebleed while in the noose."

Holmes pulled out his magnifying lens once more and closely observed the location and extent of the injury. "Excellently done," he remarked approvingly.

Martin flushed with pleasure at the praise. "My superiors will think little of it, but my thinking is that this paints a clearer picture of murder. After all, a man wouldn't waste time blooding his own nose if he was already planning to hang himself. No, this all but proves this was indeed murder."

Holmes shook his head. "It proves nothing. All that is proved is that, at some point in the hours immediately preceding his death, he received an injury that caused bleeding and subsequently the congealment we witness here. There are any number of credible explanations for the existence of such a wound. By itself, it is curious, but by no means conclusive."

He replaced the magnifying glass back into his pocket.

"I believe, if it's all the same to you, Inspector, I shall take a walk upon the grounds. Nothing like sea air to energise the body and restore the soul."

"Would you care for some company?" I asked.

"No, no. Thank you very kindly, but I shall think better for the momentary isolation. In the meantime, it would be of far more service if you were to speak with the groundskeeper and the others who may be of some interest. Facts, Watson. These, in totality, are our defence when all else fails."

And so it was that I spent most of the rest of the day mired in a series of consecutive interviews, many of which provided a number of scandalous, but hardly elucidating, observations from the townsfolk.

"He were always a bad sort!" cried Mr. Albert Hughes, a short, querulous man who operated the town's tailor shop. "Tried to court my Alicent once, so he did. But I knew his type!" The tufts of snow-white hair that hung loose from his ears quivered in indignation. "And then, not a day later, I catch him in the bar, flirting with the serving girl." He laughed harshly. "Were I but thirty years younger – Yessir, I'd have had him and given him a beating the likes of which he'd be smarting from a week from now!"

"Oh, he was a ruffian, there's no denying that," attested Mrs. Ada Fletcher, who, along with her husband, was the proprietor of a bookshop. "He was a good-enough worker. Took up a job some years back at the lumber mill, and working odd jobs here and there. A good-enough man, so it seemed. Liked to be left well-enough alone. No harm in that, I suppose. Everyone has their own little ways. Never did say a bad word to anyone, at least when he was sober. But he was a fiery devil when he be wronged. Doubly so if the drink was in him."

It only took a little time before, thanks to the inestimable authority of Scotland Yard, Mr. Evan Davis, the manager of the lumber mill, was brought forward to elucidate these various statements. "Aye, true enough, I'd wager," he declared succinctly, unconsciously flexing his powerful limbs. The chair below him creaked its protest at his bulk. "A good worker, he was. Would do twice the work of any other man on the shift. Been with me 'bout four years. I knew him by reputation, so I won't lie, I was a bit wary of him, but I needed the men, and if he didn't work out, I'd be no worse off than I was without him. Then he up and tells me he aims to leave, and not a shilling more would convince him to stay. No, no point me arguing him down.

"I thought at first perhaps he had gotten into another row of his, and didn't want word getting back to me, lest I fire him right there on the spot. He had fallen in with a bad sort when he was younger, before he sorted himself out, thanks in no small part to his father stepping in and smoothing things over. Well, as I say, there was a nervous air about him when he come to me, saying he wanted out. It was as if there were something mighty pressing on his mind. But a man's business is his own, and no affair of mine."

Martin and I questioned everyone closely. While each of them corroborated the same elementary facts, and none appeared especially surprised at the prospect of Williams' death, no one could attest for the means by which it occurred.

Aside from these brief exchanges of insight, I gleaned little else, save that Williams had, the day before his untimely end, suddenly resigned from his job without explanation. Martin and I discussed our findings at some length, but saw no way in which to further the case.

Night was rapidly setting as Holmes returned. In his hands were clenched a pair of mud-stained plain brown shoes. I read plainly, etched upon his face, the contained exaltation of the hunting bloodhound who has finally landed upon the scent.

"You have it?" I called out as he approached.

"Not quite," he responded, "but I do believe we are nearing the light at the end of this particular tunnel."

Martin and I shared our findings with Holmes. His face was indiscernible. However, I thought I detected a momentary gleam of satisfaction as we hurriedly spoke.

He spoke with Martin for a few moments and then handed him the shoes. Martin nodded and turned back to the church.

"Whatever now, then?" I asked.

"We speak with Father Lewis, and see whether he can further hasten forth the facts."

However, when we knocked upon Father Lewis' door, it quickly became apparent that this was not to be.

A young woman of slender build, hazel-eyed and with blonde hair that extended down her back in a flowing curtain, answered the door. She introduced herself as Elsie. Her beautiful face was pale, and blotches of colour proved blanket evidence of recent weeping.

"He is just gone," she told us, when we, having introduced ourselves, asked to speak with Father Lewis. Her voice was thick with emotion.

She let us in, and Holmes guided her to a chair. Holmes had ever been wary of women and, despite momentary flights of interest when acting as their agent during a case, showed little inclination to pursue even the fairest creature that crossed his path. That said, he nevertheless demonstrated the utmost courtesy and sincerest kindness in his dealings with them. While there was no duplicitous intent to his actions, it was easy, as an observer, to see how easily he could gain their confidences, which all too often had proven invaluable in any number of his cases.

"It was all so horrible, Mr. Holmes," she uttered, once Holmes had brought the conversation around to the matter at hand. "I thought I would die right there on the spot. Indeed, when all spun and went dark, for a moment I thought I had."

"Had Mr. Williams any enemies?" Holmes asked gently. "Any that might mean him harm?"

The lady hesitated for a moment. "No, Mr. Holmes. He got in many a scrap, but no. There isn't a man in his entire town who would stoop to murder."

"I never said I believed it was murder."

Elsie Lewis looked at him sharply. Her breath caught. For the span of several heartbeats, she remained statuesque as she and Holmes locked eyes – hers wide and questioning, his astute and impassive. She silently rearranged the thick necklace that lay about her neck, revealing a previously-hidden series of discoloured bruises. Then she blinked and lowered her hand, the tension leaving her limbs just as quickly as it had appeared.

"What makes you say so, Mr. Holmes?" she asked inquisitively, her gaze steady.

"Really, Miss Lewis," Holmes responded quietly, "I think it would be far better for you to make a clean breast of it here and now. You, at least, are innocent of any direct wrongdoing. Do not sully your good name through these pointless evasions."

A flurry of conflicting emotions flitted across the young lady's face as she took in Holmes's words.

"You need not speak the words," Holmes told her soothingly. "Let me tell you the facts, and pray correct me, should my conclusions be awry." He turned. "Ah, Martin," for the inspector had just walked in, accompanied by Redmond Byrne. "Very good. I shall let you know how

163

things get on. In the meantime, would you mind fetching those items that I brought to your attention?"

The inspector nodded and politely excused himself.

Byrne glanced around uneasily and opened his mouth to speak.

"It won't do, sir." Holmes told him, adopting a more-stern tone. "As I've just informed the lady, I already know. It was her own words that provided me with the final confirmation I required. You killed Clarence Williams. A pair of tracks, one larger and deeper than the other, were found in the damp soil, indicating that either a man and a younger boy, or more likely, a man and a woman of lighter build than he, had strolled for some time on these grounds. Based on the age of the prints, it was clear that they had been made the prior evening. Eventually, a far larger-sized print, matching the shoes of Mr. Williams, intercepted yours. Then there were a series of overlapping impressions. The likeliest explanation is that Mr. Williams saw the two of you walking together and, in an explosive fury of desperation and jealousy, made to confront you, Miss Lewis."

There was a knock at the door and Martin, accompanied by a second officer, walked back in, holding between them a bundle of soggy decomposing lavenders, the pair of men's shoes I had seen Holmes carrying just minutes prior, and a jagged-edged medium-sized rock. At a gesture from Holmes, he placed them down upon a table, and, departing once more, closed the door behind him. Holmes indicated the flowers.

"I found these dropped not far away, at the point where the larger footprints lengthened in distance, indicating that Mr. Williams found reason to burst into a run." He turned to the shoes. "The smaller prints, smaller than that of our deceased, were less-easily identifiable. The shape and weight present all but confirmed the owner to be a man of medium build, but it wasn't until a thorough search of all footwear in these facilities that the corresponding pair were identified. Then there was the matter of the third pair, which I already know to be yours, Miss Lewis. As if the flowers weren't indicative enough, the lightest pair of tracks led back no farther than fifty paces in this direction before fading into obscurity. Given their singular trajectory, yours was the face that Williams sought that night he strode here." While his expression remained impassive, his tone hardened. "So I ask you true: What have you to say for yourself?"

"He was a devil!" the lady exclaimed vehemently. "That temper of his! It was why I told him I'd have no more to do with him all those months ago when he came, courting my hand. I encouraged him at first. He was fine-looking, and a hard worker besides, and there was a certain boyish quality about him at times. He could make you laugh fit to bursting with just a single expression. But once I had seen the other side of him, I decided then and there to make an end of it, and to have nothing more to do with him.

"Then some time went by, with nary a word between us. I had thought that was the end of the whole business. When Reddy here – " She motioned to Byrne. " – sought me out, there was no bad business about it. He took a liking to me, and I to him, and no business ought it to have been to anyone else. A proper gentleman, he is. Nary a hand raised, nor a harsh word spoken. I honestly don't believe he has it in 'im to do harm to any man. And he wouldn't have done too, not if he had his own way about it." Her voice had risen again with passionate heat.

Byrne coughed uncomfortably and spoke up. "Elsie does me a kindness, sir. I had no grudge against Williams. Had never met him, save for an occasional glance or two during the odd service or so. When he came running at us full tilt, as if the fires of Hell were chasing at his heels, I'd be a damned liar if I said the cold sweat of fear didn't run over me, sir. 'What in blazes be you about, taking aside my Elsie?' roars he. 'Ought you to know she's spoken for?' Elsie tried to calm him, but he overrode her. 'Months I've been saving away, scrounging for every last shilling, so I could make an honest woman of you good and proper, and then you go skulking around behind my back?' It was then that he bowled past me and grabbed her about the throat and began squeezing the life out of her as easily as one would squeeze the juice from an orange." A biting anger swelled in Byrne's voice. He paused for a moment to collect himself.

"I'm not proud of what I did then, Mr. Holmes. Seeing her kick and struggle while her breath came in choking gasps, what else could I do? I strode forward and ripped his hand from her. She dropped senseless to the ground. He turned on me and bellowed. It was not a human scream. No sir, it was the roar of some untamed animal, stirred into a fevered frenzy. No thought or reason lingered there. It was a wonder that the entire town didn't hear the sound. He made a move toward me, but I was faster. My blow caught him right in the jaw. He stumbled back and fell. His neck landed on the rock you have there. I knew then what I had done.

"Moreover, I knew what it'd mean for Elsie. The scandal, the whispers that would follow her the rest of her life. That was more than I could bear. I could live with my own punishment, if it ever came out. But I told myself that if I ever had to pay the price for my sins, so would he. I took Elsie back here to recover, then carried that brute up the steps to the belfry. It was no easy thing, his weight and all, and here I was, panicking that with every creak, all might be discovered. I tied the noose around his neck and left him right along the edge, that way the moment the bells would ring, it would appear as if he took his own life. The shame of his supposed death would amount to the shame he had already committed in life."

"And the bell?" Holmes asked. "The service being underway, you could not have rung it yourself."

Byrne answered readily. "One of the older altar boys. He was just told to ring it at a certain time. He knew nothing, nor saw anything, save for that. He rang it once, then walked away. The movement of the swinging bell was enough to knock the body from the ledge, which set off the subsequent ringing. After that," he paused, "well, you already know the rest."

"Indeed," Holmes said coldly. "Whether or not it was your intent, you have caused a great deal of harm to a great number of people. The death of Mr. Williams might well be a matter of self-defence in the view of the courts. That said, the totality of the events had an impact well beyond your originally intended scope. You almost inadvertently set up an altar boy for murder, had the authorities gotten their hands on him, or had he, out of guilt, confessed by implication more than he actually committed. The unnecessarily spectacular nature of your grand display may yet claim the life of a second victim, in the way of your superior, Father Lewis. Not to mention the burden of guilt and stress you've placed on Miss Lewis's own soul, in addition to your own. Small surprise, then, that she was as taken aback as she was, when she, amidst the gaping crowd, was the only one to realise what you had done."

"What will you do now, Mr. Holmes?" Byrne asked, standing firm, although his voice shook, though whether with fear, regret, or some other emotion, or all, I could never be sure. "If you mean to walk me to the noose as well, I shall not resist. I just ask, on your word as a gentleman, that you spare any mention of Elsie's name in this matter."

"Indeed, seeing you to your end is what I should do," Holmes told him sternly, "were I employed by Scotland Yard. Despite your meek exterior, there is a callousness in the nature of your actions which repulses me. Were it not out of consideration for the lady, and the certain knowledge that such was not your intent at the outset, I should hand you over this instant." He paused and looked to Elsie Lewis. "Have you family outside of this town?"

She started. "I have an aunt in America, just outside Boston."

Holmes nodded and turned back to Byrne. "I think it's time you forfeited your position within the priesthood, something you would had to have done eventually, given your attentions toward Miss Lewis. A fresh start in America, I think, might just be well in order."

Byrne stared in amazement. "You're – You're not going to turn me in?" He asked, steadying himself by quickly gripping the back of Elsie's chair.

Holmes shook his head. "So long as you never again set foot on English soil, I think we can reasonably say the scales of justice have been satisfactorily evened." He stood up. "You have made many poor choices here in England, Mr. Byrne. Perhaps you will make better ones out of it."

As Holmes and I made our way back across the grass, we found Inspector Martin awaiting us, a mixture of impatience and rampant curiosity readily evident upon his face. "Well, Mr. Holmes? You've had your fun. Pray God have an end to it and tell me what this has all been about."

Holmes nodded with grim solemnity, although I thought I detected a momentary twinkle in his eye which escaped the attention of the inspector. "Oftimes, Martin," said he, "the strangest conundrums end up bearing the simplest fruit, and one must never make the singular mistake of twisting facts to suit theories, when the reverse is ever a more reliable process."

He winced with apparent chagrin. "A sin of which I must, in this instance, plead guilty to." He extended the wilting flowers. "Love. It is a force not merely of the physical, the mind, but also the soul. In its grasp, even the most logical of us might easily be swayed to actions that defy rationality in all its forms."

"Do you mean to say that a murderer committed these acts in the name of *love*?" Martin cried. "If so, who is he? This is no time to dawdle, if the man is still about!"

I looked at Holmes intensely, my face no doubt conveying some measure of concern, although Martin, affixed eagerly upon Holmes, didn't appear to catch the exchange.

"The murderer lies dead already. You need not chase after him, for he is beyond our reach." Holmes looked meaningfully up at the belfry. Martin followed his indication.

"It *was* a suicide, then?" he asked, with poorly-concealed disappointment.

"In a manner of speaking." Holmes went on to provide an only-slightly modified account of the facts. The involvement of Mr. Byrne in that final deadly altercation was recorded for the record as that of a gentleman coming to the aid of a lady under duress, and the exact cause of the broken neck was reattributed to the impromptu hanging witnessed by the general public. Having received a sufficient explanation for the events, Scotland Yard ultimately chose to quietly put an end to any further investigation, and the matter soon passed from the public record.

As we strode back together down the road toward the carriage that awaited us, Holmes remarked with some amusement, "It is a curious thing, Watson, that those who are perhaps most in need of a second chance are also those who, at a glance, appear the least deserving of one. The soul is indeed a remarkable thing. With time, all may not be forgotten, but it might, if we are lucky, quite possibly mend. In the words of that illustrious poet: '*Keep, ancient lands, your storied pomp! cries she with silent lips. Give me your tired, your poor, your huddled masses yearning to breathe free, the wretched refuse of your teeming shore. Send these, the homeless, tempest-tost to me, I lift my lamp beside the golden door!*'"

The Gemini Pearl Necklace
by Roger Riccard

Chapter I

The holiday season of 1898 found me accompanying my friend, the detective Sherlock Holmes, to spend Christmas in Aylesbury with his old college history instructor, Professor Christopher Nichols. I had met the professor the first time we visited his dairy farm during the Yuletide of 1882. That was the winter when Holmes had helped the newly retired historian discover the orphan his cook had taken in was, in reality, his ten-year-old daughter. [1]

It was she, the former Tina Monroe, who invited us to come spend the holidays. She was married now to the business manager of the farm, Noel Everest, and with a four-year-old daughter of her own named Marjorie, after her mother. They pretty much ran the estate now, the professor being in his early seventies and in failing health.

We arrived just before noon on the 22nd of December, under high clouds and cool temperatures. The driver from Nichols' farm greeted us warmly. "Mr. Holmes, Dr. Watson, it is good of you to come. Mrs. Everest hopes your presence will help restore the Professor's memories to some extent. He used to speak of your last visit with affection, and still marveled at your marksmanship with his Colt .45's."

"His memories are fading then?" I asked with concern as he loaded our luggage.

"I am afraid so. He can remember things from many years ago, but recent events have become difficult for him to recall."

He opened the carriage door, pointing out the traveling rugs, and said, "You'll see for yourselves, gentlemen. He has good days and bad days. The mistress hopes your presence will give him one more good Christmas to remember. Go ahead and bundle up. I'll have you out to the farm in a jiffy."

True to his word, the drive passed quickly. Coming upon our first sight of the farm, it was much as I remembered it: The same structures, paddocks, and pastureland. A light snow from a previous storm had left white patches scattered about. Coming upon the main house, the outside was festooned with holly boughs and a large wreath. One welcome addition since our last visit was a large portico which now extended out over the drive, allowing us to disembark under its shelter as we entered the house. Servants came out to pick up our luggage and, as I looked toward the open front door, I saw a beautiful young lady in her mid-twenties. I tapped Holmes on the elbow as he was looking out upon the grounds, pointed toward the lady, and said, "That must be Tina. My, she has grown into a beauty!"

Holmes turned and, for one of the few times in my association with him, froze. I noted his stare at the woman and, after several seconds, I chose to break the impasse before it became rude. "Holmes, shall we go re-introduce ourselves?"

With a quick shake of his head, he took a deep breath, looked at me, and whispered, "Sorry. I was not prepared. She is the living image of her mother."

I recalled Holmes had been socially involved with Marjorie Monroe during his college years, but she had become impregnated with her daughter when she voluntarily took to caring for Professor Nichols when he was suffering deliriums upon the death of his wife. In her admiration for the man, she had allowed herself to succumb to her own feelings when he reached for her upon calling out his wife's name during one of his delirious episodes. That action, of which he had no recollection when he recovered, had resulted in her pregnancy and leaving town. Holmes, at that age, was bitterly disappointed at her unexplained disappearance. It wasn't until we visited Nichols sixteen years earlier when Tina, newly orphaned, had arrived at the farm with her mother's diary, that he finally learned the truth.

Seeing his reaction now set my imagination at work. Could it be Holmes's Bohemian lifestyle and his utter disregard for romantic involvement was the result of that long-ago relationship? Had his feelings for Marjorie Monroe been so deep that her disappearance forever carried away his capacity for emotional attachment? Was his distrust of the fair sex the consequence of his feelings of desertion at such an impressionable point in his life?

All these thoughts flashed through my mind as I started walking toward the entrance, giving his sleeve a slight tug. Still, we approached with smiles upon our faces and grace in our manner. Tina Everest took my hand and I recalled the long fingers she had displayed as a child when she played the violin for us on that far-off Christmas. I bowed to her. "Mrs. Everest, thank you for your invitation."

"Oh, Doctor, surely you can call me 'Tina', since you've known me from childhood." She then turned to my companion. "And you, sir, if I may be so bold: Papa has told me of how you cared for my mother during your university days and suggested I should refer to you as 'Uncle Sherlock'. Do you mind?"

Holmes took a deep breath, kissed her outstretched hand, and replied, with as much emotion as I have ever seen in him, "As the odds of my ever having a niece in my bloodline are practically nil, I would be honored for you to use such an appellation, Tina."

Greetings completed, Tina hooked her arm around Holmes's elbow and led us into the house where servants took our hats and coats. "Let me introduce you to my husband. Then we'll go see Papa."

Noel Everest was seated at the desk where we had first seen Professor Nichols working on a presentation the last time we were there. Though retired, his expertise in history at that time was still sought by several universities as a guest lecturer. Everest rose at our arrival and came out from behind the desk to greet us warmly.

"Mr. Holmes, Dr. Watson! Welcome to you both, gentlemen. Thank you for setting aside your holiday plans to join us. I do hope your presence will encourage some improvement in the Professor's health."

Holmes shook the man's hand. He was perhaps two inches short of six feet, with blond hair and blue eyes which spoke of a Nordic ancestry. I would put him a bit older than Tina, perhaps thirty or thereabouts, with a lean sinewy build. As I shook his hand, I noted my companion turn his gaze upon the desk. It was a force of habit for him, as intrusive as it was, especially since we weren't on a case. Tina, of course, noted what her husband had not. "Is there something you need to know, Uncle?"

Holmes shook his head. "I am sorry, my dear. My profession often overrides my manners. Forgive me. May we see the Professor?"

She turned toward the clock against the wall and said, "I will check on him. He often naps after lunch, but he may still be awake. Follow me."

We found the professor in a sunroom in a corner of the west wing of the house. From there, one could look out upon the pastures and see the livestock through large glass French doors which opened out upon a small patio. A fire was burning brightly in a hearth on the north wall, keeping the room well-heated. Nichols sat before it, his chair at a right angle so he could view the outdoors to the west. A luncheon tray was on a small table next to him and he was just setting down a glass of red wine.

In appearance, he certainly looked more frail than the gentleman I remembered. He had lost weight and his face was thinner, now more oval than round. His hair had stopped its recession and remained a short, white fringe around his bald head. His beard and moustache had grown thicker and longer. Had he not become so thin, he might have resembled Father Christmas taking a break from his workshop. As he turned to reach for his pipe, he caught sight of us out of the corner of his eye and turned to face us.

"Hello, Tina, my dear!" he said cheerily. "Who have you brought to see me today – more teachers seeking my expertise?"

We strode forward as a group with Tina in the lead. "I have a surprise for you, Papa. This is your former student, Sherlock Holmes, and his friend, Dr. Watson. Do you remember the last time they were here? It was the Christmas you adopted me."

Nichols adjusted the bifocals upon his nose as he gazed up at us. Then, with a great smile of recognition, pushed himself up from his seat and shuffled toward us. Holmes put out his hand, but the gentleman ignored it and threw his arms around my companion.

"Sherlock, my dear boy! How nice of you to come see me!"

Holmes, unaccustomed to such displays of affection, especially from gentlemen, reacted a bit stiffly, but then warmed to the embrace and patted his old professor's back. When they parted, Nichols looked him up and down. "Still lean as an athlete and lithe as a cat."

Turning to me he cocked his head to one side as he put out his hand and said, "I know you, sir. *Doctor* Watson, you say? But that isn't it. Medicine is not what comes to mind when I look upon you. I see you more as a formidable opponent. Did we ever debate one another?"

I smiled as I shook the affable fellow's hand and replied, "I could hardly qualify to debate you upon history, sir, but we did compete against each other last time I was here. It was in your basement shooting gallery."

"Watson the pistoleer!" he cried with glee. "Welcome! Welcome! I hope you brought that Colt .45 I gave you. I should enjoy a rematch."

I smiled, bowed my head, and answered, "I should be happy to oblige, sir."

We all exchanged a few more pleasantries until Tina broke in with a suggestion. "Papa, Uncle Sherlock and Dr. Watson haven't yet settled into their rooms. Perhaps we should let them do so while you take your afternoon nap. Then, in an hour or two, you can resume reminiscing."

The old man sighed in resignation. Looking toward us, he offered, "See what I must put up with, gentlemen? A doting daughter always looking out for my best interests, whether I wish it or not. I should like to continue this conversation, but I am afraid she's right. My afternoon naps have become so habitual I start yawning even before I've finished my lunch. You two go get settled in and we'll get together later."

He paused, then added with great sincerity, "And thank you for coming. It will be a splendid Christmas with a full house."

We repaired to our rooms on the first floor. As I looked out upon the view from my window, noting the serene countryside and the holiday feeling in the air from the decorations scattered throughout the house, I thought to myself: What a pleasant way to spend Christmas, away from

172

the hustle and bustle and crime of London. A relaxing break for both of us.

I should have known better . . . .

Chapter II

I should explain to my readers that not all of the trips Holmes and I embarked on for rest and recreation ended in a case. There were certainly times when the only deductions needed were where to find the best spot to catch fish. However, when one has a mind such as Holmes's and the habit of observing every little thing, it becomes inevitable he will discover puzzles or mysteries that are beyond the ken of most mortals and lead us into some sort of adventure to solve them. This was about to turn into one of those.

With bags unpacked and a change out of my traveling clothes, I returned downstairs. Before I saw any family members, I caught the scent of something baking and followed my nose to the kitchen. There I found Holmes, seated at a table and being poured a steaming cup of liquid by the cook. I was happy to see Mrs. Ricciardo again. Her hair was completely grey, as she herself would be in her late fifties by now. Seeing me she called out in that Italian-tinged accent of hers, "Dr. Watson, a pleasure to have you join us! *Venire, sedere.* Please, come and sit, and I pour you a nice hot mug of *cioccolato.*"

I did so and returned her compliment. "It's a pleasure to be here. I'm glad to see you are still with the professor, Mrs. Ricciardo. I still remember those delicious meals you prepared for us all those years ago."

"*Grazie, Dottore,*" she said with a nod of modesty. "I can promise you are in for a feast on Christmas!"

I smiled and took a sip of the hot chocolate. It was Italian style, rich and thick. "Ah, *deliziosa, Signora!*" I said, in my rudimentary Italian.

She giggled and returned to her stove. Turning to Holmes, I asked, "What shall we do while we wait for the professor?"

His gaze turned toward the window, where we could see high grey clouds with scattered patches of blue. "I was thinking of taking a turn about the grounds while the weather is holding. Storms could arrive any day and confine us to the house. I believe this would be an opportune time to take in the fresh country air."

"Excellent idea," I agreed. Thus, upon finishing our drinks, we took up our ulsters and scarves and set off into the cool crisp afternoon. We strode westward toward the stream which separated the pastures from the woods. It was completely frozen over, and the snow on the opposite bank in the shade of the woods was still a few inches thick.

Noting the slick grey surface of the twenty-foot-wide waterway, I remarked, "It appears there will be no fishing this trip. That ice looks quite thick."

"Thick enough for a man to walk upon," he replied.

"How can you tell that?" I asked.

He pointed a short distance away and said, "Because someone has!"

I looked in the direction he held his cane. I could see some disturbance in the snow along both banks and leading into the pasture. I followed in Holmes's footsteps as he approached the scene to get a closer look. Gazing down, I could see there were holes in the mud and snow coming up the shallow slope of the bank. The actual tracks were indistinct, however. There was some curvature at each end, as one would expect of a heel or toe. Yet they were too wide and didn't leave the natural shape of a boot, merely an oblong impression.

"These are the most unusual tracks I have ever seen," I remarked to my companion. "They are too deep for a snowshoe, but what kind of boot leaves a shape like that?"

Holmes had crouched and measured the length of the print and the stride. Straightening up, he replied, "One worn by a person with nefarious purposes in mind."

I looked upon him quizzically and asked, "How can you tell he is nefarious by his footprints?"

He pointed to them and answered, "Because their shape is due to someone retracing his steps to distort the tracks. No friendly visitor would take such precautions. Let us see how far we can follow them."

Carefully we paralleled the path this strange visitor took. I should explain that the pastures weren't completely flat or level. Each had some slope to it, mostly toward the buildings, and the particular one we were in had some few mounds of boulders strewn about. Had the field been meant for crops, I'm sure these would have been cleared. As pastureland, however, there was no need. We followed the tracks to a spot where a person could crouch behind one of these boulder piles and have an excellent view of the barns, paddocks, and house.

"See how much the ground is disturbed here?" Holmes said, pointing with his stick. "The person who encroached upon this land stayed here for quite some time. Occasionally he would move around a bit, no doubt to keep from stiffening up during the cool of the evening."

"What leads you to conclude evening? Could it not just as easily been early morning?"

"Note the edges of the tracks. See how the mud has hardened? These tracks were made while the ground was still soft, then hardened with the freezing temperatures of the night. There has been some thawing today,

174

but you can still see the minute cracks caused by the expansion of the soil as the water within froze and pushed upward."

I pondered that, then suggested, "So someone, coming from the woods, hid behind these rocks in order to spy on the house. Do you suppose it was a burglar, casing the premises to learn the ways of the family, and when might be the opportune time to strike?"

Holmes leaned against the rocks and looked upon the dwellings below. "We lack data. Depending upon what the person was looking for, the target could be either the house or the barn. We also don't know if he is a thief, or even if it is a man or woman for that matter. You remarked upon Tina's beauty. This person could be an admirer. He or she may be a kidnapper after the child, or an arsonist planning a fire. All we know at this point is the watcher appears to not wish his presence known."

Holmes attempted to backtrack the intruder's footsteps. We returned to the stream, crossed it, one at a time to be safe, and picked up the tracks on the wooded side. Unfortunately, we were unable to follow them very far. The rising and falling temperatures had caused melting snow to drop from the closely spaced trees, and obliterating the tracks.

We continued our circumnavigation of the property. No other trespass signs presented themselves and we returned to the house, where Mrs. Ricciardo welcomed us each with a hot toddy. We took our drinks with us and made for the sitting room, doffing our outerwear to a servant along the way.

Chapter III

In the sitting room, we found a roaring fire. Tina was knitting in a chair, and upon the floor to one side of the hearth stood a large doll house. Playing with figures of an appropriate scale, the child, Marjorie, sat on the rug in front of it. Unlike Tina, she didn't take after her mother at all. A mass of blonde curls covered her head and hung in ringlets down the sides of her face. She wore a simple blue dress with white trim and stockings, and when she turned toward the sound of our entrance, her face bore a strong resemblance to her father.

Tina introduced us, saying, "Margie, this is your Great-uncle Sherlock, and his friend, Dr. Watson. They are friends of your grandfather and have come to share Christmas with us."

The little girl stood, walked over to us, and curtsied most properly. "I'm very pleased to meet you, gentlemen. Would you like to meet my dolls?" She reached out and took my hand, mine being the closest to her, and led the way to the dollhouse. It was quite a fanciful construct, with wings that opened up to reveal its many rooms. It was about three feet tall and just as wide. She picked up each figurine and held it up for Holmes and me to see. There was a man, a woman, a boy, a girl, a dog, and a cat, all with quite proper and fanciful names. Holmes and I congratulated her on her little doll family and moved to the sofa to delight in the warmth of the fire and our drinks.

"Did you enjoy your walk?" asked Tina, the consummate hostess wishing to see to all our comfort.

"It was quite refreshing," I answered, speaking first in my desire to assure her of our pleasure before Holmes went into his inevitable questions.

It was well I did so, for his reply to her was a request to speak with her and her husband alone, if she would allow me to watch over the child. I nodded my assent, of course, and she, tilting her head with curiosity, agreed and stood, instructing Marjorie to keep me company. She then led Holmes off to meet with Noel.

He later related their conversation to me:

Entering the study, Noel was still at work on a ledger. He started to rise when his wife walked in with the detective, but Holmes waved him back into his seat as he closed the door behind him. Seating themselves across the desk from the farm manager, Tina informed her husband Holmes wished to have a private discussion.

"Certainly, Mr. Holmes," said Everest, sitting back and folding his hands across his brocaded waistcoat. "Did you wish to discuss the Professor?"

Holmes also took up a relaxed position, not wishing to alarm his hosts. He crossed his left ankle over his right knee and also folded his hands across his waist as he answered. "Not precisely, though he may certainly enter into it. Watson and I have just returned from a sojourn about the grounds and found something of which you may not be aware."

Relaying his discovery of the tracks and their location, he enquired, "Have there been any significant changes lately? New purchases, for example?"

Everest was mulling that over while Tina spoke up. "Certainly we have purchased Christmas gifts, but I cannot imagine any of them being of such value as to make our home a target for burglars."

As she made that statement, her husband made a surreptitious movement, indicating he might have something to share with Holmes privately. Out loud, he said, "It isn't particularly recent, but we did obtain a new prize breeding bull early last month. It certainly has significant value. Do you think it may be in jeopardy?"

Holmes tilted his head. "It's far too early to tell what this perpetrator's goal might be. A bull would certainly not be an easy thing to steal, but not impossible. I trust it has been re-branded?"

"Yes, Mr. Holmes we did that the first day we came into possession."

"Does it have any other distinguishing features which might make it easily identifiable from a distance?"

Everest shrugged his shoulders and replied, "Nothing in particular, except perhaps its color. This one is a South Devon breed, solid red with no white markings at all. I haven't seen any others like it amongst our neighbors' herds, so it would likely stand out."

Holmes seized the opportunity to get Tina's husband alone and suggested they go out to take a look at it while she returned to her knitting and to tell me to meet them in the barn. Once they were out of earshot of the house, Everest revealed his secret to the detective.

"We generally aren't ones for extravagant gifts to each other, Mr. Holmes. We live simple lives and don't engage in multiple social events, being out here in the country. However, we have the most successful farm in the county and the Professor is a well-respected scholar, so we do have occasion, two or three times a year, to attend gatherings that rise above the level of a local barn dance. We own minimal formal wear, but can hold our own in fashionable attire. What is missing is any special item of jewelry for Tina to adorn herself with. Years ago, I gave her a five-carat blue topaz pendant, as that is her birthstone, as she was born on Christmas Day. It is a beautiful piece on a simple gold chain, but I wanted her to have an item really worthy of her beauty and my love for her.

"The farm has done exceptionally well the past two years, and shown enough profits for me to obtain something special. I purchased a rare six-strand pearl necklace, crafted with six-millimeter pearls. There is a large blue topaz decorated by surrounding pearls inset into a gold filigree ring, and a pair of waterdrop pearls descending underneath. The jeweler refers to them as the Gemini Pearls, as they are perfectly matched like twins. That necklace is worth fifty pounds – certainly a tempting target if anyone is aware of it."

I was just catching up to them by then and heard that final statement. Holmes asked, "Is there anyone in the household aware of it? The Professor, perhaps?"

Everest shook his head. "No. With his mental powers deteriorating, I couldn't trust that he would not inadvertently say something and spoil the surprise. I purchased it on a business trip down to London weeks ago, and told no one. I have a separate strong box for my personal papers and valuables, to which only Tina and I know the combination, and we respect each other's privacy. She wouldn't open it without my permission, any more than I would go through her purse without hers."

The Gemini Pearl Necklace

"Who was the jeweler who created it?" asked the detective.

"Yakub Goldschmidt of Hatton Garden – and before you ask, I had it insured before it ever left the store."

Holmes nodded in approval. "A wise precaution. Insurance records are kept confidential, and the chance of someone learning of your purchase through them is highly unlikely. Jewelers, however, tend to boast of their creations. Is it possible that they took a photograph of your piece to show to other potential clients?"

Everest nodded. "They did, Mr. Holmes. They even gave me a copy to give to my insurance company for their records."

"How much do they know about you?"

We had reached the barn by this time, and he opened the door so we could step in out of the cold. Securing it shut, he replied, "The jeweler only knows my last name and that I travel to London occasionally on business. They don't know what type of business I'm in, nor my address."

"What information was on the cheque with which you paid them?"

"I paid them in cash, Mr. Holmes, and the receipt was simply made out to *Mr. Everest*."

Holmes gazed upon what I must now call our client with a nod and the words, "Very good."

"My university instructors in bookkeeping emphasized the appropriate amount of detail for any given transaction. In this case, caution and confidentiality were an overriding factor." He stopped and pointed toward a particular stall. "Ah, here is our prize bull, Mr. Holmes. His name is *Samson*."

Chapter IV

The creature in the stall before us was a magnificent specimen. He was a short horn, and red as an Irish Setter. His height at the shoulder was nearly as tall as my shoulder and Everest told us he weighed over two-thousand pounds. As I took in his great size, I wondered aloud at how such a beast was kept under control.

"Fortunately," replied the farm manager, "he was raised on a small family farm where he had human contact every day from the children who cared for him from birth. He's quite tame and appears to have settled in well to his new surroundings. We aren't quite ready to have Margie around him, but Tina brushes and speaks to him every day, and he seems to understand simple commands to get him to move."

Holmes enquired, "He wasn't wary of strangers when he arrived?"

Everest smiled. "Oddly enough, only the men. He would alternately draw away from them or charge them. Tina, however, has had no trouble with him at all, and he doesn't bother the milkmaids. I suppose it may be their higher-pitched voices, sounding much like the children he was raised with."

Holmes nodded. "That may bode well for us if Samson is the target of your mysterious visitor. He would likely put up a fuss which would rouse the house, should someone attempt to lead him away."

"They would be foolish to try," agreed the young man. "The barn is kept locked, and if they did breach it, the noise of the animals being disturbed in the middle of the night would certainly draw attention to their presence."

He folded his arms across his chest and asked the detective, "What do you propose we do, Mr. Holmes? Should we set a trap? Or post a guard?"

Holmes thought a moment, and then gestured for us to follow him to the barn's entrance. He gazed toward the spot where we had found the tracks, then toward the house. At last, he said over his shoulder to our host, "Have you a telescope?"

Everest hesitated at the oddity of this request, and then realized its significance. "Yes. Yes, Mr. Holmes, we do."

"I should like to borrow it this evening. Perhaps for several evenings, depending upon our quarry's actions."

"You wish to observe him from a distance?" I enquired, questioningly. "Why not stake out his crossing point and catch him in the act?"

My friend turned to me. "In the act of what? All we could charge him with is trespassing. He could claim he merely got lost and was trying to obtain his bearings. At most, he would receive a short sentence and be free again to complete his actual crime. I suggest we observe him discreetly from a distance and see how close he dares to come, and ascertain whether it be the barn or the house that holds his object of interest."

Everest spoke up. "There is an attic window on this side of the house which would be an ideal place from which to observe. It overlooks the whole property in this direction."

Thus, it was agreed. Starting that evening, one of us would sit up in the attic with the telescope to keep an eye out for any intruder and note his or her actions. I foresaw one possible obstacle to that plan, however. "Professor Nichols will be expecting us to keep him company in the evenings. Will he not become suspicious if one of us is continually missing? I'm assuming, of course, you wish to keep this possible danger from him, so as not to aggravate his fragile state of mind."

Everest nodded in agreement and turned toward my friend. "It would be better if he didn't know, Mr. Holmes. We also need to consider the dinner hour when all of us will be expected to eat together."

Holmes, still looking out upon the pasture, was silent for some moments. Then he turned his gaze back upon us. "We, of course, must inform Tina, and, as I recall, she is a very observant person. Is there a trustworthy servant you could enlist? Someone who would take his meals at a different time than the household without notice?"

Everest immediately answered. "As long as we don't tell Tina about the necklace specifically, just that there is a valuable item on site. I would still like to keep that a surprise. Young Donny McCallum could assist us. You may remember his father, Donald, was the Dairy Foreman back when you visited before. He passed away some four years ago. The medical condition that had forced him to give up his navy career and take up farming finally caught up to him. His son, Donald Junior, is nineteen now, and has grown up here. He is a natural with the animals and treats them like his own. A stalwart lad. I'm sure we can trust him."

At this point, a loud "Halloa!" emanated from the front porch as Professor Nichols came out to seek us. Everest returned his call and waved. As the professor crossed the fifty-yard distance toward us, our client spoke softly. "I'll speak to Donny and arrange everything in the attic. When you go up to dress for dinner, I'll show you the way to its entrance."

Nichols soon reached us, only slightly winded from his effort. "Well, boys," he said, "admiring our new prize bull? A beauty, isn't he?"

"Indeed, Professor," replied my companion. "A fine-looking animal. He should prove most conducive to the expansion of your herd."

The elderly man beamed and put a hand on Everest's shoulder. "Yes, business is doing quite well, thanks to Noel here. I was lucky my daughter found such a prize herself."

The young man blushed at the praise and replied, "Our guests were just getting ready to return. I've a few things to speak to Donny about. Then I'll join you shortly."

We retreated to the house, maintaining a slow pace in deference to the professor. Once inside and divested from our outerwear, he suggested a trip down into the basement and a round of target practice. I offered to retrieve our pistols from our rooms while Holmes accompanied his former instructor down the stairs. When I rejoined them, Nichols was showing off a new item from his collection.

"Ah, Doctor!" cried the gun enthusiast as I came through the door at the bottom of the stairs. "You are just in time. Come take a look at this."

I joined them by the shooting bench and set down the cases containing the Colts the professor had given us all those years ago. He handed me a lever-action rifle with a polished brass receiver and beautifully grained walnut stock. The lever was already opened, revealing an empty breech. It was quite a bit shorter than the Martini-Henry rifle I was familiar with during my army service, but the weight appeared about the same. As I hefted it into a firing position, Nichols expounded upon the details.

"It's an American Henry Rifle, first produced in 1860 by the New Haven Arms Company. Revolutionary for its time with a fifteen-round tubular magazine plus one in the chamber, firing .44 caliber rim-fire cartridges. In spite of this greater capacity over the standard single-shot rifles, the Union Army purchased less than two-thousand during the Civil War because of its lack of a bayonet. It's widely believed, however, that some six- or seven-thousand made their way into battle through purchases by individual soldiers who felt the greater firepower would save their lives. A noted Confederate Colonel, John Mosby, was said to have cursed it, stating 'that d----d Yankee rifle that can be loaded on Sunday and fired all week'."

Holmes spoke up. "What is the effective range of this weapon?"

Nichols smiled. "The manufacturer claims over four-hundred yards, but I've read a good many articles on weapons, and my research indicates it loses accuracy at anything over two-hundred."

Holmes walked over to the gun case and picked out another ancient long gun. "I believe this Girandoni air rifle has a range of one-hundred-fifty yards, does it not? May I fire a few rounds?"

"Certainly, Sherlock, but I must warn you the capacity is currently only about ten rounds. It takes fifteen-*hundred* strokes of the air pump to power its thirty maximum shots. The main reason for its discontinuation – though I do have a spare, fully charged air container like the ones the Austrian Army used."

Nichols reached for a box of cartridges and handed them to me. "Here, Doctor. Give the Henry a try."

The steel plate backdrop for his firing range was some sixty feet from the firing line as it ran nearly the length of the house, with support beams in neat rows. Certainly, the distance was no challenge for the rifles and muskets in his collection. I loaded and stepped up next to Holmes, who was proving quite proficient with the air rifle. The Henry proved to be well-sighted in and I obliterated the center ring of the target I had chosen with just six shots. I handed it back to Nichols, saying, "A most proficient weapon. I can see why Union soldiers would pay their own money for it."

I looked toward the gun cases I had brought down. "How are your pistol skills, Professor? Care to compete with those Colts you gave us?"

I opened the cases to reveal two matched 1873 Colt Peacemaker, single-action revolvers with seven-and-one-half inch barrels for greater accuracy. These were nickel-plated with ivory handles – disturbingly beautiful for something so deadly.

Nichols picked one up gingerly, running his fingers along its long barrel before taking up a firing position to test its heft. "Ah, these are beauties indeed! I hope you and Sherlock have been putting them to good use in your pursuit of justice."

I didn't have the heart to tell him we rarely used them. Usually, when we went out armed, it was with concealment in mind and my Army Webley and Holmes's five-inch Bulldog were much easier to fit into our pockets. He checked the cylinder and saw the hammer was on an empty chamber, but the rest were loaded. He picked out a target and, using a two-handed stance, slowly put five shots into it.

"Excellent, Professor!" declared Holmes, seeing a tight pattern upon the bullseye. "Watson, I believe you've met your match this time."

I gave my friend a look, for my skills were certainly equal to the task of repeating Nichols' feat. Then I saw the countenance on my friend's face and realized what he was saying. I took up my stance and deliberately put three of my shots on the outer rim of the center circle. This pleased the elderly man to no end and gave me more satisfaction in making him happy than winning a match ever could.

We continued in this manner, testing various weapons in his collection. When at last the dinner hour was approaching, Holmes asked a question. "Professor, would you mind if I took the Girandoni for some outdoor shooting tomorrow? I'd like to test it over a longer range."

"By all means, Sherlock. Be my guest."

Chapter V

Everest joined us at the bottom of the stairs as we prepared to ascend them to change for dinner. He led us up to the attic where we were met by a handsome young lad, nearly six feet tall, yet lean as a rail. He sported long blond hair, a moustache, and the beginnings of a beard. At our introduction, he greeted us enthusiastically. "I've read your stories, Dr. Watson, and I must say, it is an honor to meet you, Mr. Holmes. I should be happy to assist in any way I can."

"Thank you, Mr. McCallum," the detective replied. "For now, your task will be strictly observation and reporting, though there may come a time when your physical assistance may be called upon."

"Anything you say, sir," answered the lad. "We've set the telescope up over here. I've kept it back away from the window so it can't be spotted by anyone far away. I'll also keep the lantern low and behind this trunk so there won't appear to be any light in this window. Just enough that we can see our way in and out."

Holmes stepped over to the telescope and sat upon the chair behind it. He peered through the lens and made a slight adjustment. "Very good. That is the exact spot where we observed the tracks come to a stop." Then he noted a pair of field glasses on a box next to the chair. "I thought those might come in handy as well," Everest offered. "We can use them to scan the area occasionally in case the trespasser comes by a different route. That way, we won't have to move the scope and try to find our way back to the location in the dark."

Holmes stood and rubbed his palms together. "Excellent, Mr. Everest! Your foresight may prove fortuitous. What time does the professor usually retire?"

The manager answered. "Generally, he's off to bed no later than ten o'clock, but with your presence, he may be inspired to stay up later."

Holmes nodded thoughtfully. "I believe we can come up with an excuse for either Watson or me to be off to bed by that time, should it prove necessary. Mr. McCallum, I presume you'll eat your dinner early enough to be on post here by dusk?"

"Easily done, sir"

"Excellent! One of us will relieve you by ten or sooner. I believe we can cease our watch by midnight. This intruder is still in reconnoitering mode and isn't likely to take any action for a day or two at least. If it is the house he watches, it will probably be only as long as lights are on."

"Begging your pardon, Mr. Holmes," said the young lad. "How do you know that?"

Holmes indulged the boy with his logic. "Our observation reveals he has only looked upon the farm one time from that spot which provides the best concealment. Whatever he is planning will require at least two or three days of scouting to learn the ways of the house before he strikes. Someone with the foresight to obscure his tracks will not act impulsively. He'll plan his action carefully, and that gives us time."

With tactics thus set, we prepared ourselves and joined the family for dinner. Discussion of the upcoming holiday was lively, especially the charming conversation carried on by young Marjorie. She had quite an extensive list of things she was hoping to receive, especially concerning her dollhouse family.

"They need a barn with animals to be a proper country squire and family," she declared in as authoritative a voice as a four-year-old can muster.

Her father, in mock seriousness, asked, "What if the father wishes to be a barrister, or a merchant, or an actor? Then they would live in town, wouldn't they?"

She looked at him with wide blue eyes and a shocked expression. "No, these are *my* family. The father is a country squire. Nothing is better than that!"

Noel chose not to argue and her grandfather, Professor Nichols, reached over and tousled her hair. "That's right, child, but a man can be many things in his life. I was a university professor before I became a dairy farmer."

"But being a country squire must be better, or you would still be a professor!" she replied with her innocent reasoning.

Knowing better than to argue with a four-year-old's logic, Nichols changed the subject and addressed my friend. "So, Sherlock, how was your walk this afternoon? Find any good fishing spots?"

Holmes politely shook his head. "I am afraid the stream is frozen over too thickly. But tell me, Professor: I know the woods across it are open to public use, how large a forest is that?"

184

Nichols pursed his lips and looked down in thought. "Oh, it's about four miles north to south and varies in width from half-a-mile to a mile."

Holmes feigned surprise. I knew he already had this information and I was wondering where this line of questioning was going. "That large? I suppose that creates a natural barrier between you and your western neighbor."

"Hatherly's farm? Indeed, it does. Not that it matters. He's a good neighbor. Mostly vegetable crops at his place. Broccoli, Brussels sprouts, and the like. We occasionally trade milk for vegetables with him."

"Have you ever had any of your cattle wander over there?"

"Never," answered Nichols. "Our livestock are content to remain on our side of the stream. There's nothing for them to eat in the woods, and Hatherley's crops are too far away to attract them."

"I suppose the woods are open to hunters, so it's probably just as well your cattle don't wander through them."

"We have an ordinance about that, Sherlock. No rifles are allowed in those woods. Hunting may only be done by shotguns using birdshot, or archery. Wouldn't want some stray bullet finding its way onto our pastures."

"A wise precaution," replied the detective.

The subject changed to more pleasant topics and little Marjorie was regaled with stories of Christmases past. After dinner, Holmes and the Professor retreated to his study where Nichols insisted on showing Holmes his latest research, while Everest and I took up a game of billiards.

As the hour approached ten o'clock, the farm manager and I quit our game, stuck our heads into the study to say goodnight, and proceeded upstairs. In the attic, we found that Tina had replaced young Donny after she had lain Margie down to sleep. She reported no sign of anyone and I volunteered to take her place to allow her and Noel to join his wife for a nightcap. I was wide awake and knew Holmes would likely be up shortly.

I settled into the chair and peered through the telescope fixed on the spot where we had seen the culprit's tracks. Nothing was to be seen there. Thus, I took up the field glasses and did a quick surveillance of the surrounding area. To quote an appropriate poem for the season, "*Not a creature was stirring*". I was just about to set the glasses aside when Holmes arrived. To my surprise, he carried the Girandoni air rifle. "Do you think that will be necessary? You certainly can't shoot a man on site just for trespassing."

He set the gun aside and replied, "Just a precaution. It's best to be prepared for any contingency. Just as I would advise you to keep your Webley at hand, should we have to pursue our quary."

"Well, our friend has yet to show himself this evening," I said, handing him the binoculars. "All seems quiet, so far."

I again took up my view through the telescope. It was well that the moon was heading into its full phase over the next few days and the sky only held scattered clouds, making for a bright view of the pastureland we were watching. As I heard the distant chime of a clock somewhere in the house announcing ten-thirty, Holmes suddenly stood and appeared to adjust the focus on the lenses of the field glasses. "We have movement," he said in a low voice. "Someone is crossing the stream at the same spot we noted earlier today."

I made a slight adjustment to the telescope and spotted a figure gingerly crossing the ice. He was well bundled against the cold so that I couldn't make out much of his physicality. The face was wrapped in a muffler and a beaver hat with earflaps was pulled low on his brow. Assuming the bulk of his body was caused by the heavy coat, it appeared that he was of average size, certainly not obese. I couldn't judge his height from this far away until he got to the same mound of rocks we had been to earlier. Standing next to them, he appeared much shorter than me – perhaps five-foot-five at most, and possibly less, depending on his boot heels.

Suddenly, as he pulled out a pair of field glasses, Holmes said, "Get back, Watson! Step to the side quickly!"

I did as he ordered, stepping out of the line of sight. As I did so, he stealthily reached over and tilted the telescope upward, then ducked out of sight backing into the dark recesses of the attic. Being well away from the window, he raised his binoculars again and trained his focus on the spy in the pasture.

"What is it?" I asked. "Why did you have me move?"

"I nearly made a blunder, my friend. I suddenly realized that the position of the moon, while being bright enough for us to see, was also lighting up this side of the house. I noticed the reflection of the telescope lens shining on the window where our nocturnal visitor might have seen it."

"He hasn't reacted?" I asked, hopefully.

"Fortunately, no," he replied. "His concentration seems to be on the house rather than the barn, but he appears to be looking at the lower floors. Ah!" he cried, lowering the binoculars and stepping back. "Now he is observing the upper half of the house."

He took a peek and again raised the instrument to his eyes and murmured, "He's writing something down. Now he's leaving the same way he came, again stepping in his own tracks." He stood up full and said, with resolve. "Come along. We should examine this new trespass while it's still fresh."

Chapter VI

We bundled ourselves into our overcoats and, accompanied by Everest, trudged out to the spot. Holmes made sure that our host and I stayed on the side of the rock-pile toward the house, so as not to leave tracks where the intruder might spot them if he came back again.

This time Holmes was able to find one footprint the trespasser had failed to smudge and measured it with his pocket tape. "A size seven boot," he said for our benefit. "That would tally with the approximate height. Unfortunately, it doesn't help us determine if it is a man or woman."

Everest reacted to that. "You think it could be a woman?" he asked with some incredulity. "How often have you run into female burglars, Mr. Holmes?"

Holmes broke a branch off a nearby bush and used it to wipe out his own tracks in the snow as he answered. "More often than you might think. Their smaller size allows them access to spaces one would normally not expect an entrance. They also use their gender to attend parties and move about freely, or to obtain positions of servanthood within a household until they can accomplish their mission."

"Well, we certainly aren't planning on hiring anyone and we aren't hosting any parties, though we will be attending one on Christmas Eve and another on New Year's Eve."

"I assume Tina will be wearing the necklace on those occasions."

"I expect she will. I am giving her the necklace on Christmas Eve so she can wear it to the Christmas Extravaganza in Oxford that night. Then there will be the M.P.'s New Year's Eve Ball in Aylesbury."

Holmes nodded, then said, "Why don't you go back to the house and get some sleep? I want to cross the stream and see how far I can follow these tracks to see which direction they go. Watson, I would welcome your company if your leg is up to it."

In truth, my old war wound was acting up with the cold, but I wasn't about to leave my friend to face an unknown intruder alone. "I'll come with you. Lead on."

We crossed the stream's solid ice and emerged on the other side. The full moon illuminated the ground for a while, but once into the shade of the trees, Holmes was forced to use the bullseye lantern and direct the light downward to keep it from giving our position away. The tracks didn't go directly through the woods toward Nichols' neighbor to the west, but rather turned northward. We hadn't gone very far when we found a spot with fresh horse tracks and signs of our visitor mounting and riding through the woods until they reached the main road. From that point, the traffic made the tracks impossible to follow.

Once back at the house and standing before a warm fire with hot tea before retiring, I asked my friend, "If this person is observing the house, shouldn't he be doing so from more than one side?"

"Yes," he replied. "Tomorrow we shall have to walk the perimeter again and see if there are other signs of his incursion. I doubt that he could infiltrate from the south, as the land is sparse with no hiding places, but the road from Aylesbury that circles the northern boundary and then turns south along the east side of the property may provide him with some observation points."

"Observing from the road seems rather risky," I noted.

"During daylight with traffic, certainly," replied Holmes. "But at night, there are ways he could manage it."

Chapter VII

Aylesbury, being the county town of Buckinghamshire, had well-paved roads throughout the surrounding area. Thus, they were ploughed frequently during the winter. However, during our sojourn the next day, Holmes found signs along the roadside where a horse had left the macadam surface and stopped in the mud perhaps one-hundred-fifty yards due east of Nichol's house. The tracks were easy to spot, as they had run into the snow shoved to the side when the ploughs had come through the previous day.

"These appear to have been made last night. Perhaps after our late-night visitor left his lookout on the west side. See how the hardened snow has cracked from the weight of the horse? It had already frozen from the cold night air."

Holmes turned his gaze toward Nichol's home and found that, from that vantage point, the top of the barn was barely visible above the roofline of the house. He pointed in that direction so I could follow his gaze. "I believe we can now be fairly certain that our trespasser was reconnoitering the house. That at least narrows the targets of whatever crime they're looking to commit."

"So," I asked, "what now?"

The detective stroked his chin in thought, then replied, "I have some further enquiries to make of the family. Then I shall have to smoke a pipe or two upon the matter. Tomorrow is Christmas Eve, and the necklace shall make its first public appearance, so we must make our plans today."

The enquiries Holmes made were to Tina, to see if she had purchased anything of significance for Christmas gifts for her family, and to Noel to ensure the Professor hadn't come into possession of some valuable object related to his academic work. Neither proved to be the case. The only other recent purchase of significant value was that of the red bull. Thus, the pearl necklace remained the most likely target for a thief.

Holmes, as was his habit when upon a case, shut himself away in his room with a good supply of tobacco and his pipe. He did make an appearance at lunch so as not to alarm the professor by his absence, but he ate sparingly, as he refuses to be distracted by digestion when contemplating a problem.

Finally, just before tea time, Holmes asked me to bring Everest up to his room for a conference. When we had all settled into place, Holmes, leaning on the window sill, began to explain his thoughts.

"I have attempted to put myself in our potential thief's place," he began. "Were I the one planning to steal this necklace, I would take much more time and many more steps to glean information, and wait until such time as most of the family is away without taking the necklace with them. Then I would have no need to subject myself to the cold weather of late winter nights, as this person has done. I would attempt to infiltrate the social gatherings where it would be worn, and see what information I might overhear about where it is kept or on what occasions it is to be worn. I might attempt to hire on as an employee during the spring when there is much more work to be done. Or, if it's a woman, to arrange to replace one of the milkmaids who come in from town to do the daily milking.

"However, as this person is spending the time to do his reconnoitering, now and under these adverse conditions, I can only assume that he means to attempt his crime in the near future.

"That said, I believe his greatest chance for success lies not in burglarizing the house, but in highway robbery while you're traveling either to or from the train station during your Oxford trip tomorrow, or while on the road into town for the New Year's Eve Ball."

My friend paused and let that sink in. Everest, after a momentary hesitation to ponder this fact, gazed up at him and asked, "What do you propose we do to stop him? Should I hire some guards for the trip?"

Holmes shook his head. "A show of force will discourage him, certainly. However, it is my recommendation that we take another tack and catch him in the act once and for all so that we might put your worries to rest."

Holmes laid out his scheme, adding, "I believe his ideal opportunity will be to confront you on the road home after the Oxford trip. The lateness of the hour will ensure no other traffic on the road, and a significant delay in your getting to town and rousing up the constabulary to pursue him. Let me suggest this . . . ."

He went on to outline his plan and, after a discussion, we all agreed as to our roles and its execution.

Chapter VIII

That evening, we were all treated to a recital by Tina on piano and Margie, who was learning the basics of the violin from her mother. I recalled that Holmes had informed me during our first visit to Nichols that Tina's mother was an excellent musician, and had taught her daughter both piano and violin before her untimely death when Tina was nine.

Christmas Eve dawn broke with blue skies and scattered white clouds with no sign of rain or snow. We spent the day dressing the tree, as the professor and the Everests were going to be gone that night to Oxford. Margie was filled with excitement and squealed with delight when her father presented Tina with the Gemini pearl necklace after lunch. Tina was taken aback by the extravagance of her gift.

"Noel, it's beautiful," she said. "But – "

He cut her off. "But nothing. It's no less than you deserve, my Love, and I wanted you to have something to show off in Oxford."

She hugged him and replied, "I have the finest husband in all Aylesbury! This is all I need to be the envy of every woman at both Oxford and the New Year's Eve Ball."

Needless to say, compliments volleyed back and forth between the couple, the professor, and the rest of us. Soon it was time to get ready for the ride into town to catch the late afternoon train to Oxford. Holmes remained in close proximity to the family as we had agreed. I stayed at the farm, on guard with the staff to protect both Margie and the house in case we were wrong about the target of whoever was spying on the farm. Donny McCallum was given a rifle to stand guard at the barn with other farmhands, and both Clinton, the butler, and I discreetly armed ourselves in case of a break-in. While remaining diligent, I still was able to have a delightful time watching over Margie, telling stories and playing games. It was a double-edged sword in that she was an adorable child and yet, still a reminder of the fact that my Mary had died before we could start our own family. I'm afraid I let my feelings give in to the child's persistence for "one more story" before I finally put her to bed, a half-hour past her bedtime.

I took up my post in the attic, searching the grounds to the west, while Clinton remained downstairs watching the eastern side of the estate while making rounds of all the ground floor doors every half-hour. The night was clear and still, befitting the Christmas carol, *Silent Night.*

It was not so, however, for Professor Nichols and the Everests.

The drive into Aylesbury to catch the Oxford-bound train was without incident. The enclosed carriage was comfortable, and the traveling rugs kept the passengers warm against the late afternoon chill.

Likewise, the train ran on schedule and all arrived sufficiently early to attend a delightful evening at the Oxford Extravaganza, a combination of student exhibits, musical performances, and ballroom dancing. Professor Nichols was welcomed enthusiastically by several faculty members, and Tina's necklace was much remarked upon.

They caught the last train out of Oxford and arrived back in Aylesbury just after midnight. The driver they had engaged for the evening was a one-armed man who was expert at the Hungarian rein style of using just his good left hand to drive the carriage while his right sleeve hung empty, tucked into his coat pocket. There had been some concern expressed over this, as there might be a need to whip up the horse for a fast getaway, but it was Christmas Eve and most of the staff had been given that evening and the next day off to celebrate the season.

The moon was still nearly full on a cloudless night, making for excellent visibility. Noel Everest kept watch of the countryside out the window in anticipation of what Holmes feared. Though he knew the detective was close by, the anticipation of danger still jangled his nerves. Just as they were passing the edge of the forest that ran south along the western border of the farm, the carriage was reined to a stop, and a voice from the opposite side of where Everest had been watching called out, "Stop right there or I'll blow your bloody head off!"

The driver might have been willing to snap the reins and make a run for it had he been alone, but he wasn't willing to risk a shot coming from behind that might strike one of his passengers, so he pulled up.

The highway robber, a stranger, was a muscular fellow, though not very tall. A black bandana covered the lower half of his face and a shotgun filled his hands. He shouted out, "Everybody out! Now! You!" He pointed to the driver. "Get down here and don't try anything!"

Speaking to all, he said. "Gentlemen, I'll have your wallets if you please." Then, staring at Tina, his eyes narrowed. "And you, m'Lady – just open up that coat of yours, and let's see what pretty baubles might be hangin' about your neck."

The professor started to protest, but Noel put a hand upon his shoulder and said, "Just do as he says, Professor."

The men reached for their wallets inside their coats as Tina undid the clasp and buttons on her coat. When she pulled the lapels apart to reveal her neckline, the robber gasped, lowering his shotgun as he stepped closer, saying, "What the bloody Hell?"

She was no longer wearing the necklace, and that element of surprise was enough to distract the bandit. Suddenly, instead of pulling out his wallet, Noel drew a Pepperbox pistol with its two-and-one-half-inch barrel that fit neatly into his breast pocket and shot the robber in the shoulder, forcing him to drop his gun. At the same time, the one-armed driver came up with a British Bulldog revolver in the right arm hidden under his coat and fired as well. Sherlock Holmes, as the driver in disguise, had shot the man near his hip, forcing him to fall to the ground.

Though we in the house must have been over a mile from this incident, the shots echoed down the glen. Knowing now that the trouble was out on the road, I charged out to the barn and mounted a horse we had saddled in the event we had to ride for the police. Donny left the barn and joined Clinton in the house to maintain guard there while I goaded the animal into a gallop across the northern pasture toward the sound of the gunfire.

I spotted the carriage lamps and approached quickly, my old Army Webley in hand in case of trouble. Fortunately, I found everyone healthy, save for the one bandit lying on the floor of the carriage, as he was to be transported back to town for treatment, arrest, and questioning. Holmes and Everest had staunched the bleeding, neither having hit any significant artery. I examined him quickly and, though wounded and in pain, the man was in no immediate danger.

After arriving at the local police station at close to one a.m., we arranged a solitary cell away from the Christmas Eve drunkards and I treated the fellow's wounds more thoroughly, removing the bullets and stitching the wounds with supplies from the police surgeon's office, while an Inspector Albertson was briefed by Sherlock Holmes. He was a wizened old veteran of the police force. Roughly five-foot-ten and fifty years of age, he was still in good physical condition, having not allowed age to let his muscular chest sink into a fat belly. He regularly walked the streets of Aylesbury to check in on his men, thus keeping his legs in peak condition for chasing down miscreants. His moustache had turned grey, but his hair was still thick and light brown, and his eyes as keen as a hawk's.

The inspector listened with great interest, but replied somewhat piqued at the actions Holmes had taken. "You should have let us know what was going on, Mr. Holmes. We could have offered protection. The professor and the Everests are among our leading citizens."

Holmes smiled indulgently. "All I had was speculation based upon rudimentary deductions, Inspector. I couldn't be sure that the criminal would strike tonight and you, I am sure, had your hands full policing the town on this night of celebrations and the abundant prizes of Christmas gifts to burglarize. This way, by seeming to be unguarded, we drew him into a trap and captured him in the act."

"So where is this necklace he was after?"

Holmes unpinned the empty sleeve from his jacket and pulled the necklace from the pocket. "Safe and sound. I knew that the sight of Mrs. Everest not wearing the actual object of his act would cause a moment of hesitation. Mr. Everest and I had agreed that was when we would take action."

Albertson inspected the mass of pearls and handed it to Tina. "I'll not deprive you of your Christmas gift at this time, Mrs. Everest, but bear in mind that we will need it as evidence for the trial."

"Thank you, Inspector," she answered, handing it to her husband to fasten about her neck once again. "We shall take great care of it."

After taking their statements, Albertson allowed me to drive the family back to the farm, while I left my horse for Holmes to follow when he was finished. He still had many questions for this bandit before he could be satisfied that the danger had passed.

Chapter IX

Upon a search of the robber's person, a short letter was found addressed to "*Parson Donner, Morrisey Inn, Aylesbury*". The fact that Donner's first name could be confused for an occupational title apparently had served him well in not being suspected often during his criminal career, but this time he was caught red-handed. The gist of the letter was that he should proceed as discussed upon the return of the *object* on the night of the twenty-fourth at the place planned upon, object to then be transported to London on the twenty-fifth and delivered for payment at the previous meeting place at three o'clock.

Cryptic as it was meant to be, should it have been discovered before the crime, now that it was found in Donner's possession after being caught, the meaning was quite clear. He wasn't acting on his own, but as the agent of a higher-up. That meant further danger for the Everests if this mastermind wasn't deterred for good.

Donner was still a bit groggy from the painkillers I had given him while removing the bullets from his shoulder and hip, but he was awake enough to answer questions – especially after Inspector Albertson told him his only chance of leniency was to name his accomplice.

193

"What sort of leniency?" asked the highway robber.

"That will be up to the Crown Prosecutor. But it could be a reduced sentence."

Donner shook his head, trying to clear the effects of the pain and medication. Finally, he replied, "Well, it weren't my idea, I can tell you that. I'll be glad to tell his name. It'll serve him right for getting me into this spot."

When he gave out his partner's identity, Holmes nodded with satisfaction and replied, "I suspected as much."

"Who is that, Mr. Holmes?" asked Albertson.

"One of the few men who knew of the necklace's existence before tonight, Inspector."

When next I saw Holmes, we were opening presents on Christmas morning. Margie was admiring the additional items for her dollhouse family and all were in good spirits. My friend appeared in the doorway of the great room and was immediately pounced upon by the young girl who thanked him for the present he had left her under the tree, a book of beginning violin music. The adults, of course, were all anxious to hear what had transpired at the police station, but didn't wish to discuss it in front of the child. At Tina's urging, Margie was off to assist Mrs. Ricciardo in the kitchen, as playtime wasn't to occur until after a breakfast of thanksgiving for the holiday.

Once she was out of earshot, Holmes described what he had learned and what steps he and Inspector Albertson were about to take. Noel was incensed when he learned who the mastermind was and wanted to join us, but my friend dissuaded him by suggesting that his place was with his family on this holy day, and that this type of work was best left to himself and the police.

Inspector Albertson insisted on accompanying us back to London. Having been denied the capture of Donner, he wasn't about to be left out of the arrest of the criminal behind the attempted theft. We had wired ahead and were met at the station by Inspector Stanley Hopkins, a frequent Scotland Yard cohort during those later years of the Nineteenth Century.

Despite Hopkins' height being nearly equal to Holmes, thus being several inches taller than Albertson, and being assigned directly to Scotland Yard headquarters, the younger inspector bowed in deference to his elder counterpart and was content merely to be representing the case via jurisdictional protocol. Both officials allowed Holmes's to present his plans for the capture of our quarry and agreed to his proposal.

The meeting place for the rendezvous was a Jewish café on Brick Lane in Spitalfields. [2] Being one of the few places open on Christmas Day, it attracted the lower classes of London's Gentiles who had no place or no one with whom to celebrate Christmas and preferred to merely drink the day away. This lent itself to both the criminal's purpose and our own. Donner wouldn't seem out of place meeting his employer, nor would those of our party who would be on hand to observe the exchange.

Fortunately, Holmes's shot to Donner's hip had struck only flesh and no bone, so my removal of the bullet and stitching it up was sufficient to allow him to walk with only a minor limp. His right arm, however, was forced to be in a sling from his shoulder wound. At three o'clock, Donner limped in, using an old bamboo cane provided by Holmes. It was sufficient to hold his weight, but should he attempt to use it as a weapon it would easily be broken. I had entered earlier and watched from a table across the room while others were in less-conspicuous locations. Donner spotted the man who had hired him and made for the table, which was situated by the kitchen door.

He sank heavily into the seat opposite, and the man sitting there immediately looked upon him with concern. He was Jewish in appearance and nearing thirty years of age with curly black hair under his yarmulke and a medium-length black beard. He immediately questioned our prisoner, *sotto voce*. "What happened? Did you get the necklace?"

In answer, Donner pulled a leather pouch from inside his sling and dropped it on the table, giving off the distinct sound of several round objects clacking together. "I had a bit of trouble with the husband. He tried to shoot it out with me. Suffice to say," he added with a wink, "one of us lost."

"You killed him?" cried our quarry, fighting to keep his voice low. "How? No one was supposed to get hurt!"

"The farm was too well guarded for a burglary," replied Donner. "I had to use our secondary plan and go for a robbery instead. I got your merchandise. Now where's my money?"

The young Jew pulled an envelope from his inner breast pocket and set it on the table in front of him. He then reached for the leather pouch, but Donner reached out with his good hand and stopped him. "Let's see what's in the envelope first."

The man, clearly shaken by the thought that the theft had turned into murder, nervously looked about the room. There were too many strangers. He began to re-think his choice of meeting places and shook his head. "Not here. Follow me."

He stood and stepped toward the kitchen. Donner hesitated, looked around, and then followed. I moved across the room to stand by the kitchen door to prevent a return to the dining area. Once behind the closed door, Donner's employer made his way toward the back door that led to the alley. It became obvious his purpose was to make the exchange and beat a hasty retreat. In a quiet corner, he stopped and opened the envelope enough for Donner to see his fee. The thief held out the leather pouch and they exchanged the items simultaneously.

Suddenly a voice spoke out in a lecturing tone. "You should have asked to see the necklace before handing over the money, Mr. Goldschmidt."

The young man spun around as a tall chef removed his hat and came toward him holding up a small revolver. "My name is Sherlock Holmes, and you are under arrest."

Goldschmidt gasped, took a quick look in the bag to find it was merely full of marbles, and then flung it at Holmes and lunged for the back door. Upon opening it, however, he was greeted by Inspector Hopkins and two uniformed constables. The inspector quickly subdued and handcuffed the culprit while Holmes and I escorted Donner out the door, rather than back through the restaurant. We all then came back around to the front through a side alley to rejoin Inspector Albertson, who had dropped off his prisoner at the beginning of this rendezvous.

Back at Scotland Yard, Hopkins locked up Donner and allowed Albertson and Holmes to question Anan Goldschmidt, brother of Yakub Goldschmidt, the jeweler who had sold the Gemini Necklace. I stood by, taking notes of the interrogation.

Albertson started by asking the obvious. "Does your brother know about this? Did he help you plan it?"

Anan, with his head down, shook it slowly, and said bitterly, "No, no, no! Yakub was not involved! He knows nothing of this."

"Then how did you find out about the necklace and where Noel Everest lived?"

"I work part-time at the store. I was the one who worked on the piece, and I overheard my brother and Everest talking about the weather, for there was heavy snow the day he picked it up. He mentioned that in Aylesbury the storm had passed south of them. So, I had a last name and a location. It took some time and a few well-spent coins, but I eventually found out where he lived."

Holmes spoke up. "Your crime appears to have been rushed. What was the hurry that you chose to go after the necklace at this time, instead of taking longer to plan something with a greater chance of success?"

The young man buried his face in his trembling hands and mumbled, "I owe money to some impatient people who aren't above using physical threats to collect. They demanded repayment before the New Year."

"Why involve Donner?" asked Albertson.

Holmes replied for the prisoner. "Look at his hands, Inspector."

Anan dropped his hands to the tabletop where they continued to shake despite his holding them together. Albertson gazed upon them and then asked, "You have a medical condition?"

The prisoner nodded quickly. "*Essential tremors*, the doctors say. It comes and goes, but I never know when, which is why my brother only lets me work part-time. I couldn't trust myself to sneak into a house and open a safe, and I certainly wouldn't attempt to hold a gun on someone. I've known Donner ever since I caught him trying to pick my pocket several years ago. I knew I could trust him to play his part for a share of the profit, as I knew enough about him to report him to the police if I ever had a mind to do so. I had learned enough information around town to discover the professor's connection to Oxford, and I learned of the Extravaganza. I returned to London to ensure I had an alibi, should I ever be suspected. When Donner informed me that burglarizing the house was impossible, I wrote him back, figuring their late return from Oxford, on the lonely highway, would be the ideal time for a robbery. Donner kept an eye on the Everests to make sure the lady was wearing the necklace that night when they left on the train. Then it was just a matter of waiting for their return. We felt sure they wouldn't spend the night in Oxford with a child awaiting Christmas morning at home. I don't know how you managed to get the drop on Donner, unless it was because his gun was only meant to scare you."

"What do you mean?" asked the inspector. "I unloaded that gun myself. He could have killed someone!"

"I think not, sir. Check the shells. They were loaded with rock salt. If necessary, he would have fired a warning shot. We didn't expect the Everests or the professor to go out armed while in their formal wear."

"Just one more question," said Holmes. "Why did you not go to your brother for assistance? Surely the profits of the jewelry store have made him a wealthy man."

"A wealthy *miser*, you mean! He may be my brother, but Yakub has had everything handed to him as the eldest son. He was always set to take over the jewelry store, but never learned to be a jeweler. He's merely a salesman with a talent for management. He pays others to do the work, whereas our father insisted that I had to learn the actual craft of jewelry-making. *I'm* the one with the talent! I was the one with the creative artistry to make that necklace to Everest's order. Yet Yakub takes the profits and pays his workers piecemeal. I was going to repay my debt and with enough left over to get out from under Yakub's thumb and go start my own shop on the Continent."

"The only place you'll be going for a while is Newgate Prison," Albertson replied.

The jeweler sunk his face into his folded arms on the table in despair while Holmes, the inspector, and I left him to contemplate his fate. Once outside the cell-block, I commented, "One could almost feel sorry for the fellow. He must have been truly desperate."

"Many criminals are desperate, Doctor," Albertson answered. "Or they're too lazy to do honest work. Or just plain evil. The law is the law and the victims must have satisfaction."

"Will he get the same punishment as Donner, who actually committed the crime?" I asked.

Albertson nodded. "It all falls under an act of conspiracy. He's just lucky no one got hurt, other than his co-conspirator. He and Donner will likely get the same sentence."

The law, however, did differentiate between the two men. Donner, as a repeat offender, was sentenced to five years hard labor. Goldschmidt was given a three-year sentence, and his medical condition allowed him to serve in a more sedentary capacity. When he was released, Holmes arranged an introduction to a jeweler in Amsterdam where Anan Goldschmidt still works to this day.

Professor Nichols, I am sorry to report, passed away in the spring following this adventure. Noel and Tina Everest still run the dairy farm, and Marjorie, though only in her teen-aged years as of this writing, is performing virtuoso violin concerts in the local theatres.

NOTES

1. Details can be found in "The Eighth Milkmaid" in *Sherlock Holmes: Adventures for The Twelve Days of Christmas* (Baker Street Studios, 2015)
2. In the late nineteenth century, Spitalfields was a largely Jewish community. Being next to Whitechapel, it lent itself to the misleading message of Jack the Ripper saying *"The Juwes are the men that will not be blamed for nothing"*.

The Conk-Singleton Forgery
by Alan Dimes

In her youth, Lady Lydia Conk-Singleton had been a noted beauty, and even now, well into her sixth decade, she was still an exceptionally handsome woman. Indeed, part of her attraction was that she had allowed herself to age naturally, without recourse to the dyes and heavy make-up so often resorted to by ladies of a certain age. Her hair was a little touched with grey, and her delicately featured face was pale. Nature had provided her with an erect carriage and a slim form, which she retained, despite having given birth to two children. Her husband, Lord Alfred Conk-Singleton, was some twenty years her senior. There were those who had expressed disbelief that he was finally giving up his bachelorhood, and presumed that he had married her because the necessity for an heir was pressing. Others found the match questionable, not only because of the difference in their ages, but also because Lydia Lilburn was the daughter of a northern industrialist rather than a product of the nobility.

But it wasn't long before all such doubts and reservations were summarily dispelled by the obvious and absolute devotion which existed between the couple. As well as serving as a shining example of marital harmony, their administration of the extensive Conk-Singleton estates was a model of aristocratic responsibility. They maintained the rents at a reasonable and affordable level and cared for their tenants, who knew that if they were in financial difficulties, or had other troubles, they could always look to the big house for help. In addition, the Conk-Singletons kept the parish church and the local school in good repair, despite the fact that there was no onus upon them to do so.

It was somewhat of a surprise, then, for both Sherlock Holmes and myself, when we received a telegram from the lady in question, informing us that she would call on us at eleven o'clock that morning on a matter of extreme delicacy and importance. What might have happened, we both wondered, to disturb the even tenor of their lives?

Lady Lydia entered our sitting room at exactly the stated time, clad in an elegant dove-grey ensemble. She took a seat opposite us and removed her kid gloves.

"Good morning, Lady Lydia," said Holmes. "You are most prompt. Would you care for some tea?"

"No, thank you, Mr. Holmes."

"You may go, Mrs. Hudson."

200

Having ushered the lady in, our housekeeper had hovered by the door in anticipation of Holmes's offer of refreshment.

"Now," said the detective as Mrs. Hudson's footsteps padded down the stairs, "how may Dr. Watson and I be of assistance to you?"

"Have you heard of Lord John Fleming?"

Holmes's thin lips pursed in distaste, and I fancy that my own expression must have displayed the extreme loathing that any decent person felt at the very mention of the fellow's name. An inveterate gambler and undoubtedly a cheat, married but an unscrupulous womanizer, he was one of the very worst men in London. He had investments in the Congo Free State and supported Leopold II's tyrannical regime in that unfortunate colony. There were even rumours, largely unsubstantiated, that he was a practising Satanist who carried out unspeakable rites of black magic at his crumbling ancestral manor in Cornwall.

"Oh, I have heard of him," said Holmes, "and considered it only a matter of time before our paths must cross. But what have you to do with such an arrant scoundrel?"

"In order to answer that question, I must go back some way into my husband's family history."

"Please proceed. I take it you will not object if Dr. Watson takes notes?"

"Not at all. It is common knowledge that the first Lord Singleton was given Hemsworth Hall, and all the lands that go with it, by Henry VII, as a reward for supporting the king at the Battle of Bosworth Field in 1485. The house was renamed Conk-Singleton Hall when the third Lord married the Duchess of Conques from southern France and combined their titles.

"In 1720, as a result of investing in the South Sea Company – which, as you may know, had a disastrous collapse – the tenth Lord Conk-Singleton's wealth was drastically reduced. In 1750, his grandson attempted to restore the family fortunes by sinking their remaining money into tea. By this time it had become the national drink, and clipper ships were making regular journeys between England and India and China. The twelfth Lord had purchased three such ships and, unfortunately they were several weeks overdue. They and their cargo were insured, but there must be definite report of their loss before the insurance company would pay up, and his creditors were becoming insistent.

"Alfred's ancestor borrowed a considerable amount to pay them off. But the man who supplied the money was one Lord Augustus Fleming, who up to that point Lord Conk-Singleton had considered a friend. Fleming took advantage of the twelfth Lord's fear of ruin and dishonour. He demanded the house and estates, which were worth at least ten times what was owed, as collateral against the debt. Should the clippers not return before a certain date, and bearing a cargo of sufficient value to cover the debt, Conk-Singleton Hall, and, as they say, 'all the lands appertaining thereto' would become the property of Lord Augustus Fleming."

"But clearly," I said, "that didn't happen."

"No. Lord Fleming disappeared shortly before the due date. Inevitably, some people claimed that Lord Conk-Singleton had murdered him, or had had him murdered. Fleming was addicted to gambling and brothels, so others thought he'd been killed in some vile den and his body tossed in the Thames."

"I have two questions," said Holmes. "First, was there any documentation, and does it survive? And second, Fleming must have had an heir – presumably Lord John's ancestor."

"I know of no surviving documentation, but Fleming claims to have a deed signed by the twelfth Lord acknowledging that he has failed to meet the conditions of the bond, and transferring ownership of the house and estate to Lord Augustus Fleming and his heirs in perpetuity. Signed by both parties. Alfred consulted his solicitor, and if genuine, it still has the force of law."

"There would have been a record at the Port Authority stating when the ships came in."

"Gone, though it isn't clear when. It doesn't seem to have occurred to Fleming's heir to try and track it down. He was Augustus Fleming's nephew, about seven years old when his uncle died, and living with his widowed mother, Fleming's sister-in-law, on a remote Scottish island. He was in his mid-twenties before he heard about any of this."

"There will still have to be civil proceedings before anything can be settled."

"I don't want that to happen, Mr. Holmes. I am here by myself because my husband is now seventy years old and in poor health. I'm not sure that his constitution could stand the strain of a public exposure of a stain on his ancestor's character. I dare not think what would follow if this document is upheld. We have said nothing to our children. How are we to tell them that they might lose their inheritance? And then there are our tenants. What will happen to them if the estate falls into Fleming's hands? I have no doubt that he will bleed them dry, raise the rents, and refuse to give them any assistance of any kind, whatever trouble they are in. The parish church is older than the Hall itself. Will a man like that do anything for its upkeep? You must help us, Mr. Holmes, Dr. Watson! You must! You must!"

Lady Lydia's aristocratic demeanour broke down in that instant, and tears welled in her eyes. I was about to go for my medical bag and obtain a sedative, but Holmes reached across to her, and she didn't demur as he took her hand in both of his and spoke in a soothing tone.

"Lady Conk-Singleton, you may rest assured that both my friend and I will do all we can to thwart this villain's plans. But what is there for us to do?"

The lady gently withdrew her hand and, after dabbing briefly at her eyes with a monogrammed white handkerchief, regained her composure.

"I apologise, gentlemen. There is one hope: We have the legal right to have the document examined by an independent agent, and as I have been informed that you have an expertise in these matters, I should like you, Mr. Holmes, to be that agent. Surely you can determine whether it is genuine or a forgery."

"I shall certainly do my utmost."

"We shall reward you handsomely, come what may."

"For the moment, I would merely ask you to defray any trifling expenses we may incur in the course of the investigation. Any additional payment you may care to make if the case is successfully concluded will be at your discretion. Now, I assume that this document is in the hands of Lord Fleming's solicitors. Their name and address?"

"Melmoth and Poole, 14 Old Fish Street, E.C. I shall arrange an appointment for you via my solicitors, Pettifer and Treadgold."

"We shall await your notification."

Lady Conk-Singleton rose.

"Thank you, gentlemen. I feel much better, knowing the matter is in your hands."

The head partner of Melmoth and Poole, Solicitors, of 14, Old Fish St, London E.C., was Sir Cecil Melmoth, a dry, cadaverous individual whose prevailing vice seemed to be the use of snuff. He sniffed a pinch of the powder into each flaring nostril of his hawk's bill of a nose and looked somewhat disdainfully across his desk at the three visitors whose arrival had upset the placid order of his morning. One of them he doubtless recognised as Donald Sedge, a junior partner in the firm of Pettifer and Treadgold.

"Sir Cecil," said Sedge, "allow me to introduce Mr. Sherlock Holmes and Dr. John H. Watson."

"Pleased to make your acquaintance, I'm sure."

"We understand that as you are Lord John Fleming's solicitors, he has left the document attesting to his ownership of Conk-Singleton Hall and its lands in your keeping."

"That is correct, Mr. Sedge."

"Mr. Holmes and Dr. Watson are here on behalf of Lord and Lady Conk-Singleton. You may have heard of them. They have assisted Scotland Yard in the solution of crimes, and the apprehension of criminals."

"I'm sorry, the names mean nothing to me. Nor do I see how any assistance they may have given to the police has any bearing on a civil case."

"Sir Cecil," said Holmes, "I'm sure you would concede that in a case of this kind, the provenance of such a document is of the highest importance, especially when so much property is in question, and after such a long time. Where was the document found?"

"At Fleming House, in an old box in a drawer containing several other papers from the same period. The box was locked and had clearly lain unopened for many years."

"Were there any others present when the box was found?"

"Lord John's wife and brother. They were also present when it was opened."

"I see."

"I thought you had a request, rather than questions. What is it?"

"We wish, as legal agents for Lord and Lady Conk-Singleton, to examine the document to ascertain whether or not it is a forgery."

"Ah," said Sir Cecil, "Lord John suspected that someone acting on behalf of the Conk-Singletons would make such a request, and, under my advisement, he is prepared to allow it – provided some conditions are met."

"Which are?"

"Firstly, that the person making such examination must do so here in these offices, in the presence of two or more witnesses appointed by his legal representatives. In other words, by us."

"I acknowledge your right to make that condition," said Holmes.

"At no point is the document to leave the sight of said witnesses."

"Agreed."

"Only one agent of the Conk-Singletons is allowed to be here in our premises to examine said document. Given that this chap here seems incapable of speech – " He looked over at me contemptuously. " – I'm assuming that will be you – What was your name again?"

"Sherlock Holmes."

Donald Sedge departed to walk the short distance back to the offices of Pettifer and Treadgold and Holmes and I hailed a cab to Baker Street

"I am afraid that Sir Cecil Melmoth is well within the law in insisting on such conditions," said Holmes as our vehicle rattled through the

204

cobbled streets of the City, "but you may rest assured that I shall give you a full report when I return from their offices tomorrow afternoon. Now, I don't know about you, but I suddenly feel a distinct need to drive the atmosphere of Number 14, Old Fish Street from my system. The Reichmann Quartet are playing in – " He consulted his pocket watch. " – twenty minutes, and I find that there is nothing like the sound of stringed instruments in harmony to sooth and invigorate the mind."

He raised his stick and thumped the roof of the vehicle.

"Cabby!"

"Yes, sir?"

"A change of destination. Wigmore Hall, and an extra five shillings for you if you can get us there before three o'clock."

Hans Reichmann and his three associates were indeed in fine form on that spring afternoon, and, as they embarked on the opening movement of Cherubini's *Second Quartet in C Major*, I turned to look at my friend as he sat, eyes closed and chin slightly lifted, totally absorbed in the performance. I marvelled, for perhaps the hundredth time, at the strange multiplicity of his nature. How, for example, the man who relentlessly pursued the criminal as the hunter pursued the beasts of the jungle might transform thence into the thinking machine whose keen logic saw through the machinations of lesser men, or into the being beside me, who could be transported to some other realm by the sublimity of music, and how, in some unfathomable fashion, each of these personae supported and strengthened the others.

The day continued in pleasant manner. We returned to our lodgings and had a splendid dinner, after which we sat and chatted in an aimless and desultory manner on various subjects – possible treatments for colour blindness, the early history of the papacy, the work of Joseph Bazalgette, and the poetry of Francois Villon – until, at about ten in the evening, Holmes stood up and glanced at the clock.

"I must bid you goodnight, Watson, for I suspect that tomorrow will tax my patience as well as my intellect, and I would be well rested."

As may be imagined, when Holmes returned late in the following afternoon, I was eager to learn what flaws he had found in the old document, and how the odious Fleming would be prevented from seizing the Conk-Singleton house and estates. But as he entered our living-room, it was immediately obvious that his examination hadn't been a successful one. I said nothing as he threw himself down into his customary armchair with a sigh and pulled his pipe from his pocket. I silently handed him his

Persian slipper and waited as he filled the bowl and applied a match to it. The first few inhalations of smoke seemed to lighten his mood a little.

"Watson", he said, "what do you know about the falsification of documents?"

"Nothing at all," I replied. "You have yet to write a monograph on the subject."

"Don't pretend that you spend any time reading my little efforts. Do you remember what you said about *The Book of Life*, the first one you ever saw?"

"As I recall, I called it the product of an armchair lounger whose theories wouldn't stand up if he attempted to put them to practical use, or words to that effect. But we have both come a long way since then."

"Then you have read them?"

"Well, I've glanced at one or two."

I was pleased to hear Holmes give a short barking laugh.

"Ha! I've had a frustrating day, and part of my irritation was that my old friend wasn't there to provide me with a sounding-board."

"I'm here now, Holmes, and you were about to enlighten me regarding the forgery of documents."

"So I was. Firstly, there is the material upon which the document is written or printed. Old vellum which hasn't been written on isn't so easy to come by these days, and it is relatively simple to discern if something is a palimpsest – that is to say, a piece from which the top layer, and the writing on it, have been scraped away and replaced by a different text. Fresh vellum is too obviously new to serve the forger's turn. In any case, the document was written on paper. I should have liked to take a flake of the page and examine it under the microscope, but I wouldn't have been allowed to do so. The paper had no watermark by which it could be dated, but it appeared to be of genuine eighteenth-century manufacture.

"Then there is the writing itself. Everyone's handwriting is ultimately based on the way they were taught at school, and the script children were taught a century or two ago is different from that which you and I use. However, my examination revealed no significant variations from the standard style of the eighteenth century. Next comes the ink. The ink of the period was made of a few very simple ingredients. In fact, many people made their own. Again, if I could have examined it under a microscope, I would have seen whether or not it contained any modern elements.

"Staying with the writing, we must consider the spelling and the style. Once more, I found nothing to arouse my suspicions. Last of all, there are the signatures, purporting to be those of the twelfth Lord Conk-Singleton and Lord Augustus Fleming. If either one of those could be proved false, it would invalidate the entire document. But with only one example of each signature, how was I to prove either false?

"I received permission to make a copy of the document, which I have here."

He produced a folded sheet of paper from the inside pocket of his jacket.

"I made a particular effort to reproduce the signatures as accurately as possible, and I flatter myself I did a fine job of it. Do you know where I took it to find signatures with which to compare my copies?"

"Somerset House?"

"Not a bad guess, but no. Fleming and Conk-Singleton were both aristocrats, members of the House of Lords, and I felt there were bound to be examples of their signatures in the archives of the Houses of Parliament. Normally one would need an appointment, but fortunately Cavendish, the archivist, was indebted to me because I had once disproved an allegation of theft which was made against him."

"Cavendish? I don't recall the name."

"It was before your time. I was still in Montague Street. My surmise was correct. Lord Conk-Singleton's signature on the document didn't seem to be exactly the same as that on a memorandum in the archive. Cavendish politely explained, however, that one's handwriting might change, temporarily or permanently, due to illness or old age. Were it not for the fact that he has been in Pentonville Prison for the last eight years, I might have thought it the work of our old friend Victor Lynch, had he decided to move from currency to documents. I am still convinced that it is a forgery. It would need an expert, or a team of experts, to carry it off, but it is far from impossible."

"How would it be done?"

"First you get an old, blank sheet of paper from the eighteenth century. There are plenty of them in existence. A page from the back of an old book, for example, where the text didn't run to the end of the section. Mix up a batch of ink using simple ingredients. Copy the script style and the writing style from books or magazines of the period – there are enough of those around, too. As to the difference between the two Conk-Singleton signatures, I can even explain that in another way to Cavendish. The signature on the document was shakier than the one in the archive. The document was written in 1752. Conk-Singleton was thirty-seven then, but his signature in the archive came from 1779, when he was sixty-four, and it was firm and clear. He died in 1792 at the age of seventy-seven. Yes, it's possible that he was ill when he signed the document, but supposing he wasn't?

"The main problem with forging signatures, or handwriting, is hesitation. It is difficult to produce something that flows in the way that the genuine article does. But this can be overcome, though the process is long and tedious. If you practice over and over again, eventually you will reach a point where you can produce a reasonable copy spontaneously. What's happened here, I think, is that the forger has done his practice, but the example he had to copy was from very late in Conk-Singleton's life, when his signature had become shaky."

"But we cannot prove any of this."

"No. But there must be something. I will re-examine this copy, and if I find nothing there, I will look at the original again tomorrow."

"Will Sir Cecil Melmoth let you?"

"Oh, I don't doubt he will puff and bluster, but the law is on my side. Remember, I am the Conk-Singletons' designated agent. I must have access to it until the civil case comes to court."

"Watson! Watson! Wake up, old chap!"

"What? What is it?"

Mrs. Hudson had cooked us a particularly fine dinner, accompanied by an excellent Chablis, and shortly after we had finished, I seem to have drifted into a light sleep.

I rubbed my eyes and saw Holmes standing before me, his face wreathed in a smile of triumph.

"Watson, luck has been on our side!"

"Luck? You have always said that a detective should never rely on luck."

"Nor should he, but when luck goes his way, he would be foolish not to take advantage of the fact."

"You've solved the secret of the forgery."

"I have indeed. I should have seen it from the very first."

"Are you going to tell me?"

Holmes's grin become positively impish.

"I think I shall take a hint from your fantastic little tales and leave the revelation until the *denouement*. In the meantime, here is my copy of the document. See what you can make of it."

"I don't need to look at the original?"

"No, no, the answer is there in front of you."

I looked at the sheet again and again but was unable to see what Holmes was driving at. After an hour, I gave up the attempt and took myself to bed.

The following afternoon found us once more at the offices of Messrs. Melmoth and Poole, nestled in one of the more archaic back streets of the City, where fish had once been on sale. Also present were Lady Conk-Singleton, Sir Cecil Melmoth, Donald Sedge, Lord John Fleming, his brother George, and his wife Lucy.

"I have complied with your wishes, Mr. Holmes, and with those of Lady Conk-Singleton," said Sir Cecil, "but this is very irregular."

"Irregular, but necessary," said Holmes. "I have irrefutable proof that the document Lord Fleming claims entitles him to the Conk-Singleton manor house and estates is nothing but a forgery."

"Impossible!" bellowed Fleming. He was a giant of a man with a heavy black beard and a red, choleric face. "The drawer containing that box with the document was opened for the first time in centuries, in front of witnesses."

"Witnesses? Your brother and your wife? Hardly impartial, or unimpeachable."

"You can't prove it's a fake, d--n you!"

"Meaning it is one?"

Sir Cecil Melmoth paused in the middle of taking a pinch of snuff.

"Lord John," he said wearily, "you are doing your case no good with these outbursts. And you, sir – Mr. Holmes – please come to the point."

"I shall very shortly, Sir Cecil, but first, I must ask your indulgence while I deliver a short history lecture. In October 1582, Pope Gregory XIII introduced the Gregorian calendar to replace the Julian calendar, which had miscalculated the length of the year by eleven minutes. Over the course of the centuries this had resulted in the date of the vernal equinox, which marked – "

"What the d----d Hell is this?" blustered Fleming. "The date of the document is *1752*, not *1582!*"

"As I said before, if you will please indulge me, the relevance will soon become clear."

Fleming's face flushed a brighter red and he sat back with a sour expression, but remained silent.

"Thank you, Lord John. Now, this error meant that the vernal equinox, which marked the first day of spring, was far too close to the traditional dates calculated for Easter. To correct this situation, Gregory excised eleven days from the month of October 1582. While this reform was accepted throughout the Catholic countries, the Protestant states rejected it, partly because it was a considered a Papist heresy and partly because it would create confusion over the correct time for the celebration of Christmas. But eventually, over one-hundred-fifty years later, Protestant countries began to accept it.

"Britain was almost the last to adopt the Gregorian system, and it is said that when the days were excised from the year, uneducated folk rioted, demanding, 'Give us back our eleven days!' This story is often told by those who love to depict the common man as irredeemably stupid, but if these riots did take place, it was probably because people were justifiably afraid that they would have to pay a full month's rent while only being paid for the smaller number of days they had worked that month. Now, Sir Cecil, I understand that the document has been placed once more in your safe. Would you do me the courtesy of removing it?"

The aged solicitor stood and went to the steel safe standing at the back of the room and opened it, carefully shielding the combination from everyone else.

He took out a manila folder and handed it to Holmes, who rose, turned back the flap, and passed it to Fleming.

"This is your document, sir?"

"You know damn well it is!"

"In that case, would you read out the date at the top, please."

"The eighth of September, 1752. What of it?"

"It may interest you to know that the year in which eleven days were finally excised from the British calendar was 1752. The month was September, the days in question being the 3rd to the 13th of that month. Could you explain to us all how this document came to be written and signed on a day that didn't exist?"

Fleming flung the paper to the floor with a snarl and rose from his chair, his face scarlet with anger, his powerful bulky body towering over Holmes.

"Well?" said the detective. "Can you?"

There was a firm knock at the door. I stood and opened it to reveal the familiar face of Inspector Lestrade, who was accompanied by two burly uniformed constables.

"Ah, good afternoon, Inspector. I trust you haven't been waiting long."

"Good to see you, Mr. Holmes. And you too, of course, Doctor. I got your note and came at once. Now, Lord John Fleming, I must ask you and your wife and brother to accompany myself and Constables Barnaby and Callaghan to Scotland Yard to be questioned on the matters of fraud and attempted extortion."

For a moment it seemed that Fleming was sizing up Barnaby and Callaghan to see if there was any chance that he could take them down and make his escape.

"Don't try it, Lord John," Lestrade said gently. "You wouldn't last two minutes. Come quietly. Cuff them, Barnaby."

Holmes bent down, picked up the document, and handed it to the Scotland Yarder.

"Evidence?" asked the inspector.

"Yes. It was evidence that Fleming thought would secure him a fortune, but now it's evidence that will send him to prison. His accomplices too, if you can find them."

Fleming lunged towards Holmes, but Callaghan and Barnaby seized an arm each and held him back.

"I'll break you, Holmes!" he screamed. "I'll snap you like a rotten twig!"

"So many have said so, but here I am, still unbroken."

"There's a Black Maria outside for you three," said Lestrade. "Let's not keep her waiting any longer."

Sir Cecil Melmoth reached into his waistcoat pocket and once more took out his little tin of snuff.

"Thank you for arranging this meeting at such short notice," said Holmes.

"You're welcome," said Sir Cecil, and sniffed up two pinches of the brown powder. "I underestimated you, Mr. Holmes, and for that I must apologise. There were a few other papers in that box of Sir John's. Might I ask you to take a look at them to check their authenticity? For your standard fee, of course."

"I would be happy to."

"Good. I shall send them 'round to you by courier tomorrow afternoon. Your address?"

"221b Baker Street."

It was pleasant to be outside once more in the spring sunshine.

Lady Lydia Conk-Singleton took the detective by the hand and said, "Thank you, thank you, Mr. Holmes! You have given our children back their future, saved our tenants, and lifted the clouds that loured upon our house. My husband can live out his remaining years in peace. All this is due to you, and here is a small token of my gratitude."

She reached inside her reticule and withdrew a folded cheque. Holmes opened it and said, "My Lady, this is most generous."

"'*The labourer is more than worthy of his hire.*' Now, here is my carriage. May I take you gentlemen back to Baker Street?"

The following day, Holmes was deeply involved in some abstruse chemical experiment when a thought struck me.

"Holmes?"

"What?"

"Something disturbing has occurred to me."

He swung round in his chair, a foaming beaker in his right hand.

"And what might that be?"

"There is no proof that the twelfth Lord Conk-Singleton's clippers actually *did* return to England in time for him to repay his debt."

"True enough."

"And for all we know, Conk-Singleton's ancestor may have actually had Lord Augustus Fleming killed."

"Again, that is undeniably possible, but what is your point?"

"Lord John Fleming's claim to the manor and estates may have been justified."

"Possibly, but would you have preferred that he had won the case?"

"Well, no, of course not."

"Then I suggest that you do not let it trouble your conscience, as I certainly don't intend to let it trouble mine. Do you know the philosophical conundrum of the drunkard with a hundred gold pieces?"

"I don't believe so."

"A drunkard has a hundred gold pieces, which he plans to spend on drink. Another man comes and steals his money, and distributes it to the poor. Who has the right of it?"

"Very well. I take your point."

The Case of the
Misbegotten Missives
by Daniel D. Victor

*For Tom Turley, who first introduced me
to the acquaintanceship
of Sherlock Holmes and Edith Wharton*

*Had ["Pomegranate Seed"] been a Sherlock Holmes story . . . the
terrified new wife arrives at Baker Street to tell her mysterious tale and
plead for help from the famous detective. But because this is an Edith
Wharton story instead, the plot advances into different territory. There
is no visit to Sherlock.*

– Ben Caps Walpole
Short Story Magic Tricks (blog)

Chapter I

"Your account of the affair was most intriguing, Dr. Watson," Edith Wharton said to me upon her arrival in our sitting room.

The American writer was referring to "The Aspen Papers", my narrative depicting the resolution of a case involving the distinguished author Henry James more than ten years before. Since the investigation concerned a professor at the University of Virginia, my account had appeared in the school's newspaper, where it had apparently caught Mrs. Wharton's eye.

"I must confess," our visitor hastened to add, "that I am not a frequent reader of *The Cavalier Daily*. But my friends know of my keen interest in all matters related to Henry James or his writings, and an alumnus alerted me to your story."

While I recognised in that last point a minor undercutting of her compliment, Sherlock Holmes viewed the matter more globally. With an encompassing sweep of his arm, he observed, "A regular French *salon* for Americans here in Baker Street, eh, Watson?"

I readily understood the sentiment. Thanks to our recent dealings with the likes of Stephen Crane, Hamlin Garland, and Richard Harding Davis – not to mention the earlier adventure with Henry James – one could easily discern the connection between a gathering of French intellectuals and the ever-growing number of American writers who have passed through the portal of 221b. [1]

As the most attentive readers know, at the time of Mrs. Wharton's visit, the latter part of May in 1900, she had yet to pen her most celebrated works – *The House of Mirth, Ethan Frome, The Age of Innocence.* Still, the lady had already produced numerous travel narratives, a number of short stories, and within the past year a novella called *The Touchstone.* What is more, within a few months, *Lippincott's Magazine* would publish her story, "The Line of Least Resistance", which would turn out to be the piece that attracted the aforementioned Henry James to her work and ultimately – as I was would later learn – lead to an abiding friendship between the two authors destined to last many years.

I should say from the start that Edith Wharton presented quite the dramatic image. Straight-backed and fashionably-dressed in a dark-violet frock of worsted with white lace at the collar, she sported a small matching hat upon a crown of coiled reddish-brown tresses. I reckoned her age at close to forty, and though a handsome woman with a barely turned-up nose and strong jawline, it was her light-brown eyes that most caught one's attention. Deeply set, they seemed to be all-knowing and, as a consequence, mournful and wise. While some might describe her deportment as stiff, I regarded the woman as stately.

In obvious tribute to the aura surrounding the American writer, it was Mrs. Hudson herself, and not our page boy Billy, who ushered the lady into our rooms for tea.

"So good of you gentlemen to see me," Edith Wharton said with a warm smile. "I'm visiting London with my husband, Teddy. World traveller that he is, he doesn't like to spend more than a few days in England, and London literary life in particular bores him." With a self-conscious chuckle, she added, "I might add that so does American literary life. Well, he's currently off yachting with some of his English friends, and I thought I'd take the opportunity to pay my belated respects to the principals who aided Henry James all those years ago."

"Thirteen," I remembered.

"One of these days," Mrs. Wharton mused, "I hope to get to Rye and meet the Master in person. Would you believe that twice we attended the same dinner parties, but on neither occasion did he notice me, and in those days I confess to lacking the courage to introduce myself."

"We're more than happy," I replied, "that you have introduced yourself to us."

With an approving smile at my salutation, Mrs. Hudson stepped back to allow me to escort Edith Wharton to the table. I should explain that whenever we had a female caller, our landlady always seemed to take extra care. Today's occasion was no different. The white porcelain sparkled, and a two-tiered serving plate boasted French *macarons* and small chocolate *éclairs*. Recognising that all was in order, Mrs. Hudson wished us well and exited our sitting room.

"Shall we?" I said, pulling out a chair for Mrs. Wharton and indicating that she help herself to the sweets.

Once our guest had seated herself, Holmes and I settled in. Mrs. Wharton carefully selected a most fetching *éclair*, and Holmes and I followed suit. My friend proceeded to pour the tea – a strong Darjeeling with a touch of Lapsang Souchong whose smoky flavour especially appealed to him – but before we could begin to savour the morsels, the tread of light footfalls climbing the steps to our door presaged an interruption. Predictably, a hesitant knock followed.

"Enter," said Holmes, and we were surprised by the reappearance of our clearly apologetic landlady.

Mrs. Hudson rubbed her hands together nervously. "I hate to trouble you, Mr. Holmes, but there's a woman come to see you. I told her that you and Dr. Watson are engaged, but she is most insistent. To be frank, she seems quite in need of your help."

"Oh, don't mind me," Edith Wharton said with the raise of her hand. "If someone is in distress, you must go on with your business."

Holmes nodded his thanks and rose. "Show her in, Mrs. Hudson. Let's see what this matter is about."

"Mrs. Alice Farthingale," our landlady announced and, after our latest caller had entered the sitting room, Mrs. Hudson exited, closing the door as she did so.

I joined Holmes in standing as he welcomed into our midst an attractive woman some thirty years of age. She was dressed in a suit of dark-blue wool and carried a black reticule in her hand. Her yellow hair was twisted into a tight *chignon,* and her wide blue eyes darted about the room, looking first at the seated Mrs. Wharton, then at me, and only finally coming to rest on Holmes who was positioned directly in front of her.

"You are Sherlock Holmes?" she asked.

"Indeed, Madam," my friend answered.

"I'm very sorry to disturb you," she said breathlessly, "but I fear I will lose my mind if I can gain no solution to my problem."

Holmes gestured in the direction of Mrs. Wharton and myself. "As you can see, Madam," he said, "we are at tea. This lady is the American writer, Mrs. Edith Wharton, and this gentleman is my colleague, Dr. John Watson. If your concerns can wait but half-an-hour, I shall devote all my attention to whatever it is that vexes you."

The woman shook her head and turned to our guest. "I have read some of your writings, Mrs. Wharton," she said. "In fact, I was especially interested in your *Decoration of Houses*. I am recently married, you see, and was hoping to make some changes in my new house like those you recommend."

"I'm flattered," said Edith Wharton, "but I'm compelled to admit that I don't consider my views on interior decoration to be part of my literary career."

"Alas," sighed Alice Farthingale, "my hopes of moving furniture about arose well before any of this current trouble came to light. In any case, I would be most appreciative of your insights."

Mrs. Wharton smiled in response.

"And not to worry, Mr. Holmes," the woman continued. "I have also read Dr. Watson's accounts of your work. I know how he has helped your investigations. I would welcome the aid of all three of you if only you can bring some sort of resolution to my problem."

Needless to say, the charming Mrs. Farthingale's appreciation of my sketches won me over. Edith Wharton nodded her participation as well, and we exchanged our seats at the table for the chairs of the sitting room. Thus it happened that, along with Sherlock Holmes and me, Mrs. Wharton also learned the details of our visitor's dilemma.

Indeed, as the psychological aspects of the situation unfolded, I could not help but imagine how, under the watchful gaze of the introspective American writer, the events of the case might very likely make their appearance in some sort of complex literary narrative, an interpretation quite unlike the more straightforward account which I myself was at that very moment beginning to commit to memory.

Chapter II

Not anticipating a three-pipe problem, I thought as I watched Sherlock Holmes withdraw a cigarette from the packet marked Bradley, Oxford Street, which I had fortuitously left on the side-table next to him. He lit the cigarette with a vesta he produced from inside a coat pocket and, tossing the match into a nearby ashtray, inhaled deeply.

At the same time, Mrs. Farthingale clasped her hands together tightly – so tightly, in fact, that her fingers were turning white. It seemed quite obvious she was bursting with the desire to tell her story.

Sherlock Holmes noted the anxiety as well. "Please explain to us, Madam," said he in a cloud of smoke, "just what it is that brought you here."

"The letters!" Mrs. Farthingale exploded. "Those infernal letters."

"Letters?" Holmes questioned. "From whom? Or should I be asking *to* whom?"

The woman let out a brief but hysterical laugh. "How foolish of me! I've put the cart before the horse. I'm – I'm not thinking straight. I must tell you my situation in order for my story to have any meaning."

"No need to hurry," Edith Wharton cautioned.

Mrs. Farthingale took a deep breath, straightened her skirt, and announced, "I am the wife of Leonard Farthingale, Q.C."

Holmes cocked an eyebrow. "The defence counsel," he said. Puffing on the cigarette, my friend leaned back in his chair in preparation for the detailed story that he expected was about to unfold.

"The same. And now he's gone missing. He left for chambers this morning, but he wasn't there when I went searching for him. That's why I'm so upset. That's why I've come to see you."

"For someone who hasn't yet been gone a full day," I offered, "*missing* seems too strong a term."

"On the contrary, Dr. Watson," countered Edith Wharton, "when a person is not where he is supposed to be – however short the time – it can be most disturbing."

Mrs. Farthingale smiled in appreciation. "I should explain," she went on, "that I am actually Leonard's second wife. He is some ten years older than I, and had been previously married. The poor man lost his beloved Margaret a year ago after nearly a decade of blissful marriage." She paused as if in contemplation.

"If I may ask," said I, "what happened to the first Mrs. Farthingale?"

Our visitor looked down and spoke softly. "She was killed – drowned, actually – in a boating accident last year. Leonard says it was somehow his fault – but before you ask, let me say that he's never given me the details."

"Farthingale," Holmes muttered. "A year ago. I seem to recall the accident."

"So do I, Holmes," I said, "There was a story in *The Times* about the tragedy. "

My friend rose and moved towards the shelf that contained his commonplace books. Pulling one down, he thumbed through the pages until he found the appropriate cutting. He raised a long forefinger and read aloud:

> "*The wife of barrister Leonard Farthingale died tragically in a boating accident off the coast at Dorset. According to her husband, the unfortunate Margaret-Anne Whish Farthingale, who could not swim, was swept overboard by a large wave.*

Not a strong swimmer himself, Mr. Farthingale was unable to reach his wife, and she drowned. Mrs. Farthingale's body was recovered the following day on a beach near Poole Harbour, where Mr. Farthingale moors his boat, the Margery-Anne. *The coroner's inquest is pending."*

Holmes replaced the book and resumed his seat. At the same time, the second Mrs. Farthingale added, "In spite of some nasty blows to the poor woman's head – no doubt the result of striking the railing when she was knocked into the water – the coroner ruled Margaret's death accidental."

Blows to the woman's head, I noted. At this hint of suspicious behaviour, I glanced at Holmes. He was contemplating the cigarette between his long fingers, but his narrowed eyes and tightly-drawn lips told me he shared the same concern.

"It's terrible to say," Mrs. Farthingale continued, "but in retrospect, Margaret's death made it most convenient for Leonard and me. You see, I first met him early last year at Covent Garden, when he was still married. As I recall, the opera was *Orpheus and Eurydice."*

"By Gluck," I remembered from somewhere.

"No," Mrs. Farthingale smiled sadly, "Monteverdi – the one with the sad ending. In retrospect, it seems fitting, no? A romantic tragedy. I was attending the performance with my aunt. Leonard had been invited by a mutual friend. Margaret Farthingale, you see, didn't fancy the opera. It was over wine during the second interlude that Leonard and I were introduced. I don't need to say that we took to each other immediately.

"Of course, it was only after Margaret's death that the two of us began stepping out together. Our social engagements were tentative at first – a dinner here and the theatre there – but inevitably one thing led to another, and after a few months, we married."

"How lovely for both of you," observed Edith Wharton.

"Indeed," Mrs. Farthingale smiled wistfully. "In truth, many of Leonard's friends had thought he would never get over the loss of Margaret. But he did, and I joined him in his beautiful house in Mayfair."

"Where, I assume," said Holmes, a shadow washing across his face, "he had lived with his first wife for many years."

"That's correct, Mr. Holmes. But aside from Leonard's desire to keep everything in its place the way Margaret had established it – all those overstuffed couches and chairs – we shared a wonderful home."

"It sounds positively stifling," Mrs. Wharton observed, comfortable with a topic more than familiar to the author of *The Decoration of Houses.*

218

"You say he wouldn't allow you to replace the furniture chosen by his first wife?"

"Indeed," Mrs. Farthingale answered. "Even though, like yourself, I prefer the simple and classical to the heavy and ornate, it wasn't any sort of problem."

"Houses, furniture," I interjected. "We're getting off the subject – though I do see Mrs. Wharton's point. Not allowing you to move things about doesn't speak well for letting go of the past."

"To be sure, Doctor, but Leonard was most decisive where it counted. Why, even before our marriage, he removed the portrait of Margaret from its position of prominence above the mantel in our sitting room and relegated it to storage."

"A good start," agreed Edith Wharton.

"I believe he simply needed more time," Mrs. Farthingale said. "We had a wonderful life together – that is, until those letters began arriving." She actually appeared to shudder. "The first one came about two months ago, and they've been arriving on an almost-weekly schedule ever since – dull, ordinary-looking grey envelopes, unfranked, dropped through the postal slot into the basket. They arrive at no particular time, so one cannot position one's self to observe who delivers them. Whichever servant discovers them puts them on the cherry-wood table in our vestibule to await Leonard's arrival. They are, after all, addressed to him."

"What is in these letters?" I asked.

"It isn't so much the letters that are disturbing, Doctor, but how they affect poor Leonard. The first time he saw one, he turned pale, and he breathed heavily. He looked agitated, frightened – like he'd seen a – a – "

"A ghost?" volunteered Mrs. Wharton.

"Exactly. Each time he finds one of those letters, he snatches it from the table and carries it with him to the library. He won't tell me whom they are from, but I have my suspicions. You see, the green ink and thin-lined handwriting look feminine to me, and I began to wonder if they were coming from a woman. It was the only explanation I could think of."

"Did you confront your husband with your misgivings?" asked Edith Wharton.

Mrs. Farthingale shook her head. "He becomes cross whenever I ask such questions. 'My business,' he claims and says no more about it. Then he goes off to the library to brood and shuts the doors. I don't dare follow."

"My word," I said.

"In the end, I decided I must take some course of action. I must do something. These letters were coming between us. Last week, another one arrived, and it was then that I reasoned a change of scenery might be in order. I hoped a bit of travel might sort things out. Thus, when Leonard

219

came home that evening, I suggested we leave London for a time, that we go off somewhere on our own, just the two of us. Frankly, I didn't know what else to do."

"And what did your husband have to say to that suggestion?" I asked.

"He told me he would have to think it over."

"Why?" Mrs. Wharton questioned sharply.

Alice Farthingale shrugged. "What I truly believe is that he had to share the idea with the woman who sends him the envelopes."

"Get permission from her, do you mean?" I asked.

"Yes, Doctor, that is precisely what I mean. Still, when Leonard returned home yesterday, he said he needed a day to set things in order, but that I should prepare for a trip to commence the day after tomorrow. Though he didn't tell me our destination, he indicated we might take the boat. I was overjoyed."

The boat again, I thought with not a little concern. Yet all I said was, "That sounds like good news – an opportunity for a fresh start."

To my chagrin, however, Mrs. Farthingale's shoulders sagged.

"Good news," I repeated, "but still you remain upset. Why might that be?"

"This morning, another envelope appeared – Number nine by my count. Leonard hadn't yet come downstairs, and I just stared at it. I know that to open someone else's mail – especially when addressed to one's husband – isn't appropriate behaviour. It's immoral. Where is the trust? But on the subject of these mysterious letters, the matter had grown too strained between Leonard and me to let it go. His legal correspondence was sent to his chambers. These have to be personal. I needed to look inside that envelope."

Mrs. Wharton nodded in agreement. She seemed to understand Alice Farthingale's motivation.

"It took but a moment to realise I had no other choice. I plucked up the envelope and hid it in the pocket of my dressing gown. I would steam open the flap, read its incriminating contents, and – if need be – paste it closed and return it to its spot on the table. Or that was what I thought at the time . . . ."

Holmes had said nothing until Mrs. Farthingale uttered these final words. Now he asked, "What did you discover?"

Mrs. Farthingale smiled wryly. "I can do better than just tell you, Mr. Holmes," she said and moved the black purse from the side of her chair to her lap. "See for yourself." Then, much to our surprise, she proceeded to open her reticule and produce a small grey envelope. From where I was seated, I could barely discern an address written in a pale-green script.

220

Sherlock Holmes flashed a quick smile, then extinguished his cigarette in the ashtray. With his steel-grey eyes shining, he secured a magnifying lens from the nearby desk and held out his open palm in front of Mrs. Farthingale. Upon it, she placed the envelope.

No sooner did Holmes begin to scrutinise it than she said, "A woman's handwriting – don't you agree? Not bold, but small and neat. Lots of curves and rounded letters."

Holmes said nothing. With his lens hovering just above the paper, he studied the penmanship. After a few moments, he raised an eyebrow. "Quite observant, Mrs. Farthingale. I have written a monograph on handwritings and can attest that your observations about a woman's script appear to be accurate.

"The thin lines are usually due to the size of the hands. Men's hands are larger and have been observed to possess shorter second fingers compared to the fourth, resulting in a less predictable and thicker script. Of course, that a woman's behaviour is expected to be more refined than that of a man also contributes to the differences in their penmanship. Yes, indeed – most feminine in its structure – and yet . . . ."

His voice trailed off as if his thoughts were flying elsewhere." A moment later, however, he resumed his commentary.

"As for the ink, there is nothing distinctive. Sherwood green – a carbon-water-gum solution. Diamine, I believe. The fact that it is lighter in colour than might be expected simply indicates that it has been blotted."

Next, he turned his attention to the paper. "Quite right about the stationery as well, Mrs. Farthingale. Nothing outstanding about it either. Like the ink, it could be bought at my local shop."

"What of the contents?" I asked.

"Yes, the contents," repeated Edith Wharton. "Do tell us, Mr. Holmes."

The envelope had previously been opened by Mrs. Farthingale, and it remained unsealed. Carefully raising the flap, Holmes withdrew a folded piece of stationery coloured the same grey as the envelope. Unfolding it, he held up the small paper by its edges for all of us to see.

"Why," observed the American woman, "it's blank!"

Indeed, for all the worry and concern shown by Mrs. Farthingale, there was no message from a mysterious lady – or from anyone else, for that matter. One could only speculate if all the other letters contained blank pages as well.

Holmes held the paper to the light. "No disappearing ink. No watermark. Nothing."

"I wondered if the blank paper might be a code or sign of some sort," said Mrs. Farthingale. "But with no message for Leonard to read, I decided to keep the envelope instead of replacing it on the table before he came downstairs. I felt no compunction about denying him some vital information arising from a blank sheet of paper. On the other hand, an empty page – assuming the other envelopes contained the same – seemed to do nothing to alleviate Leonard's agitation."

Mrs. Wharton nodded once more.

"I must also tell you that when Leonard walked into the entry hall this morning, he looked 'round – almost as if he expected the letter to be there. Upon finding nothing, he turned pale and exited."

"Strange," I murmured.

"I assure you, he looked so upset, so distraught, that I worried about him most of the morning. Finally, I hired a cab to go to his chambers – Wilfrid Forresters in Lincoln's Inn. I was determined to assure myself that he was all right. I told Emily, our maid, that I was off to look for Leonard. I also told her that if I couldn't find him, I was going to hire a consulting detective – which would be you, Mr. Holmes – to look even further.

"When I finally arrived at Wilfrid Forresters, the office clerk reported that Leonard had never come in this morning. Nor did Leonard have any meetings scheduled elsewhere. In short, my husband has disappeared. That's why I came here."

Chapter III

"Surely," I observed, repeating my earlier concern, "it's too short a time to be so distressed."

Sherlock Holmes, however, furrowed his brow and steepled his fingers. "Is there anywhere that your husband might go when he is upset? Anyone he might seek to visit?"

Mrs. Farthingale managed a facetious smile. "You mean, of course, someone besides the woman who sends him the letters."

"Quite so," said Holmes. "A friend? A brother? Some other relative? Someone you know?"

"His mother. She lives in Wilton Crescent in Belgravia. I thought of going to see her earlier, but decided to come here instead."

"All things considered, Mrs. Farthingale," said Holmes, "a wise decision. None the less, we most definitely should pay his mother a visit. Why, your husband may have done so himself – may even be there now – though I think that development to be extremely unlikely." Holmes turned to Edith Wharton and me. "I'll accompany Mrs. Farthingale to Belgravia. No sense in overwhelming her mother-in-law with the presence of all of us."

Immediately, I felt cut out of the investigation. From Edith Wharton's irked expression, I judged she felt the same.

"I'd prefer to go along," I said. "And not to speak for Mrs. Wharton, but I'm certain that she feels the same."

"Although you are indeed speaking for me, Doctor," the American lady pointed out, "I most certainly would like to accompany you, Mr. Holmes. I'd like to see this story through to its *dénouement.*"

"Agreed," Holmes said quickly. "I'll arrange for a four-wheeler. But if the two of you wish to accompany us, you must remain in the carriage until Mrs. Farthingale and I have concluded our visit. Rest assured that we will furnish you a complete report."

Chapter IV

Darkness was beginning to set in, and a chill wind blew up the road. To combat the weather, Holmes had donned his Inverness and hat. I, an overcoat and bowler. Neither woman had prepared to be out in the night air, but Mrs. Hudson had come to their rescue by offering them each a woollen coat, one black, the other navy-blue. We huddled in a group by the kerb in front of 221b as Holmes raised his hand to flag a four-wheeler, and soon a pair of black horses pulling the growler were reined in before us.

Seated in the carriage – Holmes and myself opposite the two ladies – we bounced and jostled as the brief drive began. Accompanied by the rumble of the carriage, we headed south down Baker Street, traversed Mayfair in the proximity of the Farthingale home, turned into Park Lane, passed Belgrave Square, and eventually arrived at the white, stuccoed line of terraced houses in Wilton Crescent, each home more elegant than the next.

"Quite the neighbourhood," I observed.

"Leonard's father was Sir Reginald Farthingale, baronet," Mrs. Farthingale explained. "Like his son, he too was a Q.C. He died a number of years ago, and his elderly widow still lives in the house."

The four-wheeler rolled to a halt in front of the appropriate residence, and Holmes and Mrs. Farthingale exited. Edith Wharton and I watched the pair approach the front porch, walk between its two white columns into the yellow glow from the fanlight, and come to a halt upon the black-and-white checkerboard tiles. Holmes looked to see that the carriage remained in place and then turned round to knock on the japanned outer door. A liveried footman opened it and welcomed Mrs. Farthingale and her guest. The door then closed, and the two of us in the carriage sat waiting for it to open again.

"Leonard and Alice Farthingale," Mrs. Wharton observed, "seem a most disturbed couple."

"We don't know what will be learned from this interview," I cautioned. "Perhaps, it's too soon to judge."

Edith Wharton regarded me with an expression I can only describe as pitying.

Chapter V

A quarter-of-an-hour later, Holmes and Mrs. Farthingale emerged from the Belgravia house. My friend led the lady to the growler, and she took his offered hand in order to climb in.

Just then the driver shouted down. "Where to, Guv?"

Sherlock Holmes held up a forefinger. "A moment," he shouted back.

Looking as frantic as she had before the present excursion, Mrs. Farthingale gathered her skirts and, as before, settled onto the leather cushion beside Edith Wharton. "Madness," Mrs. Farthingale muttered cryptically. "Utter madness."

"Leonard Farthingdale's mother has heard nothing from her son," Holmes reported as he seated himself next to me, "but she did say that she wasn't worried about him. 'He's probably working late,' she explained to us. 'His father maintained long hours as well,' she said. Then she asked her daughter-in-law, 'Just what makes you so concerned? After all, you saw Leonard this morning.'"

My thought exactly, I recalled.

"I hadn't intended to worry the woman," explained Mrs. Farthingale. "She's well into her eighties. But I found I could contain myself no longer." Here she became quiet.

Edith Wharton and I both looked at Holmes for an explanation.

"Mrs. Farthingale showed her mother-in-law the same letter she'd showed us," Holmes said.

"The blank paper as well as the envelope?" I asked. "How did the old woman react?"

It was Mrs. Farthingale who answered. "She never bothered to look at the blank page, for after only one glance at the envelope, she gasped, 'It is *her* handwriting.' 'Whose?' I demanded, finding it difficult to believe that my mother-in-law could discern the identity of my unknown rival so quickly. And yet her answer was even more incredible."

"Whose handwriting was it?" I questioned.

"Yes," Edith Wharton wanted to know, "who is this *femme fatale*?"

"'*Fatale*' is just the right word," Mrs. Farthingale smiled wildly, "for my mother-in-law actually stated that the handwriting on the envelope belonged to none other than Margaret-Anne, Leonard's first wife!"

"Why, that's preposterous!" I exclaimed. "She's dead."

"Quite dead, Doctor," replied Mrs. Farthingale, "which is why I told her that her claim was absurd."

Edith Wharton, appearing to sense some grander meaning in the story, murmured, "Persephone calling out from the Underworld."

"Nor does such an explanation," Holmes observed, "whether his mother believes it or not, reveal *why* her son has gone missing. Let us return to your house, Mrs. Farthingale. If your husband is to reappear, perhaps the comfort of the home he once shared with the woman now dead will serve to attract him."

Mrs. Farthingale bit her lip at Holmes's directness.

"The same home," I felt obliged to add, "that he now shares with the woman he loves."

Edith Wharton took Mrs. Farthingale by the arm. "Let me accompany you, Alice. Perhaps I may offer some sisterly strength."

"That would be much appreciated," Mrs. Farthingale said softly as she laid her hand on top of the American's.

Holmes leaned out the window of the carriage. He shouted the Farthingales' address up to the driver. A moment later, the carriage gave a lurch, and we shot forward.

Mrs. Wharton and I both shook our heads in commiseration. No envelope could possibly contain the writing of a dead woman. Obviously, there must be a logical explanation.

For his part, Sherlock Holmes scowled. "It is what I feared," he said. "An alienist would need to confirm my view, but I'm certain that Leonard Farthingale's behaviour fits that of a man suffering the pangs of intense guilt. Whether premeditated – Remember the alleged blows to the head of his first wife? – or not, in Farthingale we find a husband who quite obviously blames himself for the death of his wife."

"What reason might Farthingale have for wanting his first wife dead?" I asked Holmes.

It was Edith Wharton, however, who answered my question. "It doesn't take an alienist, Doctor, to understand that what takes place between partners in a marriage is most truly known only to the two of them. Perhaps it was time for a change."

"Quite so," said Holmes. "In any case, following his wife's drowning, Farthingale appeared to return his life to normality. He mourned appropriately and then in due time introduced to society the new young woman with whom he would share his world."

"Indeed," said Mrs. Farthingale.

"And yet," Holmes continued, "despite his second marriage, one mustn't be misled, for still he grieves. Indeed, so intense is his grief that he has tried to bring his former wife back into the real world."

"You can't be serious, Holmes," I charged.

"But I am. Leonard Farthingale may or may not be responsible for his first wife's death, but he *believes* he is, and that is all that matters."

To prove his point, Holmes held up the grey envelope with the green writing. "Notice how the '*e*' in *Farthingale* falls below the line," he said, "and how the crossbar on the upper-case '*F*' bends downward instead of parallel to the baseline. These are *masculine* tendencies. Oh, by themselves they prove nothing, but what we know about Leonard Farthingale leads me to only one conclusion: The poor man mastered his first wife's handwriting and sent himself these missives in some tragic attempt to convince himself that she is not dead. I should imagine it was enough for him to write the address – to compose an actual letter, to create the dead woman's thoughts and feelings, lay beyond his abilities."

It was this sad state of affairs that all of us contemplated as we travelled north in the growler on our way to the Farthingale home.

Chapter VI

Another row of terraced white houses. Another set of japanned outer doors with fanlights above them. Another set of entrances framed between two Romanesque pillars. Compared to the previous visit, however, this one was quite different.

"Thank goodness you've come home, ma'am!" cried the wide-eyed maid who opened the door to the four of us. She was dressed in black and wore a white cap and white apron. It was upon the latter that she now wiped her hands, hands which Mrs. Farthingale actually grabbed hold of.

"Why, Emily!" she demanded. "What is the matter?"

"It's the Master, ma'am. He came in most upset. He said he'd been walking by the river all day. Then he looked for the grey letter I put on the hall table this morning. I told him you'd taken it and that you were out searching for him, and that you were going to see a detective about the whole matter if you couldn't find him. 'No! No! No!' he shouted. But I wasn't wrong, was I, ma'am?"

"No, Emily," Mrs. Farthingale said calmly, "you were quite right."

"When he couldn't find the letter, ma'am, he locked himself in the library, and – "

The single loud gunshot startled us all, and Holmes and I quickly followed Mrs. Farthingale as, her yellow hair askew, she rushed down a corridor and came to a halt in front of a pair of oaken doors.

"In there – " she gasped.

Holmes hammered on the right-hand door. "Farthingale!" he shouted, but of course there was no answer. After he tried again with a similar result, we exchanged knowing glances and put our shoulders to the wood. It required a couple of runs, but the doorjamb finally splintered, and the doors swung open.

The scene in the library was as one feared. In a chamber lined to the ceiling with leather-bound volumes, the sulphurous smell of gunpowder filled the air. At the far end of the room stood a mahogany desk across which slumped the body of a man seated in a red-leather turning chair. His head faced left on the desktop, a spreading pool of blood beneath it beginning to drip onto the floor. Next to the growing stain of red lay a Webley pistol. It rested below the fingers of the right hand that dangled lifelessly to the side.

"Leonard!" screamed Mrs. Farthingale, running towards the grotesque figure. Fortunately, Holmes intercepted her and moved her away. At the same time, I hurried round the desk to feel the man's neck for a pulse, though I knew I would find none. In shaking my head to convey the inevitable, I noted an open briefcase lying on the floor next to the turning chair. In it were a stack of grey sheets and a collection of grey envelopes. Knocked on its side, its liquid contents mingling with the poor man's blood, lay a small, open bottle of Sherwood green ink.

As horrible as it all was, the scene served to corroborate Holmes's view of the matter. Mrs. Farthingale, who also saw the paper and bottle, must have felt the same, for as we led her out of the library, she sobbed, "Leonard's off to be with his Margaret . . . ."

There wasn't much left to do but call the authorities. Holmes made his way to the front porch and blew upon his silver police whistle. In fashionable neighbourhoods like Mayfair and Belgravia, it requires but a few short minutes for a constable to arrive – in this case, a policeman who recognised Sherlock Holmes.

"There's a man inside this house who has shot himself," Holmes told the officer. "He's quite dead. Ask for Hopkins or Lestrade at the Yard, and tell which ever one you find to come here directly."

"Right you are, Mr. 'Olmes," the constable said. With an informal salute, he marched off down the road.

Holmes and I returned to the sitting room where Edith Wharton had already secured a brandy for the shaken Mrs. Farthingale.

"On our drive back to Baker Street," my friend told the distraught woman, "we'll convey you to your mother-in-law's home. You shouldn't be alone tonight."

Half-an-hour later, the clopping of a horse's hooves and the rattle of a carriage heralded the arrival of Scotland Yard.

Pursing his lips and pushing back his bowler as he entered the house, Inspector Lestrade greeted my friend. "Not your usual murder this time, eh, Mr. Holmes? A bit strange to find you at so commonplace a death as a suicide – even if it is that of Leonard Farthingale." With a pronounced sense of importance, he added, "*Q.C.*"

Holmes cocked an eyebrow. "To a great mind, Lestrade, nothing is commonplace."

The inspector ignored the comment and, producing a small notebook, began to record the tragic details furnished by Holmes.

"We're returning to Baker Street," Holmes said once Lestrade had completed his report. "And we're taking Mrs. Farthingale, the wife of the dead man, to his mother's home in Belgravia. Your questions can wait till tomorrow."

With the maid's furnishing her a wrap, Mrs. Farthingale handed me the coat our landlady had given her earlier that day, and we moved towards the outer door. But not before Edith Wharton cast her eyes about the premises as if to assure herself that the various details – the worn armchairs, the sash curtains, the marble flagstone near the entrance – would be permanently fixed in her memory. Perhaps she was already composing the story in her mind.

We deposited Mrs. Farthingale in Belgravia and continued on to Baker Street without incident. Yet the tragedy of the evening wasn't far from the thoughts of any of us. One doesn't soon forget the bloody image of a suicide like Farthingale's – nor, if Holmes's analysis was correct, the twisted reasoning that led the poor man to pull the trigger. Whether Edith Wharton accepted Holmes's interpretation of the poor fellow's demise, I could only wonder.

"Would you believe," I informed her once we had returned to 221b, "that in connection with the Aspen case, Henry James and I actually agreed to pen our own accounts of the affair. His appears in the story he titled 'The Aspern Papers'. Perhaps, Mrs. Wharton, you and I might attempt to write our own versions of what could be called 'The Farthingale Letters'."

"An interesting suggestion, Doctor," Edith Wharton said as she removed the coat Mrs. Hudson had lent her and handed it to Holmes. Then, with her piercing, light-brown eyes levelled directly at me, she added, "but a little too soon on the heels of the horrific events of tonight to contemplate such a strategy. Besides, the tragic tribulations of the Farthingale family bear little in common with my current literary venture."

"And what might that be?" I asked, wondering where a mind like hers might lead.

"I've been working on a novel which takes place in northern Italy during the time of the French Revolution. [2] It has little in common with the mental state of a madman. And yet," she mused, "one cannot deny that the fate of Leonard Farthingale is a most haunting story – mythological in its properties really."

Edith Wharton looked quietly off to somewhere only she could see. In her silence, Sherlock Holmes and I were left on our own to ponder just what ghosts the strong-willed lady sitting before us might eventually set free. [3]

NOTES

1. To learn more about such encounters, see Daniel D. Victor's series entitled *Sherlock Holmes and the American Literati*.
2. Edith Wharton refers to *The Valley of Decision*, the work she liked to call "*the Italian novel*". Published in 1902, it was her first full-length novel.
3. Edith Wharton would not take up Dr. Watson's suggestion until 1930, a year after his death. To determine whether Wharton's supernatural interpretation of the Farthingale case probes the human soul more deeply than does Watson's "*more straightforward account*" – as he himself described it – interested readers may compare the two narratives for themselves. "Pomegranate Seed" appears in *Ghosts*, an anthology selected by Wharton. An audio version of the story may be found on *YouTube*.

The Missing
Mathematical Timber
by Ian Ableson

In his position as an investigative detective in the private sector, my friend Sherlock Holmes often filled a rather curious niche for his clients. Whereas the police in general and Scotland Yard in particular were obligated to concentrate their time and resources on only those problems that could be definitively identified as crimes, Holmes had no such restrictions. As such, much of his work through the years took place in that curious grey of difficulties – and sometimes severe difficulties – that nevertheless had little to no criminal activity involved. Certainly murder, arson, kidnapping, burglary, and conspiracy do happen, but most of the problems that people face on a day-to-day basis are of the more mundane variety. One of these in which this was most immediately apparent was the case of Tobias Longhurst, a tall, square-faced structural engineer with an impressive Franz Josef beard who came to 221b Baker Street one late summer evening.

As a note to those blessed individuals who read my writings with any degree of regularity, it will be noticed that I have not disguised the university at the center of this tale as I did with previous recounts (see "The Missing Three-Quarter" and "The Creeping Man"). The reason for this is twofold. One: There is a structure at the center of this story that will be immediately recognizable to anyone with even a cursory knowledge of the city where it is located. Secondly: The conclusion of this particular riddle (and arguably even the mystery at its core) is so innocuous that I sincerely doubt any trouble could possibly come from identifying the location where it took place, particularly after a span of time has passed.

Longhurst spoke in that curious mumbled monotone that one sometimes comes to expect from men who spend most of their days amongst drawings and numbers and significantly fewer hours in front of an audience. Nevertheless, his language was clear and concise, and he proved easy to understand.

"It's an unusual bridge, Mr. Holmes, very unusual indeed. Have you spent much time in Cambridge?"

"Oh, here and there."

"There's a bridge that spans the River Cam to connect two different parts of Queen's College. Officially they call it the Queens' Bridge –

231

although which queen I'm not sure. I'm not as well versed in history as I ought to be – but those of us who are carpenters, engineers, and architects have come to refer to it as the Mathematical Bridge. It's a wonder, Mr. Holmes, it really is. Designed back in the eighteenth century – 1749 to be precise – by a man named William Etheridge. Master carpenter, truly a genius of his time. The frame of the bridge is constructed of long wooden timbers, each a single straight piece, and yet placed at a very precise angle to give the overall bridge an arching structure. I won't bother you with the exact specifications, but it's an exceptionally efficient use of timber, and practical besides. It lets a man replace any single timber without having to take apart the entire bridge.

"Well, incredible though it may be, there's no design that can prevent wood from suffering the effects of the weather, and as it happens, it's time for some of the timbers to be retired. My lads and I were hired to take apart the bridge and replace a few parts of the structure. Not changing the design, mind you – You couldn't pay me the king's ransom to be the man who destroyed the Mathematical Bridge! – but just to replace some of the lumber with pieces of the same size and type. It's a good contract, Mr. Holmes, and we are being paid well for it.

"We arrived to begin the project just this past Tuesday, and assuming the delivery of fresh lumber arrived in a timely manner, did not expect to need more than a week for the full replacement. The university posted bulletins well in advance regarding the date that work would commence, so the bridge and the surrounding grounds were empty and free of student and citizen alike when we arrived. That was very appreciated on our part, as work inevitably moves slower when inquisitive passers-by wish to know our business, and I have no doubt it would have gone even slower if we'd had to explain that the bridge was out to some unending stream of harried students. An alternative river crossing can be found close by, not one-hundred-and-fifty feet along the River Cam. It's a cast iron bridge, put up in the early 1840's – not nearly as much character as the Queen's Bridge, I will grant you that, but perfectly serviceable all the same.

"The first two days went as smoothly as can be expected. We were able to remove the pieces in question without much difficulty, again mostly owing to the bridge's exceptional design. However, the lumber wasn't delivered on Wednesday, as it was meant to, and we received a telegram that it wouldn't arrive until Friday. I considered looking for a local source of lumber and cutting the beams ourselves, but due to the extreme precision with which each beam must be laid to ensure the bridge's stability, rushing the matter seemed unwise. Frustrating as my crew and I found the lapsed schedule to be, the unexpected respite wasn't entirely unwelcome, and we each enjoyed a day in Cambridge in our own fashion. When we returned to the mostly deconstructed bridge, two things were clear. One: That the lumber had been delivered sometime late Wednesday or Thursday, not on Friday as was specified in the telegram. The second was a much odder thing to notice: One of the beams that we'd removed from the bridge was missing.

"Now, I will grant you this seems an odd thing to notice, so allow me to first clarify that we had left the pieces of lumber that we'd removed in a neatly arranged pile, such that it would be easier to remove it from the site later. Also, because it was a relatively small number of beams, we hadn't yet removed them – if we should discover, halfway through replacement, that another timber needed replacing, it could be added to the pile, and we would take all of them away at the end. Thus, upon our arrival at the site, we determined very quickly that one beam in particular – one of the tangential members of the radial trussing, though I don't know whether those words mean anything to you – had vanished in the time we'd been away. The timbers themselves are large and unwieldly, and they would be exceptionally difficult to take away without anyone noticing. Besides, if one wanted to steal some wood, why not take one of the new, unguarded pieces, stronger as they would undoubtedly be? I have already contacted the men who delivered the fresh lumber, and they insist that they had nothing to do with the matter, being unsure whether the wood might be reused.

"I can't even say it's a crime, not in good consciousness – we ourselves likely would have put the old wood to the torch, unless the university wished otherwise, or we found a carpenter somewhere in need of some scrap. Nevertheless, it is a mystery, and one that will bother me if it isn't resolved. And even if they are scrap, they're *historical* scrap, and I feel it is my duty to put them to rest in a respectful manner. Is it a crime to steal that which no one else desires? I am an engineer, Mr. Holmes, not a historian, and thus I find myself unable to answer such philosophical quandaries. It's for this reason that I came to you rather than the police. I've heard before that you deal with an exceptionally wide variety of problems, and so it seemed that you might be the best candidate to help me find our missing timber. As an engineer, I am a man of numbers, and you may rest assured that I understand my curiosity will cost me, and I have come prepared to pay for your services, but I am nonetheless determined to see this through if I can."

Despite the strangeness of the tale, Holmes had listened to Tobias Longhurst's story with the same dedication which he brought to every case, with only the smallest twinkle in his eye reflecting the nearly farcical nature of the request. Personally, my eyebrows had raised somewhat over the course of the story. During my time with Holmes, we had been tasked with finding an astonishing variety of missing documents, jewels, weapons, personal effects, and of course people of all kinds. Never in my memory had we been asked to find something quite so innocuous as one piece of scrap wood destined for a pyre.

"Mr. Longhurst," said Holmes, "I believe you did right in coming to me. As you say, the police would likely have laughed you out of the station. You say that you noticed the timber to be missing this morning. Given the lateness of the hour, am I correct in assuming that you and your crew put in a full day's work today?"

"Yes, Mr. Holmes, we did. Despite my personal curiosity, I couldn't very well justify abandoning my lads for a day to come track you down. No matter your answer, I will be on the first train back to Cambridge in the morning so that I might direct my crew tomorrow."

"I figured as much. It is in some ways a pity. Undoubtedly the physical activity involved in bridge replacement will have tamped down most of the signs that the site would show us. Nevertheless, perhaps we'll be able to find some clue as to the fate of your missing wood. I am no stranger to flights of curiosity, Mr. Longhurst, as it lends itself well to my profession, and I well understand the frustration of a riddle unsolved."

Longhurst's honest face broke into an expression of clear relief that he hadn't been laughed out of the room. "It is a question that has grabbed hold of some piece of my mind, Mr. Holmes, and it has thus far refused to let go. As I mentioned earlier, these are large beams, and the amount of labor required to remove one of them would be staggering. Who on earth would do such a thing? Why bother stealing an old timber, and if you're going to start stealing old timbers, why stop at one?"

"I hope that we will be able to provide you some peace of mind, Mr. Longhurst. Watson, how do you feel about lunching in Cambridge tomorrow?"

"Well, there is a pub whose ploughman's I'm rather fond of."

"Well then, Mr. Longhurst, it sounds as though we will be joining you on that early train to Cambridge."

We arrived at Cambridge early the next morning, and from there it was but a half-hour's pleasant stroll to the location of the bridge in question. In my previous academic life, I had spent some time there visiting friends and attending the odd medical conference, but I hadn't been in some time. The town woke up much the same way as any other university town: Bleary-eyed students bicycling, walking, or stumbling to class, shaking off the effects of the previous night's hours-long session of hard study or even harder carousing. Very few establishments were open yet, apart from the odd café distributing coffee and light breakfasts to these academia-plagued souls.

When we reached the half-constructed bridge, we found Mr. Longhurst's laborers had already returned to the site, smoking and milling around in the manner of working men without any current instruction. They greeted Longhurst and nodded to Holmes and me as fellow professionals. Seven or eight long timbers sat in a neat pile to one side of the bridge.

"Here we are, Mr. Holmes, Dr. Watson. A rather uninspiring sight, I'm sure. I suppose you'll have to take my word for it that there was one more timber in the pile here."

"Truly, I doubt that you would bring us here under such false pretenses. Tell me, was there anything unusual about the timber in question?"

"No sir, not so far as I am aware."

Though his words were directed to Longhurst, Holmes was watching the ring of men arranged behind him. Some small shift or little change in expression in one of the workers caught his attention. He was a young lad, perhaps in his late teens, who towered over Holmes and myself and had a solid build reminiscent of a rugby player. He had an open, honest face with a square jaw and a shock of blond hair, brightened considerably by a life spent laboring out of doors. Holmes must have spotted something in it, for he singled the man out.

"What's your name, sir?" Holmes asked.

The man shifted uncomfortably, but answered nonetheless. "Eli, Mr. Holmes. Eli Benton."

"Did you notice something unusual about the timber, Mr. Benton?"

"Well . . . Yes, sir, but I don't know if I'm the best man to talk about it." He turned to Longhurst, guilt on his face. "Sorry, sir. I didn't say anything about it on account of I didn't think it'd come up."

"I'm sure Mr. Longhurst will forgive your reticence, my good man," said Holmes cheerfully. "Please, share your observations."

"See, Mr. Chatburn and I, we were the ones that did the work of removing that timber from the bridge, so I had a good amount of time to look at it. There was a carving in it, Mr. Holmes – I mean, an unusual one. You look over at these – " He indicated the pile of timbers stacked behind him. " – and there's plenty of little markings on them. Fellows with a penknife putting in the name of the girls they fancy, or their own initials on account of their vanity, or maybe rude pictures. But this one was different. It was high quality work, Mr. Holmes, the sort what's done by someone who knows proper carving and knows his wood burning, too. And it looked old to me, but it hadn't faded much in the weather like most of the other old carvings do, on account of it being properly done. But strangest of all, Mr. Holmes, was its *spot*. It was on the side of the timber facing outwards to the river, rather than one of the sides facing the bridge or upwards. It'd have been devilishly tricky to do, Mr. Holmes, if you'll pardon my language. I mean, even a tall man couldn't have reached the spot from the shore. You'd practically need to put a ladder in the river to reach it, and I don't think I need to tell you the risks involved there. It seems an awful lot of trouble just for carving, especially given the amount of time it likely would have taken."

Despite his initial hesitation, Benton's words poured out of him like water from a tap as soon as he started talking, and it was clear that he himself had put some thought into the mystery carving. Holmes smiled at him, cutting in as he took a breath.

"And this carving? What did it depict?"

At this point, Benton deflated somewhat. It was clear the wind had gone out of his enthusiasm. "Well, Mr. Holmes . . . that's why I wasn't sure if I was the best man to talk about it. Never was much one for book learning, you see, and I didn't spend a long enough time at school to really get the gist of letters. But it was letters, Mr. Holmes, of that I'm certain. Although some of them were numbers, but I didn't look too closely at them. I was never much of one for mathematics either, I'm afraid."

"Ah, I see. Not to worry, Mr. Benton. Did anyone else see the carving to which Mr. Benton is referring?" All of the surrounding laborers shook their heads, as did Longhurst. "Well then, let us start with the basics. Mr. Benton, how many separate words or numbers were there?"

"Two, Mr. Holmes. One on top of the other."

"And was there a pattern to the letters and numbers?"

"The numbers were on the bottom. The top were all letters. Fewer numbers than letters too. Three or four numbers in the bottom row, I think – I can still count! – unless the first one wasn't a number. It might have just been a line."

"Interesting. And did it appear that the letters and numbers were added at the same time?"

"The carvings all looked the same to me, so I reckon that they were."

"Anything else unusual?"

"Nothing that comes to mind." The man was still a little deflated, and I sensed that his illiteracy was causing him some amount of embarrassment.

Holmes clapped the man on the shoulder. "Thank you, Benton. Your observational skills have been a true boon to us." Benton's chest puffed up a little more at that, and some of the vigor returned to his body. Another man stepped forward, this one tall and wiry and with a substantial salt-

and-pepper mustache. He was significantly older than Benton and may have been the oldest man present. Scars on his face and bare arms indicated a long life in physical work. When he spoke, his voice was rough and gravelly, a stark contrast to Benton's light tones.

"A moment, sirs. I've one more thing to add. Name's Chatburn. I'm the one that removed the timber with Benton. There's one more thing that he, in his youth and inexperience, may have missed. Most of the timbers here are the same cut – might not be all from the same tree, but close enough to make it look right once the bridge is constructed. Wasn't the case with that one. It was different. Still looked right on the bridge – years of weathering will help with that – but it wasn't from the same order of lumber, I can tell you that much. Wood grain was wider. Lot more knots too." Chatburn trailed off, and it was clear that he had no more to say.

"Thank you very much for this contribution, Mr. Chatburn. You have both been most enlightening. Now, if I might ask all of you gentlemen to allow me the usage of the site for a few minutes, perhaps I will be able to gather some traces of our missing beam."

He pulled me aside for a moment as Longhurst and his crew turned their attentions towards discussions of the next phase of reconstruction. "I must say, Watson, this case has proven somewhat more intriguing than it seemed at the outset. When we agreed to come to Cambridge, I'd half expected to find a pile of woodchips and other signs of an opportunist with a hatchet and a need for firewood, but it seems that there may be more significance to this vanishing than it seemed. Sit tight for a moment, my dear doctor. I don't expect my investigations will take long."

Holmes's predictions proved correct. After a scant few minutes of examining the riverbank, he called my attention. "It's as I suspected: Longhurst is right that to haul away so large and awkward a timber down the middle of a Cambridge street likely would have caused something of a stir. But there is little need to carry such an item by hand in a city with such an active punting community. See here – this unnaturally square-shaped gouge out of the riverbank? They must have dragged the timber into the river from there. I'm not sure whether they tried to get it in the boat or merely let it float down the river, guiding it by hand from their own vessel, but the result is more-or-less the same. Mr. Longhurst!" he called, "have you any idea where we might rent a punt at this early hour?"

And so it was that Holmes, Longhurst, Benton, and Chatburn and myself found ourselves squeezed into a punt, rented from a small establishment a quarter-mile upstream. Longhurst had chosen to bring the two laborers along, both due to the part they played in the gathering of information, and to help haul the missing timber if it should prove necessary. Benton, with his muscled stature, took the role of punter. The long pole looked surprisingly slender in his massive hands, and he had no problem propelling the five of us and the boat down the Cam.

We must have made an odd sight, five men floating down the river, leaning out and shouting whenever we noticed the slightest abnormality along the riverbank. Poor Benton was so distracted by the search that every once in a while he forgot his responsibility in regards to steering and sent us drifting into the bank.

Unsurprisingly, despite the enthusiasm on display by the rest of us, it was Holmes who first noticed the signs of a timber dragged up the side of the bank. Benton guided the punt over so that we might examine the area more closely. Several deep, unnaturally rectangular marks in the mud – sure signs that the beam in question had been dragged, dropped, or both – were all that we needed as proof. Benton beached the punt on the riverbank, and we disembarked as smoothly as we were able.

"A step in the right direction, indeed, Mr. Holmes!" exclaimed Longhurst. It was by far the most excited I'd ever seen the man in the brief time we'd known him. He pushed his way through the bank's vegetation with no apparent regard for the mud and small tears that it left in his clothing. "But I must confess, this seems a small step indeed in the grand scheme of the mystery. We know where the timber left the river, but to find its ultimate home still seems an insurmountable task."

"Oh, I'm not so sure of that," said Holmes lightly. "If a few deductions can be accepted as the most likely solutions, then I believe we have enough information to find our missing beam. The search is afoot!"

After hiding the punt amongst the riverbank vegetation – one must never be too careful – we five climbed up the bank and set off. Holmes's keen eyes gave us an initial heading based on a few small marks, but these signs soon disappeared, swallowed by the busy traffic of university town roads. We'd emerged relatively close to St. John's College, just north of a bridge known as the Kitchen Bridge, and from there made our way to Trinity Street. Holmes seemed inexplicably confidant that the timber hadn't been taken onto university grounds.

From there, Holmes entered one business after another, with the other four of us following behind. In each of these he would take a brief look around, ask a few questions to whomever he might be able to find, then offer his thanks and take his leave, with the other four of us matching his steps like a collection of lost ducklings. We didn't enter every shop on Trinity Street, far from it. We first walked into a busy barber's, then skipped several buildings to visit a legal office, and then crossed the street to a market dealing in colorful home decorations. To my eyes, these establishments were chosen seemingly at random, but there was no doubt in my mind that our visitations were guided by a logic of Holmes's own devising.

On the sixth visit, to a small but cheerful pub known as The Gyrefalcon, we were met with success in the most blatant way imaginable. As soon as our eyes adapted to the dim lighting as opposed to the beaming morning sun, I heard cries of astonishment from Chatburn and Longhurst, and an excited laugh from Benton. There, leaning against the back wall behind the bar, was a single loose timber, nearly as high as the ceiling. Two words were ornately carved near the top of the beam, their interiors clearly charred by wood-burning:

Established
1738

Early in the day as it was, the pub was mostly empty, save for a short, thickly bearded man who I took to be the owner, a thin and lanky bartender cleaning glasses, and a few murmuring breakfast patrons, all of whom turned to face the minor commotion caused by two excited laborers and their supervisor. The bearded owner followed their lines of sight, and the moment his eyes found the timber he went very still. He sighed deeply and scratched at his face, his expression a mixture of resignation and frustration. To his credit, he seemed determined to face up to his troubles, and he put down the tray he was holding and marched over us with his head held high.

"Gentlemen," he said, addressing all of us, "might I help you with anything?"

"You've got our missing bit of bridge!" Benton boomed. His voice – nearly as large as he was – echoed through the little pub. "Chatburn and me, we pried that off the Mathematical Bridge just two days ago! What the devil do you want with it here?"

The bearded man was immediately on the defensive, although he was clearly working to hold his tongue in front of his customers. "I'll have you know, gentlemen, that this beam belongs *here*, and any persons who may have brought it to The Gyrefalcon were only returning it to its proper home."

"Perhaps we might discuss this," said Holmes, sliding smoothly into the conversation, "over some cups of morning coffee? While I believe I understand the gist of what has happened here, I must confess that I am immensely curious about some of the details. I believe you can rest assured, sir, that this is more a matter of curiosity than a formal investigation, and I don't believe anyone present is interested in pressing charges regarding theft of property that was, until recently, public. Am I correct in this assumption?" he asked, turning to Longhurst and his crew.

"No interest, no interest at all!" Longhurst cried. "I'm delayed enough on this project already without hauling the bureaucrats into this. But I must know why you've gone to all this effort, Mr. . . . ?"

"Entwistle," said the man. "Thomas Entwistle." He seemed visibly relieved at Holmes and Longhurst's statements. "Well then, gentlemen, why don't you take the table by the window, and perhaps we might have a frank discussion about all this.

We gathered and sat as Entwistle poured coffee. As he did, I noticed an additional, furtive movement around his own mug, and suspected that he may have added an additional fortification to his coffee to help him get through the conversation to come.

"The first thing you need to understand, gentlemen, is that this pub, The Gyrefalcon, has been in my family for several generations. We aren't the oldest pub in Cambridge – not when you've got a few that'll swear up and down that King Harold dined there on his way to fight William the Conqueror – but we've been around for some time. It was my great-great-great-grandfather, Robin Entwistle, that founded the pub, back in 1738, as it says on the beam back there, but it came very close to closing within his lifetime. Eleven years after he opened it, a great fire tore through this section of Cambridge, including The Gyrefalcon. Thankfully, it wasn't completely incinerated – the bones of the building were still standing, but much of the interior would need to be completely reconstructed. Now, the pub had been doing rather well, but Robin Entwistle didn't have the funds necessary to make the needed repairs, and he was considering closing shop and leaving Cambridge entirely.

"As luck would have it, this was when William Etheridge, a renowned bridge designer, made a visit to town. Etheridge was a close personal friend of Robin's, as they'd known each other as lads in Suffolk, and he had been a regular visitor to The Gyrefalcon whenever his work brought him to town. By this time, Etheridge had already made a name for himself as a master carpenter and architect and was reasonably well-to-do.

"Well, he found Robin standing in the singed remains of his pub, nearing despair, and he offered to put up the funds for the repairs on the spot. Robin, however, wasn't a man to accept charity, and would only accept the money as a loan. Etheridge disagreed, but he was a smart man, and wished not to wound Robin's pride. As the two men argued, Etheridge noticed one of the very few parts of the interior that was mostly undamaged by the fire – a support beam near the back wall. The bottom of the beam had been charred significantly, and it would certainly need replacing, but the rest of it was miraculously untouched. At the top of the beam, my great-great-great-grandfather had carved and wood burned that inscription into it back when the pub first opened.

"'Look here,' says Etheridge, 'it isn't charity. I'm going to pay you to loan me that beam back there so that I might incorporate it into the new bridge I'm designing to stretch across the Cam. It's the absolute perfect length.'

"'A loan?' asks Robin incredulously. 'See here, William, that isn't a loan! A loan would imply that one day you give me the beam back!'

"'A loan it shall be,' declares Etheridge. 'One day, many years in the future, when the structure of the bridge is in question and the whole thing needs rebuilding, you can have the beam back.'

"Well, gentlemen, that made Robin laugh, and William laughed along with him. And they struck a deal. Certainly, my great-great-great-grandfather knew that it was a joke – nothing more than a thin veneer of exchanged services to cover the generosity of a friend. Nevertheless, he was true to his word, and once enough of the interior had been fixed to ensure the integrity of the building, he and his family hand-delivered the beam to the construction site of the Queen's Bridge. Etheridge, with great enthusiasm, placed the beam front and center, facing the downstream of the River Cam.

"That means the carving's been there – why, over one-hundred-fifty years!" cried Longhurst. "It's held up remarkably well!"

"Well, sirs, I won't pretend that the family hasn't touched it up a little bit over time. Cleaned it out, added a little oil here and there for the sake of proper preservation . . . As I mentioned, it's been quite a source of family pride. Besides, charring is a wonderful way to preserve wood.

"Robin and Etheridge may have joked about it, but it was always something of a source of pride for our family, and they told the story to Robin's children, who passed it down the generations, and my wife and I have done the same. Whenever we'd take the children punting along the Cam, we'd point it out to them. 'Look, there's our family beam! That's your great-great-great-great grandpa's handywork, right there!' Soon enough, they were of an age where they'd tell it to us, rather than us to them.

"When the postings went up about the bridge's reconstruction, it was as though someone had walloped me in the gut. The Entwistle beam has been a staple of Cambridge for my entire life, and the lives of my forefathers as well. To let it be removed and destroyed was near heresy for my family, and we all had a gloomy few weeks as we waited for the inevitable.

"It was my brother that first suggested we take the beam. He isn't with me in the pub, but he runs a wonderful cheese shop down the road.

'Look here, Thomas,' he said, 'maybe it's a crime, but it's one without victims. If we let events take their natural course, the family beam will be burned or sold for scrap, which does little good for anyone. The crew who rebuilds the bridge likely won't be Cambridge folk at all. It'll mean nothing to them. We'll wait for night to fall during construction, sneak over there in a punt with as many Entwistles as we can gather, and carry it to The Gyrefalcon for safekeeping until we figure out something else to do with it.' I agreed, but on one condition: I insisted that if we took the beam into the pub, it wasn't just going to be here for safekeeping. Even if it couldn't serve its original structural purpose, we'd find a way to affix it to the back wall, to be displayed for many generations of Entwistles to come.

"Well, sirs, we did more or less exactly as we planned. We gathered as many of our cousins and uncles as we knew lived in Cambridge, took a couple of punts out in the dead of night, and reclaimed the Entwistle beam. We were sure that no one would notice, but we seem to have been mistaken. It's been a whirlwind, sirs, it certainly has."

All of us had listened to the man's tale with various levels of astonishment, but Longhurst was clearly the most enthralled of any of us, and when Entwistle finished he sat back in disbelief. "My word!" he said. "I never imagined such an intricate tale could come to light with the disappearance of a single length of wood. It's remarkable!"

Entwistle stood. "I apologize, Mr. Longhurst, for the delay that you and your crew have undergone. I will confess that we were so preoccupied with righting this perceived injustice to our family that it hardly occurred to us that our impulsive reclamation would put a pause on the work."

Longhurst, however, was preoccupied, his attention riveted on the beam that he could just barely see over Entwistle's shoulder. "Hmm? Oh, not to worry. It's a story, that's for certain, and it has made this project even more unique than it already was. But I do have some concerns about the placement of the beam. Do you intend to leave it where it is?"

Entwistle hesitantly shook his head. "I do not, sir. If possible I wish to attach it to the wall there, but I haven't yet been able to do so. I must confess my own knowledge of carpentry is limited."

"Hmm. Thankfully, mine is not," said Longhurst, standing. He strode over to the beam, testing its weight with a hand. "Chatburn! If you would please return to the work site, fetch two or three lads and our tools – I'll leave the details to your discretion – and bring them here, I'd be much obliged. Benton, retrieve our punt and take it upstream to the put-in dock, and make sure you return it to the same folks we rented it from, understood? I'm going to stay here and assess the building for a reinforced location and determine a method of attachment." Both men nodded their assent and left, Benton bounding out of the door like a birding dog with target in sight.

"You'll help me put it up?" stammered Entwistle, clearly bewildered. "But . . . the delay to your work . . . ."

"A delay of one day will hardly put us over budget, Mr. Entwistle. And as a structural engineer, I'm afraid I cannot abide the safety hazard presented by leaving a large beam leaning haphazardly against a public wall." Longhurst's serious face split, only momentarily, into a wide grin. "Which isn't to say you're getting our labor for free. What do you say to supper for the crew? It's hard work, reconstructing a bridge. A hot meal at the end of such a day is worth its weight in gold."

Holmes and I made our exit soon after Entwistle finished stammering his thanks, our part in the events of the day well and thoroughly completed.

On the train back to London, I asked Holmes to share his thoughts. While I of course couldn't deny that my friend's methods had been effective, I nonetheless was baffled by his reasoning. He gazed out the window as he spoke, taking in the beautiful countryside view as the train rumbled out of Cambridge.

"From the good Benton's description, I thought it likely that the lower string of numbers was a year. Four numbers, starting with a one – or a line, as Benton thought it may be – and below a single word. There were a few options for what that word may be, but I thought *"Established"*, or something similar, to be the most likely option. Given Mr. Chatburn's account that the wood itself differed from the rest of the bridge, it seemed very likely that the timber had been taken from some other building, one that has been around since before the bridge's construction in 1749. Very few businesses last one-hundred-and-fifty years or more, which left the possibilities limited. Thankfully, those that do tend to proudly proclaim their longevity. The next time you find yourself in Cambridge, I advise you to take a closer look at the sign on The Gyrefalcon: *'Owned and Run by the Entwistle Family Since 1738'*. Every shop we stopped in today had a similar sign outside, each noting their founding date to be sometime before 1749."

"But how did you know that the establishment itself had gone to reclaim the timber?" I asked.

"I didn't – or at least I couldn't be sure – but I thought it most likely. If a single individual, or even a small group, had an attachment to the timber, I thought it would be most likely that they would have simply chopped off the top section sporting the carving, that it might better be displayed in the home. But there were no splinters, sawdust, or any other sign of woodwork at the site. A timber like the one we saw on the bridge needs a large building for display. And it had to be connected to a local as well, for only a local could have kept such a close eye on the Longhurst team's progress. There were other options to be certain, but in this case the solution that seemed the most likely at the onset was proven to be correct."

"As always, it sounds so simple once you've explained it."

Holmes turned from the window, the smallest whisper of a smile playing on his face. "It nearly always is. Humanity is a curious beast. I know of no other animal that would exhibit such sentimentality over a piece of wood based solely on the stories of generations long gone. It is a source of great consternation for any reasonably minded soul."

"Perhaps," I agreed, "but possibly such a notion does not warrant our disdain. Through all of our adventures, I have come to view the idiosyncrasies of our species to be a subject of some affection, rather than consternation. What curious attachments we display towards items of personal or historical significance are really attachments to the people and stories that we associate with them. And that, in my mind, is a very key feature of humanity indeed."

Holmes's hint of a smile expanded. "Watson, the country's philosophers missed out on a most optimistic addition to their ranks when you chose a life of medicine. And in this case, I think your mindset is far more beneficial than my own. Perhaps I will strive to align my thinking a little more closely to it."

We enjoyed the rest of the ride back to London in companionable silence.

The Mathematical Bridge

The Adventure of the Elfrincham Maze
by Alan Dimes

The events surrounding the death of Edward Crawley in the hedge maze at Elfrincham, West Sussex, are no longer fresh in the public mind, and may therefore serve as the basis for the following narrative, which reveals, for the first time, the part played in the case by my friend, Mr. Sherlock Holmes, and, to a somewhat lesser degree, by myself.

It was a beautiful, sunny morning in late June. From the window of our sitting room in Baker Street, I looked down to see young couples stopping before the shop windows, the men dapper in their summer suits, the young women bright as new blooms in their gaily coloured dresses. No one abroad in the thoroughfare that day seemed to be in a hurry. The traffic was full but not heavy, and even the tradesmen in their carts seemed content to amble on at little more than a snail's pace. The sun beamed down on rich and poor alike, and while there was undoubtedly work to be done, its warm rays imparted a holiday atmosphere to the day's proceedings. In all, it seemed an improbable venue for the consideration of such things as murder, but having lodged with the world's first consulting detective for some years, I had become accustomed to the fact that violence and crime could rear their heads in the unlikeliest of circumstances.

The morning's glad sunshine was certainly no guarantee that all was right in the world.

Holmes was in the midst of composing a short, bright piece for violin. The mid-morning had been punctuated by little bursts of music, between which he wrote or crossed out notation on the sheet before him on his desk. I sat in my usual armchair and picked up one of H. Rider Haggard's fine adventure stories set in the African veldt.

Mrs. Hudson entered with a telegram for Holmes, who seized it eagerly and, after running his eyes over it, gave a bark of satisfaction.

"Ha! Thank you, Mrs. Hudson."

As our landlady turned to go, Holmes smiled at me and said, "Well, Watson, it is as I expected," and passed me the message. I put my book down. The telegram read:

Elfrincham Maze case proving a puzzle. Would be grateful if you could come down to assist. Have booked rooms for you and Dr. Watson at Crown Hotel in High Street.

Inspector Walcott
West Sussex Constabulary

"Walcott is a sound fellow, if a little slow," said Holmes. "You may recall, he brought us in over that business in Arundel Castle."

"The theft of the Gainsborough?"

"Exactly. Now, my friend, what do you know of this Elfrincham affair?"

"Only that Edward Crawley was found dead at the centre of the maze."

Holmes took a slim volume from his desk.

"I picked this up in Paternoster Row yesterday afternoon," he said, handing it to me. "It will provide you with all the information you need to understand the background to the case."

I looked at the spine. It read: *The Hedge Mazes of England* by H.R. Kitson.

"A train leaves from Victoria Station in – " He glanced over at the clock on the mantelpiece. " – forty minutes. I'm sure ten minutes will suffice for you to gather all the necessaries for our little trip, so I shall meet you downstairs at a quarter-past-eleven."

Soon we were ensconced in a comfortable smoking carriage on the 11:45 to West Worthing. Holmes was immersed in the last two days' newspapers, so I opened the little book by H.R. Kitson to the chapter on the Elfrincham Maze and read:

> *The hedge maze in the grounds of Elfrincham Manor in West Sussex has not achieved the same measure of fame as, for example, the celebrated maze at Hampton Court, despite its being the largest and most complex such maze in England. There are two probable reasons for this: Firstly, it was originally planted in 1594 but has not been in continuous existence since then, having been destroyed by fire in mysterious circumstances in 1726. It was replanted in 1797 in accordance with the original ground plan. Secondly, it has never been open to the general public.*

A tradition was established in 1810 whereby, on the weekend of or before each Midsummer's Day, exactly forty guests are invited to stay at the manor, and from those forty, four men and four women are chosen by lot to enter the maze at sunset. The lots are kept in two large leather bags, one for the men and one for the women, which have been replaced a few times over the years, but the majority of the wooden lots date back at least as far as the replanting. They are simple wooden discs, and four in each bag have a star painted on them. First a man picks from their bag, and then one of the women from the other, until all eight starred discs have been taken out, and then they are paired off according to the order in which the discs were picked.

The maze has five entrances. One man and one woman go in at each of four of the entrances, and the first couple to emerge from the fifth, which faces the doors of the manor house, are proclaimed King and Queen of the Maze for that year. Famous past winners include Lord Byron in 1813 (accompanied by Lady Anthea Brigstock), and Lord Balmoral and the Duchess of Abergavenny in 1865. The tradition has continued to this day, despite the purchase of Elfrincham Manor by Lord and Lady Caerphilly from its original owners, the FitzAlwyn family, in 1871.

The rest of the chapter went on at some length about the exact species of hedge used in the planting and replanting of the maze, and the similarities and differences between the Elfrincham Maze and others in England and on the Continent, in terms of the difficulty of their solutions and the nature of the patterns they formed. Before I had reached the end of this discussion I closed the book, as I deemed that such facts were unlikely to have any bearing on the solution of the case. It was enough that I had learned that since it had been Midsummer's Day the previous weekend, Edward Crawley must have been participating in the contest of the maze when he was killed.

Holmes had dispatched a telegram to Inspector Walcott just before we had left, so when we arrived at West Worthing he was waiting for us with a dogcart. Walcott was a tall, beefy man, slow of speech, with an amiable, open expression on his broad, rubicund face. He shook us both warmly by the hand and thanked us for coming. He was, as Holmes had said, a sound fellow, but while I had no doubt that his solid physique was an asset when it came to dealing with the type of criminal he was most likely to encounter, I recalled from the Arundel Castle case that he was a

247

little lacking in that faculty of imagination that Holmes considered an essential factor in the art of detection.

"Elfrincham isn't too far from here," Walcott said as we climbed into the cart. "About fifteen minutes, and then only about another five to the manor."

"I should like to examine the scene as soon as possible," said Holmes.

"Begging your pardon, Mr. Holmes, but the young woman who found the body is also staying at The Crown. She has to leave later today, as she's taking ship to America tomorrow. I was sure you'd want to speak to her."

"I would. Is she leaving for good?"

"No, she's visiting relatives in New York. She's given me a signed affidavit. And don't worry, I've made sure the scene remains undisturbed."

Holmes looked in my direction with a rueful little smile. I knew he had little faith in the ability of the police to leave the location of a crime untouched, but at the same time he didn't wish to malign the well-meaning Walcott.

A few minutes later we arrived at The Crown, a rather more impressive establishment than one would expect, considering the size of the village and, after depositing our luggage in our respective rooms, we were taken by Walcott to see Victoria Pryce-Jones.

She was a slim, pretty young woman with an abundance of thick, wavy brown hair braided into a long plait which hung over her left shoulder. I sensed that she possessed a natural vivacity which was still somewhat suppressed by the shock she had sustained a couple of days before. It is no small thing to be in the presence of a dead body, especially when one is aware that a life has left its mortal shell as a result of violence.

"Mr. Holmes! Dr. Watson!" she exclaimed. "I am so glad that you have come! Inspector Walcott told me you would be here. If anyone can solve this terrible crime, it is surely you. I am ready to answer any and all of your questions."

Holmes nodded. "My first question must be: Why are you staying at this hotel? Surely, as a participant in the maze game, you could be at the manor house. It has fifty guest rooms, or so I read, and the players traditionally stay for a few days after the King and Queen of the Maze have been honoured."

"That is so, but I could stay there no longer, Mr. Holmes. To awake every morning and see the maze – to be reminded of the horror I found there – was more than I could bear."

"I see. Now, Miss Pryce-Jones, I have some of the facts, but I would be obliged if you could take us through the events of that evening. Pray give us as many of the details as you can, then we'll trouble you no longer and you can prepare for your journey."

We sat on the four chairs in Miss Pryce-Jones' hotel room, and the mid-afternoon sun illuminated her face as she began.

"As you may know, the game begins when the sun goes down. Eight people are chosen by lot, and I was one of them. The other seven were Johnny Faulconbridge – that is, Lord Faulconbridge – Lady Vanessa Hart, Sir Michael Rutledge, Katie, the Duchess of Belminster, Max Chesterfield, Helena Broughton, and, of course, poor Edward. That's how we were paired: Johnny and myself, Vanessa and Michael, Katie and Max, and Edward and Helena. At the centre of the maze there is a circular space about fifteen feet in diameter, and of course, as soon as you reach it, *if* you reach it, you know that you're about halfway through, which gives you some idea of how long it should take you to finish. Of course, there's no guarantee that you're the first couple to reach it, or that you'll be King and Queen."

"What happens if you meet another couple at the centre?" I asked.

"Well then, there are two other openings on the other side of the centre, and each pair goes into one. I suppose it's possible that three or even all of the couples could get to the centre at the same time, but as far as I know it's never happened. Johnny and I reached the centre pretty quickly, and we were about to congratulate ourselves on how well we were doing, when I heard a sort of low moan. Johnny had heard it too. We moved further into the center and found Edward and Helena. The maze is well lit. We saw Edward lying on his back, his shirtfront was covered in blood, and – and – " She wiped away a sudden tear with the back of her hand. "His eyes were staring upward and he had a ghastly look on his face."

Her voice became quieter. "I don't think I'll ever, ever forget that look."

"Are you all right, Miss Pryce-Jones?" I asked. "We could ring for someone to bring you a coffee, or something stronger, if you'd prefer."

"No, I – Yes, please, I'd like some water. There's a glass and a carafe by the bedside."

Walcott went over and poured her a glass. She accepted it gratefully and drank half of the contents before continuing.

"Helena was lying beside him, and there was blood on the front of her dress. She was face down, and on the back of her head you could see through her hair that there was a huge, discoloured swelling. The low moan had come from her, so we knew that she at least was alive. Max and I discussed what we should do and decided that since I was younger and fitter than him, I should run through the other half of the maze as quickly as I could and alert everyone waiting at the entrance. Max would stay in the centre to look after Helena if she woke up and tell the others what had happened when they reached the centre.

"The next twenty minutes were a nightmare. I made two or three wrong turns. and my heart was pounding so hard that I thought every minute it would burst, but eventually I made my way out. Between the entrance to the maze and the doors of the manor house, a marquee had been set up. The other thirty-two guests were sitting, drinking at little tables. As I emerged, a band struck up and, at a signal from Lord Caerphilly, the night sky was suddenly full of exploding fireworks. Even the servants were all there to see the display. I had to walk the twenty yards to where Lord and Lady Caerphilly sat, but by the time I was ten yards away he saw the expression on my face, and realizing something must be wrong, sent one of his men to tell the orchestra to stop, and that there must be no more fireworks. After I gave him the terrible news, he sent another servant to Elfrincham Village for the local doctor. All the guests and the staff went back inside the house."

"How many people know the layout of the maze?" asked Holmes.

"I imagine Lord Caerphilly must have a plan of it, but I doubt he knows it without that. Of course, the maze has to be maintained, and the gardeners who do that must know the simplest way to get through it. In fact, when the doctor arrived, Lord Caerphilly sent one of them with him, to take him through – and help the other six players out."

"Have these gardeners been questioned?" asked Holmes.

"No," said Walcott.

"Whyever not? Surely it is clear that whoever committed this crime must have known how to negotiate the maze. What was to prevent one of them from entering after the game had begun?"

"That isn't possible," said Miss Pryce-Jones.

"Why do you say so?" demanded Holmes.

"About twenty years ago, there was a suspicion that the King and Queen had won by cheating – that they had come out of the maze, gone round to the front entrance and waited until they could slip forward and appear to have come through it. Nothing was ever proven, but since then a servant has been posted at the other four entrances to make sure that the players go in and do not come out again by any of them."

"That's one thing that wasn't in Kitson's *The Hedge Mazes of England*," I couldn't help remarking.

"It was written more than twenty years ago," retorted Holmes. He returned his attention to Miss Pryce-Jones. "Do you know of anyone else who would know the plan of the maze?"

Miss Pryce-Jones hesitated, then said, "Yes, there is one other person who would know. Margaret – Margaret FitzAlwyn."

"The daughter of the previous owner," Walcott informed us.

"Was she there on the night in question?"

"Yes, Mr. Holmes," said the young woman. "The Caerphillys broke a little with strict tradition by inviting her, as it meant there were forty-one guests instead of forty, but it was a courtesy to her, done out of kindness and consideration of the circumstances in which the FitzAlwyns had had to let go of the manor. Margaret's father had made some bad investments, and the family fortunes were in serious decline. Eventually, he came to the conclusion that the only way to pay off his debts and save the family from disgrace was to sell Elfrincham Manor. It was a terrible wrench, because the family connection to the Manor went back to the Thirteenth Century. Margaret was an only child, and she'd played in the maze when she was a little girl."

"By herself?"

"As far as I know. She did play with the village children, I think, but never with them in the maze. Her parents probably brought her up to respect its secret. So obviously, she didn't take part in the drawing of lots."

"Did she know Edward Crawley?"

Again, she hesitated.

"Yes, yes, she did," she replied, and drank the remainder of her glass of water.

"How well?"

"Mr. Holmes, Margaret FitzAlwyn is my friend. We were at school together . . . ."

"I'm afraid, Miss Pryce-Jones, that your duty to the truth must override your loyalty to your friend. I repeat: How well did she know him?"

"They were once engaged to be married."

"Since Edward Crawley has, or rather, had a wife, the engagement must have been broken."

"Margaret's parents had lived a very simple life after the sale of the manor. They managed to save enough for her to live fairly comfortably, and even take the occasional holiday now and then. It was on holiday, about six or seven months after her parents' death, that she met Edward Crawley. Now it seems she'd never really had a beau, even though she was a perfectly presentable girl. She fell for Crawley totally, and there seemed to be every indication that he felt exactly the same toward her. Within a few weeks, they were engaged and planning to be married in late spring. By this time, she was living in a small apartment in London. Then one day, Margaret came down with a bad case of flu and was unable to go to a gallery opening in Bond Street that they'd both planned to attend. He offered to come over and sit at her bedside, but she insisted that he go along and enjoy himself.

"At the opening, he met one of the artists, Julia Bramwell. In many ways she seems to have been the polar opposite of Margaret – confident, sophisticated, outgoing – and Crawley found himself falling in love with her almost immediately, and Julia returned the feeling. He really did try not to hurt Margaret, and struggled to control his passion, but in the end he couldn't stand it any longer, and three months before their scheduled wedding, he told Margaret that he couldn't marry her. Four months later he married Julia. Margaret was devastated. For about a year, she was walking around like a ghost, but then she recovered and entered society once more.

"Mr. Holmes, I can understand how you might suspect her of killing Edward, but I swear to you that that is impossible."

"How can you make that statement with such confidence?"

"I was sitting next to Margaret at one of the tables when the lots were drawn. She had complained of a headache and, just as I stood up to join Johnny and take my position at one of the entrances, she told me she was going back into the house to lie down in her room. I saw her walk away in the direction of the doors."

"Miss Pryce-Jones," said Holmes, rising, "I see no reason to detain you further. Thank you for your co-operation, and I wish you a safe and pleasant journey."

"I suppose," the young woman said a little bitterly, "that I am now Queen of the Maze, but as Juliet says, '*It is an honour I dream not of.*' Good day, gentlemen."

"Inspector Walcott, we have a few hours before sunset and, you may recall, I should like to examine the maze."

As the inspector had said, it was but a few minutes' drive to Elfrincham Manor. Holmes hefted one of the great brass knockers on the double doors and we were ushered into the drawing room and the presence of Lord and Lady Caerphilly by a tall, lugubrious butler.

"Good afternoon, my Lord, my lady," said Walcott with the characteristic deference of the policeman toward the aristocracy. "This is Mr. Sherlock Holmes and his colleague, Dr. Watson. I've asked them to help us out in this terrible business of the maze murder."

The Lord and Lady were in late middle age, both elegantly dressed in country clothes, and possessed of an amiable disposition.

"Holmes, eh?" said the Lord. "You're the fella who helped out the Conk-Singletons with that forgery business, right? * And that spot of trouble Backwater had a number of years ago."

"Correct, sir. Now, as we need to inspect the actual site of the murder, we shall need a guide to take us to the heart of the maze."

"Of course."

He rose from his chair and tugged at the bell-pull. The long-faced butler reappeared.

"Pearson, I believe Anderson is in the back orchard. Go and fetch him for us."

"Yes, my Lord."

"First rate fella, Anderson," the Lord continued when the butler had left. "Came with the house. Must have worked here for – Oh, what, thirty years?"

"I believe so, dear," said Lady Caerphilly.

"Ah, there you are, my good man," her husband said when Pearson reappeared a few minutes later with a short, sinewy man with iron-grey hair and a face as brown as a nut, dressed in plain work clothes. "Take these gentlemen to the centre of the maze."

"Right you are, sir."

The Elfrincham Maze was, indeed, an impressive sight. As Kitson's book had said, it was larger and more impressive than even its great counterpart in the grounds of Hampton Court. At seven feet in height, its green "walls" were taller than most men, and rising even higher was a ring of electric lamps on metal poles that served to illuminate it by night. The comparative gentleness of the curve that the front of the maze presented to us hinted at its great circumference. According to Kitson, its diameter was an impressive one-hundred-fifty yards.

"Were you here last night?" Holmes asked Anderson as we entered.

"That I was, sir," the gardener replied. "It was me as led the doctor to the centre of the maze. Horrible it was. Mr. Crawley lying there dead, blood all over his front, and that poor girl with a lump on the back of her head the size of a goose egg."

"What about before you took the doctor through? Were all the other maze gardeners there?"

"Oh yes, sir. All the servants were given the evening off. There was no one in the house. Me and the other mazers, we were at a table together, drinking from a barrel or two his Lordship had kindly given us."

I didn't take note of how long it took us to make our way through the maze, but I must confess that by the time we reached the centre, the narrow pathways threading backward and forward, the occasional unexpected curve and the towering green hedges were beginning to make me feel a little nauseous, and I was glad when we reached the open space. Holmes, as was his wont, seemed unaffected by the oddity of his surroundings.

"As I said, Mr. Holmes, no one has been here since poor Mr. Crawley's body was removed."

Holmes pressed a finger against his lips, silencing the policeman, and gestured to the three of us that we should remain where we were. For the next few minutes, he made a thorough examination of the space, at first stepping carefully, then going on his knees, and finally lying down full length. Eventually he stood and brushed down his clothes.

"Thank you, Anderson. I observed from the noticeboard at The Crown that dinner will be served at half-past seven. If you will take us to the local doctor now, Inspector Walcott, we should have ample time to question him and then get back to the hotel, to rest a little from our exertions and change for our meal."

The return journey through the maze was a little less onerous, but I hoped that our investigations wouldn't require us to enter there a second time.

It transpired that the surgery of Dr. Thomas Pocock was on a side-turning off the High Street, and thus only a few minutes' walk from The Crown. After giving us such simple directions as were necessary, Inspector Walcott departed for home with a promise that he would meet us the following morning after breakfast.

Dr. Pocock was a tall man in his late thirties with thick-lensed glasses, a full, neatly-trimmed beard, and a head of dark blond hair. His accent was, naturally, that of an educated man, but I fancied that I caught a hint of the familiar Sussex burr beneath his sophisticated tones, which suggested to me that he had returned to his home county to practice after he had completed his time at a teaching hospital.

He greeted us warmly.

"Inspector Walcott told me yesterday that I could expect a visit from you, gentlemen. I shall give you whatever assistance you need to find a solution to this ghastly business."

"If you could first tell us of the condition of Crawley's body as it was when you found it," said Holmes.

"I determined that the death had taken place about an hour or so before, The heart had been punctured several times by something long, thin, and pointed. Any one of these wounds would have been sufficient to bring about death by itself."

"And what of the Honourable Helena Broughton?"

"She was taken to the hospital in West Worthing. She was in a state of semi-consciousness, and from an examination of her head, I determined that she had probably been dealt a blow with a heavy blunt instrument at about the same time as Crawley was killed. I should say it will be a day or

254

two before she can be questioned, and even then she may well be unable to remember any of the event."

I concurred.

"That is often the case in instances of concussion."

Holmes and I returned to the hotel and came down to dinner after a short rest in our separate rooms. The meal was doubly welcome. Neither of us had eaten since our breakfast in Baker Street that morning and, like the accommodation, it was of a higher standard than one would expect of such a rural establishment. Once the first course had taken the edge from my hunger, I was keen to hear what conclusions Holmes might have reached, but as there were several other diners present, he kept his own counsel, and our conversation was restricted to trivialities.

The hotel smoking room, however, was empty of fellow-guests, and as soon as we sat down to smoke our after-dinner cigars, Holmes spoke of the matter in hand.

"I learned little from the scene and, in truth, I didn't expect to glean much. Including Anderson and Dr. Pocock, no less than eight people had tramped all over it. What do you make of it thus far?"

"Well," I said tentatively after a pull at my cigar, "I agree that whoever the culprit is, he must know how to negotiate the maze. He managed to commit his crime and escape without encountering the other six people who were in there at the time. I think he must have gone into the maze before the contest began, and thus before the guards were placed. Is it not also possible that he remained in the maze until after Crawley's body and Helena Broughton were removed? The guards would be gone, and he could escape under cover of darkness."

"A credible scenario, but do you have any ideas as to the identity of the culprit?"

"We know that Margaret FitzAlwyn was present at the drawing of the lots, and also that she returned to the house, so we can eliminate her. The maze gardeners were all together at their table, but supposing an enemy of Crawley, whoever he was – "

"Yes," interjected Holmes. "If Mrs. Crawley is still at the castle, we should question her on that point."

"This enemy bribes one of the gardeners to reveal the secret, perhaps getting him to draw up a plan, and then, as I said, goes in before the contest begins and leaves after the victims have been found and taken out."

"Again, that is possible, although if Anderson is typical of the 'mazers', as he called them, it becomes less plausible. Such men as he usually place their loyalty to their masters above mere monetary gain, but it may be prudent to meet them all and see if we can assess their individual characters, And there are one or two other factors to be considered."

"Which are?"

"Even a single blow to the heart with such an instrument as Dr. Pocock described would produce a considerable amount of blood, would it not? More than had soaked into Crawley's shirt front – and there were several such blows. Yet there was no blood on the ground. That is one fact I did derive from my examination. The only other blood was on the front of Helena Broughton's dress, and it must have been Crawley's, because her wound was on the back of her head. Had it bled, we would expect the blood to be on the back of her dress. Does this suggest anything to you?"

"That Crawley's body was moved!"

"And the unconscious Miss Broughton must also have been moved, since the pair were walking the maze together. That might explain the blood on her dress. Now, to my second point: Dr. Pocock described the murder weapon as 'long, thin, and pointed'. What could that be?"

"A stiletto!"

"Watson, you scintillate this evening! But I think it unlikely that we would find an Italian instrument of assassination in a village in the Home Counties. A far more common object fits the description equally well: A hatpin. And while I would agree that it isn't wholly conclusive, it indicates that our killer may well have been a woman."

"Holmes! Supposing it was one of the other three women who went into the maze that evening? In fact, Victoria Pryce-Jones is a friend of Margaret FitzAlwyn. She may have hated Crawley for the emotional pain he had caused her, and killed him for that reason. She claimed to be going to America to visit relatives, but perhaps she has fled, never to return."

The detective gave a deep sigh.

"Ah, Watson! You were doing so well, but this theory flies in the face of the facts."

"Why? Margaret FitzAlwyn could have given her a plan of the maze, or they may even have gone into it together when they were friends at school."

"Perhaps, but that isn't the issue. Have you forgotten that the participants are chosen at random, by the picking of lots? It is beyond the bounds of probability that both the murderer and the intended victim would be picked, and even further beyond those bounds that the murderer's partner would be an accomplice to the crime, as he would have to be if the deed were to go unpunished. Remember that the players stayed in their pairs."

"Yes, of course. My apologies."

"Don't reproach yourself. Many would have done worse, and not all your ideas were without merit. Now, I am off to bed. We shall visit the manor house again tomorrow."

As he had promised, Walcott met us again the following morning with his dogcart, and we set out once more for Elfrincham Manor. *En route*, Holmes questioned the inspector about the "mazers" and received the following answer: "I've known all of them all the years I've been in the constabulary, and I'd vouch for the honesty and loyalty of all of them."

"None of them have been in any kind of financial difficulty?"

"When you're in their position, in this kind of area, you can't keep that sort of thing hidden, and I've never heard of any of them having anything of the kind."

"Could any of them had had any kind of grudge against Edward Grawley?"

"Well, Mr. Holmes, once the players have gone through the maze at Midsummer, they're never asked back. So every year there are at least eight new guests, and this year Mr. Crawley was one of 'em, so I don't think any of the 'mazers' even knew him."

At the manor, we briefly paid our respects to the Lord and Lady and inquired as to whether Crawley's widow was still in one of the guest rooms.

"Yes," replied Lord Caerphilly. "She's staying for the inquest, which is being held tomorrow afternoon, and then I understand the body will be taken to London for burial alongside his parents in Brompton Cemetery."

"And Margaret FitzAlwyn?"

"She was at breakfast. I believe she's still here."

We found Julia Crawley, *née* Bramwell, alone in her room, and in the course of a brief interview, she stated that her late husband had been well thought of by all who knew him and she was unaware of any enemies.

We returned to the Caerphilys' private apartments only to find them empty. Pearson the butler informed us that his master and mistress had gone out shooting with some of their guests and wouldn't be back for at least two hours.

"A pity," said Holmes. "I had hoped to act with their permission, but we cannot wait two hours. The solution to this mystery lies, I believe, below stairs."

"One of the servants?" asked Walcott, but Holmes didn't reply. Instead, he went back toward the main door and began to descend the stone steps to the kitchen, which were located near the bottom of the main staircase. Walcott and I exchanged puzzled glances, then followed him down.

In the kitchen, some of the servants, mostly female, were bustling about the room, busy preparing for the next meal. They stopped and turned their heads when we entered.

"Some of you know me," said the policeman. "I'm Inspector Walcott. "You may have heard of my friends here: Sherlock Holmes and Doctor Watson."

"You all know of the bad business in the maze," said Holmes. "We are helping Inspector Walcott with his investigation, and I need to ask you some questions. First, were all of you at the Midsummer celebrations?"

"None of us would miss that," said a matronly, middle-aged woman I took to be the cook. "One of the highlights of the year, that is."

There were nods of general agreement.

"We was all there – the kitchen staff, the mazers – yes, everybody. I don't recall anybody being missing."

"So, the manor house would have been completely empty."

"Well, yes."

"My second question: Has anything gone missing from here since the celebration?"

The cook spoke up again.

"Yes, one of the big food trolleys. But how did you know that?"

"My last question: What is the lowest point of the house?"

"That would be the cold room."

"Please direct us to it."

The cold room lay at the end of a corridor that sloped gently downward. Within, piles of various foodstuffs were neatly stacked against the right- and left-hand walls, but the back wall was clear. Holmes immediately went over to it, took his magnifying glass out, and began to examine the wall and the edges of the other walls where they met it. For two minutes we were all silent. Then Holmes gave a little cry of triumph, pressed one of the bricks on the left side, and stepped back. Before our eyes, the entire wall rotated through ninety degrees on a central pivot.

Holmes struck a match, and Walcott and I followed his light down a long stone corridor for about thirty yards until we reached a great circular hall supported by concrete pillars. At this point, Holmes's match died down. I reached into my own pocket for my box of vestas and struck one. By its light, we saw that as well as the pillars, there were four sets of spiraling stone steps that seemed to lead only to the ceiling. At the foot of one of them was what could only be the missing food trolley. Holmes climbed to the top, even as my match began to fizzle, and I saw him push upward with both hands. My vesta went out, but at the same moment a shaft of bright summer sunshine burst in upon us. Walcott and I followed Holmes up the steps, and found ourselves in the centre of the Elfrincham Maze.

Holmes pushed back the block he had removed and pointed at it.

258

"I saw this when we were in the maze yesterday," he said, "but I didn't make the connection. It looks as if a tree has been cut down and its trunk levelled without being uprooted, but it conceals this secret entrance, and I have no doubt one would find something similar at the other three."

"I begin to see that in some way this was how the murder was carried out," said Walcott, "but who is the culprit?"

"And what is the purpose of that underground chamber?" I asked. "I can't believe it was built to facilitate murder."

"No, indeed. If I am correct, it was constructed for the preservation of human lives, rather than their destruction. The FitzAlwyns became High Church Protestants during the reign of Charles I, but before that, they were one of the richest and most prominent Catholic families in England. In the sixteenth century they were recusants, refusing to attend Church of England services and remaining loyal to the Pope and to the 'Old Religion'.

"For some time, *'recusant'* was just a label, but in 1593, Elizabeth I passed a statute which gave the term a legal definition and made recusancy a crime. There were four basic forms of punishment: Fines, confiscation of property, imprisonment, and execution. You were fined if it could only be proven that you weren't attending Church of England services, but if it could be shown that you had attended a clandestine Roman Catholic service, your property would be confiscated, and if you went on attending, you would be imprisoned or possibly executed. Rich families like the FitzAlwyns, who could afford to pay the fines, went on not attending C. of E. services, but were very careful not to be found attending Catholic services. Instead, they had their own priests to cater to their spiritual needs. If this was discovered, both the priest and at least the head of the family were likely to be executed. So the priests were lodged in secret chambers known as 'priest-holes'.

"There was a Jesuit priest called Nicholas Owen who specialised in designing and building them until he was executed in The Tower of London in 1606. In 1594, he was arrested and heavily fined. A wealthy Catholic family paid the fine and he was released. He then disappeared for three years until he rescued the Jesuit John Gerard from The Tower in 1597. Now, there's no record of which family paid his fine, but it's a reasonable assumption that it was the FitzAlfreds, and that a little later he embarked on a special project for them."

"1594 – that's the year the maze was planted," I interjected. "Are you saying he designed the maze?"

"No. I believe that at first the maze was nothing more than a blind, an explanation as to why there were so many people coming and going on the Elfrincham estate. I suspect that the reason why it's so large and complicated was so that it would take a long time and continue to be a cover for what was really being done – the construction of the underground chamber beneath it, which would provide a safe haven for not one but many priests. The stairs and concealed openings which give access to the maze were probably placed there so that if the chamber were discovered, the priests would stand a chance of escaping. They were doubtless informed how to negotiate the maze so that they could hide there until there was a possibility of escape, or until whatever danger there was, was over.

"When the FitzAlwyns became Protestants, the underground chamber became redundant and was eventually forgotten – until, that is, someone discovered it, presumably by accident."

"This is all very interesting, Mr. Holmes, but who is there for me to arrest?"

"Margaret FitzAlwyn. Here is how I read it, and how I reached that conclusion: She heard Edward's name called out as one of the maze walkers, and within a few moments had formulated a plan. From the order in which the names of the walkers were called out, she knew which entrance they would use to enter the maze, and therefore which paths they would be using until, as was likely, they reached the centre. So she went into the house, down into the cold room, through the secret door, and into the underground chamber. Using one of the concealed entrances, she went up into the maze and hid until she saw Crawley and Helena Broughton.

"I don't know what she hit Miss Broughton with, though I expect we shall find it if we examine the chamber. Crawley was probably too surprised to defend himself, and we know the first blow was fatal. That she went on stabbing him testifies to her hatred of him. Then she dragged them back down into the chamber. But how had she transported Crawley's corpse, and the unconscious Helena, to the concealed entrance nearest the centre? No woman would be strong enough to drag two dead weights through the chamber. That was why she took the food trolley. She must have put Crawley and Helena next to each other on the trolley, which, incidentally, explains the bloodstains on Helena's dress, and pushed them through the chamber until she reached the concealed entrance nearest the centre. Now she did have to drag them, but it wasn't too far. She likely took them up the steps one at a time."

"But," I remarked, "from what you have said, it couldn't have been premeditated. How did she know to have the trolley ready?"

"No, she didn't premeditate it, but she was thinking and acting quickly. All the servants were at the ceremony, so the house would be empty. She went straight down into the kitchen and took the trolley along the corridors, and down into the cold room and through the secret door.

After she'd committed the crime, she went back upstairs and probably went to bed. And now, let us return to the underground chamber, since that will get us out of here more quickly than going through the maze."

Margaret FitzAlwyn was formally charged with the murder of Edward Crawley when her luggage was searched and found to contain the dress she had worn on that fateful evening. It was covered with bloodstains which she could not explain, and on being questioned by Inspector Walcott, she confessed. Her mental health was examined by a board of doctors, who determined that she should be placed in an institution rather than executed. As usual, Holmes allowed the police officer to take the credit for solving the case.

A few days later we read in *The Daily Telegraph* that Lord and Lady Caerphilly had decided that the Elfrincham Maze, and that singular underground chamber, should at last be open to the public. Holmes turned his attention back to his musical composition and produced a gentle air which, to this day, I still enjoy hearing him perform.

NOTE

*   See this volume for more about "The Conk-Singleton Forgery".

The Bewildering
Bicycle Business
by Craig Stephen Copland

The headline of a brief story on page three of *The Times* of 17 July, 1902 read:

> *Two Two-Wheeled Barons Murdered Two Times by Two*
> *Thugs with Two Weapons*

In between sips of coffee and bites of toast, I read about two barons, a father and his son-in-law, who had been found in their office at the Brunswick Bicycle Works in Vauxhall. They had both been shot in the back of their heads, and their throats had been cut.

The motive was obvious, the paper said. On 15 July, the firm was going to conclude the purchase of its greatest rival, The Empire Bicycle and Tyre Enterprise. Clearly, someone did not want that transaction to take place.

I put the newspaper down and looked across the room to where Sherlock Holmes was reading yet another journal.

"Did you see this?" I asked. "It looks interesting. Are you going to see if Scotland Yard needs your help?"

Without looking up, he replied. "Of course not. I'm too busy with two other cases to even think about it. The only proper course of justice would be to murder the editor who wrote such a banal headline . . . twice."

"Oh, come now, Holmes. He's just doing his job of selling newspapers. You must admit, the method of the murders is out of the ordinary."

"Other than using both a gun and a knife, there is nothing unusual about it. Murders within the small world of British industry are invariably motivated by reasons of commerce and greed. The suspects are, therefore, limited and easily investigated. Scotland Yard will catch and charge the villains within a week. There is no need for my particular skills."

I could see that he wasn't interested in any further discussion, and I flipped the pages of *The Times* until I found the accounts of the previous day's horseraces and rugby scores.

Two weeks later, Holmes and I were once again sitting in the front room of 221b, having enjoyed a pleasant Saturday morning breakfast lavished upon us by the indefatigable Mrs. Hudson. We chatted off and on about the coming coronation of our new king, Edward VII. It was to be quite the spectacle.

The bell rang at the front door, followed by odd-sounding footsteps ascending the stairs.

They were heavy enough to belong to a man, but moving slowly and ponderously. Whoever it was took two or three steps and stopped. Then another two or three.

I looked over at Holmes, and he turned his palms up and shrugged.

"Perhaps an overweight patient of yours," he said.

"Or a new client of yours who has been shot," I said.

It was neither.

Through the door came a bowed over and exhausted Inspector Lestrade. He didn't bother to remove his coat and hat and shuffled to an open armchair. He dropped his body, placed his hands over his stomach, and stared into the unlit hearth.

"Good Heavens, Inspector," I said. "Are you ill? Let me get you a brandy. Do you need something to eat? You look like you haven't slept in days."

"Ah, thank you, Doctor," he said. "A brandy would hit the spot."

"What's wrong?" I asked.

Before Lestrade had a chance to reply, Holmes spoke up.

"It is rather obvious, is it not? Our dear inspector has been worn down by some case he is working on night and day, but has gotten nowhere. The only question is, which case? There have been none reported in the recent past that struck me as not amenable to rudimentary investigation. Has there been something that has been kept out of the press, Inspector?"

Lestrade took several sips of his brandy and put it down on the side table. Then he lit a cigarette, took several slow puffs, and replied.

He sighed. "It's been in the press. The murders a fortnight ago of Baron Stepford of Sodenleigh and his son-in-law, the Baron Bampfylde of Galtimore."

"My dear Lestrade," Holmes said, "how can that not have been solved by now? It was obvious that all you had to do was ask *cui bono*. There couldn't have been more than three or four possible parties who had a reason to want them dead. Just interrogate all of them and pick the one who cannot offer a decent defense or alibi."

Lestrade gave Holmes a look of annoyed impatience.

"Please, Mr. Holmes, enough of being condescending. We do know something about asking who would benefit and pursuing an investigation.

Unfortunately, every one of the obvious suspects has a watertight alibi. The same is true for the less-obvious ones. We've left no stone unturned. Do you think I would come here if it had been as straightforward as you think it should have been?"

Holmes softened his gaze. After more than twenty years of consulting with Scotland Yard, he and Lestrade had developed not what anyone would call a friendship, but there was strong mutual respect. I thought it much like the respect the captains of Northampton and Leicester rugby teams had developed for each other, irrespective of their eternal rivalry.

"I stand corrected," Holmes said. "Please. How may I be of assistance to you and Scotland Yard?"

"You can go over the same ground we have. Even if we've raked through every scrap of paper, talked to everyone, and conjectured a hundred possible ways it happened, your new set of eyes and your unconventional methods may help. Regardless, they can't hurt."

Lestrade reached into his suit jacket pocket and took out several sheets of folded paper.

"Here's a list of every possible competitor in England . . . and those in Europe and America. And here are the names of every manager and assistant manager in their factory in Vauxhall. The other pages summarize what we've learned so far. Have at it, Mr. Holmes. They should be enough to get you started."

Lestrade stood up and prepared to leave.

"Before you go," said Holmes, "may I trouble you for the home addresses of the two victims? I assume they both had houses and wives."

"They're on the back of the first sheet. Both of them lived in the same street in Belgravia. I had Inspector Lanner and my men go through their houses with a fine-toothed comb. They found nothing. The wives – lovely women, both of them – are understandably distraught and are doing whatever they can to keep the doors of the factory open. But I'm told they are terrified. They've hired guards to follow them around everywhere and have them posted at their houses and the factory. Best let Dr. Watson question them. You're likely to get yourself thrown out to the pavement."

"I shall be the soul of gentlemanly consideration."

"I'll believe that when I see it. Just do what you can, and let me know."

"As always, Inspector."

"Well, Holmes," I said after Lestrade had departed, "fancy a jaunt down to Vauxhall?"

"I think not. First to Belgravia. Wives and widows always know things. Give me a few minutes to read over the pages Lestrade gave me, and then I shall be ready to go."

A half-hour later, we hailed a cab on Baker Street and gave the driver an address in Eaton Square.

"Anything in Lestrade's note strike you as unusual?" I asked.

"No. But that didn't surprise me. Had something singularly odd existed, he would have investigated it thoroughly. Any questions on your part?"

I gave my chin a rub and nodded. "Only one so far: He said the widows were distraught and terrified. Being overcome with grief, I can understand, but why are they in fear? Why hire guards?"

"Ah, the answer was in his notes. Inspector Lanner assisted him – not the sharpest knife in the drawer, if you recall – and he managed the search of the houses and interviews with the widows. For some reason, known only to Lanner, he suggested to the two women that the killer might have been one of their employees, and he urged them to arrange protection."

"That may have been good advice."

"Quite possibly, as long as he didn't furnish the guards from amongst his unemployed cousins and friends."

"Really, Holmes. You have no right to say such a thing. You should never start by impugning a man's integrity."

"Oh, his integrity is quite all right. It's his intelligence I wonder about."

Eaton Place in Belgravia boasts a line of terraced houses, all fronted by balconies supported by Doric columns. The inhabitants are known to be rather well-off, and these fine homes often double as the city residences of members of the landed gentry who have estates scattered around all corners of the British Isles.

"Which house is it you're wanting, sir?" asked the driver.

"Kindly look ahead. Do you see the door with two large men standing in front of it?"

"Can't miss those two blokes. They look like they could scare off a troop of Royal Marines. You're quite certain that's where you want out?"

The two guards were indeed imposing. The one on the left was a young African chap who was tall enough and black enough to have been a member of the Watusi tribe. The man across from him was an older Lascar whose face may have been of a lighter hue, but was crisscrossed with scars that surrounded a misshapen nose.

"They don't look to me," I said, "like cousins of Inspector Lanner. Quite the fearsome chaps."

"Our widows aren't taking any chances," said Holmes. "That would suggest they truly are in fear of their lives. Come. Let us have a chat with them."

The two guards moved and blocked our way as we approached the porch.

"Who are you two?" said the African fellow. "What do you want here?"

He moved directly in front of Holmes and towered over him.

"My name is Sherlock Holmes. I am assisting Scotland Yard in bringing to justice the criminals who caused your employer to become a widow."

The dark scowl on the dark face vanished and was replaced by a wide grin.

"You Sherlock Holmes? Hey, Rohan, we get to meet Sherlock Holmes. And you? You be Dr. Watson?"

"I am, indeed, my good man," I said.

He put a gigantic hand at the end of a very long arm on my shoulder.

"Rohan and me, we read all your stories. If we let you in and you solve the crime, we get our names in the story. Rohan and Gichinga. We help you, you help us. You agree?"

"Agreed," I said.

He opened the door and announced us. A maid met us and curtsied.

"C'mon in," she said in a distinctly American accent. "I'll tell Mrs. St. Aubyn you're here."

"Pardon me, Miss," said Holmes. "We are here to meet with the Baroness Stepford of Sodenleigh, not the woman you named."

"Same one. I worked for her for ten years before she crossed the pond and bought herself a title. So to me, she's always Mrs. St. Aubyn. Or just plain Gloria. I'll get her. Go sit in the parlor."

The front room was filled with sunlight from the large windows and furnished with the latest in fine furniture, paintings, and *objets d'art*. A side table supported a decanter of brandy, several bottles of select imported vodka, and a bottle each of Scotch, Irish whiskey, and bourbon.

There was, however, an odd, though not unpleasant, odor in the room.

Holmes gazed around the parlor, leaned down, put his nose against the top of the sofa, and sniffed.

"Brand new," he said. "The style isn't so much English as American. Possibly imported from the state of Vermont. Ah, and the portrait of George Washington above the hearth has been hung here recently."

He gestured to a painting of the first American president, and I could tell by the slight difference in the shading of the paint behind it that it had replaced a larger painting.

"Is this lady an American?" I said.

"Apparently, she is," said Holmes. "That wasn't in Lestrade's notes. I suppose I shouldn't be surprised, as Lanner inspected the house, and goodness knows what else he failed to note."

Any further observations of the room were cut short by the arrival of two women. They were both dressed in black, but their dresses were slender and more form-fitting than is common amongst English widows. I assumed that America must have left our dowdy mourning fashions behind, as they had so many other aspects of civilized culture.

A cursory glance at the two women revealed they were mother and daughter. Both had the same comely facial features that rendered them attractive, although not what one would call stunning. The older woman's hair, neatly arranged on her head, was dark blonde and tinged with silver. The younger one's blonde hair was let down and swayed back and forth across her shoulders. Both greeted us with warm smiles.

"Good morning, gentlemen," said the mother. "Please, do sit down, and I'll have Betty bring some coffee and a bite to eat. As we used to say in Vermont, you both look like you could use a bit more fat on your bones. Judy, darling, will you ask Betty to bring something for these two?"

The younger woman nodded. "Certainly, Mother." And then she got up and walked back into the house.

She returned a moment later. "I hope coffee and crumpets would be to your liking. I'm terribly sorry we don't have anything better to offer. But crumpets topped with Vermont maple syrup is something we are awfully fond of."

From somewhere several rooms removed, a voice called out, "I'll be there in a second. I found a new bottle of Vermont Gold."

"Vermont Gold is what we call our maple syrup," said Judy. "I hope you enjoy it as much as we do."

They sat on the sofa, and Holmes and I each occupied an armchair.

Holmes was about to speak when the Baroness, now known as Gloria, took over.

"Gentlemen, you cannot imagine how good news it is to learn that Mr. Sherlock Holmes is now working on this . . . this horrible, this dreadful mess. Frankly, Sherlock – I'm sorry. You don't mind if I call you that, do you? Forgive my being too . . . too, well American. In Vermont, I'm Gloria. This is Judy. We can't stand anyone calling us 'My Lady'. Well, like I said, it's good news. The best we've heard in a while. Frankly, Mr. Holmes – Sherlock – the two of us are scared stiff. Whoever shot and cut the throats of our husbands is as ruthless as they come. We are living in terror. Anything you can do to help would be a godsend. Anything you need to know from us, please, just ask. Isn't that right, Judy?"

The younger woman nodded. "It is, Mother."

"Allow me to begin," Holmes said, "by complimenting you on securing two excellent guards for your home. Their presence should help you to be less frightened."

"Oh, yes," said Gloria. "They are fine men, those two. And we have four more at the factory. They're every bit as big and strong as Rohan and Gichinga. Oh, yes, they do help us be a little less frightened."

"The factory?" said Holmes. "Why would you need more guards there? Are you afraid of theft? Arson? Vandalism?"

"No, my dear Sherlock. I know it must make us seem hopelessly fearful, but we are afraid for our lives. Our necks. We go in there every day, and that's . . . that's where our husbands were murdered."

She choked on her words and dabbed her eye with her handkerchief.

"You go there?" said Holmes. "But why? Do you not have managers to look after the place?"

Before she could answer, Betty, the maid, appeared with a pot of coffee and a plate of warm crumpets. "Here you go, gentlemen," she said as she placed the tray in front of us. "Some of our best American coffee for our guests, and warm cakes right off the griddle. In that little pitcher is what we call our Vermont Gold. It's pure maple syrup. Please, enjoy."

The four of us each took a small side plate to which we added a crumpet and poured a layer of maple syrup on top of it. I cut off a piece with a fork and gave it a taste. I had to admit, it was highly delectable. I looked over at Miss Judy, who had also poured a serving of maple syrup over her snack and then, somewhat to my surprise, she cut off a piece, stuck it on her fork, closed her eyes and placed it in her mouth. As her jaw moved ever so slowly, the expression on her face bordered on ecstasy.

I smiled at her. "You appear to be fond of this dish," I said to her.

She swallowed and smiled at me. "You bet I am, Doctor. Wonderful reminders of home are about the only thing these past two weeks that has brought us any happiness."

"Could we return to my questions?" said Holmes, who had only sparingly topped his crumpet with syrup. "I had asked about your managers."

"All good men," said Gloria. "But we aren't about to rely on them. We can't. What happens over in Vauxhall is our problem now. *Our* responsibility. *Our* duty. We have over one-hundred men working for us. We can't allow them to be laid off. They all – Well, the married ones – have wives and children to feed and look after. The single boys will never find a girl to marry if they don't have a job."

"And," said the young woman, Baroness Bampfylde of Galtimore, from here on to be known as Judy, "we have a dozen girls working in the front office doing typing and keeping the books and handling all the mail. I'm afraid I know what happens to girls who lose their jobs in New York. They have no choice but to . . . to sell themselves. Horrible though it is, it is what they have to do to survive. It's no different here in London, is it?"

I nodded. She was right about that.

Holmes agreed and then asked, "Are you familiar with the business of manufacturing? I take it you are."

"Sherlock, my dear," said Gloria, "as we say in America, business is business. It doesn't matter what you make and sell, and it doesn't matter where you do it. Back home in Vermont, my granddad started with lumber. My dad expanded into furniture. My husband – my *first* husband, that is, God rest his soul – He was a brilliant man, a wonderful man – he took the company and expanded it so we exported furniture and maple syrup and textiles and carpets all over the world, and he worked for years to get us listed on the New York Stock Exchange. We ran our companies together. So yes, I have learned quite a lot about running factories and selling anything there's a market for."

"And I have been trying to help her," said Judy.

"And she's as smart as they come," the mother added.

"And, no doubt," said Holmes, "you are becoming experts in the manufacture and sale of bicycles."

"Bicycles?" Gloria said. "Bicycles, you say? No, Sherlock, my dear man. The day of bicycles is as dead as the dodo. We are in the age of *motorcars*. And motor trucks, or whatever you call a truck here in England. *Lorries*. Imagine naming a big machine the same as the lovely name of a girl. No, Sherlock, Brunswick is leaving bicycles behind and striving to claim a share of the massive new market for motorcars."

"Have you started to make motorcars?" asked Holmes.

"Oh, Heavens, no. That is beyond our ability. We are simply acquiring the licenses to import them. We will bring them in from France and Germany and the United States. And we will try to sell them all over the world. Well . . . that's what we would have done. That's why the barons wanted to buy Empire Bicycles. They have distributor offices all over the British Empire. But what with the murders, that plan has gone."

She stopped again and dabbed her eyes.

"Everything now is . . . it's a *mell-of-a-hess*. Excuse my French, but that's what we say in Vermont. That's why we go over to Vauxhall every day, and that's why we need the guards. That was your question, wasn't it, sir?"

"It was, Madam. Kindly permit me one or two more. I trust you will not be offended in any way, as knowing everything I can about what took place is essential to my bringing the criminals before a judge."

"Charge ahead. Judy and I are open books. Aren't we, Judy?"

"Entirely, Mom."

"In whose interest, amongst the managers within your firm, was blocking the acquisition of your competing firm?"

The two women looked at each other. Both made a face that said I haven't any idea and shrugged.

"Well, now," said Gloria after another nibble and sip of coffee, "our husbands, the barons, had five men who served as their managers: Eddie Swanson is in charge of the plant where they made things. Stuart Pearson manages the sales. Paul Dovecote orders all the supplies and materials, and Jeffrey Smith is the most recent to join. He heads up the new importing and exporting division."

"Mom," said Judy, "don't forget the accountant."

"Oh, yes, him. What's his name? Forgive me, but I call him 'Haggis MacBagpipe'. That isn't his real name, but it's something like that."

"Mom, he's Hamish MacBaird, and he's a smart man. You said so yourself."

"I did, I know. But he's also awfully frugal. He wouldn't even let me send a hundred pounds from our petty cash to the Children's Hospital. All I wanted to do was help a few poor children get treated. Like I said, he can be a bit of a skin – "

"He's a socialist, Mom. He says charity only keeps the working class dependent and subservient."

"Oh, yes, he does have some strong views. All right, Sherlock, those are our managers. Every one of them could lose their jobs if Brunswick were to amalgamate with Empire. The same would be true of the managers over at Empire. Unfortunately, no firm needs two managers for every position. Any one of them might not want the merger to go ahead. But I know that not one of them would be capable of murder."

"How well do you know them?" asked Holmes.

She tapped her fingernails on the wooden arm of the chair and shook her head. "I suppose, now that you ask . . . not at all. What have I forgotten? Is there anything else you want to know?"

"I need to ask about matters that are considered indelicate."

Gloria laughed quietly. "Oh, Sherlock. We're Americans. Everything we do and say over here is considered indelicate. Ask away."

"Are you, either of you, aware of any sexual impropriety? Might there be a jealous husband whose wife became too close, shall we say, to either of your husbands?"

Gloria looked at her daughter. "You go first, sweetheart."

Judy raised her head and looked up at George Washington. "On Bampfylde's part? Not a chance. I know it isn't good manners to tell tales out of school, but, if you must know, he preferred the company of his pals and his classmates from Oxford."

"And on your part, Miss Judy?" said Holmes.

She blushed. "I might have gotten kind of bored at times. I may have flirted now and again. But nothing to cause some man to kill my husband."

Holmes gave her a hard look and then turned to the mother.

"I believe it is now your turn," he said.

"My marriage to Baron Stepford of Sodenleigh was one of, shall we say, mutual convenience. If you must know, I am still far more distressed over the loss of my beloved Freddie five years ago than I am about what happened two weeks ago. Freddie was everything to me . . . as I was to him."

"Please explain 'mutual convenience'."

"He got the cash he needed to expand the plant. I got an irresistible way to make all those snobbish society matrons who parade up and down Fifth Avenue have to call me 'Lady Gloria', or 'Baroness Stepford' instead of treating us like country bumpkins from Vermont. We both got what we wanted. Our conversations were limited. Passion more so. Are we done now? I'm sorry, but I am finding this conversation difficult. Have you learned enough, Mr. Holmes?"

She looked as if she were about to say more but caught herself. She took a mouthful of her coffee and smiled.

"I'm sorry. I shouldn't be so lacking in fortitude. I know you're just doing your job. Please forgive me. These past two weeks have been terribly trying. The life Judy and I had hoped to find in England has vanished. As soon as this whole awful mess is over, we're going back to Vermont, where we belong. Isn't that right, Judy, darling?"

"For sure we are, Mom. The Green Mountain men might be missing a tooth or two, but they know how to make a girl feel wanted. I never thought England would be so full of choir boys."

I was tempted to suggest she become a supporter of the nearest rugby team, a reliable cure for whatever was causing her sullen disposition. However, I refrained, as I could tell Holmes was ready to leave.

We bade the baronesses a good day and departed.

"Quite the pair," I said to Holmes when we were on the pavement. "I must say, they don't lack for pluck and gumption. Have to give them credit where it's due."

"If we were to admire all the bank-account countesses who come from America with money and arrive here seeking a titled husband, then those two certainly qualify. But pray tell, Watson, did you have the impression they were entirely candid? Or might they have been playing a role – posing as it were?"

271

"They're Americans, for Heaven's sake. They all take on roles and start acting the minute they step onto the dock in Southampton. They act like . . . well, like *Americans*. They all pretend to be rich, disdaining class distinctions, subject to strong emotions, and liberated, even if they are nothing of the kind."

"An excellent point. All right, we shall grant they aren't dissolute reprobates. Are they rich? Or was that also a pretense?"

"Didn't Lestrade's notes confirm that the factory had undergone a large expansion recently? The money for that must have come from somewhere. And if they have helped the firm move into the importing and exporting of motorcars . . . well, there is a fortune to be made doing that. They certainly seem to me to have come from money. They seem to know a bit about how to make it."

"Some excellent observations. Yes, excellent. But enough of them. There is still time this afternoon to visit the bicycle factory in Battersea."

"Don't you mean Vauxhall? Their factory is in Vauxhall, not Battersea."

"Not their factory, their planned acquisition. The Empire plant is a little farther up the river."

The Empire Bicycle and Tyre Enterprise was housed in an ancient-looking red-brick building adjacent to the south bank of the Thames. The sign on the building was somewhat faded, but clearly stated in smaller letters: *Building Fine Transport since 1650*. A short wharf behind the building extended into the river, but no one was on it, and no boat moored.

We opened one of the tall oak doors and entered the building. The foyer was spacious and entirely covered in marble. A row of marble pillars topped with Corinthian capstones supported a mezzanine floor. Paintings of distinguished-looking English gentlemen hung on the walls, filling up all available space.

The only furniture in the room was a single desk near the back wall. There sat a silver-haired, well-dressed man who was reading a book.

He looked up, somewhat surprised, as we entered.

"Oh, well, my goodness. I don't recognize you, so you must be visitors. What brings the two of you gentlemen to the hallowed halls of the Empire Bicycle and Tyre Enterprise?"

"Indeed, we are visitors," said Holmes. "We have come to visit Viscount Smithers of Abington-Under-Severn."

"And forgive my having to ask, gents, but whom shall I say is paying the visit?"

"My name is Sherlock Holmes, and this is my colleague, Dr. Watson."

"Oh, Sherlock Holmes, you say. Well, well. The viscount will find a chat with you to be rather amusing. Kindly wait here."

He vanished and reappeared within two minutes, followed by a portly gentleman clad in a dark suit, waistcoat, and spats, and sporting a large walrus mustache. He looked very much the viscount.

"What ho! Sherlock Holmes, you say! And the famous scribbler, Dr. Watson! What a jolly fine surprise. Come, please, back to my office. I have some excellent brandy, and more questions than you could imagine about that horrible hound on the Grimpen Mire."

His spacious office boasted a stone hearth, a credenza bearing, at least fifty decanters of fine liquor, and several sofas and armchairs, all surrounded by panels of walnut on which hung a dozen or more prints of dogs and horses and men riding to the hounds. Except for an ivory inkwell and a leather-edged blotter, his desk was bare.

The viscount strode directly to his decanters and started pouring.

"Never too early in the day for a decent cognac, what say? Had this one sent over from France last month. Top drawer, if I do say so. So, Mr. Holmes, about your encounter with that gigantic hound. Now, if I had been you – "

"*You* would have had a burning interest in a more recent, more tragic event that struck much closer to home," said Holmes.

The viscount was advancing toward us, bearing a generous snifter of cognac in each hand, and he stopped.

"Oh, yes, well, if you must. You came to chat about that dreadful business over at Brunswick. Quite awful what happened, eh? Soderleigh and Bampfylde were fine chaps. All the documents were ready to be signed. Terrible thing to do to our solicitors. All that work for naught. Can't think of anything I know about it that would be of use to Sherlock Holmes. But a glass of cognac or two stimulates the brain. So be good fellows and enjoy a sip or two first and then some questions."

Any chance of posing our questions straight away was squashed, and the three of us sipped and chatted about rugby, and then Holmes and I listened as the viscount cursed the government.

After his second full snifter, he looked ready to talk about something else, and Holmes pounced.

"Who was opposed to the merger? Who would have lost out had it gone ahead?"

Viscount Smithers frowned and became more serious. "Quite frankly, old chap, no one from our side. The price they offered for our entire enterprise was beyond all we could ask or imagine. I had promised to share it with my team. Fine lads, every one of them. Not a man amongst my managers who didn't bear at least a minor title."

"Any on their side?"

"Their wives. Only their wives. Those American women. They were opposed at first, but they came around. They were so concerned about not putting their working men or women out on the street that they forced their husbands to promise in writing that there would be no layoffs for at least five years. Jolly decent of them. Really, quite the impressive ladies. Terribly charitable. It was good for us, of course. I was quite the hero to the boys in our shop when I told them about the promise. Mind you, it struck me as bloody stupid. These working blokes are used to being laid off and scampering around for another position. They would have got along well enough. So . . . what was it you asked? Ah, yes. Who was opposed? Forgive me, but your more correct question would be who was so *violently* opposed that they would commit bloody murder. Quite so, eh?"

"That is quite so," said Holmes.

"Not a soul in either party. Their penny-pinching accountant was, and he drove the initial price down, but it was still a fair deal for all. But there was one group who had reason not to be happy. Would you like to know who that was, Mr. Sherlock Holmes?"

"Of course I would, Viscount."

"Those Indian boys over at Brilliant Quality Bicycles. They are quite the striving up-and-comers in this trade. They started only five years ago and have already grabbed a share of the market. Mostly at the lower end, of course. But they work like slaves, they do. Start early, work late. The merger would have sent them running for cover faster than a scared cat runs from a constable's dog. All their work would have been for nothing. The rumor was they wanted to cut into the motorcar enterprise that Brunswick had started. But what with both our firms combined, they would have to say goodbye to that dream. Can't fault them for being ambitious. That spirit is good for the nation. But really, Mr. Holmes, these boys from the colonies should be warned that they were up against two firms owned by men of noble birth. What chance would they have had? Obviously, they didn't want it to happen. You can see that, can't you, Mr. Holmes?"

"Yes, I suppose I can." Holmes took a final sip of his brandy. "And I thank you for being so helpful. But would you mind doing me one final favor?"

"Of course. I assume you would appreciate some insights on that awful case of the trained snake. I could have told you – "

"Something much more important."

"Oh, and what might that be?"

"As you are as exceptionally familiar with the cases I have worked on, you will know I always strive to acquire as much pertinent data as possible. Yes?"

"Yes . . . yes, I guess I am. I've read every one of the Good Doctor's stories in *The Strand*, and – "

"Then you will have already discerned that it behooves me to know as much as I can about this business of making and selling bicycles. As you clearly have splendid knowledge of your industry, would you mind taking a few minutes of your valuable time to give Dr. Watson and me a tour of your plant? That would be of enormous usefulness to me in trying to solve this horrible case."

"Oh, yes, well, of course. I'm . . . I'm flattered that you would find our modest endeavors to be useful. But come along. Always happy to show off what we do here. Must say, the boys in the shop will be tickled pink to know that Sherlock Holmes wanted to see what they're up to. Cripes, they will be pleased as punch to know they helped you solve that wretched nonsense over at Brunswick. Please. Come along. Follow me."

As we followed him out through the front office, the viscount made a bit of a show of stopping and chatting with the men at the desks, patting each on the back as he passed. We exited through a set of doors and entered a spacious factory. It was well-lit both from rows of high windows and newly installed electric lights. The scattered pieces of equipment struck me as far from modern in their design but well-cleaned and polished. Half were dormant, but the others were clicking and clacking along smoothly.

The men all seemed cheerful as they pushed and pulled on the machinery. Half of them, though, were either shutting down their machines and getting ready to go for tea, or on their way to the tea room, or having tea, or coming back to their machines after tea.

The viscount made a point of stopping and chatting often and introducing his men to Sherlock Holmes.

"Mr. Sherlock Holmes asked for our help," he told his employees, "in solving that horrible disaster over at Brunswick. Do you hear what I said, boys? Sherlock Holmes needs our help. Something to be bloody proud of for all of us here at Empire."

As soon as our tour ended, Holmes stood at the factory gate and lit a cigarette.

"Tell me, my dear doctor," he said to me, "if you were the owner of Brunswick, would you buy this firm?"

I thought about it. "There's no problem with the workers. All seem as happy as clams. Not even a hint of a union. Not the busiest factory I've ever been in, but they've been in business for a long time. So, as the price was right, it might be a decent purchase. What do you think?"

"I wouldn't offer more than five pounds for the entire operation. They are fifty years behind in their production facilities, and even so, they are running at well below half capacity. That viscount is putting in no more than an hour or two a week. He probably spends most of his time at his club or the racetrack. Brunswick would be buying a pig in a poke. Within a year, this place will be bankrupt."

"If you say so. Then would I be correct in assuming you have decided there was no one here who had any reason whatsoever to oppose the merger? Doing murder to block it is inconceivable?"

"Precisely."

At the ungodly hour of six o'clock the following morning, Holmes hustled me out of bed and through a hurried breakfast.

"We need to be in Southwark before half-seven," he said. "That's when the doors of Brilliant Quality Bicycles open. It is always a useful time to observe whether employees are angry or content."

A cab took us south and across the Thames before the streets were clogged with traffic. The building of the bicycle firm wasn't quite what one would call a factory. Rather, it was more a conglomeration of various edifices that had been connected by passages and temporary structures. We arrived at the gate at a quarter-past-seven and were surprised when, immediately after the whistle, workers began to pour out of the plant.

"Do they run the factory at night?" I asked.

"It would seem they do," Holmes said, pointing to a group of workers lined up ready to enter, "and during the day as well. We can join them and wait in the front office."

There was no front office. Crammed in one corner of one of the buildings, a small cluster of nine desks was manned by six women. The remaining three were unoccupied. Every desk bore small piles of files.

"Pardon me, Miss," I said to the woman at the nearest desk. "Would you be so kind as to direct us to the owner of this establishment?"

"Which one?" she said without missing a stroke on her typewriter. "Do you want Brother Muhammed, Syed Sahab, or Bob?"

"Whichever of them is the owner."

"All three are. Wait here. I'll fetch them. It'll take a minute or two. Mo's at the metal press, Syed's over in the paint room, and Bob's at one of the drafting desks. But let me warn you: They won't like being hauled away from work for more than a minute. Truth is, they won't like even that. Oh . . . who's wanting to see them?"

"Please tell them it is Mr. Sherlock Holmes and Dr. Watson."

"Who? You must be one of the newest customers or suppliers. That's a good thing. They're always happy to talk with one of you. Well, as long as you don't talk too long."

We stood for several minutes before she returned, followed by three not-dark-but-not-light-either-skinned men. They all had jet-black hair and were walking quickly.

"Hello, hello," said the one who was the shortest but clearly the oldest. "I have heard about you two. You must be the detectives Scotland Yard hired to find whoever did those terrible, nasty murders over at Brunswick. We were very, very upset to hear about that. Oh yes, very upset indeed. We are eager to do the necessary. What do you wish to know?"

"Permit me to introduce myself and my friend," I said. "I am Dr. Watson, and this is Mr. Sherlock Holmes. Would you mind introducing yourselves?"

"Of course, of course," said the senior of the three of them. "I am Muhammed, but everyone calls me Mo. On my left is Syed, and on my right is Bob."

The chap he identified as Bob didn't look at all like a Bob.

Mo read the confusion on my face.

"Yes, yes, my Good Doctor," he said. "Of course, his true name, given to him by his father, isn't *Bob*. He is *Bankebihara*, but that was too difficult for you Englishmen to remember, so we call him Bob."

Holmes stepped forward until he was facing Mo directly.

"As you aren't ones to waste time, the necessary is for you to explain why you shouldn't be the three primary suspects for the murder of the Barons of Brunswick?"

Shock was followed an instant later by outrage that swept across their faces. But those looks were followed by a burst of convulsive laughter, first from Mo and then from the other two. They slapped their thighs and each other's backs and then crossed their arms over their abdomens.

"Gentlemen, I fail to see the humor," said Holmes. "Two men were heinously murdered. There is nothing funny about that."

"Oh, please, please, Mr. Holmes, sir," said Mo. "The murders weren't funny. No, no, not funny at all. But what is hilarious is that you think we would have wanted them dead. They were our promise to untold wealth, to undeserved thousands of pounds. To every prayer we prayed, we added an addendum begging whichever god or gods we worship that the foolish, silly merger would be consummated. Did we not do that?"

He looked first at Syed, who nodded vigorously. "Oh, yes. Yes, we did. We couldn't believe our good fortune."

"But it wasn't to be," said Bob. "Except for the Christian god, no god gives undeserved and unearned gifts. And the only thing He gives is eternal life. He doesn't give wealth that does not come from diligent labor. It was too good to be true."

I was confused and by the look on his face, so was Holmes.

"Please explain," he said.

Mo looked over to Bob, who gave us a condescending smile. "Had they joined their firms together, they would both soon be bankrupt. They have no idea, no, none at all, of how to run a profitable company. Those two women tried to stop the men from doing something so stupid. They are very very smart women. Very smart . . . and charming. Try they did, but it was too late. Empire is swimming in debt and will close its doors within three months. They tricked the fools at Brunswick into agreeing to acquire all their shares."

"You must be fair, Bob," said Syed. "They were not tricked. They were lied to. Their fault was believing that just because another man's blood was as blue as theirs, they must be honest. Had it not been for those two American women, they too would already be gone. We would have taken over the market share of both of them. It would have been a gift, but now it will not happen."

"Yes, yes," said Bob. "Now those women are in charge, and they put a stop to all the nonsense at their firm. Maybe we will get a share of Empire's customers when they collapse. But we will have to work hard to beat those women to that prize. They can do things we cannot possibly compete with."

"To what are you referring?" said Holmes.

"We must spend many, many pounds advertising our bicycles. They get everything for free. It doesn't cost them a farthing."

"No one gives away free advertisements."

"That is very very true, Mr. Holmes, sir. But they donate five bicycles to Barnardo's Homes, and the Press come and take pictures of them giving the bicycles, and they are in every newspaper in the country. Last month, they loaned, for no charge at all, not a penny, three very very expensive German limousines to the Prime Minister. Daimlers. He and his cabinet members now drive them in all the parades. They had a contest in which a single bicycle messenger boy could win a new bicycle – just one bicycle for one boy – and even *The Times* told the story and had a photograph of the smiling winner."

"But you could do the same thing."

"Oh, no, no, no, Mr. Holmes. We could not. They are *Baronesses*. Their firm is run by those whose blood is blue. The Press follow them around like lap dogs. We are three immigrants from India. We would have to kidnap and torture a reporter before we ever appeared in a story in the newspapers."

278

Holmes pursed his lips and nodded, but I sensed his growing suspicions and felt somewhat the same.

"How," Holmes said, "do you know so much about the state of your competitors? Do you have your spies working for them and reporting to you?"

"Oh, goodness, no," said Mo. "But at least a quarter of our employees used to work for one or the other."

"You mean to say," said Holmes, "you have been poaching workers from your competitors. That is hardly fair cricket."

"Poached?" asked Mo. "Oh, no. no. We do not poach."

"What do you do, then? Offer a higher wage?"

"Only for those who work through the night. During the day, the hourly wages are the same. All we offer is more hours. The men at Empire only work five days a week and have the weekends off. The same for Brunswick, except they work eight hours a day. Our men and women work twelve hours during the day and twelve at night."

"Some of our more liberally inclined politicians," said Holmes, "would consider those hours inhuman and exploitive."

"Oh, sir, sir. There are men and women all over London who are eager to work harder than their neighbors and to enjoy the fruit of their labor. These people come to us. We don't have to advertise for any workers."

"I presume you have them work through the weekend as well," said Holmes.

"Oh no. We live in a Christian country, and therefore we all take Sundays as a day for rest and family."

"But they work all day Saturday?"

"No, no. Only Saturday morning. And only those who sign up to work those extra hours."

"Why not Saturday afternoons?" asked Holmes.

I knew the answer to that one, and I smiled and winked at Mo. He returned a sheepish smile and a wink.

"We confess, Mr. Holmes," he said, "Saturday afternoons are sacred. That time is reserved for playing and watching cricket."

Holmes paused his questions, and the three of them shuffled in such a way as to make it clear they were anxious to get back to work.

"Who," he asked, "in your world of bicycle manufacture had any reason to block the merger? If not you, who?"

He gave them a hard look, and they gave helpless looks to each other.

"We have talked about this very very much during the past fortnight," said Mo. "The only answer we can offer is that it must be some foreign agent. Those barons and their wives had their fingers into every German and Frenchman and American who had anything to do with making and selling costly motorcars. And we all know, those chaps shouldn't be touched with a ten-foot barge pole. That entire nasty business runs on bribes and extortion."

"Do you believe cash was changing hands under the table?" asked Holmes.

"Some cash, yes, But also motorcars. They make very very good bribes."

In the cab back to Baker Street, Holmes muttered a few impolite words of frustration.

"I am like a dog chasing its tale, Watson. Every possible suspect merely but logically exonerates himself and points a reasonable finger at someone else."

We rode the rest of the way in silence. As soon as we were back in 221b, Holmes began to smoke and pace and smoke and pace some more.

Eventually he stopped. "If we eliminate the competition and those in fear of losing their employment, the only avenue we haven't explored is the foreign agents."

"That was what those Indian chaps suggested," I said. "And regardless of what one thinks about recent immigrants from the Raj, they struck me as awfully clever. And their insights into English people and business affairs were spot on."

Holmes strolled over to the window and peered out for a full five minutes before responding.

"I have no choice but to spend the next few days making inquiries in the City, at the docks, and in the Customs Houses. I need data on what they're doing."

He promptly strode toward the door and disappeared down the stairs.

For the next week, I saw nothing of him. Twice, a half-empty cup of cold coffee on the breakfast table gave evidence that he had come home late at night and departed before dawn. A note beside one of the cups read:

My dear Watson:

Kindly do not fret. I am engaged in a highly informative pursuit of appropriate data.

Holmes

On the morning of 8 August, however, he was sitting at the table and sipping a hot cup of coffee.

"Remind me," he said as I entered the room, "to thank our dear Mrs. Hudson for her everlasting goodness to us in providing fresh poached eggs and coffee. Don't you agree, Doctor?"

"Yes, and where have you been? You haven't eaten or slept adequately in days."

"Ah, but what an adventure of learning I've been on. Do sit down, have some coffee, and I shall tell you all about it."

"Fine. Go ahead."

He rose from the table, lit a cigarette, and paced back and forth while preparing to expound.

"That very capable woman, Baroness . . . What was her name?"

"Gloria."

"Yes. Gloria. She made a passing reference to the enterprise Brunswick Bicycles had developed in importing and exporting motorcars. That aspect was only the tip of the iceberg. What I learned is that for the past three years, they have been up to their eyeballs in buying, trading, and selling all sorts of goods all over the world. They may buy a fleet of motorcars in America and sell them in Brazil, but such a transaction is child's play by comparison with the machinations they have been through. Why, on one set of transactions alone, they purchased wheat from Russia and shipped it to Italy, where they exchanged it for silk textiles. Those were then sent on to France in exchange for some excellent Bordeaux wine, which was then sold in Sweden. The Swedes paid them in dynamite and TNT, which they shipped back to Russia as payment for the wheat."

"How could you possibly have discovered all the details of that business?" I asked. "Those who ply that trade would prefer, I would think, to keep it secret."

"Oh, they most certainly would. But in between every agreement and trade and shipment, there sits the same inevitable man: A banker. Money and letters of credit and insurance premiums have to move back and forth. Bankers make that happen. It so happens that several chaps in the City sit in the corners of some of our most reputable banks and owe a favor or two to a Mr. Sherlock Holmes. In months and years past, I have rescued them, their children, their wives, and even a grandchild or two from being victims of extortion, blackmail, theft, and kidnapping. It was time to call in a few favors, and they were thrilled to help. If you must know, they were eager to brag about those accomplishments they must otherwise keep secret. And the complications and twists and turns they engineered were beyond belief."

"Does that type of business go on these days?" I asked.

"All over the world. The largest portion of it is used to disguise the sending of arms, ammunition, and armaments from countries that manufacture such goods to countries the makers of those goods don't want their products shipped to."

"Ah, and that is what those barons were doing, and that must be what got them murdered."

"Yes . . . and no. Everything was done in the name of Brunswick Bicycles, but the work was all directed by a certain Baroness, known to us as Gloria, with the capable assistance of her daughter, also Baroness, and known to us as Judy."

"You don't say. My, but those two are rather more clever than they let on."

"They are indeed," said Holmes as he continued to meander around the room. "Every man I spoke to about them commented on what a pleasure it was to work with them. They are both brilliant and charming. I dare say, you found them that way as well, didn't you."

"Oh, entirely. Two of the most winning women I ever met."

Holmes stopped pacing.

He froze in place for several long seconds and then turned his face toward me.

His lips were parted, and his eyes wide open. For several more seconds, he said nothing.

Then he gasped. "No. No. They couldn't be. No. Not possible."

"What couldn't be? What isn't possible?"

"What you just said. I used those same words years ago."

I racked my memory. "Oh, yes, something about 'the most winning woman I ever knew' . . . Something like that."

"Yes. She was hanged for poisoning three little children for their insurance money. Those two are every bit as winning."

"Oh come, come, Holmes. That is impossible. You've met scores of murderers over the years. Those two are just not the type. Besides, no woman puts a gun to a man's head, blows his brains out, and then cuts his throat. Female killers abhor violence. They use poison. One or two might drug a man with brandy and laudanum and drown him in the bathtub, but scattering blood and brains? Impossible."

"My dear Doctor, when you eliminate – "

"Yes, yes. I know. You've said that several times a year since I met you. But those two committing murder? That is one more impossible for you to eliminate."

"Probably true, but . . . ."

He marched toward the door. "Until tomorrow. I need to do some eliminating."

Then he descended the stairs, taking two at a time.

At three o'clock in the afternoon, he returned and ascended the stairs, two at a time. He strode into the room, his face smugly beaming and his eyes sparkling. I knew that look. I likened it to that of a cat that has cornered the mouse and is about to pounce.

I sprang to my feet, stepped over to the hearth, and turned my back to the decanter of brandy.

"Oh no, you don't," I said. "You want to reward yourself for whatever you've accomplished. But no reward until you talk. Come on, my friend. Out with it."

He laughed, something he didn't do often. He was clearly pleased with himself.

"Oh, *et tu*, Watson? Oh, all right. Sit back down, and I'll tell you. But then I deserve a reward."

"Fine. Out with it."

He collapsed into his favorite armchair, sloped toward the hearth, and stretched out his long legs.

"My first stop was the American Embassy down in Victoria Street, where I had a friendly meeting with the Ambassador, Joe Coate. Splendid chap, and doing a fine job of keeping America and Great Britain from each other's throats, mending fences, and helping all to get along. He was happy to chat, as he has read all of your sensationalized accounts of my cases. He called in his First Secretary for commercial affairs and had him check out the Vermont connection."

"Was it legitimate?"

"Most certainly. Vermont Consolidated Industries of Burlington did indeed start over a century ago in lumber, and then expanded into maple syrup, furniture, textiles, and carpets. It was started by a Mr. Pierre Leblanc and expanded by his son. But the son didn't have a son. He had only one child, a daughter named Gloria – "

"Who we already know."

"Not so fast. I'm getting to her. The daughter marries a fellow named Frederick St. Aubyn – "

"Gloria's beloved Freddie," I said.

"Technically correct. Gloria and Freddie have a daughter, Miss Judy, and everything is going along swimmingly. Until – "

"Until what?"

"Until my conversation with the Ambassador ended, and everything appeared to be on the up-and-up. Neither he nor his First Secretary had any more recent knowledge and could only pass along what they had on file. News from a small city in Vermont isn't included in diplomatic pouches. I, however, still had deep suspicions about this entire affair, so I sent a long telegram across the pond to Burlington's current mayor, Mr. Berkley Sandercock. I had read about him in the American press. He is known to have socialist leanings, but is generally regarded as a decent fellow and a man of integrity. I asked him if he had any more recent data on Vermont Consolidated and the St. Aubyn family."

"Going by the look on your face, Holmes, he must have sent something that set the underseas cables on fire."

"Oh, that he did. He informed me that on a glorious summer day five years ago, Gloria and Judy went on a sailing outing on Lake Champlain accompanied by two other women and a local lad who served as the captain of the sailboat. A fierce storm came up, and the boat capsized. All five were thrown into the water. And the boat sank."

"That would have been quite the terrifying experience," I said. "A good thing Gloria and Judy knew how to swim."

"They didn't. They drowned. So did the captain. The two women friends of theirs, however, did know how to swim and made it to shore."

He stopped speaking, lowered his head, and looked across at me from under his furrowed eyebrows.

I sat in stunned silence and then rose, walked over to the hearth, and poured two generous snifters of brandy. I placed one beside him and sat back down with the other in my hand. After a large gulp, I had to admit, he had earned his reward.

"Who were the other two women, and is it possible we have already met them?"

"Possible, but not yet confirmed. The two of them claimed they had tried valiantly to save the others, but that they were wearing heavy clothing and boots, didn't have the sense to strip them off, and sank beneath the waves. The captain was an African fellow who couldn't swim a stroke. It was a terrible tragedy. It affected the entire town and was devastating to poor Freddie, who had a heart attack soon after and died. The firm is now in the hands of his son-in-law, the young widower husband of the real Miss Judy, and the business is doing quite well, thank you very much."

"And the friends in the sailboat? The ones who knew how to swim and how to rip their clothes off in the water? Who might they have been?"

"Their names, mother and daughter, were Katerina and Zinada Pavlova."

"Russians?"

"Daughter of a father who had fled Russia after being part of a plot to assassinate the Czar. They grew up in a revolutionary home in Burlington and are thoroughly American."

284

I took another gulp of brandy. "Where did they get their money? Gloria – *our* Gloria, that is – said the barons used her money to expand the plant. That would have taken at least a thousand pounds."

"And here the tale becomes even more interesting, if perhaps somewhat sordid."

"Go on."

"There was a rumor, heard by everyone right up to the mayor, that dear Freddie St. Aubyn had a mistress, a charming local woman of Russian descent."

"Named Katerina, by chance?"

"Correct. However, he had *two* mistresses. The other was named . . . Miss Zinada."

I gasped. "No. Say it wasn't so. The mother *and* the daughter? That's . . . that's utterly depraved. What is that degenerate colony coming to?"

"Let us agree that the Americans are endlessly, shall we say, *non-traditional* and *innovative*. Now, the next chapter: Not long after the funeral of the two who drowned, and only a few days before Freddie died, the Russian women left town accompanied by what was suspected to be a very substantial amount of cash."

"Hush money?" I said.

"Also called blackmail."

Holmes lit a cigarette, and I poured myself another brandy. Nothing was said for the next five minutes, and then I posed the inevitable question.

"Mind telling me what comes next?"

"A necessary step. I have to confirm the data I have been given. We shall pay another unannounced visit to Belgravia and say hello to Madames Katerina and Zinada."

"This should prove interesting," I said. "But all you have learned is that two American women of Russian descent may have used false names to attract and marry a couple of naïve English barons. That might not even be a crime, and it doesn't move us any closer to solving the murder."

"One thing at a time, my dear Watson."

"Very well then. Off to Belgravia first thing tomorrow morning?"

"No. Now. The element of surprise always favors those making use of it. With every passing hour, the possibility of surprise lessens. So, come Watson, our Russo-American ladies await our attention."

We hailed a cab and made straight for Belgravia. The two fearsome guards were still standing at the door of the house on Eaton Square, and they stepped aside as we approached the door. The Lascar made a slight bow.

"Hello, Mr. Holmes and Dr. Watson. Both Baroness Stepford and Baroness Bampfylde are in. Please enter, and I will call for them."

He opened the door, and the two of them followed us inside. There was no need to call anyone, as the two women were immediately visible and sitting in the front parlor.

We stepped into the room, and they rose to greet us.

"Good evening, Baronesses," said Holmes, "or should I say *dobryy vecher, samozvantsy*, Katerina and Zinada."

They didn't look at all surprised, and the woman Holmes addressed as Katerina gave a slight nod first at Holmes and then at me.

I heard something move behind me, and then my entire world went black.

"Watson, Watson, try to wake up. Please, don't be hurt so badly that you cannot come to." I felt a hand slapping my face and another holding my head up.

"Yes, yes. That's it, Watson. Deep breaths. Yes, and another."

I shook my head and forced my eyes to stay open.

"Holmes?"

"Yes, yes, it's me. Oh, thank God you've regained consciousness. My apologies, my dear friend. That was a foolish blunder on my part."

"What happened?" I asked.

"They were expecting us."

"But how?"

"I should have known they would have their spies and accomplices in the mayor's office or the telegraph desk in Vermont. No mayor sends his own long telegrams. Someone there must have sent a wire off to those women minutes after one was sent to me. How could I not have known such a thing would happen?"

"I'll tell you how," I said. "You were too pleased with yourself for getting such a resounding confirmation of your suspicions that you forgot to think."

That was perhaps not the kindest remark I had ever made to Holmes, but I had just been knocked senseless and now found myself in a dank, dark room and wasn't feeling inclined to be charitable.

"Yes, you are quite right. But kindly put that aside until a later day. Right now, we have to find a way out of here."

"Where are we?"

"We are in a basement. Locked in tight. There is one high window that is too small for either of us to reach. I can hear the sounds of ships' horns, so we cannot be far from the Thames. It's impossible to be certain, but I assume we're in a lower cellar of the Brunswick Bicycle plant."

"Is there a door?"

"Oh, yes, of course. It's securely fastened. I already tried to pick the lock, but it's barred from the other side."

I looked around, but in what little light came through the window, I could scarcely see my hand in front of my face.

"How are we going to get out?" I said, and I reached into my pocket and took out a box of matches. I lit one, and in the few seconds of light it provided, I confirmed what Holmes had said.

"Is there anything in those crates?" I asked, gesturing toward a small pile of sturdy packing cases.

"No. And no need to look inside. I lifted them. All are empty. But if we stack them up and you stand on top of them, I will be able to stand on your shoulders and see out the window."

"Why am I always the one who gets stood upon?"

"Nothing personal, my dear Doctor. Physics, my friend. Physics. You are built closer to the ground and have a lower center of gravity. You make a more stable base than I would."

I might have engaged in a lively argument had we been sitting in 221b, but under the circumstances, I couldn't be bothered. I staggered to my feet and stumbled over to the pile of cases.

"Do you have another match?" asked Holmes.

"The rest of the box. But I can't hold it lit and move the cases at the same time."

"I only need a second. Some labels on the cases caught my eye. I would like to take a closer look."

I lit another match, and the two of us bent close to the sides of the cases. In red paint, the words *Caution – Explosives. Handle with Care* were clearly visible and printed on all sides, the tops, and the bottoms.

"You're entirely certain they are empty?" I said.

"Quite certain. Come. Let's get them into a pile."

We made a small pyramid, and I clambered up to the top of the third level. Holmes followed me and, using my knee, my clasped hands, and then my shoulders, he raised himself up. I straightened my legs until he had a clear view outside the window.

"Ha! The Thames is right next door. And yes, I can see the wharf Brunswick must use to load and unload their bicycles, and whatever else they are importing and exporting."

I bent my knees and balanced myself against the wall as he worked his way down my body and then leapt the final few feet to the floor.

"Brilliant," I said. "Now we know where we are. How does that help us?"

"It doesn't yet. But do give me a few minutes to think. I suspect we shall have no other alternative but to engage in physical battle with whoever first opens that door."

"That would be when they come to kill us?"

"Most likely. We had best be ready."

"Are you so sure they won't just leave us here to rot?"

"Our baronesses may be women, but they are still villains. I have yet to meet a villain who cannot resist the temptation to chat with his or her opponent and expound on how he or she bested him . . . before killing him. To date, no opponent of mine has succeeded in doing so."

That fact Holmes was alive and telling me this made his comment patently obvious.

"There's always a first time," I said, and sat back against a wall with my knees pulled into my chest.

He was right on one thing. Several hours after the final light had vanished from the small window, we heard a movement outside the door.

A small wooden slide moved to the right, allowing a shaft of light through a slot that couldn't have been more than two inches by eight inches.

"Welcome to my parlor, Sherlock," said a now-familiar voice.

"And a fine evening to you, Gospazja Pavlova. How considerate of you to bid us farewell before you flee the country and run home to Mother Russia."

"Why, how clever you are, my dear. By this time tomorrow, our mission in England will indeed have been accomplished, and we shall move on to our next assignment."

I now knew that this woman was an absolute master of deception, but I was surprised by what she said. Her spontaneous reply had a ring of truth to it. I felt Holmes's hand gripping my wrist and sensed he felt the same way.

"Tomorrow?" he said. "My dear *prostitutka*, tomorrow is a holiday. There will be no factories to steal from, no rich men to seduce, no unions to organize. All those common working men and women will have the day off to celebrate."

"Oh, how little you understand, my dear Sherlock. We have no use for any more ineffective trade unions. They have been taken over by the Labour fakirs. They have been seduced by the power of officialdom and the pride of public office. No. Like my father before me, we know that the only way to win a revolution is by direct action. Do I need to teach you a lesson on how effective we have been in cutting off the heads of the oppressors?"

288

"Such action accomplishes nothing."

"Oh, but it does. We who are courageous enough to engage in violent struggle have removed McKinley in America, Daza in Bolivia, George Brown in Canada, Carnot in France, Cavendish in Ireland, Castillo in Spain, the Empress of Austria, and the Czar himself in Russia. Tomorrow, we will add England and the British Empire to our list."

A chill of horror swept through my body. They were going to kill our new King during his coronation. I cried out in anguish. "No! You can't do that! He has never been crowned king. He hasn't done anything to oppress anyone."

She laughed merrily. "Oh, my poor, foolish Doctor. Not King Edward the Caressor. He is useless. Nothing but a fat philanderer. No, we will strike where the power of England is held. By tomorrow afternoon, your Prime Minister and most of his Cabinet will be blown up and scattered into little pieces. And we will have disappeared. Do have a pleasant night, gentlemen."

"You had better," Holmes said, "kill us as well. If you harm any official of the Empire, be assured I will pursue you to the ends of the earth and see that you are hanged, preferably on a public gallows."

"Kill you, Sherlock? No, we would never do that. We are not murderers. We are soldiers fighting a revolutionary war. You bring criminals to justice, regardless of whether or not their victims are rich or poor. And Dr. Watson provides medical care to the indigent and the homeless as well as the bourgeois. Neither of you are oppressors. Within a few days, someone will find you here, and you will be free to go on with your lives. But you will never find us."

The wooden slot slammed shut, and we were alone again.

Holmes was on his feet, lighting matches and pacing and smoking and then pacing faster and smoking more. The pinpoint light from the end of his cigarette danced up and down and back and forth in the darkness.

"Watson! The female of the species is your department. Tell me, was she making an idle threat? Was that nothing but vain puffery? Did you believe her?"

"I did. She is enhancing her personal pride by boasting about what she and her accomplices are going to do. If anyone – a man or a woman – brags about what they are going to do and then nothing happens, they become a laughing-stock. I firmly believe she was utterly serious."

"About killing the Prime Minister and his Cabinet? You believe she was serious about that?"

"I do."

"But how? The coronation route will be lined with police constables. Crowds will be kept well back from the carriages carting dignitaries, from the bands and the marching soldiers, from the King and Queen in their Gold State Coach, and certainly from the open landaus bearing the politicians."

He returned to pacing and smoking, stopping only to light another cigarette or, very briefly, to rest his forehead against the cold cement wall.

"Umm . . . Holmes?"

"What?"

"Didn't someone – one of those Indian fellows – tell us Brunswick had loaned the Prime Minister's Office three large Daimler limousines to use in parades?"

He was silent. The glow of his cigarette was motionless.

"Yes, Watson. Why . . . Yes, that's it. All they had to do would be to stuff those Daimlers with explosives and set a timing device. They could explode anywhere along the route. No army of constables, not even the Royal Marines or His Majesty's Army, could do anything to stop that. The country will be thrown into chaos. Relations with Germany would be destroyed. Another mile along the road to advancing the anarchist cause and fomenting revolution. How utterly, diabolically brilliant."

"Those timing devices may already be set," I said. "The Coronation Procession starts tomorrow morning. I must say, that doesn't leave us much time."

"We have to get out of here," he said, and lit another match and resumed pacing and smoking.

I refrained from observing that his conclusion was beyond obvious.

He paced, and I sat down against the wall in a corner of the room. I soon became aware of a gentle draft wafting up beside me, accompanied by a distinctly unpleasant odor.

"What smells in here?" I asked.

"There's a manhole cover beside you," he said. "I noticed it while you were still unconscious."

"Does it lead anywhere?"

"Only to a pool of water. I pried it open and dropped a farthing down it, and it returned a splash, not a clink that it would have had it landed on the hard base of a sewer pipe. Had it been dry, I would have suggested we descend. But it is of no use."

I thought about that for a while he resumed his pacing.

"Umm . . . Holmes?"

"What this time?"

"When you were standing on my shoulders, and you looked out the window, you said this building was situated immediately beside the bank of the Thames. That was what you said, wasn't it?"

"Yes, that is indeed what I said. Why are you bringing that up?"

"How far was that window above the level of the ground that surrounds this building?"

"Perhaps ten feet. The floor of this room is ten feet below that. Why?"

"If when you tossed the farthing down the drain, and you heard a splash, that must mean the Thames Tide was high when you did that."

He stopped moving. The pinpoint glow of his cigarette fell to the floor.

"And six hours later," he said, "the Thames Tide will have gone out. The level of the Thames will have fallen by twenty feet. The end of the sewer pipe will be above the water, and whatever is in the pipe will spill out onto the mud flats. Watson, there are times when you – "

"If the diameter of that pipe is large enough," I said. "We might – "

"Oh, good old Watson! Yes! As long as we can stretch ourselves out, hands and arms above our heads, we should be able to wriggle through it. Oh, well done, Watson! Here, help me lift the grate off this drain."

The manhole cover was about two feet in diameter and made of cast iron. Fortunately, we only had to lift it far enough to slide it over. Once we had done so, I lit another match and stared into the darkness.

The prospect of crawling on my stomach along a sewer pipe that would still have effluent flowing wasn't the most pleasing image I had ever conjured in my mind. I remembered a time in my life when I had crawled through mud, blood, and stench. That was in Afghanistan. It was a long time ago, and I never expected I would have to do it again.

"Umm . . . Holmes?"

"Yes. What?"

"Can you not think of a less miserable way to get us out of here?"

"No. Can you?"

Holmes knelt beside the drain grate.

"Please, be quiet and listen. I'll try another farthing."

He dropped a coin through the grate. In less than two seconds, I heard a distinct plunk, followed by an uncharacteristic word of profanity from Holmes.

"The water is higher than before," he said. "It was on its way *in* when I tried earlier. We may be stuck here for another six hours. It will be close to eight o'clock in the morning before we get out."

"When does the procession start?" I asked.

"At nine."

"I saw a map of the route in *The Times*," I said. "It goes from Parliament Square up the Embankment, and then across Northumberland and over to Pall Mall, Piccadilly, and along Oxford. We may have a little more time if they don't explode the Daimlers until farther along the route."

"I fear not," said Holmes. "If she said anything I can believe, it is that they don't wish to harm the common working people. The thinnest crowds will be at the start. They can only line up a dozen or more bodies deep along one side of the Embankment. The other side is the river. That is where they will set off the bombs. They will be there by ten minutes past nine."

We sat there. Every so often, Holmes lit another cigarette and tossed another farthing down the drain as if by doing so, it would worry the tide to move faster.

It would be another six hours before the tide had fallen far enough to make a passage possible.

The final farthing he dropped delivered a distinct plink and not a plunk.

"Let's go," said Holmes.

The walls of the drain hole had the usual hand and foot holds fastened into the concrete sides. Holmes worked his body around until he was able to drop his feet and legs into the hole and then wriggled some more until his torso was over the edge. Then he moved quickly down into the abyss.

I did the same and followed him.

I was about fifteen feet down when I felt a firm hand grasp my ankle.

"I'm standing on the horizontal pipe," he said. "There isn't room for both of us to stand. Stay where you are while I twist myself so I can lie down and move. Some light would be useful. I have run out of matches. Can you light another one?"

"Umm . . . Holmes?"

"What this time?"

"It takes two hands to fetch the box of matches out of my pocket and light a match. Unless you want me to drop on top of you, I cannot let go with both hands."

"Quite so. I will feel my way."

He grunted and shuffled and squatted until he squirmed into the lateral drain. I then let myself down to the bottom, took out a match, and lit it. In the light, I observed a sewer that was about two feet in diameter, with Holmes's calves and boots disappearing into it.

As a young, athletic man accustomed to twisting my body into a rugby scrum, I would have had no problem getting down and moving from a squat to a prone position. Those days were long gone, and it took me several painful minutes to contort myself until I was lying on my stomach. Fortunately, the drain was wide enough that I could crawl on my elbows and slightly bent legs.

Unfortunately, there was still a slow stream of water moving through the pipe. I was getting soaked, but it was still early in the morning, and there was no one in the factory building.

Ten minutes later, I tumbled forward out of the end of the drainpipe and onto one of the many mud flats that line the Thames at low tide. Holmes was already well in front of me and standing beside the edge of the water. He was splashing handfuls on the front of his jacket and trousers in a vain effort to wash away the smell of the sewer. I did the same, also to little effect.

"Quickly please, Watson," Holmes said as he splashed a final few handfuls of water from the Thames on the front of his clothing. "We have a little less than an hour to stop the Coronation Procession."

"And just how are we going to do that?"

"I don't yet know. I will think about it in the cab on our way to Parliament Square."

There were no cabs.

It was early on a Saturday morning of a national holiday, and over a million Londoners were on their way to line the Procession route. We had no choice. We had to walk and partly run from Vauxhall, across the Lambeth Bridge, north on Millbank, past Westminster Abbey, and up Abingdon until we reached Parliament Square.

The entire square and the roads leading in and out of it were packed cheek-to-jowl with representatives of every regiment and corps of our Army, Navy, and Marines. There were at least twenty regimental bands all tuning up, and several hundred horses supporting red-coated, gold-braided, white-plumed riders. According to *The Times*, over thirty-thousand men in uniform would either be marching or lining the route.

I would have stopped and let my heart swell with pride at the site had not Holmes been desperate to find the man in charge of the gigantic spectacle.

"I cannot see any limousines or the Prime Minister and his gang. We have to find Viscount Esher. He's in charge of this chaos. He'll know where those motorcars are."

Reginald Balioly Brett, the Second Viscount Esher, was a sufficiently close confidant of the new King that they chummed around as "Regy" and "Bertie". Observers of the powers-that-be had dubbed him an *éminence grise*. Holmes considered the epithet ironically amusing as there was nothing at all *grise* about his shining bald pate.

We found him, all ribboned and medalled in the uniform he acquired during the Boer War. He was surrounded by sycophants, all vying for improved visible positions in the Procession. Holmes strode up to him, planted himself a few inches from the Viscount's shiny toes, and looked down on him from his advantage of several inches in superior height.

"Viscount Esher, my name is Sherlock Holmes. You must stop what you are doing and listen to me. It is a matter of overwhelming importance to you, the Government, and the British Empire."

The viscount took a step back and looked Holmes up and down. Then he gave an obvious sniff and screwed up his nose.

"You're Sherlock Holmes, you say? If you're Sherlock Holmes, then I'm the King of Siam. Now, whoever you are, old sport, run along. Have yourself a hot cup of tea and you'll be fine."

He turned and resumed barking orders to his minions, who were coming and going furiously.

"Viscount! You must listen. Bombs have been planted in the motorcars carrying Prime Minister Balfour and his Cabinet. They will explode while they are in the Procession. You must stop them!"

That got his attention.

"That, my good man, is a very serious charge. Now, whoever you are, prove to me you aren't some lunatic and that I should listen to you. Who planted a bomb? Where is it planted? How do you know?"

"I assure you, sir, I am Sherlock Holmes, and you know I was the one who rescued your daughter, Dorothy, from the clutches of that wild Bohemian artist she met at Slade."

The Viscount's head snapped back. "How did you know about . . . Right. What about this bomb? Speak up man! The Procession is due to start in fifteen minutes, and I won't have it late. Speak!"

"It was put there either by or under the direction of Baroness Stepford of Sodenleigh and her daughter, Baroness Bampfylde of Galtimore. They are impostors and anarchists, and they are going to wreak havoc on the Coronation and the Empire by murdering Prime Minister Balfour and the members of the Cabinet."

Viscount Esher's face changed entirely. He wasn't shocked, though. He was furious. He sputtered his words.

"How . . . how *dare* you! How dare you slander that woman – that *poor widow*! I know her. She is a lady of sterling character. And so is her daughter. They are in mourning and bereaved. Have you no decency?"

"You have been deceived, sir."

"I beg your pardon! The dear lady is the most winning woman I know. How dare you . . . *Constables*!"

Three police officers in uniform rushed forward.

"Get this man away from here, and do it now, and don't let him come anywhere close to the Procession! Now!"

294

Strong, rough hands were laid upon Sherlock Holmes, and he was lifted, dragged, and carried out of the square and unkindly tossed onto the pavement on the far side of Parliament Street.

I followed him and helped him to his feet. He was shaking, trembling with anger and fear. But he took several deep breaths and regained his composure.

"Lestrade," he said. "We have to find Lestrade. Scotland Yard is five minutes from here. Run."

He took off, and I tried to keep up with him, cursing the pain in my leg left behind from a nasty Jezail bullet of years ago.

We burst through the doors of Scotland Yard, and the officer behind the desk looked up in alarm. Fortunately, he recognized Holmes.

"Why, Mr. Holmes! Good Lord, sir, what's happened to you? You look like something the cat dragged in."

"It is imperative that I speak to Inspector Lestrade immediately. I wouldn't be here and looking like I do if it were not of critical importance."

"Right you are, Mr. Holmes. Now, be a good fellow and sit down and relax yourself. Shall I have one of the secretaries bring you a hot cup of tea?"

"No! My apologies. I mean, no thank you, Officer. Please, just get the inspector and, I beg you, do it now."

"I'll be back in two shakes of a dead lamb's tail."

And off he went.

"Holmes," I said, speaking quietly, "he's going to ask you who killed the barons. That's why he hired you. You still don't know who did that."

"I do know. They did."

"The women?"

"Yes."

"No, you said they couldn't. I heard you. We agreed that women don't cut throats, blow brains out, and leave blood and flesh all over an office desk. Only men do that. How can you – "

"When you served in the war, did you observe nurses performing deeds you thought no woman was ever capable of?"

"Of course I did. They were magnificent. What they did was marvelous. But . . . but they weren't women. They were *nurses*."

"And these women are combatants in a revolutionary war. They will do what they believe they have to do to win a battle."

"But why would they do it?"

"Elementary, my dear Watson. Their husbands may have been privileged dilettantes, but they weren't stupid. They must have realized what their wives were up to and tried to stop them. There is no stopping anyone, man or woman, who has given their souls to the revolution."

295

The desk officer returned in less than three minutes with Inspector Lestrade in tow.

"What in the name of all that's holy do you want, Mr. Holmes?" said Lestrade. "You look dreadful. And you smell. What is it?"

Holmes dropped his voice to a whisper. "Inspector, I give you my word based on everything you know about me for the past nearly thirty years. What I have to tell you is serious . . . and terrifying."

"If you say so, Mr. Holmes. Try to be concise and precise. I'm hoping to get out of here soon so I can watch the Procession."

Lestrade sat down and listened as Holmes succinctly reviewed the plot. He was barely under control when he demanded Lestrade stop the Procession and get the politicians out of the Daimlers.

Lestrade's posture changed. First, he straightened his back, and then he rose to his feet.

"All right, Mr. Holmes, all right. I'll grab a couple of my men and we'll do something. But I hired you to find out who killed the barons. Who did that?"

"Their wives."

"That's what I thought."

"You did?"

"Of course. They're Americans. Think of all the American women who betrayed King George and helped kill all our fine British soldiers during their rebellion. They're like that."

Lestrade commandeered four uniformed constables. We rushed out of Scotland Yard and pushed our way through the crowd who were lined up on the land side of the Embankment. Hundreds were watching and cheering on the soldiers and sailors and the marching bands that were approaching.

In the wake of a flying wedge of burly constables, we crossed over and worked our way through the smaller crowd lined up along the edge of the Thames.

"There they are, Inspector!" shouted the constable at the head of the wedge. "I can see what looks to be three big motorcars coming our way. About fifty yards up there, Inspector, sir."

"Good work, son," said Lestrade. "Now, all of you, get yourselves out in front of the first car and make them stop. I'll talk to the Prime Minister."

We shouldered our way through the line of cheering spectators. Some were clearly annoyed with our poor manners, but the sight of constables in uniform and the rousing sounds of the band of the Coldstream Guards kept them from pushing back.

The constables ran out to the middle of the road directly in front of the first long, black Daimler. The Prime Minister of England, Arthur Balfour, sat beside a uniformed driver. Behind him on two bench seats were the Chancellor of the Exchequer and the Secretaries of State for the Home Department, Foreign Affairs, the Colonies, India, and War.

"Terrible sorry to be such a bother to you, Mr. Prime Minister, sir," said the constable, "but we have to ask you to step out of the car."

"What is the reason for this?" demanded the Prime Minister. Then he noticed Lestrade. "Lestrade? Scotland Yard? This is the Coronation Procession! Why are you interrupting it?"

"All for your safety and well-being, sir," said Lestrade, looking woefully serious. "Scotland Yard has just received secret intelligence that there is a band of mad jingoes somewhere up ahead, and as soon as you and your Cabinet appear, they are going to pelt all of you with rotten eggs, ripe tomatoes, and moldy cabbages."

"Nonsense. I've only been Prime Minister for less than a month. I haven't done anything to offend anyone – Well, not yet."

"Oh, it isn't you, sir. It's the *cars*. They're made in Germany. And there are some chaps, and ladies too, who aren't inclined to like anything German these days. It started, as you know, sir, with Kaiser Billy sending that silly letter to cheer on the Boers, and that fellow Tirpitz stole the plans to our battleships and is bragging about *Weltpolitik* and besting the Royal Navy, and – "

"And they are mad enough to attack us because we are being driven in German cars? Nonsense. We are Englishmen and made of sterner stuff. We can fend off a few eggs and tomatoes. Stand aside, Inspector."

"You might want to reconsider, sir. They also have members of the press and photographers with them. You can be sure, sir, that tomorrow morning, your photographs, all covered in egg yolks and tomatoes, will be on the front page of every newspaper in the land, and all over the Empire within a month after that."

Balfour leapt out of the car and shouted to all three motor cars. "Listen up, all of you. Umbrellas under your arms. Bowlers on your heads. We are marching the rest of the way. Chop, chop, out you get!"

Twenty men quickly made up a formation and began marching up the Embankment behind the Prime Minister, leaving three large limousines parked in the middle of the road.

Holmes hopped into the driver's seat of the first car. "Watson, into the next. Inspector, take the third. Constables, there is a set of Watermen's Stairs ahead on the right. Clear a way. We're driving down them."

The four constables all looked at Holmes as if he had arrived from another planet. But then they looked at Lestrade, already sitting in the third car.

"Do it!" he shouted.

They forced an opening in the lines of spectators, and one after the other, we banged and bounced our way down the cement steps to the wharf that was used by those who work on the River Thames. At high tide, the boats would pull up to the wharf. But the tide was still some ways out, and Holmes roared along it at top speed, flew off the end, and landed with a resounding splash in the soft mud. I followed him, careful to turn just enough to avoid landing on top of him. Lestrade was right behind me and a few feet to the left.

Holmes waived his arms frantically. "Get back from the cars!"

We stomped our way through the mud and back to the shoreline. I looked up and saw four constables gawking at us, shaking their heads in disbelief. A few of the Procession spectators had watched us, but they were soon distracted by a loud band that was blasting out Rule Britannia. They turned back and lent their voices to the joyful chorus.

We clambered up to the top of the Watermen's Stairs and looked down at the semi-submerged limousines.

For a full five minutes, nothing happened.

"Mr. Holmes . . . ." said Lestrade. "Mr. Holmes, if those motorcars just sit there until high tide washes over them, you and I are going to have to have a not-very-friendly conversation."

For another five minutes, nothing happened.

Then it did.

The Daimler Lestrade had driven off the wharf exploded. We threw ourselves to the ground, faces down, to avoid being struck with flying pieces of metal and covered in mud. Then Holmes's motorcar burst apart, and finally mine. Blobs of mud flew as far as the top of the bank, landing on a few of the spectators, who didn't like it at all.

Lestrade was already up and holding his palms in front of his chest and gesturing to the angry recipients of portions of the Thames mud flat.

"Sorry folks, just a small political stunt. His Majesty's Government wanted to send a message off to the Kaiser to let him know what we English think about their cars. Politicians, these days. What can I say? Please, enjoy the Procession. Get your children up onto your shoulders. It's the opportunity of a lifetime."

Several small bodies were hoisted up, and the mud forgotten.

"Constables! Mr. Holmes! Doctor!" said Lestrade. "Follow me back to the Yard. I'll have a police carriage take us over to that house in Belgravia. If we move quickly, they won't know we foiled their plot."

298

"Begging your pardon, Inspector," said the largest constable, "but what with those Germans motorcars out of the way and blown up, we were thinking it would be a bit of all right if you could let us kind of stand guard over them, and that way we could watch the rest of the parade."

"All right. Fine. Stay here. Mr. Holmes, Dr. Watson, come with me."

We exited Scotland Yard from the Parliament Street side of their headquarters, jumped into a police carriage, and hurried through the near-deserted streets to the Birdcage Walk, past Buckingham Palace, and south into Belgravia.

The two guards who had proven to be highly skilled in the art of applying blackjacks to the backs of our skulls were gone.

The door of the elegant terraced house was open.

We rushed inside, split up, ran upstairs, and into every room and closet.

There was no one there.

Not a baroness, not a maid, not a cook . . . no one.

"Their clothes are gone," Lestrade called from one of the bedrooms. "Only the dead husband's clothes left behind."

The three of us came to the obvious conclusion. Our birds had flown.

"I'll get back to the Yard and send out a wire to all the stations and all the ports," said Lestrade. "If they're still in England, we'll find them."

"It's too late," said Holmes. "They will have traveled last night to Dover and be on the Continent by now. All you can do is send a warning to the Crowned Heads of Europe. Tell them to beware of two exceptionally winning women."

"Where was their factory?" asked Lestrade. "Somewhere in Vauxhall? We should go there and see if there are any clues as to where they might have gone."

"Or," said Holmes, "where they plan to strike next."

The police carriage raced through the deserted streets of Belgravia, across the Vauxhall Bridge, and stopped in front of a factory that bore the sign Brunswick Bicycle Works.

"You've been here before, I take it," Lestrade said to Holmes.

"Only to the cellar and the storm sewer."

Lestrade looked at Holmes, opened his mouth as if to say something, closed it, and shook his head.

The front door was open, and we entered the building. There wasn't a worker on the floor or anywhere. It was Coronation Day, and all work had ceased to welcome the ascension of our new king.

Lestrade opened the door to one of the offices. Inside, sitting at a table, a man was bent forward, his head buried in his hands. He looked up at us as we entered. His eyes were glowing red as if he had been weeping for hours.

"Aye, and who might ye be?" he asked.

"My name is Sherlock Holmes. This is Inspector Lestrade of Scotland Yard, and this is Dr. Watson. And might you be Mr. Hamish MacBaird?"

"Aye, that I am. And sorry to say that you've come too late. Lady MacBeth has done her foul deed. You'll read about it tomorrow in the press."

Holmes walked over to the miserable fellow and put a hand on his sagging shoulder.

"At ease, my friend. Her best laid scheme ganged agley. No one was hurt."

A wave of relief swept over the reddened face.

"Auch, are ye telling me the truth? Oh, but that's a sore relief."

But then he shrugged and sighed. "But ye may as well lock me up. For I was the one who caused it."

"I do not believe that to be the case, sir. Why do you say that?"

"Auch, because it was me that saw the numbers that had been fiddled with. I brought it to the attention of the two barons. I dinna ken what happened after that, but they ended up dead. I shoulda gone to the coppers, I should."

Lestrade sat down across from Mr. MacBaird. "There is no reason to charge you with any crime, sir. You are free to keep doing your job."

"Ow, but they'll be closing it down, won't they? After the murders and what those two Jezebels tried to do. And all our fine lads and lassies will be out of work and heading for the poorhouse."

Holmes glanced at Lestrade. "Inspector, Scotland Yard can exert some authority in a situation like this, can it not?"

"Can you vouch for this man, Mr. Holmes?"

"I can. I know him to be honest and frugal."

"Right. Well then, Mr. MacBaird, in the name of Scotland Yard, I am appointing you as trustee of this factory. I suggest you get to work. Come Monday morning, your employees will be coming through your door."

The Scotsman looked up, his face now beaming. "Oh my, I canna say I ever dreamed I'd be the laird of anything, let alone a firm like this one."

"I suspect," said Holmes, "that not far from where we sit, there is a bottle of fine single malt whisky waiting to be opened and a wee draught poured to celebrate. But no more than one."

We bade Mr. Hamish MacBaird a good day and returned to the pavement. Lestrade climbed into his carriage and headed back to Scotland Yard.

It was a fine summer day, and it was wonderfully quiet so far from Westminster. We walked back to Baker Street.

"Are you going to go after her and her daughter like an obsessed hound?" I asked Holmes as we strolled over the Vauxhall Bridge.

"No. Doing so would only serve to salve my wounded pride. It would be an inefficient use of what time I have left to work as a consulting detective. I have a chap coming over to Baker Street this evening, and he promises to be an interesting case."

"Does he now? What? Murder? Treason? Robbing the Bank of England?"

"Not at all. He is a wealthy fellow who wishes to be a philanthropist with a quarter-million to donate to a worthy cause. He wants me to investigate several charities that claim to help London's poor and make certain they are up to scratch."

"You don't say. Well, I might like to meet him. Sounds like a capital fellow."

"He isn't. He is the second most repellant man of my entire acquaintance."

Death at the Diogenes Club
by Tim Newton Anderson

I had just arrived at 221b Baker Street when I encountered Holmes exiting his lodgings. It had been several days since I'd had an opportunity to visit, as my practice and marriage had kept me busy and I had been looking forward to catching up with my friend and his latest cases. Instead of sharing one of Mrs. Hudson's meals and a bottle of brandy, however, Holmes bustled me towards a waiting cab.

"I'm glad you're here, Watson," he said as we sat in the cab which immediately moved off. "I've received an urgent summons to attend my brother, and the last time we met we had a disagreement. I believe your presence will inhibit any continuation of our argument."

"Then we're off to the Diogenes Club?" I asked.

"Far from it," said Holmes. "We are hastening to meet my brother in prison."

"Is he visiting a prisoner?" I asked. "Some kind of enemy of the state?"

"It is Mycroft who is the prisoner," he said. "He is under arrest for murder."

"That's unbelievable!" I exclaimed. "What has happened?"

"That is all I've been told," said Holmes. "Doubtless we'll find out more when we reach our destination."

I wanted to ask Holmes more, but he turned away and stared out of the cab at the swirling mists that filled the streets. The smoke of ten-thousand chimneys had combined with a thick mist rising from the river to form a London Particular fog that was thick enough to sear the lungs and make the streets echo with a chorus of coughs, as well as the sound of the hooves and wheels of our carriage. The toxic fog was one of the reasons my practice had been so busy of late, and I was aware from the newspapers that its concealing gloom had also hidden crimes which my friend had played his part in solving. The Spitalfields Strangler and the spate of burglaries in Bond Street were just two of the cases in which he had been engaged.

I had expected that we would proceed to the Whitehall Police Station, and was therefore surprised to find we were travelling in the opposite direction. After fifteen minutes moving through the largely empty streets, we pulled into the gates of The Tower of London. Its red crenulated towers peeked above the low-lying fog.

Although the holding of prisoners in The Tower was now rare, the last being the Cato Street Conspirators in the 1830's, the cells were kept ready to hold traitors against The Crown. That was an additional reason why I was heartily shocked to find Holmes's brother being held there. Mycroft Holmes had an undying loyalty to Britain and its government. It was hard to hold the thought that this bastion of the state should be wrenched from his habitual environment and incarcerated in a cell, let alone that he should have committed a crime worthy of that imprisonment.

In recent years, almost as many visitors have desired to tour the cells and execution site at The Tower as have viewed the Crown Jewels and the building's architectural splendours, in the same way people flocked to see the insane at Bethlehem Hospital in the eighteenth century. It is my understanding that the unscrupulous have already commenced walking tours of the East End to point out the sights where the Ripper carried out his crimes to lollygaggers. If they had dealt with the real horror criminals inflict on the public as Holmes and I have, I don't believe they would be as fascinated by death and destruction.

We were greeted by one of the Beefeaters in his traditional uniform, and escorted to the second floor of one of the buildings. I had expected to arrive at a cell with bare walls, stone floor, and thick bars on the windows, so I was surprised to enter a well-appointed suite of rooms furnished in the style of the seventeenth century. The carpets, wall hangings, and chairs were faded with age, but the room was light and airy, and Mycroft was sitting at a large oak table enjoying a meal of pork chops and potatoes.

"Welcome to my temporary abode," he said as we entered. He had placed his bulky frame in one-half of a love seat. "I hope you will allow me to finish my meal while I brief you on the reason for my incarceration."

"I confess that I was expecting less-luxurious surroundings when I heard that you had been arrested and taken to The Tower," I said.

"Understandably," said Mycroft. "However, as Richard Lovelace said: '*Stone walls do not a prison make, nor iron bars a cage*'. Some of my predecessors in this accommodation were high ranking members of the House of Lords imprisoned for political or religious indiscretions, and the authorities permitted them to pass their time in comparative comfort."

"As I could not explain on our journey for fear of inquisitive ears," said Holmes with a smile, "Mycroft is in The Tower so that certain people cannot get in, rather than to prevent him from getting out. At the present moment, this provides far safer accommodation than the Diogenes Club."

"I don't understand," I said. "Surely as a senior member of Her Majesty's civil service, the police could provide a secure guard on any premises."

"I thought so too," said Mycroft. "Until I was first shot at as I took a carriage from my lodgings to Westminster, and then was nearly poisoned by a meal at the Diogenes. If my intelligence is correct, and I have every reason to think it is, I'm threatened by an assassin with considerable resources and resourcefulness. At first, I was reluctant to make such a drastic change in my habits, but the Head of Scotland Yard himself suggested this was the only safe course of action."

"But what about the murder you are supposed to have committed?" I asked.

"A murder there has certainly been," said Mycroft. "Although I didn't consume the poisoned food that was destined for my plate, one of the kitchen staff who was tasting it died. It was his collapse from the effects of the poison that alerted the chef that all wasn't well and stopped him sending the plate out. If I hadn't been observed in the club afterwards by several members, I would have started the rumour that I was the one who had expired. Instead, the charge of murder was a convenient excuse to remove me from danger. Although I have to say it isn't proving at all convenient, as there are many things I need to attend to, and this isn't an appropriate venue from which to do that."

Holmes and I had taken a seat opposite Mycroft – I in a gilt chair and Holmes on a chaise lounge. Mycroft's manservant had accompanied him in his exile and brought us brandy and cigars which he placed on a low table, together with an ashtray. I clipped the end of my Havana and lit it from a spill that had also been placed on the table, along with a box of matches.

"I assume you wish me to find out who is behind the attempts on your life?" said Holmes.

"I am already aware of his identity," said Mycroft, putting down his cutlery and leaning back in his chair. Mycroft always appeared at ease in his habitual surroundings, and he had carried this *sangfroid* with him to this unusual location. "What I need you to do is track the villain down and arrest him."

"If you know who he is, cannot the police do that?" I asked. My cigar had gone out as I concentrated on Mycroft's story.

"Do you remember the matter of the Eddystone Lighthouse?" [1] Mycroft asked. Holmes and I nodded. We had managed to avoid an international incident by arresting the German spies who had killed a Russian diplomat. "The assassin is the brother of one of the German's you apprehended."

"Another German spy?" Holmes asked, leaning forward in his seat. He had also abandoned his cigar to the ashtray.

"Quite the opposite," said Mycroft. "His brother, Hans Burgholz, died in prison after his trial for spying. The Germans tried to have him released to their custody in exchange for one of our agents, but he succumbed to pneumonia before that could be negotiated. Wolfgang Burgholz has sworn revenge, despite having taken a very different career path to his brother. He is wanted in a dozen countries, including his native Prussia, for anarchist atrocities. Indeed, it's surprising that his brother managed to retain his position in the secret service with such a notorious criminal in his family. Bombings, assassinations, kidnap, bank robberies, and attempted coups have all been attributed to Burgholz and his associates."

"I assume you have a description you can give me?" said Holmes.

"Unfortunately not," said Mycroft. "I'm aware you consider yourself to be a master of disguise, Sherlock, but I suspect even those skills you learned in your brief career as a thespian pale in comparison to those possessed by Burgholz. No two descriptions of him match, from either his colleagues or those who have witnessed his crimes. Each time he has been spotted, his appearance is radically altered and for many years his deeds were attributed to several people rather than a single mastermind.

"I am aware you hold the Russian spymaster, Pyotr Rachkovksy, [2] in low esteem for his duplicitous dealings – as do I – but I do have high regard for his intelligence network. He has been tracking Burgholz for a number of years and unearthed evidence of his part in numerous plots. It was Rachkovsky that alerted me to his presence in England and his plans for revenge."

"Tell me more about the attempts on your life, Brother," said Holmes. The worry he had over their previous argument seemed to have evaporated to be replaced by concern for Mycroft's safety.

Mycroft picked up some papers from the round side table by his chair and handed them over with a casual gesture to Holmes as if it was a matter of little consequence.

"You'll find all of the details in these files – the statements of witnesses as well as my own," Mycroft said. "In brief, the first attempt took place when I was taking a cab along the Mall towards my club. A cyclist drew alongside with a pistol in his hand and was about to fire into the cab when the quick action of my driver, who struck his arm with his whip, disarmed him. The man quickly sped off. Unfortunately, he had covered his face with a bandana so he was impossible to track down.

"The more worrying incident took place at the Diogenes. As you know, I have my colleagues carry out extensive vetting checks on everyone who is employed there. I'm not the only servant of Her Majesty who is a member, and I'm well aware of the dangers posed if any of our enemies find their way inside its walls. This includes all of the kitchen and serving staff. The head chef – Gustave Laurent – had prepared me a meal of *Moules Mariniere*, and the mussels had been hand delivered from Kent this morning. He assured me that he knew the fisherman who had harvested them and the courier, and had personally overseen the cooking of the white wine cream and tarragon sauce made from ingredients that had also been personally vetted. At no time was the kitchen left unattended, and if the assistant chef hadn't taken it upon himself to check the dish as some of the mussels had failed to open, I wouldn't be here to relate what happened.

"All of the kitchen staff and anyone who had the opportunity to interfere with the fresh produce, as well as the suppliers and the men who delivered the ingredients, were extensively interviewed by Inspector Gregson, and all seemed above reproach. It is therefore a mystery how the deadly gypsum weed was administered. As I'm sure you are aware with your extensive knowledge of poisons, it tastes like liquorice, so wasn't detected against the aniseed flavour of the tarragon."

"While I have a great deal of respect for Gregson," said Holmes, "I shall make my own inquiries. Of course, I'll require access to the kitchens at the Diogenes Club and free rein to search the building."

"Impossible," said Mycroft. "The members were disconcerted enough with the police trampling around. Those walls contain many official secrets and cannot be breached."

"Nevertheless," said Holmes, "they must. It is the best hope of tracking the trail from the crime back to Burgholz."

"Shall I accompany you?" I asked.

"I fancy not," said my friend. "We need to track this anarchist from both directions. I would like you to go to the Rose Street Club in Soho. Although it is less active since Johan Most departed these shores for the United States, it is still frequented by German anarchists, and you may be able to pick up some useful information there."

"They are hardly likely to confide in an associate of Sherlock Holmes," I said.

"That is why we need to provide you with a different identity," Holmes said. "I'll conjure up something on our way back to Baker Street."

As soon as we had entered our cab and pulled away from the entrance to The Tower, I questioned Holmes on my assigned role.

"I'm unsure how well I'll be able to sustain a role," I said.

"Never fear," he said. "I have complete confidence in your abilities. I have in mind that you will present yourself as a doctor who has been treating the immigrant community in the poorer parts of our metropolis and feels some common ground with their plight – a scenario that isn't too

306

far from the truth. You were drawn to the Rose Street Club to see if there is more you can do in your medical capacity to help their community. There is no need to pose as an anarchist – merely someone with philanthropic aims."

I was somewhat reassured by Holmes words. The main challenge would be remembering my false name and address.

"I must say, Mycroft seems to be coping well with his situation."

"As I've said a number of times," said Holmes, "you see but don't observe. At first glance, you could be excused for coming to that conclusion, but if you knew Mycroft as well as I do, you would think very differently. The most obvious was the fact that he has called me in rather than rely on his extensive network of contacts to deal with Burgholz. My brother only summons me when there is a problem that requires my unique talents to find the solution. The second indication, which even you should have spotted, is that he abandoned his meal after a few bites. It takes a lot for Mycroft to lose his appetite, especially his favourite dish. No, he is extremely worried indeed."

Although Holmes had suggested I would need little preparation for my role, he couldn't resist making me change my clothes to some which were shabbier than my current dress – he found some of my old attire in a wardrobe at Baker Street that dated from the penurious period when we had first shared rooms and I was pleased to find that they still fitted. He also smeared my face and neck with dirt to suggest that I cared more about my profession than my appearance, although I insisted my hands remain clean. No doctor would allow himself to treat a patient without that essential step of hygiene.

The German anarchist club was in a side street off Shaftesbury Avenue in Soho. A banner in German hung over the entrance proclaiming support for working people against the Kaiser, and inside a number of poorly dressed men and women were busy compiling a newsletter from lead type, ready for printing. They all turned towards me as I entered, and a large man challenged me in his native language. He was around five-foot-ten inches in height but had the solid body of a manual labourer and a bushy red beard. Like the others, his plain clothes showed signs of having been mended many times.

"I'm afraid I have little German," I said. "I have learned a few words from my patients, but am far from fluent."

"A doctor, then," said the man in good English. "There is no one here in need of your attention."

"That isn't my purpose in visiting," I said, "although I would have been happy to provide medical services to any who needed it. I have been working with some of your fellow countrymen in the East End of London and been touched by their plight. My grandfather was from Saxony and came to this country half-a-century ago to live in a more liberal country. I have been fortunate enough to have a number of wealthy clients who provide me with a good living and I wanted to help those who cannot afford a doctor."

"We don't need your charity," said the man. "We look after our own."

He turned and walked away, back towards the table where the newspaper was being assembled. One of the ladies who had been preparing food for the workers came over and spoke to me.

"Never mind Shultz," she said. "He is fiercely loyal to the anarchist cause and suspicious of anyone who isn't part of the group."

"Given the attention of the police after recent incidents in Germany and London, I can understand his concerns," I said. "However, my intentions are purely as I have stated. I want to give something back to those who, like my grandfather, found a safe haven in this country."

"I'm sure there will be people who would welcome this," said the woman, who had introduced herself as Helga. "Our more fortunate compatriots employ many of us – when he isn't editing the newspaper and organising demonstrations Shultz works for a wine merchant importing product from the fatherland – but there are also many who aren't able to find work. Many thousands have made Britain their home."

I looked around the room again and saw several cases of Rhenish wine under a table, no doubt destined for German homes across the capital. Another table was laden with produce which Helga told me was distributed for free to poor households.

"I will leave you my card," I said, taking one Holmes had prepared for me from my waistcoat pocket. "It has my surgery hours on it, indicating the times when I'm able to take free patients. I look forward to being of service."

I waved a farewell to the people still busily bending over the newspaper and left the building.

Holmes had requested I report to the Diogenes Club after my investigations, and I got a cab at the cab station in Soho Square. I had been careful to ensure I wasn't followed and relieved to see that I wasn't under observation.

At the Diogenes Club I was shown into the Stranger's Room – the only place where conversation was permitted outside of the bedrooms. As usual, there was a roaring fire in the grate which dispelled some of the chills of the autumn air and dried the fog which had penetrated my clothes. After a few minutes, a waiter in the club's uniform entered and asked what I would like to drink.

"I will take a glass of your excellent brandy," I said.

308

"Certainly, sir," he said. "And would you like a sandwich, Watson?"

With a start I looked more closely at the waiter and discerned Holmes features under the wig and makeup.

"I hope your time has been as productive as mine," he said, taking a seat opposite me. He removed the distinctive club jacket and his wig and the putty that had disguised his aquiline nose. "I feel we're getting closer to the truth in this affair, although I also believe that the level of danger from Burgholz is moving towards a climax."

I told Holmes what I had found in my visit to the Rose Street Club as a real waiter arrived with the two glasses of Courvoisier that Holmes had previously ordered.

"Then you have met our assassin," said Holmes. "The pieces of the puzzle fit together nicely."

"Shultz is our man, then?" I asked.

"That is merely one of his identities, I'm sure," he said. "His work for a vintner confirms it. As you are aware, one of the puzzles was how the poison was administered in Mycroft's meal. My brother is very particular about his food, and had specified every detail of the dish. As he told us, the ingredients had been carefully sourced, and the police had tracked back through the chain of supply to see where the deed could have taken place."

"And you have been able to answer the question?" I asked.

"Indeed," he said, sitting back in his chair with a broad smile on his face. "Suspicion naturally fell on the staff within the Diogenes Club, but I believe they are completely innocent. A careful examination of the cork from the wine bottle showed a syringe had been used to inject a powerful distillation of gypsum weed. Mycroft is the only member who favours that particular vintage and grape variety, so I believe he had been waiting for weeks for his plan to work, and resorted to a more crude attempt when he became impatient."

"The shooting came second rather than first," I said.

"Exactly," said Holmes.

"Then surely we must inform Gregson about Burgholz's identity so he can arrest the devil."

"As I said earlier, that is merely one of several identities he will have established," said Holmes. "The chances of finding him amongst the German community are slim, especially as he will have allies in the anarchist cause. No, to get our man, we simply have to sit here enjoying our brandies and wait for the next part of his plan to take place. I have also taken the liberty of ordering us a steak pie to eat while we sit."

"You believe he will strike again?"

"Assuredly," said Holmes. "I would have thought you would anticipate Mycroft wouldn't be the only target for his revenge. You and I played no small part in his brother's eventual demise."

I confess I had assumed the veil of secrecy Mycroft had drawn over the whole affair would obscure the part Holmes and I played in it, but if what Holmes said was true, we were also targets. My eyes scanned the room anxiously in case there were any infernal devices placed ready to blow us all to kingdom come. I interrogated my memory to see if any of the furnishings were out of place or hadn't been present at our last visit, but couldn't be sure. My eye for detail was sadly not the equal of my colleagues', and I felt a sense of dread rise in my stomach as I examined each item, any one of which could contain explosives.

By contrast, Holmes seemed completely relaxed, as if he was enjoying a social occasion rather than waiting for an assassin to strike. He cradled his brandy globe in his right hand and inhaled its aroma. His broad grin had softened to a gentle smile.

I was still looking around the room nervously when I jumped as the door opened. I was relieved that the room was entered by a waiter rather than a gun-brandishing anarchist. He carried a silver tray with two plates and condiments and placed them on the table between Holmes and me.

"Will you gentlemen be requiring anything else?" he asked.

Holmes sat upright.

"There is," he said. "I wonder if you would be so kind as to sample the pies for us. After the unfortunate incident last week, one cannot be too careful."

The waiter took a step backwards and threw quick glances around the room before reaching behind his back under his frock coat and drawing out a pistol. However, Holmes had sprung to his feet and held his own weapon at the waiter's temple."

"If you wish to be a martyr to your cause, Burgholz," he said, "I would be more than happy to oblige you. Otherwise, I would let go of your pistol and let it drop to the floor for my colleague to retrieve."

I could see a moment's hesitation on the anarchist's face as he weighed the options, but to my relief he let go of his gun. Holmes kicked it to the side of the room and I bent over to pick it up, turning to point it at Burgholz's back.

"Watson," Holmes said, "if you reach into the pocket of my coat on the chair, you'll find a pair of handcuffs. Kindly place your hands behind your back, Burgholz, so Dr. Watson can secure them."

Again, I could see the German calculate whether he could disarm Holmes and me and make his escape, but he realised the situation was hopeless and complied with Holmes request. As soon as I had locked the cuffs on his wrists, Holmes rang the service bell, and within ten seconds the door opened to two uniformed constables and Inspector Gregson.

"Here is your man, Gregson," said Holmes. "If you have the food tested, I'm sure you'll find enough poison to fell a horse. There are more meals in the kitchen which are similarly tainted, and the poison itself should also reveal itself."

"How did you know his plan?" I asked as the constables escorted Burgholz to a waiting police wagon.

"I'd like to know as well," said Gregson.

"You and your colleagues made the false assumption that Mycroft was the only target," said Holmes. "Hardly surprising, as that is also what my brother assumed in his vanity. What I realised was that revenge was only part of what Burgholz had in mind. Mycroft is an important part of the Government, but few of us are indispensible. However, a strike against *all* of the members of the Diogenes Club would be a very severe blow against not only our government, but those of our allies who are fighting against Burgholz and his ilk. The initial poisoning wasn't aimed at Mycroft. It was designed to kill the person who did in fact succumb to the poison. If he was able to kill the *sous chef*, Burgholz would be able to take his place. I believe he has been ingratiating himself with Gustave Laurent for some time to be able to step into the dead man's shoes."

"To carry out a mass poisoning?" asked Gregson.

"As a first step," said Holmes. "The chaos which would have ensued as the club's members collapsed all over the building would have allowed him to set off the explosives, now disarmed, which you'll find placed in various hiding places throughout the club. A score or more key individuals in the civil service and the world of finance and commerce would be wiped out in one atrocity. A major coup for Burgholz, which he would flee from in the confusion."

"I'm sure your brother and the nation will be grateful," said Gregson.

"I'm sure the nation will never get to hear of it," said Holmes. "Mycroft and his colleagues will want to spirit Burgholz away and interrogate him about his network before the anarchists hear of his arrest. And while I'm certain that Mycroft will be grateful, he isn't one for acknowledging any indebtedness – especially to his little brother."

In this instance, Holmes usual infallibility was incorrect. Two days later, a package arrived at Baker Street with a pound of his favourite tobacco mix and a bottle of his favourite brandy. Mycroft hadn't attached a card, but the delivery boy confirmed it had been sent by a large man at the Diogenes Club. I declined to share the foul-smelling tobacco that Holmes favoured, but was happy to taste the brandy.

"How did you enjoy your undercover assignment?" my friend asked as we sat in his study.

"It is not my *forte*," I said. "I believe I shall leave disguise and dissemblement to you and Burgholz in future."

"Perhaps that is wise," he said, lighting his pipe and filling the room with clouds of smoke that echoed the fog which still billowed outside the window.

NOTES

1. See "The Keeper of the Eddystone Light" in *The MX Book of New Sherlock Holmes Stories – Part XXXVIII: 2023 Annual (1889-1896)*
2. See "The Unlikely Assassin" in *The MX Book of New Sherlock Holmes Stories – Part XLII: Further Untold Cases (1894-1922)*

Gruner's Diary
by David Marcum

"Ah, Watson," said Sherlock Holmes when I opened the door. "My strong right arm. Now we can continue."

I blinked as I sought to understand why I had been summoned. Holmes's wire had contained a note of urgency, and fortunately my practice was quiet enough, and it was late enough in the afternoon, that I was able to quickly divert the last of my medical responsibilities to a willing neighbor for whom I often did the same favor, explain to my wife that Holmes had requested my presence, and find a fast cab in Cavendish Square.

There was, however, some delay from that point. The distance between Queen Anne Street and Scotland Yard, could one traverse it in a straight leap, was just two or three miles, but at that time of day, the main thoroughfares were rather choked with vehicular traffic. My cabbie was seasoned enough to know the secondary routes – but there are many seasoned cabbies in London who know the same tricks, and they, too, had opted to avoid Regent Street, Haymarket, Trafalgar Square, and the other major paths. Nevertheless, despite delays and irregular turns that often seemed in the wrong direction to avoid congestion, I arrived at the Yard as quickly as I could and strode inside.

A small part of me, I suppose the remnants of that young boy who – if a fellow is lucky enough – is never entirely eradicated by the responsibilities of taking on adulthood, is always a bit secretly amazed that my path has led me to be so easily recognized, and even welcomed, by the officers of Scotland Yard. A quarter-century earlier, as I neared the completion of my medical studies, I never envisioned the life I would eventually lead. At some point I'd conceived the idea of joining the Army and, in the vague way that the young have of seeing the future, I pictured that type of life, based on the little I knew of soldiers. I would travel. There might be battles, but they would be successful, and then I'd return, having made lifelong comrades-in-arms, to great stretches of calm and orderly sameness in life.

But then came Maiwand, and injuries, and the unexpected severance of my Army association. I met Sherlock Holmes, thinking that ours would be nothing more than a temporary and expedient acquaintance while I husbanded my meagre funds and regained my shattered health. Then, on the fourth of March, 1881, he'd revealed to me his curious profession and, almost as an afterthought, asked me to join him when summoned by Scotland Yard to a murder investigation.

"We may as well go and have a look," he'd said, but I had no inclination that he actually meant for me to join him. "I shall work it out on my own hook. I may have a laugh at them, if I have nothing else. Come on!"

As he put on his coat, I still had no sense that he was truly inviting me to join him and observe his methods – about which I'd shown such skepticism only a moment before.

"Get your hat," he pointedly advised, this time making it clear that he expected me to join him.

"You wish me to come?" I considered what I'd planned for the day – perhaps a walk to some as-yet unexplored neighborhood as I labored to regain my strength. But Holmes really meant for me to come along.

"Yes, if you have nothing better to do."

At the lonesome and shabby house where the dead body had been discovered, we found two of the Yard's inspectors, Lestrade and Gregson. I'd met the former some weeks earlier on occasions when he stopped in to visit Holmes, but then I'd had no idea of his profession or the reason for his visits. In those early days, both Lestrade and Gregson had been great rivals – though perhaps not quite so much as Holmes liked to think, as it amused him to classify them as "a pair of professional beauties", jealous of one another and their successes. It was only as the years passed that I realized the two of them, while so different from one another in physical description, background, temperament, and method, actually had a grudging respect for one another that grew through time, and as Scotland Yard Professionals, they used their jealousy and one-upmanship to keep themselves sharp, honing themselves like knives, and working together toward doing the best job that they could.

My good opinion – and Holmes's too – had grown quite a bit toward both men in the nearly twenty-two years since that morning at No. 3 Lauriston Gardens, off the Brixton Road, where my life had unexpectedly pivoted away from being a young and aimless invalid, still mistakenly believing that I might return to Army life. I'd had no idea that Holmes's simple command to get my hat and join him, almost an afterthought which, to him, wouldn't have mattered one way or another, would be one of those moments where my life would change forever. That day, I'd simply thought Lestrade and Gregson to be a couple of strangers, met once in those terrible circumstance, and never to be re-encountered. As so many say when looking back at the twisting paths of their own lives, "*Little did I know* . . . ."

Now, on that afternoon in late 1902, I'd opened the door to Lestrade's office to find my three good friends – Holmes, Lestrade, and Gregson – with most-concerning looks of worry on their faces.

"Doctor," said Lestrade, while Gregson only nodded. The former was seated behind his small crowded desk, while Holmes and Gregson were in a couple of wooden chairs on the other side. I settled into a third and started to lay my hat upon some sort of wooden club resting on Lestrade's desk – a peg-leg, I realized, with some suspicious splintering around the lateral stabilizer and a dark stain at the end.

"I wouldn't," said Lestrade, raising a hand. "That's what Wooten used to kill his mistress. Her blood and brains are dried upon the end there. Your hat will stay cleaner if you just put it on that stack of papers."

I nodded, readjusted where I placed the hat, and looked expectantly at the trio, who looked back at me. Certainly they had been talking with one another before I arrived, but now they seemed to be at a loss for words.

The day outside was chill, as would be expected for that time of year, and the small coal fire in Lestrade's grate did little to counter it, even here, deep in the building. But it was better than nothing, and I trusted that I would soon feel warm enough.

In the short silence, I could see that both Lestrade and Gregson looked worried, while Holmes's mouth was tightened in irritation. Seeing that each party, the professionals and the consulting detective, were waiting for the other to begin, I chose the alternative and spoke first. "What has happened?"

Lestrade opened his mouth, but Holmes beat him. "Gruner's diary – it's been stolen."

With those few words, I immediately recalled the events of the previous September: A most illustrious visitor to Baker Street, representing the Crown itself. A noble old soldier's daughter in terrible deadly jeopardy. Holmes suffering a terrible beating, and the subsequent justice rendered upon the odious and wicked murderer behind it. And in the middle of it all, like some squatting cancerous toad, was a book – something like a journal or diary, but so much more vile and evil, and very much like the man who had written it.

Baron Adelbert Gruner was a killer. That should have been enough to outweigh any other factor about him. The Austrian nobleman had managed to murder his former wife without being caught, saved only by a legal technicality and the suspicious death of the only witness. Afterwards, he'd relocated to London and turned his sly attentions upon Violet de Merville, the only daughter of the famed hero who had made his name in the Khyber region. Before the general realized what was happening, Gruner had gained entrance into his daughter's life. The old soldier had been helpless against the reptilian fascination Gruner exerted upon the girl, and she would hear nothing against him. In fact, every delineated crime only made her cling to him more firmly. Marriage to Gruner, as everyone realized but the young lady, would lead to her complete and total ruin, both physically and spiritually, and she was racing toward that certain eventuality with a willing heart and open arms. For she loved the black-hearted sinner, and she would hear nothing against him.

Friends – both hers and her father's – tried to make her listen, but she believed that any stories against Gruner were either jealous exaggerations or total lies, and every effort that was expended to convince her otherwise only made her that much more stubborn. Even the testimony of one that he had cruelly wronged, a sad young woman named Kitty Winter, had no effect. From Kitty, Holmes learned of Gruner's diary – a dark chronicle of his perversions, written with cold and clinical precision and describing in graphic detail the defilement and destruction of every woman with whom he'd had substantial contact. Holmes realized that this book alone might be the only thing to convince Violet de Merville of the Baron's intent toward her – another page in his diary as she was systematically destroyed in every sense.

But before anything could be done, Gruner's men attacked Holmes, retribution for his efforts to dissuade the girl from the Baron. In desperation, as the Baron was leaving soon for America and would take the book with him, Holmes devised a rickety scheme in which I would distract the Baron, a noted collector of Chinese pottery – with a saucer from the Royal collection while Holmes searched for and retrieved the diary elsewhere in the Baron's house. But the plan nearly failed when he perceived my false position and then heard a faint sound from Holmes's search. All would have been lost if Kitty Winter had not rushed forward just then and flung vitriol into the Baron's snarling face, ruining his cruel handsome features forever.

My duty was clear: I had to stay and treat the patient, writhing in agony, no matter how justified his punishment. Holmes, meanwhile, escaped with the diary, and I saw it later in Baker Street. I did not wish to examine it, for Holmes explained that it was explicitly deranged in its exactly described details, with sketches and photographs tucked between the leaves. I was shocked to learn just how many notable women, many that I'd heard of and some that I knew, were in Gruner's collection – as if he were a butterfly collector who had pinned, corked, and carded them. At some point in our conversation, Holmes had looked at diary, the ugly brown book resting on the octagonal table by his chair, with distaste. "The Devil's pet bait," he'd murmured, although I hadn't understood his meaning then. It was only later, when Kitty Winter came to trial for throwing acid in her persecutor's face, that I followed his thought: There were secrets in that book to rock the nation, and if it fell into the wrong hands, the damage would be incalculable. That was one of the reasons that Kitty's sentence was no more than a slap on the wrist – fear that her lawyer would introduce the book into evidence. (The other reason was that so many people were grateful for what she had done.)

After the trial, there was much discussion about what to do with the book.

It seemed to me that, after it was used to break Gruner's hold on Violet de Merville, the only answer was to destroy it, but more influential minds – that is to say, *scheming* minds – saw some value in preserving it, the way that the government builds bigger and more deadly bombs – "*Not to use them! No sir! We'd never do that! They're only here as a* deterrence *– in case some situation means that we* have *to use them. But we never will. But just in case there's no alternative, we'll have them . . . .*"

I was not privy to those conversations, and I had only heard about the decision to preserve the diary when Holmes described, with great disgust, how he had unsuccessfully taken the same position I held – that the book should be burned immediately. He was overruled.

I was unaware of what happened after that, and in truth had given the diary no further thought until that November day, in Lestrade's office, when I was told of its theft. The implications were immediately apparent.

"Has someone already made a blackmail attempt?" I asked.

Holmes shook his head. "If so, the chances that we would know about it this quickly would be nearly nil. The diary has only been gone for less than a few hours."

Still uncertain as to why I'd been summoned, I asked, "Where was it kept? How was it taken?"

Gregson sighed and replied. "The '*where*', Doctor, is *here*. In Lestrade's safe. The '*how*' has yet to be determined. That's why we asked for Mr. Holmes's help – and yours too."

I struggled to catch up, and to perceive the implications of such a theft occurring in the deep heart of Scotland Yard.

"Why . . . why was it kept here?" I finally chose as my first question. "Surely – "

"'Surely there were better places for it'?" interrupted Lestrade with disgust. "There's no denying that. But them that are smarter than the four of us thought that it would be safe here." He muttered a short curse under his breath. Then, "'*Safe*'," he repeated, shaking his head.

"It was felt that," explained Holmes, "for whatever reason, the book could not be simply destroyed. Without anyone actually making the statement aloud, it seems that Gruner was too good at describing . . . what he described, and those with devious and scheming minds saw that such information might be useful somewhere down the road – God knows how – to blackmail a minister into coming 'round to a certain opinion, perhaps, by threatening that his wife's complete degradation might be revealed. Alternatively, they might force an industrialist to knuckle under to a government demand, lest his daughter's reputation be publicly destroyed by showing those pages in the diary devoted to her to a few influential and noisome individuals. My disgust knows no bounds in this affair. This is beyond any evil that was ever perpetrated by Milverton."

At that, the inspectors' gazes, previously unfocused and imagining the Government's dark intrigues, were both suddenly aimed rather sharply at Holmes, and I knew that they still had their suspicions about the true events on the night of Charles Augustus Milverton's murder, nearly four years before. Lestrade, who had investigated the brutal killing of the noted blackmailer, had hinted on more than one occasion that he'd still be looking for the middle-sized, strongly built man with a square jaw, thick neck, and moustache, nearly caught by the under-gardener as the fellow was escaping over Milverton's six-foot wall, if the blackmailer's death hadn't removed such a blight from the capital. I would probably tell him the truth someday over a couple of pints at The Ship in Wardour Street – but not yet.

Diverting attention from that topic, I stated, "Surely your brother wasn't involved in such a revolting scheme."

"Thankfully, he was not," Holmes replied. "Mycroft is devious, but honorable. However, even his influence was checked in this matter. All he could do, when it was apparent the diary would be preserved, was to insist that it be removed from the Halls of Power and deposited in a safer place – unknown to those who would use their influence to gain access to the book for their own purposes. When he achieved consent on that point – and such a compromise was no easy thing to wrest from those who are used to finding obsequious agreement with their every statement – Mycroft took the book and left it with Lestrade and Gregson."

"A most singular honor," growled the tall fair-haired inspector, while Lestrade fumed.

"Do you know how offensive it was," the smaller man asked, "to have that . . . *thing* in my safe? I buried it under papers and evidence so that I wouldn't have to look at it, but I still knew that it was there."

"And how long has it been here?" I asked.

"A month – or nearly so. After you and Mr. Holmes obtained it in mid-September, the politicians had to work through the great disagreement about what to do. Then Kitty Winter's attorney wanted to subpoena it for the trial – " He stopped abruptly and looked at Holmes. "And I have my suspicions as to how he got that idea."

"No need to wonder," replied Holmes. "Kitty deserved the best defense possible. I advised him to take that course."

Lestrade nodded, and Gregson said, "Would have done the same myself – as would Lestrade, if he doesn't mind me saying so."

"Wish I'd thought of it," Lestrade declared, and Gregson added, "He and I, as you might imagine, have discussed that filthy book a great deal."

"After Kitty's defense threatened to drag the diary into evidence, Higher Powers intervened." Lestrade's tone became rather bitter and somewhat sarcastic. "They argued for weeks before Mr. Mycroft Holmes, with his famed Solomon-like wisdom, dropped the whole mess onto the Yard – specifically the two of us."

"You should see it for the honor that it is," countered Holmes. "Mycroft knew that you were both above reproach, and that it would be safe here, of all places."

"And yet," growled Gregson, "it was *not* safe." He stood from his chair and walked to the side of the room, adding some coal the fire. "No reflection on Lestrade. If the two of us had instead decided to keep it in my office, it might have fared no better. He and I have the same type of locks upon the doors, and the same types of safes – brought with us from the old Yard when we moved here to the new building a dozen years ago." He gestured toward the old iron safe to the right of Lestrade's desk. "Mycroft Holmes asked us to keep the diary in a secure place, but where could we put it? Neither of us wanted that thing in our homes. There's no one we would have trusted to hide it for us except the two of you, and we didn't want to shift that burden onto your backs. Nor did we want to be seen putting it into a lock-box at a bank. Powerful men would give much to have that diary. It wouldn't take much influence for one of them to ask a favor of a bank president or director, and a way would be found to open the lock-box and remove it."

"And we didn't want to be checking on the lock-box once or twice a week," Lestrade, continuing Gregson's thought, "just to make sure it was still there while drawing attention to both us and the diary. It was much safer for it to simply disappear – and where better than deep in Scotland Yard? But even here, we had to be careful. We couldn't just bury it downstairs in the old evidence files, or jam it behind some loose brick in a little-used hallway. There was always the chance that it would be found. And the same as with the lock-box – we couldn't constantly check on it, which would draw too much attention. We finally thought that simply putting it in one of our safes and paying it no mind and attracting no interest, but able to verify regularly – and privately – that it was still there, was best."

"Who knew that you both had the diary?" I asked.

They looked at one another, and Gregson replied, "No one – but us and Mr. Mycroft Holmes." He looked at Sherlock Holmes. "I don't believe that you even knew what had become of it – or so I understood from your brother."

"That is correct," Holmes answered. "I was not told, and that was satisfactory. Now, for Watson's benefit, please repeat how you discovered that the diary was missing."

Lestrade pinched the bridge of his nose and, with eyes shut, related those events. "I know that the diary was in the safe last night. I had to put away the letters threatening Lord Rawchester's sister, and I took a moment – as I often do, to lift aside the other items resting on the diary and make sure that it's still there. It was. I re-covered it with the other files, put away the letters, and locked the safe. And I'm certain that I did so. I always make certain, but I'm also aware of just how often people *think* that they do something – a thing that has become an unthinking routine – and then actually forget to do it. But last night, I recall that when I spun the combination dial, it stopped exactly on the number *ten* – and as yesterday was November tenth, the moment stuck in my mind. Then, being finished for the day, I straightened my desk, extinguished the light, and left through the door. As is also my routine, I pulled the door shut and locked it – making sure several times that it was fully closed and locked. I don't have a corresponding fact to confirm it like the ten on the safe combination, but I absolutely recall closing the door. Wait – I do remember something. I had a newspaper in hand as I checked the door lock, folded open to yesterday's birthday honors. John Winthrop Hackett was knighted. You recall him, Mr. Holmes? The Australian newspaper proprietor who received that pair of horse eyes in the bloody box five years back?"

"So the doors to both the room and the safe were locked. I'm sure that it doesn't need to be confirmed that you were alone when this all occurred – checking the presence of the diary, re-covering it and locking the safe, and departing from the office?"

"That's correct. And the door was shut and the office empty when I verified that the diary was in the safe. This afternoon was the first time I needed to open the safe and retrieve a document. I unlocked it as usual, verified the fact that I needed, returned the document, and then made sure, as I nearly always do, that the diary was there. But it was *not*. I summoned Gregson."

"Lestrade and I looked at the safe," offered Gregson, "but we saw nothing. After much discussion, and before we notify Mr. Mycroft

Holmes, we decided to consult with you, Mr. Holmes. Would you mind having a look?"

"I was about to suggest it."

As he rose and moved to the safe, Lestrade shifted his chair away to provide more room, while Gregson stepped back in the other direction.

How curious, I thought, to see how easily and willing the two seasoned inspectors were to seek Holmes's assistance. I was again reminded of that day in March 1881 when I first accompanied Holmes on an investigation. He had approached the body, lying in the ground-floor dining room of the empty house. The dead man's eyes has been open, and he was staring upward through the ceiling toward eternity. The corpse was twisted and rigid, and his expression bore a horrific and malignant rictus of agony, even in death.

After some discussion of the scene, and Lestrade's discovery of a telling word written in blood upon the wall, Holmes had finally begun his enthusiastic inspection of the room, moving here and there, making small noises and clicks and mutters, and entirely focused upon what he was observing – certainly so much more than the rest of us would ever see. Throughout, I looked away from whatever Holmes was accomplishing to glance at the two inspectors, seeing their expressions occasionally displaying curiosity, but more often a great deal of contempt. In later years, I was proud to note that I had recognized from that first encounter with Holmes's method that his ends were practical and directed, while it took some years for the official force to come around to that same way of thinking.

Now, with the same intensity he'd shown over twenty years earlier, Holmes examined Lestrade's old safe, its door open for his perusal. When he was done, he shut and locked the door, and then tried to open it this way and that without success. Afterwards, he examined the room around it, forcing us to shift aside when he needed to be where we were sitting or standing. Meanwhile, Lestrade and Gregson watched quietly and respectfully, as if – even at this late date – they might learn something useful.

After ten minutes, Holmes asked to see Gregson's office. Although he and Lestrade exchanged a look of confusion, and I could almost see the words, *"But Mr. Holmes, it was stolen from* my *safe!"* forming on the latter's lips, he bit his tongue. While they were out of the room, neither Lestrade nor I exchanged a word.

It wasn't long before Holmes and Gregson returned. I looked for any sign of encouragement, but even Sherlock Holmes's many skills were of no use just then, as he shook his head.

"There is nothing but coal ash in the fireplace, and not much of that – he didn't burn it. There are no footprints that one wouldn't expect – Lestrade, you keep your office far too clean. Not a speck of dust on the desk or safe, or even on the floor in the out-of-the-way corners, to retain a mark. Obviously there are no signs of forced entry to the room, or to the safe. As you say, it's an old model, and given enough time, there would be no difficulty using a physician's stethoscope to listen to the tumbler's falling into place, but there's nothing to indicate that occurred either."

He looked as if he wanted to pull out his pipe and think, but he restrained the impulse.

"Do you maintain that no one could get into the office or the safe except yourself?"

Lestrade shook his head. "I don't maintain that at all. The lock is nothing special, and there are other keys to the office. There's a duplicate in the Superintendent's safe, and Gregson has one as well."

"And Lestrade also has a key to my office," added Gregson. "It has saved a lot of time."

"And this has been your office since the Yard moved here from Whitehall Terrace," agreed Holmes, "so there wouldn't be a key in the hands of a former tenant. What about the safe?"

Lestrade's brow wrinkled. "You see how old it is. I inherited it from Dockery when he retired, back before I met you, Mr. Holmes. The old safes came with us from the old building when we moved here – it was determined that buying new ones would be too expensive." He had resumed his seat after Holmes's investigation, and he leaned forward, arms crossed upon his desk. "What are you thinking?"

"I'm thinking that this may not have been a planned theft, specifically targeted toward obtaining the diary. I'm satisfied that Mycroft didn't tell anyone that he was leaving the diary in your possession, and that neither of you have told anyone either."

Lestrade gave a firm shake of his head, and Gregson replied in a low tone, "Not a word."

"Then no one would know to look for it here," I said, rather obviously.

"I'm convinced," reiterated Holmes, "at least for the purposes of progressing forward, that only three people – Mycroft and you two, Gregson and Lestrade – knew that the diary was coming to Scotland Yard. And as you say, Mycroft didn't know where you intended to keep it once it was here. He trusted you –"

Lestrade snorted. "That turned out to be misplaced."

"He *trusted* you," Holmes repeated with emphasis, "and rightly so. But my point is this: No one but the two of you knew where the diary was hidden, so no one could come looking for it – intentionally and knowingly – here, in this office, and specifically in that safe. Therefore, it would be better to consider who has access to the office and might have discovered it accidentally and understood what he or she had found, rather than trying to determine who knew of the diary."

Gregson nodded. "Whoever found it, realized what it was, and impulsively took it away."

"That is how I read it," agreed Holmes. "So the question becomes who has access to this office and your safe, Lestrade – which one would ideally hope might be impregnable. Who would have *reason* to enter your office and access your safe?"

Lestrade shook his head. "Not impregnable. You've seen that door lock, Mr. Holmes. Even if there are only three *known* keys, there's nothing there that would keep out a determined man or woman. And as I said, the safe is old, and the combination, as far as I know, is the same as it was when it was first installed in the old Yard."

Holmes nodded. "It's a fair assumption that someone went to this trouble for a reason, before unexpectedly finding the diary. Perhaps this person came here to see one of the other documents in your safe? What else of a sensitive nature in there, related to a current investigation? Have you looked to see if anything else is missing?"

Lestrade frowned, and I could see that he was both irritated and embarrassed with himself for not having made that examination earlier. But I could understand his thinking. If I'd been the keeper of such a dangerous object and noticed that it was gone, it would never occur to me that something of lesser value or importance was taken as well.

He rose and stepped to the safe. Holmes joined him, watching over his shoulder as Lestrade spun the combination without thought, and apparently with no hesitation at Holmes seeing and learning it. I considered the relations between the two of them when I first met both in early 1881 – the consulting detective holding the professional in contempt who, along with Gregson, was "the pick of a bad lot", while Lestrade would acknowledge Holmes's sometime assistance and usefulness to the Yard, but not much more than that.

Now, Holmes accepted Lestrade's limitations while admiring his many admirable traits – particularly his doggedness and his integrity – and Lestrade had said it best a couple of years before, while congratulating Holmes after a particularly neat piece of work, stating, "We're not jealous of you at Scotland Yard. No, sir, we are very proud of you, and if you come down tomorrow, there's not a man, from the oldest inspector to the youngest constable, who wouldn't be glad to shake you by the hand." If, as a young man of twenty-eight, I'd been swept forward nearly two decades in time and clapped down in front of Holmes and Lestrade and shown that scene, I wouldn't have believed it possible.

Lestrade had reopened the safe and lifted out a stack of papers, returning with them to his desk. There was a variety of envelopes, large and small and varying in shade, mixed in with a few worn manila folders. The entire collection was no more than five or six inches high, and none of the packets were any thicker than the others. Lestrade began to go through each with great diligence, sheet by sheet, and, while one might have expected such a thorough inspection to become tedious, we three – Holmes, Gregson, and myself – remained fixated upon the inspector's secret files.

"The Whittaker forgery, and the true heir's identity," he explained with the first envelope opened. It was no more than five or six sheets, which he examined individually, replaced, and set aside. "The Russell Square Ripper," he said, opening a folder. This had a few clipped pages and one smaller envelope, containing a single sheet. "The confession," Lestrade said, holding it up with a grimace. "It wasn't accepted, as a 'better' solution was found implicating a dead man, and The Crown wanted to save one of their own." He closed that folder and set it aside with obvious disgust.

He continued to look through each set of papers – "The Templeton Plague. The Dutch Monkey Incident. The Stolen Greystoke Inheritance – you can bet we'll hear more about that one. That nasty business in the Dorset Street sewers. Milverton's shooting – " He paused to look toward Holmes and then me with a knowing expression and a raised eyebrow. "These are just the public facts, you understand. I haven't recorded my own theories – about the two men who escaped and were blamed by the servants, or the evidence I found of a lady in very expensive shoes who was on the scene. Bloody footprints, you understand – one of them on Milverton's face." Then he dropped his gaze back to the papers and resumed his examination. "The Siamese Quintuplets and their pet constrictor. The terrible business at the artificial knee-cap factory . . . ."

Five minutes later, he restacked all of the envelopes and folders and stated, "Every file is complete, to the last sheet and photograph and scrap. Only one is missing in its entirety: The Clissold suicide."

I recalled the terrible affair. Six weeks before, Floyd Clissold, a low-level agent of the British Government, suspected of taking payments from other interests, had been found dead in a Hackney room, which he'd apparently rented under an assumed name. He was supposed to be out of the country, and it was uncertain why he was back in London. If the body hadn't been recognized by one of the investigating sergeants who knew Clissold when he was a thieving lad roaming the streets, he might have been buried as an unknown in a pauper's grave. But when the dead man's name was revealed, someone within the Government who had dealings with him saw it in the newspaper and recognized it. There was some concern that he was in London without permission, and why Scotland Yard, escalating the investigation because of the Clissold's sudden apparent importance, had Inspector Youghal approach Holmes for assistance. After he'd made some initial inquiries, Holmes was warned off the case by his brother Mycroft – "In the national interest" Mycroft had cryptically explained – and thus the matter stood, unsolved.

"It was clear," said Lestrade, "that – in spite of the obvious evidence – it was murder and not suicide. In spite of the official position to step back and leave it be, I was asked to take over from Youghal and continue a low-level investigation, despite our efforts being quashed from higher up."

"And who asked you to do this?" asked Gregson, rightfully curious as to who within the police hierarchy would make such a command.

"Superintendent Blevins," Lestrade said, his eyes taking on a knowing look. Gregson nodded with understanding as well, and even Holmes seemed to comprehend the implications of Blevins' involvement. As usual, it was left to me to ask for help catching up, trying not to sound like an ignorant but curious child while the adults whispered above me about things that were none of my business.

"What is the significance of Superintendent Blevins?" I asked after all three had pondered for a silent moment.

Holmes deferred to the two inspectors. Gregson sighed. "He has been here forever, it seems. Not quite one of the original Peelers, but you'd be forgiven for thinking that he was. He was here when Lestrade and I arrived, and sometimes I wonder if he'll be here when we're gone. He's a big man, but not in an unhealthy way. His hair had gone gray when I met him, and it's slowly whitened. Likewise, his ruddy complexion has faded over the years, and now he moves through the hallways, slower than he once did, like some black-suited ghost."

"Understand," added Lestrade, "he's a good officer. He worked his way up, and he understands the . . . complications of being a policeman, from the lowest constable walking his set rounds to the inspectors being pulled between finding the truth and finding what the politicians want us to find. During the search for the Rippers, [1] he was our strong advocate against what the Masons were demanding from us more times than I can count."

"He was already a superintendent when I first started associating with the Yard," offered Holmes, looking in my direction, "and to his credit, he didn't discourage the first inspectors who sought my assistance – Plummer and Penner, for instance. A wrong word from him, and my opportunities would have been sharply limited." He turned his head back toward Lestrade. "Are you surprised to find that Blevins could have entered your office and opened your safe?"

Lestrade's arms had been resting on his desk, fingers intertwined. Now he unwound them, leaned back, and rubbed the heels of his palms on his eyes. "I suppose not. Nothing surprises me."

"The safe was the most secure place we could think of," Gregson said in Lestrade's defense. It was many years since their rivalry had defined their friendship. He felt the need to re-explain what they had already excused. "My office and safe would have been no more secure from such an . . . attack from within. Neither of us could have taken that . . . thing home with us. I wouldn't want it defiling where I live, and neither would Lestrade. And we couldn't tuck it away here in the building, for anyone to find. If a man can't trust the safe in his own office – "

"Peace," said Holmes, holding up a hand. "I am not faulting you – either of you. The question is, now that it seems likely to have been Blevins, does it make sense? That he was able to open your safe?"

"Yes," said Lestrade. "Yes to having a key to my office, and also to knowing the combination to the safe. Blevins was probably around when these safes were first purchased."

"Then it simply remains to confirm that he was the one who took the diary, and why. Will you take this matter to Sir Edward? Shall I now involve Mycroft?"

Lestrade and Gregson glanced at one another and silently reached immediate agreement. "Not your brother," said Gregson. "And not Sir Edward, either. He's approaching retirement, and not as . . . shall we say, *involved* in day-to-day affairs as we might wish."

I knew Colonel Sir Edward Bradford, the Metropolitan Police Commissioner, rather well, having encountered him a number of times by way of Holmes's investigations. He had taken the post in 1890, during that thankless period following the tenures of Sir Charles Warren and James Monro. Sir Charles had overseen the Yard during the Bloody Sunday riots, as well as the search for the Rippers, and when he resigned in late 1888, poor Monro had been left to pick up the pieces. Although popular with the Force, Monro's service had lasted just eighteen months, the shortest time of any commissioner. His replacement, Sir Edward, had served as a calming influence after the tumult of the following years. The man's vast military experience – he'd gone out to India around the time I was born, and was still there after I was invalided home after Maiwand – had given him the administrative skills to manage the police force in a successful way. But Gregson's comment implied that, after a dozen years, Sir Edward might not be the man he once was.

"If we go to Sir Edward half-cocked," added Lestrade, "we may disrupt something we don't understand – some reason that Superintendent Blevins took the diary."

Holmes shifted in his seat, leaning back as if he were getting comfortable and about to watch a play. "Well, then, perhaps you might have him step in satisfy our curiosity."

"Mr. Holmes – " said Gregson, while Lestrade said, "It might be better if – "

Holmes shook his head. "Now that you see a possible solution, you're ready to send Watson and me away, so that we won't observe the Yard's dirty laundry. It won't do. We're involved now, and with – I believe – a legitimate interest in finding out what happened to Gruner's diary. Watson and I didn't work that hard to retrieve it, just to lose track of who has it next. And if you need another reason, consider me to be Mycroft's representative – officially undesignated just now, but that can be fixed with a quick telephone call, should you require it."

Lestrade and Gregson didn't need to confer, or even look at one another. They knew how stubborn Holmes could be. With a sigh, Lestrade pushed a button on the side of his desk, which was electrically wired to a bell in a nearby room. I knew that there were always a few constables there, and that one of them would answer momentarily. And within half-a-minute, a young officer – And they looked so young to me these days! – leaned in and was told by Gregson to please find Superintendent Blevins and ask him to step around to Lestrade's office.

Gregson, who had been standing for much of the time, reclaimed his own seat after setting another chair in place for Blevins, in a position where all of us could see him. None of us spoke, apparently agreeing that there was nothing left to say until we'd heard the superintendent's story. We only had to wait in silence for a couple of minutes before there was a slight knock upon the door, followed by the entrance of the elder policeman.

After he entered, I realized that I had seen him in the past – quite a few times, actually. I was rather surprised, after learning of the long occupancy of his position, that I hadn't actually met him during one or more of Holmes's investigations.

As described, he was a big man, but he moved with the carefulness that one acquires with age. I was then just turned fifty years old, and I had already noticed that I was more careful when going down stairs, or when crossing wet or icy pavement, having begun to realize that I was past those strong young and middle years when one feels indestructible.

327

Blevins shut the door behind him and took a moment to look around. He didn't exactly seem surprised to find four of us there, but an eyebrow did lift fractionally upon spotting Holmes and me. I didn't know if he would have recognized me in the street, but my being there along with Holmes probably gave him a good idea who I was.

"You asked to see me, Inspector Lestrade?" he asked, his voice soft, and rather rough with age. Lestrade only then decided it was a good idea to stand, and he did so, followed by Gregson. My long-ago military training urged me to do the same before I really gave it a thought, but I saw that Holmes remained seated, leaning back with one leg crossed over the other, and so I matched his response.

"I did, Superintendent. Umm, we did, actually. I . . . ."

It was only then that I – and I think Lestrade and Gregson as well – noticed that Blevins carried something in his hands, wrapped in a cloth. It was eight or nine inches long, five or so wide, and a couple of inches thick. I glanced at Holmes and saw that his eyes were also focused on the object. He had probably seen it as soon as Blevins entered. A small gleam was in his eyes.

Without being told, Blevins turned and seated himself in the empty chair like a witness in an interrogation, the object held in one hand and resting upon his lap. He gave a weary sigh, and he seemed to settle in upon himself, as if a bucket of stiff concrete was dumped upon the ground, slowly slumping from a cylindrical shape into a vague spreading mound.

The old man looked at Lestrade. "You wish to question me about the intrusion into your safe."

"Umm . . . ." Lestrade was clearly nervous – a condition which I've rarely seen him evince. I cut my eyes to see if his old rival was taking any pleasure in it. He was not.

Lestrade soldiered on. "In your position," he said, his voice becoming clearer as he spoke, "you have the right to enter any room here at the Yard, and to look into any safe. It's only that – "

Blevins raised his free hand. "A quick explanation is best, isn't it? We're all very experienced in this sort of thing. Any protestations upon my part are a waste of everyone's time." He turned his head toward Holmes, who was still sitting in a relaxed but interested manner.

"It's good to see you again, Mr. Holmes. I'm not surprised that Lestrade and Gregson sought your council. You have worked very well together over the years."

Holmes nodded. "I was honored to be asked by my friends to offer advice, but I really didn't have that much to give. An examination of the safe's papers revealed one set of missing case documents, and those were associated with you."

"Nevertheless," Blevins countered. He looked back at Lestrade. "That was my safe once, you know. When I was an inspector – years before you and Gregson came along – even before old Dockery. That old scratch on the front? That's where Darrell Finney tried to kill me with a wicked jack-knife as I interviewed him in my office. Just missed me and hit the safe door, before sliding off and giving my constable a terrible gash in the leg. I should have known better than to interview a killer like Finney in those circumstances without having him searched." He fell silent in the reminiscence, but then his fingers squeezed the object in his hand and he returned to us.

"The safe combination? Zero-seven, zero-two, thirty-five? That's my birthday, you see. When they bought the safes, the safe-maker let each of us pick a number that we could remember. That's how I was able to get into the safe this morning to retrieve the Clissold file." He shook his head. "You won't have heard yet, Lestrade, but it's being swept under the rug. Not a surprise, eh? I was ordered to retrieve all materials related to the matter and turn them over to the Commissioner. Apparently there are some Royals who might get burned if too much more about what Clissold was up to is discovered, and I'm rather on the hot seat for continuing to pursue it. I've made sure, however, that your name was kept out of it. They have no idea that you were keeping the file, or that it was you asking more questions."

Lestrade nodded, and the superintendent continued.

"I came down to your office to get the file, only to find your door locked. Quite right, of course, but I couldn't wait. Since the file was supposed to be in my keeping, and I was supposed to be retrieving it right then from my office to turn it over to Sir Edward and a palace representative waiting with him, I was forced to open your door with my master key. I knew that I could open the safe as well, so I did it. I was rooting around, looking for the Clissold file, when I unexpectedly found this . . . ."

And he held up the object in his hand, letting the cloth fall away.

It was a book.

I had only seen it once before, when Holmes showed it to me after he'd stolen it from Baron Gruner's private office while I distracted him in the adjacent room. I'd never seen inside it, and I didn't want to, but even without confirming the contents, I knew what it was. It was brown leather, with a lock on it. The cover was decorated with Gruner's Coat of Arms, a hideous red-and-yellow mess that appeared rather like something a sick animal would expel. There were feathers around the edges that looked more ichthian than bird-like, and some sort of knight's helmet in the top half which looked more like a low-headed eyeless chicken head. Below that was a red shield with a backward-facing Turkish crescent. I found it offensive, and would have done so even if I hadn't known anything about the book's original owner.

Holmes had described it as Gruner's "lust diary". He had first learned of the volume from the poor debauched girl, Kitty Winter, who told him that Gruner "collects women, and takes a pride in his collection, as some men collect moths or butterflies." She explained that it contained names, details, photographs – everything about the women he'd captured. *Souls I Have Ruined* was the title that Kitty suggested should be on the outside cover – but no such wording was there. Just that hideous Coat of Arms that seemed to illustrate so well with everything that I knew about Baron Adelbert Gruner.

Perhaps sensing that questioning their superior would be awkward, Holmes took the lead. "Once you found it, you had to read it?" He asked. "You'd heard of it and wanted to see just how bad it was?"

Blevins lips tightened in what might have been a gentle smile, or perhaps it was a grimace. The skin on his face was loose with age, and it was difficult to determine just what he meant to express. I saw that there might have been a tear in his eye – or perhaps it was just an old man's rheumy dampness.

"Correct, Mr. Holmes," Blevins replied. "I had to read it – and I had to know how bad it was."

He stopped, his voice having broken as he finished speaking. We were silent as well, sensing that some dark undercurrent was about to be exposed. Then Holmes said softly, "Someone you know is in that book."

Blevins' fingers tightened upon the volume, the old chalky knuckles turning even whiter. His lips tightened, and he just nodded – once in acknowledgement, and then again, with more decision. He looked up, now facing Holmes, as if my friend were to serve as the old man's confessor.

Blevins tried to speak, but his voice failed him. Then, with effort, he tried again, and as he talked, his voice became smoother, but the strain was not lessened.

"My wife," he rasped. "My dear, beautiful wife is in this book. Gruner took her and . . . My wife is in this book."

Once Blevins began his story, it seemed to pour out, for he had likely never had anyone with whom he could share it.

"I married late. Lestrade and Gregson may know – but then again, they might not." Both shook their heads. "I thought so. When I was an inspector, I could barely keep track of my work, let alone my own personal life. For so long, the work was enough – but then I met Elizabeth.

"She is Sir William Cress's youngest daughter – widowed in her forties. She was attending one of those social functions that occasionally require the presence of a police superintendent, and from the moment I saw her, it was as if I had awakened for the first time in my life – or as if my eyes had been covered and I was then just seeing sunshine.

"We talked that night, and I was thrilled that she was willing to entertain my presence. Having never held any interest in social functions, I found myself making excuses to be at parties where she would be in attendance, and contriving further ways to have conversations with her. Long ago, such a one as me wouldn't have been welcome at some of these events, but times had changed, and I also began to understand that, because of my position, I'd gained more respect over the years than I'd realized, having limited myself before then by remaining focused solely upon my work, and not understanding how empty and lonely I was.

"One can't be a policeman and also be a coward, so I found the nerve to request her hand in marriage. At her age, there was no real objection, and I gave little thought to the difference in ages between us. And perhaps back then, it didn't seem as obvious. That was ten years ago, and I've had something of a steady collapse since then, while Elizabeth is still as beautiful as the day I first saw her. That's why, I fear, she soon became bored with our marriage.

"I was never under any illusion that she loved me as strongly as I loved her, but she did feel that it was a good match. I don't believe she came to fully regret it, but I did know that she didn't reciprocate my feelings. I didn't care. I still don't care. She has my heart, until the end.

"If she was having affairs, I didn't know. I didn't want to know. I was promised to her – My *lady*! – and that was the beginning and end of it. I had *promised*! But then . . . then Gruner set his sights upon her.

"I knew that she was different than she had been – at first, a bit happier, and then upset – but I didn't know why. And then she told me. It wasn't blackmail, and Gruner was through with her. She had nothing else that he wanted. But his . . . his true enjoyment didn't begin until he'd told her about his book . . . and that she was in it. It seems that he has a special type of cruelty that way. He doesn't demand money, or anything of value. He simply has to remind his victims, from time to time, what they did and how he has it recorded. He revels in their shame and pain. Finally, when she could stand it no more, she told me . . . ."

Blevins drifted in to silence, and Lestrade quietly asked him if he'd like some water. The old man shook his head, and his gaze drifted toward the fireplace, where the flames, ignorant and disinterested in the affairs of men, danced greedily upon the small mound of coal.

Then Blevins refocused on Holmes. "I understand that you've been to Gruner's house out in Kingston," he said. He cut his eyes in my direction. "And you too, Doctor Watson. You've seen what a beautiful

331

place it is – the long drive, surrounded by shrubs, and the open space before the house dotted with statues. The architecture is peculiar, but I believe that it's what the former owner, Coetzee, wanted when he moved here from South Africa. In any case, there is a stateliness to the place, and one would never have suspected the cancer that dwelled within.

"Gruner welcomed me affably when I went to see him, and he offered no apologies that my wife was in his book. He told me . . . He shared specific details. Apparently my shame also pleased him. I demanded that he surrender the book. He refused, and gleefully told me specifics of other women that were also included – 'Of course, I shan't share names, Superintendent,' he murmured, his manner giving one the cold shivers, as if being too close to a serpent. 'It wouldn't be discreet, would it? But I can generally tell you about the M.P.'s wife, or the daughter of one of the Queen's cousins . . . .' He went on and on, and I was given to understand that any attempt on my part to retrieve the book would meet with failure, and prompt the very real chance that names and details would be made public.

"'Do not fear, Superintendent,' he said, clearly enjoying the power he held. 'I am neither a Milverton nor a Carruthers. I have no interest in blackmailing anyone. I derive my enjoyment from the fact that my ladies never forget that I *know* them, perhaps more than anyone else ever has or will, and that with my extensive notes, I shall never *forget* them. Now, the night is passing, and I have other appointments. Do give your lovely wife my best regards, and let her know that I think of her – quite often.'

"It seemed all that I could do to keep from killing him right then, but he knew me, too – he could see into me as easily as any of the women he ruined, and he understood that I wasn't a murderer. I hated myself as much as him as I slunk away, like some defeated lick-spittle cur.

"I returned home, and my wife knew before I spoke that I'd been beaten. I fear that she lost a great deal of respect for me that night – possibly whatever was left of any she'd had before. When you retrieved the diary, Mr. Holmes, and that girl threw acid in Gruner's face – Well, we knew then that others would read it, and our shame was increased exponentially, but no one has ever said a word, or approached me about it. We've gone on with our lives, and my love for my wife is still as certain as before. And yet . . . and yet . . . ."

"And yet," Holmes said softly, "you had to know. You didn't simply toss the diary into Lestrade's fireplace as soon as you found it."

"I did," whispered Blevins. "God help me, I had to know."

Then, as if hearing Holmes's words again, hearing the slight emphasis that Holmes had made, Blevins' mouth tightened, a decision made. He looked at Holmes, who nodded, almost imperceptibly – as if giving him permission.

Blevins stood, looked at Lestrade and Gregson, and me as well, to see if anyone would challenge him. When there was no response, he took two steps, leaned over, and laid the opened diary face-down upon the coal fire.

I think I expected Lestrade or Gregson to rise and make some protest, or to lurch forward to save the wicked thing from the flames. I was already tensed to rise and place myself in front of one or both of them, defending the old man and letting the thing burn. But neither inspector made a move, nor made a sound. They, like Holmes, were watching the hungry red-and-yellow tendrils first licking the book, and then hungrily consuming it. The leather cover curled quickly, throwing up a strong plume of black smoke, and then the pages that I could see browned and burst into flame. The room filled with hints of a terrible odor, as if some vile trapped spirit was being consumed.

Leaf by leaf, the sadness and grief that the book contained rose with the smoke. One might naively hope that such would erase the pain, but in truth, many in the book would never know that they were now free. Perhaps, somehow if there was any greater mercy, Gruner's victims could sense that their secrets were now burned, traveling in the air, never again to be discovered. But I doubted it.

Blevins had positioned the book in such a way that it settled deeper into the coal as it collapsed, insuring that it didn't fall out of the grate.

I don't know how long we watched – perhaps five minutes – before it was obvious that the volume was nearly gone. What was left was something made of ash that held the shape of a book. Only then did Lestrade rise and step quietly past Blevins. He reached for his small poker and prodded and flattened the remains, scattering them forever.

Replacing the poker, he turned to his superior and asked, "Did you find everything that you needed when you retrieved the Clissold file, sir?"

"I did, Inspector," replied the old man, still standing by the fireplace. "I did." And then he offered his hand, and Lestrade took it.

Nothing else was said as Blevins shook hands with Holmes, Gregson, and me before walking out of the office and pulling the door softly shut behind him.

No one said anything for several moments, until Holmes finally muttered, "Poor helpless worm. There, but for the grace of God . . . ."

Lestrade looked at him curiously. Holmes had said something similar to me long ago, when old John Turner had confessed how he'd killed his persecutor at Boscombe Pool. Lestrade had investigated the case at the time, but hadn't learned the truth until years later, when he and I had discussed it just before the narrative was published in *The Strand.* We both thought that Holmes was dead then, and I'd related to Lestrade how Holmes had chosen to show mercy to old Turner, as the old man was believed to be dying. [2] Lestrade had nodded then, confessing to me that he was often pulled between his sworn professional duty to catch and punish lawbreakers and his innate instinct see that actual justice took place, even if it meant turning a blind eye to the law.

That day, in Lestrade's office, both inspectors had wisely chosen the latter.

"I'll explain to Mycroft," Holmes added, and the inspectors nodded in gratitude. Then Holmes turned to me.

"Sorry it wasn't more of a chase, Watson," he said, his tone rather jovial after the gravity of what we'd just heard and seen.

I waved my hand, reluctant to simply close the subject. "The Superintendent – " I said. "Burning Gruner's diary hasn't really solved anything for him, has it?"

Gregson shook his head. "God help him. He loves her. You saw it. He's risked his career – even prison – if what he just did comes out, or if Mr. Mycroft Holmes takes a dim view of what has happened. He loves her – but to know what he knows now, having read it, and still – . The specifics and the details . . . ."

"Why did he have to look at it?" asked Lestrade. "He could have just burned it here, as soon as he pulled it from the safe. Why did he have to look – to *know*? It seems it would be the last nail in the coffin of his love."

"I can't pretend to know anything about love," said Holmes softly, "but I believe he had to set and pass one final test for himself. He said, 'God help me, I had to know.' I don't think he meant that he needed to see every explicit fact recorded in the diary about Gruner and his wife. He had to know if, after seeing that, he could still love her.

"He already knew that he loved her when she didn't quite love him back in the same way. He still loved her when she possibly had affairs, and even when the affair with Gruner was confirmed. He still loved her when the full shame of it became apparent. But with all of that, he had one more obstacle to overcome: To see just how great his love has to be. And I believe him when he said that, even after today, he still loves her. I believe that he will until his dying day – although I fear that this experience will hasten that event sooner than it might have been. I just hope the lady understands and appreciates what she has, instead of testing him even further before he's gone."

My friend often claims to lack an understanding of the human heart, but he's mistaken. Lestrade and Gregson nodded in agreement with Holmes's supposition. Then, with nothing left to say until next we met, hands were shaken, thanks were conveyed, and Holmes and I stepped outside, pulling Lestrade's office door shut behind us.

NOTES

1. For more information about Holmes's overall investigation into the massive Rippers Conspiracy during the terrible Bloody Autumn of 1888 can be found in "November, 1888", published in *The Collected Papers of Sherlock Holmes – Volume III: Accounts*. It was originally published in *The Watsonian* (Fall 2015, Vol. 3, No.2) and in my online blog, *A Seventeen Step Program* at:
   https://17stepprogram.blogspot.com/2017/02/sherlock-holmes-versus-jack-ripper.html
2. Further facts about John Turner's supposed death are revealed in "The True Account of the Bushell Street Killing", in *The Collected Papers of Sherlock Holmes: Volume V – Chronicles* and *Beyond the Adventures of Sherlock Holmes – Volume II*

The Tsushima Legacy
by Mike Adamson

Occasionally, I am struck by the way some things change, yet others never do. Quiet revolutions have come upon society during my lifetime, and the details of our comfortable, familiar England have drifted gradually. In the 1880's and 1890's, when I accompanied Holmes upon his errands of investigation and justice, we most frequently travelled by horse-drawn vehicle or train. But as the new century gathered momentum and the days of our lost and dearly-missed Queen Victoria were replaced by the reign of King Edward VII, the internal combustion engine grew gradually more ubiquitous. While the clop of shod hooves is a sound as old as this land, it is now overlaid by the mechanical emanations of the machines that whir by upon the highroads, whether the hum of Walter Bersey's electric taxicabs – known as "hummingbirds" for their sound – or the rattle-and-drone of reciprocating engines. The motor vehicle has come to London, and London will be forever marked by this evolution.

I had received a cable from Holmes, and nothing was more certain to extract me from my practice and the convivial quarters of my marriage than the sort of cryptic missive he was wont to transmit. While we had kept up a lively correspondence since his retirement to the Channel coast some four years earlier, our paths had crossed many a time since. His invitation – *"Possible fun in the offing. Do partake of it!"* – drew me to meet his train up to London with a thrill of old times and the feeling that the inevitability of Sherlock Holmes applying his keen mind to some problem was beyond question.

The 10:26 service from Eastbourne to Victoria Station was on time, and I raised my stick in greeting as I saw Holmes's always-spare frame emerge from a first-class compartment. He was unbowed by retirement, though perhaps a touch greyer than I remembered him, and he wore his deerstalker and Inverness coat against the chill and blustery late January of this year of 1907 like the badges of his own distinguished office.

We shook hands with the pleasure of old acquaintances renewed, and I took one of his cases to escort him from the echoing hall of the station to what had been the yard where we hailed countless hansoms in the old days. A rank of black taxicabs now predominated, and we boarded with Holmes's curt "Admiralty" instruction to the driver.

The vehicle purred out of the yard, turned right into Victoria Street, and proceeded up towards Westminster Abbey. As we regarded the shadowy aspect of the city in this cool, grey season, Holmes nodded shallowly and acknowledged that there were fewer horses than he recalled from previous visits – and more motor vehicles. Truly, though there yet lingered a feeling of strangeness in the sounds and sights of such machines, they proceeded with an alacrity unknown in the old days.

The driver took us through Parliament Square and across into Parliament Street, thence up to Whitehall, and before we knew it, we were turning into the great old Admiralty buildings behind Drummond's Bank – the very spot where Oliver Cromwell's London residence once stood.

A Naval attaché was waiting for us and paid the fare, giving instructions for Holmes's luggage to be delivered to the Metropole Hotel – around the corner on Whitehall Place, backing onto Great Scotland Yard, original premises of the London Metropolitan Police.

"Mycroft has spared no expense," Holmes mused as the vehicle departed, and we were shown into the Admiralty buildings. Polished timber, whitewash, dark old furniture, and portraits of the illustrious officers of centuries past flowed by as we ascended to the next floor and at last paused by an imposing door. A knock, and we were hailed.

"Mr. Holmes and Dr. Watson, sir," the aide announced before standing back.

Within, by a cheerful hearth, Mycroft Holmes occupied an armchair. An immaculately uniformed senior officer rose from a seat on the opposite side to offer us his hand.

"Sherlock, Dr. Watson," Mycroft began in his breathy rumble, "I'd like you to meet Admiral Sir Rupert Billington." Hands were shaken, and the aide took coats and hats before stepping out.

Billington was the sort who made one think of salt water at his mere appearance – crisp silver waves framed a face beaten to leather by sun, wind, and spray. He had obviously begun his career in the days of sail and matured to command as steam had come to predominate in the forces he served.

The office was elegantly furnished, and two glass-cased dockyard models caught my eye. One was of a classic line of battleship under full sail: A three-decker of Napoleonic times, the sort of ship that remains, even today, a symbol of British pride and prominence. The other was a modern warship, her lines made ugly by the rake and jut of innumerable guns. Her aspect was ominous, forbidding, with her weight of armour and the crowded top-hamper of masts, funnels, searchlights, platforms, and other nautical stock in trade. At once, my innards tightened somewhat. If the business afoot had to do with the British battlefleet, it was of national import.

"I was happy to accept Mycroft's invitation for a foray out of retirement," Holmes said mildly, though his manner was reserved under the sparkle of pleasure in simply being here. There had been times, I knew, when Holmes would not have been pleased to get back into harness – times when his reasons for retirement were all too clear in his mind – but when matters were dire, he placed the security of the nation ahead of such concerns, and it seemed now was such an instance.

"I have indicated to Brother Sherlock the gravity of matters," Mycroft added. "It remains to go into detail." His attention turned to me. "As always in such cases, Dr. Watson, any future chronicle will be subject to official approval."

The aide brought in a tea trolley and served with a swift economy of motion. "Thank you, Geoffrey. I'll take it from here." At the admiral's smile and nod, the young officer departed, closing the door soundlessly. When we had sunk into richly upholstered chairs around the hearth, the admiral gave a troubled glance to Mycroft. He produced a pipe and began to stuff it from a pouch. "Smoke if you wish, gentlemen," he murmured.

I had cut back considerably, and my lungs felt the better for it, so I was gratified that Holmes also settled for tea rather than nicotine. He hooked one knee over the other and raked our hosts with a piercing look. "Mycroft, Admiral, you have my undivided attention. *What is wrong?"*

The elder Holmes gestured genially, and the admiral took up the narrative.

"Two years ago, on the night of the 27th to the 28th of May, 1905, the Imperial Japanese Navy won a decisive victory in the Straits of Tsushima over the navy of the Czar. There are many lessons to be learned from this conflict for all concerned and, leaving aside enmity between the warring parties, the technical aspect is very much in focus at this time. You see, Japan's capital ships came out of *our* yards – Thames Ironworks' and Armstrong-Whitworth's, to be precise – and we are eager to absorb every possible morsel of information about their performance against the equivalent ships of other nations. The Emperor has a diplomatic mission in this country to that end – but also to expand the Japanese fleet.

"As you would expect, the Tsushima ships are now obsolete. Japan is just as aware of this as is Russia. The difference is that Japan is seeking to modernise its fleet from *our* builders, which ever-so-slightly makes us partisan to their disagreement with Russia – an embarrassment, given the genealogical ties between our own royal family and that of the Czar."

Holmes nodded gently, absorbing the information, but I was somewhat at a loss as to the point. "Obsolete?" I asked. "Two years makes so radical a difference?"

Admiral Billington smiled indulgently. "More like ten years since they were launched, Dr. Watson. And, more importantly . . . ." He gestured at the gaunt, grey monster in the display case. "British audacity. The march of progress. There she is, in all her glory: *HMS Dreadnought*. She was built in just one year – 1906 – and she rendered every other capital ship in the world obsolete at a stroke. Twelve-inch main armament – *ten* of the beasts in revolving, enclosed turrets. The first all-big-gun battleship. Even her secondaries are three-inch – twenty-seven of them! What this means is that every major navy in the world is scrambling to catch up. The Germans, the Americans, the French, the Italians – they're all eyeing this ship with a mixture of trepidation and envy. She might officially be in service, but, believe me, she's still going through exhaustive trials. She points the way to a complete revision of the formula by which capital ships are designed and built, and no country is in a better position than ours to exploit this imperative change."

"We have a lead," Holmes observed, "but it's a precarious one."

Mycroft gave a vast shrug. "If we were to relax for even twelve months, we would lose the initiative. Now, our Naval planners are keenly aware of the balance of power that the so-called 'battleship race' constitutes. Theoreticians have speculated on the likelihood – even the inevitability – of a conflict between the Great Powers at some point in the future, and it stands to reason that the technical edge Britain enjoys at this moment must not be squandered." He gave us a pensive look, folding his hands. "Japan is an ally at the far end of the world, and it is considered wise to court her as such. In a conflict on the scale of that which may lie ahead of us, a strong ally is always good to have. I can tell you that His Majesty's Government favours continued technical assistance to Japan, and doesn't rule out the sale of *Dreadnought*-type ships at some point."

"This will not please Czar Nicholas," Holmes murmured, sipping his tea.

"Indeed," Admiral Billington agreed softly. "Nor, indeed, the Americans, given that new-generation ships could appear in the Pacific as easily as an agreement being reached." He sighed, his expression grim. "We believe a situation has arisen out of these concerns."

"Now we come to it," Holmes said with an icy smile.

Mycroft stirred in his seat and looked hard at his brother. "Over the last few weeks, a further round of talks has been hosted in this building between the delegation from the Japanese Naval Ministry and our own experts – tacticians absorbing their reports of Tsushima, engineers analysing the performance of the ships in action, diplomats assessing the state of relations between our nations. These men report directly to the First Sea Lord, Admiral Sir John Fisher – 'Jacky' Fisher, as he's known to an admiring public – who has a vested interest in these proceedings. The talks were chaired by Sir Edwin Patterly, one of our most experienced men when it comes to delicate negotiations and the handling of the most sensitive information. Things were moving well, and the outlook was that we would be reequipping our Pacific friends in due course. However . . . three days ago, Sir Edwin disappeared."

Silence rewarded that bombshell for long moments, then Holmes settled back in his chair, steepled his fingers, and half-closed his eyes – a pose I had seen him adopt times without number when the moment came to absorb the framework of a case. "Tell me," he said simply.

"It was Sunday last," Admiral Billington went on gravely. "Patterly lives in Mayfair and was taking the air with his family in Hyde Park. The weather was bright that morning, so the place was thronged with walkers and riders, children at play. A band was playing at the rotunda – just like any glorious Sunday morning for centuries. The family was watching children sailing model boats upon the Serpentine. Sir Edwin parted from his wife and children to buy a newspaper . . . and never returned."

"Taken in broad daylight?" I murmured.

"Indeed," Holmes agreed. "Audacity, it seems, is not a uniquely British trait."

"Foreign agents, then?"

Holmes's glance reminded me not to belabour the obvious. "An act rehearsed in detail – to encounter Sir Edwin, overcome him in some way, then take him unobtrusively to transport. After all, who notices one specific group of gentlemen walking together in a thronging crowd who, after all, broadly fit the same description?"

Mycroft nodded, his jowls flattening against his starched collar. "The best place to hide a tree is always in a forest."

"Tell me about Sir Edwin."

"He is a fit fifty-six years of age," Mycroft replied from memory. "Of aristocratic stock, with lands in the west. He rides and shoots. He was briefly in the military in this youth – was recalled in his thirties and served in Gordon's Egyptian campaign. A solid fellow in every way."

Holmes absorbed the information, building his mental picture of the man, but Mycroft moved on to the consequences of the matter.

"The occurrence has the gravest overtones. Sir Edwin chaired the full series of discussions and is thus privy to the essence of every matter under discussion: The performance of our battleships. First-hand knowledge of the *Dreadnought*. Our intentions towards the future of the naval balances in the Far East. The Japanese delegation is especially concerned that the consequences of this event could jeopardise their own regional stability.

But the fact is, any naval power in the world would welcome the chance to interview Sir Edwin Patterly at this juncture in time."

"And by *interview*, you mean *interrogate,*" Holmes added with a flinty expression. "They have had him for three days. Under the sort of pressure that may be brought to bear, we cannot expect a politician, a diplomat, to resist their coercion. Few men could. We may also expect that when they have drained every last shred of information he might reasonably be expected to hold, he will be disposed of, and the agents responsible will make their escape with their treasure trove of technical, tactical, strategic, and political data." He brought out his pipe, the better to cogitate with, and stuffed it with methodical motions. "And the steps taken to date?"

The admiral went on. "Well, Mrs. Patterly raised the alarm when he had been missing for some ten or fifteen minutes. She approached a policeman on patrol, and he ran to the nearest telephone. Scotland Yard was brought in, as were the Navy and our more secretive departments. They all agreed that so professional a job would have spirited away its subject in good time to avoid any move to seal the park – not that such would really be practical. Mrs. Patterly gave a statement, but to all intents and purposes, the gentleman had vanished."

"What are his usual security precautions?"

"He is collected from home by a Naval staff car each morning and delivered home the same way in the evening. A bodyguard accompanies him at all times. His home is watched very discreetly from a neighbouring house owned by the government. Even his children receive such services at school to guard against the possibility of them being used as leverage by an unscrupulous party to the same ends."

"Where was the bodyguard on Sunday morning?" Holmes's question was blunt, his eyes hard as he sparked his pipe to life.

"Mr. Holmes, Sir Edwin is a man who has never suffered an 'incident' in his life. He follows protocols to the letter, but one thing he asks is a few hours in which his family life can come before his national obligations. And that is their Sunday walk in the park. For those few hours out of the week, they can be a family rather than a branch of government."

"He refuses protection, then," Holmes whispered.

"Close protection, on that occasion only. A bodyguard *is* present during their walks, but at a distance, and, with the crowds so thick on that day . . . Sir Edwin's habits were obviously observed and exploited."

"I take it no government official will be permitted such latitude in future." Holmes was as scathing as his reputation specified when he perceived simple stupidity at work, and he didn't spare the dignity of government or military in his expression. "Unfortunately, nothing is to be gained, no matter how firmly the stable door is slammed." He blew smoke towards the hearth and enumerated the facts so far. "The potential course of capital ship development is in the balance, as are our relations with our various neighbours and friends. A man in a key position of privileged knowledge was snatched in broad daylight from the heart of London and is, as we speak, doubtless being pressured to divulge that knowledge to the detriment of all concerned. This is an espionage situation, which is – as ever – a prelude to war, somewhere, sometime."

Holmes spoke with a steely quality. He was in the best position to understand the responsibility he unhesitatingly accepted. This wasn't a missing masterpiece nor some criminal enterprise. This was "The Great Game", where statecraft became a matter of life and death. If the information in play escaped to the attention of other powers, then the next time British battleships came up against their counterparts, the story might not be to British liking.

"And to return to Watson's point," Holmes added, "what do we know of foreign agents in Britain at this time?"

Mycroft gave the ghost of a shrug of his huge shoulders. "They are present. We are aware of German, Russian, and American agents entering the country over the past month. We lost contact with the American almost at once, likely on account of her ease of blending with the 'old country'. We were in sporadic contact with the others for weeks. One German we were able to intercept and repatriate – we were confident he knew nothing of value to us, as he was a recent recruit and too junior in their hierarchy. We already know more than he did."

"And the others?"

"Their whereabouts are presently unknown." He smiled for a moment. "The game is forever in play, Sherlock."

"Then the odds favour our man having been abducted by one or other of those groups. Each is a naval power. Each fields capital ships. To steal a march on us is also to steal a march on every other player."

"Admiral Fisher is gravely concerned," Mycroft added. "Sir Edwin is in possession of details of the First Sea Lord's plans for our own Naval policy. I can tell you that Admiral Fisher has masterminded a whole new class of warship based on 'protected cruisers', but more developed in every way. He calls them *battlecruisers. Dreadnought's* impact is essentially a *fait accompli,* and he intends to build, in the next year alone, *four* new monster battleships that exceed even *Dreadnought* in capacity. So, you can see that it is imperative that whoever has abducted Sir Edwin not escape with his information. I need hardly say that recovering our man alive, though of course desirable, is secondary to obstructing the escape of his captors – a sentiment Sir Edwin would be the first to endorse."

"I would expect no less," Holmes admitted, allowing the man the dignity of recovering his honour in the face of the security blunder. "Still, until we know otherwise, let us assume Sir Edwin can be rescued from his predicament." He streamed smoke with a hard look. "So, tell me what became of his newspaper. Not the one he went to buy. The one that should have been delivered that morning but evidently was not."

My expression betrayed my confusion, and I realised ruefully that I was out of practice at the art of Holmesian thought. My friend took pity and explained without short temper. "It is inconceivable that a statesman in an exclusive district wouldn't be a subscriber to the papers of his choice. That he would need to buy one is our guarantee that it wasn't delivered. It is also a subtle way to draw a target to a particular place."

"Three Mayfair streets missed their morning delivery," Mycroft returned, as though Holmes's observation were the most matter-of-fact thing in the world. "The paper boy was waylaid and assaulted, apparently without motive, but clearly this was to force the situation the abductors wished. All they needed do was place a man to attract Sir Edwin's attention and, if appropriate conditions prevailed, perform their abduction. Clearly, the conditions of confusion and separation from the family were acceptable. Also, when Scotland Yard searched the park for evidence, they found a satchel containing unsold papers – likely the very ones taken from the delivery boy – plus a cloth cap and false moustache placed surreptitiously in a waste bin."

"Examination of which has yielded what?"

"Nothing. Both are of local manufacture and purchase, like countless others of their sort. And before you ask, the paperboy was unable to be of any help. He caught only a confused impression of his attacker in the dawn light."

Holmes huffed a frustrated sigh. "The ground isn't very fertile. One point may provide us some purchase upon the problem. No scuffle was reported, correct? From the moment of confrontation, Sir Edwin yielded to them, yet we know him to be a sterling sort who by no means wilts at danger. How did they overcome him? Was it some overt threat to his family? Or perhaps a drug was administered to weaken his spirit. Either is possible, and the latter would be less demonstrative – a hand on the arm, a fine needle passing through clothing – such that passersby wouldn't necessarily notice anything. Then the paper seller would pass him along to one or more other agents and quietly disappear himself. They would walk Sir Edwin to the park gates, into an automobile, away into the anonymity of the city – or indeed anywhere in due course."

"Not much hope, then, Mr. Holmes?" Admiral Billington asked, his expression grave.

"Never say die, Admiral. But this will not be easy."

The grist of Holmes's deductive mill was information, and his next step was to assimilate the details – the tiny, inconspicuous ones – sifting them for anything of use, no matter how peripheral. To that end, we were given the use of an office in which numerous files had been collected – the personnel records of all concerned, including the Japanese delegation. Before we began this arduous task, Admiral Billington called in two extra fellows whom he and Mycroft seconded to our service.

Inspector Bertram Kent of Scotland Yard was the keen sort, experienced but with youth's flush of enthusiasm not yet dulled by time. He was a dark-haired chap with the bearing of a boxer, always watching for the next morsel of information on which he would pounce, with the alacrity of an advancing pugilist. The other was the tall, uniformed figure of Commander Clive Forbes-Branscombe, Naval Intelligence – the solid sort of chap one expects in a position of gravity.

We four gathered in the office and were provided coffee as we began the process of examining the documentation. The place opened off an operations room where secretaries received and sent signals by telegraph and telephone, and typewriters clacked as reports were transcribed. Against this background, Holmes began to study the paperwork pertaining to the main players in this affair, from Admiral Fisher down. Admiral Billington's file was also on the desk, though I noted with interest that no document pertained to Mycroft. It seemed the elder Holmes was to remain forever an enigma.

Now the tedium set in, and I didn't see how I could help. I contented myself with noting my observations of our interview as the others worked through the files. Each was viewed in turn with reference to a London map upon a corkboard, where the routes taken by each party had been marked in coloured pencil. Holmes mused upon the map for a time. I saw his eyes moving from place to place as he considered risks and strategies – what other plots might the abductors have considered, and which might offer some avenue of investigative approach?

After a while, Mycroft hove into the office, a stick supporting his mass, and eyed us with a spark of excitement. "Gentlemen, a report just to hand. I emphasise that it is tentative, but it may bear upon the situation. A field agent on routine work made a sighting of a face he would swear belongs to one Captain Grigori Sidorov. Not a naval man, as you might assume, but an officer in the Czar's secret intelligence organisation. Sidorov is an expert interrogator."

We shared glances filled with a sudden optimism, but Holmes raised a hand to quell our enthusiasm. "Where and when?"

"On the Great Northern Railway. The man left the train at Hatfield, and our agent was able to maintain touch for a while, but was evaded skilfully. That in itself suggests it was indeed Sidorov. However, the agent is currently on his way back to London to review file photographs and make his mind up. We can have a likeness printed and get agents onto the streets in a matter of hours."

"If it *was* Sidorov, he will be aware he was recognised, even tentatively, and will go to ground," Holmes added tersely. "Conversely, if the identification is in error, we cannot afford to commit resources to wild goose chases."

"I'll brief you the moment we know more." With that, Mycroft stepped out.

But it seemed we weren't to be without options. A second pot of coffee was disappearing, and the hour had passed noon when Holmes looked up from Sir Edwin's army record with an alert, pensive expression. He blinked once and asked mildly, "Correct me if I'm wrong, Watson, but doesn't stress exacerbate recurrent malaria?"

I was dumbfounded by the oblique nature of the question for a long moment, then my medical training took over. "Correct. It's well known that in old malaria patients, periods of personal difficulty can bring on a bout."

Holmes rose at once. "Commander, I need a telephone."

He was escorted into the dispatch office, where a device was made available to him, and I saw him speak with great precision, enunciating clearly to whomever he addressed. Then he returned and drafted a message swiftly in a clear hand. "Commander, I need your staff to send this message at once to all appropriate companies. Request reply by telephone at their earliest convenience."

I frowned as the wheels of bureaucracy swung into action, the message being copied and passed to several telephonists who thumbed through the London Telephone Directory and addressed operators far away.

Holmes perched on the edge of the desk and filled his pipe. "It's a long shot, but it's got to be worth taking."

"What is?" I asked

"All in good time," he returned with a wink, and settled to smoke with his coffee as he waited on replies.

They began to arrive within the hour, and the telephonists delivered slips from their message pads one by one. Holmes would scan them and crumple them into a waste basket, then continue to browse the files, but when one particular report reached him, he sat back with an expression I knew well – that the game was afoot. He brandished the paper, turned to the map, and traced northward from London. At its upper edge, he stabbed a finger at a country town.

"Will you keep us in suspense forever?" I exclaimed.

He turned and put his hands behind his back to explain. "Sir Edwin contracted malaria during his service in Egypt – it's recorded in his service file. As we know, it follows one through life. I placed a call to Mrs. Patterly, and she told me that he has suffered a number of recurrences during their marriage. It's been some while, so another might have been on the cards. However, the stress of his abduction is more than likely to provoke a bout, and a man in the throes of a malaria attack is quite useless, nigh insensible. It's easily treated, of course, so if his captors wanted to continue to press him for information, they would find themselves in the position of having no choice but to provide him the appropriate medication."

"Quinine," I remarked. "It's commonly available through chemists."

"But not universally stocked. It's only of use to those who have been overseas so as to contract the disease. I took that long shot I mentioned and had all the main drug distribution companies called to check whether any of them had received a rush order for quinine from a pharmacy they hadn't previously supplied with the stuff." He raised the slip. "One has. An order was placed yesterday morning for quinine by one John Forest, Chemist, in New Town, which is immediately west of . . . Hatfield."

We came to our feet as the connection asserted itself. "It's still circumstantial," Inspector Kent cautioned. "A man who looks like such-and-such, and then someone takes a bout of malaria . . . ."

"I agree, Inspector, but two such occurrences in the same place, twenty-four hours apart, shorten the odds. It's a desperate gamble, but it's all that has emerged so far from the data. There are men moving into the area already?"

"To follow up the sighting, yes," Commander Forbes-Branscombe assured us.

"Then we are in the best position to explore both options." Holmes turned to fetch his cap from a hat-stand by the door. "To King's Cross, Gentlemen, and the first service north. And may I impose upon the Navy to have a car at our disposal when we get there?"

Trains were their familiar, busy selves, racing to connect the corners of Britain, and our party occupied a first-class compartment as the service butted through the grey January day. Our Naval chap had exchanged his uniform for civilian dress to attract less attention. Mycroft had alerted the agents already in Hatfield that they had company and a fresh lead on the way, and we proceeded with optimism – though I couldn't shake the feeling that the identification could turn out to be all wrong, and the malaria case perhaps an elderly female missionary recently returned from Bechuanaland. If so, we were no better or worse off than with no lead at all, and it was distressing to think that the situation could be so far out of hand.

My first hope was to return Sir Edwin to his family, and I was keenly aware of the weight of the Smith and Wesson .44 that I had been issued, in my deep coat pocket. Holmes and I were very definitely on His Majesty's Service in this moment, as surely as I had served Her Majesty when I wore the red coat.

The train had us in Hatfield by two-minutes-past-two, and we walked through to Great North Road, which ran north-south alongside the extensive passenger and goods stations, then around the corner to Salisbury Square and the Great Northern Inn, where Holmes and I had stayed so many years ago, during one of his seminal earlier cases. Here, we were hailed by the driver of a nondescript black Hillman, by which we hovered a few moments in discussion.

"Commander, Inspector, would you take the car over to New Town and cover the chemist, then contact the agents already in place? Watson and I will make inquiries at the estate agency. Let us meet back here in half-an-hour."

We parted and put best foot forward through the blustery afternoon as rain threatened.

We walked freely at this time. The station was unlikely to be under surveillance, as our quarries had to keep their heads figuratively tucked low, attracting no attention. Thus, it was doubtful that more than a few hands were involved. Theirs was a very daring venture, and I had to give credit where it was due – they didn't lack for courage, considering the treatment they could expect at the hands of our own security services, should capture befall them. It was a war, but one where the guns were silent and the tensions below the level of public awareness: A war of espionage, second-guessing, and eternal positioning to take advantage of future possibilities. In such a conflict, there are no battles, but most certainly losses.

Hatfield is a small town, a reminder of Tudor days with the last vestiges of Henry VIII's palace and the great national monument of Hatfield House, ancestral home of the Marquesses of Salisbury, overlooking its ancient parkland. The town was growing gradually with its new urban development to the west, near the St. Albans railway spur. As yet, only one estate agent served the town, and business was slow, such that we secured an interview with the proprietor without difficulty.

"Recently leased property?" Mr. Garvey mused. He was a small, bespectacled man in late middle age, with a shining pate surmounting a chubby countenance adorned by a modest moustache. "I don't believe there's been much trade in the last month or two. A farmer seeking to sell. A few cottages have changed hands for the railway staff, and just one or two houses." He opened a filing cabinet, drew out a folder, and rummaged through the contents.

Holmes and I remained pleasant as the minutes went by. The agency was an office in the village, almost within sight of Hatfield Park, old-world charm in its every stone and beam. I found myself aware that the new century would likely sweep away so much that had characterised the nineteenth, whose ways and institutions had so shaped us as people. Places like this were islands of the past where one could yet feel the old and the comfortable. A portrait of Queen Victoria looked down from one wall, and I felt it would probably hang there until this gentleman departed the world.

"Likely a private house," Holmes added quietly, "though anything is possible."

"For the famous Mr. Sherlock Holmes, I would scour my filing system from top to bottom," Mr. Garvey replied with a beaming smile. "But I don't think that will be necessary – as I said, only a couple of properties have passed through our hands recently." He took out some papers, stapled at their top left corners. "A shop in the village, one street over from here. I believe it's a grocer's. No? Then it'll be No. 10, St. Albans Rd. That's over in the New Town, a few doors along from The White Horse public house." He passed us a sketch of the property, which we saw was a house in the midst of a considerable allotment that ran back from the road. "We let it a couple of weeks ago to a gentleman by the name of Haskins – a surveyor for the railway, as I recall."

Any such details given would be false, and Holmes brought out the printed likeness of Sidorov. "Do you recall seeing this gentleman at any time?"

Garvey fingered his glasses as he turned the paper to a better light. "No, I don't think so . . . it certainly isn't the gentleman who concluded the lease."

"Very well, Mr. Garvey. Thank you for your time."

We stepped out, and Holmes clicked open his watch. "Back to Salisbury Square."

Lights burned in shops as the afternoon grew dark. We had scarcely two hours' daylight remaining, but the January weather was inclement, and heavy cloud on the angry easterly threatened an early dusk. The car was back in the square when we arrived, and we four shared our reports. Inspector Kent told us that the chemist had a record of the order for quinine, that it was a rush delivery the previous day, collected in the evening. When shown the printed face, he assured us it wasn't the man who placed or collected the order. However, no supervising physician had been mentioned, merely that the ailment was "an old one", and the patient knew precisely what to do. However, the chemist did recall that the client was a newcomer in the village, had something of a foreign look, and a strangely flat sort of accent and way of speaking.

"A schooled speaker of English, then," I observed, "rather than a natural one."

Holmes proffered the address we had found. "We still have no definite connection between the man observed on the train and the malaria case," he said flatly. "At this moment, the odds are probably . . . sixty-forty, in favour, that Sir Edwin Patterly is confined at No. 10, St. Albans Road. After less than twenty-four hours since receiving medication, he will not yet be feeling well. Nevertheless, he will be pressed, as hard as they dare, to answer questions, write out information, sketch plans and diagrams. We can expect his captors to be ready to dispose of him, lest he relate anything of use about them to his own side. This means we need to infiltrate the house either quietly and unnoticed, or with such suddenness that the agents have no time in which to react. But that calls for prior knowledge of their disposition." He looked hard from face to face. "How many men do we have, Commander?"

"Six are present, all armed. There'll be two more in an hour."

Holmes checked his watch. "This miserable weather is at least providing us a modicum of darkness in which to move. We need to act decisively, but if we are to extract Sir Edwin alive, we cannot do so precipitously. I move that we should at least *try* to effect his rescue." All heads nodded at once. "Thank you, gentlemen. If such shouldn't be possible, our wider objective remains unchanged: To prevent the foreign agents escaping with their data."

Inspector Kent turned up his topcoat collar and thrust his hands deep into his pockets. His breath was wispy in the air. "I need to advise Hatfield Police Station. They can provide assistance, keeping the locals away in case of gunplay at the very least."

"At once, please, Inspector. Then we must reconnoitre our target as surreptitiously as we may." He eyed me oddly for a moment, then exchanged his deerstalker for my bowler, reached into the car, and took up a clipboard from beside the driver. On it were logged mileages and expenses. He fished out a pencil from an inside pocket to complete the illusion of officialdom, plus a grubby and illegible business card, which he flashed peremptorily. "Sam Boggins, Council Works Inspector," he began in a creditable Midlands accent. "Followin' up details on these new properties. Are the privies working a'right?"

I had seen Holmes perform his transformations countless times, but it never ceased to amaze me when he became someone else entirely. Even his gait changed. His straight, tall frame became round-shouldered and somewhat bowed, and his manner brusque, as if he hated the job in which life had trapped him.

We went along St. Albans Road in the car to size up the target. The allotment was a fair size, a good thousand square yards, and had been planted with trees and the beginnings of a vegetable garden, with a greenhouse under construction at the time the property changed hands. Rough grass decorated the frontal area, and the two-storey stone-and-brick house was set back fifteen yards behind a picket fence. All windows were shuttered, and light showing at the odd crack alone suggested occupancy.

The driver took us back around in a circuit behind the New Town area. Holmes prepared for his performance like a thespian about to take the stage, clearing his throat and checking his appearance in the rearview mirror.

I waited with the inspector and the commander at The Gun public house on the corner of French Horn Lane. I nursed a warming whisky as we heard a train go through on the St. Albans line, and I knew Holmes was making good his part by calling at other houses in the row. No. 9 was also set back from the road on an allotment, and he would walk up the gravel path with a view over the hedge of the house next door. I knew he would carry off his act with the lady or gentleman of the house, making notes that meant nothing. Then he would doff the bowler to him or her, and bustle off through the early twilight of racing black clouds that seemed to threaten snow, and enter the property in question. From that moment on, it was all down to his skill.

We gave him twenty minutes, and then the car circled around again and picked him up by the smithy on the western corner and had him back at The Gun for a libation in a twinkling.

"We were right," he said softly, under the general hubbub of the bar, where we gathered by a cheerful hearth. We exchanged hats once more. "The door was answered by a fellow disinclined to be helpful, and though his English is schooled to perfection, some trace remains of Continental enunciation."

Commander Forbes-Branscombe nodded over his naval pink gin. "German? Italian?"

"Russian." Holmes nodded with certainty. "Understandably, they're still smarting over their defeat at Tsushima, and eager to even the score

351

any way they can. Their Baltic Fleet's feat of seamanship – taking capital steamships halfway round the world in battle order to engage an equal foe – has already been forgotten by history. All that will be recalled is that their expedition resulted in a tactical failure. Czar Nicholas clearly seeks a rematch, and on more even terms. It is imperative his naval planners be apprised of Japan's situation, which by default means *our* current developments. Thus, the situation we now face."

"How will we do this?" Inspector Kent asked quietly.

"Light showed from the hall through panes beside the front door, and a sliver of light was visible between shutters at two upstairs rooms, both at the front of the house. One of those is probably Sir Edwin's place of confinement. We need to get inside quietly and overcome the guards." Holmes sketched quickly, in pencil on the back of an envelope, a rough chart of the property. "There's a gate to the back premises on the left. No dogs appear present on this or adjoining streets, which is a mercy. Though there is a carriage lantern by the front door, they don't keep it lit at this hour, which affords darkness. From the general appearance of the house, the stairs will be in close proximity to the front door, so . . . ." He smiled tightly. "Commander, how are your men at staging a diversion?"

Very good, as it turned out. The Navy driver participated in the scheme, and one of the Intelligence agents, who had visited around the village in pubs and cafes to keep watch on the passing trade, was more than eager to provide the victim of the piece.

The roads were damp as a patter of rain developed, misting around the newly-lit streetlamps. The end of day made a show of reds and yellows over the fields westward, and we were in position, hearts racing, with a skerrick of daylight remaining. Moving with cat-footed tread, Holmes and I, accompanied by the inspector and the commander, cleared the picket fence rather than chance the squeaking of a gate. We advanced over the rough grass for quiet and flattened out around the corner of the house, our pistols drawn. Now, all we needed to do was provoke the occupants into opening the door.

The braying of a car horn and a squeal of brakes cut through the evening quiet, and a cry went up as the drama unfolded. The agent lay in the damp and dirt by the roadside and rolled as if in agony, clutching a leg, while the driver left his vehicle with a noisy slamming of his door. Voices were raised, then the driver ran back and honked urgently at his horn for attention.

A couple of other agents were poised to respond, hurrying along the street from the forecourt of the White Horse pub, and a few locals naturally followed. A moment later, lamps brightened at the intervening houses, and onlookers appeared. In moments, someone was asking if they should fetch a doctor.

As the "accident" was *almost* opposite No. 10, it would have been bad form – therefore perhaps suspicious – for no one to show a face. A light shone in the hall, its glow spilling through the glass beside the door. Locks clacked open and the door went back. Then a dark figure emerged in the wash of lamplight, stepped onto the gravel way, and peered into the street. Holmes moved like lightning, darting from concealment to clip the fellow across the back of the head with his gun butt. The man went down without a sound. The inspector dragged him out of sight and snapped cuffs into place – there was one agent out of action. No one in the street noticed our byplay, and we four melted into the house in seconds.

Now, speed and silence were key, and my heart thudded behind my ribs with the surge of the moment. I hadn't done anything like this in years and was keenly aware I had a wife to go back to, so I let the others take the lead. Holmes advanced up the stairs on silent tread, and Inspector Kent covered the upstairs hall with his pistol outstretched in both hands. Then Commander Forbes-Branscome followed Holmes up, and they beckoned us to follow. The stairs were new, sturdy, and didn't creak. Carpet muffled our tread, so we reached the upstairs hall unopposed.

Light showed in two front rooms at the end of the hall, where their doors stood ajar, one at the end of the passage, the other opening to the left. In the room into which we could see, I caught the impression of a bulky figure as a hand reached to turn down the gaslight. Then the fellow went to peer out between the slats of a shutter. Holmes advanced soundlessly along the carpet, pistol upraised, and the tension was almost too much to bear as we neared the end of the hall. The spell couldn't last forever and was broken by a creaking floorboard – under whose foot I had no idea – that brought the man staring into the street turning in a whirl.

Things seemed to happen in slow motion, one event piling atop another. First, consternation in his face as he saw us through the part-open door – strangers, when he would have expected his friend from downstairs to have returned. Then he snatched for a weapon in a cross-draw and bellowed, *"Ubit' zaklyuchennogo!"* Holmes raised his weapon and triggered in the same instant, outdrawing his opponent and sending him thumping back into the closed window with a sudden shattering of glass. Holmes whirled and kicked open the half-closed door to the adjoining bedroom, which opened off the same landing.

"Nyet!" was the roar, and from the door we saw Sir Edwin Patterly, wrapped in a blanket and looking very unwell, hunched at a writing bureau, many sheets of paper before him filled with notes and drawings. He was held in the crook of a powerful arm, and a pistol was pressed to

353

his temple, clutched in a hard fist. The broad, fair-haired Slavic features that snarled over his shoulder belonged unquestionably to Sidorov. "Back!" He shifted easily to English. "If you would have your man alive, make no sudden move, or his prospects will be cut short rather drastically!"

We huddled in the hall behind Holmes, who hugged the door jamb for cover, his pistol extended around it. "There is nowhere for you to go, Captain Sidorov. Your man below is cuffed and in custody by now. Your compatriot in the next room isn't coming to your assistance. You are outgunned and surrounded. Your only logical action is to surrender."

"It is easy to ask a man to surrender, but so hard for him to perform the deed." A Russian accent had returned, now that Sidorov must maintain a pretence no longer. "I was under no illusion about risks when I entered this country. I can take solace from the fact that, but for Mr. Patterly's illness, I would have concluded interrogation yesterday. He is politician, after all. Not spy. Not engineer. There is only so much he can possibly know, and my comrades drained him of policy matters within the first three hours, long before I arrived. The rest is all technical." He cast an eye over the sheaves of paper. "Such a shame it will never reach those waiting so eagerly for it."

Holmes held his weapon steady on the Russian's forehead. "I repeat, Captain, you are without options here. You must submit to captivity."

"And find myself on the receiving end of the same or worse?" He smiled, icy and unamused. "We Russians are called brutal, but few countries in this world can match the British for ruthlessness in pursuit of their national interests."

I had a crooked angle of view into the room and watched what transpired via the reflection in a dressing table mirror. I saw Patterly – ill and afraid, his eyes hooded and desperate – where he sat, the Russian's arm around his neck, and my heart went out to him in his ordeal. Clearly, he expected to die even now in some last gesture of defiance from his captor. But fate worked a little differently today.

"Captain, we're waiting," Holmes grated, his weapon unerringly on target and his patience duly thin.

"Indeed. You must pardon a man savouring his last breaths." Sidorov smiled for a moment. "Please tell His Majesty the Czar that I served him honourably to the last." Then he transferred the pistol from Patterly's temple to his own.

And fired.

"There was no talking him around," I offered a little while later, when we sat on the end of a bed and listened to rain on the roof.

354

"I know. He was a seasoned professional who had lived with the necessity of avoiding interrogation his whole career through. He knew better than most what the process entails, how 'experts' like him are used to break down even the strongest mind and body. His sacrifice was preferable to him, and denied us an intelligence coup of our own."

"By the way – What was it the fellow you shot called out?"

Holmes raised a single brow. "'*Kill the prisoner.*'"

The local police were on hand. A constable guarded the door below, and a call had been placed to London. A special would be sent up the line after commercial services concluded to bring back our party, plus Sidorov's body and his cuffed companion. The man Holmes had shot was in fact alive and might well pull through, having been deprived of nothing more vital than his spleen. He had been taken under guard by motor-ambulance to the General Infirmary in Hertford, a little under eight miles distant. There wasn't even a cottage hospital locally. The Naval Intelligence fellows wouldn't leave his side.

A burly police sergeant rustled up tea and biscuits from the kitchen below and brought a tray. We accepted it with thanks, and I looked into the other room to find Sir Edwin awake, seeming a little dazed but otherwise in surprisingly good condition, given his ordeal. We delivered a cup to him where he rested in bed, the blanket around his shoulders against the January chill, and he cradled the mug of tea as if it were ambrosia.

He brushed at an abrasion on his left cheek where "persuasion" had been dealt. A lip was also split. "Please don't think me ineffectual, gentlemen," he murmured. "I could have done the noble thing and utterly refused to cooperate – but that would have seen me reduced to wreckage, unfit to be returned to my family, and likely hastened my despatch at the point of a gun. Besides, I had faith that I would have help sooner or later."

"Please don't distress yourself, sir," Holmes soothed. "We are entirely aware of the choices with which you were faced. You were in an impossible situation."

"But not, I am happy to say, without means to affect it." Patterson gestured to the bound parcel of papers on the bureau. "The Intelligence section will have a field day going through those. You see, I had the presence of mind to introduce over a hundred technical errors in the information I was giving them: Overestimating the capacity of our own ships, the reach of their guns, the resilience of their armour, their possible top speed. I was giving the Russian designers an impossible target for their obligatory engineering response, which would have nigh bankrupted the Czar's treasury, had he felt compelled to aim for it." He sipped his tea, nursing it around his split lip. "It was the most, and the least, I could do."

I laughed and nodded my approval. "Well done, Sir Edwin! Once a redcoat, always a redcoat." I raised my mug in salute, which he returned.

Commander Forbes-Branscome came up to take official charge of the documentation, promising a coal fire in the parlour and a meal sent in from a restaurant to tide us over until the train arrived for us, which would be around one of the morning. Inspector Kent stepped in to sit with the knight, and Holmes and I excused ourselves.

In the hall, we chinked rims, and I gave a faint shake of the head. "Do you miss it, Holmes?" I asked softly.

"The game?" He paused a moment, then shook his head also. "Not quite the way you mean. Times have changed, and I retired for good reasons. More than twenty-five years a consulting detective was a good run. But yes – there are times I look back on cases, on our adventures, and wish there had been just a few more." He gestured at the house around us with an inclination of his deerstalker. "And occasionally, those wishes come true. But the motor-car has replaced the hansom, Her Majesty is a memory, and we live in fascinating and foreboding times when men have learned to fly and the weapons of war become ever more terrible. From my solitude down on the coast, I can view it with a detached impartiality, balancing the world we knew with the one that is coming. These Edwardian times have their own flavour, to be sure, but they feel *impermanent*, if you follow."

I made a bit of a face at that. "Don't tell me that Sherlock Holmes is a thing of the past. You've just demonstrated that he is not!!"

"I'll be here when needs must, Watson," he replied mildly, but with an edge of introspection. "But let us not try to imagine that The Great Game, as they call it, will necessarily save us from the conflagration of some world-wide confrontation. *That's* what troubles me. And in the race to build bigger and better ships, we see the shape of things to come for all areas of human endeavour. Who knows what times we may live into?"

With that sobering thought, we put the case behind us and went down to indulge in a pipe on the front doorstep as the rain beat gently from the chill darkness, and, much as I had enjoyed serving with Holmes once more, I thought fondly of home and hearth and of my good lady.

The Problem of the
Locked Room
by Daniel D. Victor

"That docteur *anglais* – what did one call him –
Doyle? Pouf! He was an echo [of Poe] . . .
What was Sherlock Holmes beside this Master Dupin!"
– M. Duclos in Melville Davisson Post's *The Nameless Thing*

Editor's Note: According to the Fall 2009 Newsletter of the University of West Virginia, Melville Davisson Post (1869-1930) was "extolled by Ellery Queen, imitated by William Faulkner, adored by Teddy Roosevelt and . . . considered by many to be the greatest mystery writer of all time." The headnote above comes from The Nameless Thing, *Post's fictional version of Dr. John H. Watson's account that follows. By insulting Sherlock Holmes with a comparison to Poe's fictional Dupin, Post's equally fictional Duclos provided Post the opportunity to distance himself from the original history.*

– D.D.V.

Since 1890, the year that marked Sherlock Holmes's recovery of the missing racehorse Silver Blaze, Holmes and I have always cherished the notion of attending the heralded horserace for the "Wessex Cup", the competition originally held every year in late September at Worthy Down in Winchester. After all, as reported in the sketch I titled "Silver Blaze", it was Holmes's success in the investigation that ultimately allowed the horse to compete in the venerable event.

Although the original racecourse in Winchester was demolished many years ago, the run for the Wessex Cup has continued. Like numerous other competitions previously held at Worthy Down, the storied contest was relocated on Dartmoor, much closer to such estimable stables as Lord Backwater's Mapleton and Colonel Ross' King's Pyland.

As a consequence, rather than travelling by railway from Waterloo to Winchester, as one would have done to watch Silver Blaze run, Holmes and I made the same journey we had made on our initial visit to King's Pyland – that is, from Paddington to Tavistock by way of Exeter. There were not many motors on Dartmoor in those days, so we hired a dogcart for the final drive to Tavistock Down.

Not that we made the trip every year. As appealing as racecourses can be, I am forced to confess that our attendance had become a tradition more

357

honoured in the breach, for Holmes and I soon discovered that his detective work and my medical practice seldom allowed us the annual opportunity for a day at the races.

Still, once Holmes retired and moved to the South Downs, we did find the occasional opportunity to make the trip. We would meet at Paddington – my friend, a little greyer, coming up via Brighton from his cottage and beehives. I, a bit more hobbled, driving by hansom from my home in Queen Anne Street in London.

It was in the early fall of '07 that the seventeenth anniversary of the rescue of Silver Blaze provided us the chance to watch a running of the Wessex Cup once again. Though the surroundings at Tavistock Down may have differed from the original course, the bracing aroma of animal and earth was the same – as was, I should add, the Siren call of wagering to which Holmes and I always succumbed whenever we approached the turf.

A horse appealingly called Baker's Dozen was our champion that day, and beneath grey skies we stood by the rails of the single grandstand cheering him on as he thundered past the waving touts, the well-dressed toffs, and the shouting commoners on his way to winning the Cup. With the favourable odds posted on various slates about the grounds, we headed through the crowd for our bookmaker's stall to collect our winnings.

It was on the footpath to the exit that the first of two encounters interrupted our high spirits. The initial intrusion arrived in the form of a loud "Halloo!" produced by a smartly-dressed, Saville-Row-tailored gentleman. He looked like a Londoner, but from the twang in his tone, one could easily discern that he was an American. Greying sideburns suggested his age to be near forty. Of average height and stature, he sported a *pince-nez,* which presented a serious and academic look, rather striking in the bucolic atmosphere of a racecourse.

"You're Sherlock Holmes," he said to my companion. The sharp timbre of his voice made the words sound like an accusation. "I can tell from that deerstalker and your profile."[1] To me he said, "And you must be Dr. Watson, his Boswell. I've read most all of your stories about Sherlock Holmes, sir, and I don't mind telling you that I like them. I don't read much beyond crime fiction these days, but I also enjoyed those other stories – oh, but wait – " Here he held up his forefinger. " – Those were written by your agent – also a writer – weren't they? Arthur Conan Doyle?"

"I'll be sure to tell him you liked them," I replied rather coolly, "but I'm afraid we're at a disadvantage. You've correctly identified *us*, but we don't know who *you* are."

"Come now, Watson," interjected Holmes. "I'm sure Mr. Post would be disappointed to learn that we didn't recognise the illustrious author of the Randolph Mason stories – and also a novel or two, if I'm not mistaken. *Dwellers in the Hills*, the account of your boyhood in West Virginia, is reputed to have done quite well here in England."

The animated American was suddenly speechless. "My God," he said, "it's true! You are indeed clairvoyant, Mr. Holmes! How could you possibly know who I am? We've never met before."

"Elementary, my dear Post," Holmes explained, obviously enjoying the simplicity of the answer he was about to provide. "Your photograph, along with that of your charming wife, appeared in all the prints as a result of her presentation to King Edward at Buckingham Palace last June. She wore quite the elegant gown by Redfern. I recall in particular the three white plumes in her headdress and the eleven-foot train." [1]

Mr. Post's face reddened. "Why, that's quite correct. I'd forgotten – the photograph, that is, not meeting the King."

"Just who is this Randolph Mason?" I wanted to know.

"Watson," Holmes said, "I think you'll find that at least in his fiction, Mr. Post, a lawyer by profession, is quite adept at dancing round the law. Randolph Mason is an unscrupulous American attorney who makes it his business to advise his clients how to evade legal responsibility. In 'The Corpus Delicti', for example, culpability for murder is avoided because the body of the victim has been effectively disposed of."

"That's right," said Post, clearly impressed with Holmes's awareness, "but it was only fiction, let us not forget – something my critics can't seem to manage."

To me, of course, Holmes's familiarity with Post's work was far from surprising. My friend may never have claimed mastery of the classics, but his knowledge of sensational texts was unrivalled.

"Your King is quite the horseman, you know," said Post. "In fact, it's due to him that I've come out here to Dartmoor. I'm a polo fanatic, you see, and he and I exchanged a few comments on polo ponies. When he was the Prince of Wales, he kept Dartmoor ponies in Princetown. They're well suited for polo – quite sure-footed, you know. I was out at the Royal Stables yesterday having a look. I even rode one out on the Moor. I love their thick, long manes."

Post waved his arm about. "All of this is part of a grand trip my wife, Bloom, and I are in the midst of. We left the States in September of last year. Our son of eighteen months died of typhoid fever in August, and we're trying to put all that behind us. Bloom was happy enough to remain in London to do some shopping while I pursue the horses."

A typical American, it seemed to me. We had known the man for but a couple of minutes, and already we had learned of a family tragedy and his relations with his wife.

Nor was Mr. Post finished. "When I learned that today was the running of the Wessex Cup, gentlemen – Well, I just knew that I had to come to the track. I've read 'Silver Blaze', you see, and appreciate the connection. Can't say I expected the good fortune of running into its two central figures, of course."

"Quite," said Holmes. Obviously ready to move on, he consulted his pocket-watch and added, "It's time for us to be returning to town for our trip back to London."

"Oh, allow *me*," said the American gesturing towards the road. "I'm staying at the Bedford here in Tavistock – I love all your historic places – and the station's in the same direction. I hired a carriage at the hotel to meet me after the final race, and I can deposit you both at your train."

We nodded our thanks and followed Post through the dwindling knots of people to the roadway where stood an open landau with "*The Bedford Hotel*" lettered discreetly on the side. As the American instructed, the driver conveyed us to the Tavistock North Railway Station.

It was there that occurred the second significant encounter to which I previously referred. No sooner had we exited the landau in front of the red-brick and grey-granite station than we saw a moustachioed gentleman in bowler, suit, and long coat determinedly zigzagging his way among the white posts and milling passengers. In Tavistock, as well as in London, such attire was the recognizable uniform of a Scotland Yard detective. As he hastened towards the road, he suddenly noticed my friend and came to an abrupt halt.

"Is that Sherlock Holmes?" he asked.

"Why, yes," Holmes replied.

"Inspector Marcus Henry," the man said, extending his hand. "I thought I recognised you. We've never worked together, but I'd seen you on the job before you retired. Lestrade has filled me in on your work."

Though cocking an eyebrow at the reference, Holmes shook the inspector's hand and dutifully introduced him to me and to Post, who nodded from the landau. Holmes took the opportunity to consult his watch again and, explaining that we had a London train to catch, proceeded to move forward.

The inspector, however, raised his palm and brought my friend to a halt.

"Actually, Mr. Holmes," said the policeman, "I've been called here on a murder investigation. In point of fact, it sounds like a case that might interest you. A man-servant, who's now in custody at the scene of the murder, couldn't rouse his master late last night and reported his concern to the local constabulary. As it turned out, his master was dead. Skull crushed. At first glance, it seemed like a clear case of murder. Yet the Tavistock Police wired the Yard late last night, and here I am today."

"Quick work," said Melville Post, who had been listening over the rail of the open landau.

All business, the inspector produced a notebook from his coat pocket. "The deceased is one Albert Bingham," he read. "The local police had no trouble identifying him, but here's the rub: His body was in a room whose door and windows were all securely shut. In fact, they had to break down the door to gain entry. Everything was locked from the inside, Mr. Holmes. Just the sort of challenge I should imagine that a detective like yourself might find engaging."

Holmes smiled wryly. "A *retired* detective, may I remind you."

"But a locked-room mystery, Mr. Holmes!" marvelled Post. "The very best kind."

"Perhaps in popular magazines," I felt obliged to add.

Post ignored me. "I'd love to accompany you, Mr. Holmes," he went on, "should you decide to investigate, of course. Such cases provide inspiration. Though my mystery stories are fiction, most all of them are based on some real crime I've read about or been involved with in a legal capacity. I like to call each such case the 'germ' of my narrative." [2]

Holmes arched his bushy eyebrows, then looked at me. "What's your pleasure, old fellow? Care to spend some time on an investigation?"

I recognised the familiar spark in my friend's steel-grey eyes, the spark that accompanied the arrival of a new case, especially a challenging one. Actually, current investigations were nothing new to me. After Holmes had retired and left London in '03, I continued providing medical advice to Scotland Yard whenever called upon. Attentive readers will remember that I did similar work following Holmes's assumed death in '91.

In a word, I agreed immediately. "Of course, I'm ready," I told him. "'The game is afoot,' as you used to say."

Post pointed at himself questioningly.

"With your legal background, Post, why not join the group?" said Holmes. "That is, if Henry here will have you."

Inspector Henry narrowed his eyes as he seemed to be calculating – the value of Holmes's help in the investigation versus whatever the cost of bringing along the American writer. "Very well, then," the policeman said at last. "Agreed. Let us be off."

Melville Davisson Post climbed out of the landau and sent it back to the Bedford. The three of us then followed Inspector Henry into the police van that had been sent to the railway station to pick up the Scotland Yarder, and together our *ad hoc* team of investigators set off for the Dartmoor countryside.

Negotiating the rise and fall of the moor's western inclines, we journeyed some two miles east of Tavistock. As the landscape grew ever more barren, Inspector Henry shared a few of the details he had learned about the deceased from the telegram the local police had sent to London.

"Albert Bingham moved here three years ago," Henry said, "profession unknown. Besides the servant who reported the murder, he lived by himself."

"What do you know about this servant?" Holmes asked.

"Thrush, he calls himself. Leo Thrush. Former military down on his luck. He was detained at the house once Bingham's body was found."

The van turned into a dirt road that led into a small valley. The only structure visible in the desolate landscape was the location of the crime. Blanketed in brown vegetation, the surrounding hills did little to protect the single-storey building from the wind, and a series of tree stumps and cleared-away brush made the structure appear all the starker.

A uniformed constable stood at the outer door and raised his right hand to his helmet in a semi-formal salute.

"Inside, sir," the constable directed Henry. "Collins is with the suspect. The deed was done in the library. Bars on the windows. A door of solid oak bolted on the inside with an iron crossbar. It took three workman a couple of hours to break the door down so we could reach the victim. I placed a chair at the entrance so no one would go in by accident."

The detective grunted acknowledgement, and we all entered the house. Though Henry had informed us that, aside from Thrush, the victim lived alone, we could have reached the same conclusion by simply looking about. Bookcases lined the sitting room. A gun rack hung on one wall, and a pipe rack stood on the mantel. Models of various sailing ships adorned available tabletops and shelves. In a word, it looked to be a masculine retreat.

A second uniformed constable – the aforementioned Collins, I assumed – was in the midst of searching the sitting room. Upon our entry, he straightened up, tugging at the skirts of his jacket to sharpen his appearance. In contrast, occupying a chair beside him sat a slight, little man with a drawn, sallow-cheeked face whom I took to be the servant, Leo Thrush. Despite the coolness of the day, he was dressed in baggy shirtsleeves and rough trousers.

362

Henry introduced himself to Collins, informing the constable that the three of us were police consultants. In return, Collins handed Henry the notes the local police had taken while questioning the man.

Henry glanced over the pages, then said to Thrush, "You aren't the ordinary butler-type. Not unused to spending nights in Trafalgar Square, it says here."

"Yes," agreed Thrush. "That's where I met Mr. Bingham – Well, close by anyway. On a street near the Thames, it was, a few months back. I was sleeping on a bench near the Embankment one night – always on the lookout for coppers, I was – and I caught sight of this bloke standing too close to the water. I run over to him, didn't I?

"To this day, I swear to you that I prevented Mr. Bingham from drowning himself. In thanks, he hired me as his 'man': His valet, his gardener, what have you. Basically, I did whatever he needed me to. After a week, he dismissed his cook and a groom – their responsibilities becoming my own from then on. Mainly, though, I was a watchman."

"What were you watching for?" Henry asked.

"Never was told, was I?" said Thrush. "All I know for certain is that Mr. Bingham wanted to be alone. He used to get invitations to dinner, but he turned them down, and after a while people gave up inviting him. He used to ride a horse about the moor, or march through the brush with a rifle on his shoulder looking for the odd fox or wild rabbit. But as the months went by, he gave all that up as well.

"Weeks ago, it was, I helped him cut down trees and shrubbery round the house to give him a clearer view of the countryside. When you drove in, you must have seen the results. We built higher fences, put in shutters, attached large padlocks to his outer door, and two-inch iron bars in all the windows.

"Sounds like he turned the house into a sort of fortress, eh, Thrush?" Henry asked. "As if he was trying to keep someone out."

"Can't really say, sir, can I?" replied Thrush. "Except that he did loads of exercising, and he always walked about armed."

"And last night, when he died?" Henry queried. "Where were you?"

"Out here, sir, cleaning up. Mr. Bingham went into the library. It was about ten o'clock, it was. I'd had a few drinks with him before, so I wasn't moving too quickly. Suddenly, I heard shouting in the library, then lots of gun shots. I had no clue what was going on in there, but it sounded bad. There was no getting through that oak door, so I figured the smart thing to do before anyone came after me was to get out, which I did. There wasn't no one around, so I went to town and told the police."

363

"Right," said Henry, patting his moustache. "Now it's time to have a go at the body." He pointed to Thrush and said to Collins, "Keep an eye on this one."

A corridor led into the sitting room. At its far end, a bow-back Windsor chair blocked a splintered portal. Despite the darkness within the chamber beyond, however, one could discern enough books to assume a library. As was his wont, Holmes attempted to prevent anyone from contaminating the scene, but the inspector, not used to my friend's methods, side-stepped him and, easing the chair out of the way, motioned for the rest of us to follow him into the room.

Ten-foot-high bookcases framed the interior, interrupted only by the door through which we had just passed and by two casement windows that looked out over the moor. While the windows were shuttered tightly on the inside, any number of small holes perforated the solid-oak slats at odd intervals, allowing numerous fingers of twilight to penetrate the darkness. In fact, there was enough light to reveal not only that the glass panes had shattered, but also that someone had ransacked the library. Chairs lay helter-skelter. Ashtrays, pens, and inkwells littered the oaken floor. A bookcase had been knocked over, and various volumes lay scattered about.

"No point in looking for a push-button," Henry informed us. "We aren't in London. There's no electricity out here." On a desk stood a lantern which the inspector, having produced a vesta, proceeded to light. The flame was strong enough to illuminate the corner of the room containing the dark-grey blanket, beneath which was situated the corpse. A large rifle lay on the floor a few feet away.

"Doctor?" Henry said to me, extending his arm by way of invitation to examine the body.

Stepping around an array of splayed books, I removed the blanket and bent over the victim, his twisted body lying on its side. Clearly, the man had been dead for hours. *Rigor mortis* was beginning to set in. Still, as a matter of professional routine, I checked for a pulse, and finding none – nor, for that matter, any bruises – examined the deep gash at the top of the poor fellow's head. Though it had done nothing to cushion the blow, his black hair had been left thick on the top and cut short on the sides – in typical military style.

A muscular young man, probably in his twenties, Bingham had been viciously struck at the juncture of the two parietal bones on the top of his skull. There was no slant to the wound, just a powerful downward blow, which had produced a vast quantity of blood. Death would have been near instantaneous. Although I didn't speculate aloud, I thought a hammer could have been responsible for such damage, a hammer in the hands of a strong, tall, and determined assailant.

"Could he have done this to himself?" Post asked as I replaced the blanket over the body. "That business by the river – it sounds like Bingham was suicidal."

"Coshing oneself on the head?" Henry said. "Not the usual method for topping oneself, I'm afraid."

"That's why you think Thrush might be responsible," the American said.

"More a person of interest," replied Henry. "Thrush doesn't appear tall enough to have inflicted such a wound. Of course, one can never be sure. Bingham might have been bending over."

Instead of examining the body himself, Holmes cast his eyes round the room, checking every possible point of entry. "The door was clearly locked," he observed, "and the chimney is too small for passage. Both windows have their bars in place, and the latches of their shutters remain fastened."

Post nodded sagely. "A true locked-room mystery," he said in awe.

"The perforations in the shutters are bullet holes," Holmes continued. "The projectiles head outward – shot, I venture to say, from the gun on the floor, a Lee-Enfield bolt-action repeating rifle common to the military. It would appear that our victim was attempting to keep someone out."

"Someone – or some *thing*," Melville Post added melodramatically.

Holmes proceeded to the bookcase that had been knocked over. "Do you have a magnifying lens, Inspector? I anticipated no need to bring mine to the racecourse."

Henry produced a glass from an inner coat pocket and handed it to Holmes.

Holding the lens over the fallen bookcase, Holmes examined each of the wooden shelves, running a finger lengthwise along the middle of each one. He then turned and scanned the books on the floor. "Many of the classics," he read aloud. "Dickens, Shakespeare, Thackeray."

"The poor fellow had good taste in reading," Post observed. "But notice," he added, as adjusting his *pince-nez* he too looked over the titles, "how many of these novels deal specifically with warfare – *The Red Badge of Courage, War and Peace, The Four Feathers, The Charterhouse of Parma*."

"Interesting indeed," murmured Holmes.

It was I who spotted the strongbox. "What's that?" I asked, pointing to the heavy wooden coffer on the floor. It stood in the shadows about a yard from the man's head. "A clue? A target for thieves, perhaps?"

With small leather handles at both ends and standing about a foot tall, a foot wide, and two feet in length, the box looked not unlike a miniature traveller's trunk, and inch-for-inch was no doubt just as heavy. Positioned as it was so close to the dead man's head wound, its bottom-most edges were steeped in blood. Holmes peered at the coffer from all angles, employing a pencil to poke at the red clots near its lower edges. Only after completing his examination of the exterior did he attempt to open it and discover, not surprisingly, that its impressive black lock at the front was latched.

At that moment, however, Constable Collins, who had been searching the sitting room, came into the library. In his hand was a small silver key. "I saw the box earlier, sir," he said to Inspector Henry. "I just found this key in a drawer that might fit the lock."

The policeman handed the detective the silver key and, stooping over, Henry confirmed that it did indeed fit. "Excellent work," he said to Collins before sending him back to the sitting room.

"There's a wax seal over the lock," Henry announced, "and it's covered with dust. No one's has opened this box – or even tried to – in a long time." He then scraped off the seal with his forefinger, inserted the small key into the lock, and gave it a turn. The motion produced a gratifying click, and the lid elevated a quarter-of-an-inch. Henry proceeded to open it all the way.

"What's inside?" Post wanted to know. And of course, so did Holmes and I.

Still bent over, the inspector reached in and, withdrawing three large envelopes, placed them on the table next to the lantern.

"Nothing else inside," he said, and we watched him open each envelope.

The first one contained a group of twelve photographs – all sepia-coloured faces of young men with the same dark background – taken, no doubt by the same photographer in the same studio. All were dressed differently – some in suits, some in simple white shirts, their hair long on top of their heads, shaved round the sides.

It took Henry but a moment to discover the face of Albert Bingham among the twelve. Like the others, he was staring seriously into the camera lens, an image far different from the blood-riddled face of the dead man lying beneath the blanket on the floor just a few feet away.

Once Henry had looked at all the photographs, he handed them to Holmes, who turned each one this way and that, front and back, unsuccessfully seeking any marks that might indicate their origin.

The second envelope contained dozens of newspaper cuttings, some very old and, I hesitate to add, doubtlessly removed surreptitiously from libraries or museums with the aid of a scissors. A glance at the headlines revealed their gruesome commonality – vessels of the Royal Navy that, along with their entire crews, had sunk in various oceans round the world.

A sampling should suffice to indicate the macabre nature of the collection: *HMS Redwing* went down off the west coast of Africa in June of 1827. *HMS Sappho* was lost near Australia in February of 1858. *HMS Atalanta* sank near Bermuda in January of 1880. Most recent was the story of *HMS A1,* the first British-designed submarine, that sank in March of '04 off the Isle of Wight, just three years before Bingham's death. Also in the aggregation was a cutting about *Resurgam II*, the ill-fated British submersible which sank in 1880 in the Irish Sea. Unlike in the case of the other ships, however, none of *Resurgam II*'s three-man crew was aboard.

The third envelope contained a different assortment of cuttings. Though more numerous and common, they too were unified by a central theme: Justice triumphant. There were stories of murderers hanged, thieves jailed, debtors imprisoned. The fate of Charles Peace, executed in February of 1879 for killing at least two men, one of whom was a policeman, should serve as an example.

"Ah," said Holmes when he saw the article, "my old friend Charlie Peace again." It was a comment he had made once before, [3] but now, as then, he was referring sarcastically to Peace's violin virtuosity, not the man's deadly murder campaigns. Musical talent notwithstanding, justice caught up with Charles Peace on the gallows.

It was a curious assortment of memorabilia that Albert Bingham had kept locked in his strong box. One could only wonder what it all had to do with his murder.

Upon setting down the last envelope, Inspector Henry said, "The coroner will arrive shortly to remove the body. In the meantime, I must ask, Mr. Holmes, if you have any thoughts concerning who might have done this deed?"

"Oh, yes," said Holmes. "I've worked that out."

Wide eyes and open mouths greeted Holmes's announcement. "Who?" we asked in unison.

"I wish to establish motive before I make my deductions public," he said. "A phone call to my brother Mycroft in Whitehall should help me on that front."

Following Holmes's cryptic comment, we exited the house. Until a more satisfactory suspect was presented, the local police would continue detaining Thrush. For our part, we took advantage of Henry's offer to have the police van drive us to the Bedford Hotel, where Post was staying and where Holmes and I assumed we too might secure rooms for the night. Although the rates at the Bedford might be a bit dear, we assumed our stay would be but for a single night. Besides – though it seemed a long time ago, had we not become flush at the racecourse earlier that very day?

After agreeing to return to the Bingham house the following morning, Holmes and I did in fact procure rooms in the crenelated old hotel. With much of Dartmoor having been influenced by the Duke of Bedford, an antique-looking reproduction of the Bedford Coat of Arms, complete with red lion, hung above the desk in the lobby. Fortunately, the hotel was fashionable enough to possess a telephone, and Holmes made private use of it to ring his brother in London.

Sherlock Holmes was already seated in the hotel dining room when I came downstairs for breakfast. Over ham and eggs, he told me in the most general terms of the early-morning phone call from Mycroft. "All will be explained when we see Inspector Henry," he assured me as we drank our coffees.

To convey us back to the location of the murder, Melville Post hired the hotel carriage, an elaborate, ancient-looking four-wheeler replete with brass *accoutrements* and a reproduction of the Bedford Coat of Arms on each door. The two tawny horses, while serviceable, would probably not be employed by the Duke himself. Still, they delivered the three of us to our destination and, as previously agreed, we met Marcus Henry in the sitting room.

The inspector wasted no time in getting directly to the point. "All right, Mr. Holmes," he greeted my friend, "you said you know the party responsible for this crime. That must also mean you know how it was committed – committed, I need not remind you all, in a room that we found locked tightly from the inside."

Before taking a seat, Sherlock Holmes withdrew his briar and matches from a coat pocket, filled the bowl with his usual dark shag, and lit the tobacco. After inhaling deeply, he let loose a cloud of smoke. Only then was he ready to speak:

"We all sensed Bingham's connection to the military – the rifle, most significantly, but also his hair style and muscular physique. The model ships surrounding us, as well as the cuttings about disasters at sea, suggested the Royal Navy. Last night I rang my brother, who works for the Government, and asked him if he knew of any suspicious but unpublished naval activities – including underwater events. if you recall the submarine report – in the last three years."

"That would be just before Bingham moved here to Dartmoor," Henry observed.

Holmes nodded. "My brother said he would ring me back this morning."

"And did he?" Henry asked.

"He did. And he furnished me with the following information that strikes a chord with the cuttings we viewed: Recall the story of *HMS A1*, the first British-designed submarine. In March of 1904, she was involved in a practice attack on another ship near the Isle of Wight. In a colossal accident, a third vessel, a steamship carrying the Royal Mail from Southampton to Hamburg, struck the starboard side of the submarine's conning tower – a palpable hit, for the encounter was fatal to the submarine. She went down so quickly that, as we know, the entire crew was lost – all eleven of them, according to the public announcement."

"Shocking," I said, "no matter how many times it is reported."

"Quite so," said Holmes. "Save that according to Mycroft, there were in reality *twelve* crew members aboard the vessel."

"*Twelve*," murmured Post. "Why, then, I imagine it is more than coincidental that *twelve* is the same number of photographs that are contained in Bingham's envelope."

"An excellent observation, Post," said Holmes, "save that the victim's name isn't *Bingham*. It's *Harris*. Rupert Harris. What is more, as a highly confidential matter, one *Rupert* Harris was listed as a member of the crew of the *A1*."

"But all were lost," Post pointed out.

"Not all," said Holmes. "Before the crippled submarine went down, someone was seen swimming away from the wreck. Yet this survivor never came forward to identify himself, and the Admiralty, to avoid distracting from the tragedy of the affair, simply set the number of drowned seamen at eleven. If my supposition is correct, however, the body in the library was that of the *twelfth* man, Rupert Harris."

"But *why* was he killed *now*, Holmes?" I asked. "Are you suggesting that his murder is somehow related to the tragedy of the *A1*?"

"The tragedy of the *A1*, Watson, as you so aptly call it, is at the centre of this entire business. For among the possessions of the lost seamen, Mycroft identified a signed document containing the names of all twelve members of the crew. Each one pledged his devotion to his shipmates, all vowing on their lives to go down together if it ever came to that. The twelve men, whose portraits we have already seen, signed the oath and faced their destiny in unison."

"Except that one didn't," said Post. "Not that I blame him if he had the chance to save himself."

"Yes, yes," said Inspector Henry impatiently. "But Bingham or Harris – What does all this have to do with the man's murder?"

Holmes rose and extended his arm in the direction of the library. "Let us return to where Harris's body was found. Then all shall be made clear."

Pipe in hand, Sherlock Holmes led the three of us – Henry, Post, and myself – back to the spot where Harris's corpse had lain. We entered the darkened room and Holmes proceeded to open the bullet-riddled shutters, allowing, as it were, greater light on the subject. The library wasn't a very large room, and we four crowded together. Holmes's pipe had gone out, and he cradled the bowl in his hand, using the stem as an abbreviated pointer.

"Rupert Harris did his best to forget the recent past. Hence, his name-change. In particular, he was trying to eradicate from his mind the solemn agreement into which he had entered with his shipmates. For a period, he was successful. Those were the days when people saw him on horseback out on the moor. But his guilt was overpowering, and he shut himself away. The greater the solitude, the more time he had to dwell on his sense of betrayal. So great was his shame that I should imagine he feared the dead crew of the submarine were coming to claim him."

"Preposterous!" exclaimed the policeman.

"On the contrary," Melville Post said, "quite the intriguing tale. It makes sense of that mass of clippings about justice. The man's conscience was at work."

Holmes pointed the pipe stem at the American. "Quite so, Post," said he. "As the newspaper cuttings indicate, Rupert Harris was consumed with a fear of retribution – tortured by it, one might say. In this case, retribution for escaping the fate of his dead shipmates."

"A religious soul might call it *Providence*," Post observed.

"An alienist might term it remorse at surviving," I said.

"So many theories," said Post shaking his head. "Quite the basis for a story." As if to give himself time to ponder such a thought, he removed his *pince-nez* and polished the lenses with a handkerchief.

Inspector Henry cleared his throat. "Gentlemen," he said forcefully, "we aren't here to postulate philosophical interpretations, fictional plots, or psychological theories. Who killed the man? That is the question."

"That's right, Holmes," I agreed. "Whatever his state of mind, you still haven't told us who killed Rupert Harris."

Holmes now aimed his pipe stem at me. "Better to phrase the question, '*What* killed Rupert Harris?' That is the *real* question, Watson."

I believe we all looked puzzled.

"Rupert Harris," Holmes explained, "feared the wrath of his dead comrades. As time went on, his dread increased, and he took measures to keep them away. The removal of trees allowed him greater opportunity to see anyone approaching the house. The taller fences, the latched windows, the closed shutters, the locked door – all manifestations of his attempts to keep away the avenging spirits."

370

"Avenging spirits," I repeated incredulously. "You can't be serious, Holmes. Avenging spirits from the Other Side – That's more in Conan Doyle's bailiwick."

"The Greeks called them the *Eumenides*," Post offered. "The *Furies* in English."

"Spirits! Furies!" Henry stormed. "Utter nonsense! Is there no end to this philosophical humbug? For me, the only question is how a murder could have taken place in a locked room."

"Alas, Inspector," said Sherlock Holmes with a grim smile, "I am afraid that, like many a locked-room mystery before this one, when the truth is discovered, it detracts from the romantic delusions the scene may have originally conjured."

With a look of concern, Melville Post asked, "Just what is that supposed to mean, Mr. Holmes?"

"Recall the wound to Harris's head," replied my friend.

"A severe blow to the top of his skull," Henry reminded everyone. "Obviously struck by a tall assailant."

"Or rather," Holmes countered, "by a falling heavy object. I suggest to you, gentlemen, that in reality, the recoil of Harris's powerful rifle, the Lee-Enfield – said by those who know to provide quite the kick – propelled the man forcefully backward. So often did he fire at whatever he thought he saw at the windows that he knocked over the various pieces of furniture we see about us, including, most significantly, that wooden bookcase lying on the floor.

"For amidst the chaos, the heavy coffer, which Harris had placed at the very top of the bookcase to prevent anyone from finding his secrets, plunged from the uppermost shelf, struck Harris on the top of his skull, and killed him. By chance, it came to rest upright, looking as innocent as any murderer could wish."

Henry shook his head. "And how do you know, Mr. Holmes," asked the sceptical policeman, "that the box was positioned in just such a manner on the shelf as to cause so much damage?"

"Because, Inspector, while you were examining the body and the books on the floor, I was examining the dust on the bookcase – or rather the lack thereof in a rectangular form on the top shelf. The dust-free space has the same dimensions as the box.

"Oh, it is quite clear: The box fell, the box hit Harris, the box killed him. No window or door need have been opened to allow for such a circumstance. Furthermore, as you will discover for yourself when you examine the lower edges of the box, there are bits of hair and scalp imbedded at the bottom of the left-front corner where the pointed edge crashed into Harris's head."

371

"Quite the weapon," said Henry.

"Pushed by some unseeable hand," marvelled Post.

Holmes would have none of such speculation, however. "Not unseeable! The man fired his rifle, fell backward, and dislodged the object that killed him. An accident, yes, but all the logical result of his own actions, all quite consistent with the laws of physics."

"Still," added Post, "caused by some nameless force."

"If you believe that sort of thing," I said.

"Well," observed Inspector Henry, "I believe it enough to release Leo Thrush."

With the close of the case, Holmes returned to the South Downs and his bees. I returned to London. Melville Davisson Post re-joined his wife, Bloom, and together they continued their European travels for another two months before returning to their home in West Virginia. For his part, Inspector Henry remained in Tavistock to complete the report of Harris's death.

One could not but agree that the investigation into the death of Rupert Harris had produced a fascinating story. Yet according to Mycroft, the Admiralty demanded that the details of the submarine disaster remain secret. As a result, however much the death of Harris continued to haunt him, Melville Davisson Post was forced to re-focus his literary energy on American themes – in this case, the creation of a new character: An austere Virginian, the Bible-carrying defender of justice whom Post called *Uncle Abner*. [4]

When Mycroft finally did lift the need for secrecy a few years later, I made public my own account of the tragedy, which the reader now holds before him. It took Post a full five years to produce his own version of the case, and when it appeared, its details differed significantly from the facts.

In the first place, Post inflated the relevance of the victim. Not only did he enhance Harris's social standing, but he also made him the commander of the submarine. In addition, he moved the Dartmoor house to America, omitted any reference to the Wessex Cup, and identified a different submarine as the vessel that went down with her crew.

Post also failed to mention key figures in the investigation. Perhaps, given the controversies raised by the amorality of his fictional Randolph Mason, it was with the hope of shielding actual figures like Holmes and myself – not to mention Conan Doyle – that prompted the American to eliminate us entirely from his narrative.

Yet even with all the changes he made, Post couldn't diminish his fascination with the ambiguous causality behind Harris's death. It was no doubt this keen interest that prompted him to intersperse his account of Harris's demise with similar stories of fate provided by three additional narrators. The philosophical discussions of a priest, a doctor, and a judge entertain a variety of possible catalysts for an outcome like Harris's – Providence, conscience, and chance, to name but a few. In the end, of course, Post admitted his own inability to identify such a cause when he chose to title his own version of the locked-room mystery, "The Nameless Thing".

Despite his literary departures from reality, however, Melville Davisson Post remained impressed with the actual Yarder he had encountered in Dartmoor, for in some of Post's later stories, tales he actually set in these islands, he no doubt had in mind the very real police detective he had met in Tavistock. In those new accounts, what attentive reader cannot hear the echo between the names of Inspector Marcus Henry and the Scotland Yard Chief of the C.I.D. whom Post called Sir Henry Marquis?

In the end, of course, one is tempted to conclude that the American author ultimately settled on *Marcus Henry* as the namesake for his so-called "Sleuth of St. James's Square" because the name Sherlock Holmes was already spoken for. Needless to say, C. Auguste Dupin, the appellation of Poe's master detective, wouldn't quite fit in at Scotland Yard.

NOTES

1. Thanks to the influence of Mrs. Whitelaw Reid, the wife of the American ambassador, Post's wife, Ann Bloomfield Gamble Schoolfield (whom he called "Bloom"), was presented to King Edward VII on June 6, 1907. According to Charles A. Norton's *Melville Davisson Post: Man of Many Mysteries*, during this period the Posts leased "*a baronial-style house where they could entertain their many English friends and acquaintances in a very British manner.*"
2. In *Melville Davisson Post: Man of Many Mysteries*, Charles A. Norton reports one such "*germ*" that sparked Post's interest: A news story concerning a suicide victim who had hoped to make his death seem like murder so his family could garner the insurance money. While standing on a bridge, the man employed a gun, a cord, and a stone in such a manner that, once the trigger was pulled, the gun would disappear into the water and eliminate the charge of suicide. Post appreciated a good story when he heard one, but on reading "The Problem of Thor Bridge" that deals with just such a set-up, he is said to have commented about Watson's literary agent: "*I knew then that Doyle had beaten me to it.*"
3. See "The Adventure of the Illustrious Client".
4. In *Melville Davisson Post: Man of Many Mysteries*, Norton credits the Uncle Abner stories begun in 1911 as helping establish Post "*as one of the highest-paid authors of magazine material of this period.*" Even more effusive was John Cuthbert in the Fall 2009 newsletter of the University of West Virginia. Dubbing Post "*the Arthur Conan Doyle of America,*" he identified the author as "*one of the most widely read writers in the nation.*"

The Beast of Birling Gap
by Paul Hiscock

"It sounds like we have company," said Holmes.

I looked up in surprise, as I hadn't noticed anyone knocking. All I could hear was the howling of the wind as it blew across the South Downs, and the rain pounding on the roof of Holmes's cottage. I was grateful to be inside, sat in front of a roaring fire with a warming glass of brandy and a pipe full of good tobacco.

There was another knock at the door, and this time I heard it too. We both stood up to see who was calling at that late hour.

When Holmes opened the door, there was a man standing there. In the dark and the rain, it was hard to make out any details, except that he was as tall as Holmes, but broader, and was holding a tall walking stick.

"I'm sorry to intrude," he said, speaking loudly to be heard over the storm. "Do you think I could come in?"

"Of course," Holmes said, and stood back to allow the stranger through, then closed the door behind him.

Now that he had stepped into the light, I could see that the visitor was wearing a flat brown cap and long waxed coat. Water dripped off him, forming a large puddle on the floor.

"Please make yourself comfortable," said Holmes, pointing to the hat-stand in the corner. "You can hang your coat there."

"Thank you," said the stranger. "The rain is coming down hard. I'm soaked through."

He removed his hat, revealing dark-brown curly hair which matched his bushy eyebrows and thick moustache.

"What brings you to my cottage on a night like this?" asked Holmes.

"It's embarrassing. I'm afraid I got lost on the Downs in the dark and rain. I must have been walking in circles for hours. The light in your window is the first sign of civilisation I've seen all night. I hoped you might be able to offer me shelter for a bit, and point me in the right direction."

"Certainly," said Holmes. "We're always happy to assist a man in need. Come through to the parlour. You can warm yourself by the fire."

"Thank you. You're very kind."

We returned to the parlour and I poured our unexpected guest a drink, before sitting back down in my chair by the fire.

"Now that you are comfortable, I think some introductions are in order. I am Sherlock Holmes, and this is my friend, Dr. Watson, who is staying with me for a day or two."

"I'm sorry to interrupt your time together," said the stranger. "My name is Harold Stevens."

"It's a pleasure to make your acquaintance," I said. "I am glad you found your way here to take shelter, but whatever were you doing out in such foul weather in the first place?"

"Mr. Stevens is visiting from Belgium," said Holmes. "He is here on a walking holiday."

Stevens looked at him in surprise. "You are correct on both counts. However did you know?"

"It's quite simple. Although you speak very good English, you cannot conceal every trace of your accent. Your native language is obviously French. Your surname is common in England, but not France, and is Germanic in origin. This, and the way you pronounce the letter '*R*' with a more guttural sound, tell me you are actually Belgian. As to the purpose of your visit, it's obvious from your sturdy boots and hiker's walking stick."

"Indeed," Stevens said, clearly impressed, as people always were, by Holmes's deductive skills. "I came here planning to explore the coast and the South Downs. My plan for today was to head up to Beachy Head. However, before I set off, I stopped at the Tiger Inn for a spot of lunch."

"A good choice," I said. "We know it well."

"Now that I think of it, Mr. Holmes, I think I might have seen you there."

"You might have done. I dropped in earlier to have a word with the landlord."

"I thought I recognised your face. Well, anyway, I enjoyed my lunch immensely, but I spent longer over it than I had planned. It was already mid-afternoon when I left. Nevertheless, I felt confident that I could still make it to Beachy Head and back before supper. The walk up there was most pleasant, but the trouble started when I turned back. The easterly wind, which had been at my back on the way there, was now driving towards me, and the rain was starting. At first it was a light drizzle, but quickly grew harder and harder until I could barely see the path in front of me."

"I've walked that route on many occasions," said Holmes. "It's a beautiful stretch of countryside. You were unlucky that the weather turned, but also should be grateful that you weren't hurt or killed. The ground near the cliff edge is treacherous, and in some places can give way under the slightest weight."

"I worried about that, and I'm very glad to be safe inside at last."

"Well, you're very welcome to stay here as long as you need."

"Thank you. I appreciate your hospitality. It isn't just that I am relieved to be out of the rain, or away from the cliffs. Just before I arrived here, I thought I heard The Beast."

"A beast?" I asked.

"Yes, a creature that has been stalking the area at night. The locals are calling it 'The Beast of Birling Gap'."

I laughed. "Let me guess. It's a huge creature, luminous, ghastly, and spectral. Oh, and people have found the footprints of a gigantic hound. I am sorry, Mr. Stevens, but you aren't the first to try that prank. Ever since *The Hound of the Baskervilles* was published, people have been enjoying the same joke. I was at dinner with friends the other night, and after reciting that ominous description, they produced a small white poodle, to the great amusement of the whole company."

"This isn't a joke, Dr. Watson. No one has described it as luminous, and I haven't seen any gigantic footprints. However, I can vouch for the fact that sound of its roar can freeze a man's blood in his veins."

While a joke among friends was one thing, I was beginning to think that this stranger was taking it too far. I looked across at Holmes to gauge his reaction, and was surprised to see that, rather than being amused or annoyed, his expression was grave.

"Mr. Stevens is telling the truth, Watson. I was about to tell you about it when he arrived. For the past week, something dangerous has been terrorising the area around East Dean. They're afraid to venture outside at night."

"I heard about it when I first arrived here," said Stevens. "I fell in with a couple of fellow hikers, and they asked if I had heard strange noises in the night. I told them that I had heard nothing, and dismissed it from my mind. However, that evening, as I lay in my bed at the boarding house where I am staying, I heard it too. Not the howling of a dog, but the dreadful roar of some far more fearsome beast."

"Did you hear it," I asked, "or did you just *think* that you did? The power of suggestion can be strong, especially when one is tired."

"In the morning light, I wondered if it had just been a dream. However, when I went downstairs for breakfast, I discovered that my fellow guests had heard it too."

"I've also heard it," said Holmes. "It was an unnatural sound, quite unlike that made by any creature I've ever encountered."

"Very well," I said. "I can see why some kind of animal making noises in the night might be unnerving, but why are people scared to go out in the dark? It sounds like a case of mass hysteria."

"Everyone was slightly concerned, but not really afraid until yesterday," said Stevens. "I set off that morning, planning to walk around the coast up to Beachy Head. However, as I approached Birling Gap, I was stopped by a policeman.

"'You'll have to turn back,' he told me. "We are investigating a death.'

"At first I thought that someone had fallen, or jumped from the cliff. But then he told me that a local girl had been attacked by a wild animal. He warned me to stay alert and sent me back the way I had come."

"A dead girl," I said. "That puts a different complexion on things. I am beginning to understand why people are afraid."

"Indeed," said Stevens. "Anyway, since my plans for the day had been thwarted, I decided to adjourn to the inn. I bought myself a pint, then settled myself at a table in the corner. From snatches of overheard conversation, I quickly learned that the dead girl's name was Katie Summers, and that she had been a teacher at the local school. More disturbingly, people were saying that she hadn't just died, but been badly mauled. A creature had raked across her face with its claws, and torn apart her body, leaving her to bleed to death on the ground!"

"A gory spectacle," I said, "if it's true. However, village gossips are liable to exaggerate – especially when they have had a pint or two to drink."

"Sadly, in this instance, their accounts were accurate," said Holmes. "When the body was discovered, Constable Anderson immediately sent for me. I have rarely witnessed a bloodier scene. Even Anderson avoided looking at her as much as possible, and someone had been sick nearby. It had clearly been a vicious and frenzied attack. It was hard to deduce much more than that from the extensive wounds across her torso, but there was less damage to her face – just three long gashes made by a set of evenly-spaced razor-sharp claws."

"What else did you learn?" I asked.

"She had clearly run away from The Beast. Her shoes had fallen off during her desperate flight. One lay on the ground a short distance from her body, while the other was further away, near the cliff edge. Her body had been discovered not long after dawn by a man out walking his dog. He was sitting some distance away, waiting for the police to let him leave. There were traces of vomit on his clothes, and he was clearly traumatised by what he'd seen. I briefly questioned him, but it was clear that he wasn't responsible for the attack and knew nothing more than I could see for myself."

"What did you do next?" I asked.

"While Anderson called in additional men to scour the South Downs for The Beast, I took upon myself the sad task of visiting the dead woman's mother.

"While Miss Summers had lived in a small cottage owned by the school where she worked in East Dean, her mother lives to the north in Friston. When I arrived there and knocked on the door, I heard someone call from inside for me to come in.

"I entered the house and discovered a woman sitting there. Although I judged that she was only in her forties, she seemed frail, and there was a stick propped up next to her chair.

"'Please forgive me for not standing,' she said. 'I had a nasty fall a few weeks ago and damaged my hip. Ever since, I've had difficulty getting about.'

"'I am sorry to intrude,' I said. 'However, I'm afraid that I'm here with bad news. A body was found near Birling Gap this morning, and we believe it is that of your daughter, Katherine.'

"Mrs. Summers broke down in tears, and I went over to comfort her. I chose not to describe the condition of her daughter's body. There are some things a mother doesn't need to hear.

"After the initial shock had passed, I offered to make us both a cup of tea. I then sat down opposite her and asked about her daughter's movements on the previous day.

"'Kind girl that she is, she's been coming over in the evenings to help me after school,' said Mrs. Summers. 'We had dinner together, then stayed up later than we should, playing gin rummy. Finally, she helped me get into bed and set off for home. I told her to stay the night, because it was so late, but she insisted that it wasn't that far.'

"'Can you think of any reason why she might have been near the cliff edge?' I asked.

"'No. She would have had to walk past the school to get there. Besides, she would never go near the Gap in the dark. She knows how dangerous it is there, especially with the recent rock slides.'

"I stayed a little longer to comfort the bereaved woman. She told me all about her daughter's childhood and how she had enjoyed teaching at the school. However, she said nothing that could help me to explain the poor girl's death.

"After I had left her, I made my way back to East Dean, calling at the houses nearest to where Miss Summers had lived. From the accounts that people shared with me, I established that The Beast starts roaring at about ten in the evening, and continues until around three in the morning. The night that Miss Summers was attacked, they had briefly wondered if the creature had moved on, since there was no sound of it at the usual time.

However, around half-an-hour later it started up again, as loud as before. Everyone in the area seemed to have heard The Beast, but I couldn't find anybody who had caught even a glimpse of it."

"Did no one go out to investigate?" I asked.

"Some looked out of their windows, but the nights have been stormy this past week. I'm not surprised that they weren't inclined to venture out in the such conditions in search of a fearsome-sounding animal. I might have investigated myself, but I'd been away and didn't return until the day of the attack. I heard the noises for the first time that night, but paid them little heed. I regretted that when I saw the bloody body of Miss Summers the next morning. If I had ventured out, perhaps I might have saved her life."

"Of perhaps you could have been killed yourself," I said. "There is no point in speculation and self-recrimination now."

"Quite right, Watson. At this point, our priority is to prevent any further deaths."

"Is Miss Summers the creature's only victim?" I asked.

"Thankfully, yes."

"I wondered if the police searching in the area might scare it away," said Stevens. "Yet it still seems to be out there."

"So you said, but I haven't heard it yet tonight," said Holmes. "Have you, Watson?"

"No, although with the wind howling as it is, I could easily have missed something."

At that very moment, as if prompted by our conversation, I heard a terrible sound in the distance. Stevens and Holmes had been correct. This wasn't a howl, like that of the hound we had encountered on Dartmoor. It sounded more like someone had tipped a bucket of gravel into an automobile's engine.

Holmes looked at the clock on the mantelpiece. "Quarter-past-eleven," he said. "Later than before, as I suspected it would be."

"How did you work that out?" I asked.

"The Beast only comes out at low tide, once the waves at the foot of the cliffs have receded, and that time has been getting later every night."

"That makes no sense," I said. "It clearly isn't a sea creature, as it attacked Miss Summers on the land."

Stevens stood up and walked over to the drinks cabinet. "You don't mind if I help myself to another?" he asked as he poured himself a large measure. He took a sip and then said, "I've heard stories about creatures affected by the phases of the moon, in the same manner as the tides. Perhaps it is one of these that is responsible."

"Do you mean a werewolf?" Holmes asked. "Such creatures are the stuff of myth and legend. I have no interest in such outlandish suggestions."

"What do you think it is then?" Stevens asked, sounding irritated by Holmes's sharp rejection of his idea. "A lion or a bear escaped from a zoo, or a travelling circus? Where has it been hiding during the day, and why has no one reported it missing? Surely there is something supernatural about this creature?"

"You're wrong," said Holmes. "It isn't a creature, supernatural or otherwise. It's a *machine*, operated by ordinary men, digging into the rocks at the bottom of the cliff. All the rumours about a beast are a smokescreen intended to conceal their activities. This afternoon, I crept down to the beach, just before the tide came in, and saw where they've been excavating."

"And Miss Summers?" I asked. "What killed her?"

"Not *what*, but *who*? She wasn't attacked by an animal. She was brutally murdered by a man."

While I was concentrating on Holmes's explanation, I failed to notice Stevens moving to stand beside his chair until it was too late. Stevens reached into his pocket and pulled out a metal tool. It appeared to be a gardener's hand fork, with three sharp metal tines. It glinted wickedly in the firelight, and I realised that it must be the weapon used to inflict the vicious wounds that had killed poor Miss Summers.

I started to shout out a warning, but before I could say anything, Stevens placed the fork by Holmes's neck, its deadly tines pressing into, but not quite piercing, his skin.

"I advise you not to move," Stevens said. "And you should stay where you are too, Dr. Watson. The points on this tool are very sharp, and I wouldn't want it to slip and cut open Mr. Holmes's throat – at least not yet."

Holmes seemed calm, despite the danger he was in. "I wondered when you were going to show your true colours," he said. "I realised as soon as you removed your overcoat that you were the murderer I was hunting."

Stevens looked surprised. "How did you know?" he asked.

"You have spent the last few nights on the beach excavating a chalk cliff face. Drilling into those rocks will have thrown up a lot of white dust, a fine layer of which can be seen coating your clothes. In addition, your weapon is too sharp. It cut through your pocket and I spotted the tip poking out."

"What could you be looking for on the beach that was worth the life of that poor young woman?" I asked. "And why did you need such powerful digging equipment?"

"I suppose it doesn't matter if I tell you now. There's a small cave at the bottom of the cliff at Birling Gap. We hid some valuable goods there, while we made arrangements to sell them. However, before we could get back, part of the cliff collapsed and blocked the entrance. Shovels and pickaxes weren't enough to shift the debris, so we brought in a powerful drill. However, as soon as we started using it, we realised that the noise would be heard from miles around. So, the next morning, while my associates hid in an abandoned cottage further up the coast, I disguised myself as a hiker and started to spread rumours about a terrifying beast roaming the South Downs at night. It seemed to be effective, and the story quickly took on a life of its own. People kept adding their own embellishments. I hardly had to say a word."

"Let us see," said Holmes. "There were three major robberies in the week leading up to the first appearance of The Beast at Birling Gap. The first was a gold heist in York, but I think it unlikely that the criminals responsible for that would have chosen to bring their haul, all the way down here. The second was a robbery at Sandown Park, where the thieves made away with the day's takings after a major race. That was much closer to here. However, having heard your accent, I am now sure that you were actually responsible for the theft of four panels from the Van Eyck altarpiece at St. Bavo's Cathedral in Ghent. It was an audacious and violent robbery which left three men badly injured and created an uproar in Belgium. Presumably you smuggled the panels into England by boat, planning to sell them here, where people were less likely to be looking for it."

Stevens looked shocked. "I don't know how you figured that out, but clearly I was right to come here to silence you. My friends and I need time to finish our work, and we cannot afford to have anyone poking around until we do."

"That's why you killed Miss Summers," I said.

"Yes. The foolish girl heard the noise of our equipment, and rather than minding her own business, she decided to investigate. She came right up to the cliff edge and saw what we were doing below. I had no choice but to chase her down and kill her."

"But you always expected that you might have to kill in order to protect your secret. Otherwise, you wouldn't have been carrying a weapon intended to imitate a creature's claw marks."

"It's true. Her death served a dual purpose. It silenced her and helped to convince people that there really was a dangerous animal. Once the people round here learn that The Beast has killed you too, no one will dare leave their homes at night until we are long gone."

"Why didn't you kill us as soon as you arrived here this evening?" asked Holmes.

"I was curious to find out how much you had worked out. However, it is clear that you know too much, and I certainly cannot let you speak to the police in the morning. It is unfortunate that you chose to visit this evening, Dr. Watson, as it means you will have to share your friend's fate."

"It isn't a coincidence that Watson is here tonight," said Holmes.

"What do you mean?" asked Stevens, looking worried for the first time.

"I invited him to come down from London specifically to join my investigation, and witness the arrest of a murderous gang of criminals."

"The police won't be arresting us. You didn't have a chance to tell them what you had found, and now you never will."

"Why do you think that?" I asked.

"Remember, Mr. Holmes: I was in the Tiger Inn at lunchtime. I heard the landlord complaining about how The Beast had been bad for business, because his customers were afraid of staying after sunset. You told him not to worry, because it wouldn't be a problem much longer. You had solved the mystery and were planning to speak to the police."

"So, you also heard me explain how Constable Anderson had been summoned to Eastbourne to report on his progress with the case," said Holmes.

"Yes, I heard everything. You didn't trust that whoever you left in charge would listen to you. Instead, you planned to wait until the morning when Constable Anderson returned. It was foolish of you to speak about your plans so publicly."

"On the contrary, everything worked out exactly as I planned," said Holmes. "If we wanted to be sure to arrest your whole gang, we needed to catch you digging for your treasure. I realised that the police presence might scare you away, but refused to let you get away with Miss Summers' murder. Therefore, I decided to offer a small window during which you would be tempted to try to complete your work. I anticipated that there would be someone at the inn listening out for gossip about the investigation and that word would get back to you. One indiscreet conversation was all it took to lure you into my trap."

"That was very clever, Mr. Holmes, but not clever enough."

"I admit that I hadn't anticipated you coming here to kill me. I have learned a lot from our conversation, but now you need to turn yourself in. Your 'claws' are no match for Watson's revolver."

Taking my cue, I drew the gun from my pocket. Holmes has suggested that I should bring it with me, knowing that we would be facing a gang of violent criminals that night.

The appearance of my weapon surprised Stevens, and for just a moment, he let his weapon stray slightly from its place on Holmes's throat. This small lapse was all that Holmes needed. He grabbed Stevens's arm and twisted it painfully, causing the killer to drop the deadly tool. It fell to the floor with a clatter.

Stevens freed himself from Holmes's grip and quickly moved out of reach. However, I kept my revolver trained on him.

"It's over," Holmes said. "You might as well surrender. The police have been hiding near Birling Gap all evening, waiting for your friends to start up their drill. Even as we speak, Constable Anderson and his colleagues will be preparing to move in and arrest them. You cannot get there in time to help them"

"Perhaps," said Stevens, "but I can still try."

With a cry intended to startle us, he threw the sharpened fork towards my head. I ducked out of the way, but in the process took my eyes off him for a moment. That was all the opportunity he needed. He dashed through the door, then ran from the cottage, out into the dark.

"Was what you said true?" I asked Holmes. "Are the police waiting to arrest his accomplices at Birling Gap?"

"Yes, but they don't know about Stevens. He could disappear into the night if we don't pursue him ourselves. Come, Watson! There isn't a moment to lose!"

He ran into the hall grabbing his cape and hat as he passed the stand. I picked up my own coat as quickly as I could and, without waiting to put it on, followed Holmes out into the night.

If anything, the weather had deteriorated since Stevens's arrival at the cottage. The wind drove the rain towards us, and I was already soaked by the time I finished fastening my coat.

"I cannot see him!" I shouted to Holmes.

"We know he's trying to warn his friends," replied Holmes. "He must have gone this way. Follow me."

I wasn't sure how Holmes knew where he was going, but I was happy to follow him, and we set off, as fast as we could, down the narrow road towards Birling Gap.

As we neared our destination, I saw the flash of lights up ahead and heard the sound of a police whistle on the wind.

"We're just in time," said Holmes. "Anderson is making the arrest."

"Where is Stevens?" I asked. "Do you think he made it down to the beach?"

"No, look. There he is, hiding on this side of the wall. The police at the cliff edge haven't spotted him."

We ran towards the murderous leader of the gang, but at the last moment he spotted us approaching. He stood up and vaulted over the wall, then started to run towards the cliff edge.

"Where does he think he's going?" I asked. "There are police officers everywhere. Surely he cannot still think that can get away?"

"He is panicking, yet he might still succeed. The police weren't expecting anyone to come from this direction."

Sure enough, for a moment it looked like Stevens had caught the officers unawares. There were lots of shouts of, "*Stop!*" and "*Hold there!*" – yet he managed to run past them all.

There was just one officer left between Stevens and freedom. He was a burly man and he knelt down as Stevens approached, as though he was playing in a rugby match.

Stevens quickly adjusted his course, running to the left and passing just inches away from the officer's outstretched arms. However, in doing so, he strayed perilously close to the edge. I watched in horror as the ground gave way underneath him and another part of the cliff was reclaimed by the sea. The officer who had blocked his way nervously approached the new edge and looked down at the beach below.

"He's gone," the officer said. "There is no way he survived that fall."

"Who was that man?" asked Anderson, who had come up behind us, "and what was he doing here?"

"That was Mr. Stevens," said Holmes. "He was the leader of the gang, and the one who murdered Miss Summers."

"In that case, I for one will not be mourning his passing. Although I suppose that I'd better send some men to fetch his body and check that he didn't, by some miracle, survive that fall."

"What of his accomplices?" I asked.

"They tried to escape by sea, but didn't get very far. Their boat has run aground on the rocks, and if you look hard, you can just about see them out there."

I looked where he pointed and thought I could just about make out two men waving for help. More than once, the waves crashing against the rocks knocked them from their feet.

"They are going to get swept away by the storm," I said.

"They might at that, and it would be some sort of justice if they did, but they may yet survive. The Coast Guard are about to mount a rescue attempt. They should be firing the rocket at any moment now."

There was a flash of light from the small hut on the cliff edge and the sound of a loud bang. An object, much like a firework, came shooting out of the building, leaving a blazing trail in its wake as it headed out to sea.

"There it goes," said Anderson.

"Whatever are they doing?" I asked.

"That building over there is the Rocket House," said Anderson. "It's there to help stranded sailors. A line is attached to the rocket they just fired. The Coast Guard will use it to pull those men ashore using a life buoy. Once they've been dragged back to the beach, I'll lock them up. They'll get to dry out in a nice warm cell, which is more than they deserve."

Holmes and I watched for a while as the rescue proceeded exactly as Anderson had described. However, it was clear that there was nothing else for us to do there that night, and so before long we headed back to Holmes's cottage to dry out and get some sleep.

The next morning, we returned to Birling Gap. The rain had stopped and the sun had come out. Nevertheless, we were still cautious as we made our way down the steep and slippery path to the beach. Neither of us had any desire to meet the same fate as Stevens.

At the bottom, we found a group of men hard at work, under the supervision of Constable Anderson. He greeted us as we approached.

"Gentlemen, you are just in time. I think we are going to break through the last of the rocks quite soon."

"You've made swift work of it," I said.

"Those thieves had almost broken through," he said, "and it is far easier for us, working in the daylight. What do you think we'll find in there?"

Holmes started to explain about the robbery in Ghent, but we were interrupted by a cry from over by the drill. Looking around saw that it had started a small rock slide. For a moment, I was afraid that the whole cliff was about to fall down on our heads, but then the dust settled and we saw that it had actually made it through the last of the rocks to reveal the entrance to the cave.

Anderson handed each of us a torch and we headed inside. The four stolen panels had been wrapped separately in oil skins to protect them from the water, and were stacked at the back of the cave, just waiting to be collected. They were far larger than I had imagined, and I wished that I could open them up to see what all the fuss was about.

"How did they hope to get these to the top of the cliff?" I asked.

"I don't think they did," replied Anderson. "I suspect that they planned to load them into their boat and bring them ashore elsewhere. Now if you will excuse me, I need to make arrangements to do the same, before the tide comes in. I imagine that the authorities in Belgium are eager to get these paintings back."

We let Anderson get on with his work and headed back up the path to the top of the cliff. I stood for a moment, looking out to sea. Now that the drilling had stopped, all I could hear was the sound of seagulls flying overhead and the waves lapping at the shore below. The Beast of Birling Gap was silent at last.

The Worker
by Marcia Wilson

Spring 1912

Some accident had befallen the honeybee, and it lay dying with a crumpled wing in the clover lawn. With the utmost delicacy of touch, Sherlock Holmes lifted the drone up, and with a thoughtful expression, pressed it to his shoulder, exactly where his violin rested. The little forager took the indignity as a challenge, as bees do, and promptly impressed its venom into its captor's skin.

"I suspect," the detective said with a strange, half-quirk of amusement to his lips, "that you would never think to see me injecting one more drug into my bloodstream, Watson."

"And I would suspect," I countered, "that you would be aware that I am well-versed in the effects of bee-venom on aging joints."

Holmes waited until the poison was completely within his veins, his expression never changing from its silent, almost compassionate features. When the attack was finished and the bee quite dead, he picked it up again with the same delicacy, and dropped it with a final glance into the shimmering net of a spider's web. His fingers, although occasionally stymied by the stiffness that comes with the chill sea-fog, are as sensitive and refined as ever. With only a touch, he had the spider fooled into thinking the bounty in its trap was alive, and he accomplished this without tearing a single line of silk. His smile was one of amused pride to fool a predator into believing in his little deceit.

"A spider is less watchful for my bees if it carries a well-stocked larder," he observed. "And the bee fulfils one last purpose in the defence of her hive."

I have long known my friend's complex thought-processes were adorned with his own peculiar philosophy – a mental web as intricate as any spider's and tainted with his special sort of sympathy. That he would eschew the comfort of his own aching body until a dying bee could happen under that sharp grey gaze was no surprise to me, nor was I astonished that he would finish its use as a spider's meal to prevent a future hunt on his precious colony.

It was a warm day amongst the Downs, and I well recalled my first visit of the season as a continuous salt breeze blew off the Channel, stirring the grasslands to life in stages. Holmes's dormant vegetable-plot had been carpeted with purple dead nettle, though he insisted on the more poetic name of "Red Archangel". The dusty-rose flowers created an early feast for Holmes's hives, and he was content to celebrate the end of the cold winter in a lawn chair under the full exposure of the sun, watching the colonies gorge on nectar from the strange flowers that smelt of bitter maroon earth.

I think of him now, wondering what business compelled him to leave his beloved home, and I remember that at least late in his years, he was finally able to set aside his great energies and his greater mind, and merely content himself within the moment of being.

After some long moments had passed, and slowly, Holmes began working the muscles in his rejuvenated shoulder, his concentration replaced by a smile of satisfaction as mobility was restored. "As I recall, my good fellow, I once asked if you wished one of my injections."

"And I naturally refused," was my response. "But in the matter of bees, I am much less against the treatment." So saying, I rose up, pipe in hand, and finally walked to the clump of native flowers he had painstakingly cultivated for the sake of the small yellow butterflies that shared their living-quarters with the bees. Here were many spider webs, and in the early hours the sea-dew collected an artificial shine, like leaded crystal beads. "I plea the folk-remedy of my upbringing, Holmes. If one wants to ease the rheumatism quickly, there's nothing as swift as a sauna, with a flagellation of stinging nettles among the limbs."

Of course, he knew I was teasing him, for his eyes narrowed in a laugh in that strong summer sunlight. The spring flowers had bowed to purple lavender among the fescue, planted in thick rows along his little road of crushed seashell and coral. It had made visits inadvisable until the bloom had passed for the profusion of the hungry bees. It was now that time of year when the world might be seen as white: Never were the yarrows and Queen Anne's Lace as plentiful as they were this year, and they grew in confusions against minor hedges of brilliantly white and yellow Ox-eye daisies and sweet chamomile. In the heat of the sun, the chamomile released its oils, creating a tropical scent of pineapples, and the birds found the atmosphere as agreeable as I.

"You are concerned," Holmes said to me. I thought to myself that his voice had changed over time, growing deeper, as if from lack of use. I knew he had his neighbors. Some he was even on intimate terms with. But this was not London, where one couldn't pass a day without having to speak.

Holmes planted many succulent foods for his bees – his own enjoyment of his labours came after his hives'. There was one happy accident in a slender cabbage rose, emerging one day without warning and blooming ever since. I paused to examine the pattern of the waxy petals.

"I should never have wrung that promise out of you," I answered. "I am sorry, Holmes."

His long hand – once white, now brown, lifted in a maneuver that he didn't have before he was forced to flee from Moran.

"I have heard from Mycroft," he said at last. "His alleged retirement was merely a freeing-up of his time and energies, as you suspected to me years ago. At the time, there was little point in confirming or denying it." Some long-ago memory sent a twist to his lips. "We both have our duties, both base and higher." A solitary bee slid past his gaze, and he smiled at it. "A Monarch, or a drone? That is truly the question."

"I do not completely understand," I confessed. "If you are leaving, I trust it is for the best. I only regret that publishing "The Second Stain" might cause the wrong person to remember you. I can only hope enough time has passed for *The Strand* to fade in the public memory."

Holmes paused and lifted his head for a moment to that nearly cloudless sky. I saw him smile at the distant cry of a peregrine falcon, high upon the winds. "Those were the end of my salad days," he said. "When I was green in judgment. How did you ever tolerate all my foibles?"

"How did you ever tolerate mine?" I tried to laugh, pretending it was a light matter, but our conversation had irrevocably gone down a dark road. Holmes wasn't of a maudlin turn of mind, even in his days when the drug had him firm.

"You choose not to understand." He spoke without the least rancor. "Very well, that is a fair enough response considering our history

"Holmes!" I cried. It was a protest without an argument. I didn't wish to pursue this line of thought, for sad experience taught me that while Holmes had stepped away from the Black Moods that tormented him in London, they were no more vanquished than the drug he had once been slave to. "I fail to see what this conversation has to do with my publishing 'The Second Stain'."

It was a desperate act of circumlocution, and as the moments ticked away, I thought I had failed. Holmes remained standing, his attention oriented upon his bees but he was also completely aware of how I stood by his volunteer rosebush, waiting for an answer as he waited for that answer to come.

"Good old Watson," he said at last, with great fondness in his voice, and the way he turned to regard me as if I was a particularly beloved part of his garden.

December 1912

Once the Diogenes Club had been polished and suave, populated by the most antisocial men in London. The club now had the air of advancing age and comfortable neglect when I handed my coat to the silent page. The lamps were low – so low that I wondered if dust had collected while the staff and patrons passed by unawares.

London was changing. It would always change. I wondered to myself what new face the next generation of misanthropes would don – for it went against reason to think they would blindly copy their forefathers' example.

Mycroft Holmes had changed little since our last acquaintance. He hadn't gained in weight, but the power he carried that added to his sense of corpulence had very much grown. If the late Moriarty was a spider sitting in his web, attuned to the least stirrings of his prey (to be fooled by the likes of Holmes and his deft touch), then Mycroft Holmes was a sharp-eyed falcon who observed the world from a height so extreme no one else could have the hope of sharing his vision.

It takes more than being merely above the world. One must possess the ability to *see*. Mycroft was as sharp as a hawk. Whatever faculties he possessed that made him separate from his brother, he also shared his love of his chosen comforts. This epiphany struck me as we adjourned to the club's meeting room, to see nothing about it had changed since I had first entered it.

Perhaps it is these very gifts that limit him, for as his brother has told me, Mycroft has his lines, and he lives upon them. A mind powerful enough to absorb the cause and effect of every country in the world cannot be omnipotent enough to vary the singularity of his humdrum life. He always struck me as a man who drew relished repetition, perhaps for the same reason why his brother found the same pleasure in playing the same arias for hours: They throve in complexity, but found peace in their patterns.

"You look well, Doctor," he said as he offered me a glass of brandy. Outside the window of the Club, the wind whistled with tiny sheets of freezing rain and sharp, small grains of soot from the factories that gave the city its life. "How are Mrs. Watson and the family?"

I knew it was a preliminary with him. He knew as surely as he knew everything about me. Yet I smiled with the pride of my answer. "All are well," I informed him. "I fear it looks as though I deserted them. They have gone to ground in the warmer clime of Kent."

"A minimal difference can be a great thing," he answered with a philosophy that reminded me of his brother. "You are wondering if there is any news of Sherlock."

391

"Yes," I agreed.

His thick lips pursed thoughtfully, and he didn't answer me directly. "This isn't like the first time he vanished off the map," his voice was modulated to expand under the least effort. "On occasion, one catches a glimpse of him in some scrap of news or an event that rings slightly out of true, as visible and yet elusive as Ahab's Whale."

I knew Holmes wouldn't contact me – whatever this mysterious business was, he refused to jeopardize a family man, and he had made that clear. Still, the months had passed and there had been no word. It was no effort to return to my old boroughs and re-acquaint myself with past friends this close to the holidays.

"Hence my need to deliver this in person," I placed the small box on the table. "You will, if given the chance, tell your brother that if he wants his own Christmas greeting, he can come and get it himself."

Mycroft grunted one of his strange, half-stifled laughs. No doubt he has already divined the cufflinks, which are plain and unadorned as he is. "So I shall," he answered. "I confess, it is good to see you again, Doctor. Feel free to visit me any time."

I was a tie to his brother, and despite their lack of overt affection, the two were close in ways the salt is close to the pepper. Sherlock Holmes is a difficult man to call friend, but like mining for opals, it is worth the effort. In his own way, Mycroft Holmes was telling me he knew and understood what I had done for his closest kin.

"The world is changing," he announced, as if to himself. "We have seen many changes in our lifespan, have we not?"

"I have no doubt there are many more to come," I answered.

His smile was strange to my sensibilities. Small and wondering, the same expression I had caught upon Holmes countless times – the look of a man who admires something he doesn't quite fathom.

"You accept change with aplomb," he observed.

"I fail to see what else I can do." I shrugged with my better shoulder, not knowing what he meant. When I was young, I had resisted change unless it had been at my direction – the arrogance of youth knows no limitations, after all! But my wounding had taught me I wasn't so much in control of my destiny as I was my own adaptation. With the loss of my loved ones, I had vowed to never lose my perspective on such a hard lesson.

"Let me ask it of you, then." Mycroft looked at me expectantly. "What if the unthinkable would occur – that say, England was conquered by an enemy? How would you accept that?"

"I would not," I answered firmly. "Nor would many people I know. We would fight, and if fighting was taken from us, we would resist."

"Well, then! What about your friends at Scotland Yard? They are collecting their years, same as we are. What would happen if they were to be replaced with a newer sort of policeman, one that felt no urge to assist those in my brother's profession? What if they felt it their duty to hinder those who sought to help in their own ways?"

I was a moment in responding. "There will always be someone willing to help," I said at last. "Holmes and I couldn't rely on everyone at the Yard, even when he was at his height. But there were a few who could always be counted on – and those few were worthy men."

Mycroft made a chuckling sound, deep in his chest. "What if someone you trusted committed a betrayal against your country?"

"It has happened before," I answered. "Not someone I personally knew, but there were people who I trusted by rights of their position. Working with your brother taught me it isn't often as simple as a weak man seeking to escape his debts. Sometimes it is a vulture preying upon an innocent."

Again, he chuckled, and rose to his feet, adjusting the watch-chain at his waist as he did so. "You are thinking of the unfortunate Trelawney Hope, and perhaps his equally unfortunate wife, Lady Hilda."

I didn't ask how he knew. His mind was sharper than his brother's, and I knew how clear my thoughts were to him.

"You are a man of conviction, Doctor. For that reason, I believe you were my brother's inspiration."

I stared at him, the brandy hot in my brain while the empty glass was forgotten in my fingers. Mycroft was staring out at the darkening glaze of the winter storm, and I felt that he had momentarily withdrawn, his mind seeking a solution to a puzzle too vast for my comprehension.

"Perhaps," I heard him murmur, "we are all less intractable than we believe."

I left the Diogenes Club with no lessened puzzlement at our conversation. Outside, the storm had grown to the typical form of misery that seems to be the lot of London in the heart of winter. Even Edinburgh hadn't been as mixed in its ability to remove one's sense of comfort.

My umbrella was greatly appreciated by the time I huddled up against the shelter of New Scotland Yard, and I struggled to break the glaze of ice off the canvas before shutting the ribs. It did occur to me that I might have read more into our conversation than had truly existed, but Mycroft was a deliberate creature – lazy, Holmes had called his brother, and there was truth in that. But Mycroft was too lazy to not speak accidentally, and his mention of the Hopes couldn't be a coincidence. There was only one other person in London who would be in a position to understand some aspect of that particular case.

The Yard was a drastic change from the huddled up, piled-up chaos of the past in its old address. For one, it was brightly lit with more electric lights, and I knew too few of the new faces. The ones that knew me were gratifying in the quickness of their greeting.

"What can we do ye for, Doctor?" I recognized Constable Murcher – Sergeant now, content with his position, and growing quite grey about the chops. "Good as it is to see you!"

"It has been a while, hasn't it?" I looked about, politely ignoring the curious gazes. I had often chided Holmes for his complaints about being seen in a "fanciful light", but I confess I had difficulty taking my own medicine when those awestruck gazes came my own way.

"Aye, it has, and no lie," Murcher chuckled. His body was stiff, but he glowed with that stubborn vitality common to the Englishman who takes pride in his work. "You just missed Mr. Bradstreet. He was here to stop by, saying hello to the Chief Super not an hour ago."

"I am sorry I missed him."

"Well, he's no doubt back with his boys in Bow Street. We were right proud of his promotion, right proud. Couldn't be a finer man in charge of that crowd. Doesn't like when he has to ride a horse, but can't have everything!" Murcher chuckled deeply. "Even Gregson admitted he was suited where he is. Weren't you at his retirement party? Thought so. I suppose it doesn't matter – he'll be retiring in a few years. He'll go a world of good while he's here."

"I couldn't agree more." I leaned on my umbrella as a walking-stick, for my wounds still ached on such fiendish nights. "Who else is here, sir?"

Murcher grinned at me, showing that a surprising amount of his natural teeth had survived his profession. "Well, there's old Lamps of course. I'm sure he'd like to say hello to you."

Lestrade's promotion had come as a shock to all of us – no one had doubted his ability to be a Detective Chief Superintendent. Anyone who could bully the most recalcitrant mob into obeying the Crown laws by sheer force of will was someone born to lead. But Lestrade's intractable will had left a trail of well-connected enemies as well as allies, and the former had been more concerned with watching his failure.

When I think of it now, it was thoughtless arrogance that led to my astonishment. The police had ever been staffed with people who were determined to rise above their limitations. While Lestrade would concede defeat when he was wrong, he never had been known to give up. Against his superior foes, he had merely ignored them to concentrate on his duties, maintaining his work while they battered themselves senseless in their efforts to dislodge him. Even Holmes had said once, in the most grudging of tones, that his willpower was "enviable".

I hadn't seen him in almost eighteen months – twice the amount of time since I had last seen Holmes. My practice and my family had caught up much of my attention, but the span meant nothing when Lestrade looked up from his desk and his first reaction was to smile.

"Well, Dr. Watson! What brings you here on such a wretched night?" He rose and we shook hands across his desk while the storm sent the electric lights to flickering. He wasn't a handsome man, nor did he pretend to be. But he had a personality that compelled, a simple force of will through those remarkably dark eyes that bade one listen to him. For the first time, I could see his temples had grown quite silver, sweeping back like bird wings.

"It is good to see you," he added, "though I shudder to think it would be work that would force you out on the streets now!"

"Not business, so much, Detective Chief Superintendent." I emphasized his new title, and he grinned at me. "I am late in paying my respects."

"Not at all. You have a life to live like everyone else." He dropped his ink-pen and leaned back, stretching for a moment within the confines of a new wool uniform. "There was an assembly today," he explained, "hence the fancy togs . . . but I'll confess, the new cut is a great improvement from the stuff we used to patrol in!" His hand slipped to his deep blue sleeve to touch it self-consciously. "How is Mr. Holmes? Still keeping to his bees?"

I hesitated slightly, and Lestrade's eye met mine in silent knowledge. I cannot describe the moment in a way to do it justice. The little man's hair had greyed, which too often is a sign of age and not wisdom, but there was a wisdom in his gaze that I was certain hadn't existed in the old days.

"Have you heard nothing from your comrades in Sussex?" I asked, already scenting the answer.

Lestrade tilted his head back slightly, a faint smile flitting at his mouth. "Other than there are occasional visitors to tend to the bees, and the villa is kept up? No doubt his fancy brother at work."

"No doubt." And now that I was here, I was suddenly unsure of my next steps. "I was just to see Mycroft Holmes today, to be honest."

"Ah." Lestrade turned and turned up the light in a small oil lamp. "Electricity is all very fine, but it tends to go brown in the bulb when you need it the most," he complained. "My wife still prefers her old-fashioned cook-stove and bake-ovens. Can't say I disagree. What is one to do when the juice goes out?" He warmed his hand over the lamp-flame for a moment, and straightened. "You're looking well, John." He used my given name, as I had offered it freely some years ago. "You're worried about him, of course. I can't blame you a jot. He's the sort of man who inspires worry, though he's unaware of it himself."

Faced with such candor, I was embarrassed. "I'm sure he's being careful."

"No doubt." Lestrade answered dryly. "It is a strange world, is it not? I finally rise above Detective Inspector. You inherit a small fortune and need not work ever again . . . and Mr. Holmes has learned caution. Which of the three was the least likely?"

"We had faith in you," I protested.

He sent an eyebrow up at that. "John, do you know how old I am?"

I thought about it. When we had first met, in '81, he had mentioned being in the force for twenty years. At the minimum, that put his birthday to 1843 . . . I had been a heady youth just facing the prospects of my thirtieth year at our first meeting. He had well been within that decade.

"I am just turned threescore and ten, John." At my surprise he smiled, honestly amused. "My lineage speaking, I'm afraid. We finish up growing so quickly that we seem to be adults longer than anyone else. Very well, better late than never. I can stay long enough to do some good here, just as Bradstreet is doing in Bow Street. I suppose we'll be buried together, as long as we've served." He folded his arms across his chest. "Thank you for that vote of confidence, though." He made a slight movement. His in-turned foot was less noticeable here, and I wondered if he was wearing a corrective shoe of some sort to treat his old infirmity.

"I apologize. I suppose I let my worry for Holmes override my usual sensibilities." I sounded less than convincing, even to myself.

Lestrade cocked his head to one side, still a spry grasshopper of a man who kept his grandchildren's faces within the case of his watch, and knew the value of his wife as well as he knew the laws he served. "Did I ever tell you why a Copper's coat is blue, John?"

Surprised, I stared at him. "No. No, I am afraid you did not."

Lestrade examined his fingernails almost absently. "It was designed out of fear, you know," he said conversationally. In the newly-brightened lamplight his lean, strong features looked to have been carved of iron. "The people were afraid we would show loyalties to the government, which they were greatly fearful of at the time . . . and everyone knew the soldiers wore the red. Unlike the government, most of us never carried anything rougher than a truncheon. What I had to go through for permission to carry an iron! But that would be a story for another day. Our whistles alert the authorities. The only rank we carry that parallels the military is the detective sergeant." His lean face dipped into a look that had seen much and for long. "Anything to keep from being confused by the public we served, for being the military they feared all the more. I once ciphered out how many of us had died in the first ten years of duty, how many of us were dismissed for petty corruptions, or the drink . . . how many of us were wounded too badly to keep serving. It was never easy, Doctor, but it was necessary. Slow steps. Slow, painful steps."

"I have never doubted the bravery of the Yard, you know," I told him.

"I know. We know." His smile was closer to a grin now, the look of a man who knows more than his opponent thinks. "You never once impugned our honesty in your writings. You never once accused us of being selfish, or weak, or greedy. No one else did that for us. At first, we cared a great deal that you made us look like fools against Mr. Holmes. Then, though . . . Well, who wouldn't look a fool next to him? But everyone else was doing much worse. You treated us more honestly than any newspaper, and Mr. Holmes, for all his high birth, gave us a fair deal. For the first time, the public we served was seeing us as if we *cared* about them. Did you know, after Mr. Holmes became famous, our recruitment came up?"

The little man clasped his hands behind his back and peered out at the blackening stripes against the window. "And for all our lack of parallels with the military," he said carefully, "we do know the military exists. We answer to the Home Secretary more often than not, you know. They still need our small help from time to time. We are permitted to give them that help, so long as we never forget we aren't supposed to work together." His eyes gleamed suddenly, a quiet triumph after years of silence. "Playing the fool is the task of the politician."

"Do you know where he is?" I asked against hope.

Lestrade shook his head, and I believe he wouldn't lie to me. He might suspect, and perhaps even be right . . . but he wouldn't send me on a false trail of hope. "No," he answered, "but he is Sherlock Holmes. I daresay it's an important matter he's on. More important than the little affairs of my people. Whatever did Mr. Mycroft say to put such a look in your face?"

"It was just a strangeness . . . I believe he was trying to tell me something. He asked me what I would do if . . . England was ever conquered by one of her enemies."

"To be conquered?" He repeated softly, and interest crossed his face. "An interesting question, isn't it? What did you tell him?"

"Something trite, I fear, about how I would find some way to resist if I couldn't overtly combat. What would you have told him?"

He laughed under his breath. "You're asking the wrong person, John . . . but England has been invaded before, has she not? Your people to mine, and the Romans to us both after that . . . and then the Normans. For all that, we're all here." He tucked his hands inside his loose sleeves, for a slight chill was growing about the corners of his office. "But as a policeman . . . ." He shook his head from side to side. "I would resign," he said softly. "It's difficult to make an example of a person if they refuse to wear a uniform, you know. And from there, I suppose that I would find some . . . constructive way to while away my retirement."

"Sabotage?" I chuckled. "That would be just as dangerous, would it not?"

"For you, perhaps. For a man who has been called 'a complete imbecile' by the very best? It truly is astounding what one can get away with, if that is the common consensus."

"As some of us learned during a particular incident involving a stained drugget."

Lestrade shrugged in a mighty gesture. "One cannot eat pride, John. Only crow. As I said, more important than the little affairs of my people."

"There are no little affairs in England, Lestrade," I found myself saying. "Nor are there little people." He smiled to hear me say such, and when we shook hands again in our parting, it was to promise to remain in touch. It pleases me to say we have both kept our ends of that bargain, and we are likely to do so until one of us dies.

December 1913

One year has passed since my conversation with Mycroft. The second approaches, and I feel something in my bones that says Holmes will return. It's a military sensation, a peripheral touch that is bred in the arena of survival.

I didn't want to come to the inevitable conclusion that Holmes, who has worked for the heads of Europe, is now working against them in defence of his people. The dangers are astounding, and yet when has risk ever influenced his nerve? Lestrade's regular letters support my beliefs. He is as careful as anyone I have ever known, yet behind his plain hand, when I recall how often he has played the fool, I see a very different accounting.

We both play the fool, he and I. So well we have been in these roles that neither of us fully suspected the other's gift in the deception until this late hour. In the newspapers he thoughtfully mails me, I find stirrings of discontent where people are choosing sides, and not all of these sides are for England. There are arrests, and there are displays of behavior that would have been unthinkable in my youth. Somewhere, Holmes is in this – in what country performing what chore, I will not say without proof. But the signs are as clear as tracking a wind by watching the birds that ride the currents.

My question is, what will Holmes do? He has ever chafed at the bonds, real or imagined, when they were placed upon him. This task he is upon – he might serve it, but I believe he will remove himself from it. By what means, I don't know, but he is a master of obfuscation and deception, and he is lastly, a man not to be manipulated.

After a life of searching the world and his soul, my friend found the one place where he would be content. He was happy among the Downs, where his villa caught the different environs of field and forest, stream, beach, and marsh. Surrounded by a metropolis of flora and fauna every bit as interesting as the heart of London, he had come to see himself as its keeper, the way he had once kept London. Only Moriarty's gang had been able to uproot him from the city he had bound himself too. For three years he had survived as a nomad, and reliant on his brother for funds. They had used him then, as they needed to. His bright mind had been perfect for observing the world and reporting the first stirrings of this burgeoning war. He must have loathed that sort of mindless obligation, but to survive, to return home, he had bowed to it.

A monarch or a drone, eh Watson?

A ruler . . . or the servant of a ruler? Holmes would obey his Monarch . . . but would he obey the Monarch's servants?

Once in service, always in service. I knew that as deeply as any man who took the Queen's shilling. Holmes's survival during his "death" had depended on the support of the Government. They must have collected his debt to them for this. I feel the pain of how that long-withheld obligation took his hard-earned peace.

His word, when given, will be followed through, but he will go no further. I know this much of him.

And I will be there for him, as I have always been. I will watch his villa, knowing it isn't likely that he will return to it before his time, but I am a soldier still, and I know to wait until it's time to be deployed. Holmes will know where to find me. And he knows that he will find me.

And perhaps, when this mysterious affair is finished, I will see him again the way I remember him – content, and surrounded by the sleepy croon of his bees in his home facing the coast of France.

NOTE

I wanted to do something with "His Last Bow", but mostly I wanted to intimate that Holmes's apparent goofs – enough to make most government aids and diplomats flinch – were due to the fact that he wanted out of this job he was in, and he wanted out right now. Why else would he blow his cover six ways from Sunday, and create so many *faux pas*? One has two choices: The quick choice, which is to say that "His Last Bow" is a forgery, or the harder choice of plumbing for the logic of an apparently illogical action. The first option creates the problem of a simple answer followed by a complicated explanation – *Who wrote it, then, if it was a forgery?* But I've taken the second option, and I hope it is satisfactory.

– MW

The Lambeth Twin
by Martin Daley

Chapter I

While recognising the physical limitations of a sixty-two-year-old man, I nevertheless answered the call for retired officers to re-enlist as the clouds darkened over Europe. In 1914, I rejoined my old regiment and – given my age and location – was asked to assist with casualties in London hospitals who were returning from the front. By the summer of 1916, these same hospitals were being overwhelmed with soldiers, suffering with all manner of injuries and ailments, to the point where staff were struggling to cope without such assistance. Far from *de*creasing, I found my workload *in*creasing, as I was being asked to help with basic care from changing dressings to simply offering a kindly ear.

I will never forget a visit in late July of that year. I had read about the disastrous offensive on the Somme where tens of thousands of men had been lost. I then witnessed for myself some of the broken survivors who had been shipped home. My task in all the chaos was to go around the wards with an orderly, attempting to identify men who had no formal identification and who were in such a traumatised state that they were unable to speak. Some wore identity tags but had no regiment associated with them, while others had no tags or papers. Some poor souls just lay there staring, unable to unsee the horrors they had witnessed. Others couldn't contain themselves as they screamed out their mental agonies. In that first morning, we managed to identify soldiers from as far and wide as New Zealand to Scotland, from Canada to Northumberland.

As summer bled into autumn, I gradually found myself a little less distressed by my visits, despite the fact that the numbers of incoming wounded were seemingly endless. It was during a visit to Guy's Hospital in late September when I was astounded to run into a character from my old Baker Street days.

I entered a ward to find a dozen beds crammed in against the side walls, each containing soldiers with various wounds and traumas: Burns, broken limbs, missing limbs. Some with bandages covering their eyes, others swathed in a Mummy-like gauze. I had witnessed suffering myself in Afghanistan decades earlier, but observing these men, I struggled to imagine what fighting conditions were like on the Western Front. Family members crowded round many of the beds, trying to comfort their husbands, sons, and brothers.

Looking round the ward, I suddenly had the sensation that I was being watched myself. I turned to see one of the patients looking directly at me, as if he knew me. He seemed little more than a boy.

"Doctor Watson?" he asked.

"Yes," I said, glancing down at the board on the end of his bed. "Private William Cates, London Regiment."

"Don't you recognise me, sir?"

I felt a little embarrassed. "I'm sorry, Private, I don't."

"It's me – *Billy*."

I looked again and saw the features of our young page who would scamper up and down the stairs of Baker Street, carrying out our errands and messages. I should say at this point, by way of an explanation to my readers, that this young man was one of no less than four separate boys who acted as our page, during our years at 221b. The first, employed in our early years, happened to be called Billy. Much to my shame, I was never entirely sure of the Christian names of the next two young lads who filled the position, as Holmes and I had settled into the habit of calling our page "Billy" and, rightly or wrongly, we continued to do so during their tenure. It just so happens that the young man before me now was the final lad to wear out the stair carpet in our lodgings, and he did, in fact, have that same name.

"*Billy!*" I cried, unable to contain my delight. Further to my embarrassment, everyone stopped talking and turned around.

"Sorry," I announced to the ward in general. "Billy, how wonderful to see you!" I shook the young man's hand with such vigour that the poor lad winced with pain, and I realised how inappropriate my actions and words were in the circumstances. "Oh, I'm so sorry. I must apologise. I'm so surprised to see you. The last time must have been when we left Baker Street over ten years ago. You would be around – ?"

"That's right, Doctor, I was eleven at the time."

It was a stark reminder, if one were needed, that most of the men in this war were children just a few years earlier. How sad it was to see young men cut down so needlessly.

"What did you do afterwards?" I asked.

"Well, after you married and Mr. Holmes retired to the country, and Mrs. Hudson followed not long after, I got a position with Mr. Benjemin Briggs, a solicitor in Hanover Square. He was a good man, was Mr. Briggs. He treated me and the other servants well. He even paid for me to receive an education, and I ended up passing my exams and getting a place at the University of London. When I left, I obtained a position as a solicitor's clerk at Mr. Briggs' office. Then war broke out. Although I had no connection to anyone south of the river, I was allocated a place in the Lambeth Pals."

I looked on the young man with great fondness. "You've done well for yourself, Billy. I'm so proud of you."

My pride for him was equalled by a feeling of great sadness. He had worked so hard to achieve something for himself, only for his career to be interrupted.

"I hope you'll be able to resume your employment now that you're back," I said.

"Yes, I hope so, Doctor, although I'm not sure how fit enough I am to start work. We got caught in a gas attack."

At that moment, the young man started to cough. I reached for the cabinet beside his bed and poured a glass of water.

"Lie back, Billy. Try not to exert yourself."

He waited until he regained his composure before speaking again. "It's so strange that I should see you today, Doctor. Only yesterday, I was talking to my friend and saviour here – " He indicated to the young man in the next bed. " – about the days when I used to run errands for you and the great Sherlock Holmes. I was saying how we could use Mr. Holmes's skills right now."

"In what way?" I asked.

"Well, Scotland Yard has been asking soldiers about some murder that was committed earlier this year. A policeman was here yesterday wanting to speak to John."

I turned my attention to the next patient: A young lad with a shock of blonde hair, whose fresh face was now marked and troubled with his experiences. Before I could speak, a plain-clothed inspector entered the ward. It was obvious he was a policeman, as he was accompanied by a uniformed colleague, who pointed towards Billy's friend. The policeman referred to the soldier's details on the board hanging from the end of his bed, and then addressed the lad himself.

"Now, Private Watkins, I believe you were too unfit to answer my constable's questions yesterday. Well, I am here to tell you that my name is Inspector James Styles of Scotland Yard, and I am investigating the murder of Silas Emery in Lambeth in June of this year."

"I've been in France," said the wounded man irritably.

Before he could elaborate, he began coughing and reached for a bowl on the small cabinet beside his bed.

"I think the murder took place the night before you left for France, Private Watkins. We have a description of the suspect as being in uniform and with blonde hair. We are speaking to every soldier who may have been here around that time. I believe you have a twin brother? Can you remember where you both were?"

"This is outrageous, Inspector!" interrupted Billy. "John here saved my life and lost his brother in the process."

"I'm sorry, lad," said the inspector, "but I am duty bound to investigate such a crime, regardless of the circumstances."

"Surely you can show some compassion for these men," I interjected.

"And who are you, sir?" he asked.

Momentarily, I was unsure what to say. Retired doctor? Former soldier? Friend and colleague of the great consulting detective Sherlock Holmes? "My name is Dr. John Watson," I said finally, believing it to be the less confrontational option. "I am a retired medical officer attached the Royal Berkshire Regiment, and helping here at the hospital."

"That's very commendable, Dr. Watson," replied the man, rather dismissively, I thought, "but I am Inspector James Styles of Scotland Yard and, as I said to these two lads, it is my job to investigate the crime of murder, a crime for which this man may be able to help with my enquiries."

"I don't know anything about it," said John Watkins.

"Again, son: Where were you the night before you left for France?"

"We were down at The King's Head."

"Were there any witnesses?"

"Probably the whole of the Lambeth Pals!" he replied. "Everyone was there for a final send off."

"Were *you* there?" Styles asked Billy.

"I was," replied our former page.

"And?"

"And what?"

"And did you see Watkins here and his brother in The King's Head?"

"Well, there was a lot of people crammed in that night, Inspector, but I'm pretty sure they would have been there."

I thought Billy hesitated somewhat in his answer. I sensed the inspector thought the same thing as he looked from one to the other. Before he could speak, however, there was a disturbance further down the ward. One of the poor wretches – no doubt haunted by what he witnessed just a few short weeks earlier and unable to control his mental agony – started screaming and shouting. I rushed down the ward and was quickly joined by two nurses and an orderly. Between us, we managed to calm the man down and settle him back against his pillow.

By the time I returned to Billy's bedside, Inspector Styles had left. Billy explained. "He said it wasn't the time or the place to carry on his questioning, so he left to explore 'other avenues of his investigation'."

"I should think so, too," I said, a little chagrined at the inspector's manner and lack of appropriateness.

Watkins appeared to be younger than Billy, and the exertion and excitement of the policeman's visit obviously tired him out. He began to doze before falling asleep completely. This allowed Billy to speak without him hearing.

"I knew John and his twin brother Jim by sight – they were like peas in a pod – but it wasn't until we were trapped in a waterlogged shell-hole in No Man's Land that I became attached to him."

Billy adopted the characteristic stare of the battle-hardened soldier as he recalled the horrors of his experience – a stare I have witnessed and experienced many times in my long life.

"We were standing on the fire step, waiting to go over the top. I've never been so terrified in all my life, and I hope to never again experience such a sensation. I wasn't sure who was around me. As the whistles blew and we climbed the ladders, dozens of men were falling back down into the trench under the merciless machine gun fire. Those of us who actually made it into No Man's Land found ourselves in a chaotic blur – smoke, shell, and shot everywhere. I was blown off my feet at one point, nearly losing a leg in the process. I landed in a large, waterlogged shell-hole along with a dozen or so other men. John and his brother Jim were among them, and I could see that Jim was in a bad way. The two exchanged a few words and John was beside himself with grief as his brother died in his arms. It was just then that a group of four or five German soldiers appeared above us at the mouth of the crater. John went berserk and charged up the muddy face, killing them all. No sooner had he slid back down into the base to see if he could do anything else for his brother, when the cry of 'Gas!' went up. Seeing that I was the only one left alive, he proceeded to half-carry me back to the British trenches while we struggled to share a gas mask."

My blood ran cold at the thought of such an action, and I found myself empathising with young Billy as I recalled my own similar experience when my orderly Murray got me back to the British lines after being wounded at Maiwand.

"So, this inspector is referring to something Watkins allegedly did before he went across to France?" I asked.

"*Allegedly*," Billy repeated. "Yes."

"On what does he base this allegation?"

"Well, his constable yesterday said that a witness saw a blonde-haired soldier leaving the home of the victim on the night the murder was apparently committed. Because John and his family live nearby, they seem to be paying particular attention to him."

"And this was the night before you all left for France?"

"Yes."

"But didn't you say that you were all in The King's Head public house the night before you left?"

Billy hesitated before answering.

"Well yes, but I couldn't swear to seeing the Watkins brothers there. It was crowded, and I didn't stay very long. You see, Doctor, all the Lambeth lads know each other. When I was conscripted into the Army, I was just assigned to the Battalion to make up the numbers. I've only got to know John since we got out of that hell-hole. Although I saw them from afar, I can't say I ever spoke to his brother."

"You mentioned Mr. Holmes earlier. Presumably you would want him to use his skills to clear your friend's name?"

"Exactly, Doctor. Judging by the attitude of the inspector and his constable, it's as though they are just looking for someone to blame. I think it's so unfair that a man should give his service to King and Country and be treated in this way."

"Well, I wonder if you may be in luck," I said. "It so happens that Mr. Holmes makes regular visits to London, and he happens to be coming up again this weekend. I could ask him to look into this matter for you if you like?"

Billy looked across at his friend who was still sleeping.

"That would be wonderful, Doctor. Thank you."

Chapter II

I had endeavoured to keep in touch with my friend Sherlock Holmes as much as I could since his retirement, making several weekend visits to his bee-keeping farm when my own schedule allowed. But as the years passed and my Queen Anne Street practice burgeoned, it became increasingly difficult to get away, and we saw less and less of each other. That was until my assisting him with his trapping of Von Bork on the eve of the war. Following that affair – and given his knowledge of espionage and the Irish problem – it became clear to me that the government had continued to request his help and advice and, on several occasions, my friend therefore asked for my own assistance. This invariably brought him to London on many occasions, sometimes staying at our old rooms in Baker Street, the lease of which he had retained after Mrs. Hudson moved out, and sometimes even accepting my dear wife's invitation to stay with us.

The one thing that Holmes shared with me following the Von Bork affair was that the government had re-appointed his brother Mycroft as an advisor, to contribute his own expertise. I must say, as the dark days of the conflict closed in on the country, it gave me some personal comfort knowing that the brothers' two great brains were contributing to the war effort.

Holmes had sent a telegram regarding his forthcoming visit two weeks earlier. Ysaÿe was giving a recital at St. James's Hall, he informed me. I was aware that the great Belgian virtuoso had fled to London at the outbreak of the war – and had given the occasional concert to acknowledge Britain's support for his country – but I suspected the reason given for Holmes's trip was more a pretext to visit Mycroft and help with another Matter of State. When he didn't go into any further detail regarding his visit – something that was unusual in itself – and I then learned that he was staying with his brother at his Pall Mall lodgings, I was sure of it. Always respectful of my friend's work, however, I didn't pursue the matter and took what he told me at face value.

It was two days following my surprise encounter with Billy and his comrade that I met with Holmes at his brother's home. I found that in his years of retirement, he had become more relaxed from the unpredictable flat-mate I had known in Baker Street. Many is the time when I have witnessed him too irritable for conversation, too restless for sleep. I've heard him prowling round our apartment after dark, or perched on a chair shrouded in tobacco smoke while he wrestled with a problem. There was no evidence that such behaviour was adopted in his rural idyll. Despite the sombre mood that hung over London in those dark days of war, I found Holmes full of enthusiasm when I called to see him.

"Watson, my dear fellow!" he cried when the maid took me through to the study where he was reading. "How wonderful to see you!"

"As it is you," I replied taking his hand. "You look well." My comment was genuine – the long thin face had a good colour to it and despite his sixty-two years, the sharp sparkle of eager anticipation still burned brightly in his eyes.

My old friend, gestured that I take the seat opposite him. "Brother Mycroft summoned me to Whitehall on something he always calls 'Official Business'."

"Which," I added, "no doubt results in you getting involved in some role?"

Holmes smiled at my perspicacity, "Yes. On this occasion, it was easier for me to lodge with Mycroft." He subtly changed the subject. "So, tell me, Watson, what brings you here at this early hour? I suspect Mycroft isn't the only one who wishes to avail themselves of my opinions."

I returned his smile. "Indeed. I ran into an old acquaintance of ours the other day, when I was assisting at Guy's. You remember Billy, our page – the last one, before you moved out?"

Holmes's face lit up momentarily as he recalled the little boy, scampering up and down the stairs at Baker Street, delivering telegrams and running errands. His visage altered as quickly, however, as he instantly calculated the number of years it had been since we had known the little lad, which in turn informed him that Billy was now a young man of fighting age.

"You saw him in hospital?" I nodded. "He has returned from the front?"

"He had been gassed and wounded, but still has the same jolly expression as he had as a child. I'm ashamed to say I would never have recognised him had he not seen me and introduced himself."

"There is something else, Watson."

"He asked if you would help him and his friend with a problem."

"Problem?"

I knew that Holmes had refused many an investigation after moving to Sussex, as his time became more and more involved before and during the war by serving the British Government, but I asked anyway.

"Billy was saved by a young lad who is now being questioned by the police about the murder of a money lender in June."

"Silas Emery."

"Yes. How did you know?"

"Oh, I keep abreast of things," he replied enigmatically.

I then remembered that on one of my visits to his cottage, I saw the latest editions of several London newspapers. Holmes obviously had them delivered and this is where he would have read of the murder.

"Apparently, this young lad and his twin brother lived near the dead man, and the police say there was a witness who saw someone resembling their appearance at Emery's premises the night he was killed. This was shortly before they and Billy travelled to France. The police seem intent on seeing the matter to a conclusion, and Billy was hoping you would look into it and clear the lad's name."

"Who is the inspector in charge of the case?"

"James Styles."

The name meant nothing to either of us, used as we were to Lestrade, Gregson, *et al*, all of whom had now retired or passed away.

"My consulting days are behind me, Watson," said Holmes after a little thought, "but I'm willing to make the odd exception and considering the assistance Billy has given us in the past – not to mention his service to

King and Country. It's the least I can do to help him and his friend in their time of need."

"I'm sure he will be delighted," I announced.

That evening, I accompanied Holmes to the recital given by Ysaÿe and arranged to meet him at Guy's the following morning. Billy was overjoyed to see us and it was clear Holmes was equally so, although his pleasure, like my own, was tinged with sadness at the thought of this young lad, and thousands like him, being sacrificed indiscriminately.

"This is John Watkins, Mr. Holmes," said Billy, after a few minutes reacquaintance and indicating towards the patient in the next bed. "My friend and saviour."

"Hello, Private Watkins," said Holmes. "I believe you're being questioned by the police regarding the Emery murder?"

"That's right, sir," said the young man.

"Did you know Emery?"

"Everybody knew Silas Emery," he replied, scornfully. "He was the scourge of our area."

"And where was that?" asked Holmes.

"All round Lambeth, Kennington, and the Elephant and Castle."

"Incidentally, my friend Watson here informed me of the loss of your brother. Please accept my deepest condolences."

The young man nodded his acknowledgement, clearly pained by his recollections.

"I'll look into the matter of Silas Emery for you," assured Holmes, "and see what we can do."

"Oh, you don't have to do that, sir!" said the young lad.

"No, as a favour to Billy here," said Holmes. "I insist." Later, as we left the hospital, my friend asked, "Are you free tonight, Watson?"

"Why yes," I replied. "What do you have in mind?"

"I think a trip to Lambeth is in order. We need to find out a little more about this Emery character and the hold he had over the people there. If my instincts are correct, any one of a number of people could be responsible for his death."

I thought back to Holmes's tried and trusted methods in such a circumstance. "To the local public house, perhaps?" I asked.

Holmes laughed in the hearty noiseless fashion which was peculiar to him. "You're coming along, nicely, Doctor," he said at last. "If people know more than they're letting on, that's the one place where they'll talk freely about other people's business.

I called at Holmes's temporary lodgings at seven o'clock and we took a cab to the Lambeth Walk Inn. Under Holmes's instruction, I had dispensed with my collar and tie and slipped on an old jacket and flat cap. We entered, bought a pint of beer each, and wandered over to a seat in the corner. I picked up a discarded copy of that morning's edition of *The South London Press,* while my friend simply sat back with the air of a man who'd had a little too much to drink already, all the while observing everyone and anyone who entered the premises.

Within half-an-hour, the pub was starting to fill up, and after an hour, it was crowded with locals, cheering and laughing amongst each other, seemingly putting the troubles of the war behind them for the night. As the night progressed, the atmosphere became more raucous and, at one point, someone shouted, *"A toast to absent friends!"* This was met with a loud cheer in which we both joined in, not wishing to attract attention to ourselves by appearing different to everyone else.

"Get the old Joanna going!" cried one man and another sat at the old, battered instrument and, much to everyone's delight, started belting out *"It's a Long Way to Tipperary"*.

Scouring the crowd as discreetly as I could over the top of my newspaper, I pointed to a man who appeared to be extremely popular amongst his fellow patrons. "I'm sure I heard someone call him 'Eddie Watkins' at one point above the din," I said to Holmes. "Perhaps he's a relative of Billy's young friend? If you'll allow me."

I left Holmes seated and moved closer on the pretext of making my way to the bar through the crowd. While looking the other way and feigning a joke with a couple of other men, I listened in to what was being said between the man and his friends.

"Them two boys of yours should have got medals before they even went to France, if you ask me," I heard one say. The rest of the men on his table chorus their approval by raising their glasses.

"Here's to the Watkins boys!" shouted one as the rest cheered. Watkins himself just sat with his head bowed.

I reported my observations when I returned to our table. Shortly afterward, Holmes stood up and knocked into the table next to him, spilling one of the drinks in the process. Before the owner of the drink could get up and voice his displeasure, Holmes acted quickly to defuse any incident.

"Oh, I'm sorry, mate," he said, putting his hand and the man's shoulder and swaying back and forward for effect. "I've had one or two meself. Let me buy you and your friends another one." Before the man could respond, he added, "I insist," and headed for the bar.

The man and his friends – similar in age to ourselves – shrugged and were presumably prepared to ignore the incident, given that no damage was done. Their ambivalence turned to delight however a few minutes later, when they saw the man they took for a drunkard return to the table carrying a tray with four tankards of ale.

"There you go, my friends," said Holmes, still swaying from side to side, while skilfully avoiding spilling any beer. "No hard feelings, eh?"

"*Hey-hey!*" cried the man. "Thank you, old son. You're a true gent!"

Holmes continued to engage with the man as the evening wore on. And *as* it wore on, and the man's friends gradually dispersed, he became increasingly inebriated. Far from discouraging this, Holmes contributed to his condition, flashing me the odd glance and knowing that information could be gleaned from such a character. Finally, and unknowingly, the man created the crack in the door for which Holmes was looking.

"I take it you got your money back as well then?" he said, pointing to the empty tankards on the table in front of them.

"Money?" asked Holmes.

"Aye," slurred the man. "From old Emery."

It was at that point that both Holmes and I appeared to have the same thought: The reason so many people were in the pub was because they had excess money. And the reason that they had excess money may have been because whoever killed Emery must have also robbed him and distributed it to the people in the area.

"Emery," said Holmes. It was neither a question nor a confirmation, simply an attempt to encourage the man to expand on his comment. Holmes's method proved successful.

"Aye," continued our new friend, staring into the bottom of his drink. "Nasty piece of work. Got what 'e deserved, if you asked me."

"Aye," agreed Holmes.

"Couldn't believe me luck when the envelope dropped through the door."

"Envelope?"

The man looked at Holmes. "Aye, the one with the money!"

"Aww, the envelope, o'course. You know something? I can't remember when I got mine."

The man thought for a while, as if he was deliberating a question in Parliament.

"It must 'ave been . . . it must 'ave been . . . I think it must 'ave been the day after we 'eard of Emery's killing."

"That's right," agreed Holmes. "It would have been one of those white envelopes, wouldn't it?"

411

"No," said the man, as if offended by his companion's error. "It was one of them brown ones with *G.R.* on the back." He laughed to himself. "I remember because everyone was shouting '*Good old George Roper!*'"

"That's right," said Holmes, joining in the laughter. "I remember now."

"I think I've just about 'ad enough," said the man, whose head was shaking as he tried to focus on what remained of his drink. "You couldn't 'elp me 'ome, could ye? I just live round the corner."

We thought it was the least we could do, given that Holmes was effectively responsible for the man's condition.

After we assisted the man to his door and watched with some amusement as he tried to select the correct key, Holmes announced. "We'll leave you now, my friend."

"You're a real couple o' gents and no mistake," he muttered as he struggled to get the key selected into the lock. "If you ever need anything in the future, just you come and see old Sammy Watts."

With that, having succeeded in opening the door, he stumbled into his house and shut it behind him.

Holmes noted the address on the cuff of his shirt – *3 Gibson Road*. As he did so, I had an overwhelming feeling: It was though I was being transported back in my own mind twenty years, when I would accompany my friend around the streets of London and on many an obscure investigation. Not for the first time in our long in intimate friendship, it was as though Holmes read my mind.

"Just like the old days, eh, Watson?"

I smiled. "Yes," I said simply, before referring to the case itself. "Our friend's comment about the money is interesting, don't you think? If those envelopes were delivered after the Pals left, then young Watkins couldn't possibly have committed the murder."

"I agree," said Holmes, "although something tells me there is more to this than meets the eye. However, I think that will do us for this evening," he said. "Let us make our way back and pick up the trail again tomorrow."

Chapter III

"This case troubles me, Watson," said my friend when I called on him the following morning.

"What aspect exactly?" I asked.

Holmes sucked on his cherry-wood and pondered. "The letters *G.R.* What do you think they stand for?"

"I'm not sure."

412

"Surely *George Rex*. And if that is correct, why would government envelopes full of money be delivered through the doors of ordinary people in Lambeth who had previously repaid the money they had borrowed to a lender, embezzler, and thief?"

"A lender, embezzler, and thief who had recently been murdered," I added.

"Precisely."

"What do you propose we do?"

Holmes thought for a while.

"Ordinarily, I would follow the money," he said at last, "but not knowing exactly which department provided those envelopes, that would be difficult at this stage. Instead, I think we'll visit the War Office and see what we can find out about the Lambeth Pals."

I followed Holmes up the steps of the grand building in Whitehall. Upon entering, my friend adopted the air of an authoritarian figure as he approached a man at the front desk.

"Good morning," he said, without waiting for a response. "My name is Holmes, you have probably heard of me regarding government matters. I'm here to carry out a preliminary audit of the stationery used by the government departments in the last twelve months. My colleague and I would also like information about the movements and whereabouts of the Lambeth Pals Battalion, presumably attached to the London Regiment. Thank you."

The man was clearly flustered by Holmes's confidence and authority – so much so that the ridiculous reasons for given for our visit didn't seem to register with him.

"Erm . . . Good morning, sir. Yes, I'll just get my supervisor."

He disappeared momentarily behind a screen at the rear of the desk. We could hear muffled voices before one exclaimed. "Mycroft Holmes?" I looked at my friend and saw a smile pluck at his lips. The man and his supervisor appeared, the latter adjusting his jacket and appearing to wipe tea from his lips with a handkerchief.

"Mr. Holmes?" he said. "I am Sydney Male. I'm sorry, I wasn't expecting such a visit. I've heard so much about you in government circles. How can I help?"

"Envelopes, Mr. Male, envelopes."

"Envelopes, sir?"

"Yes, we believe a consignment of envelopes has been stolen, and if they were to fall into enemy hands – Well, who knows what it might lead to."

"Yes, sir, I perfectly understand. Have you any idea as to when they might have been taken?"

"The matter has only come to light recently, so we estimate it would have been about two months ago."

"If you could follow me, Mr. Holmes, we may have some records here." As we followed Mr. Male down a corridor, he continued. "We don't actually keep any stationery here at the office. It's kept in a warehouse in Lambeth."

Holmes stopped. "Lambeth?"

"Yes. We used to have a store at the Woolwich Arsenal, but as the factory had to be extended because of the war, we obtained a warehouse in Lambeth."

"That is very interesting," said Holmes, much to Mr. Male's confusion. "Tell me, do you have a list of people who work at your Lambeth warehouse?"

"Yes, of course," said Male. "Specifically for the security purposes you alluded to a few moments ago."

We changed direction and he took us into an office where a dozen or more men were drawing on maps of the Western Front. He opened a cabinet and took out a thick buff-coloured file marked *"Warehouse Staff"*. At that moment, one of his colleagues called him over.

"You can have a look through that if you like," he said, as he acknowledged his colleague. "I will be right back."

Holmes took the file and started running his finger down the names that, from what I could see, appeared to be in alphabetical order. He turned two or three pages without showing any signs of interest before stopping on the final page.

"Watkins," he said. "Eileen Watkins of 6 Gibson Road, Lambeth."

"What a remarkable coincidence," I said.

"Coincidence? The matter may be beyond coincidence."

"In what way?"

Holmes didn't answer. Instead, he stared into the middle distance contemplating his discovery. Just then, Mr. Male returned.

"Did you find anything of interest, Mr. Holmes?" he asked.

"Yes," said my friend, "but inevitably it has led to a further point of enquiry. Would it be possible to access the recruitment papers of an individual soldier – Two soldiers, in fact."

His question was met with a stunned silence. It was clear Mr. Male was torn between acceded to the request of someone he believed to be Mycroft Holmes, senior government official, and the logistics involved in identifying individual soldiers among the hundreds of thousands recruited in the previous two years.

"There are a lot of papers to wade through, Mr. Holmes," was all the poor man could offer.

"I understand that Mr. Male," said Holmes, ignoring the mild-mannered protestation and writing down the information he wanted, "but it is of the utmost importance. A man's life may depend on it."

"Which regiment are they in?" asked Male with a sigh as he took the piece of paper.

"The Lambeth Pals. I would imagine they would be attached to the London Regiment."

"Yes, quite probably. Being local men, we should be able to access the regimental records and, assuming they are categorised in alphabetical order, we may have some luck."

"When could you have the information available?" asked Holmes, ignoring Male's reference to the element of good fortune.

The official referred to the piece of paper. "I will get one of my men on it straight away. If we can locate the records of the battalion they are attached to, we may have something for you by tomorrow afternoon."

"Splendid, Mr. Male, thank you. My colleague here – " He indicated to myself, whom I noted he had never introduced throughout our time with the War Office official. " – will come by and pick them up at two o'clock."

With that, we left the strained official to that and his many other duties.

"Are we going to Lambeth now?" I asked as we left.

"No, I think that's for tomorrow," replied Holmes. "There is little we can do there today. Instead, I think we shall return to the hospital, update our erstwhile page, and test a theory at the same time."

We found Billy and his accused friend sitting up in their beds, having just received a cup of tea from the nurse.

"Mr. Holmes! Doctor Watson!" cried Billy with great enthusiasm, as we entered. "Have you had any luck?"

"A little," said Holmes. "We hope to identify the killer of Silas Emery very soon."

"That's excellent news, eh John?" he said turning to his friend.

"Yes," said the young lad.

"Tell me, Private Watkins," Holmes said, "has Inspector Styles made any further visits since we spoke?"

"No, sir," he replied.

"He has obviously made no further progress in his enquiries then," Holmes said, almost to himself.

He then addressed the patient again. "One other thing – " He took a pencil and a piece of paper from his pocket and handed it over. "Could you give me the address of this Silas Whoever-he-Was character?"

"Yes, sir," said Watkins, taking the offering. "Emery was his name."

"Yes, of course. Emery. I would like to visit the location of the alleged crime to see if that could throw any further light on the matter."

Watkins spoke as he wrote. "*Silas Emery, No. 46 Kennington Road.*"

"Tell me, Private Watkins: Did you have any dealings with this man before his death."

"No, sir."

"Thank you. I shall update you further on our progress as soon as there is something to report."

I had put in a further three hours work at the hospital the following day before lunch. Afterwards, I carried out Holmes's instruction of enquiring at the War Office to see if the papers he asked for were available. It so happened that Mr. Male was near the front desk when I arrived.

"Ah, er . . ." he said, recognising me, but realising that we hadn't been introduced. ". . . I have found the information Mr. Holmes was looking for."

He reached down behind the desk and brought out a large envelope containing some papers.

"Thank you," I said, taking them from him. "I'm sure Mr. Holmes will find them of great use."

Without inspecting the contents, I took them directly to the Pall Mall lodgings where Holmes was staying. There was no sign of his brother and, judging by the poisonous atmosphere of the sitting room, it appeared as though Holmes had been sitting smoking all morning.

"Good Heavens, Holmes! It's as thick as a river fog in here. I can barely see you!"

"I suppose it is rather thick," he said, apparently oblivious to the foul environment.

"Here are the papers you asked for," I said, laying them down on the table beside his chair and going over to open a window.

Holmes didn't say anything, but opened the envelope.

"As I suspected," he said quietly.

"To whom do they refer?" I asked.

"They're the recruitment papers and medical reports on James and John Watkins."

"What did you want them for?"

He handed them to me. "Tell me what you see."

I studied the papers for a few minutes.

"They seem fairly regular to me: Names, address, age, physical condition."

Holmes handed me the piece of paper he had taken from Private Watkins the previous day.

"And now?"

I referred to the paper that had the address of Silas Emery written on it and compared it to the official army documents.

"Yes, this writing appears to match one set of the documents."

"Indeed, it does," said Holmes. "I think we should visit Private Watkins's family."

"What will they be able to tell us that we don't know already?"

"Not very much, I would suggest. Perhaps their role would be to listen rather than speak."

Chapter IV

It was a pleasant late summer afternoon as we crossed the river once more. In Gibson Road, a group of children were playing in the street with an old bicycle wheel rim that had been stripped of its tyre. A woman was on her hands and knees scrubbing her front step, while a couple of neighbours were passing the time of day on the other side of the road. As I looked down the street, it occurred to me how the brilliant blue sky was in marked contrast to the blackened buildings and deprived streets of impoverished London . . . and the fact that a few hundred miles south of where we stood – across the Channel – thousands of men were fighting in a war many knew little about. My thoughts were broken as something knocked lightly against my ankle – it was the wheel rim the children had been rolling between each other."

"Sorry, Mister!" said a small boy as he ran over to retrieve it.

"That's quite all right, young man," I said, smiling at the innocence of these children, shielded as they were from the injustices and difficulties of the adult world. "Enjoy your game."

The boy returned to his friends and joined them once again in their own imaginary world. Meanwhile, I followed Holmes as we prepared to continue in our own very *real* one. He knocked on the door of No. 6.

"They aren't in!" cried one of the neighbours from across the street.

"Is it Mr. and Mrs. Watkins who live here?" asked Holmes, going over.

"Yes, that's right," said the woman as her friend disappeared into her own house. "They've gone to see their lad who's in hospital."

"Yes, Private Watkins," said Holmes. "That's what we wanted to speak with them about. We were talking to him only yesterday. It's so sad about his brother."

It was clear that Holmes had pricked the curiosity of the woman, who was now fully engaged and apparently keen to find out what our business was.

"Lovely boys they are," she said. "Both work with their dad down at the coal yard."

"Yes. Do you know if they have been gone long?"

"About an hour or so, I would imagine. Do you want me to pass a message on?"

"We're from the War Office and have some of their son's belongings – the one who was so sadly killed. We had called to return them."

I felt Holmes's fabrication was rather distasteful, but I had known him long enough to realise that, as far as he was concerned, every action was a means to an end. The woman knew nothing of the deceit, of course, and her eyes widened at Holmes's comment in anticipation of valuable gossip.

"Perhaps you'd like to come in and wait. They shouldn't be too long."

"Oh, that's very kind," said Holmes without looking at me for approval.

We followed the woman into a humble living area where a man was sitting reading a newspaper.

"Here, George," she said. "Sit up straight. These gentlemen are 'ere from the War Office."

"Blimey!" he cried. "You 'aven't come to recruit me, 'ave you?"

"No, they aren't that 'ard up!" said the woman, laughing. "They're 'ere to see the Watkins about their lad."

"Yes," said the man, bowing his head in sorrow. "I'd 'eard that one of them had been killed."

"Lovely lads they were," agreed his wife. "John and Jim, they're like peas in a pod."

"Yes, it's a terrible business," said Holmes.

"A good family like that an' all," said the man. "They've 'ad their fair share of problems."

"Really?" asked my friend, sensing the couple's propensity for gossip.

"Well, it wasn't long ago that poor Eddie – the father that is – got a good 'iding on his way 'ome from the pub."

"Oh, yes, we've heard about that," said Holmes, seeing an opportunity to probe for more information. "Wasn't it suggested that it was in connection with that money lender?" He furrowed his brow in mock ignorance. "What was his name again?"

"Emery," said the man.

"Yes, of course, Emery. I read something about his murder in the newspaper."

The improbability of an official from the War Office knowing the details of a local man being beaten up didn't occur to the couple who were clearly more intent on gossip-mongering.

"I believe the man Emery loaned money to many in need?" asked Holmes.

"Yes. Evil man 'e was. Nobody mourned 'is loss around here. Most people loaned money from 'im. The 'arder things became following the outbreak of the war, the tighter the grip 'e had on the place. Wasn't afraid to set 'is dogs on people either," added the old man.

"His dogs?"

"Well, 'is 'enchmen that is. 'E had a gang of ruffians who could get nasty when people were late with their repayments."

"And did you ever fall victim to these 'dogs'?"

"Thankfully I didn't," he said. "I always made sure I paid back what I borrowed. Others weren't quite so lucky, mind you – Eddie Watkins being a prime example. Reckon 'e was late with 'is payments and got a terrible 'iding for his troubles."

"Tell me, Mr. – er . . . ?"

"Roper. Call me George."

"Tell us, George: Can you remember when this incident involving Eddie Watkins took place?"

Our host thought for a while. "Yes, I can," he said, snapping his fingers in recollection. "It was just before those lads came back from their training." He thought a little more. "That's right. The young lads in the Lambeth Pals were away doing their basic training when Eddie was set upon. When their training was done, the lads all came back briefly to say their goodbyes before being shipped over to the front. It was just after they left that news of Emery's murder came out. Then we all got the money delivered by some guardian angel."

"Money?" asked Holmes.

"Yes. The whole street had an envelope pushed through the door a day or two later. In it was the money we all paid Emery. It was funny really because the initials *G.R.* were on the back, and everyone thought it had come from me!"

I remembered the man in the pub referring to this. Holmes ignored the point.

"And you're sure this *after* the battalion left for France?" he asked.

"Yes, I'm sure. There was a bit of a parade to send the boys off on the Sunday, and it was a day or two after that when we received our money and 'eard about Emery."

Holmes rose. "Mr. and Mrs. Roper, I think we should be leaving. Perhaps we could try the Watkins family another time. Thank you for your help and hospitality."

As we were leaving, we saw the door close at No. 6. It was clear that the Watkins family had just returned from visiting their son.

"We seem to be in luck after all," said Holmes, indicating that we cross the street.

"Mr. Watkins, is it?" he asked the man who answered the door a few moments later.

The man was still levering himself out of his coat. Despite the fact that several weeks had passed since his beating, he still had a sticking plaster across the bridge of his nose and above one eye that appeared to be gradually recovering its shape after presumably being completely closed. He looked at us suspiciously.

"Who are you?"

"My name is Sherlock Holmes. This is my friend and colleague, Doctor Watson. We're looking into the matter of the murder of Silas Emery, and the possibility of it being committed by one of the Lambeth Pals."

The man appeared nervous. "Are you the police?"

"No. We were asked to look into the matter by a friend of your son who, like him, is currently in hospital. And may I also express my sincere condolences regarding the loss of your other son in the fighting."

Watkins never said anything.

"May we come in?" asked Holmes. "It would be easier to speak inside."

Reluctantly, the man stepped aside and allowed us to enter. His tenement was a mirror image of the one belonging to Mr. and Mrs. Roper across the road.

"This is my wife, Sarah, and daughter, Eileen," said Watkins as the two women came through from the kitchen to see what the occurrence was. "These men have come to ask about Emery and the boys."

Mrs. Watkins gave a look of concern.

"I assure you, Madam, that we are not he police. Nor are we retained by them to supply their deficiencies. What we say here will remain between us."

Mrs. Watkins reddened, but never said anything.

Holmes continued. "We were asked by the friend your son saved – the young man beside him in the hospital – to look into the police's investigation into the death of Silas Emery, and the subsequent questioning of your son regarding the matter."

Neither of the lad's parents said anything. It was as though they knew something of the issue, but were reluctant to divulge what it was until Holmes revealed his hand. My friend therefore obliged.

"This young man was our page when my friend and I shared lodgings in Baker Street many years ago. It grieved us both to see him now – still with his life ahead of him – in such a paltry condition. If we feel that about him, we cannot begin to imagine what you must be going through, having lost one son, and now having the other suspected of the most serious of crimes. When Billy told us about the heroics demonstrated by your son on the battlefield, we were only too pleased to help. Can I ask if either of you have been questioned by the police regarding the murder?"

"No," said the man of the house.

"That is good," said Holmes. "For once, I think we can rejoice in the deficiencies of our friends from Scotland Yard. Tell me, Mr. Watkins: Where did you get that bruising on your face?"

"I . . . I had an accident at work."

"It's been suggested to me that you were beaten up on your way home some weeks ago. Before your two boys left for France in fact."

The man didn't reply. Holmes then turned his attention to Watkins's daughter.

"Would I be correct in stating that you work in the stationery stores at the Lambeth warehouse, Miss Watkins?"

It looked as though Miss Watkins's mind was racing. "Yes," she said at last, apparently wondering what else Holmes knew.

Instead of continuing his questioning, Holmes instead indicated to a photograph that stood on the mantel. It was of the two Watkins boys. They stood side by side, in full uniform and in perfect symmetry, with their rifle butts in the crook of their elbows.

"Two fine lads, Mrs. Watkins. You must be so proud."

Mrs. Watkins followed Holmes's gaze and began to sob into a handkerchief. "Yes," whispered.

The boys were indeed alike, indistinguishable to any but their immediate family and friends. Much to my surprise, Holmes drew the meeting to a close.

"I don't think there is a need to prolong the matter any further," he said. "If the police haven't been here by now, I think your son's secret is safe. Be assured that neither my friend nor myself have any intention of divulging it to anyone else. We will bid you good day and, once again, express our deepest condolences for your loss."

I followed Holmes out of the Watkins's residence, somewhat baffled by the events of the afternoon. Strangely, however, I noticed that none of the Watkins family showed any emotion – anger, shock, offence – at my

421

friend's apparently haphazard questioning. The sun had faded to the point where there was a slight chill in the air. It seemed to reflect Holmes's mood. He sat in silence with his eyes closed as we travelled back to his brother's lodgings. It was only when the maid served us some tea that I questioned my friend on his strange behaviour.

"I must confess, I'm not sure I really understand your approached to investigating this case."

"It is a sad situation," was his melancholic reply, as he stared into the fire.

"Do you think you will be able to clear young Watkins's name?"

He looked up from the flames. "That *is* the sad situation."

In response to my furrowed brow and slight shake of the head, he explained.

"The description the police have of their suspect is that it was a man in uniform who had a shock of blond hair. Our man and his brother therefore both fit the description, which puts them both under suspicion."

"Along with potentially thousands of other soldiers who are moving through London at the moment," I added.

"Quite. But most of them have little knowledge of, or dealings with, the Lambeth money lender. We need, therefore, to explore a motive and the chronological sequence of events. Emery was killed during the period between when the Lambeth Battalion returned from their training camp, but before they left for France. It was also during this period that Mr. Watkins was beaten up by Emery's gang."

"I'm not sure I like what you're hinting at."

My friend ignored my interruption. "Days after the murder, the people in the area all received money anonymously. It was for the exact amount they had paid to Silas Emery. Whoever murdered the scoundrel also took the money from his house and arranged for it to be returned to whom he saw as its rightful owner."

"Hardly the act of a heartless villain," I said.

"Precisely. But if it was one of the Lambeth Pals who committed the murder, he must have had an accomplice, as the battalion left for France the day after the murder. And yet, the money wasn't delivered until the following day."

"The envelopes . . ." I said, almost to myself.

"Exactly, Watson. The envelopes. They were all marked *G.R.*"

"*George Rex*. Government issue."

"And who had access to government issue stationery?" He didn't wait for my reply. "Miss Watkins, the sister of the two boys, who works at the Lambeth warehouse."

"If it was one of the Watkins twins," I said, "and I stress, *if it was one,* then which one? There is no proof, other than an uncorroborated claim that a blond-haired soldier was in the area at the time."

Holmes thought for a while. "The police clearly haven't made the links in the chain that we have. I think we shall visit young Watkins in the morning, when I will share my theory with him and see what his reaction is."

When we arrived at Guy's the following day, we found Billy – despite his injuries and dreadful experiences – in his usual disposition of eagerness and excitement.

"Have you solved the case, Mr. Holmes?" he asked as we appeared.

"I think we have, Billy," Holmes replied in a more subdued tone. "I wonder if it is possible to speak with your friend here alone."

Private Watkins expression had been ambivalent during the brief exchange. Holmes turned to me. "Watson, could you use your influence to find a quiet room somewhere?"

I left briefly and found a nurse who – once I had explained the need to speak privately with a patient – kindly gave us permission to use a small office to the rear of the busy nurses' station, where a constant flow of patients was being checked in and out. I returned to the ward with a wheelchair and we helped Watkins into it and wheeled him into the room.

"Could I get you a glass of water?" I asked as we sat down beside him.

"No, sir, I'm fine," he replied, continuing to look at his lap.

"You have no need to fear us, Private Watkins," said Holmes. "We aren't the police, and we are neither here to condemn or convict. But we are here to share some information with you. I speak for my friend Watson here when I say that what is said in this room will never be repeated elsewhere. I therefore believe that no action will be taken against you or your sister."

It was at the mention of his sister that caused the young man to look up.

"I believe I know what happened before you went to France. Your father, like so many of your neighbours – borrowed money from Emery – money he was either late or unable to pay back. For this, he received a severe beating from Emery's gang of villains. When you and your brother returned from your training camp to find your father in such a condition, you took matters into your own hands, believing that you had nothing to lose, given that you were going to the Western Front. You went to Emery's home, probably gained entry by suggesting you were there to settle your father's debt, and, once inside, you stabbed him with your bayonet –

removed from your rifle and discreetly hidden in the inside of your tunic. Presumably, you then searched the premises and discovered a ledger listing the money paid to him by his debtors. Further searching uncovered his store of funds. You took the monies paid to him by your friends and neighbours. You then took your sister Eileen into your confidence and, after you had left for France, she pushed the money through the doors in envelopes she had taken from her place of work."

Watkins didn't challenge any of Holmes's narrative, but for the first time, he looked at my friend in the eye. His look wasn't one of defiance, but neither was it one that showed any regret. I decided to clarify a point of my own.

"Even if the police do follow your process, Holmes, and come to the same conclusion, there is no way of proving which of these two boys murdered Emery."

"You're right, Watson. Scotland Yard has crudely resorted to questioning every blond-haired soldier returning from the front. I think we'll allow them to continue such an approach, it will sadly become increasingly overwhelming, as more young men are shipped back."

He turned back to Watkins. "As I said earlier, your secrets are safe with us. I can only hope you'll learn to live with the violence and tragedy you have experienced in your short life. And if you do, I believe you will be living with it under your brother's identity." I turned and looked at Holmes in amazement. He added, "You aren't *John* Watkins, but *Jim* Watkins."

For the first time, the young man opened up on the subject. "When we got to France, I told John what I had done. He said if we got out of that hell-hole and the police found out, I would hang. He therefore said that if he didn't make it, I should assume his identity, his thinking being that if the police did discover that *Jim* Watkins killed Emery, they couldn't touch him 'cause *Jim* Watkins would be lying dead in France."

At this, the young man broke down and wept – wept at the thought of his brother's sacrifice.

"Your brother was an honourable man, Private Watkins . . . as are you. We don't condemn you for your actions."

We allowed the young man to compose himself before wheeling him back to his bed and assuring the ever-enthusiastic Billy that the matter was now resolved.

"A desperately sad case, Watson," said my friend as we travelled back to Pall Mall.

"Yes, I agreed. "How did you know about the brothers' change of identity?"

"Young Watkins overplayed his hand and gave the police too much credit regarding their investigative skills. He returned to England as *John* Watkins, but when I asked him to write down Emery's address and then compared the handwriting to that of the recruitment forms, it was clear it was the writing of *Jim* Watkins. That of John was the distinctive crab-like style of a *left*-hander. I don't believe it was necessary for the boys to do this, as the police don't have the wit, the wherewithal, or the resources to work out the identity of the killer."

"But why then did he ask you to get involved?"

Holmes looked at me. "He didn't! If you recall, it was our erstwhile page who couldn't contain his natural enthusiasm when he saw you. At no point did young Watkins ask for our help. Little did *he* know that the man he saved on the battlefield was the same man who was inadvertently putting his own life in danger by getting us involved."

"Of course, poor chap." I thought for a while longer. "A few months ago, he was nothing more than a lad going about his business. Now, he will have to carry this around with him for the rest of his life."

"Indeed. What reaction might you expect when you take a boy and train him to be a cold-blooded killer, and then send him home for the weekend before he ships out? I'm sure, had this happened before the war, no murder would have occurred."

"Now he and his family will keep their secret between them and no one else will ever know."

"Yes. It's difficult to know who should be called a victim in the whole sorry affair."

"Now Comes the Mystery"
by Brett Fawcett

"Frederick Sander's *Reichenbachia: Orchids Illustrated and Described* was published in London from 1888-1894. It is considered by many to be the greatest illustrated work on orchids ever published . . . *Reichenbachia* was named in honor of Heinrich Gustav Reichenbach, a well-known German orchidologist."
– Beth Monroe
Public Relations and Marketing Director,
Lewis Ginter Botanical Garden

"Regular Anglican Services in Meiringen were started for British tourists in 1850. The English Church was built in the garden of Hotel Sauvage in 1868 and visited by Queen Victoria in the same year . . . Destroyed by fire in 1891, a new church was constructed on the same site . . . [It] is currently used to house The Sherlock Holmes Museum."
– Paul Schniewind
Anglicans in Switzerland, Past and Present

"The ways of Fate are indeed hard to understand. If there is not some compensation hereafter, then the world is a cruel jest."
– Sherlock Holmes
"The Adventure of the Veiled Lodger"

"Now comes the mystery."
– Henry Ward Beecher's last words

Sussex, November 1917

Two letters lay on the table before Sherlock Holmes that morning.

Both had come from British Military Intelligence. One, sent from Mycroft's office, was written by a "*Henry M.*", Mycroft's right-hand man. The letter had arrived in a thick envelope which also contained three photographs. In it, "*M*" outlined the evidence that one of the three men in these pictures was providing munitions materiel to German spies in England through dummy corporations. Would Holmes be so good as to review the evidence and provide his opinion on who was the most likely suspect?

Holmes's grey eyes that had penetrated so many dark mysteries skimmed over the letter again. It provided a detailed explanation of everything that "*M*" considered to be relevant evidence.

He felt himself growing irritated. His back hurt from some recent beekeeping work on his farm – which was happening more frequently as he grew older – and reading this retinue of "evidence" only made his mood worse. To Holmes, it was mostly a heap of irrelevant trivialities. If he *did* choose to solve this case, he'd need to look for evidence elsewhere.

He looked at the photographs again: The round, bearded, eager-looking face of the London-based financial speculator Arthur Farebrother, the thin, sharp-featured, clean-shaven face of the Swiss banker Conrad Trollinger, whose high eyebrows gave him a supercilious look, and the irritated, wolf-like, moustached face of the French merchant Napoleon Lamar. With a grunt, Holmes looked away and picked up the other letter.

It was from his nephew, Siger, [1] son of his older brother, Sherrinford. The young man worked as a codebreaker for the British Government in Room 40. His letter also asked Holmes a question, but his query was of a rather different nature.

> *Dear Uncle Sherlock,*
>
> *[. . .]*
>
> *You will remember that, ten years ago, I followed your lead into the profession of consulting detection. When the war began, I had to leave my practice behind when Uncle Mycroft recruited me to solve the micro-mysteries of espionage.*
>
> *I anticipate this war to end within the year. Although I sense British Intelligence's anxious desire to keep me on when this is all over, I find myself again attracted to taking up consulting detective work similar to your own, which will come as no surprise to you. And, since I'm one who likes to plan ahead – one learns that from playing chess – I'm also thinking about what I'll do once I retire from* that *work.*
>
> *[. . .]*
>
> *I've always been intrigued that you retired from detection – rather early in life, all things considered, if I may make so bold as to say – and chose beekeeping as the focus of your attention.*
>
> *Would you be willing to share a bit about why you chose to retire when you did, and how you chose that particular pursuit to occupy yourself with in your leisurely latter life?*
>
> *Consider your answer to be a bit of avuncular counsel to one who is discerning his mission in this world.*

427

Holmes stared at the letter for a full minute. His irritation had evaporated. Something about the language of that last sentence triggered a memory which pulled him out of his bee farm and threw him back many decades.

The inky words on the page before him began to bustle and cluster in his imagination and slowly transformed into a swarm of bumblebees as memories flooded into his mind . . . .

Yorkshire, Summer 1867

Yes, it was a great swarm of bumblebees he saw, all busily at work flitting from and climbing into flower after flower in the bright sunshine.

Thirteen-year-old Sherlock Holmes sat on the grass watching them. His face looked melancholy and thoughtful. Next to him, in full ecclesiastical garb, was a scholarly but kindly-looking priest with an aquiline nose. This was the boy's godfather, Sabine Baring-Gould. [2]

The lad was in the process of recovering from a severe illness, and his clerical godfather had come to visit. One reason for this was so that he could keep Sherlock company. Another reason (one that was never stated aloud) was that, if things took a turn for the worse, Sherlock's parents wanted to have someone on hand who could promptly perform the office of anointing the sick.

"There's a bluebell," Baring-Gould murmured, pointing at the flower patch, "and that purple plant there is a particularly lovely Southern marsh orchid."

Baring-Gould would later be described by historians as the last man who knew everything. His friendly but distractible personality, which often caused him to appear absent-minded or even naive, concealed the fact that he carried around an incredible amount of information in his memory. The way that knowledge could spill out of him at times struck some people as mere chattering, but Sherlock always responded well to it.

"Ah, and that's an *alba maxima*," he continued, "the white rose of York, Bonnie Prince Charlie's Jacobite flower, and the longest living of all roses. It can last for up to fifteen years."

"But, after fifteen years, it dies," Sherlock said gloomily.

Baring-Gould turned and gave the boy a long, meaningful look.

"Are you afraid you might stop existing after your death?" he finally said in a quiet voice.

Sherlock looked startled. The boy had no idea how Baring-Gould had deduced this, since he had kept his recent religious doubts extremely private. Church was deeply important to his mother, Violet, and she saw

428

great significance in the fact that Sherlock had been born on January 6th, the Feast of the Epiphany, which commemorated a star leading the wise men to Jesus.

Baring-Gould smiled reassuringly. "I saw Winwood Reade's *The Martyrdom of Man* at your bedside," he explained. The priest cleared his throat and closed his eyes to concentrate. He then quoted the book's conclusion:

> *The following facts result from our investigations: Supernatural Christianity is false. God-worship is idolatry. Prayer is useless. The soul is not immortal. There are no rewards and there are no punishments in a future state.*

He opened his eyes. "It's quite a dreary view of the world, isn't it? But perhaps it's a possibility that troubles you, all the same."

Sherlock shuffled uncomfortably. It was true. Ever since he'd read Reade, whenever he thought about death, it appeared to him, not as a blissful paradise, but as a kind of suffocating endless darkness, an unending, flailing plunge into a terrifying and merciless black emptiness.

"I've learned my catechism," he said. "You've taught it well. But my talent is observation, and only the material world – the empirical – can be observed. If something is not empirical, I . . . struggle with it. And I don't know what empirical evidence there is for an afterlife."

"My boy, you're looking at it now."

Sherlock looked at Baring-Gould with surprise. The priest was leaning over a flower with a curious but pleased expression.

"Could it be? Why, yes, that's a delightful specimen of bird's-eye primrose! – Ah, yes, well, you have expressed interest in *investigation* of crime, no? The word *investigate* comes from *vestigium*, meaning '*footprint*'. To investigate is to recognize and follow footprints. St. Bonaventure said that creation is covered with God's *vestiges*. We can recognize His footprints everywhere." He gestured at the bees and flowers before them. "So let us *investigate* these particular footprints.

"If the bees do not pollinate, the flowers will die. But they will die without propagating. Death without pollination brings their existence to utter finality – much like Reade's view of *our* death. *The Book of Job* talks this way somewhat: '*Man that is born of a woman is of few days and full of trouble. He cometh forth like a flower, and is cut down: He fleeth also as a shadow, and continueth not.*'

"But pollination, the work of bees, results in new life for the flowers. Their nectar nourishes the bees. The bees, in turn, propagate the flowers.

There is a grand design that shows the workings of a master intelligence behind it all.

"And Mr. Darwin's speculations do not discredit any of this. In the preface to *The Origin of Species*, he acknowledges that death and suffering are what give rise to new life, and that this is all the purpose of God."

Baring-Gould again closed his eyes to concentrate on his quotation:

> *Thus, from the war of nature, from famine and death, the most exalted object which we are capable of conceiving, namely, the production of the higher animals, directly follows. There is grandeur in this view of life, with its several powers, having been originally breathed by the Creator into a few forms or into one.*

"In other words, the survival of the fittest means that out of suffering, war, and death come new life, as part of the Creator's design.

"We can see all this in what God has written in *The Book of Nature*. And, in *The Book of Scripture*, we find that the grotesque suffering and death of Christ was prelude to His resurrection, and ours. [3] Yes, God's plan involves death, and pain, but death leads to new life, and we learn and grow through pain."

"But – is it a good plan, if it involves so much death and pain?"

"Nothing is more certain! We can see the goodness of it in beauty, especially the beauty of the flowers, such as this lovely buttercup . . . ." Baring-Gould crouched to examine a yellow flower from which a bee had just flown.

"But isn't beauty subjective?" Not every schoolboy would have asked the questions that Sherlock Holmes was asking, but Baring-Gould was used to this from him. "Different cultures have different aesthetics. How can we say something like a mountain is truly beautiful, and not simply that it elicits beautiful feelings in me?"

"Yes, certainly a meadow buttercup!" Baring-Gould remarked with glee before turning back to Sherlock.

"When a necklace is stolen," he explained, "three different policemen may have three different views of who the thief is, all based on the same evidence. Does the fact that they differ in their interpretations mean there is no correct interpretation? In the same way, the fact that some people disagree about what is beautiful does not mean beauty does not exist.

"Look at those flowers. If someone told you they were not beautiful, would you truly believe this is just a difference of opinion, or would you conclude that person was objectively wrong? I would suggest the same of music, and there is a reason musicians often have a kind of spirituality that

430

radiates from their countenance – because they are constantly participating in the production of beauty.

"And, of course, one cannot discount the evidence of love. Love is tied up with beauty. Love either creates beauty in the other – this is the case with God's love for us – or it is a response to beauty, either physical, intellectual, or moral, in another." A dreamy look passed over Baring-Gould's face as he thought about Grace Taylor, the woman he hoped to one day marry. "Our senses tell us about the objective truth of the material world, but love tells us about the objective spiritual truth of beauty. You'll know it if you ever fall in love yourself."

Sherlock frowned. "But how does this prove immortality?"

"We can tell there is a cosmic plan, and we can tell from the existence of beauty that it is a good plan. That means death and suffering must serve towards some good purpose and have some higher outcome.

"Yet, in this life, we do not always see a just or beautiful resolution to violence and sorrow. That means that the resolution to it all must exist in some other world than this one, '*a new heavens and a new earth wherein dwelleth righteousness*'. There, those souls who suffered unjustly will be rewarded, and those who escaped justice in this life will be punished. All will stand before the just Judge – which is why it's so important to carry out the mission God has for us in *this* world so that we can give a good account of how we used our lives when *we* are judged.

Baring-Gould plucked a bluebell and sniffed it deeply. The smile on his face was one of transcendent, almost beatific peacefulness.

"Do you understand?" he asked gently.

The boy nodded silently and resumed looking closely at the flowers.

Oxford, 1874

During his first year at Christ Church College, Holmes had become engrossed in chemical research. He debated whether he wanted to become a purely theoretical chemist and lecturer in chemistry or whether he would use chemistry for practical purposes, perhaps as in an industrial context. His youthful curiosity about crime solving had been almost completely forgotten.

Early one morning during his second year, Holmes was pondering this on his way to chapel. Christ Church Cathedral is unique: It is not only the diocesan cathedral, but it also provides daily chapel services to the college. It is a large, looming structure, and Holmes was able to see its cross-topped steeple from a ways off.

As he looked at the cross, he thought of Baring-Gould's counsel to him. He would be accountable to God for however he used his abilities once he left Christ Church. It wasn't something to take lightly, or to make a mistake about.

Holmes sighed and offered a brief prayer asking for a sign to guide him in the direction he should go. He didn't like offering these kinds of prayers. After all, how could one be sure what was a legitimate divine answer and what was a meaningless coincidence? He took another breath and added another petition: *Make the sign unmistakably clear to me.*

Before he could even finish this thought, Holmes heard aggressive barking that sounded as if it came from a small dog. Turning towards the sound, he saw a bull terrier charging towards him and a worried-looking young man chasing after it.

The fierce dog's destination was unmistakable. It headed right for Holmes.

Before he had a chance to react, the dog's teeth sank into Holmes's ankle.

The pain was incredible, and Holmes was laid up in his rooms for the next ten days. During that time, the young man, who had been the creature's owner, often visited him to offer condolences. His name was Victor Trevor. Appreciative of his solicitude, Holmes came to befriend Trevor.

That summer, Holmes visited Trevor's home in Norfolk and met his father, a Justice of the Peace. Simply by looking at him, Holmes was able to deduce that the senior Trevor was a former boxer who had done much digging in his youth, had visited New Zealand and Japan, had recently been in fear of his life, and who had been associated with someone with the initials "*J.A.*" whom he now wished to forget.

Mr. Trevor was so flabbergasted by this string of inferences, particularly the last deduction, that he collapsed into a faint. When he recovered, he told Holmes, "I don't know how you manage this, Mr. Holmes, but it seems to me that all the detectives of fact and of fancy would be children in your hands. That's your line of life, sir, and you may take the word of a man who has seen something of the world."

The instant he heard this, all Holmes's youthful ideas about becoming a solver of crimes floated from the subconscious where they had been buried and bubbled up to the top of his mind. He couldn't stop thinking about this suggestion, and, by the end of the summer, his vocation was clear to him. As he set out from Norfolk, Holmes realised that God had, indeed, immediately sent an answer to the prayer he had offered on his way to chapel.

It took a painful bite from a dog for Holmes to learn his mission, but, as Baring-Gould had said, "We learn and grow through pain."

Hopefully, thought Holmes, *that will be the last time I have an alarming supernatural encounter with a vicious dog.*

Initially, Holmes's study of detection was built on this religious foundation. The basis of his empirical method was the theological idea that the universe was a book that could be read, and the monograph he wrote on scientific observation and inference bore the Biblically-inspired title *The Book of Life.*

But after he set up his detective practice in Montague Street, which later moved to Baker Street, such devotional life as he had began to slip. When one was looking at a bloody corpse, what mattered was chemistry, biology, and, sometimes, psychology. Study of Scripture didn't seem especially relevant in this bleak world.

Further, the more gruesome violence, crime, and corruption he encountered, the harder it was to believe in a meaning to it all. Christ's crucifixion, the ultimate example of God drawing a positive outcome from a seemingly pointless murder and injustice, still glowed dimly in the back of his mind, but it was obscured by the thickening darkness of human misery he encountered nearly every day.

In practice, the transcendent and the supernatural faded from Holmes's mental world. Perhaps the best that could be hoped for was to eke out some measure of justice in this life.

That meant that, when he wasn't at work, life seemed rather dreary, especially when his intellect had no problems to wrestle with. Before long, he turned to cocaine to deal with this *ennui.*

By the mid-1880's, Holmes had begun to notice similarities between different crimes. What seemed like random, unconnected lawbreaking and anarchy to the police was, to Holmes, evidence of a great controlling intelligence behind it all.

The thought occurred to him that this was just like what Baring-Gould had said: The workings of the natural world showed evidence of God's overseeing wisdom. But Holmes had discovered vestiges of an intelligence that was malevolent and evil in the underbelly of society. In contrast, the footprints of the universe, such as flowers, proved that *its* mastermind was benevolent and good.

Encouraging as that thought was, it didn't seem relevant to his work, so Holmes shoved it from his mind. For now, what was important was that he dealt crime a severe blow by defeating the Napoleon who ruled over it.

The first step was to identify who this Napoleon was. Soon, he had a suspect: Professor James Moriarty, mathematician and author of *The Dynamics of an Asteroid.* The challenge now was to prove it.

May 1887

The freshly married Watson [4] had bought a medical practice in the Paddington district from Dr. Farquhar and returned to his profession. In May, the King of Bohemia, who was engaged to be married to a Scandinavian princess, approached Holmes about the American actress Irene Adler, with whom he had once been involved and who was blackmailing him with a photograph of them both that he gave her during their relationship.

As part of his investigation, Holmes disguised himself as a groom and found himself in St. Monica's Church, watching Adler marry the lawyer Godfrey Norton – a much nobler man than the king. It was Holmes's first time in a church in some time, and something affected him about witnessing this sacrament of love taking place. Moreover, it was clear even from this brief encounter that Adler was an impressive and formidable woman. He could tell what the king saw in her.

To get into her home and ascertain the location of the photograph, Holmes disguised himself as a simple-minded Nonconformist clergyman. Perhaps being in the church gave him the idea. He got into character by mimicking his godfather, another clergyman who sometimes came off as absent-minded and amiable. Doing so made him reflect, once again, on that pivotal conversation they had shared twenty years before.

In this disguise, Holmes pretended to have been injured so that Adler would bring him into her home to help him. There, he successfully determined where the photograph was hidden. However, when he came to collect the photograph the following day, Adler had already departed. Holmes found a note addressed to him from Adler with another photograph: She had deduced that the clergyman was actually him, and had even followed Holmes in disguise. The letter concluded:

I remain, my dear Mr. Sherlock Holmes, very truly yours,

Irene Norton, née *Adler*

It wasn't the first time Holmes had recognized the limits of his intellect. He had also been humbled in the case of the yellow face. While it stung, he appreciated the rebuke to his pride. He knew the dangers of hubris. (He hoped Moriarty did not.)

But this was different. There was another emotion involved, or rather a mixture of emotions. Admiration. Affection. Even longing.

434

It was painful. But he somehow felt wiser from it. After all, "we learn and grow through pain."

In his account of the story, Watson had said that the emotion Holmes felt for Adler was not love.

But, if this wasn't love, then what was it?

7 January, 1888

One of Holmes's greatest breakthroughs in his campaign against Moriarty came as a birthday present.

On the morning after Holmes's thirty-fourth birthday, "Fred Porlock", an alias for one of Moriarty's agents, sent Holmes a coded message warning him about an upcoming plan of Moriarty's. The message consisted of a series of numbers, which Holmes deduced referred to pages and words in a particular text. The question then became *which* text. It must be, Holmes inferred, "a large book, printed in double columns and in common use."

"The Bible!" Watson exclaimed.

"Good, Watson, good! But not, if I may say so, quite good enough! Even if I accepted the compliment for myself, I could hardly name any volume which would be less likely to lie at the elbow of one of Moriarty's associates."

Saying this aloud made Holmes reflect momentarily on how long it had been since *he* had read the Bible. The fact that inattention to Scripture was something he had in common with Moriarty and his gang gave him pause.

Instead, the book was the almanack, and Holmes was able to deduce that Moriarty meant to do harm to someone named Douglas. While that case initially seemed to end happily, with Douglas' life being saved, two months later Holmes received a telegraph from Moriarty himself: "*Dear me, Mr. Holmes, dear me!*" Shortly afterwards, he heard the news that Moriarty had finished the job, and Douglas had been killed after all.

That was the situation, Holmes realised: If you stood in Moriarty's way, he would kill you.

And the largest obstruction in Moriarty's way was himself.

All the fears and anxieties of that childhood illness came back to him. He knew he was now walking alongside the Valley of the Shadow of Death, into which he could fall at any time. The figure of Moriarty loomed over his imagination and haunted him like an avatar of death. Even his name seemed to threateningly whisper the Latin infinitive *mori*: "*To die*".

And if Holmes *did* die by Moriarty's hand, what had been the point of it all? What had his life's work amounted to?

Perhaps, he reflected, that earlier conversation with Baring-Gould was more relevant to this current work than he had recognized.

And so Sherlock Holmes, who had previously focused so exclusively on the study of crime that he didn't know whether or not the earth went around the sun, began a program of personal study to try to determine the ultimate philosophical truth about the universe.

He undertook extensive research into Tibetan Buddhism, and found he was sympathetic to its view that all human existence was suffering. He was also intrigued by its thesis that we shouldn't hope for an afterlife but rather aspire to a kind of non-existence. However, when he learned that Tibet's Buddhist monks also admitted to being afraid of death, he determined that he would ultimately need to look elsewhere for intellectual and spiritual satisfaction. [5]

He also studied mediaeval Catholic culture, which, thanks to the plague, was all too familiar with death. But, while death was omnipresent in popular art and devotion, it was also largely defanged of its terror by Jesus' death, harrowing of Hell, and resurrection, all of which were often depicted in the mystery plays of the time.

And, sure enough, he reread Winwood Reade.

September 1888

Holmes finished rereading Reade, who had so affected him twenty years before. While he appreciated the breadth of Reade's historical knowledge, and was happy to recommend *Martyrdom of Man* as one of the most remarkable books ever penned, he also found that Reade contradicted himself.

For example, Reade notoriously claimed that there was no immortal soul. This would mean that humans are purely material beings. Yet Reade also stated that, while the behaviour of masses of men was law-like and predictable, it was impossible for a statistician to predict what an individual would do in a given situation.

This, Holmes thought, clashes sharply with materialism. His work in chemistry had taught him that inert material matter operates according to laws. It has no will of its own. But if a human being is, in practice, unpredictable – not because their mind is random, like a dice throw, but because of the power of free will and the conscious choices that they make – the human mind must consist of something other than the purely material. It must be *immaterial*. It must be a soul. And that meant that it was capable of surviving the death of the material body.

436

Ironically, it was Reade, the enemy of religion and denier of the soul's existence and immortality, who convinced Holmes of the soul's existence and immortality.

Thus, Holmes could say of a group of yard workers, "Dirty-looking rascals, but I suppose everyone has some little immortal spark concealed about him. You would not think it, to look at them. There is no *a priori* probability about it. A strange enigma is man!"

"Someone calls him a soul concealed in an animal," Watson replied. *"Someone,"* Watson mused to himself. *"Could that have been Plato? I really ought to reread him!"*

"Winwood Reade is good upon the subject," Holmes replied.

May 1889

One afternoon, Wiggins and the Baker Street Irregulars informed Holmes that they had seen new and powerful-looking safes being brought into the stockbroking house of Mawson and Williams's, and that there was now always an armed watchman guarding the building. That was suggestive to Holmes. It practically announced that expensive securities were being held there. And Holmes suspected that if he could deduce this, Moriarty could, too.

Holmes decided to call in a favour from Inspector Patterson. Having failed to convince the usually dependable Inspector MacDonald to suspect Moriarty, he had focused his energies on persuading Patterson of Moriarty's guilt, and this seemed like a promising opportunity to add a key piece of evidence to this case. The two detectives went into Mawson and Williams's to speak with the manager about their security measures.

"You're right that we have recently acquired some important new bonds, particularly in American railways," admitted the balding, well-dressed manager, "and that's why we've hired three new armed guards to keep watch over them."

"Was there anything odd or noteworthy about the hiring process?" Holmes asked, his smooth tone concealing the urgency he felt.

The manager rubbed his chin and thought. "Well, I suppose it's worth mentioning that Ben Hogg was the last one to be hired. We were originally going to recruit a different guard, one Hamilton Street, but he had to withdraw from the position when he sustained some injuries in a carriage accident. Fortunately, Hogg applied for the position the same day Street declined the role."

Holmes and Patterson exchanged a look.

"Has Mr. Hogg requested to work on any particular days?" asked Holmes.

The manager furrowed his brow. "Just one, I think. He made a point of asking to work on Saturday, June 22nd – he was scheduled to work the Friday before, but said he had a commitment then and absolutely insisted that he work the next day instead."

The two men thanked the manager and took their leave.

"I suggest," said Holmes to Patterson as they left the building, "that you have a couple of good officers watch Mawson's on June 22nd."

"I'll be sure to put Sergeant Tuson and Constable Pollock on the job," replied Patterson. "We'll see if you're right, Mr. Holmes."

June 1889

Holmes and Watson travelled to the countryside to investigate the murder of Charles McCarthy in the Boscombe Valley. Although McCarthy's son was accused, Holmes discovered that the real killer was McCarthy's landlord, John Turner.

Turner was a former bushranger in Australia who had attempted to reform his life, but McCarthy knew about his past and blackmailed him, which was why Turner allowed McCarthy to live on his land. When McCarthy wanted to force Turner's daughter to marry his son, Turner lost control of himself and killed McCarthy.

Turner was already dying of diabetes when Holmes found all this out. After hearing Turner's testimony, Holmes had a moment of moral rumination.

He believed in the immortality of the soul. There would be a realm where justice was done. He didn't need to try to force it here.

"Well, it isn't for me to judge you," Holmes said, his mind going back to the *Our Father* he had recited as a child. "I pray that we may never be exposed to such a temptation."

"I pray not, sir. And what do you intend to do?"

"In view of your health, nothing. You are yourself aware that you will soon have to answer for your deed at a higher court than the Assizes."

And so Holmes allowed Turner to face the judgement of God rather than of men, still puzzling over the curious and seemingly cruel ways of fate, which put men in difficult situations that often almost forced them to break the law, and fully aware that, "There, but for the grace of God, goes Sherlock Holmes."

On the twenty-second of the month – the day Holmes expected a break-in at Mawson and Williams's – Hall Pycroft came to Holmes with a story that *also* involved Mawson and Williams's.

Pycroft had gotten a job at Mawson's. Before he could assume his role there, he was offered a position as business manager to the Franco-Midland Hardware Company Ltd. by a man calling himself "Arthur Pinner". That company, "Pinner" claimed, operated "a hundred-and-thirty-four branches in the towns and villages of France, not counting one in Brussels and one in San Remo." Pycroft accepted this offer, and "Pinner" encouraged Pycroft not to tell Mawson's that he wouldn't be taking their job.

Pycroft went to their office the following day. He met "Harry Pinner", Arthur's supposed brother. The office was bare. Apparently it had only been rented the previous week. Pycroft was given menial and time-consuming work to do. This made him grow deeply suspicious of this new occupation, which led him to consult Holmes.

It was difficult for Holmes to contain his excitement. His prediction that a theft would occur at Mawson's on this day was all but vindicated, and now he knew the mechanism of that robbery. And, whoever this Pinner was, he must, like Ben Hogg, have been an agent of Moriarty's. Since the police were already watching Mawson's, Holmes decided to go with Pycroft and Watson to see "Pinner" in the hopes that this would allow them to catch one of the criminals involved in this scheme – and get hold of another thread that could lead the police to the master weaver, Moriarty.

On the way over, Watson observed Holmes nervously biting his fingernails. Watson assumed he was deep in thought over Pycroft's story. In fact, Holmes was thinking about the robbery he anticipated was being attempted at that very moment. Normally, when Holmes determined that a crime was about to be committed. he would be present along with the police to apprehend a criminal in the act. He wasn't used to entrusting this duty entirely to others, and was finding the experience rather nerve-wracking.

Holmes and Watson caught "Pinner" in time to save him from successfully hanging himself. The *Evening Standard* newspaper on the table revealed the truth: The "Pinner" brothers were actually the Beddington brothers, who had just served five years of penal servitude. Their plan was to keep Pycroft from going in to work so that one of them could impersonate him, thus gaining access to Mawson's and cracking the safes so as to access the securities inside.

The Beddington brother impersonating Pycroft had killed the watchman, Hogg. Holmes suspected this was to avoid having to split the loot with him. However, Sergeant Tuson and Constable Pollock were on the scene and able to arrest Beddington. (The author of the *Evening Standard* article didn't note how unusual it would be for a sergeant to be walking the beat. If they had, they might have drawn the obvious conclusion that Tuson only happened to be on hand because someone had arranged for him to be there at that time.)

Holmes's plan had been a massive success. The robbery was thwarted and the culprits captured. Of course, Holmes knew they would say nothing about Moriarty. But that didn't mean there was nothing else to glean from this incident.

He asked Patterson to look into who had rented Beddington's office for him. They found it had been rented in the name of *"FMHC, Ltd."*

Two things struck Holmes.

The first was: If Beddington, or Moriarty, had created a false company for the purpose of this ruse, why not rent the office using the full name of that fictional business? Why use the acronym?

Could it be, Holmes wondered, that Moriarty maintained a dummy company for purposes like this, and that it had an acronym rather than words in its name so that it could be used for different purposes without raising suspicion? Perhaps the name "Franco-Midlands Hardware Company" had been chosen to fit the acronym, rather than the other way around.

The second thought was: When Beddington had described the location of Company's stores, he mentioned not only France but also San Remo and Brussels. Why include those?

Pycroft worked in stockbroking. If he suspected he was being tricked, he could potentially look into whether "FMHC, Ltd." had a presence in Europe. If the Beddingtons wanted to fool him, their lie had to have some authenticity. This made Holmes strongly suspect that FMHC, Ltd. *would* have operations in France, Italy, and Belgium. That meant Moriarty had agents there, and not just in England.

Holmes felt strongly that he had made a breakthrough in his war against Moriarty. But that placed him that much closer to the risk of death. A cold darkness descended on his mind and sent a cold chill down his spine.

July 1889

Watson brought Holmes to see his old schoolmate Percy Phelps of the Foreign Office, who had been bedridden with brain fever for weeks. Phelps had undergone a kind of nervous breakdown when a critical naval treaty in his keeping had gone missing. (Holmes didn't disclose that his brother Mycroft had already informed him about this missing treaty, though he did let slip that he had already made inquiries about the situation.)

As Holmes listened to Phelps' testimony, his mind stole in the direction of Moriarty, and of his own anxieties about the possibility of the professor taking his life. When Phelps was done explaining what had happened, Holmes noticed something by the open window of his bedroom: A beautiful red-and-green moss-rose.

Contemplating that rose, he once again heard the reassuring words of his godfather recounting the lessons we learn from flowers: That death can have meaning. That God has a plan for everything. That beauty, like the beauty of flowers, proves that this plan is fundamentally good. The moss-rose had a message for Holmes: *Do not fear Moriarty. Do not fear death. Be strong and courageous.*

That message engulfed Holmes with an enthralling comfort, and he couldn't stop himself from exclaiming, "What a lovely thing a rose is!"

Ignoring everyone in the room, who were looking at him with startled bewilderment, Holmes strode over to the flower and picked it up by its drooping stem. He had fallen into a mystical reverie. After all, he mused, it wasn't just that beauty had a strong emotional impact: It was a piece of evidence from which a theology could be deduced, just as any other piece of empirical evidence provided data from which rational conclusions could be drawn.

"There is nothing in which deduction is so necessary," Holmes pronounced, "as in religion. It can be built up as an exact science by the reasoner."

He leaned against the shutters, contemplating the rose, while those around him stared in incredulous confusion.

"Our highest assurance of the goodness of Providence," he continued, "seems to me to rest in the flowers. All other things – our powers, our desires, our food – are all really necessary for our existence in the first instance. But this rose is an extra. Its smell and its colour are an embellishment of life, not a condition of it. It is only goodness which gives extras, and so I say again that we have much to hope from the flowers."

This homily was so perplexing, and yet, Watson thought, so moving that it left the others silent for a few full minutes before Phelps' fiancée sharply asked, "Do you see any prospect of solving the mystery, Mr. Holmes?"

"Oh, the mystery!" Holmes said with a start, before reassuming his normal sharp demeanour. But he had undergone a kind of transformation from that flower, which reminded him there was more to reality than bloodstains and the contents of chemistry tubes.

Baring-Gould had said that God revealed Himself in *The Book of Nature* and *The Book of Scripture*. Holmes had just read a word from *The*

Book of Nature. He resolved to study that Book more carefully and learn its teachings.

(The treaty, it turned out, was in the room in which they were standing all along. Sometimes, Holmes reflected afterwards, what we seek has been hidden close to us this entire time. He thought about his childhood and the Word of God that his mother had taught him to hide in his heart, a Word which had laid quietly waiting for him for years.)

August 1889

The following month, Holmes investigated the death of Colonel James Barclay. His wife, Nancy, was suspected of the crime because they had been overheard having a row in which she angrily shouted the word "David".

One of the facts of the case was that Nancy Barclay was a devout churchgoing Roman Catholic who was involved with charitable work. Holmes didn't immediately recognize the significance of this for the case.

It emerged that, before James and Nancy were married, she was in love with another soldier, Henry Wood. On the battlefield, Barclay betrayed Wood's location to the other side so that he would have no rival for Nancy's affections. Wood was captured and tortured until his body was left crooked and broken.

It was assumed that he had been killed on the battlefield, and Nancy had married Barclay instead, but Wood had recently returned and told Nancy what actually happened. This led to the heated argument between the two which. When Wood revealed himself to Barclay, it startled him to the point that he died of a fit of apoplexy.

Watson was still perplexed about one thing. "If the husband's name was James, and the other was Henry, what was this talk about 'David'?"

"That one word, my dear Watson," Holmes explained, "should have told me the whole story, had I been the ideal reasoner which you are so fond of depicting. It was evidently a term of reproach."

"Of reproach?"

"Yes. David strayed a little occasionally, you know, and on one occasion in the same direction as Sergeant James Barclay. You remember the small affair of Uriah and Bathsheba? My Biblical knowledge is a trifle rusty, I fear, but you will find the story in the *First* or *Second* of *Samuel*."

Nancy, the fervent Catholic, reproached her husband with language from Scripture, which told the story of how King David abandoned the soldier Uriah to death on the battlefield so that he could take Uriah's wife, Bathsheba, as his own. Had Holmes been more Biblically conversant, perhaps he would have recognized this sooner.

So the Bible is relevant to my work after all, he mused.

And so, in addition to resolving to read *The Book of Nature* more closely, Holmes also resolved to take another look at *The Book of Scripture*.

Later that month, Watson brought Holmes the engineer Victor Hatherley, whose thumb had been chopped off.

Victor Hatherley had been hired by someone calling himself "Colonel Lysander Stark", whom Hatherley took to be German, to fix a machine he claimed was for making bricks out of Fuller's Earth. Hatherley described Stark as exceedingly thin, with skin pulled tightly over the sharp features of his face.

"Stark" brought Hatherley to an estate in the countryside near Reading. Once there, Hatherley was introduced to his "secretary and manager", a plump and taciturn Englishman called "Mr. Ferguson", and a young woman named Elise, whom Hatherley also assumed was German and who begged him to flee. It became clear that the machine was actually for printing counterfeit half-crown coins, and, when Hatherley realised this, "Stark" – whose real name he overheard was Fritz – tried to kill him, severing Hatherley's thumb in the process, though he was able to escape.

When Holmes and Watson came with Hatherley and Inspector Bradstreet to the house to investigate, it was burning to the ground, apparently because of a lamp knocked to the floor in the course of Hatherley's flight. They learned that the Englishman "Mr. Ferguson" was really named Dr. Becher, that this counterfeiting operation had been going on for at least a year, and that the three conspirators had fled in the direction of Reading, which Inspector Bradstreet had already determined was where the counterfeit coins were funnelled to the rest of the country.

Holmes once again saw the footprints of Moriarty in this case. And, thanks to the Pycroft incident, he had a clue where those footprints led.

He asked Bradstreet to see if any businesses in Reading used properties that were rented by an "FMHC, Ltd." A few days later, Bradstreet reported that he had found one: The firm of Financial Markets and Held Capital, which engaged in money lending and converting foreign currency. Needless to say, such a business was the perfect engine for distributing counterfeit money.

Holmes informed Bradstreet about how FMHC had already been linked to financial crime and suggested the inspector check the firm's coffers for counterfeit coins. Unsurprisingly, within a week, the management of Financial Markets and Held Capital was arrested.

This, in Holmes's mind, was proof positive: FMHC, Ltd. was Moriarty's shell company. The fact that this Reading business was engaged in converting foreign money seemed like further confirmation that FMHC had to do with Moriarty's European connections. Now he had to determine where this company was headquartered.

Holmes's mind turned back to Dr. Becher. He was an Englishman who owned a longtime property in Reading, so he wasn't European himself, but he didn't have an especially English name, and was somehow able to be controlled by a European criminal. Was it a coincidence that a German-sounding foreigner would work with an Englishman with a German-sounding surname? But how would this European criminal have found this European-descended Briton? Holmes theorised that "Colonel Stark" – or rather, Fritz – may have been a relation of Becher's.

Hatherley thought "Stark" was German, but also admitted his ignorance of the German language, which presumably meant he was also ignorant of different kinds of German accents. Was it possible Fritz and Elise were of a different nationality?

To find out, Holmes went to the Diogenes Club. He was looking for Douglas Tukey, a rodent-faced man with a dropping moustache and a long, thin beard. Tukey was inevitably curled up in a chair by the bookshelf reading thick volumes of dry statistics or actuarial tables. When Holmes found Tukey in his usual spot, he silently passed him a note:

> Are you able to find out where the surname "Becher" is most popular?

Holmes knew that no remuneration would be necessary. Tukey took pleasure in this kind of arcane research, and his delighted smile and nod confirmed that he would do this for Holmes for the sheer joy of the hunt. The next day, Holmes returned to the Diogenes Club library, and the rat-like statistician handed him back his note. The following was scribbled beneath Holmes's message:

> "Becher" must be a shortened form of "Becherer".
> "Becherer" is the 470th most popular surname in Germany,
> and the 6th most common surname in Switzerland.

So the odds were that Becher was of Swiss descent.

With that knowledge in hand, and testing Holmes's hypothesis that the "Colonel" and the doctor were relations, Holmes and Patterson contacted the Swiss police to ask whether they knew anything of a Friedrich or Frederick "Fritz" Becherer.

The reply came back: Friedrich Becherer came from a Swiss banking family. He had a brother, Lars, who worked as a banker. Lars had a teenaged son, Nicklaus. Becherer also had a cousin, Dr. Malcolm Becher, the son of Becherer's uncle who had moved to England and changed his surname. Becherer, who had served, like all Swiss men, in the military, had been linked to financial crimes, but had fled the country before he could be apprehended for them. The best evidence indicated he had fled to Belgium.

Belgium.

Beddington had told Pycroft that FMHC had a store in Brussels.

Holmes's feeling of certainty grew stronger. Brussels must be where FMHC, Ltd. was based.

The net around Moriarty tightened. But, Holmes knew, so also did the rope around his own neck. Yet, when he thought of the moss-rose, he feared that rope less and less.

September 1889

The case of the cardboard box containing two severed human ears sent to Susan Cushing was one of the more grotesque in Holmes's career. The facts he discovered were awful: Susan's sister, Sarah, fell for Jim Browner, the husband of a third sister, Mary, but, when Browner rejected Sarah's advances, she took revenge by convincing Mary to think poorly of Browner and pushing her into having an affair. This drove Browner to a kind of temporary insanity in which he murdered Mary and her lover. The ears in the box were the victims', and were intended for Sarah, not Susan.

Contemplating this disgusting display of human sinfulness, Holmes was moved to soliloquize.

"What is the meaning of it, Watson?" he asked solemnly. "What object is served by this circle of misery and violence and fear? It must tend to some end, or else our universe is ruled by chance, which is unthinkable. But what end? There is the great standing perennial problem to which human reason is as far from an answer as ever."

"Unthinkable, Holmes?"

"In two senses. One is that it is impossible for a rational mind to accept. If human reason can comprehend the universe, then the universe itself must be rationally structured. If it were indeed chaotic and meaningless, we wouldn't be able to use reason to navigate it. The universe is a book, and a book has an author.

"It is also unthinkable in that it is objectionable on an aesthetic level – the mind is repelled by it as an ugly and obnoxious thought."

"But surely one cannot reject an idea as untrue simply because it isn't beautiful!"

"On the contrary, Watson: Aesthetic judgement is perhaps as important a criteria in the scientific mind as explanatory power is. Indeed, a theory is beautiful and elegant but fails to explain all the relevant evidence should often be preferred to one that saves all the phenomena yet is aesthetically unappealing. [6]

"When you met me, I was unacquainted with the scientific model of the solar system. I have since learned that when Galileo asserted heliocentrism, he didn't have enough evidence to prove his theory. The Tychonic model explained all the evidence that the Copernican system did, and avoided some of the problems that Galileo's theory fell into. Yet in the end, heliocentrism won out, even before it was fully established by evidence and experiments, because it was more compelling than its rivals – it was, it seems, more aesthetically satisfying. The human appetite for truth seeks the flavour of beauty just as much as it seeks the substance of evidence." [7]

"But Holmes, isn't beauty subjective?"

Holmes looked introspective. "Some would say that the experience of love proves the objective truth of beauty. I have never loved, so I cannot say. I *can* say, however, that anyone who doesn't see beauty in the polyphony of Lassus' motets is simply mistaken."

He paused.

"But there is still the question of what end it all builds towards. There seems to be no justification for much human suffering in this world. If we can persuade ourselves of the immortality of the soul – and, if memory serves, we have done so before – perhaps we can hope there is a better ending for it all in another, spiritual world."

"You make me want to revisit Plato," said Watson, remembering his earlier desire to study the great philosopher again. "I rather enjoyed his dialogues – They are, after all, stories, and I appreciate any well-told story. I think he tackles that problem of immortality and a higher realm after death in one of those dialogues."

Holmes didn't respond. Instead, he reached for his violin and began playing thoughtfully.

1890

Inspired by his discussion with Holmes about the immortality of the soul, Watson reread Plato's dialogue *Phaedo*. It recounted the last words of Socrates before he was unjustly executed.

Socrates explained that he did not fear death. The fact that the human mind was rational and could comprehend truth showed that it was immaterial, and the fact that it grasped eternal truths like those of math and

446

geometry showed that it was eternal, too. Yes, there was injustice in this life, such as his trial had been, but he went to death confidently knowing that his immortal soul was going on to a realm of truth, goodness, and beauty. With that confidence, Socrates boldly drank the hemlock he was given by his enemies.

The dialogue ended thusly:

> *Such was the end, Echecrates, of our friend, a man, I think who was the wisest and justest, and the best man I have ever known.*

Meanwhile, Holmes, using the same skill in cryptography that would later enable him to solve the case of the dancing men, began developing his own personal code for containing large amounts of information in small symbols. He experimented with geometric symbols, Chinese characters (which stand for entire words rather than letters), and other succinct representations of complex words and ideas. During this time, he had a visit with his young nephew, Siger, who had been fascinated with the code Holmes had developed. Holmes had no idea he was sowing the seeds for Siger to one day work as a code-breaker.

Instead, during this time, the seeds that Holmes focused on were those of the flowers he had begun to study. He especially became fascinated by orchids, and often pored over the *Reichenbachia* to learn more about them. The word *"orchid"*, he was reminded, derived from the Greek word for *"testicles"*, since some orchids have rhizome-tubers resembling that body part. Because of that, orchids were often linked to love and sexuality in mythology.

For some reason, orchids made him think of Irene Norton.

He would always remember the day he and Watson learned from the newspaper that Godfrey Norton had been killed in Montenegro valiantly protecting his wife, noted actress Irene Adler, from a gang of bandits. Irene had gone missing and was presumed dead.

Holmes still sensed a pang of some sort of emotion when he thought of her. He would maintain to his dying day that he had never experienced romantic love. But, if this wasn't love, then what was it?

He would feel this emotion most acutely during the Christmas season, which, ever since the rekindling of his faith some years ago, he had celebrated more heartily. Its religious overtones had even influenced his decision to let the thief of the blue carbuncle go free – (*"I suppose that I am commuting a felony, but it is just possible that I am saving a soul . . . Besides, it is the season of forgiveness"*) – and its culmination in his birthday made it even more enjoyable now that he found new meaning in his life, and more to celebrate in the fact that it had begun during such a holy festival.

That year, with Watson's help, Holmes successfully undertook to curb and eventually conquer his cocaine habit. And, in the privacy of his heart, while he took more relish in life, he also prepared for the possibility of death.

April 1891

By this time, Holmes had collected enough information to expose Moriarty and put him and his entire gang in prison. (Well, his entire English gang, at least.)

But he knew what this meant. His life was in danger like never before. And, as he predicted, Moriarty's agents began making attempts on his life. Moriarty himself even came into his Baker Street rooms to threaten him.

It was time to flee to Europe – not just because England was unsafe right now, but also to try to root out what might have remained of Moriarty's power there. He sent a telegram ahead to the Brussels Police asking for the address of FMHC, Ltd.'s office. After receiving their reply, and after having another close scrape with death, he went to Watson, explained the situation, and proposed a trip to the Continent.

When he met Watson on the train, he was, for the second time in his career, disguised as a clergyman. This time, he went as an Italian Catholic priest.

Later, he would ponder why he chose that particular disguise. Perhaps, he thought, it is because the Catholic priest is consecrated as *alter Christus* – "another Christ". Their highest purpose in life is to offer the Eucharist, the re-presentation of the sacrifice of Jesus Christ, when he laid down his life to defeat the Devil. Perhaps that symbolism had been buzzing in his subconscious.

As the train started moving, Holmes and Watson saw a tall, thin man with a large forehead and sunken, angry eyes viciously struggling through the crowd towards them.

Breaking through the crowd, Professor Moriarty snarled angrily as he watched the train, and its passengers, pull out of the station and beyond his grasp.

Brussels, April 1891

The office out of which FMHC, Ltd. operated was intentionally small and unassuming. It wasn't meant to draw attention. Indeed, it was intentionally as obscure and ignorable as possible. Even the bookshelf, stuffed as it was with dull-looking directories, was mostly unremarkable, except for one book: The French translation of *The Dynamics of an Asteroid*. To look at this little office, one would never guess how many major criminal projects were run from within its walls.

There were only a few clerks who worked in this office, and their job was primarily to serve as mediators between Moriarty in England and criminal operatives here in Europe. The work consisted mostly of relaying instructions, making travel arrangements, and transferring finances. The young man seated at the desk right now was new and was still getting accustomed to the responsibilities of the role.

The clerk looked up as the door swung open. He had to raise his head, for the man at the door was very tall, and he found himself staring into a pair of glaring, moving eyes. They were floating from side to side, for the head which carried them oscillated like that of a serpent, and they glared back at him with icy, superior contempt. The visitor turned to look at the bookshelf, walked over, and pulled *Dynamiques de l'Astéroïde* off it.

"I am glad to see my employees regularly read Scripture," the man said coldly in French, slipping the book into his pocket. It was an unmistakable gesture of ownership.

"Professor Moriarty!" The clerk jumped to his feet. He had never met his employer and felt utterly unprepared for it.

"Holmes has found all," the man hissed. Even the way he talked was like a snake. "England is too hot to hold me now. I'll relocate here. But I'm sure that pestilent rogue has learned about this office and is on his way here with the police. There can't be anything here that would betray us when he arrives. Give me all incriminating documents. I will relocate them and contact you soon."

The clerk panicked and hastily collected a variety of papers from his desk, stacked them, folded them, stuffed them into a large envelope, and handed it over with a shaky hand.

"You have been most helpful, young man," said Sherlock Holmes, turning on his heel and marching out the door.

An hour later, Professor Moriarty appeared in the office. When the clerk realised he had been duped, he nervously began to explain to the professor what had happened.

He did not get a chance to finish his explanation. "A man pretending to be you – " were the last words he uttered in this life.

Two Hours Earlier

"There was nothing at the address listed for the FMHC offices, Monsieur Holmes," explained the Police Commissioner to the tall

449

Englishman in his office. "It had all been abandoned. Tables overturned, chairs knocked over – and a thick layer of dust covering everything, at that. This criminal gang must have heard we were onto them and fled before we got there."

Holmes's face took on a look of impatience. "It has been but a few days since the movement against Moriarty began in earnest," he declared sharply, his voice growing louder with each word, "and the Belgian police were only contacted very recently, yet you accept that a layer of dust has already had time to accumulate? Furthermore, life is seldom as clunkily dramatic as the penny dreadfuls. Upon hearing that they need to flee, any criminal gang – let alone a well-organised one – is not going to be so frantic that they'll be knocking tables and chairs over in their haste. They already have escape plans. Their escape would never look so haphazard. No, Commissioner, I'm afraid you have been duped. My prey rented that space long ago and listed it as FMHC's office, but that was entirely to serve as misdirection in a situation like this. And now we have no idea where they might actually be!"

He practically bellowed these last words to the sheepish looking policeman before him.

"We will search the city, sir!" the Commissioner insisted. "No doubt by this point they have had time to relocate to the opposite end of Brussels, and I can have my best men there right away!

Then came a more gentle voice from behind Holmes, intoning softly: "If I may, *mon ami?*"

Holmes turned to see a rotund but strongly built young policeman with a formidable pair of moustaches who had opened the door quietly and poked his egg-shaped head inside. No doubt he had heard Holmes's fury and had stopped to listen in, and his modest but knowing expression suggested he had already formed an opinion based on it.

"Speaking of my best men," grumbled the commissioner with thick sarcasm, "Hercule here has a propensity for looking beyond the material facts and trying to peer into the invisible, psychological origins of crimes in an attempt to solve them. It's terribly unscientific, but it comes from still believing in the *soul*, I suppose. You'd have been better off as a priest, Poirot."

Holmes raised an eyebrow and scanned the well-manicured young policeman. Sure enough, he detected the outline of a rosary in his breast pocket. The policeman, in turn, seemed to sense this scrutiny, and smiled and bowed a bit in response.

"Do you have thoughts on this matter?" Holmes asked Hercule. He did not see the commissioner's surprised expression behind him, though he knew it was there.

Hercule bowed again. "Monsieur, suppose you wish to hide something from the intrepid hunter. First, you make a deliberate – How do you say? – *misdirection*. The false clues leading to the false location. The avid hunter follows the clues, finds the spot you have deliberately misled him towards, triumphantly flings open your concealment, only to be crestfallen – Nothing is there!

"What do you predict this hunter will now do? Recognizing you have misdirected him to this location, and knowing you wish to keep him from his quarry, he will assume, *naturellement*, that you would have only led him here to keep you as far from that quarry. That must mean that the treasure he seeks is somewhere distant – somewhere as far as possible from this false location! He gallops off with all his speed in the opposite direction.

"Now, remember, your purpose is to keep the hunter away from what he seeks. What better way to keep your hunter as far as possible from his prey than to put it in a spot he will not look for it – namely, a spot near the one he has just abandoned and left far behind? The wise hunter will stay right where he is and search the immediate area of the false treasure spot."

"See what I mean?" groaned the commissioner. "All psychologizing. No facts."

Hercule shrugged. "It is a fact that, two offices away from the one we raided – I so happened to be there and observed this myself – was a sign for the offices of '*De Smet and Janssons Consulting*'. The little grey cells of this poor policeman – they strain, but they fail to imagine a more generic pair of Belgian surnames, and a more unremarkable name for a business. There is nothing in this nomenclature to tell you what these consultants do, so you would not think to contact them if you had a particular need, since you have no idea what they take consultations about! Yet it is also not a name that raises any suspicion. The eyes scan this name, the mind assumes that someone in some line of work must know who these people are, and the brain forgets about it. Whatever is there is effectively hidden from the world.

"If I were this, eh – Dr. Moriarty, is it? – that is what I would do: Rent one set of offices as a misdirection and leave it looking hastily abandoned (that way it looks like it was recently used and left in a hurry), and then rent an office nearby to actually run my operations, confident that this would slip under the nose of anyone who went on the hunt for FMHC, Ltd. If *le bon Dieu* had put me in this office, De Smet and Janssons is where I would send my best men." And he smiled in a way that seemed simultaneously humble and arrogant.

And Holmes thought of a principle he had recently remembered:
Sometimes, what we seek has been hidden close to us this entire time.

The commissioner gave an exasperated sigh. "The Belgian Police can't go pestering local businesses based on a tenuous line of reasoning like that," he shot back.

"Perhaps not," said Holmes, rising from his seat with a new fire of excitement in his eyes, "but I can."

Holmes and Hercule exchanged a look that was a kind of mutual recognition of greatness before the consulting detective marched out of police headquarters, leaving the astonished commissioner behind without a farewell, and headed to De Smet and Janssons Consulting. On his way over, he began practising his Moriarty impression.

Strasbourg, April 1891

Holmes couldn't risk mailing the FMHC documents to the authorities of any country. It could be lost in the mail or somehow intercepted by one of Moriarty's European agents, and, even if it did reach its destination, it was written in a code Holmes had yet to crack, a combination of words and numbers.

Seated at the desk of his hotel room puzzling over this while Watson went for a walk, Holmes reflected on the morning he cracked the code from Porlock. Watson had suggested the Bible might be the key to the code. Holmes thought of his own quip upon picking up *Dynamics*: "I am glad to see my employees regularly read Scripture."

The thought struck him: Just because FMHC was an office of Moriarty's organisation, why would Moriarty's book on galactic physics be on the shelf? What relevance would it have to the work that went on there?

Holmes pulled the copy of the book he had taken from the office out of his suitcase and started checking pages and words that matched the numbers in the documents.

Eureka.

He quickly learned that FMHC not only controlled small cells throughout Europe, but that all its financial resources were in a bank in Switzerland.

Holmes began scribbling furiously in his notebook.

Switzerland, April-May 1891

"I think that I may go so far as to say, Watson, that I have not lived wholly in vain," Holmes told Watson as they hiked through the Gemmi. He was thinking about the account he might soon have to give for his life at the great Judgement Seat, though he chose not to make this explicit to his friend.

He thought again about the orchids of the *Reichenbachia* and how he had been toying with the idea of leaving detection behind to focus on horticulture – if he returned, of course. "Of late," he continued, "I have been tempted to look into the problems furnished by Nature rather than those more superficial ones for which our artificial state of society is responsible."

But, of course, there was work to do before then, and Holmes was anxious to finish that work. Surrounded by the beauty of nature, he once again offered the prayer of his youth:

> *Give me a sign of what to do, Lord, and make it unmistakably clear.*

Then they came upon Meiringen. It had a strong English population, to the point where it had an English hotel, the Englischer Hof, and in that hotel's garden was one of the only Anglican churches in Switzerland. Immediately, Holmes wondered if this might be somewhere an English criminal like Moriarty might have established some connections.

Meiringen, Holmes learned, also had an incredible waterfall he couldn't afford to miss.

It was called the Reichenbach Falls.

Reichenbach. The name he saw every time he looked up an orchid.

Once again, God had answered promptly. Once again, Holmes heeded the sign.

They arrived at Meiringen on the third of May, a Sunday, in time to attend the Anglican liturgy. There was a large stack of hymnals at the back of the church, and Holmes and Watson each picked one up as they went in.

Holmes had difficulty listening to the sermon. His mind was elsewhere. But, as the liturgy came to an end and he opened his songbook to the recessional hymn, he felt his heart rise with confidence within his breast. The hymn was "Onward, Christian Soldiers", with its reassuring second verse:

> *At the sign of triumph,*
> *Satan's host doth flee;*
> *On, then, Christian soldiers,*
> *On to victory!*

It was a stirring hymn in its own right, but what was even more comforting was the name of the song's author: *Sabine Baring-Gould.*

Once again, Holmes' godfather had a reassuring message for him.

Meiringen might be his Gethsemane, but this church was the angel sent to minister to him. He prayed for what was about to happen, and that Watson would be kept safe and comforted before slipping a wad of paper in the hymnal to serve as a bookmark for the hymn and exiting the church with his best friend.

The next day, they went hiking by the Reichenbach Falls. The roaring chasm reminded Holmes of his childhood apparitions of the bottomless pit of death. Yet he was not afraid.

As they walked, a thin Swiss boy with a long, sharp-featured face ran up to them. His eyes seemed wide with panic, and his eyebrows seemed to go all the way up his forehead. He carried a letter on the letterhead of their hotel begging Dr. Watson to come and care for a sick Englishwoman.

"I cannot refuse such a request from a countrywoman in a foreign land," Watson said, "but I dare not leave you, Holmes!"

"Never mind, Watson. This lad can serve as my guide and companion until you arrive."

Mollified, Watson hurried off. Holmes gave the lad a long, hard look.

"Nicklaus Becherer?" he asked.

The boy started. "How did you know?" His face now bore a distinctly unpleasant expression, and his high eyebrows seemed less startled and more condescending and even cruel.

"You bear the same features I once heard your uncle described as possessing. Also, I had a feeling your father might have work near here. He is, after all, Moriarty's European banker, is he not? Why, speak of the very devil!"

The scarecrow-like personage of the professor was now standing behind young Becherer, his oscillating face a mask of silent, lethal fury.

"You've taken to getting children to run errands for you, too?" chuckled Holmes, leaning his walking stick against a nearby boulder. "I ought to have trademarked the idea and charged you royalties for it. Care for a cigarette? And might I leave Watson a final note?"

Barely waiting for a reply, he produced his notebook and silver cigarette case. As he scribbled in the notebook, Moriarty muttered to the boy, "Go finish your other job." Nodding, and looking nearly as malicious as the professor, Becherer rushed off.

Holmes finished writing, tore three pages from his notebook, folded them, and set them down on the boulder, placing the cigarette case on top of them. Then he turned and stared down Moriarty. The screaming waterfall roared in his ears.

Here it was.

Here was the enemy that had haunted him these recent years, and the greater enemy that had haunted him since that childhood sickness.

He still felt the tingle of fear. But out of the corner of his eye, he saw a flower by the side of the path into which a bee was crawling.

There was a plan. A good plan. Of this, Holmes was confident. And he was ready to face his Judge.

The next instant, the two men lunged at each other.

Watson rushed back to the spot he had been when he received the forged letter. He saw Holmes's stick leaning on a large rock jutting onto the path and caught the glint of his cigarette case atop it. Lifting it, he found Holmes's note to him, and mournfully read the message that ended:

> *Tell Inspector Patterson that the papers which he needs to convict the gang are in pigeon-hole M., done up in a blue envelope and inscribed "Moriarty". I made every disposition of my property before leaving England, and handed it to my brother Mycroft. Pray give my greetings to Mrs. Watson, and believe me to be, my dear fellow,*
>
> *Very sincerely yours,*
> *Sherlock Holmes*

Watson was deeply grieved, but, in a strange way, was also proud. He had seen men give their lives in acts of self-sacrifice on the battlefield, and his friend had just performed such an act with aplomb and grace.

The words with which Plato described Socrates came to Watson's mind. Without a doubt, Holmes was *"the best and the wisest man I have ever known"*.

Nicklaus Becherer was frustrated. Knowing that they would both be empty, he had raided both Holmes's and Watson's rooms at the Englischer Hof hotel in search of the FMHC documents. He'd found nothing. He knew the papers were on neither of their persons. There were too many of them to simply conceal in one's pocket. They must have been hidden somewhere else. But where else had Holmes been since he arrived?

Then it struck him.

Becherer slipped out of the hotel and made his way into the garden where the Anglican Church was. He shattered a stained glass window and climbed into the church. At the back of the building was a large stack of hymnals. Undoubtedly, Holmes must have hidden the papers in one of these books.

But how to discover which one?

Becherer panicked. Watson would surely raise the alarm soon, if he hadn't already. There was no time to go through them all.

Then he had an idea.

He ran to the vestry. There were candles there.

And matches.

Maybe he wouldn't need to go through all the hymnals, after all.

Holmes ran.

He had survived both Moriarty and his right-hand man, Colonel Sebastian Moran. He frankly recognized this as a miracle. As he would later tell Watson, he managed this only "by the blessing of God".

He had defeated death in his heart by overcoming his fear of it. Perhaps that gave him the courage to defeat death on the slopes of the Falls.

Now, he ran. He ran towards the church, his impromptu hiding place for the FMHC papers, hoping he could retrieve them before anyone saw him.

But before he got there, the smell of smoke in the air already told him it was futile. Sure enough, when he arrived, he could tell from a distance that the church was ablaze. Nicklaus Becherer, Holmes thought grimly, had rendered Moriarty one last service.

Conscious that he might be seen by Moran, Holmes turned and ran in the opposite direction.

Montenegro, June 1891

There was a knock at Irene Norton's door. As always, when she went to answer the door, she held a loaded revolver behind her back.

She and her husband had made enemies. They'd already gotten to Godfrey. Thanks to her actress' skill with makeup and disguise, she had been able to escape and elude her pursuers, and was now living in hiding and under a false name. It helped her that other actresses, hoping to gain credibility, had been using "Irene Adler" as a stage name since her disappearance, which only muddied the waters about her location even further. But she was not a woman to take chances, and she never answered the door unarmed.

She cautiously opened the door to reveal Sherlock Holmes, the only man capable of tracking her down. He wore a knowing smile and carried a bouquet of orchids.

In response, Irene Norton smiled in a way she hadn't smiled for almost a year.

Watson had said that what Holmes felt for Irene was not love. But, then, what was it?

All Holmes knew was that coming this close to death had made him realise he needed to see her again.

Within the week, Holmes and Adler would, for the second time in their lives, be in a church together.

During the time Holmes spent with her in Montenegro, he put the knowledge he had learned from *Reichenbachia* into practice by cultivating orchids, particularly ophrys orchids, the most common variety of orchids in the area. (Their colour scheme makes them look like bees, and thus they are more commonly called "bee orchids".)

Eventually, however, they both recognized that this was not a safe or sustainable existence for either of them, and that ultimately Holmes's place was in London and he was bound to return there. They promised to remain in close contact and to regularly visit each other, and Holmes left Irene, and his orchids, in Montenegro.

Decades later, a consulting detective with Montenegrin roots consulting detective working in America would also cultivate orchids. He was skilled with them, for he had grown up around them.

Holmes went on to travel the world under the alias "Sigerson". Much of that time was spent in Tibet, where he spent time with the Dalai Lama. While he did learn some valuable things about meditation from the Lama, the visit was less about seeking enlightenment and more, as he put it, for amusement. After all, he had already found spiritual meaning and intellectually satisfying theology elsewhere.

And, eventually, it came time for him to return home.

London, April 1894

The season was spring, when the world comes back to life – thus read *The Book of Nature*. In the liturgical calendar, it was Easter, when Christ rose from the dead – thus read *The Book of Scripture*. And it was the season Sherlock Holmes left the world of death and returned to life.

After revealing himself to Watson, solving the locked room murder of Ronald Adair, and capturing Sebastian Moran, the last remnant of Moriarty's English gang, Holmes asked Watson if he still had the three-page note he had left him at Reichenbach. Of course, Watson had, and kept it in a place of privilege on the wall.

"Might I see it?" Holmes asked with just a touch of slyness.

Watson obligingly fetched it.

Each page only had writing on one side. The other was blank. Watson had observed at the time how odd it was that Holmes would be so uneconomical with his use of paper, but had thought nothing more of it.

"During our travels on the Continent," Holmes explained, reaching for a pencil, "I obtained documentation of Moriarty's European machinations, but knew there was a risk of it being stolen or destroyed."

He started shading the back of the first page of his note with the pencil. As he did so, geometric symbols, Chinese characters, and other exotic shapes began to appear on the paper.

"So," Holmes continued, "I transcribed the most important pieces of information here using my own special code – invisibly, in case my notebook were searched, and leaving the opposite side of each page blank, in case I had need to – Well, do precisely what I did. When death looked imminent, I wrote my final testimony down, not only to communicate with you, dear friend, but also as a way to entrust these notes to your safekeeping. I could not tell you openly about them, of course, but I hoped you might deduce on your own that the back of each page was only blank because a hidden message lay within it."

"I, erm . . . can't say that I did, Holmes." Watson looked sheepish.

"If your inability to find these jottings meant that Providence had to keep me alive in order to show them to you," chuckled Holmes, "then I am grateful you did *not* find them."

Several Europeans were arrested when Holmes made his findings available to the police of their various countries. One of the first to be apprehended was the banker Lars Becherer, though his son Nicklaus fled and was never found. Unlike Moriarty and Moran, it did not appear that young Bercherer would ever face justice for his crimes.

September 1903

Nine years later, Holmes dealt with the strange case of the sixty-one-year-old Professor Presbury, who behaved like a monkey. Holmes unearthed that he had been taking injections of monkey hormones to try to de-age himself, and, in so doing, to indefinitely stave off death.

In the light of all Holmes had considered about death and the afterlife during his battle with Moriarty, he was appalled at this. Within this life, all was meaningless. As he had remarked a few years before to Watson, in this life, everything is futile, like *The Book of Ecclesiastes* says. So why would anyone choose to stay in this world *forever* rather than go on to another spiritual realm where a higher goodness and beauty dwell?

This did not mean disdaining this world. In fact, love of goodness and beauty meant savouring it in this world as much as possible. But choosing these shadows over the realities? It would take a base mind to do that.

"When one tries to rise above Nature, one is liable to fall below it," he mused aloud. "The highest type of man may revert to the animal if he leaves the straight road of destiny."

He had defeated many villains who had deigned to put themselves above the normal laws of human conduct, who saw themselves as somehow beyond good and evil, Moriarty among them. He had learned that goodness lay in walking the straight and narrow path of human nature, which destiny, or fate, or God, had laid out for us.

"There is danger there – a very real danger to humanity. Consider, Watson, that the material, the sensual, the worldly would all prolong their worthless lives. The spiritual would not avoid the call to something higher. It would be the survival of the least fit. What sort of cesspool may not our poor world become?"

But speaking this way and ruminating on this case made him realise that aging is nothing else but moving down the straight and narrow path towards death. And, if death is not to be feared, what is there to fear about aging?

And Holmes *had* been feeling his age. Even his exercises, which included boxing and baritsu, had left him feeling more sore lately. Why ignore this? Why pretend to be a younger man than he was? Because he *had* to keep solving crimes? It was hubris to think that he was the only thing standing between the world and criminal lawlessness. He thought of the well-groomed policeman he had met in Belgium, and the memory reminded him that knew there were other great investigators out there – many of whom had learned from him. And, of course, he trusted there was a greater cosmic plan that went beyond his or any other human design.

Yes, Holmes reflected, everyone ages. It was something to accept and remember.

November 1917

Everyone ages.

Holmes jerked forward in his seat as he remembered this thought.

He reached over and pulled over the photograph of Conrad Trottinger, the Swiss banker accused of using false businesses to funnel weapons. He looked over the man's long, thin, tightly drawn face and high, arrogant-looking eyebrows.

Holmes cast his mind back to a youthful visage he had seen twenty-six years ago. It did not look exactly like the man in the photograph before him, but, after all, everyone ages. Looking closely at the picture, there could be no doubt. "Trottinger" was Nicklaus Becherer.

He grabbed some foolscap from his drawer and scribbled a quick note to "*Henry M.*" So there *would* be justice in this world for that wicked lad, after all.

1903

The last time Holmes had been in Sussex, he had made sure to observe the flowers. There had been a lot of bees among those flowers. It was impossible not to remember his youthful conversation with Baring-Gould about how the bees were the instruments of propagating the flowers and how this revealed God's organising plan. It was a foregone conclusion: When Holmes retired to Sussex, he bought a farm at which he could keep and study bees. They kept him grounded in something more bright and real than the shadows of crime.

He produced some scholarly work at this farm, including a study into the preservative effects of Royal Jelly. Certainly he hoped that it would lengthen his own life. The world remained wonderful and interesting, and he was in no hurry to leave it. But, if he had any inkling that Royal Jelly would ever serve as some sort of elixir of endless youth, he would have marched to Beachy Head cliff and thrown all his jelly and all his research into the sea. He wasn't about to make the same mistake Presbury had made. Perhaps one day people would fantasise about Holmes being some kind of earthly immortal. He himself had no interest in the idea. His hope lay elsewhere.

August 1914

During the years of his retirement, Holmes finally had a chance to read the Bible as carefully as he had wanted to. On the eve of the Great War, he read the passage in Genesis in which the pharaoh has a dream about heads of corn on a stalk: "*Seven ears of corn*" are consumed by seven empty ears which are "*blasted with the east wind*". Joseph interprets the dream as meaning that "*the seven empty ears blasted with the east wind shall be seven years of famine.*" The moral Holmes gleaned from the story was that, while calamity would fall a great empire after a period of prosperity, it was all part of the purpose of God.

When the Great War came, it seemed to put all the pointlessness and emptiness of human life – and human death – on display. The greatness of the Victorian Era was decidedly over, and Britain's best young men were horrifically destroyed *en masse* for reasons many found nebulous. It looked like God's curse rested on the world, and it led many to lose, or at least question, their faith.

But not Holmes. He'd been through that crisis before. And he'd come out of it confident that even the most horrific suffering had some greater goal in the purposes of Providence, and he said as much to his best friend.

"There's an east wind coming, Watson."

"I think not, Holmes," replied Watson, missing the Biblical allusion. "It is very warm."

"Good old Watson! You are the one fixed point in a changing age. There's an east wind coming all the same, such a wind as never blew on England yet. It will be cold and bitter, Watson, and a good many of us may wither before its blast. But it's God's own wind none the less, and a cleaner, better, stronger land will lie in the sunshine when the storm has cleared."

God's own wind, Holmes thought again. All the suffering tends towards us becoming cleaner, stronger, and better. A better land in this world, or a promised land in the next.

Sussex, November 1917

God's own wind, Holmes thought again. *All the suffering tends towards us becoming cleaner, stronger, and better. A better land in this world, or a promised land in the next.*

He took up another piece of paper and began to write:

My Dear Siger,

Let me endeavour to explain to you how I created the consulting detective business, why I chose to exit it, and why I chose to keep bees afterwards – and why I recommend the same path to you . . . .

461

NOTES

1. Siger Holmes was the son of Holmes's older brother, Sherrinford Holmes. At times, Sherrinford had used the alias "Asenath Pons", and Siger, therefore, used the *nom de plum* "Solar Pons" in his own detective work. For more on this, see David Marcum's "The Adventure of the Other Brother" in *The Papers of Sherlock Holmes* and *The Collected Papers of Sherlock Holmes – Volume I: Narratives* (MX Publishing). It appears that Siger would indeed also go on to take up beekeeping when he retired. (See Allen J. Hubin's introduction to The Chronicles of Solar Pons).

2. Laurie R. King first discovered that Sabine Baring-Gould was Holmes' godfather, a fact revealed in her novel *The Moor*.

3. The image of nature being a book that reveals God and which serves as a companion to the Bible goes back to St. Augustine, who wrote and preached in the late fourth to early Fifth Century. For example, in his exposition of *Psalm* 45, he says: "*There is for you the book of the divinely inspired page, so that you might hear these things. There is for you the book of the wide world, so that you might see these things. Only the literate can read the books, but even the illiterate can read the book of the world.*"

4. This was Dr. Watson's first marriage, in late 1886, to the ill-fated Constance Adams of San Francisco. Although her existence can be deduced from Watson's writings, we know her name and some details about her life from William S. Baring-Gould, who, in turn, learned them from his grandfather – who was none other than Holmes' godfather, Sabine. (See chapters VII-X of Baring-Gould's *Sherlock Holmes of Baker Street: The Life of the World's First Consulting Detective*).

5. A more recent study corroborates this: "*We predicted that the denial of self would be associated with a lower fear of death and greater generosity toward others. To our surprise, we found the opposite. Monastic Tibetan Buddhists showed significantly greater fear of death than any other group*" (Nichols *et al.*, "Death and the Self," *Cognitive Science* 42(1), 314-332 (2018)).

6. This is very close to what the twentieth century mathematician Paul Dirac would later assert: "*A theory with mathematical beauty is more likely to be correct than an ugly one that fits some experimental data.*" Various scientists and philosophers of science have said similar things. A good example would be Pierre Duhem discussing how experiments do not prove a scientific theory, but "*good sense*" (*bons sens*) does.

7. Arthur Koestler, *The Sleepwalkers: A History of Man's Changing Vision of the Universe*.

About the Contributors

The following contributors appear in this volume:
The MX Book of New Sherlock Holmes Stories
Part XLV – 2024 Annual (1898-1917)

Mike Adamson holds a Doctoral degree from Flinders University of South Australia. After early aspirations in art and writing, Mike secured qualifications in both marine biology and archaeology. Mike has been a university educator since 2006, has worked in the replication of convincing ancient fossils, is a passionate photographer, master-level hobbyist, and journalist for international magazines. Short fiction sales include to *Metastellar*, *Strand Magazine*, *Little Blue Marble*, *Abyss*, and *Apex*, *Daily Science Fiction*, *Compelling Science Fiction*, and *Nature Futures*. Mike has placed some two-hundred stories to date, totaling over a million words. Mike has completed his first Sherlock Holmes novel with Belanger Books, and will be appearing in translation in European magazines. You can catch up with his journey at his blog "The View From the Keyboard"
http://mike-adamson.blogspot.com

Ian Ableson is an ecologist by training and a writer by choice. When not reading or writing, he can reliably be found scowling at a clipboard while ankle-deep in a marsh somewhere in Michigan. His love for the stories of Arthur Conan Doyle started when his grandfather gave him a copy of *The Original Illustrated Sherlock Holmes* when he was in high school, and he's proud to have been able to contribute to the continuation of the tales of Sherlock Holmes and Dr. Watson.

Tim Newton Anderson is a former senior daily newspaper journalist and PR manager who has recently started writing fiction. In the past six months, he has placed fourteen stories in publications including *Parsec Magazine*, *Tales of the Shadowmen*, *SF Writers Guild*, *Zoetic Press*, *Dark Lane Books*, *Dark Horses Magazine*, *Emanations*, and *Planet Bizarro*.

Donald I. Baxter has practiced medicine for over forty years. He resides in Erie Pennsylvania with his wife and their dog. His family and his friends are for the most part lawyers who have given him the ability to make stuff up just as they do.

Brian Belanger, PSI, is a publisher, illustrator, graphic designer, editor, and author. In 2015, he co-founded Belanger Books publishing company along with his brother, author Derrick Belanger. His illustrations have appeared in *The Essential Sherlock Holmes* and *Sherlock Holmes: A Three-Pipe Christmas*, and in children's books such as *The MacDougall Twins with Sherlock Holmes* series, *Dragonella*, and *Scones and Bones on Baker Street*. Brian has published a number of Sherlock Holmes anthologies and novels through Belanger Books, as well as new editions of August Derleth's classic Solar Pons mysteries. Brian continues to design all of the covers for Belanger Books, and since 2016 he has designed the majority of book covers for MX Publishing. In 2019, Brian received his investiture in the PSI as "Sir Ronald Duveen." More recently, he illustrated a comic book featuring the band The Moonlight Initiative, created the logo for the Arthur Conan Doyle Society and designed *The Great Game of Sherlock Holmes* card game. Find him online at:
www.belangerbooks.com and
www.redbubble.com/people/zhahadun and
zhahadun.wixsite.com/221b

Craig Stephen Copland confesses that he discovered Sherlock Holmes when, sometime in the muddled early 1960's, he pinched his older brother's copy of the immortal stories and was forever afterward thoroughly hooked. He is very grateful to his high school English teachers in Toronto who inculcated in him a love of literature and writing, and even inspired him to be an English major at the University of Toronto. There he was blessed to sit at the feet of both Northrup Frye and Marshall McLuhan, and other great literary professors, who led him to believe that he was called to be a high school English teacher. It was his good fortune to come to his pecuniary senses, abandon that goal, and pursue a varied professional career that took him to over one-hundred countries and endless adventures. He considers himself to have been and to continue to be one of the luckiest men on God's good earth. A few years back he took a step in the direction of Sherlockian studies and joined *The Sherlock Holmes Society of Canada* – also known as *The Toronto Bootmakers*. In May of 2014, this esteemed group of scholars announced a contest for the writing of a new Sherlock Holmes mystery. Although he had never tried his hand at fiction before, Craig entered and was pleasantly surprised to be selected as one of the winners. Having enjoyed the experience, he decided to write more of the same, and he has now written new Sherlock Holmes mysteries related to and inspired by each of the sixty stories in the original Canon, along with a number of others.

Martin Daley was born in Carlisle, Cumbria in 1964. His thirty-year writing career has seen over twenty books and numerous short stories published. Inevitably, Holmes and Watson remain his favourite literary characters, and they continue to inspire his own detective writing. In 2010, Martin created Inspector Cornelius Armstrong, who carries out his police work against the backdrop of Edwardian Carlisle. With the publication of the first *Inspector Armstrong Casebook* (published by MX Publishing), Martin became a member of the Crime Writers' Association. Most recently, he published *The Selected Cases of Sherlock Holmes.* He lives with his wife Wendy, in Kirkcudbrightshire, in Southwest.

Alan Dimes was born in Northwest London and graduated from Sussex University with a BA in English Literature. He has spent most of his working life teaching English. Living in the Czech Republic since 2003, he is now semi-retired and divides his time between Prague and his country cottage. He has also written some fifty stories of horror and fantasy and thirty stories about his husband-and-wife detectives, Peter and Deirdre Creighton, set in the 1930's.

Sir Arthur Conan Doyle (1859-1930) *Holmes Chronicler Emeritus*. If not for him, this anthology would not exist. Author, physician, patriot, sportsman, spiritualist, husband and father, and advocate for the oppressed. He is remembered and honored for the purposes of this collection by being the man who introduced Sherlock Holmes to the world. Through fifty-six Holmes short stories, four novels, and additional Apocryphal entries, Doyle revolutionized mystery stories and also greatly influenced and improved police forensic methods and techniques for the betterment of all. *Steel True Blade Straight.*

Steve Emecz's main field is technology, in which he has been working for about twenty-five years. Steve is a regular speaker at trade shows and his tech career has taken him to more than fifty countries – so he's no stranger to planes and airports. In 2008, MX published its first Sherlock Holmes book, and MX has gone on to become the largest specialist Holmes publisher in the world with over 500 books. MX is a social enterprise and supports three main causes. The first is Happy Life, a children's rescue project in Nairobi, Kenya, where he and his wife, Sharon, spend every Christmas at the rescue centre in Kasarani. They have written two editions of a short book about the project, *The Happy Life Story*. The second is Undershaw, Sir Arthur Conan Doyle's former home, which is a school for children with learning disabilities for which Steve is a patron. Steve has been a mentor for the World Food Programme for several years, and was part of the Nobel Peace Prize winning team in 2020.

Brett Fawcett is a humanities and Latin teacher at the Chesterton Academy of St. Isidore in Sherwood Park, Alberta. He lives with his wife and son in Edmonton, where he is a member of The Wisteria Lodgers (The Sherlock Holmes Society of Edmonton). He vividly remembers the first time he finished reading the Sherlock Holmes stories in Grade 6, and has been a student of Holmesian literature and scholarship since then. He is also a frequent author of columns and articles on topics like theology, education, and mental health, as well as the occasional mystery story.

Mark A. Gagen BSI is co-founder of Wessex Press, sponsor of the popular *From Gillette to Brett* conferences, and publisher of *The Sherlock Holmes Reference Library* and many other fine Sherlockian titles. A life-long Holmes enthusiast, he is a member of *The Baker Street Irregulars* and *The Illustrious Clients of Indianapolis*. A graphic artist by profession, his work is often seen on the covers of *The Baker Street Journal* and various BSI books.

John Atkinson Grimshaw (1836-1893) was born in Leeds, England. His amazing paintings, usually featuring twilight or night scenes illuminated by gas-lamps or moonlight, are easily recognizable, and are often used on the covers of books about The Great Detective to set the mood, as shadowy figures move in the distance through misty mysterious settings and over rain-slicked streets.

Arthur Hall was born in Aston, Birmingham, UK, in 1944. He discovered his interest in writing during his schooldays, along with a love of fictional adventure and suspense. His first novel, *Sole Contact*, was an espionage story about an ultra-secret government department known as "Sector Three", and was followed, to date, by three sequels. Other works include seven Sherlock Holmes novels, *The Demon of the Dusk*, *The One Hundred Percent Society*, *The Secret Assassin*, *The Phantom Killer*, *In Pursuit of the Dead*, *The Justice Master*, and *The Experience Club* as well as three collections of Holmes *Further Little-Known Cases of Sherlock* Holmes, *Tales from the Annals of Sherlock* Holmes, and *The Additional Investigations of Sherlock Holmes.* He has also written other short stories and a modern detective novel. He lives in the West Midlands, United Kingdom.

Paul Hiscock is an author of crime, fantasy, horror, and science fiction tales. His short stories have appeared in a variety of anthologies, and include a seventeenth-century whodunnit, a science fiction western, a clockpunk fairytale, and numerous Sherlock Holmes pastiches. He lives with his family in Kent (England) and spends his days taking care of his two children. You can find out more about Paul's writing at: *www.detectivesanddragons.uk*.

Roger Johnson, BSI, ASH, PSI, etc, is a member of more Holmesian societies than he can remember, thanks to his (so far) 16 years as editor of *The Sherlock Holmes Journal*, and thirty-two years as editor of *The District Messenger*. The latter, the newsletter of *The Sherlock Holmes Society of London*, is now in the safe hands of Jean Upton, with whom he collaborated on the well-received book, *The Sherlock Holmes Miscellany*. Roger is resigned to the fact that he will never match the Duke of Holdernesse, whose name was followed by "*half the alphabet*".

Daniel Lenois graduated with a Bachelor of Arts in English Literature from Central Connecticut State University in 2023. A lifelong appreciator of Sherlock Holmes since reading the original stories as a child with his father, Daniel currently moonlights as a graduate student while also pursuing his real passion in the area of literary achievement. Prior and forthcoming publications include *The Helix*, *Blue Muse*, *Unleash Lit*, *Savage Planets*, and *Shacklebound Books*.

Jeffrey Lockwood spent youthful afternoons darkly enchanted by feeding grasshoppers to black widows in his New Mexican backyard, which accounts for his scientific and literary affinities. He earned a doctorate in entomology, and worked as an ecologist at the University of Wyoming before metamorphosing into a Professor of Natural Sciences & Humanities in the departments of philosophy and creative writing. He considers Sherlock Holmes a model of scientific prowess, integrating exquisite observational skills with incisive abductive (not deductive) reasoning.

David Marcum plays *The Game* with deadly seriousness. He first discovered Sherlock Holmes in 1975 at the age of ten, and since that time, he has collected, read, and chronologicized literally thousands of traditional Holmes pastiches in the form of novels, short stories, radio and television episodes, movies and scripts, comics, fan-fiction, and unpublished manuscripts. He is the author of over one-hundred-twenty Sherlockian pastiches, some published in anthologies and magazines such as *The Best Mystery Stories of the Year 2021* and *The Strand*, and others collected in his own books, *The Papers of Sherlock Holmes*, *Sherlock Holmes and A Quantity of Debt*, *Sherlock Holmes – Tangled Skeins*, *Sherlock Holmes and The Eye of Heka*, and *The Collected Papers of Sherlock Holmes* – six volumes and more to come. He has won back-to-back first place fiction awards from *The Arthur Conan Doyle Society* (2023 and 2024) and the Nero Wolfe *Wolfe Pack*. He has edited over 1,100 Holmes adventures and eighty books, including dozens of traditional Sherlockian anthologies, such as the ongoing series *The MX Book of New Sherlock Holmes Stories*, which he created in 2015 to promote traditional Canonical Holmes. This collection is now at forty-five volumes, with more in preparation. He was responsible for bringing back August Derleth's Solar Pons for a new generation with his collections of authorized Pons stories, *The Papers of Solar Pons* and *The Further Papers of Solar Pons*. Pons's return was further assisted by his editing of the reissued authorized versions of the original Pons books, and then several volumes of new Pons adventures. He has done the same for the adventures of Dr. Thorndyke, and has plans for similar projects in the future. He has contributed numerous essays to various publications, and is a member of a number of Sherlockian groups and Scions, as well as *The Mystery Writers of America*. His irregular Sherlockian blog, *A Seventeen Step Program*, addresses various topics related to his favorite book friends (as his son used to call them when he was small), and can be found at *http://17stepprogram.blogspot.com/* He is a licensed Civil Engineer, living in Tennessee with his wife and son. Since the age of nineteen, he has worn a deerstalker as his regular-and-only hat. In 2013, he and his deerstalker were finally able make his first trip-of-a-lifetime Holmes Pilgrimage to England, with return Pilgrimages in 2015 and 2016, where you may have spotted him. Another is planned in mid-2024. If you ever run into him and his deerstalker out and about, feel free to say hello!

Mark Mower is a long-standing member of the *Crime Writers' Association*, *The Sherlock Holmes Society of London*, and *The Solar Pons Society of London*. His pastiche collections include *Sherlock Holmes: The Baker Street Case-Files*, *Sherlock Holmes: The Baker Street Legacy*, *Sherlock Holmes: The Baker Street Epilogue*, and *Sherlock Holmes: The Baker*

Street Archive (all with MX Publishing). His non-fiction works include the bestselling book *Zeppelin Over Suffolk: The Final Raid of the L48* (Pen & Sword Books). Alongside his writing, Mark maintains a sizeable collection of pastiches, and never tires of discovering new stories about Sherlock Holmes and Dr. Watson.

Sidney Paget (1860-1908), a few of whose illustrations are used within this anthology, was born in London, and like his two older brothers, became a famed illustrator and painter. He completed over three-hundred-and-fifty drawings for the Sherlock Holmes stories that were first published in *The Strand* magazine, defining Holmes's image forever after in the public mind.

Tracy J. Revels, BSI, a Sherlockian from the age of eleven, is a professor of history at Wofford College in Spartanburg, South Carolina. She is a member of *The Survivors of the Gloria Scott* and *The Studious Scarlets Society*, and is a past recipient of the Beacon Society Award. Almost every semester, she teaches a class that covers The Canon, either to college students or to senior citizens. She is also the author of three supernatural Sherlockian pastiches with MX (*Shadowfall*, *Shadowblood*, and *Shadowwraith*), and a regular contributor to her scion's newsletter. She also has some notoriety as an author of very silly skits: For proof, see "The Adventure of the Adversarial Adventuress" and "Occupy Baker Street" on YouTube. When not studying Sherlock, she can be found researching the history of her native state, and has written books on Florida in the Civil War and on the development of Florida's tourism industry.

Roger Riccard's family history has Scottish roots, which trace his lineage back to Highland Scotland. This British Isles ancestry encouraged his interest in the writings of Sir Arthur Conan Doyle at an early age. He has authored the novels, *Sherlock Holmes & The Case of the Poisoned Lilly*, and *Sherlock Holmes & The Case of the Twain Papers*. In addition he has produced several short stories in *Sherlock Holmes Adventures for the Twelve Days of Christmas* and the series *A Sherlock Holmes Alphabet of Cases*. A new series will begin publishing in the Autumn of 2022, and his has another novel in the works. All of his books have been published by Baker Street Studios. His Bachelor of Arts Degrees in both Journalism and History from California State University, Northridge, have proven valuable to his writing historical fiction, as well as the encouragement of his wife/editor/inspiration and Sherlock Holmes fan, Rosilyn. She passed in 2021, and it is in her memory that he continues to contribute to the legacy of the "*man who never lived and will never die*".

Dan Rowley practiced law for over forty years in private practice and with a large international corporation. He is retired and lives in Erie, Pennsylvania, with his wife Judy, who puts her artistic eye to his transcription of Watson's manuscripts. He inherited his writing ability and creativity from his children, Jim and Katy, and his love of mysteries from his parents, Jim and Ruth.

Alisha Shea has resided near Saint Louis, Missouri for over thirty years. The eldest of six children, she found reading to be a genuine escape from the chaotic drudgery of life. She grew to love not only Sherlock Holmes, but the time period from which he emerged. In her spare time, she indulges in creating music via piano, violin, and Native American flute. Sometimes she thinks she might even be getting good at it. She also produces a wide variety of fiber arts which are typically given away or auctioned off for various fundraisers.

Robert V. Stapleton was born and brought up in Leeds, Yorkshire, England, and studied at Durham University. After working in various parts of the country as an Anglican parish priest, he is now retired and lives with his wife in North Yorkshire. As a member of his local writing group, he now has time to develop his other life as a writer of adventure stories. He has published a number of short stories, and he is hoping to have a couple of completed novels published at some time in the future.

Daniel Stashower, BSI, is an acclaimed biographer and narrative historian and winner of the Edgar, Agatha, and Anthony awards, as well as the Raymond Chandler Fulbright Fellowship in Detective Fiction. His work has appeared in *The New York Times*, *The Washington Post*, *Smithsonian Magazine*, *AARP: The Magazine*, *National Geographic Traveler*, and *American History*, as well as other publications. His books include *The Ectoplasmic Man*, *The Hour of Peril*, *Teller of Tales*, and *The Beautiful Cigar Girl*.

Daniel D. Victor is a retired high school English teacher who lives with his wife in his native Los Angeles, California. His doctoral dissertation on the assassinated American writer David Graham Phillips led to Victor's first Sherlock Holmes pastiche, *The Seventh Bullet* (St. Martin's Press) and ultimately to his ongoing series, *Sherlock Holmes and the American Literati*. Each novel in the series introduces Holmes to an American author who was writing during the period Holmes was detecting. Victor has also recently published *Cruel September*, a novel based on his many years of teaching in Los Angeles.

Emma West joined Undershaw in April 2021 as the Director of Education with a brief to ensure that qualifications formed the bedrock of our provision, whilst facilitating a positive balance between academia, pastoral care, and well-being. She quickly took on the role of Acting Headteacher from early summer 2021. Under her leadership, Undershaw has embraced its new name, new vision, and consequently we have seen an exponential increase in demand for places. There is a buzz in the air as we invite prospective students and families through the doors. Emma has overseen a strategic review, re-cemented relationships with Local Authorities, and positioned Undershaw at the helm of SEND education in Surrey and beyond. Undershaw has a wide appeal: Our students present to us with mild to moderate learning needs and therefore may have some very recent memories of poor experiences in their previous schools. Emma's background as a senior leader within the independent school sector has meant she is well-versed in brokering relationships between the key stakeholders, our many interdependences, local businesses, families, and staff, and all this while ensuring Undershaw remains relentlessly child-centric in its approach. Emma's energetic smile and boundless enthusiasm for Undershaw is inspiring.

Marcia Wilson is a freelance researcher and illustrator who likes to work in a style compatible for the color blind and visually impaired. She is Canon-centric, and her first MX offering, *You Buy Bones*, uses the point-of-view of Scotland Yard to show the unique talents of Dr. Watson. This continued with the publication of *Test of the Professionals: The Adventure of the Flying Blue Pidgeon* and *The Peaceful Night Poisonings*. She can be contacted at: *gravelgirty.deviantart.com*

The following contributors appear in these companion volumes:
Part XLIII– 2024 Annual (1874-1888)
Part XLIV – 2024 Annual (1889-1997)

Mike Adamson also has a stories in Part XLIII

Gretchen Altabef has authored five Sherlock Holmes novels. Her stories, though murder mysteries, are full of hope and the bonhomie of friendship. Her fictional journeys grow out of her historical research. She shares with her main character a half-humorous perspective on the world and the creative application of imagination, and intuition. She is a member of *The Sherlock Holmes Society of London, The Adventuresses of Sherlock Holmes, The ACD Society, The John H. Watson Society*, and *The Sherlock Holmes Society of India*.

Chris Chan is a writer, educator, and historian. He works as a researcher and "International Goodwill Ambassador" for Agatha Christie Ltd. His true crime articles, reviews, and short fiction have appeared (or will soon appear) in *The Strand, The Wisconsin Magazine of History, Mystery Weekly, Gilbert!, Nerd HQ*, Akashic Books' *Mondays are Murder* web series, *The Baker Street Journal, The MX Book of New Sherlock Holmes Stories, Masthead: The Best New England Crime Stories, Sherlock Holmes Mystery Magazine*, and multiple Belanger Books anthologies. He is the creator of the Funderburke mysteries, a series featuring a private investigator who works for a school and helps students during times of crisis. The Funderburke short story "The Six-Year-Old Serial Killer" was nominated for a Derringer Award. His books include *Sherlock & Irene: The Secret Truth Behind "A Scandal in Bohemia", Murder Most Grotesque: The Comedic Crime Fiction of Joyce Porter, Sherlock's Secretary, Of Course He Pushed Him, Nessie's Nemesis, Ghosting My Friend*, She *Ruined Our Lives*, and *The Autistic Sleuth*.

Mike Chinn's first-ever Sherlock Holmes fiction was a steampunk mashup of *The Valley of Fear*, entitled *Vallis Timoris* (Fringeworks 2015). Since then he has written about Holmes's archenemy in *The Mammoth Book of the Adventures of Moriarty* (Robinson 2015), appeared in several volumes of *The MX Book of New Sherlock Holmes Stories*, and faced the retired detective with cross-dimensional magic in the second volume of *Sherlock Holmes and the Occult Detectives* (Belanger Books 2020).

Alan Dimes also has stories in Parts XLIII and XLIV

Paul A. Freeman is an English language teacher. He is the author of *Rumours of Ophir*, a crime novel which was taught at 'O' level in Zimbabwean high schools and has been translated into German. In addition to having two novels, a children's book and an 18,000-word narrative poem (*Robin Hood and Friar Tuck: Zombie Killers!*) commercially published, Paul is the author of scores of published short stories, poems and articles. He is a member of the *Society of Authors* and of the *Crime Writers' Association*. He lives and works in Mauritania.

Arthur Hall also has stories in Parts XLIII and XLIV

Paula Hammond has written over sixty fiction and non-fiction books, as well as short stories, comics, poetry, and scripts for educational DVD's. When not glued to the keyboard, she can usually be found prowling round second-hand books shops or hunkered down in a hide, soaking up the joys of the natural world.

Stephen Herczeg is an IT Geek, writer, actor, and film-maker based in Canberra Australia. He has been writing for over twenty years and has completed a couple of dodgy novels, sixteen feature-length screenplays, and numerous short stories and scripts. Stephen was very successful in 2017's International Horror Hotel screenplay competition, with his scripts *TITAN* winning the Sci-Fi category and *Dark are the Woods* placing second in the horror category. His three-volume short story collection, *The Curious Cases of Sherlock*

Holmes, will be published in 2021. His work has featured in *Sproutlings – A Compendium of Little Fictions* from Hunter Anthologies, the *Hells Bells* Christmas horror anthology published by the Australasian Horror Writers Association, and the *Below the Stairs*, *Trickster's Treats*, *Shades of Santa*, *Behind the Mask*, and *Beyond the Infinite* anthologies from *OzHorror.Con*, *The Body Horror Book*, *Anemone Enemy*, and *Petrified Punks* from Oscillate Wildly Press, and *Sherlock Holmes In the Realms of H.G. Wells* and *Sherlock Holmes: Adventures Beyond the Canon* from Belanger Books.

Kelvin I. Jones is the author of six books about Sherlock Holmes and the definitive biography of Conan Doyle as a spiritualist, *Conan Doyle and The Spirits*. A member of *The Sherlock Holmes Society of London*, he has published numerous short occult and ghost stories in British anthologies over the last thirty years. His work has appeared on BBC Radio, and in 1984 he won the Mason Hall Literary Award for his poem cycle about the survivors of Hiroshima and Nagasaki, recently reprinted as "Omega". (Oakmagic Publications) A one-time teacher of creative writing at the University of East Anglia, he is also the author of four crime novels featuring his ex-met sleuth John Bottrell, who first appeared in *Stone Dead*. He has over fifty titles on Kindle, and is also the author of several novellas and short story collections featuring a Norwich based detective, DCI Ketch, an intrepid sleuth who investigates East Anglian murder cases. He also published a series of short stories about an Edwardian psychic detective, Dr. John Carter (*Carter's Occult Casebook*). Ramsey Campbell, the British horror writer, and Francis King, the renowned novelist, have both compared his supernatural stories to those of M. R. James. He has also published children's fiction, namely *Odin's Eye*, and, in collaboration with his wife Debbie, *The Dark Entry*. Since 1995, he has been the proprietor of Oakmagic Publications, publishers of British folklore and of his fiction titles.

Naching T. Kassa is a wife, mother, and writer. She's created short stories, novellas, poems, and co-created three children. She resides in Eastern Washington State with her husband, Dan Kassa. Naching is a member of *The Horror Writers Association*, *Mystery Writers of America*, *The Sound of the Baskervilles*, *The ACD Society*, *The Crew of the Barque Lone Star*, and *The Sherlock Holmes Society of London*. She works in Talent Relations at Crystal Lake Publishing and was a recipient of the 2022 HWA Diversity Grant. You can find her work on Amazon.
https://www.amazon.com/Naching-T-Kassa/e/B005ZGHTI0

Susan Knight's newest novel, *Mrs. Hudson Goes to Paris* (2022) from MX publishing, is the latest in a series which began with her collection of stories, *Mrs. Hudson Investigates* (2019), the novel *Mrs. Hudson goes to Ireland* (2020), and *Mrs. Hudson Goes to Paris* (2022), and *Death in the Garden of England* (2023) She has contributed to many recent MX anthologies of new Sherlock Holmes short stories and enjoys writing as Dr. Watson as much as she does Mrs. Hudson. Nine of these stories comprised *The Strange Case of the Pale Boy and Other Mysteries* (2023). Susan is the author of two other non-Sherlockian story collections, as well as three novels, a book of non-fiction, and several plays, and has won several prizes for her writing. Susan lives in Dublin.

Daniel Lenois also has stories in Parts XLIII and XLIV

David MacGregor is a playwright, screenwriter, novelist, and nonfiction writer. He is a resident artist at The Purple Rose Theatre in Michigan, where a number of his plays have been produced. His plays have been performed from New York to Tasmania, and his work has been published by Dramatic Publishing, Playscripts, Smith & Kraus, Applause, Heuer

Publishing, and Theatrical Rights Worldwide (TRW). He adapted his dark comedy, *Vino Veritas*, for the silver screen, and it stars Carrie Preston (Emmy-winner for *The Good Wife*). Several of his short plays have also been adapted into films. He is the author of three Sherlock Holmes plays: *Sherlock Holmes and the Adventure of the Elusive Ear*, *Sherlock Holmes and the Adventure of the Fallen Soufflé*, and *Sherlock Holmes and the Adventure of the Ghost Machine*. He adapted all three plays into novels for Orange Pip Books, and also wrote the two-volume nonfiction *Sherlock Holmes: The Hero with a Thousand Faces* for MX Publishing. He teaches writing at Wayne State University in Detroit and is inordinately fond of cheese and terriers.

David Marcum also has stories in Parts XLIII and XLIV

Kevin Patrick McCann has published eight collections of poems for adults, one for children (*Diary of a Shapeshifter*, Beul Aithris), a book of ghost stories (*It's Gone Dark*, The Otherside Books), *Teach Yourself Self-Publishing* (Hodder) co-written with the playwright Tom Green, and *Ov* (Beul Aithris Publications) a fantasy novel for children.

Will Murray is the author of some 75 novels, including some 20 posthumous Doc Savage collaborations with Lester Dent, and 40 books in the long-running Destroyer series. Other Murray novels star the Executioner, Tarzan of the Apes, The Spider, Pat Savage and the Mars Attacks characters. His book, *Nick Fury, Agent of S.H.I.E.L.D.: Empyre* (2000) foreshadowed the 9/11 terrorist attacks. Murray has penned more than 45 Sherlock Holmes short stories. Twenty of Murray's Holmes short stories have been collected as *The Wild Adventures of Sherlock Holmes*, Vols 1 and 2. His novelette, "The Adventure of the Vengeful Viscount", in which Tarzan of the Apes, otherwise Lord Greystoke, hires Sherlock Holmes to solve a mystery, was approved by both the Estate of Sir Arthur Conan Doyle and Edgar Rice Burroughs, Inc. Murray is the author of the non-fiction book, *Master of Mystery: The Rise of The Shadow*, which is an exploration of the famous radio and magazine character, and a sequel, *Dark Avenger: The Strange Saga of The Shadow*. *The Wild Adventures of Cthulhu* Vols 1 & 2 collect Murray's Lovecraftan short stories. For Marvel Comics, Murray created the Unbeatable Squirrel Girl with legendary artist Steve Ditko. Website:
www.adventuresinbronze.com

Ember Pepper was born and raised in San Diego, CA. She has an M.F.A. degree in Creative Fiction Writing. She has been a fan of The Great Detective since she was a pre-teen and her greatest artistic enjoyment is challenging herself to write quality pastiches of Sherlock Holmes and his stalwart biographer and friend, John Watson.

Tracy J. Revels also has stories in Parts XLIII and XLIV

Jane Rubino is the author of *A Jersey Shore* mystery series, featuring a Jane Austen-loving amateur sleuth and a Sherlock Holmes-quoting detective, *Knight Errant, Lady Vernon and Her Daughter*, (a novel-length adaptation of Jane Austen's novella *Lady Susan*, co-authored with her daughter Caitlen Rubino-Bradway, *What Would Austen Do?*, also co-authored with her daughter, a short story in the anthology *Jane Austen Made Me Do It*, *The Rucastles' Pawn, The Copper Beeches from Violet Turner's POV*, and, of course, there's the Sherlockian novel in the drawer – who doesn't have one? Jane lives on a barrier island at the New Jersey shore.

Jonathan Schneer is an *emeritus* professor at the Georgia Institute of Technology, where he taught modern British history for thirty years. He has written nine history books published by university and commercial presses. His work has been translated into Russian, Chinese, Turkish, Estonian, French, and German. He has held many visiting fellowships at Oxford and Cambridge Universities, and elsewhere, has spoken about his books on radio, television, and podcasts, at seminars, conferences, meetings, book fairs, community centers, museums, libraries, book stores, etc. Now that he is retired, he divides his time between Williamstown, MA, and Decatur, GA. He certainly enjoys writing about Sherlock Holmes.

Fifteen of **Brenda Seabrooke**'s Sherlock Holmes pastiches have been anthologized in MX Publishing and Belanger Books, six in *Best Crime Stories of New England*, one in *Destination: Mystery* and *Mystery Tribune*, and twelve in literary reviews such as *Yemassee, Confrontation*, and one in *Redbook*. Twenty-two of her books for young readers have been published at Penguin, Clarion, etc., and won awards such as a Notable from the National Council of Social Studies, Junior Literary Guild, Hornbook Honor, an Edgar finalist, etc. She received a grant from the National Endowment for the Arts, and The Robie Macauley Award from Emerson College. In 2022, MX published her collection, *Sherlock Holmes: The Persian Slipper and Other Stories*.

Shane Simmons is the author of the occult detective novels *necropolis* and *Epitaph*, and the crime collection *Raw and Other Stories*. An award-winning screenwriter and graphic novelist, his work has appeared in international film festivals, museums, and lectures about design and structure. He was born in Lachine, a suburb of Montreal best known for being massacred in 1689 and having a joke name. Visit Shane's homepage at *eyestrainproductions.com* for more information.

Peter Shumway is a retired computer professional residing in Pennsylvania with his wife, Patty. They have been married forty-one years and have two daughters and four grandchildren. In the early 1970's, Peter performed magic with Bill Baker's World of Magic, John Bundy's Magic Concert, and traded secrets with David Copperfield when they were teenagers. Peter read the original Sherlock Holmes stories while in college in 1979, and has enjoyed rereading them many times since. He published his pastiche *Sherlock Holmes and The Kiss of Death in* 2005 and *Gullible's Journey* in 2023. When he was offered the opportunity to write a short story for the MX Series, he picked up his pen one more time.

Hailing from Bedford in the South East of England, **Matthew Simmonds** has been a confirmed devotee of Sir Arthur Conan Doyle's most famous creation since first watching Jeremy Brett's incomparable portrayal of the world's first consulting detective, on a Tuesday evening in April 1984, while curled up on the sofa with his father. He has written numerous short stories and his first novel, *Sherlock Holmes: The Adventure of The Pigtail Twist* was published in 2018. A sequel, *Sherlock Holmes: The Adventure of The Found Note* was published in November 2023. Matthew currently co-owns Harrison & Simmonds, the fifth-generation family business, a renowned County tobacconist, pipe and gift shop on Bedford High Street.

Denis O. Smith's first published story of Sherlock Holmes and Doctor Watson, "The Adventure of The Purple Hand", appeared in 1982. Since then, numerous other such accounts have been published in magazines and anthologies both in the U.K. and the U.S. In the 1990's, four volumes of his stories were published under the general title of *The*

Chronicles of Sherlock Holmes, and, more recently his stories have been collected as *The Lost Chronicles of Sherlock Holmes* (2014), *The Lost Chronicles of Sherlock Holmes Volume II* (2016), *The Further Chronicles of Sherlock Holmes* (2018). He also wrote a Holmes novel, *The Riddle of Foxwood Grange* (2017). Born in Yorkshire, in the north of England, Denis Smith has lived and worked in various parts of the country, including London, and has now been resident in Norfolk for many years. His interests range widely, but apart from his dedication to the career of Sherlock Holmes, he has a passion for historical mysteries of all kinds, the railways of Britain and the history of London.

Robert V. Stapleton also has a story in Part XLIII

Kevin P. Thornton has had a varied career. He has been a soldier, a military contractor, a logistics consultant and, at various times, a forklift driver and a barman. It was not a well-thought-out path. He has played rugby, cricket, and other games of violence with virtually no success but plenty of gusto, and has the aches and scars to prove so. He has also had a varied writing career. In his time, he has written for *The New York Times* on the wildfires in Alberta, as well as a long running column in the *Fort McMurray Today*. He has had poetry published in more than a dozen collections, some of which have even sold commercially. He has also edited a journal on a military base in Afghanistan, and is currently the chief and only writer of a magazine for a Dene and Cree First Nation in Canada. He has written about half-a-dozen books, all of which were shortlisted in the *Crime Writers of Canada* unpublished awards, all of which are still unpublished. He has had rather more success with short stories, with somewhere around thirty anthologized. Many of these involve Sherlock Holmes and, while he would hesitate to call himself a Sherlockian – just as he hesitates over such titles as author, poet, journalist, columnist, editor – he is quite fond of the gentlemen of 221b. "They allow me to write crime stories succinctly, and if I were to title myself, I would take that as a starting point; if forced to take a stand I would describe myself as a storyteller." Kevin is one of the founding members of the *Northwords Literary Mag*azine of Fort McMurray, Alta. and a current or former member of the CWG, WGA, CWC, CWA, MWA, ITW, S-in-C, MofM, and the IACW. Decoding available on request. In 2015, he was accepted as a member of *The Keys*, the London based organization of writers founded by G.K. Chesterton and Ronald Knox. He has two sons of whom he is enormously proud, and a wife he adores, and who in turn seems to love and tolerate him, depending on the mood and the moment.

Thomas A. (Tom) Turley has been "hooked on Holmes" since finishing *The Hound of the Baskervilles* at about the age of twelve. However, his interest in Sherlockian pastiches didn't take off until he wrote one. *Sherlock Holmes and the Adventure of the Tainted Canister* (2014) is available as an e-book and an audiobook from MX Publishing. It also appeared in *The Art of Sherlock Holmes – USA Edition 1*. In 2017, two of Tom's stories, "A Scandal in Serbia" and "A Ghost from Christmas Past" were published in Parts VI and VII of this anthology. "Ghost" was also included in *The Art of Sherlock Holmes – West Palm Beach Edition*. Meanwhile, Tom published two collection of historical pastiches entitled *Sherlock Holmes and the Crowned Heads of Europe* (2021) and *Watson's Wives and Other Tales of Sherlock Holmes* (2024). Although he has a Ph.D. in British history, Tom spent most of his professional career as an archivist with the State of Alabama. He and his wife Paula (an aspiring science fiction novelist) live in Montgomery, Alabama. Interested readers may contact Tom through MX Publishing or his Goodreads author's page.

DJ Tyrer is the person behind Atlantean Publishing and has had fiction featuring Sherlock Holmes published in volumes from MX Publishing and Belanger Books, and an issue of *Awesome Tales*, and has a forthcoming story in *Sherlock Holmes Mystery Magazine*. DJ's non-Sherlockian mysteries can be found in anthologies such as *Mardi Gras Mysteries* (Mystery and Horror LLC) and *The Trench Coat Chronicles* (Celestial Echo Press), and on *Mystery Tribune*.

DJ Tyrer's website is at *https://djtyrer.blogspot.co.uk/*

DJ's Facebook page is at *https://www.facebook.com/DJTyrerwriter/*

The Atlantean Publishing website is at *https://atlanteanpublishing.wordpress.com/*

I.A. Watson's first professional publishing credit was with a Sherlock Holmes story. The tale in this book will be his 50th (counting his novel *Holmes and Houdini*, and one or two short stories in publishers' queues). He is constantly surprised at how many ways there are to tell Sherlock Holmes adventures, which he holds to be a sign of Sir Arthur Conan Doyle's genius in developing so flexible and resilient a format for such a compelling cast of characters. A full list of I.A. Watson's 100+ published works including twenty or so novels is available at:

http://www.chillwater.org.uk/writing/iawatsonhome.htm

Marcia Wilson also has stories in Parts XLIII and XLIV

The MX Book of New Sherlock Holmes Stories
Edited by David Marcum
(MX Publishing, 2015-)

"This is the finest volume of Sherlockian fiction I have ever read, and I have read, literally, thousands." – Philip K. Jones

"Beyond Impressive . . . This is a splendid venture for a great cause!"
– Roger Johnson, Editor, *The Sherlock Holmes Journal,*
The Sherlock Holmes Society of London

Part I: 1881-1889; Part II: 1890-1895; Part III: 1896-1929

Part IV: 2016 Annual

Part V: Christmas Adventures

Part VI: 2017 Annual

Eliminate the Impossible
Part VII: (1880-1891); Part VIII: (1892-1905)

2018 Annual
Part IX: (1879-1895); Part X: (1896-1916)

Some Untold Cases
Part XI: (1880-1891); Part XII: (1894-1902)

2019 Annual
Part XIII: (1881-1890); Part XIV: (1891-1897); Part XV: (1898-1917)

Whatever Remains . . . Must be the Truth
Part XVI: (1881-1890); Part XVII: (1891-1898); Part XVIII: (1898-1925)

2020 Annual
Part XIX: (1882-1890); Part XX: (1891-1897); Part XXI: (1898-1923)·

Some More Untold Cases
Part XXII: (1877-1887); Part XXIII: (1888-1894); Part XXIV: (1895-1903)

2021 Annual
Part XXV: (1881-1888); Part XXVI: (1889-1897); Part XXVII: (1898-1928)

More Christmas Adventures
Part XXVIII: (1869-1888); Part XXIX: (1889-1896); Part XXX: (1897-1928)

2022 Annual
Part XXXI: (1875-1887); Part XXXII: (1888-1895); Part XXXIII: (1896-1919)

"However Improbable . . . ."
Part XXXIV: (1878-1888); Part XXXV: (1889-1896); Part XXXVI: (1897-1919)

2023 Annual
Parts XXXVII (1875-1889), XXXVIII (1889-1896), and XXXIX (1897-1923)

Further Untold Cases
Part XL: (1879-1886), Part XLI: (1887-1892) and Part XLII: (1894-1922)

2024 Annual
Parts XLIII (1874-1888), XLIV (1889-1897), and XLV (1898-1917)

In Preparation *. . . Part XLVI (and XLVII and XLVIII as well?)*
and more to come!

The MX Book of New Sherlock Holmes Stories
Edited by David Marcum
(MX Publishing, 2015-   )

Part VI: *The traditional pastiche is alive and well . . . .*

Part VII: *Sherlockians eager for faithful-to-the-canon plots and characters will be delighted.*

Part VIII: *The imagination of the contributors in coming up with variations on the volume's theme is matched by their ingenious resolutions.*

Part IX: *The 18 stories . . . will satisfy fans of Conan Doyle's originals. Sherlockians will rejoice that more volumes are on the way.*

Part X: *. . . new Sherlock Holmes adventures of consistently high quality.*

Part XI: *. . . an essential volume for Sherlock Holmes fans.*

Part XII: *. . . continues to amaze with the number of high-quality pastiches.*

Part XIII: *. . . Amazingly, Marcum has found 22 superb pastiches . . . his is more catnip for fans of stories faithful to Conan Doyle's original*

Part XIV: *. . . this standout anthology of 21 short stories written in the spirit of Conan Doyle's originals.*

Part XV: *Stories pitting Sherlock Holmes against seemingly supernatural phenomena highlight Marcum's 15th anthology of superior short pastiches.*

Part XVI: *Marcum has once again done fans of Conan Doyle's originals a service.*

Part XVII: *This is yet another impressive array of new but traditional Holmes stories.*

Part XVIII: *Sherlockians will again be grateful to Marcum and MX for high-quality new Holmes tales.*

Part XIX: *Inventive plots and intriguing explorations of aspects of Dr. Watson's life and beliefs lift the 24 pastiches in Marcum's impressive 19th Sherlock Holmes anthology*

Part XX: *Marcum's reserve of high-quality new Holmes exploits seems endless.*

Part XXI: *This is another must-have for Sherlockians.*

Part XXII: *Marcum's superlative 22nd Sherlock Holmes pastiche anthology features 21 short stories that successfully emulate the spirit of Conan Doyle's originals while expanding on the canon's tantalizing references to mysteries Dr. Watson never got around to chronicling.*

Part XXIII: *Marcum's well of talented authors able to mimic the feel of The Canon seems bottomless.*

Part XXIV: *Marcum's expertise at selecting high-quality pastiches remains impressive.*

Part XXVIII: *All entries adhere to the spirit, language, and characterizations of Conan Doyle's originals, evincing the deep pool of talent Marcum has access to. Against the odds, this series remains strong, hundreds of stories in.*

Part XXXI: *. . . yet another stellar anthology of 21 short pastiches that effectively mimic the originals . . . Marcum's diligent searches for high-quality stories has again paid off for Sherlockians.*

Part XXXIV: *Mind-bending puzzles are the highlight of Marcum's fully satisfying 34th anthology, which again demonstrates that multiple authors are capable of giving Sherlock Holmes and Watson innovative mysteries to tackle while staying in character. Marcum's inventory of canonical pastiches shows no signs of being exhausted any time soon.*

The MX Book of New Sherlock Holmes Stories
Edited by David Marcum
(MX Publishing, 2015-   )

An Investees' Anthology
Edited by David Marcum
(MX Publishing, 2022)

Selected Contributions to
The MX Book of New Sherlock Holmes Stories
by Members of
The Baker Street Irregulars

*All royalties from this collection are being donated
for the benefit of the preservation of Undershaw,
a school for special needs students located at
one of the former homes of Sir Arthur Conan Doyle*

Stories, Forewords, and Poems in this volume
have previously appeared in Parts I – XXXVI of
The MX Book of New Sherlock Holmes Stories

Featuring Contributions by:

Mark Alberstat, Marino C. Alvarez, Peter Calamai, Catherine Cooke, Carla Coupe, David Stuart Davies, John Farrell, Lyndsay Faye, Sonia Fetherston, Jayantika Ganguly, Jeffrey Hatcher, Roger Johnson, Leslie S. Klinger, Ann Margaret Lewis, Bonnie MacBird, Stephen Mason, Julie McKuras Nicholas Meyer, Jacquelynn Morris, Otto Penzler, Christopher Redmond, Tracy J. Revels, Steven Rothman, Nancy Holder, Mark Levy (and Arlene Mantin Levy), Nicholas Utechin, and Sean M. Wright (and DeForeest B. Wright, III)

MX Publishing

MX Publishing is the world's largest specialist Sherlock Holmes publisher, with over five-hundred titles and over two-hundred authors creating the latest in Sherlock Holmes fiction and non-fiction

The catalogue includes several award winning books, and over two-hundred-and-fifty have been converted into audio.

MX Publishing also has one of the largest communities of Holmes fans on Facebook, with regular contributions from dozens of authors.

www.mxpublishing.com

@mxpublishing on Facebook, Twitter, and Instagram

www.ingramcontent.com/pod-product-compliance
Lightning Source LLC
Chambersburg PA
CBHW032258020726
47495CB00001B/153